Carry the Light

Stories, Poems and Essays
from the San Mateo County Fair
2015

SHRP

Sand Hill Review Press

Carry the Light
Vol. IV
Stories, Poems and Essays from the San Mateo County Fair
San Mateo, California
© 2015

Library of Congress Control Number: 2015940345
ISBN: 978-1-937818-33-3

Published by Sand Hill Review Press
www.sandhillreviewpress.com
P.O. Box 1275, San Mateo, CA 94401 (415) 297-3571

Front cover art: Light in the Night, by Peche Turner
Back cover art: Woman of the Sun, by Randie Marlow
Cover design by Joanne Shwed, Backspace Ink
(www.backspaceink.com)

SHRP
Sand Hill Review Press

INTRODUCTION

"You can't depend on your eyes when your imagination is out of focus." -

—Mark Twain

As we move into the 4th installment of the San Mateo County Fair Anthology, I am impressed at the amount of vision and imagination that has taken place to get us to this place. What started as a conversation and dream has now become a true reality; a composition of a publication and clearinghouse for local writers to become judged by their peers, presented to their friends, and published in this anthology.

Each year, I have had the chance to read a sample of the works submitted and continually come away impressed at the increased skill and writing ability that is in our hometown. What started as a chore years ago has now become a personal highlight in my responsibilities. I am touched with the opportunity to browse the writings of your imagination nation.

While I am allowed the easy role of being your audience through the submissions, a heartfelt "Thank You" needs to be given to Bardi Rosman Koodrin and her team. Individuals like Tory Hartmann, Sue Barizon and Laurel Anne Hill are key leaders in this entire endeavor. Not to mention all the judges, helpers, and volunteers who have shared their time in the creation and continuation of the Anthology. One last person who has had an integral impact on our dream is Boris Koodrin. Without his focus and involvement, none of this would be possible. He has been the driving force for the Fine Arts Galleria and the push to grow the Literary Department under the guidance of Bardi. He does not get the recognition that is due, but he, most assuredly, is deserving of all of our gratitude.

Additionally, the Board of Directors for the San Mateo County Fair needs to be commended for their support and guidance of the Fair. Through their advice as well as the direction of SVP and General Manager, Chris A. Carpenter, the Fair has seen continued growth in all levels. The mantra "Where Tradition Meets Innovation" has proven to be more applicable than originally planned, with evidence in this newest edition of the Literary Anthology Series.

As a closing note, I entice all of you to continually share your dreams. Our past may be blurred with the passing of time and our future may be uncertain, but our imagination will be the lens that keeps our focus. Write off the pages and your words will materialize right before your eyes.

Live life to your fullest imagination!

Matt Cranford, CFEE
Fair & Festival Manager
San Mateo County Fair

FOREWORD

We are excited to announce the San Mateo County Fair received almost three hundred literary contest entries this year—our highest total to date! Thinking back, we had thirty-seven entries in 2009, my first year as director. The San Francisco/Peninsula branch of the California Writers Club (CWC) embraced my experimental concept: a stage upon which to present free literary workshops at a county fair. That first year we put on perhaps five or six workshops. We booked close to sixty events in 2014. My, how our collaboration has grown.

Speaking of booking events, I must thank my two outstanding stage managers Laurel Anne Hill and Dave Hirzel. They continue to amaze me. Sue Barizon is my tried and true sidekick. Our fourth anthology would not be possible without our Sand Hill Review Press publisher Tory Hartmann, who has gone with the flow of dealing with increased entries each year. I can't imagine how anyone could manage to compile a top quality, four hundred page anthology of contest entries and get them printed in a mere six weeks and yet, Tory does it with good-natured aplomb. We enjoy watching the entrants' smiles at seeing their work in print, some for the first time, during our annual autograph party. Without the ongoing support of the Fair & Festival Manager Matt Cranford, none of this would be possible. Thank you Matt!

We offered something new and wonderful this year: Lotteries for free critiques of memoir, essay, and short story entries. Over fifty eager participants vied for the professional editing services of Darlene Frank (memoir), Audrey Kalman (essay) and Lisa Meltzer Penn (short story). We will post the before and after results on our literary fair page.

Our theme for the 2015 literary stage events is "Writers Helping Writers Through Mentoring." This goes hand-in-hand with our Carry the Light philosophy of uplifting oneself by helping others, which in turn challenges us all to dream a better dream.

There is a saying, "It takes a village." Well, I say it takes TWO villages to run the literary and fine arts departments known as the Fine Arts Galleria. We rely on volunteers and in fact, I must brag: the Fine Arts Galleria, under the directorship of my husband Boris Koodrin, won a 2014 Western Regional Fair award for our outstanding volunteer programs. The literary stage relies on the generosity of our volunteers so to honor their commitment we will again offer our volunteer raffle during the 2015 San Mateo County Fair. One lucky volunteer will win a year's free membership to the

San Francisco/Peninsula branch of the CWC. Bette Houtchens won last year and now she's an active member of the CWC board of directors.

In closing, I must say that this anthology would not exist without the talented writers who submitted their poems, essays, memoirs, novel chapters, and short stories. We've even stepped into the digital world of blogs and podcasts. Everyone has a story. Tell me yours...

Bardi Rosman Koodrin
Literary Director

Table of Contents

The Winners

We think everyone who entered is a winner, but here is the official list. There were over 15 judges. Not all judges awarded first prizes or gave honorable mentions. A few of the entries were not published in this volume because of the author's wishes. They have been indicated by an asterisk. *

Div. 350 Sand Hill Review Press, Publisher's Choice Novel Chapter
Winner: *Winds of Change*, Colleen Fliedner
HM: *The Occupation of Joe*, Bill Baynes
HM: *The Last Storyteller*, Audrey Kalman

Div. 351 Genre Novelist First Chapter
First Place: *The Rainbow Warriors*, Lisa Boragine*
Second Place: *A Murder Foretold*, David Wolf*
Third Place: *Under*, Missy Kirtley
HM: *The Dog of Pel*, Mary Holland
HM: *The Animal Group Home*, Yukari Sakura*
HM: *Fanboys Shrugged*, Dave Strom

Div. 352 Best Blog
First Place: *Freshmen Say the Darndest Things*, Laura Deck *

Div. 355-01 Personal Memoir
First Place: *Wisteria*, Kathleen Canrinus
Second Place: *Eight Letters*, Louise Lenahan Wallace
Third Place: *Eating My Heart Out*, Sue Barizon
HM: *A Single Stroke of a Pen*, Sheena Arora
HM: *Learning the Bones*, Laurel Anne Hill
HM: *Taking My Imagination for a Ride*, Marjorie Bicknell Johnson
HM: *The Ol' Button Place*, Linda Brown

Div. 355-02 Lifestyle Memoir
First Place: *Home on the Range*, Laura Deck
Second Place: *Liva and Let Liva*, Sue Barizon
Third Place: *Needle Shy*, Jamie Miller
HM: *Cups of Tea*, Gloria Bares
HM: *Education on a Greek Island*, Shelley Buck

Div. 356 Heroes Arise: Heroic Deed Novel Chapter
First Place: *House of Comedy*, Edie Matthews
Second Place: *Squirrel in the Intersection*, Luanne Oleas

Div. 357 San Francisco/Peninsula Writers Club: CWC Writer of the Year
Winner: *In Plain Sight*, Anami Sheppard

Div. 358 "I'm Dying to Tell You" Mystery Novel Chapter
First Place: *Righteous*, Ezra Barany

Div. 359 The Immigrant Experience: Novel, Memoir, Short Story, or Monologue
Third Place: *Customary Madness*, Bernadine Fornesi

Div. 360 Parenting on the Peninsula Children's Novel, Chapter or Story
First Place: *The Fairy Garden*, Kimberly Schultz
Second Place: *The Drawing Lesson*, Nanci Lee Woody
Third Place: *One Fog-Knit Night*, Bill Baynes
HM: *A Carton for Barton*, Stanley Gedzelman
HM: *Ruben's Tales of the Amazon Jungle*, Audry Lynch

Div. 361-01 Free Form Poem, Exhibitor 54 or Younger
First Place: *Stock*, T.R .Poulson
Second Place: *Brave*, Nicole Justine Cavanaugh
Third Place: *Poetry Before Language,* Michele Jessen
HM: *Summertime*, Jeannine Gerkman

Div. 361-02 Senior Free Form Poem
First Place: *Gladiolas in a White Vase*, Evie Groch

Second Place: *The Ephemera of Memory*, Mary Heneghan *
Third Place: *So Here I Come*, William Baldwin
HM: *The Oddball Dancer*, William Baldwin
HM: *The Invisible Synagogue*, Evie Groch
HM: *Worship*, Martha Clark Scala

Div. 361-03 Structured Poem, Exhibitor 54 or Younger
First Place: *Long Hair*, Michele Jessen

Div. 361-04 Senior Sturctured Poem
First Place: *Honor Student*, Dorsetta Hale
Second Place: *Villanelle for a Coffee Queen*, Evie Groch
Third Place: *The River That Sings*, Ken Owen
HM: *Again. Again.*, Frank Saunders

POETRY BEST OF SHOW
Gladiolas in a White Vase, Evie Groch

Div. 362-01 Persuasive Essay
First Place: *Whack A Mole*, Stanley Gedzelman
Second Place: *The Dream Can Survive*, Rudie Tretten
Third Place: *The Pain of Passion*, Evie Groch

Div. 362-02 Literary Essay
First Place: *Seeing Jerry Winters*, Katie Burke
Second Place: *Steinbeck and His Wives*, Audry Lynch
Third Place: *Beyond Wonder*, Rudie Tretten
HM: *Dazed and Confused*, Mary Heneghan*

Div. 363-01 Short Story, General Fiction, Under 55
First Place: *In Plain Sight*, Anami Sheppard
Second Place: *Serenade*, Lisa Meltzer Penn
Third Place: *Tile Store*, Lisa Meltzer Penn

Div. 363-02 Short Story, General Fiction, Senior
First Place: *The Quest*, Lisa Johnson
Second Place: *The Boat Ride*, Valerie Stoller
Third Place: *Remnants*, John Hotson

ESSAY BEST OF SHOW
Seeing Jerry Winters, Katie Burke

Div. 363-04 Short Story, Science Fiction/Fantasy, Senior
First Place: *The Once and Future Queen*, Carolyn Donnell
Second Place: *Light at the End of the Tunnel*, Thomas Kirkpatrick
Third Place: *The Final Stage*, Judith Shernock

Div. 363-05 Short Story, Mystery/Thriller, Under 55
First Place: *Campsite 39*, Kimberly Schultz

Div. 363-06 Short Story, Mystery/Thriller, Senior
First Place: *Haunted by the Past*, Edie Matthews
Second Place: *Homicidal Blueprint*, Bernadine Fornesi
Third Place: *The Trolley*, Judy Jette-Hanson**

Div. 363-08 Short Story, Western Up to Modern, Senior
First Place: *Weenie Roast*, Marjorie Bicknell Johnson

Div. 363-09 Short Story, Humerous, Under 55
First Place: *Pluto's Republic*, Jack Rosman
Second Place: *Reginald Van Flautmeister*, Thomas Kirkpatrick
Third Place: *What Are Tampones For?*, Pastor Bejinez

Div. 363-10 Short Story, Humerous, Senior
First Place: *Why Gladys Stuben Turned to Crime*, Luanne Oleas
Second Place: *Stalking Elizabeth George*, Valerie Stoller
Third Place: *Blue Man of Morocco*, Linda Brown

SHORT STORY BEST OF SHOW
In Plain Sight, Anami Sheppard

Div. 800 Notre Dame De Namur University $20,000 Creative Writing Scholarship
The Light of My Future, By Elizabeth Seter

2015 LITERARY EXHIBITOR OF THE YEAR
Anami Sheppard

Div. 313 Fine Arts Galleria Book Cover Art Contest: "Carry the Light" for the San Mateo County Fair Literary Anthology
First Place: Front Cover: *Light in the Night*, Peche Turner
Second Place: Back Cover: *Woman of the Sun*, Randie Marlow

Div. 314 Fine Arts Galleria Book Cover Art Contest: "Fault Zone, Transformation" for the San Francisco/Peninsula Writers, a branch of the California Writers Club (CWC)
Winner: *Transformation*, Donald Shernock

CONGRATULATIONS TO ALL OF THE WINNERS!

*Not published in this volume due to the wishes of the author.
**We regret the accidental omission of our 2014 Short Story 3rd prize winner, *The Trolley*, by Judy Jette-Hanson. We are proud to publish it in this volume.

350: Publisher's Choice Novel Chapter

Winds of Change

By Colleen Fliedner

PART ONE – MANHATTAN, NEW YORK

March 2, 1915

CHAPTER ONE

The morning air was heavy with an icy chill that crept clear to Sophie's bones. Winter seemed to be dragging on longer than usual this year. It was mid-March, for heaven's sake. The fact that St. Patrick's Cathedral was a cavernous edifice of stone and marble and stained glass windows didn't help either. Besides, this was the first Mass of the day. At 7:00 a.m., the heating system, such as it was, hadn't yet warmed the massive structure. Even worse, each time a late arriving parishioner opened the entry doors at the end of the long corridor, the breeze off Fifth Avenue swept down the center aisle and swirled beneath the hard wooden pews. Even the myriad of candles in graduating levels on each side of the altar seemed to object to the gusts.

They flickered so erratically that it must have taken some sort of miracle to keep them burning.

Sitting at the end of the pew on the far left side of the Cathedral beside her twin sister and mother, Sophie fought back a yawn. Her gaze traveled to the two stoic-faced altar boys, who stood nearby like good soldiers ready to enter battle, prepared to relight any wayward candle that dared to snuff out in St. Patrick's, the most divine of churches in New York. A third boy, older from the look him, carried the brass incense burner, swinging it just enough so that the gray-tinged, pungent smelling smoke escaped in curling puffs. The altar boys all looked so...so serious. More than likely, they would rather be outside playing with other children. Tossing a baseball about or...good heavens...anything besides this pomp and circumstance, she thought.

Dressed in his long purple robe, Bishop Hayes struck a commanding figure. "Sanctus, sanctus, sanctus," he said in monotone Latin, interrupting her wandering thoughts. He made the sign of the cross, then steepled his hands at his chest. This was one of the holiest times of the year in the Catholic faith. The weeks of Lent were underway, and most of the parishioners were at St. Patrick's to say their morning prayers. But for Sophie, Mother, and Yvette, there was an even greater need to pray today. They had come to receive the body and blood of Christ in communion and, most especially, to mourn the death of a young man who had been a part of their family's life for well over a decade.

Not only was the local priest at this morning's Mass, the Cathedral's own Bishop Hayes would say a special prayer for Julian Laurent. An honor to be sure. Julian had been killed in the fighting in France. In spite of the fact that America was still a neutral country, young men living in the United States were signing up to fight the Germans and their allies...and dying. Like poor Julian.

Sophie's mind flashed back to envision Julian. Handsome. Broad-shouldered. He was nearly eight years her senior. As children, both families had spent time every summer on the Cape. Julian and his sister, Emma, had played games – mostly croquet and kick-the-ball–with Sophie and Yvette outside the Laurents' grand mansion situated on the edge of the sea. They swam and fished off of the pier, though the girls all left it up to Julian to thread the wiggling worms onto their hooks.

For years, Sophie had a girlish crush on Julian. He, on the other hand, obviously thought of her as a child. And when he reached his late teen years, he fell in love with a pretty girl from a private school. Sophie saw less and less of him as time passed. Still, the thought of him dying in some muddy trench in the French countryside had become unbearable. Unthinkable. There was no grave to mark where his body lay. A mass grave had been dug. Too many victims to bury the day he died, they told his grieving parents in a telegram. Thousands had been killed that day, the reports said. All his parents knew was that he was gone. Not how he died. Not if he had suffered. Nothing more.

Early morning light beamed a rainbow of colors through the stained glass windows, scattering a diffused glow over the nave and rows of pews. It was as if the sun was trying to break through the overcast skies to send its warming rays into the Cathedral. And yet, even as the air warmed ever so slightly, Sophie was glad she wore heavy stockings, high-top shoes and her gray woolen tweed suit. As usual, Yvette hadn't used good judgment. Sophie glanced at her sister, shivering in her flimsy pink chemise dress and ridiculous, silky crepe de Chine jacket.

Appropriate for the warm summer months, but certainly not for a chilly New York spring morning. She had tried to reason with Yvette when they were dressing that morning, but her sister was all about fashion and coifs and trying the newest ladies' make-up products at Macy's.

It serves her right, Sophie thought. She and her sister weren't silly young girls, for heaven's sake. In fact, they would both be twenty in June, only a year away from legal age. They were nearly grown women, for heaven's sake. Yvette should have used better judgment.

Sophie, on the other hand, didn't have time for such frivolities as fashion. Nor did she care what the other parishioners thought about her outfit. Anyway, with the exception of Mr. and Mrs. Laurent, most of the people attending the Mass didn't know her or her sister. They were Mr. and Mrs. Laurent's or her parents' friends, not hers; associates from various social organizations to which her father and mother and the Laurents belonged.

Pulling her knitted neck scarf tighter, she gazed around the magnificent old cathedral.

The saints were all draped in silky dark purple fabric in recognition of Lent. The service was in Latin. With the exception of a few words here and there, it might as well have been recited in Greek or Russian or some other language that Sophie didn't understand. Eyelids suddenly heavy, she fought to stay awake.

Her mother turned, cleared her throat a little too loud, and shot Sophie her "I'm not pleased with you" look. It was what the girls called mother's evil eye: glaring stare, eyes narrowed, mouth set hard. Sophie straightened in her seat, moving her gaze back to the splendid altar where Bishop Hayes and Father Murphy, the local priest, stood in front of the large golden cross while reciting the liturgy.

A gentle bell tinkled. Sophie lifted her skirt and undergarments and maneuvered herself to the kneeler, closing her eyes in prayer. Other than the occasional Mass, Christmas, Easter, and a smattering of holidays, church was something that received little attention in the Rogers' household. Thankfully. Sophie had little time or inclination when it came to things like confessions and long, knee-abusing services.

The Bishop recited long Latin prayers that seemed to drone on for hours, not minutes.

Finally, he signaled the congregation to rise. Crossing herself, Sophie rose and slid back on the seat. At last, he began to give the eulogy to Julian in English. Bishop Hayes included prayers for the thousands of soldiers on both sides who had already been killed in the sweeping French countryside. He spoke of Julian's deep religious beliefs and the fact that he was certainly in God's heavenly paradise. The lad, said the Bishop, fought on the side of right and for justice and, as a good and faithful Catholic, he was surely resting in the arms of the Holy Mother.

Although she was sitting a few rows in front and to the right of Sophie, the sound of Mrs. Laurents' sobs stabbed into her heart like a lance. The war had begun a mere seven months ago. Tens of thousands of soldiers—no one knew exactly how many—had already died. It was impossible to even imagine such carnage.

According to Sophie's mother, Julian' parents had begged him not to sign up as a soldier for the French army. But when he had read the newspaper accounts of how the German army had marched across Belgium, a neutral country, and laid waste to its capital, murdering innocent citizens in the process, it was the last straw for the conscientious young man.

It was difficult for Sophie to understand why an American-born boy would volunteer to fight in a foreign land. Yes, his parents had immigrated to New York from Belgium before his birth, and yes, he had relatives still living there; but signing up for the war was tantamount to a death sentence. Or so just about everyone believed. Of course, he wouldn't listen to reasoning. He was stubborn...and determined to make a difference.

And what difference did his death make? Sophie thought, swiping at a tear straddling her cheek. None, except for the terrible grief for those left behind. Losing Julian caused nothing but misery for those who knew and loved him. *Where was the sacrifice and pride in that?*

Tears filled her eyes and then streamed down her cheeks. Opening her handbag, she pulled out a freshly laundered lace-edged handkerchief. As she dabbed her face, Sophie heard a strange swishing sound that caught her attention. To Sophie's left, in the aisle, three scrub women had appeared out of nowhere. One was rather large. Not fat, really, but broad shouldered. She casually dusted the wood trim of the pew's end panels with a soiled towel, then squatted and continued to clean an area close to the floor. The other woman was much taller and quite thin. The third was a homely girl with a large nose. The poor dear was dressed in a faded blue skirt and loose white blouse. Her dull red hair was braided and hung down her back. The other two looked to be middle-aged, perhaps because they both wore old-fashioned, baggy dresses.

The bigger woman carried a metal bucket and a string mop. Sophie fought back a smile when she saw that the woman's crisp white apron barely fit around her torso and that the bow on the back of her rather thick waist was coming untied. When the woman set the bucket on the marble floor, it made a hollow clink, followed by a splashing sound. A wave of water spilled out. Looking disgruntled at the mess, she let out a huff. Sophie giggled, diverting her eyes forward once again for fear that she would break out in an inappropriate laugh.

Yvette and her mother had been disturbed by the activity. Mother shot a questioning glance at Sophie. With a shrug, Sophie tipped her head to the left a few times, signaling to her mother that something seemed amiss. People simply didn't clean the cathedral during services. It was all so strange. So unusual. So amusing watching their utter clumsiness. Her mother frowned and returned to her prayers. It seemed that most everyone else, still deep in prayer, didn't notice the odd disturbance. One elderly woman a few rows in front of Sophie, however, turned and shot an angry, disapproving glance at the scrub women before looking forward again.

Footsteps echoed as a man wearing a long brown coat walked down the side aisle. He was almost bald, though the thin fringe of very dark hair around the bottom of his head made him look a bit like a monk. Something caught Sophie's gaze as he passed by. He carried a lit cigar in his right hand. Good heavens! No one dared to smoke inside the cathedral. Everyone knew that. As he settled in the empty spot on the end of row in front of her, Sophie scooted directly behind him and tapped him on the shoulder. He half-turned to look at her.

"Excuse me, sir," she whispered, just as the organ music resumed. Raising her voice slightly, she added, "You need to snuff out your cigar."

When he twisted around and scowled at her, Sophie drew back. She was sorry she had said anything. Those eyes. Dark. Cold. So angry. Then he turned forward again, raised the cigar to his mouth, and drew in a mouthful of smoke. She couldn't believe it. How dreadful! The ill-mannered lout blew out a murky gray puff. It was as if he were defying her...and disrespecting the church. Maybe even God.

21

Surprised at the man's arrogance, Sophie scooted to the right, as far away from him as she could, so that her body was smashed into her sister's. "Can you believe that?" she whispered to Yvette.

Yvette was also watching him. Shaking her head, she said, "What in the world is going on?"

Sophie shrugged.

Another man approached, pausing in the aisle beside the rude man. Both men were fairly dark-complected. Italians, she surmised, noting their coloring and features. This one, much younger, had a full head of curly coal black hair and long sideburns. Did they know each other? And then she noticed that he, too, carried a lighted cigar. She and Yvette exchanged confused glances.

Before Sophie could say anything to him about the matter of smoking, a bell sounded signaling the parishioners to kneel again. Both her mother and sister went back to the kneeler. But not Sophie. Instead, she watched as the balding man motioned to the younger man, indicating that he should continue walking. With that, he ambled forward slowly, stopped, crossed himself and kneeled to pray. But why there? In the walkway? Why didn't he move into one of the empty pews? She moved to the end of her row, craning her neck to see what he did next.

The curly haired man kneeling in prayer wore a long black woolen coat. It had frayed elbows and looked as if it had faded several shades. And the bottoms of his shoes, visible as he knelt, were riddled with holes and the heels were worn away on the edges. Obviously, he was one of city's poor who had come to seek solace.

Suddenly, the scrub woman wearing the apron leaned her mop against the wall and quietly moved towards the kneeling man. So did the woman with the dust rag. The third one with the large nose had been busying herself in the vestibule. She joined the other two women. They exchanged quick looks, nodded, and edged forward in the direction of the altar. The Italian in front of Sophie rose, his gaze now fixed on the three women. He stood, frozen it seemed, his gaze moving from the man kneeling is the aisle and the scrub ladies.

Why were the cleaning women acting so strange? And why was the man in prayer holding that horrible cigar? He seemed to be so deep in prayer that he was unaware of their approach. Then, in a sudden move, he lifted his head, reached inside his coat and pulled something out, placing it on the floor against one of the huge marble pillars. He touched the glowing tip of his cigar to a thick cord protruding from the packet. It only took a few seconds for the cord to ignite. In an instant, the curly haired man was on his feet, racing up the aisle in Sophie's direction. The realization of what was happening struck her. "Oh my God! It's a bomb!" she said with a gasp. She stood up, only half aware of the words that escaped her lips.

The next moments were a blur. The rude man standing in the pew in front of Sophie made an abrupt move into the aisle, bolting back towards the main entrance. One of the parishioners, a handsome middle-aged man with a mustache and short brown hair, tackled him before he could make his escape. "You're under arrest!" he yelled, pinning down the Italian.

One of the cleaning women shouted, "Stop!" She grabbed the man who had lighted the bomb and was joined by the younger woman in an effort to wrestle him to the floor.

Yvette and her mother were now standing, watching, utterly confused by the scene.

Pointing forward in horror, Sophie could see that the fuse was still burning. "Run!" she shouted, as she began to scurry to the back of the cathedral.

The elderly usher, the man who had been bespectacled, bearded, and hunched over as he showed parishioners to their seats that morning, raced past them at breakneck speed.

In the melee, the white wig was sliding off, revealing his light brown hair. The old man wasn't old at all. He was an undercover police officer. Of course!

Her mother and sister were out the door. Sophie stopped momentarily, glancing back just in time to see the half-disguised policeman pounce on the explosive and snuff out the burning fuse.

"I simply can't believe so many of the parishioners didn't know what was happening," Sophie commented to one of the police officers, a rotund young man, outside on the landing at the top of the front steps. "How could that be? I mean, it was total chaos for a while."

He shrugged. "I think the folks all the way across, on the other side of the church, didn't hear the ruckus. St. Patty's is like a gigantic cavern, isn't it now, miss?" His Irish brogue was quite evident.

"Yes, but—"

He shrugged, his lips puckering. "What with the bells sounding, and the organ hymns, and the Bishop talking loud like he has to, and the echoes and all that. Folks that was sitting closer to where you was over there on the north side where all of the commotion was going on. Well, I think theys the ones what got out, like you ladies, here." He motioned to Sophie, Yvette, and their mother with a sweep of his hand.

"And those cleaning ladies? They weren't women at all, were they?" Yvette asked.

"Oh no, miss. They was all undercover New York Police officers. At their finest, I might add." He straightened his back and smiled, his pride simply oozing out. "The Department has been watching those two Sicilians for quite a while. Months, from what I'm told." He nodded, wearing a confident expression. "They won't be planting no more bombs, ladies. I can promise they'll be locked up for a long time to come."

Sophie said, smiling. "I cannot imagine what would have happened if it weren't for your fine work. Most especially, the officer who put out the bomb before it exploded."

"That certainly took a lot of courage," Yvette added. "Please thank all of the police officers on our behalf. We all owe them our lives."

"Ah. That was Detective Willie Durant hisself. I will certainly pass

23

your message along to him, miss," he said. With a tug on the brim of his cap, he descended the stairs to a waiting vehicle.

For the past twenty minutes, their mother had been silent. Now, standing between her two daughters, she muttered. "*Mon Dieu, Mon Dieu!*" It was as if she finally realized the reality of what had happened.

"It's all right, Mother. It's over now," Sophie reassured, reaching out and squeezing her mother's arm.

"But we didn't have time to finish our prayers." Mother blinked several times, her brow furrowing. "We should go back inside, *n'cest pas?* To finish Mass."

"No, mother. We should go home now. You need to rest," Yvette said, gently stroking her mother's cheek with the back of two fingers. "You do look faint."

"And what about the Laurents?" With a puzzled, distant expression, their mother shook her head. "I should be there to comfort Marie. I should go to their home later, don't you think? Poor, dear Marie. For a mother to lose a child." She shook head, her eyes suddenly misting. "It's simply unthinkable."

"We'll see the Laurents at their home for the memorial tomorrow," Sophie assured. "Remember?"

"Oh...*oui*," she said with a vacuous gaze, brushing away a tear that escaped her left eye. "I suppose you're right. *C'est bon. C'est bon.*"

"I'll get a taxi. Mr. Mueller wouldn't be here to pick us up to take us to the restaurant for another hour," Sophie said. "We need to go home now. We'll have lunch there."

Yvette nodded her agreement. "Come, mother." She slipped her arm around their mother's back and guided her down the steps to the sidewalk.

The threesome made their way to the curb in front of the grand cathedral. All but one of the police cars were gone. The sidewalk that had been cordoned off to the public was now open again. The ever-present throngs of pedestrians pushed their way along Fifth Avenue at a hurried pace, late for this or that, as if nothing had happened. Motor cars and trucks rattled along, horns blaring out their "a-ooh-ga's." Life, it seemed, had already returned to normal.

And yet, as Yvette and Sophie helped their mother into the back seat of the taxi, Sophie knew that it might be a long time before life in New York City would truly be normal again. She read the newspaper, much to her father's displeasure. "Girls shouldn't trouble themselves with politics and the woes of the world," he would tell her.

Which immensely annoyed Sophie and made her all the more determined to keep up on the latest happenings. She simply refused to bury her head in the sand. She knew that the economy was terrible. Too many men were unemployed. People, and especially the immigrants, were starving... and angry, like the men who tried to blow up St. Patrick's and other Catholic churches. On top of that, the war overseas was claiming the lives of a generation of young men not only from England, France and Russia. The Germans and their allied countries were suffering greatly as well. The United States, the world, everything was in turmoil. At that moment, Sophie set her mind to find a way to help. But what could she, a woman who hadn't quite yet reached the age of majority, hope to do?

Vain Ambition's Cure

By Stanley Gedzelman

Is poetry better than prose?
I'm quite sure that nobody knows.
Should poems have meter and rhyme?
Yes, I think, most of the time.
My poems are witty and light.
I find that they're easy to write
Why then have I not won a prize?
They're not that good I must surmise.
In any case I should feel great.
For anything I can create.
I can't compose like Bach or Brahms.
My lectures don't inspire psalms.
My science is middling to fair.
I don't build or even repair.
I can't paint a portrait or draw.
I'm not fit to practice the law.
I neither can heal nor can cure.
My visage excites no allure.
In swimming, in biking, or track.
I find myself back in the pack.
I'm not shrewd and can't play poker.
My humor is mediocre.
Yet I have no cause to complain.
My life's filled with more joy than pain.
And though my skills are far from great
Its enough to appreciate.
The great things that others can do.
And most of all how I love you.

The Last Storyteller

By Audrey Kalman

HONORABLE
MENTION

The world begins to reflect again in the storyteller's eye. It is as if a veil had covered that aqueous, convex organ, a veil brought down by weariness: twenty- two acclaimed works of fiction written over thirty years, twenty-two stories read and re-read, well-thumbed, wept over by groups of earnest, literature-loving women. Some even turned into screenplays and eventually movies. Coming down the other side of the arc of her career to land in this cozy, retired life, leaving others to wound and entertain.

Now she sits before her tiny desk staring out over the city day after day.

The HomeAssist Bot was sent away weeks ago. Her apartment is high and tranquil as it has always been. The pigeons trill outside the window; ambient music wafts from the room's EnviroSystem.

She has typed to the end of the single sheet of paper, covered it front and back with words crowded side to side and top to bottom. She was never meant to use this single sheet; she had finished with all that nonsense years ago. But this obviously is merely a prologue.

Rima has begun to suspect that something about the surgeon's hands has brought back this creative urge. She presses her abdomen where the transecting scar has already all but disappeared. Daily, her suspicion grows. What did the dear doctor leave behind inside her? He could not have, would not have, augmented her without her knowledge. In that case, she could have him arrested!

Besides, he seems too thoughtful and backward-looking to have perpetrated such a crime. Coincidence, then?

All this speculation is not moving her writing forward. She faces the forked tongue of destiny—or some such nonsense—a path leading here and a path leading there, with "here" and "there" equally murky. In no way is she ready to take this on. The words choose her. Without paper, they flitter from synapse to synapse and disappear in the aging and disconnected segments of her brain. She can't tell her family of her dilemma; her daughter would only shake her head. "You could fix all of that, Ma," she would say, and dial up the schedule of the nearest Augmentation Clinic. "You're so goddamn stubborn."

And she is. Obstinacy is one of her most enduring personality traits. Also: *inflexibility, perseverance, contumacy, pigheadedness*. The storyteller pictures herself with the head of a pig and smiles. How Andrea would hate to have a pigheaded mother.

Rima leaves the table and stands before her apartment's one big window. Her view extends to the ocean over an angular forest of buildings. Most people don't want windows in their dwellings. They would rather have enormous walls covered with ViewScreens so they can feel as if they are anywhere in the world or the universe. Rima rents this place cheaply because the building owner has not yet removed the large windows left over from a bygone era. The window faces west and on clear evenings she likes to watch the blaze that precedes the sun's nightly extinction. But today's sky is murky and the sun is no more than a green-yellow smear behind the clouds.

It only makes sense, Rima thinks, staring out the window into the descending darkness, to contact the blasted doctor who, she is coming to believe, got her into this mess in the first place. She turns from the window to the interior and reluctantly switches on SearchAssist, although she turns it to speaking mode. "Locate Dr. Dean Connaster," she says aloud to the empty apartment.

SearchAssist whirs for a moment, then speaks back to her. "Located." "Contact," says Rima, and sits once more at the desk before the full sheet of paper to await the connection.

"Doctor? It's Rima Marginaux. Do you have a minute to talk?"

Her call has taken him by surprise. "I—yes. Of course. Is everything all right? You're feeling better?"

"Yes, yes."

"No pain?"

"Not that kind of pain."

It's clear the doctor isn't sure how to respond. From his side of the connection Rima hears a high wailing sound followed by the doctor's laugh. "A sea bird," he explains. "I'm out walking."

Rima jumps into the conversational opening. "Hadn't taken you for a walker."

"Oh yes," the good doctor says. "I have my mother to thank for that. A real fresh-air fanatic. I'm sure you haven't gotten in touch to talk about fresh air, though."

"No."

Rima has turned AutoAmbiance off in her apartment and it is growing dim with the gathering darkness outside. She takes a breath. There is nothing for it but to forge ahead.

"I've been writing again," she says.

Dr. Connaster feels a tingle of nerves not unlike the anticipatory prickle he used to feel before a date with Terilyn. He is not sure why he asked Mrs. Marginaux to meet him in his office. He will have to fix the billing codes so the visit is compensated. A café would have been too public and his home too private, although this will be a most private transaction.

He glances down to the box at his feet. What possessed him to keep the ream of paper for more than twenty years? The printer for which it had been intended had been long ago recycled. Yet he has lugged the ream of

27

paper with him as he moved from one apartment to another.

Paper is not illicit, simply irrelevant. Dr. Connaster knows there are societies of collectors who make it their life's work to preserve the past, as if steam ships and microwave ovens still had purpose. He has always thought of himself as a man of progress, who prefers to set his gaze ahead and not behind, which makes his attachment to the paper even more anomalous.

And now he is about to give it away to Rima Marginaux, simply because she asked. Rather than seeming surprising, his inclination to give her what she has asked for appears to be a natural outgrowth of the un-ease he has been feeling lately. He remembers how ordinary he felt after his augmentation, completely himself, to such a degree that he wondered whether the procedure had actually been done. Then, as his memory sharpened and his brain buzzed with a singleness of purpose he had never experienced, even in the halcyon days of his youth, it became clear that something other than his own blood ran through his veins.

Dr. Connaster finds himself now in the grip something impenetrable.

He hears a rap on his door and smiles to himself. The woman who refuses augmentation and contacts her surgeon in search of paper chooses also to circumvent the hospital's announcement system and rely instead on the strength of her knuckles, making a hollow, human sound with the tap of bone against laminate. To honor her, Dr. Connaster foregoes the auto-open, rises from his desk, and crosses the room to admit her himself.

He realizes he has never seen her standing up, their previous encounters having been as doctor and patient, with her seated or in bed. She is a foot shorter than he, and slightly stooped, so he looks down at the top of her head with its halo of thin white hair and spotted skin showing through. She looks good for a hundred and seven, but her spry figure might conceal the deep interior spread of mental incapacity.

Dr. Connaster stands aside and ushers her in. Her step is firm and her balance good, he notes. "Sit, sit."

She settles into the guest chair and looks up at him. "All right, then. You got the goods, bub?" Her mouth wrinkles into a smile and Dr. Connaster sees again the woman on the book jacket cloistered behind the older Rima Marginaux's face.

"Right here." He lifts the paper from the box and sets it on his desk.

Together they contemplate the brick of processed wood pulp.

"I'm sorry to ask this," she says. "Could we open it? I don't imagine anything would have happened to it but I'd rather not lug it all the way home and find out—"

"Of course." Dr. Connaster wishes now for the cup of tchochkes that long ago adorned his desk, filled with useful items: scissors, pens, pencils, even a slim silver letter opener Terilyn had given him. He keeps those at home now, in his bedside drawer. No need for such physical items these days, when anything can be opened with a word, a whisper, a thought.

Not the ream of paper, though. He slips his finger inside the flap at the end. The glue has dried and the flap lifts easily. Gently, so as not to wrinkle the remaining paper, he slides out the top sheet and places it on the desk. It's perfect, white and opaque, corners pleasingly squared.

Rima Marginaux nods. "I believe this will do just fine. What do I owe you?"

Dr. Connaster waves his hand. "It's yours. I don't have any use for it. I'm not even sure why I kept it." He leans back in his chair. "Although maybe I could keep this one sheet?"

"Of course."

Rima Marginaux busies herself refolding the flap of the package and lifts a briefcase from the floor to his desk. Dr. Connaster hadn't noticed the briefcase until now, another relic, smooth black leather with the initials RSM inlaid in silver beneath the handle. She pops the clasp and nestles the paper inside. Dr. Connaster feels time running down. Their transaction is nearly complete. Words jumble in his head. He's glad he muted the Emo-Sensor or it would be going crazy now, desperately playing soothing tones to pacify his agitated brain.

"Mrs. Marginaux," he says finally, desperately, as she snaps the briefcase shut and prepares to stand.

"Oh, call me Rima, please. You've seen my gall bladder. I hardly think we need to be on such formal terms."

"True. Rima—" The name feels oddly intimate on his lips. "I—"

"You're wondering what I'm working on, aren't you?"

"Yes. That, and I—well, I'm hoping to keep in touch. I know it's highly unusual. Of course, only if you want to."

"I would enjoy that," Rima Marginaux says. She has made her way to the door. The weight of the paper in the briefcase seems to have tugged her downward another few inches. She looks back at him expectantly.

"Dean," he says. And then, to give her an option, "If you'd like."

Rima Marginaux nods and lets herself out. Dr. Connaster sits for a long time staring at the rectangular white sheet on his desk.

Rima places herself once more before the typewriter. The stack of paper rises beside her. She rolls a sheet into the platen, relishing the zipping sound as the gears feed the sheet into position. Now she can really begin.

Except now she is not sure where to go. She finds herself thinking of Dr. Connaster—Dean—and his very handsome face as he earnestly asked if he could keep in touch. Why had he done that? "Don't be foolish," she murmurs aloud. "He's fifty years younger than you at least."

A love story, then? Why is her old blood surging as if with the hormones of adolescence? But love stories lead inevitably to heartbreak, and she can't survive that. Her mind ranges over the other great themes: war and peace, betrayal and forgiveness, sin and redemption. Not even the most grand seems equal to the insistence throbbing within her. And so she begins where she always used to: with a sensation, a single thought, the merest scrap of a memory.

Once upon a time she loved a man who died. She threw her body in with his. They made love, as it was fashionable to call such couplings in those days. They spent long Sundays in bed feeding each other toast and coffee, brushing away the crumbs that pinpricked their bare skin beneath the sheets. They went to the beach. Once she grabbed his hand and shouted over the roar of the waves: "I want to come back here with you when we're seventy." He laughed in his happy, indulgent way, leading her into the surf. His young body was hot and the water was cold. Twenty years later he left her alone with their two teenage daughters.

She ran after his body, down the long hallway of a hospital that was the predecessor and the prototype of the one where Dr. Connaster now works, but it was too late.

The lonely years accumulated and when her seventieth birthday approached she flew away by herself to one of the few beaches on the continent still hospitable to human feet walking in the sand. She raised a hand to block the molten lozenge of the sun. As her last day of being sixty nine rolled away, Rima spoke a single word that she would never say again, her dead husband's name.

The first sheet has rolled all the way through and emerges patterned with grief. "Really, Rima," she says aloud to herself, going so far as to make a "tsking" sound with her tongue. She grasps the page and rips it from the typewriter's clutch, a bit too forcefully, perhaps, then crumples it and throws the irregular ball in a gentle arc toward the kitchen.

"Now that you've got that sentimental mush flushed out," she mutters, selecting another blank sheet from the pile, "You can begin."

Rima's writing rushes forward with the steadiness of rain beating on a tin roof. Words fall from the ends of her fingers. She barely thinks.

The lights begin their scheduled glow as dusk falls. Hunger carves an emptiness under her ribcage and her scar throbs, but she keeps at it with the homophonic clacking of the keys and the satisfying *scritch* of the carriage back at the end of each line. She wonders during a brief pause how she was able to write her entire first novel this way, with every word ossified as soon as she spits it onto the page. But she finds great satisfaction in keeping her ideas to herself until she feels ready to share them, the paper an extension of her brain and not mixed up with all the other connected brains of the world.

At last, her empty stomach drives her to stop.

Based on his newfound interest in *Le Malaise,* Dr. Connaster has added himself to the list to receive a daily research précis. This streams in with the rest of his news and is read out to him as he prepares for his day, showering, drinking his coffee, riding the tube to the hospital. It's mostly the usual dry stuff— statistics, numerical indicators. He has chosen a scientific briefing rather than the titillating synopses intended to enthrall members of the public with the stories behind the numbers. Dr. Connaster has always believed in the inherent danger of anecdote, the way a story can get inside you and obscure the truth.

Oddly, he has heard nothing more about the International Committee for the Study of *Le Malaise* since its announcement at the medical conference. But, like so many interests sparked and attended to briefly, his interest in it has been subsumed by the greater urgencies of daily life, the flow of patients into and out of his office, mornings in surgery, afternoons in rounds, evenings spent with colleagues or, if he is feeling melancholic, alone in his favorite chair with gloomy music as accompaniment.

One morning while stepping out of the shower he hears something that stands out from the rest of the stories. It's a notice of an upcoming *in-person* event to be held in his city. "Interested parties should contact Dr. Robert Tipton for details." Dr. Connaster recognizes the name of the lecturer who led the session at the medical conference, the one who got him interested in the first place. "Bookmark," he says, rubbing the towel over his back once more before dropping it into the bin for the CleanerBot to launder.

He returns to his office that afternoon after rounds and pulls up the item. "Contact Dr. Tipton," he says.

The young doctor's face appears on his screen a few minutes later. Dr.

Tipton's features are impassive; he looks as if he could be an advertisement for skin smoothing gel. "Dr. Connaster," he says. "Thank you for contacting me."

"I heard about the meeting. I'd like to get the details."

"Of course. We have a few forms for you to fill out first. I'll send them over and we'll get you the details as soon as you've returned them to us." "I appreciate that. I'll watch my mailstream for them."

Dr. Tipton's smooth face cracks into a smile so slight it might merely have been a cramp in his cheek. "I'm afraid we're requiring—how shall I put it—*old fashioned* forms. Of course we'll send over a pen as well!" he finishes, and a small chuckle escapes his cramped smile. "Do you have a problem with that?"

Dr. Connaster leans back in his chair. "Not at all," he says. "I have my own pen, though."

"Excellent!" Dr. Tipton says, and smiles slightly more widely before cutting the connection.

The papers arrive at his apartment the following afternoon, presented by a painfully thin bicycle courier. Dr. Connaster accepts the package, artfully disguised as a delivery from a kitchen decorating company. He watches the courier's flat backside retreat down the hall to the elevator. How can such work still be allowed? He remembers the days of drones clogging the sky, hovering outside windows, delivering everything from toilet tissue to bourbon, and he remembers the legislation that banned them, the rise of the League of Human Workers, which sought to wrest a few professions from the clutches of the automata.

Two nearly transparent sheets covered in tiny printed words lie in the bottom of the box. Dr. Connaster scans them quickly to the end and finds a line where his signature is intended to go. What he will be doing, he sees, is swearing himself to secrecy. The idea makes him slightly uncomfortable. For all his retro hobbies and fondness for the accoutrements of the previous century, those are harmless pursuits. Where authority is concerned—the hospital administration, the government—he has never strayed from the proscribed path. He has learned to discipline his thoughts.

Very occasionally, alone in his apartment, Dr. Connaster talks to Terilyn. If he forgets to turn off the Sensor array he will be assaulted by a stream of responses and suggestions that are laughable in their inappropriateness. This oversight reminds him of the need for vigilance. Now, scanning the thin sheets, he certainly remembers, and flicks the switch. As always, without the array, the apartment feels somehow even emptier, devoid of an imperceptible hum, the way the kitchen of his childhood felt when the refrigerator motor cycled off.

The thin sheets awaiting his signature feel far weightier than any nostalgia for the past. He fingers them and lets his eyes absorb the words. He cannot help the feeling that he has been *selected*, despite the fact that he contacted Dr. Tipton and not the other way around.

"What do you think?" he asks Terilyn, or his memory of her. She never knew this world—it has leapt forward at such an accelerated pace in the fifty years since her death—and yet Dr. Connaster feels certain she would have known exactly what to do in this situation. He sits in his favorite chair and closes his eyes, lets the sheets flutter to the floor, consciously relaxing his digits, limbs, trunk, central nervous system. It is an ancient technique of meditation and it serves him well, he has learned, when he wants to open his mind to his dead wife's voice. After a few minutes he senses her answer. It comes not in the form of words but as a sensation traveling through his relaxed body.

This will be your life's work.

Harlem Blues

By Judith Shernock

In 1953 Harlem Jammed.
Not rocked, baby, Jammed.
As in close together
Making sweet , red jam music.
I, a little white girl
Adoring long, brown fingers
Tapping silver drums.
Pink mouths
Blowing brass trumpets
Planting rhythmical seeds
In a fallow heart.
Today, when down and out blues
Invade my soul
I conjure up red jam seeds
Sprouting an elixir of sound.
Music, mixed with blackness
Forces the sun out.
So yellow, so warm.

The Occupation of Joe Isamu

By Bill Baynes

The radio seemed so certain. The voices were so proud, so stirring. The sacred war was going well. It was nearly over. It made his chest swell.

Father would be home soon, Mama promised. He would take them to a bigger place, one with space for Hana-*chan*, who never stopped crying. Mama said the baby was hungry. Who wasn't?

Who isn't?

Six months later and the radio is silent. No good news. No songs to glorify the Emperor.

No electricity.

No Father either. Mama doesn't talk about him any more. Not since that day a few weeks ago when the soldier knocked on the door and delivered that telegram.

Now no food.

Mama hasn't eaten in days and she's gone dry. Nothing for Hana-*chan*. No milk and no money to buy any. He has to do something.

Huddled in the corner, his arms around his knees, he looks around the room, murky in the wan light from a single window. Not much remains of their meager belongings.

His stomach hurts.

He watches Mama giving his sister water. Hana-*chan*'s cries don't seem as loud lately.

Maybe he's getting used to them.

Mama glances at him and smiles gently. "Isamu—I love you."

He pushes himself to his feet and shrugs his skinny shoulders. He feels a little shaky.

"I need to move around," he says in his high-pitched voice. "I'll be back in a couple hours."

Mama purses her lips and nods. "Be careful."

He clatters down the rickety stairs. He crosses the shabby lobby and pauses, watching the street through the warped glass in the ornamental door. It's empty. It's early, barely light.

He turns up the collar on his thin shirt and steps outside, his bare feet in sandals. The October wind is icy. Unusual. It's often warm this time of year. It still smells like smoke.

Better than babyshit.

He looks around carefully. No rats. No dogs. Does he dare?

He has to. Mama, she has to take care of the baby. It's up to him to find some food. He has a plan. He has to go now.

He sets out across the ruins. It's the first time since that night six months ago when he and Mama dashed across the streets, dodging the burning buildings and the desperate neighbors. He's stayed close to home since then.

He used to roam as far as the docks, exploring and playing with the other children, but nothing looks familiar now. He keeps to the side of the dirt road, away from the holes and piles, trying not to draw notice. He trots past the temple his family used to attend. Two walls are standing.

That pile there, the one with the charred cart, that was the Sasaki family. He remembers the mother trying to save the baby strapped to her back, the padding smoldering, then her trousers flaming, her husband's too. They fell where they stood.

He tries to concentrate on what he's doing, but he can't keep the images from flashing across his mind.

The bombing was bad enough. Hearing the sirens every night, the drone of the B29s.

Never knowing the target. Waiting for the explosions.

Then the fire, the night it happened everywhere, the entire city filled with live sparks and then bits of burning wood and paper. It felt like it was raining fire.

Bursts of light flashed high in the sky and fell to earth, whistling. A huge glow spread over the city, showing the big planes, flying low, their wings slicing through columns of smoke rising from the ground.

The voice blaring through the intercoms was calm as always. "Take shelter. Do not panic. Take shelter. More attacks coming."

People stood in gardens and watched, spellbound by the spectacle. Red puffs of anti-aircraft guns sent dotted red lines across the sky. Thousands of cylinders dropped with a rushing sound like a downpour and then exploded into flames. Frail wooden houses bloomed alight.

He realizes he's been running. He stops and leans over, hands on knees, breathing hard, fiery images flooding his memory.

He spots a group of bigger boys in the distance. He heard they ran in packs now. He hides behind a water barrel outside the husk of a house.

That night, the night of the fires, he remembers he jumped in a water barrel because of the intense heat. He splashed Mama and his sister until they were soaked.

Then they ran across the streets, where telegraph poles and overhead trolley wires fell in tangles, him pulling his mother by the arm, her other arm holding the infant.

Today the wind is stiff, but nothing like the night of the fires. He saw a burning plank sail through the air and hit a man, killing him instantly. Fanned by heavy gusts, the flames spread as fast as people could flee.

Coils of black, choking smoke surrounded them, but there were unexpected open spots, where he and Mama coughed and gulped the good air. They couldn't hear each other over the roar of the firestorm.

Now the breeze blows the ashes like dirty snow over the acres of crumbled structures and charred rubble. When the bigger boys pass out of sight, he hurries past a shuttered shopping district. He waves to Mrs. Kuraki, mother of his friend Kenji, who died of the burns he suffered that night.

Isamu steers clear of the homeless in their lean-tos built against standing walls. He stays away from the few remaining brick or block structures, fearing the desperate people who shelter in the hollowed-out interiors.

He cuts across another block of desolation, girders in gestures of supplication sticking out of the blackened ground.

His feet are completely gray.

He catches sight of the Sumida and trots over the bridge spanning the river. When he looks down, he sees the thousands of bodies that clotted the water that night, living people splashing among the burned and drowned. The ghastly smell—will it ever leave? He retches and runs.

The next thing he knows he pulls up again, gasping. He's missed the last minute or two, caught up in what took place months ago.

After that night, he refused to leave the room for more than a few minutes. Stunned and numb, he spent those months staring at the walls and waiting for the awful announcements to begin again.

Instead the soldier came, saluting and bowing to Mama, leaving behind the yellow telegram and the awful emptiness.

"I'm sorry, Isamu. I know you miss your father."

Mama opened her right arm for him. She was holding Hana-*chan* with her left. He shook his head.

And then a day came, not long ago, when the air over Tokyo filled with airplanes, hundreds and hundreds of them, bombers and smaller fighters all flying over the city at the same time. He was terrified. He was convinced his life was over. He was almost glad.

But they didn't drop any death. Just leaflets. The Allies were celebrating the Emperor's surrender.

He reaches the port and the wind shifts, replacing the smoke with the smells of tar and rust, the metallic tang of water.

He spies a different gang of local boys, six or seven of them, dragging and shoving a heavy box. He ducks behind a huge container until the sounds of their struggle fade away.

He peeks around the corner and studies the scene. It never seemed so large before. Each the size of a large truck, the containers are arranged in long rows. They stretch as far as he can see.

He can barely glimpse the docks.

Large, pale men are working about 50 yards away, lifting and loading wooden crates. As he gets closer, he can hear them talking to each other in a language that sounds to him like spitting.

They must be Americans.

He feels a wave of revulsion. These are the men who destroyed his life.

But his plan is to find them. Waiting in line for the toilet yesterday, he heard two merchants talking about the invaders.

"Joe has so much food he doesn't know what to do with it all," one said. Isamu means to get some.

He swallows his disgust and approaches the men, wending past piles of equipment and large carts. One yells at him and waves him away, but he smiles and keeps coming.

Suddenly, a bulging net slams onto the asphalt, barely missing him. He jumps to the side.

Other men shout angrily. They shoo him and two begin to chase him. He scoots out of their reach. Clumsy and ugly, they can't catch him.

He continues until he reaches the piers. He wraps his arms around his chest against the chill and gazes out at Tokyo Bay. All the ships that arrived in the past few days, hundreds of them, fill the harbor. Isamu is amazed. Giant battleships, dozens of smaller ships, little boats zipping from one to another. So many Americans.

How can he get one to pay attention to him.

The Party

By T.M. Caldwell

I ought to be holding a tray of some kind.

A soft December breeze wafted a mixture of food and floral scents past Maria, chilling her slightly; she clutched the expensive beaded shawl Ana had lent her around her shoulders—a match for the gorgeous silk dress she'd borrowed—and tried to look like she belonged.

Ana belonged. Ana was the whole reason Maria had come to this party. Her best friend looked back at her in exasperation, grabbed her free arm, and leaned in close so she could be heard over the noise of the party. "Come on, Maria! You need to get used to this if we're ever going to hang out again."

Trust Ana to think that. Sometimes her best friend could be downright naive in her single-mindedness. But despite her reservations she let Ana tow her into the crowded back yard. After all, this could be the last time she ever saw Ana. She better make it count.

Tomorrow morning Ana and her once-in-a-generation face would be on a plane to Rio de Janeiro, off to start her modeling career thousands of kilometers away from Honduras and her best friend. And I will be finding Giselle's shoes, doing laundry, and waiting tables for Mom.

She paused, forcing Ana to stop as well, and gestured to the enormous house behind them. "Are you sure my sister is going to be safe up there? Really, really sure? She's only four—she could be getting into trouble."

"Of course! And she was sleeping by the time we finished tucking her in. How much trouble can a sleeping kid get into?"

"Lots." Maria crossed her arms. "I don't know about this. Do we have to be here? Can't we go somewhere else?"

"For the last time, stop being such a spoilsport. Would I put Giselle in danger? She's practically my baby sister, too."

If you really wanted to hang out with me before you leave forever, you could have done it at my house. You know Mamá will kill me when she finds out I brought Giselle here. But this was so important to Ana. She'd spent their whole final week of high school talking Maria into agreeing to go. Most of her little tricks don't work on me any more, and I thought when Mamá told me I had to babysit that would be the end of it. But when Ana started crying...she never cries. Not unless it actually is important. Though why she wants me to meet these people...

Maria sighed and looked around again, trying to see the event with objective eyes. Most of the people here were older than her seventeen years. This looked more like a society party than a drunken brawl. Everyone here was so well dressed, attractive, clearly wealthy. Maybe Giselle would be safe.

"You're right." Maria sighed. "But Mamá... "

"I don't think you'll need to worry about that." Ana took her by the arm and pulled her along. "I saw a nice quiet couch where you can sit until you've gotten over yourself. Then I'll introduce you to some people."

Maria plopped down and rolled her head around on her neck, hoping to loosen her shoulders. Their couch was only one of many; Maria could see a number of couches and seats set about for conversation, many of which were occupied. She wrinkled her nose at a couple making out, only partially obscured by pots of plants. "They ought to get a room."

Ana followed her gesture and laughed. "God, Maria, don't be such a prude."

"I'm not a prude. He's going to leave some huge hickeys, the way he's sucking on her neck."

Ana leaned back into the couch cushions and scrutinized the couple for a moment. Her brows drew down. "Yeah, don't watch that. Ew." Her expression lightened. "Oh, hey, here's Uncle Pablo. I was hoping to introduce you two."

These people don't care who I am and I won't remember them next year. But it would make her friend happy. Maria steeled herself and smiled as a man, probably in his forties, approached them. He wasn't much to look at, but his clothing had to be high fashion and expensive.

"Ana!" He beamed as he saw her.

She stood to greet him and clasped his hands in both of hers, greeting him effusively. They kissed each other on the cheek. "Uncle Pablo, it's good to see you. Thank you for inviting us. Can I introduce you to Maria?" She gestured toward Maria.

Maria rose, and he took the hand she extended to him, his grip firm and dry. "A pleasure," he said. "Ana has told me so much about you. It's nice to meet you at last." He kissed the back of her hand, his lips slightly damp, his eyes never leaving hers.

She flinched. Despite his friendliness, something about him stopped her breath and made her heart race. What has Ana been telling him about me? "Likewise." She bit her lower lip. "Ana said you're helping her start her career. That's very kind of you." Awkward, but at least her words had the benefit of being polite.

"Anything for my girl." His eyes slid to Ana, whose shoulders had inexplicably tightened. "Are you certain you have everything you need?"

"Yes." Ana's nod was a shade too fast. "Just like we discussed. No changes."

"Very well." His eyes slid back to Maria and for an instant his smile turned sardonic, though his expression resumed its open friendliness so quickly that Maria wondered if she hadn't imagined the harsh expression. "Feel free to enjoy the party. Have anything you wish. I hope you both have a pleasant evening."

Maria nodded as Ana thanked him and kissed his cheek again by way of parting. Laughing softly to himself, he wandered away.

"Why did he kiss my hand?" Maria asked Ana once she thought he was out of earshot. She rubbed the cooling damp spot against her thigh.

"I don't know. Maybe because you're too standoffish to be normal. Do you think you can handle getting a drink? I'm thirsty."

Maria's lips thinned. "Just because I don't let every guy slobber all over me doesn't mean I'm standoffish. You know how much I don't want to be here."

Ana sighed and pinched the bridge of her nose. "Okay, I'm sorry. You're right. I just want you to get used to this. It's important." She put on the pleading look that worked on all their teachers at school. "Please? For me?"

Maybe Ana felt overwhelmed, too. Flying off to another continent, moving away from her family and friends and everything she knew to live on her own...Maria resolved to be more patient. She only had to endure this for a few more hours. "Okay," she said, and attempted a smile. "And yes, I'm thirsty, too."

"Good!" Ana beckoned to a servant and ordered something unfamiliar for both of them. "Friends forever!" Ana toasted once the drinks arrived, and they clinked glasses and sipped.

Fruity. She couldn't even taste the alcohol. She could sure feel it, though. Her pulse thumped in her neck. She sipped again. The lights illuminating the back yard started to smear, and the stars above them spun slowly. The drink made her stomach gurgle. Sweat beaded her hairline and she pushed her shawl back onto the couch. "Wow. What did they put in this?"

Ana shrugged, faux-innocent and red-cheeked. "Alcohol, of course. It's not the first time you've had a drink."

"Yeah, but I don't drink whole drinks." Maria's lips tugged up. If they all tasted and made her feel like this, though....

"Only because you know your mom would kill you. You want another?" Ana fanned herself with one hand.

Maria sank into the soft comfort of the couch. "Sure. Maybe with a little less alcohol in it?" It wouldn't do to get too drunk. She should still check on Giselle.

Ana summoned over the same server, and with a mischievous look and a sidelong glance at Maria, whispered instructions in the man's ear. He nodded and left for the house.

"What was that all about? You're not having him bring me milk, are you?"

"No." The faux-innocent look was back. "I just asked him to get us something Pablo suggested earlier. It sounded delicious, so I wanted us to try it before you chicken out and go home."

"Less alcohol, right? Because I'm a little drunk already and I don't want to be puking in the potted plants by the end of the night."

"It'll be fine! You'll like it. I promise."

The servant returned with a tray containing two small vodka glasses filled with some red liquid, like a cross between tomato and pomegranate juices, and garnished with bits of greenery. Each girl took a glass. Maria thanked her and the servant glided off toward the bar on the other side of the yard.

The glass was warm, and the drink smelled salty, not sweet. "What's this?"

"House special." Ana tossed hers back, licked her lips, sighed, and set the little glass down on the ground. "I love you, Maria. You're my best friend and much more of a sister to me than any of mine. I want us to be friends forever. Please promise me you'll never leave me."

Maria sat back and regarded her friend with astonishment. Ana never spoke like that. Maybe she'd been right, and their upcoming separation was getting to Ana more than the girl would let on. She ought to put aside her discomfort and be there for her friend. "I'll never leave you. I promise." If only it could be true. She pulled the sprig of cilantro out of her glass and drank the contents down.

It was not like the fruit juices it resembled at all. The warm, tangy, savory drink felt almost as if it were passing directly through the thin membrane lining her mouth and throat, straight into her blood; wherever it touched tingled. Giddy, she licked her lips and the inner rim of the glass. Ana's face was flushed, her eyes sparkled, and when Maria looked at her she started to giggle.

Feeling unaccountably happy, Maria joined in.

She laughed until her belly hurt and then she laid back against the couch cushions and stared for a while at the smeared lights, her head spinning, before she flopped her head over to look at Ana. "What was that drink? Ana, I—"

The mirth slid off Ana's face. Her mouth gaped, her eyes opened wide, and she clutched at her stomach. "Oh," she breathed, and fell forward.

Maria didn't think. Her body, conditioned by four years of toddler rescue, slid off the couch, hit the grassy ground just as Ana's chest collided with hers. But Ana weighed more than a toddler, and between that and Maria's disorientation they both fell over. Maria used the couch to pull herself upright.

What on earth is going on? Ana's face was too pale. The girl curled around her belly and her lips drew back from her mouth in a rictus of agony. She kicked and writhed as a deep groan issued from the depths of her stomach. And then her muscles tightened and a flood of watery vomit surged from her mouth. The bile-and-alcohol smell made Maria's eyes water.

"Help! Please! Anyone!" But the party clamor trapped her words, and the party itself whirled around her. Nothing about this felt good any longer. Ana vomited again and Maria started to shake.

Maria's stomach turned to iron and collapsed in upon itself. She retched and slumped to the ground, narrowly avoiding Ana. Everything continued to rotate around her even after she landed on the cool grass; wretchedly she turned her head before she vomited again. A dark cloud gathered at the edges of her vision and flowed toward the center, obscuring the partygoers until all she could see were the lights, and the music became nothing more than cacophony, pressing in like fingers on her eardrums. Her mouth and sinuses burned. Her stomach contracted again and she coughed to empty her throat. The clogged feeling in her ears abruptly cleared and the music crawled into her head like some invading parasite and thumped her skull from the inside. Light pierced her eyes until all she could see was the red of the blood flowing through her eyelids. She could not close her eyes enough. Her mouth filled with saliva; she welcomed it, swallowed it down, hoping to clear away the toxic vomit, but her stomach sent it all back up again and a deep hunger replaced it, wracking her bones. She shivered in shock and horror as her hearing clouded again.

Are we dying?

"Here."

Maria opened one watering eye. Uncle Pablo had returned. Thank God. He'll help us, get us to a hospital. Save us. Hoping he could hear her through the noise, she croaked out a word. "Help."

"In due time." He watched her suffer, his face composed despite the avarice that lingered around his eyes.

Her relief dissipated, pulled under by the riptide of her pain, and despair replaced it. He did this on purpose. No one's going to save us. She clawed at the wet grass and gritted her teeth as another horrendous cramp struck. "How ... could you do this ... to her?" Ana's body twisted helplessly not far away.

He squatted down beside her and smoothed a piece of hair from her sweat-soaked forehead. "She asked me to. She drove a hard bargain, too. She insisted I take you as well." He shrugged. "I was going to feed you to her, but she wouldn't have it." A forest of legs muddled into view; he looked up and gestured past her. "That one first."

There was a wet, crushing, ripping sound.

A new, intoxicating smell permeated the night air, driving all of her questions right out of her head. It was like inhaling hope; it pushed aside her despair. Oh. Whatever that is. It will help. I just need...I just need...some of that. Her convulsions eased and left her muscles aching and abused. Ana pushed herself up and crawled away from her, obscuring the source of the scent, and Maria struggled to roll to her side so she could better see.

I'm hallucinating. It was the only possible explanation.

Ana, who'd somehow lit on fire and burned without exhibiting any pain, had dragged herself a meter or so away to neck with a tall, skinny, unappealing-looking man. He had enormous, white-rimmed eyes and a recessed, quivering chin and he panted for air as he burned, but neither of them made any effort to put the fire out.

Ana wasn't kissing him. No, she had bitten him. The delicious smell came from a bloody, gristly chunk of his flesh that she'd spat onto the grass. Her mouth moved rhythmically on his neck.

Maria gasped and pulled herself upright despite the tearing ache in the abused muscles of her belly. She leaned forward, stretched out one hand to warn Ana about the fire, but caught herself—red, flickering light, like flame but without heat or pain, rose from her skin as well. The fire isn't real. Her burning hand planted itself in the grass and she shifted her weight onto it without thinking, hauling her suddenly ponderous, clumsy weight after, as her mind uprooted itself to float, tethered, behind her.

She's drinking his blood.

The scrap on the grass would do her no good. She passed it.

I need to drink from the source.

She could smell him, rich and savory. Her tongue wet her lips.

No. Wait. What am I doing?

The man gasped and melted under Ana, releasing his breath in a long sigh. A shock like a nine-volt battery touching her tongue surged from Maria's tailbone up to the base of her skull. The entrancing smell trickled away, and her mouth made a tiny sound of protest. I lost my chance.

Ana, still on fire, dropped the body and turned to look at Maria. Her mouth was a gory slash in her face and dark blood spotted and stained the front of her vermilion dress. Her eyes were a strange and startling black, a darkness that had spread from lid to lid, corner to corner. She closed her eyes and tilted her head, displaying her graceful, blood-spattered neck. Shoulders rolling in ecstasy, she sighed as she exhaled much as the dead man had. "It was the drink," she murmured, almost as if she spoke to herself.

Darkness enshrouded Ana in her own endless night. She rose to her feet, her grace inhuman.

Minuscule changes to her face and skin smoothed out her few flaws until her beauty became surreal. Terrible. "Sister," she intoned through bloody teeth, her voice impossibly sweet. Maria pressed her hands to her eyes.

"Excellent," Pablo said behind her. She'd forgotten him. "Bring the kid over and remove the body."

Ana, smelling of old blood and bile, crouched next to Maria. "Here comes Giselle," she said as she stroked Maria's hair. Her voice descended like dandelion fluff, soothing and light. "All drugged for you. She won't feel a thing. And all you have to do is drink her blood. All the pain you're in will go away. Then we'll be young and beautiful and together forever. Like you promised me."

Horror crushed Maria's heart. I didn't promise you this. Never this. Her mouth moved but no sound came out. She tried again. Her voice sounded like a screwdriver scraping raw wood. "No."

More movement, and Giselle's limp little four-year-old body settled beside her. The child's skin radiated red, heatless fire. Ignoring the pain of torn muscles, she gathered her little sister to her, curling protectively around Giselle's boneless body. The monsters'll have to come through me first.

Her nose and mouth drifted down to the petal-soft skin of her sister's neck. Giselle smelled – her baby smell—like peace, like love and happiness. All the times she had fed Giselle, changed her, found her shoes, carried her around, combed her hair, played with her, read to her, survived the girl's tantrums flickered through Maria's mind. Too precious to lose.

But hunger, as unremitting as the beat of her sister's heart, shriveled her stomach and tore at her resolve. All she had to do to make the pain and hunger stop was break just a little of that tender skin and pull that happiness into herself. It wouldn't hurt anyone.

The succulent child shifted and smacked her lips. Maria froze, her mouth on the girl's neck. This isn't food. This is my sister. If I bite her, I'll kill her—just the same way Ana killed that man. With difficulty she turned her head and swallowed an excess of saliva. "No. Please, Ana. Not my sister."

Ana's brown eyes narrowed and she snarled. "I am your sister. She is nothing more than a half-sister, and you complain about her constantly. I have been with you since we were born. I will always be with you. Do it—show me that you love me forever, like you promised." The blood staining her skin emphasized her maniacal expression and Maria shrank away from her, clutching Giselle close.

Ana's fingers curled around Maria's upper arm. She pulled, her impossibly strong hands leaving deep bruises as she wrestled Maria's arm off the child. She stared straight into Maria's eyes, her bloody, savory breath washing over Maria's face. Maria inhaled deeply, helplessly. The blood on Ana's face and neck would do her no good; licking it off wouldn't satisfy the hunger beating at her from within. What kind of monster am I? She recoiled from herself in disgust and squirmed to better place her body between her best friend and the child, but Ana yanked at her arm. Maria yelped as muscles and tendons stretched. "Do it, or I will do it, and I will make it hurt. Like this." Ana closed both hands hard around Maria's arm and jerked.

The bone snapped. Maria's sight, hearing, and her sense of smell all vanished, replaced by pain that radiated so quickly from her arm to the rest of her body that in the first few seconds she could not tell what had broken. Her stomach rocked and leapt, and air exploded from her lungs in a shrill, thready scream. Ana twisted her arm, relocating the nexus of that pain, and then dropped it. Her useless limb struck her hip and side and she lost consciousness.

She woke to the smell of fresh blood, dance music booming in her ears. Hunger wore her like a second skin. Pain swamped her when she tried to move her arm, and her hot tears obscured her vision, turning the garish lights of the party to rainbows. Where was the blood? It smelled so close....

Where's my sister?

She sat up so quickly that she gasped and swallowed against vomiting up whatever might still remain in her stomach. But there was no time for that. Ana sprawled over Giselle, and the little girl's red-rimmed body rocked as she fed from it. Maria gritted her teeth as jealous, insane anger bubbled up. Ana was poaching her prey.

No. She's killing my sister!

She howled her rage and rocked herself to her knees, hobbled the meter or two that separated them, and seized Ana by the hair with her good hand. "You can't—"

"None of that." Pablo hurried forward and shoved her with casual strength. She fell back, her rear hit the ground and her head followed. Her arm and shoulder rocked against her and agony made the world uncertain for a moment. Something near her burst. Large, chunky drops of fetid wetness spattered her face and chest.

As her vision cleared, Pablo's body turned and slammed into the grass and goo leaked from his ruined head. She shrank back in horror. What on earth was that? But Ana did not react.

Giselle's red aura vanished just as an electric shock sent a surge of energy up Maria's spine and throughout her body. Through the music she heard a strange sound—a crack, or snap, like a tree limb breaking. Someone screamed, and then gunfire filled the air.

The party dissolved into chaos and the music abruptly stopped. Bullets struck the ground around Maria at random, and she rolled onto her stomach, screaming into the fouled lawn as the ends of her broken bone ground against each other. Shock after shock, as if someone tapped her with jumper cables just to watch her suffer, abused her nerves. But the shocking energy didn't dissipate into the grass below her. It built up, lessened the pain in her arm, cleared her head, and took the edge off the hunger that had turned her belly into a seething pit.

She turned her head, the better to keep Ana in sight. Another shock buzzed through her just as someone a few meters past Ana fell, dead, to the ground. Ana prostrated herself on the grass just past Giselle. Her little sister—

A gaping, raw wound marred Giselle's neck. Her thin brown hair matted to her neck and her open eyes stared up. She did not move.

I'll kill her! I'll kill her for this!

The unruly energy within her agreed. She pushed herself up—she could kick Ana to death— but something hot and fast passed right over her head and she dropped back to the grass, heart thumping in her mouth. A bullet. That had been a bullet and she'd nearly been shot. Fear consumed her unruly energy, wrung her between crushing hands, and dropped her attenuated body to the dirt. Blood and bits of bone—

Like popcorn in a microwave, the gunfire tapered off and then stopped. For a moment everything was quiet.

I Come From

By Maria Barr

I come from teenage migrant parents from acres and acres of cotton waiting for the endless rows of white to end, working in the blazing sun from morning until dark. I was old before I was young

I come from working for the rich man living in his huts, barns and shacks, from dog fights, and cock fights. From, there-are-no-tortillas-for-dinner. God please provide, once my tummy is full I thank Him a hundred times

I come from absence of dictionaries not one book, no math to learn. An almost complete Sears Catalog, the only school I know

I come from a family of illiterates, and me—that made one more yet.

I come from kindness...sublime. A story telling father, a warrior for a mom

I come from Elsa, in the great big state of Texas accordions, harmonicas and guitars, accents all around me, in word and in song.

I come from the land of the corridos, where stories are sung without books

I come from a long line of field laborers, I help my father build the canals to irrigate the cotton by moonlight with shovels, hoes and spades

I come to grow a perfect country garden—rows of tomatoes, okra and corn

I come from endless hours of labor, with no joy, a never-ending thirst for heavenly sleep—the perfect respite from the misery of working in the cotton fields from morning until dark with no hope and yet

I prayed

Heidi

By William Baldwin

When I look into your soul
Is it surprising that I want you,
Want you with all my being,
Want you with all my heart;
Because your goodness is so evident,
Because your power is so clear?

Parlor Tricked

By Shannon Brown

CHAPTER One: Confessions of a Reluctant Psychic

"So what are you thinking of doing with your life?" Mom asked yet again. I sighed and ignored the question. It was our usual routine. We were sitting in what everyone with a normal house would describe as a living room but what Mom always referred to as the parlor.

The room has been parlor-ized to the hilt, complete with a bay window surrounded by heavy drapes, and throw pillows scattered all over the place. A large round antique oak table sat in the middle surrounded by an assortment of mismatched antique chairs. Mom was sitting in one and I was across the table from her. As usual we were forgoing the parlor couch which was shaped in that Victorian style where comfort was a distinct afterthought. Next it was a smaller round table which held the haunted mansion lamp. A huge 1890s monstrosity, it had a heavy lampshade supported by a base made up of a large glass ball. I wished you could open the globe up so you could fit a goldfish inside. Sadly you couldn't.

"I know you don't like the question Victoria," Mom said. I shifted my eyes from the lamp back to her, hoping she didn't notice my lack of attention, but of course she did. "It's just that, you seem so directionless lately. I can't believe your spirits haven't been guiding you more."

"We've been over this Mom," I said, as I crossed my legs and shifted against my chair. "I didn't receive the family gift. I'm not psychic, or intuitive, or even particularly touchy feely. Nobody's guiding me."

"Of course you are, sometimes our gifts take their time manifesting," Mom said, then launched into her everyone has a spirit guide whether they know it or not speech, and I went back to pretending to listen to her.

If you haven't guessed by now my mother is the town psychic. Ironic since I am the town skeptic. She has the gift, her sister has the gift, all my cousins have the gift and my little sister Charlotte has so much of the gift she once appeared on an episode of the reality show *Mysterious Children*.

I didn't get the gift. I must have inherited my traits from my father's side of the family. We don't talk much about him since Mom is angry that she didn't have the foresight to see that he was going to pack up and leave when I was twelve.

Mom and Charlotte refuse to believe what is completely obvious. They are convinced I am in denial about my psychic abilities, but trust me, if I had any I'd be using them. I wouldn't have to study, because the answers would just come to me, and I'd be able to get money anytime I wanted just by hitting the track instead of toiling away at my job at Andy's Linen Outlet.

Only my mother would see going to school and working a nearly full time job as being directionless. Mom doesn't get the concept of general education either. Yes I assume at Harvard or something you have a major and you only take classes in your major but at Stallings Community College you have to take your G.E. classes first then pick a major later.

The reason why Mom is down on my attempt at getting an education is because she wants me to go into the family business. She has convinced herself that since my dormant psychic abilities have been so late in manifesting, I'm even more psychic than her or Charlotte. She's sure I'll have the strongest gifts of any of the Wiltons in at least three generations. Of course I am always quick to remind her that thanks to her quick elopement at age nineteen, I am only 50% Wilton. Half of me is Maldene, and like most of my father's family I have no psychic abilities whatsoever.

Mom's delusions came about one day when I was seventeen. She was watching Mitch Boudreaux on a talk show. He's that psychic who tries to reunite people with their dead relatives. While she was watching Mitch tell a woman her husband's stroke was not her fault, Mom's main spirit guide Claude informed her that I had stronger gifts than Mitch and if I wanted to, I could also help the world with them. Mom interpreted—help the world with my gifts—as have my own TV show and make lots of money to share with the family.

I'm convinced my family is crazy but I have to defend the whole psychic thing seeing as how it's our family's way of putting food on the table. My father's alimony is pitiful at best.

Darien Maldene is currently an unsuccessful lawyer living with his new family 45 miles away in the thriving metropolis of Trainfork, Ohio. I'm currently the only one on speaking terms with him. Charlotte only sees Dad on holidays and Mom has never forgiven him for cheating, or almost cheating on her. To be honest, I don't remember exactly what happened. Maybe my nonexistent spirit guide blocked it all out or something.

I am secretly convinced there is no Claude but if my mother's spirit guide is real he's pretty confused. Clearly Charlotte's the horse to bet on. She even almost had me convinced with her appearance on *Mysterious Children*. Especially the part where they were down in the basement and she entered a trance where she kept talking about getting the mail when it turns out that the town's postmaster was shot and killed in that same basement.

The grandfather clock chimed and I looked up. Crap four o'clock. I had been half listening to my mother drone on for 45 minutes. "Nice, talk Mom, but I gotta get to work, Liz is managing tonight, so I can't be late," I said.

I started my job at Andy's Linen Outlet my senior year of high school. At first it was easy, just 4 hours a day 2 days a week, but the second I turned 18 and started taking college classes, Andy's became convinced that now that I was a legitimate adult, and they could feel free to make my schedule nearly full time but without the benefit of having actual benefits.

I filled out the availability forms and clearly stated I had classes whenever I had them or didn't want to be scheduled. If anyone asks I do have classes on Friday night and Saturday morning. Not that this stopped them from trying to schedule me when I'm not supposed to come in. Everyone who works there is a little flaky and they're always trying to call me and have me take over their shift. I have a ringtone that is specifically from work that I never answer, but now they try to text me too. What a total invasion of my phone plan.

I was taking a late shift because I traded with Mandy so she could go see some terrible boy band in concert. I don't normally like working nights but I figured it would be good to have her owe me in case I need to rearrange my schedule on the fly.

After I clocked in I spotted an ancient jean jacket draped over one of the chairs in the break room. That meant Darrel was working. He's one of the older guys and a lot of my coworkers find him annoying, but he's always seemed cool to me. I usually try to get along with everyone here. I mean you can't choose your coworkers right. Anyway Darrel has never once mentioned that my mother is the notorious Madame Maldene or the ugly neon psychic sign outside our house so he is alright with me.

Out on the floor my manager told me to restock the kitchen section and I started making a lovely pyramid of coffee grinders when Darrel walked up.

"Hey where's Mandy tonight?" He asked.

"Yeah we traded shifts 'cause she wanted to go to a concert tonight" I told him with a shrug.

"Oh yeah a concert, cool, cool," he said. "Who's playing?"

"*The Funkay Monkeys*, I think, Mandy has terrible in taste in music."

"Oh yeah no shit," Darrel said, then realizing he just swore on the sales floor, glanced around looking for any hovering managers. "I used to go to concerts every weekend back in the day, real concerts, great bands, I got kicked out of some classic shows for smoking weed, it was worth it though." Darrel turned around once again to make sure nobody heard him say weed. I was beginning to change my view on casual drug use after talking to Darrel. Maybe pot really did fry your brain, after all Darrel was old and he still worked at an Andy's Linens. Well, whatever it wasn't my problem.

"I used to see a lot of shows here," he continued. "Great shows, I mean yeah everyone was past their prime but a good song live is always worth the price of admission."

"Wait, what do you mean, here?" I asked, trying to imagine a scenic towel side concert in our lovely bathroom department. It's not really a guitar solo unless it's performed atop a fake bed perched next to a display of body fat analyzing scales.

"You know, here at the Dead End," Darrel said. I gave him a confused look. "The River's End Theatre. Come on, you can't be that young."

"Oh yeah right, I forgot that used to be near this shopping center," I said, as I adjusted the sale sign in front of the grinders.

"It was this shopping center; they tore it down to build this Andy's Linens. So now there is one less venue in the world and one more boring ass place to get towels." Darrel forgot to turn around to see if a manger had heard his last slip up. "Of course I don't blame them the reputation it had.

I wouldn't be caught dead playing the Dead End."

"So why do you keep calling it the Dead End?" I asked Darrell. I had finished my pyramid of coffee grinders and now the both of us were restocking spatulas and wooden spoons.

Back in the eighties everybody who played here would die soon after. It was notorious for being the place where you played your final show that was never meant to be your final show. Ray Cordan, Stevie Mark Slicktone, Ken Kennedy of the Nowtones. Of course Johnny Billingsley was the most famous. He had a massive heart attack at the Carlton Lodge the night after his show here. Just when he was starting his comeback. Put this town on the map back in 87."

"Oh yeah, I remember hearing about that, I just didn't realize other people had died too." I said.

"Well nobody died on stage or anything like that, but still everybody started calling it the Dead End."

Just as Darrell was finishing his sentence, the lights flickered and went out for half a second. This happens a lot at our store. The managers keep telling us that there is some sort of faulty transformer outside but some of my coworkers are convinced that it's faulty wiring and the place is going to burn down at any second. My own theory is that it's the managers deliberately doing it to keep us employees on our toes. Darrell must have had the same theory because he mumbled something about restocking bath accessories and wandered off.

I spent the rest of my shift thinking about the River's End Theatre. I'd seen a show there once with my Dad. It was a magician and as far as I knew he hadn't fallen over and died the next day though if he had that's not the kind of thing you tell a five year old.

Johnny Billingsley died before I was born, but everyone in this town knew the story. At first it seemed like it was just a heart attack but then there were rumors that he was back on drugs and he overdosed. His autopsy came back inconclusive however.

One time as a kid my mom, sister and I all stayed at the Carlton Lodge. It was fun during the day playing in the pool but that night I got annoyed because we could have been home where we got good channels on TV and instead my sister Charlotte and I were forced to help my Mom hold a séance for Johnny on the floor of our room with the Ouija board she got at Target. You would have thought Mom would get some sort of psychic grade spirit board doused in holy water to keep the evil spirits away, but no ours was the kind they sell for sleepovers.

Neither Johnny nor any other spirits graced us with their presence that night. I think it's either because spirits don't exist or they don't like mass market discount store conjuring supplies. Mom was convinced it was because we were unable to book room 232. The room where Johnny died is always booked. It's become the lone tourist attraction in our suburban corner of Ohio.

When I got home from work that night Mom was still up, I could hear her banging around in the kitchen and there was no way to sneak by. I entered through the garage door and headed her way.

Thankfully the parlor is the only place in our house that resembles the Winchester Mystery house, the rest of our place strictly suburban Midwest. The house itself is over 90 years old but has been done and redone over the years. The kitchen was remodeled in the mid 1980's thanks to the money from my father's one big case. Though it looks shabby compared to the new houses with granite counters and Sub-zero appliances they built over by the newer high school it looks a lot more functional than the old forties era kitchen I have seen in pictures.

Mom was sitting at the table under the ceiling fan with lights that look like buttercups. "Hey, how come you're still up?" I asked as I pulled up a chair.

"I was having trouble sleeping," she said. "Things are about to break for us. I have the feeling."

I knew from vast experience that *the feeling* was something never to be questioned even though I never really knew what exactly it entailed. Mom coming up and talking about her spirit guides or paranormal messages I could understand. I've imagined a spirit whispering in her ear thousands of times, especially when I was growing up waiting for my own spirits to whisper something in my ear, but a feeling, crap everyone has feelings.

In my experience feelings are not something a mysterious dead person is whispering in your ear. The last time I had a bad one, it wasn't Harry Houdini's spirit telling me I was going to get a D on my last math test instead it was just my gut telling me that no matter how much I studied I was never going to grasp quadratic equations and that whole stupid order of operations thing.

I started to yawn and feign extreme exhaustion in order to get away when Mom started in on me again.

"I wish you were at least open to experiences," she said "I am," I said. "I just don't ever have any."

"Do you know how much of a struggle it is to have a daughter who doesn't believe in her own gifts? Sometimes I think you don't believe in any of it."

That's 'cause I don't, I thought to myself but I didn't dare say.

"I do believe in them Mom I have been standing up for this family my entire life, how can you say I don't believe?" I said, my eyes slipping past her to the hallway and our worn out stairs. What I wouldn't do to be upstairs lying in my cozy bed right now.

"Because I see the skepticism in your eyes and in your choices, I think it's the strength.

You are afraid of your own strength. Why can't you just trust me on this?" Mom said. "Trust you on what?" I asked.

"Things are finally going to break for us, and you are instrumental in that. Do you know how frustrating it is to have real gifts and have the town treat you as a joke? Just someone to appear at parties? Our family could do some real good around here if we only had the chance. Think of what we could do if the local police were not so narrow minded for example."

"Come on Mom, we've been over this. Nothing ever happens in this town. If there is a murder or disappearance I am sure you or Charlotte will sense something then you will go to the police and be vindicated." I sighed. Only my family would be disappointed in living in a crime free and quiet suburb.

"Mitch Boudreaux is getting a daily TV show," Mom said. "Christ Mom, is that was this is about?" I asked.

"He has the same type of gift we do. Mitch has never solved a crime or predicted one but he helps people, the same way Charlotte and I do when given the chance." Mom paused and took a sip of her tea. "Look I'm not saying we are worthy of having our own TV program or radio show or anything like that, but being able to pay the bills on time would be nice. The property tax is coming up too, if we can't pay it we lose everything."

Shit, the property taxes, every year the same worry popped up. "I'll start taking more hours at work Mom" I said.

"Do whatever you feel you need to. I really do think something positive is going to happen." She said. "I have the feeling."

Paradise Now

By Nader Khaghani

Remembering my father's favorite verses of Omar Khayyam

He Only Knows-
Edward J. Fitzgerald (Fitzgerald) translation
The ball no question of ayes and noes
But right or left as strikes the player goes
And He that toss'd thee down into the field
He knows about it all-He knows-He knows!

Universal Potter-My translation
Hey, you, thrown in this game like a polo ball
Hit hard from left to right you thrust
The one who threw you into this ball game
Why, He knows, He knows, He only and He

Part I.
The Heart Attack and the Fear of Death
This paradise not that one-My translation
This heart of mine, you will not unravel life mystery

All those learned theories of yours will fall short
Here and now with the cup and wine make your paradise
There and that paradise, you may find or may not

1 Awake?

Awake-Fitzgerald translation
Awake! For morning in the Bowl of Night
Has flung the stone that puts the stars to flight:
And lo! The hunter of the East has caught
The Sultan's Turret in a noose of Light

Before break of dawn, in the dark room, I had awakened to an excruciating pain in my lower chest, upper chest, all over my chest. At four AM the heart attack had hit me with vengeance. I was dying and did not know it.

Your Heart is in Slumber-My translation
Give me wine my heart inundated
This short-lived life can only end
Seize the moment life's fervor is short-lived
Awake, you seem awake, but your heart is in slumber

Two major arteries were blocked. My heart frantic for food and oxygen shot waves of pain through my chest. The struggle was for survival. The hardest working muscle wanted to live, to beat, and to nourish the rest of the body with a rich blood. Instead, it was choking, and was taking me to the land of the dead.

In the darkness of night, the underworld had thrown its doors open to my psyche. Its dead residents of Hades were urging me to cross over.

"Listen to the Nightjar blaring inside: a wounded heart. Release your soul. Get over here, join us in Hades."

As usual, I had locked the door to my apartment. Somehow, the spirit of death had found a way. Had the pain invited him in? He was there with a nightjar on his dark shoulder. The red-eyed bird was scrutinizing every pain in my chest. The reaper's flat hand frozen in a horizontal gesture induced a deeper stupor—a deadly sleep of which no awakening.

"Shut your eyes to the pain dear one; soon subsides. A dead senseless body feels no pain. Go deep. Let your spirit enter the dark tunnel of infinity. Stay in bed and meet with eternity in the second wave of heart attack. Rest assured the dead of my world are beyond every imaginable pain. Come."

In that condition and unknown to my conscious mind, the dark figures of my own inner world, had surfaced to negotiate the terms of death. My own painful body had it with the irregular heartbeat and throbbing pain; it was also urging me to end it once and for all.

The reaper sniffed me. Was I ripe to harvest?

"Good, you are stinky enough. The underarms are secreting the right stuff. Soon the life tension is gone, your whole body dies into a relaxed state. The ugliest smile of your life is coming. Dead folks always grimace. At birth, the face is God given, at death, the face is what you have earned while living. Let's see your stiff smile, charming, is it coming up?"

Another jab brings me back to the demands of the heart and pain of the body, not in my chest, but in my guts—a gut wrenching pain. Doubling into a fetus position did not help. I wanted to burp. I needed to burp this mother out.

To ease the pain I took a deep breath. Useless. Pain mixed with the pungent smell of my underarms. Earlier that night, I had also noticed it, an usual strong odor despite the underarm spray. The pain stopped the nose and kicked me in the guts harder. Was the reaper getting impatient?

I think to myself. "Goddamn gas must be trapped. What the hell did I eat?"

Little I realized the cause agony as other than food. No ordinary ulcer pain, never occurred to me the sting was the harbinger of death. Never thought the aching chest was foreshadowing a journey to down under of the underworld. Never realized that night I had a date with the reaper.

The invisible spirit of death had come to choke my heart and to squeeze out the multicolor white light of living. The self-delusion was killing me. Had I remained in bed long enough, it would have been my deathbed.

Now a heavy feeling in the pit of my stomach, burp, for relief I must burp. Let's get it out. I tried. Despite my efforts, the thing did not balk; it was not going anywhere, not up or down, just stuck. I threw up on the bed. As my stomach turned, I vomited more violently. Each time more stomach enzyme poured out. Still, something heavy in the pit of my stomach weighing a ton. Not subsiding, feeling worse, I cursed the damn ulcer acting up again. Then I had a smart idea, I am throwing up: this got to be an intestinal blockage, oh, yeah it had to be that. Blockage alright, but hardly intestinal.

A heart in slumber, a mind in deep sleep of self-delusion, I stayed in bed with my illusions, felt pain, and dreamt up self-diagnosed ailments. Then with all the energy I could muster, I forced myself to the bathroom. I found the medicine cabinet, ignored the bottle of the Aspirins, and swallowed a handful of Tums. Tum, tum, tum ran through my mind, I would be fine and pain free any minute I promised myself. Tum would do the trick. It always did in the commercials. Nope. The next three hours the imaginary ulcer pains persisted despite popping the blessed Tums like candy.

Getting no relief at nine AM, five hours after the onset of the heart attack, my sister drove me to the emergency room. At the hospital, I self-diagnosed again complaining of ulcer pains or intestinal blockage. The chest x-ray told a different story. The emergency physician broke the news. His words shocked me.

"Hey, your lungs are full of fluid. You are having a heart attack."

2 Hard Life/Easy Death

How Long-My translation
How long depressed whether I have or not
How long worry whether I have fun or not
Fill up the cup that I don't know
This breath, that I inhale, I shall exhale or not

At the hospital lying on gurney waiting for my turn to be wheeled into cath lab (cardic catheterization laboratory) for angioplasty, I found dying too easy. All I had to do was just lay there, eyes closed, breathing stopped, heart blocked, and gone.

A lifetime of anxiety and worry ends in one brief moment of time. Death was easy life hard. Why is it so? Should it not be the other way round?

Easy-My translation
If I could rule the fate like God
I would eliminate this scheme of things entire
Would remold the fate entire so that
To get to the heart's desire would be far easier

Dragged into cardiac catheterization theater ended my life and death thoughts. Earlier I had signed the angioplasty consent form. The doctor had explained a long list of risks. They boiled down to three major ones: sudden closure of the coronary artery, another heart attack, and death.

For the angioplasty to proceed I had to accept all those risks or the alternative was to die in the next attack. I had witnessed my ex-father-in-law dying from the second wave of heart attack following the first one in matter of hours. The paramedics had misdiagnosed the initial attack, after the Thanksgiving Dinner, as indigestion. With the next attack he died.

The emergency angiogram revealed two major blockages 97 and 95%.

The surgeon could stent only one, due to the weakened heart, and the stressed physical condition of the body post heart attack. I pinned my hope on the catheter to carry the angioplasty balloon (and or stent) to the narrowed coronary artery. If widened, the blood can flow to the heart tissue once again. Could it enliven the heart tissue that had already died during the heart attack?

The next procedure for the second blockage had to wait for a month.

This one-month waiting period posed its risks. The other narrowing may cause another heart attack or stroke, even death. No choice though, the body could not tolerate two stents in my condition. The waiting period was essential to the next operation. A period in limbo had begun not knowing I would die or survive.

For me it took a shock of death and a damaged heart to wake up.

I was in sleep-My translation
I was in sleep a wise person said
From sleep no happy flower blooms

53

Why sleep when with death forever you must lay
Drink up since below the dark earth shall you abode

Once Blown for Ever Dies-Fitzgerald translation
Another voice, when I am sleeping cries,
"The flower should open with the morning skies."
And a retreating whisper, as I wake—
"The flower that once has blown for ever dies!"

I had a pile of art books on my nightstand next to my bed. I used to joke with my siblings, that I kept them handy for a reason: in case I die in the middle of the night, I would place one hand on an art book. That way, I would end up in the picture land where I could meet Vincent van Gogh and a few other of my favorite painters, the Fauves included. That fateful night, I had read an art book, and had gone to sleep, but this time no sweet dreams about Fauve colored landscapes, jut a rude awakening to a painful heart attack. In no shape to place my hand anywhere except on a painful chest.

The heart attack also shocked me out of my heart slumber that the routine of everyday life had wrapped me in. After the first stent, the one-month waiting period began. A life in limbo followed. Die or live another day? The next and the next day to the next procedure? I did not know.

In this period, unlike the sudden heart attack, the inner waking came soft and slow. To get more oxygen into the lungs and the damaged heart, the cardiologist had advised to sleep with two pillows. The elevated head position would improve the oxygen intake. The side benefit was it also perked up my hearing. The sounds from the adjacent apartment were coming too clearly sometimes mixing with my own depressed thoughts causing insomnia.

One night, a loud music from next door caused me to suffocate all the external sounds. Concentrated on inner sounds of my own breathing, I slipped into a meditative state. Silence. A sound of hush spread all over my inner universe. Within the stillness, I heard a distant sound like the buzz of TV. Unlike the TV noise that I often heard from the next door, this particular sound was deep. From within? Could not tell, but I was relieved when it diverted my thoughts from the fear of death, my constant bedmate, to somewhere distant in time and space. A soft captivating whisper, I listened closer. Muffled sounds of my childhood, intermixed voices. I could hear them but the meaning was lost on me. Would I make it the end of the month? The pinch of anxiety of death barred the clarity of the voices within.

Was there a message, something I had to hear in the jumbled up voices? Curious, I listened. No, could not make anything out. I listened again, even closer with all my might. Fed with close attention, the voices grew stronger. Then a few words of poetry; the broken words and stanza were about human fate and death; the questions on my mind relating to the state of my consciousness.

Khayyam? The poet that father recited often at dinner table as a five year old? When I listened well, I recognized the warm voice belonged to my father reciting his favorite. Then, I remembered.

The fear of death kicked in. I had read somewhere before death, the past life parades before the mind's eye and ear like a movie. Was this the second heat attack? Was I dying? Filled with blood thinners, and having felt no pain, I relaxed and listened.

Rose-Fitzgerald translation
Look to the rose that blows about us—
"Lo, Laughing, "she says, "into the world I blow:
At once the silken tassel of my purse
Tear, and its treasure on the garden throw."

Then more verses. They came like a lamb but devoured me like a lion.

The words hit the interior of my mind, touched my soul, and literary knocked me out of deathbed. I sat up thinking. If I were to tear the silken tassel of my being, would it scatter any treasures? I had lived all those years ignoring Dad's favorite poems only experiencing them as earworm. Never before in father's voice though, even if it was him that did the reciting, his voice had been lost in the maddening rush of everyday events.

Now in bed, in the quietude of my mind, and the stillness of my thoughts his warm was unmistakable. With his way of reciting only unique to him, the verses were pouring into my head announcing their presence stronger than ever before. Dad had quite a repertoire of Omar Khayyam poems. I tried to find some organizing order. No way, too many loose ends, unconnected dots, verses scattered all over my inner canvas in reds, yellows, blues, and greens. Some times in dark hues, other times light and sunny, a few bright, others pale.

The poems pushed my soul every-which-way and up. Could they put distance between Hades residents and me? The favorite verses of my father had resurrected themselves when I needed to divert my thought from dark depression. But can they recharge my soul? Restore life-force?

Post heart attack, the fear of death that I had always felt throughout my life grew stronger. I needed an epiphany, something to bring back the living sizzle that I was losing to depression. The cause of melancholy was all those constant thoughts of my own morbidity and mortality. The prospect of dying was daunting; and fear of death sucked my life sap dry.

When the poems appeared, I found a respite from contemplation of death. I allowed them to echo in my head, despite the confusing chaotic manner in which they came. Then I thought to myself, look, if you are going to die, go entangled with the verses. It beats the reaper showing up again with his nightjar. God, those red-flaming eyes ready to snatch my living soul and carry me to Hades. No, not now, first I must make some sense of the father's favorite verses of Omar Khayyam floating in my head.

The Silence of God

By P. John Anderson

CHAPTER ONE
La Milice comes to *le Bois Bailleau*

Adair could not believe how dry her mouth had gone when she heard the news.

Wasn't it to avoid such horrors that she and her daughter Celia had fled Paris before the occupation and come to their home from home, here in this blessed city of Chartres, to their little place in rue Chanzy. This house, this room, had been a refuge from the cruelty of a world gone mad. They had survived three years, at times even been happy, such as when Celia married her childhood sweetheart. Now her daughter and her daughter's beloved Shanoé stood before her to deliver their news: this world was at an end. Everyone in the camp, including Shanoé's parents, had been murdered by la Milice.

The young ones had escaped the attack because they had ventured out into the field, hunting mushrooms. Then they heard the fusillade. It kept on repeating erratically, finally thinning into silence. Sickened and distraught, they had run to the shelter of the woods, but dared go no further. If it was the encampment under attack, there was nothing they could do right now. However much the heart hurt and bled by not rushing straight to the settlement, they would be no help if they too were shot. Still, it was not long before they began to hasten through the trees

Hearts pounding, they slowly approached the camp. There was a stench of burning but little evidence of flame. Still they crept; the camp could be under watch for people returning, like they were returning, step by hesitant step, trying to make out what had happened, still not being able to believe the horror of what they would find.

One more step brought them in sight of the camp. The caravans were just smoking relics – charred spars and beams. Abandoning any pretense at caution, they raced into the camp and toward the family caravan. On the way, they saw the empty cans of fuel left by the Gestapo; it had to be Gestapo. La Milice wouldn't have access to so much fuel. But then they saw a surviving caravan with a crudely painted slogan: "Down with the gypsy leper." La Milice – beyond a doubt.

A few more steps and there was the caravan, with two familiar shapes lying on the ground, just short of the steps leading up into the refuge that was no refuge.

Shanoé rushed to the inert form of his mother. The body was still warm, but the gaping wound in the back of her head... He fell, pressing his face into the body and screamed silently into the bloody clothing around her neck. Celia had knelt beside the body of Shanoé's father, bent down and kissed his neck. Then she moved over to comfort Shanoé.

"It's getting dark. We must go."

"Where shall we go? To whom will we bring the kiss of death?" Celia had to strain to decipher Shanoé's muffled rhetoric.

"To my mother's place. Chartres isn't so far from here – and if we're careful and not too slow, we can reach the house in the dark. Come! We're wasting time. We have to make our goodbyes. We don't honor them by getting killed ourselves."

"We have to bury them. Then I want to die. I want to join them." Shanoé's voice was still muffled.

"Not till I'm bearing your child. You're not allowed to die until then. And then, of course, you have to live for your child, for your posterity, and for theirs." Celia shook him gently, kissed him softly on his neck, then stood up. "I'm going to look for a shovel."

"There's one slung under the caravan." Shanoé had lifted his head. "I'll look under the Lagrène's. They always had one too."

The desolate pair dug and sobbed, sobbed and dug as hastily as they could. It seemed hours before they felt the graves were deep enough, but the soft earth had yielded quickly. A shallow grave would have to do. Just pray that there would be no foxes to dig them up. They picked up his mother's body first and laid it in the cramped slot in the earth. Shanoé had found some clothing, scorched and reeking of the fire, but it served as a grave cloth to cover the body. Then they tenderly lifted his father's body and covered it too with what clothing could be found. Celia went to start filling in but Shanoé stopped her with a look of alarm. He picked up a water jug, and speaking in Romany, sprinkled water over the bodies, invoking the name of Saint Sarah and Ceferino Giménez Malla. It lasted perhaps a quarter of a minute. Celia was a little surprised and found the liturgical language hard to follow.

"Now let us complete the burial." Shanoé started in right away. It did not take long, but when it was finished, Shanoé stayed, standing over his mother's grave, leaning on his shovel. Celia became alarmed.

"Shanoé!"

He dropped onto the grave. "You go. You go. I will only endanger you."

Celia rushed and knelt by his side, pulling at his clothing. "Give me your child, then I can smuggle you out in my belly."

Shanoé rolled over and seized her in a furious embrace, starting to unbutton her down her back. Celia unbuttoned him, almost tearing off his clothes. They collided in a rage of love.

Celia and Shanoé, having arrived at the house in rue Chanzy and told their story, it was clear that the house was no more a refuge than the camp in Bois Bailleau. Even if the hunt had not yet begun, it soon would. It was a moonlit night and it's a long walk down rue Chanzy. It was quite possible that someone saw them violating curfew and reported them. Celia maintained that it was she who had to try to make contact with the group planning to head south to Spain. It was she who had made the initial contact, had the phone numbers, and the codes to get information. If they hadn't gone already, they might well come down through Chartres.

The road is good but is not a major road. If we can't get in touch, we have to do it on our own. Then we're in trouble but not as bad as staying here.

Shanoé was finally persuaded that it had to be Celia who went. If she ran into a patrol, she had a chance to talk her way out of it. With la Milice on alert, Shanoé would be shot on sight. It was a long and painful leave-taking, but finally Celia slipped out the door, closing it quietly behind her. Wordlessly, Adair and Shanoé clung to each other and cried themselves to sleep.

Adair had been awake a while. Shanoé was still asleep, leaning on her arm which had gone quite dead. She slowly extricated it, while it burst into such violent tingling that it hurt. Shanoé stirred slightly, but thankfully did not wake. She soon stopped gazing at him. It was too painful, as now everything seemed too painful. What a beautiful boy. A gypsy of legend, but that's not what concerned her friends – what friends? She thought that they'd get over it, the wedding, but so many stopped speaking to her. The intensity of the prejudice surprised her. So much at variance with the national myth.

"But they've been childhood sweethearts. 'So much the worse.' Wasn't that what they had said, or thought at least? All except Martine and André. Well there were a few others I suppose."

Adair thought back to when she was Celia's age, sixteen and the world at her feet. 1921: the war to end all wars—over. Now, twenty two years later, I'm sitting here waiting for this door to open—and fearing the worst.

Waves

By Don Rogers

Rolling in ... breaking on the shore
Receding ... white foam abounds
Observing the back and forth ... calming comes through
Becoming one with the motion ... a sense of meditation
Becoming one with the greater ...
a sense of experiencing the One

Early Years in the Tenderloin

By Jo Carpignano

Downtown San Francisco was a relatively quiet place in the late seventies. The political and social turmoil of the sixties and early seventies had died down. The beat generation had just about worn itself out, and hippies had either grown up or given up. Most of those who had given up were being identified as "street people," sleeping on sidewalks and lining up for free meals wherever they could be had. "Working the system," became a way of life, and that was all I knew at age twelve.

We lived on Larkin Street, a few blocks north of Market, in a two room apartment in a third floor walkup. The place was a pig sty. Ma didn't think picking up dirty diapers was worth the bother, since another would follow within a short time. Thy just stacked up in the corner.

Ma was a single parent with four children. We were on welfare, and Charlie found us the cheapest apartment in the city. There was a small stove, refrigerator, and table with four chairs in the biggest room; a bed, cot and dresser in the other. We also had a small bathroom with an old tub in one corner, and a sink and toilet in back of the door. At thirty-two, Ma already had four kids, and one on the way. I was the oldest, so it was my job to look out for my two younger brothers. Three-year-old Emily was just learning to talk. She was a bit slow getting started with things, and Ma was growing impatient as her belly got bigger by the day. Even though the rooms were big, there were too many of us for that confined space. *I like the word "confined." I think it sounds better than "cramped."*

"The more the merrier," Charlie would say when he made his weekly visits. We heard that it was his routine comment with the others too. He would bring in the groceries, and collect Ma's welfare check. Sometimes he stuck around for a few hours, and he and Ma would lock the door to the bedroom. We kids would ignore the noise, and turn up the TV, and that was O.K. with me. Ma was not happy for long though. She came out of the bedroom a tousled mess, grumpy and mean the rest of the day.

But even when Charlie was not around, she was grumpy and mean. As soon as I could get my two little brothers dressed, I was always eager to get out the door. There was a hot breakfast waiting for us at school, and that was O.K. with me too.

Weekends were not so easy, other food would just about run out, and oatmeal was the usual fare for everyone. It was at meal three times a day on Saturday, and sometimes on Sunday too— if Charlie did not show up. One Sunday morning I got snippy with Ma, telling her I was getting tired of eating oatmeal all the time, and she didn't like that at all.

"You Goddamn brat, what do you mean you don't LIKE oatmeal," she bellowed. "How' d you like it if there weren't no oatmeal? Huh? How'd you like that!"

I sat in silence with my chin on my chest. My brothers stopped eating, alert to what might happen next..

"You know what? YOU don't get to eat no oatmeal today missy, that's what! If you don't like oatmeal, you stand over there by the door, and you can watch US eat the oatmeal."

Stupid me, I froze and refused to move away from the table. That really made her mad.

Standing up, she reached out and slapped me across the face.

"You do what I say, WHEN I say," she growled clenching her teeth, and pushing me off my chair.

"You stand against the wall by that door, NOW, just like I said, you hear?"

I crawled to the wall, my cheek burning, and tears starting. I stood by the door as I'd been told. Ma sat down at the table where the other kids started eating their oatmeal, silent and watchful. I could tell that Ma was still fuming, as she stumbled returning to her chair. It had been the wrong time for me to complain.

She's been drinking again, I thought. I'd forgotten that Charlie had brought a bottle with the last delivery.

I stood and waited, hoping my silence would keep Ma from another outburst. Instead, she smiled. It was not a happy smile.

"So, you're tired of eating oatmeal? Well then, let's see if *this* is better for you."

Carefully she scooped a spoonful of oatmeal from the bowl and turning, flung it at me from across the room. Her aim was perfect, and the oatmeal hit my shoulder.

"Is that better now? If you don't want to eat it, you can wear it, O.K.?"

Another spoonful landed on my forehead, and a third on my chest. I cried while my brothers looked on, fascinated by the oatmeal assault.

Just then the door swung open pushing me to the side, and Charlie walked in. Never before was I so pleased to see Charlie arrive.

"What the hell is going on here?" he exclaimed with a puzzled frown.

"The brat got tired of *eating* oatmeal," Ma said, "so she's gonn'a wear it instead." With that, she flicked another spoonful at me.

"Well Goddamn woman, you gonna turn her into a oatmeal statue, you keep this up" he said, starting to laugh.

Ma quit throwing the oatmeal, and began laughing too. My two brothers laughed along with them. Everyone was laughing except for me. I was still crying.

"Well, you stupid kid, don't just stand there. Go get cleaned up!" Ma yelled. "Hold up there, honey, let me he'p get that mess off a' ya," Charlie offered.

I finally found my voice, "No! I can do it by myself! No Charlie, I don't need help, thanks anyways."

I turned quickly into the bathroom, before Charlie could say anything more. Shutting the door behind me, I gave in to a tearful humiliation.

Charlie must have felt sorry for me that Sunday, 'cause he was awful' nice to me the rest of the morning. He thanked me for helping him bring some of the groceries up from his car, and started talking to me about how sorry he was that Ma got so mad at me. "Y'a know he'a baby due soon, and yo'a ma, she's jus' about wore out with takin' care o' Emily. Don't know wha's wrong with tha' lli'l one, she don' seem so quick as your brothers was at three yea's. You jes' gotta he'p your ma the bes' you can, 'til the baby gets bo'n."

I wasn't sure what Charlie thought I could do—any more than I was already doing with taking care of Tom and Jimmy. And I was not looking forward to another baby either.

"What if things get worse after the baby comes, what then?" I asked.

"Why Honey, we get da social work'a out hea', and find somebody to he'p out. 'Sides, the welfe'a check, it be big'a an' we can do some thin's to make it mo'a easy fo' yo' ma," he said smiling.

So that's why Charlie was so eager for the baby to arrive, I thought. The welfare check would get bigger!

In the meantime, I was to continue taking care of my two brothers who attended the same school as I did. Jimmy was not so bad, he was in second grade now, and doin' O.K. keeping up with the other kids in his class. He liked his teacher, and got along with everybody. Tom was another story. His fifth grade teacher was always tellin' me how he was fightin' with other kids—all the time.

"He just doesn't seem to be able to get along with others. He insists on being first all the time, even when they play games. And that's not how we do things, you know," Mrs Brown complained.

"Sorry Mrs. Brown, I'll talk to him about taking turns," I apologized.

Then, using a much more serious tone, Mrs Brown said, "I really don't think that's your job, Nadine. This is not the first time you've tried to help. Your mother needs to be dealing with this problem. Do you think you could ask her to come to school for a conference some time soon?"

I took a deep breath and tried to think of something that would explain why Ma could never make it to a school conference. If she got a report about Tom being so bad that the teacher had to see her about it in person, Ma would get out that long wooden spoon, and make him all black and blue again.

"Well, you know, my mother is going to have a baby soon, and I don't think she could walk all that way."

John Muir Elementary School was a good six or eight blocks from where we lived, so I wasn't really telling a lie. Ma could never walk that far now.

"Well, couldn't she take a bus or get a ride from someone?" Mrs Brown suggested. "No ma'm, there's no money for bus fare, and Ma don't have any friends with cars. Let me tell her about Tom, then she will talk to him about being good, 'specially on the playground." I hoped this would satisfy Mrs. Brown, and that she would let me take care of it again.

But Mrs. Brown was not to be satisfied by the assurances of a twelve year old. "I think I'll talk to her on the phone, then," she said.

"But we don't have a phone," I answered quickly. "And I'm sure that when I tell her how serious the problem is, Ma will find a way to get Tom straightened out."

"Oh, you don't have a phone?"

Mrs. Brown seemed to be running out of options, and I was hoping that she would settle for my latest suggestion. But no, not Mrs. Brown. She was determined to make that parent contact, and though I'd been able to deflect her other attempts, she found another possibility.

I'd just learned the word "deflect" in a book I read, and lie to practice using it.

"Well then, I think I'd better consult with Miss Gray and see if we can think of another way," she said pursing her lips and shaking her head as she walked away.

After talking to Tom's teacher about his problem behavior, I thought Mrs. Brown would probably find more important things to think about. I had scolded Tom thoroughly, and warned him that I would have to tell Ma if he got in a fight again. Since we had no phone, I knew there was no way for the school to reach Ma, unless they sent a letter. It was my job to bring in the mail, so I'd know if they tried that. I could always say that the letter got lost, if I had to. So I stopped worrying about Tom's problem.

Early morning the following week, the boys were getting dressed for school, and Ma was in the bathroom with Emily. As usual, I cleared the breakfast dishes from the table, sliding a good portion of my oatmeal into the sink. I wondered how long it would take for the drainpipes to get clogged. I was pretty sure that someday they would, oatmeal is really sticky.

I forgot about that problem too as I speculated about what kind of breakfast might be waiting for us at school.

As I was collecting my homework from the table, I noticed Ma's purse sitting on the chair. She usually kept it in the bedroom in the bottom drawer of her dresser. She had mentioned being short on cigarettes, and probably planned to go shopping as soon as Tom, Jimmy and I were gone. So the purse was there ready for her to grab as soon as we were out the door and she got Emily cleaned up.

I don't know what made me do it, but I did know how to be quick, so I gave it a try, not even thinking about what might happen if I got caught. The coin purse was waiting just inside the first section of the handbag, so I opened the clip, grabbed a coin, and slipped it into my pocket. The coin purse went back in the bag, and everything looked the same.

"'Bye Ma!" I said, as I herded the two boys out the door and down the stairs. We were on the sidewalk in no time, and hustling towards school and a decent breakfast.

"I saw what you did," Tom said softly, looking straight ahead.

"What did she do?" asked Jimmy, curious, but oblivious as usual, to what was going on around him. Sometimes I thought he was trying not to know, and that was O.K. with me.

"She took money out 'a Ma's pocketbook," Tom said with a sly grin.

"Wow, are you goanna get in trouble when Ma find' out," Jimmy added looking worried. "And how's she gona find out?" I asked smugly.

"Well, I bet she knows how much money she had in that purse. And if she don't remember, I'm gonna tell her," Tom threatened, raising his eyebrows.

"Now why would you manna do that?" I asked. "You think Ma's gonna do you a favor for tellin' on me?"

"Maybe not. But you boss us around all the time, and I think maybe it'd be fun to see what happen when Ma find out you's stealin' from her purse."

"Naw! Come on Tommy. Don' tell. You don' hafta tell," Jimmy said, worry in his voice again. This was getting really serious, and I thought I better do something pretty quick or we'd *all* be in trouble.

"Well, let's see how much I got, and then figure what we can do with it," I said, reaching into my pocket. "Hey, look here, a whole dime. What do you think we can buy with a dime, you guys? Got any ideas?"

"Ain't nothin' much we can get with that," Tom offered hesitantly. But now he was using *we* instead of *you*, so I was making progress in the right direction. I'd known Tom as a baby, and it had always been easier to get him interested in cooperating—if there was something in it for him.

"How about on our way home from school we stop at the corner store and see if we can find something we all like, then we can share," I said. And so the conspiracy was formed. *I really like the word 'conspiracy.'*

After school we stopped at the store as planned, and after looking around agreed to buy a pack of gum, We happily chewed on Wrigley's Spearmint all the way home. At the front door to our own apartment we found a clean spot on the molding to park our gum, ready to pick up the following morning. I put mine the highest 'cause I was the tallest, Jimmy's was at the bottom, 'cause he was the shortest, and Tom's was planted firmly between the two. It gave us all something to look forward to, I thought.

When we walked in the door to our apartment, I could see that Ma had her new pack of Lucky Strikes, and was puffing away. She didn't say a word about missing money from her purse.

Tom kept his silence, Jimmy was the good boy he always was, and I got away with taking something I wanted - even if I did have to share.

It had been easy getting that dime for gum. Taking a chance in stealing it from my mother's purse was dangerous, but I enjoyed the excitement of succeeding at something like that. Getting away with it had made me feel powerful, and I liked that feeling. For once I had been in control of something in a different way than taking care of my brothers. Besides, I'd enjoyed my deception. *'Deception' is such a neat word.*

I wanted to try it again, but I had something to work out, in keeping the boys from knowing. Jimmy would be no problem, but Tom was the sneaky one. He wouldn't hesitate to make the most of squealing - unless I shared with him of course. But if they were not around, and there was another opportunity? Hmm... Maybe?

Pantheon

By Kennon States
(Where Rest Our Honored Heroes)
9/19/2014

Rise up, fallen warrior.
Grasp once more your broken lance and hobble homeward,
where your *compadres* gather and await you.

We need you still.

Despite your wounds and weakness,
your life-spirit and *esprit de corps*
still smolder, ever incandesce.

We stand together one final time,
shoulder-to-shoulder, back-to-back,
faithful to the end, the bitter end.

We need you now,

as once we found in you, so unexpectedly,
a hero's attributes.

We used you then,

and you sacrificed yourself on our behalf,
fought on with shattered spear and broken body,
exceeding all endurance, and showed uncommon courage.

For that, we loved you, honored you,
raised you up and blessed your name.

Come home this one, last time,

if only to bid us all farewell,
while we avow your noble deeds and give you thanks,

and wish you well, and say to you: *"Va con Díos."* – Go with God –

Good-bye.

The Ballad of Billy Shay

By Sylvia E. Halloran

Bo Jenkins came back to life one piece at a time.

Clunk of a stove grate. Creaking floor. Rain on the roof. Door latch.

Food cooking. Smokey stove. A breath of moist air. A whiff of clean linen and hay. Like back home.

The hurt woke up in a rush. Bo's head pounded. His back and shoulders throbbed.

His ribs stabbed at him. His arms lay at his sides, aching and powerless. His hip launched a scream that lost its way to his mouth. Only came out a whimper.

Heavy steps crossed the room. "Has he come to yet?" a man's voice asked. "Just now, maybe. Groaned a little," a woman replied.

"Lucky we noticed he was still warm when Springer brought the first load over."

"Surprised he wasn't smothered under that pile."

"Springer says he's got another load coming, soon as they get them dug out. Three, maybe four more."

The woman waited before she spoke again. "That Blackjack mine went in way too fast. Careless timbers don't like this wet weather." A clink of dishes. "Think killing a dozen men will close it for good?"

"Springer says old Boatwright's already figuring how to sink a new entrance from the north. Stinking greedy bastard."

"All of California runs on greed," the woman's voice said.

"Good business for us, sorry to say." More heavy footsteps, a scrape of a chair. "See what you can do to pull that one through. Maybe he can be some use around here." The chair creaked. The man gave a little snort of laughter. "It worked for the dog."

The woman laughed, too, but kept her low tone. "That was a champion mutt, for sure. Looked about as bad as this one when he first showed up, remember?"

"You did well by that one, all right. Bandaged him up, warmed him by the stove, fed him good. Turned him into a right nice little ratter," said the man.

"Fine dog, that was," said the woman. "We'll give this one the same treatment. See what we get."

A ladle clonked and the food smell wafted toward Bo. Dishes being filled. "Here you are," the woman's voice said.

Not to Bo.

If she sees I'm awake, maybe she'll feed me.

But his eyelids stayed clenched over his gritty eyes. His arms refused to move. His mouth couldn't make words.

I'm clear shut down.

Footsteps padded up from behind where he lay, and Bo felt a bolster being pushed in behind his head and shoulders. A hand came alongside his head. It surprised him and he jerked away. The pain in his hip exploded.

Quiet fingers stroked his whiskery cheek while the other hand guided a spoon into his mouth. Weak broth.

It's a start.

A second dose, a trickle greasing his dry tongue and slipping across the dust in his throat. It choked him. Broth sprayed everywhere.

Cheek hand patted his chin with a cloth. Spoon hand came at him again and ladled a dribble more. Bo managed better this time and swallowed it down.

"There you go," the woman's voice purred.

Steady footsteps crunched outside and clomped up a few stairs to a resonant floor. The pounding on the door made Bo twitch. The woman hastily wiped him with the cloth again and rustled as she rose.

"We got the last of the Blackjack bunch dug out," said a raspy voice. "They're in the wagon."

"What's the count?" asked the man's voice. "Any of them got kin hereabouts?"

"Five in this load," Raspy Voice replied with a weary tone. "Ed Moyer, Bill Burns, Turk Canton."

"God, Springer," said the man. "That's half the Methodists."

"And there's a couple others that will just need pine boxes. No fuss. Some of that bunch that came in yesterday from working the placer mines up north. No idea who the hell they are."

"Boatwright thinks they all need proper buryin'?"

"Said he'd pay you for the plots and coffins. Don't want nothing fancy, of course. But the bastard's all show. Thinks just dumping them into a hole and liming over might loook bad to the town."

Bo's shiver made him hurt more.

"Well, pull the wagon around back," said the man. "We can stack them on the porch till I can get the coffins built. That'll keep them out of the weather, at least."

"Smells real good in here," Springer said. "I ain't had my supper yet." Stony silence. Springer kept at it. "Smells like Miz Swanson's outdone herself. Is that rabbit stew?"

"Believe so. But I don't reckon she needs another visitor just now. She's got her hands full with that one poor feller you brought in earlier."

"The warm one? That him over by the stove?" Springer asked. "Looks like he'd have done better to stay dead. The work up north didn't feed him too good, did it?"

"Pretty scrawny, alright. But Mrs. Swanson's good with such. If there's any life left in him, she'll find it."

Probably ain't worth it.

"Well then, I guess I'll just run the others around to the porch for you. Oh, 'evening Miz Swanson. Didn't see you there in the shadow."

More silence.

"I'll just be going, then." He paused. "Sure is a miserable night." Bo heard the last hope for supper fade in Springer's sigh. "Well, evening', Miz

66

Swanson. Mr. S."

As he listened to Springer shut the door and walk away, Bo's gut took hold of the dabs of stew juice and started grinding on them. He didn't plan the moan that eased out of him. The fit in his innards got his eyes open, though.

He was facing a corner, lying on a straw tick. Stiff white sheet on it. Shadows from lantern light played on the pine wainscot. He couldn't see who the voices were. Didn't much care.

Someone put a cracker in his hand. "Eat that real slow," said Mrs. Swanson from behind him. "It'll help your stomach."

It took some doing for Bo to bend his sore elbow and get the saltine to his mouth.

He held it on his tongue till he had enough spit to swallow.

Maybe I can live through this.

His leg didn't ease up any.

Maybe I don't want to.

The rain pounded. The fire in the stove crackled.

Mrs. Swanson busied about, always out of sight. She brought a cup of water, and he took a few sips. She brought him another cracker and a doll-sized bowl of the stew.

Good thing she was so miserly. It only took two heaves to puke it all up.

Bo heard the men grunting with effort outside, followed by some heavy thuds as they unloaded the wagon. Goodnights and so-longs. One of them let out a low whistle.

When the last rattle of the wheels had rolled away, Mrs. Swanson left the room and joined the man on the porch. Bo eavesdropped best as he could. Couldn't make out all the words.

"...if you think so, then I'll head out and fetch him," said the man as they both came in. "It's rainy enough, nobody will see." His heavy footsteps approached Bo.

The man's rosy face leaned over Bo. "I see you've had a little trouble, friend," he began.

You could say that.

The old man noticed the fresh mess on the patient's shirt and reached for a rag to mop him up. "Maybe more than just a little. You have a name?"

Bo heard the question just fine. Trouble was, his mouth wasn't reconnected yet. His head strained forward as he struggled for words, but the man settled him back with a gentle hand on Bo's shoulder. Didn't hurt much.

"Never mind, friend."

I'm your friend?

"There'll be time for all that. Just stay put. We'll do what we can for you." The white-haired man gave Bo a smile and left.

Bo couldn't remember the last time he'd seen a smile on a man.

Weariness more demanding than hunger overwhelmed him, and Bo's eyes drifted shut. His own stink and the cry of his bones promised misery even in sleep, but he didn't think of resisting.

Cold hands prodded Bo everywhere. Under his shirt, up his pants, behind his neck, down his socks. Before he could fight them off, clever hands found the places he hurt the most, and warmed as they worked his battered flesh. Fingers sought the hollows beside his ankles and wrists and breastbone, and around his pelvis. They manipulated each spot and pressed deep enough to bring tears to his eyes. When the hands found his sore hip and leg, Bo tried to kick them away. The torment of moving smacked all the fight right out of him.

Just kill me now.

The hands were fiery hot by the time they settled around his rib cage. Bo was quaking all over.

He heard a tongue clicking, and the hot fingers tightened on the back of his waist. "Bad kidneys. Sick liver. Many angry points," said an accented voice. "Also leg gone out. We fix."

Bo looked at the slight man with the busy hands.

Have they carried me back to the camps?

The Chinaman's round forehead sloped back to his blue-grey pigtail. Round spectacles magnified his glittering eyes. His long silk brocade garb carried the scent of rain.

"Drink tea," he told Bo, offering a tiny, thin-walled cup. Bo took a sniff and gagged.

"Drink, not smell. Small drink. Will fix."

Bo turned his head to the wall.

From behind him, Mrs. Swanson rustled as she sat. With surprising strength, her hands eased Bo's face around, and the Chinaman put the cup to his lips. "Not smell. Drink."

The warm tea was gluey as tree sap and tasted like his shirt smelled. It coated his tongue and expanded in his mouth. A second sip was every bit as bad as the first.

"Once more. Drink," said the Chinaman.

The man stood after Bo's third sip and padded away from the corner. Mrs. Swanson followed after him. Their patient on the straw tick began to sweat. The heat rose in him like dry pine igniting. He expected sparks to shoot out of his ears. A shudder radiated from the inside out, starting deep in his gut and finishing with a spasm that pretty nearly threw him on the floor.

The Chinaman returned to his side, smiling broadly. "Working," he told Bo. "Good fix." He pulled a thin dagger from a small wooden chest and came at Bo with another smile.

Bo froze at the sight of the knife. With the awful tea poisoning his digestive system, he was a sitting duck for this butcher.

"Now fix leg," he said, and in an instant had split Bo's pants leg clear to the pocket.

Blistering hot and strong as iron, those hands took hold of Bo, one at the thigh and one at his hip. With a quick, sickening pop, the Chinaman slipped Bo's joint back into the socket.

When Bo came to, he kept his eyes on the Chinaman at the table as the little man arranged a vial of milky liquid and a folded paper packet. In the lantern light, the little man tucked his peculiar ingredients into the chest and pushed the corner levers that locked it.

"Give twice more, then soup. Watch for anger in leg." The Chinaman noticed that Bo was conscious and padded over to his side. "Good fix," he said, smiling. He lay his hand over Bo's heart and let it rest there. "Strong heart. Good bones." His face crinkled into another smile and he bowed. Bo wanted to give him what for about the tea, but the man's touch soothed him somehow, and he relaxed into the tick.

Mrs. Swanson walked the man toward the door where Bo couldn't see. "Thank you for coming, Yi Ben," she said. "We are once more beholden to you. "

"Good fix. Now sleep," he said.

"Come on, Yi Ben. I'll fetch you back home," said the white-haired man. "We'll need to move fast to use the last of the rain as cover. Looks like it may be letting up."

"Be careful," Mrs. Swanson warned, and she closed the door behind them. The Chinaman's fix was having a powerful effect on Bo's eyelids...

When he woke up, the shaking had stopped. He was still sweating rivers, but his gut had settled. His hip merely throbbed.

Must've fed me opium.

He'd seen Chinese herbalists cure nasty outbreaks in camp. Seen men reduced to shells, too, begging from the shadows with empty eyes.

He turned his head to take in the rest of the darkened room. The woman crossed to the stove with a light step and banked the fire. Bo gazed at her profile in shadow. The lantern light showed the edge of a simple dress and apron strings on a trim figure.

Not a bad looker.

The man came in from the porch, and she turned to face him so Bo could only see her back.

"You're back sooner than I expected."

"Didn't run into any trouble on the road. But I'll need to head over to the mill come morning," the man said. "Just poked through our stock on the porch. Thought we'd have enough to finish up that crowd Springer brought in. But looks like we've lost a few things."

"What's missing?"

"Coffin lids, is all. Maybe a few pine planks. From what I can tell, anyway." "Things walk away with themselves these days," she said.

"I'd prefer it if they were growing legs. Hate to think that darned kid is coming right up to the house and stealing from us."

"Maybe thinks we have enough to spare." "Maybe we do."

Bo watched the woman kiss the man on the cheek. "You are a generous man, Toby Swanson."

"You are more than kind, my dear." Toby Swanson wrapped a hand around the woman's waist and pulled her into an embrace. "More than kind." He nuzzled the woman's hair. "You'll stay up with him?"

She nodded.

The man nudged the long curtain hanging in the doorway opposite the porch and bid her goodnight as he stepped through it.

"Goodnight, Mr. Swanson," replied the woman. As she turned to the table, the full beam of the lantern lit her face.

A sour oath jumped over Bo's lips into the room. The woman flinched and turned away.

"I didn't know you were awake," she said, still facing away from Bo.

He'd had no business eavesdropping on their intimacy, and now he'd given himself away. But his rudeness was not the reason for his profanity.

Mrs. Swanson had only half a face. A smudge of shiny pink flesh stretched blankly where her right eye should be and rode the little rise where a nose must have been. Made her look like a rag doll with a button missing. Waves of chestnut shrank back from the injury.

"So sorry, Ma'am," Bo croaked.

The woman trimmed the wick in the lamp and the room went dim. She brought over a cool damp cloth and a short stool, intending to sit and swab Bo's face. "Yours is a common reaction," she said.

He waited for her to continue, until it was clear she would say nothing further. By then, it was too late for him to say anything, either.

She stayed up with him, cooling his face with the rag and giving him little sips of water into the early morning. He listened to the rain come and go, and floated in and out of knowing about it.

From Within

By Ryann Murrin-DeSouza

Your true self comes,
From inside yourself.
The true spirit,
Comes from within.
Keep the faith,
You can believe in yourself.
And if you believe in yourself,
Then you have found the true person inside of you,
That person from within.

Deeper Colors

By Carolyn Donnell

Gina leaned back in her chair and gazed past the easel by the French doors to a garden overflowing with purple dwarf irises. Mild iris scent mixed with the delicate flowers of the crab apple trees blooming at the rear of the garden to proclaim the arrival of Vermont spring. The tabby cat ignored her mistress and the signs of spring as she catnapped in a shaft of sunlight. *Not the most appropriate setting for a funeral,* Gina thought.

She unfastened the clip that held her hair away from her face. Honey-colored tresses cascaded halfway down her back. She ran her fingers through her hair before turning back to the Priority Mail envelope that lay on the kitchen table. The package contained several items: an unopened envelope marked *Return to sender,* a letter from the diocese, and an 8x10 manila folder. She picked up the letter and read it a second time.

Dear Miss Martin,
We are sorry to inform you that Father Bernard is no longer with us. His heart gave out on him last month. Your letter arrived after he went into hospice. The other materials were found in his belongings with your name on them. We have enclosed everything and offer you our condolences.

May God, the Father of all consolation, be with you in your sorrow and give you His light and His peace. Amen.

"Ohh." A rough sigh escaped Gina's lips. Father Bernard dead. Just like that. She crumpled the letter. Consolation? Light? Peace? The only person she had ever known, in or out of the Church, who had any of those qualities was Father Bernard. And now he was gone.

She pitched the letter on the table and opened the folder. A child's drawing fell out, the one she had given to Father Bernard the first time he had peeked in on the children's group at the orphanage.

The social worker pulled him aside and pointed to the corner table. "That's Ginette. I can't get through to her. She doesn't talk much. Just draws all day long."

They walked over to the little girl who sat bent over a sheet of paper. "What do we have here?" Father Bernard reached for the drawing.

Ginette jerked the paper away from his outstretched hand. "She's not very cooperative," the worker complained.

"That's OK," the priest said in a quiet voice. "She doesn't have to show me if she doesn't want to. I can wait." He sat on one of the child-sized chairs and smiled.

Ginette stared at the man for a long time. "Who are you?" she finally asked. He offered her his hand. "I'm Father Bernard."

She looked at his hand and wrinkled her nose. "You have red paint on your finger." She pointed to his index finger.

"You're right. I was painting this morning and I didn't get all the paint off. Thank you for telling me."

Ginette tilted her head to one side. "Are you an artist?" He nodded. "Yes, I am."

"Me too." She handed him her drawing.

He looked at the paper. "This is very good, Ginette." "My name is Gina."

"Of course, Gina. May I have this?" "Why?"

"I like it. I would like to frame it and hang it in my office." "You want to put my picture on the wall?"

"Yes, I would, if I may." "You may." Gina smiled.

That day Father Bernard became her first art teacher, her mentor, and her only friend for many years. She felt a sudden chill. Her hand trembled as she picked up the second letter—*To Ginette Martin,* addressed in his spidery scrawl. She opened the envelope.

My Dear Ginette,

I know you said for everyone to call you Gina, but I still think of you as Ginette. Such a lovely name. It's French, you know. I have tried to locate your records and I have discovered that your name before you entered the foster system was Ginette Marden. (Both names are French, by the way). Somehow it got changed to Martin when you were put in the first foster home with the Fergusons. Looks like Mr. Ferguson died of cancer not very long after they took you in and the wife died shortly thereafter.

You were then put in the orphanage where I found you that day working away on your drawings. Oh, and it looks like you may have been born French Catholic, which could be a reason for not fitting into the Irish Catholic community. It is perhaps why you and I always got along so well. God works in mysterious ways.

I have two friends who are into French genealogy in the Vermont area digging through their resources to see if we can find anything else for you, but at this time this is all I have.

I'm so grateful to have been able to help you. It has been a great gift to me. I want you to go to France and see firsthand the homes of the Impressionists you love. Learn from your French ancestors. Perhaps you will find the missing pieces of your heart there. Remember that God loves you, even when people can't.

I have enclosed a small check to help with that as my final bequest to my favorite student. I wish it could be more, but my wealth is my spirit and my greatest treasure is in Heaven.

Your friend, now and in the eternity to come,
Father Bernard.

Gina shook the folder again. A travel brochure and a check fell out. She stared at the check. How had Father Bernard managed to put that aside for her? She walked to the back door and looked out again over the sea of purple-tipped green. Maybe the scene was fitting for a funeral after all. Father Bernard had loved the colors of Vermont and painted them many times. He taught her to paint the landscape in all its seasons.

Vermont spring colors were as perfect in their own way as the glorious swirls of sunlit orange, deep reds and shimmering yellows of a New England autumn. Both seasons provided her with many inspirations. Some of her work had been judged good enough to win a few small awards. Everything she was able to do today was thanks to Father Bernard's instruction and later his help in getting a scholarship to college.

She had never achieved complete satisfaction in her paintings though. Somethingwas always missing. Father Bernard used to say perhaps her whole heart wasn't with her when she painted. She glanced at two landscape paintings on the far wall: a field of hazy gold spikes backed by a line of trees so dark that the green faded into purple and black; the other, ash and smoke birch trees, complete with the reds and oranges of full-blown autumn reflected in the backwash of an abandoned beaver dam. One of her best, she thought. When she painted it, however, it was as if someone else had taken over her hand and she had been a mere observer. She hadn't created anything that good since.

Her attention turned back to the half-finished canvas on the easel. "Crap." She kicked the foot of the easel and the canvas clattered to the floor. The tabby jumped straight up and landed on all fours with her fur all fluffed up. She hissed at her mistress.

"Sorry, Moochie. It's just that the tree doesn't look like a crab apple, not even an impressionistic one. Looks more like damned psychedelic cotton-candy," she muttered to herself as she cleaned up the mess and placed the canvas back on the easel.

The travel brochure stared up at her from the tabletop.

Tour the Art Museums of Paris

Our tour group prides itself on organizing tours to achieve the maximum benefit in the allotted time. Whatever you want, Tour France can find the perfect museum for you. We only work with experienced guides, university-educated French national guides.

Highlights and Secrets of the Louvre: From the Da Vinci Code to the Crown Jewels.

The Louvre.

Gina stared at the word. A place, people said, where you could stay for days, even weeks, and never see it all. She looked back at Father Bernard's letter. ...*go to France. Learn from your French ancestors.* Paris. The name was popping up everywhere.

"I'm French," she addressed the cat. "What do you think about that?

The tabby yawned. "I know, you know exactly who you are, don't you?" Gina thought about how she had never felt like she belonged anywhere. Her art had always been her refuge. Her French ancestors, the letter said. Could it be that she belonged somewhere after all?

Gina made a call on her cell phone. "Charlotte? Yes. I'm taking you up on that offer—the art tour. Yes, really. I want to go. Why now?" Gina's voice broke. "No, Charlotte, I'm all right. It's just that—. You remember, I told you about Father Bernard, the priest who helped me so much. That's right. I just got a letter. He's dead." She began to cry. "Yes, I'm crying. No, you don't need to come over right away. I'll tell you the details tonight at supper. Just book that tour to Paris. Yes, my passport's up to date. I'll talk to you later." She grabbed a paper towel and wiped her face.

She slapped the phone shut and looked over at the cat. "Next stop—Paris. Let's hope it does some good." It seemed Father Bernard was managing to help her even after he was gone. "Thank you, Father Bernard," she whispered. She dropped her forehead into the palms of her hands and sobbed.

The doorbell rang twice before Gina reacted. When she opened the front door she found her friend Charlotte on the porch. "I thought we agreed you'd be here for supper."

Charlotte stepped inside. "You didn't think I was going to leave you in tears until then did you?"

"I'm all right."

"You're not all right. Look at you. Your nose looks like a Christmas light." Gina peered cross-eyed at her nose.

Charlotte took Gina by the arm. "Come on, girl. Time for some of Charlotte's tea." She led her back to the kitchen.

Gina sipped a cup of Irish Breakfast tea while Charlotte read through the letters. "French, huh? Well I'm not surprised. Lots of French descendants live in this state. So your Father Bernard mandated this trip, huh? Find your heart in France. Sounds good to me. I would like to have met him. He sounds like a nice guy.

"The best."

"Do you know who his friends are, the ones into French genealogy in Vermont?" "Not a clue."

"Maybe your diocese will have some ideas."

Gina shook her head. "I don't know anyone there."

"Well, I do. We'll ferret all this out. But later. Here." She handed Gina a packet of papers. "I reserved a place for you on the tour. They leave next Friday from JFK."

"Friday? Gads. I know you're a great travel agent, but this is fast even for you." "I had all the information in the database when we talked about the tour earlier.

The form is pre-filled. All I had to do was hit enter." "You'll take care of Moochie?"

"Of course. Don't I always? She can come back and visit her siblings. Now you have no excuse to change your mind. I know what you're like. I'll help you pack."

The Social Contract

By Mary Heneghan

Waking early on Sunday morning
we take the path to Junipero Serra where
cone-shaped eucalyptus gumnuts on hairpin
bends plot Nascar schemes to catch the unaware.
Some days discretion is the better part of valor.
Deaf to terrier demand I cross the road to circle back to the open
space upland of the town park,
wetly green after the night soaking.
Ivy glistens against the dark of Mission Oaks,
whose muscled branches flex and arc
above the dry ravine slopes,
purposed and tenacious as aging body builders.

In the green space: sweetness,
trills, ripples, whistles, birdsong in dynamic,
form and rhythm as variable as tryout pitchers,
and yet a symphony no less.
The wicker cages hang, half-hooded, semi-circle in the Oaks:
the isolate divas, compatible duets and trios.
The Asian men who meet here stand unstudied in mirror groups,
as if on stage around the decorated twanging space and like shadow
boxers, move and shout and laugh in their own language.
Each group a transplant, hobbled, burdened,
they celebrate in mutual delight.

Note: The Social Contract, Jean J. Rousseau, 1762
"Man is born free and everywhere..."

Diagrams

By Suda Miller

I'm washing a window. It's already clean. I've been washing it for the last hour. You would think they'd be suspicious by now – but no, the teams are still wandering around, in clumps of two's, three's or four's – looking at their last clue, which is a scrambled acrostic that led them to this falafel place on Hollywood Boulevard, and to me, washing the falafel joint's window. But they don't look at me, they look beyond and around me. They look down, at the inlaid stars in the sidewalk on which we all stand: the Hollywood Walk of Fame, then wander away a short distance to scratch their heads and confer. Those star memorials, with their brass borders – if you squinted, they could be Stars of David – like what a Jewish person might wear on a necklace, instead of a cross or a saint. David was one classy guy from the ancient times, but instead we have today, on these sidewalk stars: Ernest Borgnine, Sally Struthers, Alfred Hitchcock. Who were they? Beats me, though I should know by now, because my father goes on endlessly about all the Hollywood luminaries: number of marriages, affairs, visits to rehab, offspring, awards, plastic surgery, credits. He knows every celebrity star and its location mapped out on all fifteen blocks. He also knows all Best Picture winners going back to the first year, 1929: these are etched on the columns of Hollywood & Highland's mall entrance. His knowledge is so voluminous and ever-present that I can only retain a tiny portion of it at any one time.

Consider David, though, who got his star more than seven hundred years ago. He was not only an awesome entertainer but killed Goliath when he was just a wee lad, was related to Jesus, and was the King of Israel – hello? Yet his star is not among the ones on the sidewalk. My dad would say, "But Mary Jane, Orson Welles played Goliath in 1960, and his star can be found at Hollywood and Vine."

I happen to know, and this is not via my dad, but due to my own research, that you just need to throw some cash at the Hollywood Chamber of Commerce and boom, you get a star. That's what Absolut Vodka did. Theoretically, we could all have a star on the Walk of Fame, so why not David, too?

If I had the cash, would I want a star? The idea makes me stop washing my window for a second. I stare at Agnes Ayres's star at my feet. Under Agnes's name is an icon indicating that her achievement was in film. I stare at Agnes's star long enough to see my own name in her place: Mary Jane Mack. Under my name, the icon changes from a film camera to a squeegee.

Agnes won't mind, I don't think, if I temporarily hang out atop her star. I doubt the star made up for her dying alone, despondent, and penniless. I think you'd have to be over eighty to even know who she was, but I do because my dad knows and is a walking encyclopedia about everything Hollywood, and up until last summer I hung onto his every word. Since I'm only thirteen, knowing who Agnes Ayres was and how she died makes me pretty much a social pariah, so mostly I keep it to myself. That's not too hard to do since I don't have any friends. And if you are wondering why I don't have any friends, may I point out that I'm in eighth grade, e.g. middle school. There's not much room for loving kindness in middle school, is all I'm saying, so I mostly keep to myself. Anyway. At the beginning of last summer, I was happy to help my dad by being a clue on the Exciting Hollywood Scavenger Hunt, which my dad invented, owns, and runs. He's also an actor of course, just like my mom was before she became a shaman. But that's another story. I had no idea what it meant to be a clue, but now I do, and I'm dying a slow death here, or at least it feels like it.

The conveyor belt of tourist bodies bears down on me, four people across, and one hundred people deep, shuffling along. Ten million people a year visit this street, to shuffle along in the same manner.

Inevitably I am bumped. People aren't looking where they're going, they're looking at the ground. No matter how often it happens, I feel like a space station bombarded with space junk. The tiniest impact can send my squeegee flying. I really should use a firmer grip. You'd think I'd be prepared by now, for the bumping. But I never am, and anyway, there's nowhere to go. I'm supposed to stay here and wash the window, and get bumped for my trouble.

Here comes Team 6 again. They've clued into my existence finally, but they're not sure about me; I threaten them, though there is nothing about my person to inspire such feelings: acne, glasses. Small footprint. I'm minding my own business, washing this window – or I was before the squeegee went flying. Innocuous. Yet they're uncomfortable, it's plain to see, as they clump together on the other side of the tourist river, near the curb, consulting their clue book and the falafel place. Duh. Of course it's not me making them uncomfortable; it's just that there are still too many undesirable people all around us on this sidewalk, such as addicts, tramps, panhandlers, and the mentally ill, in addition to the so-called desirable tourists. The city couldn't quite clean the place of the undesirables when they restored the stars and planted trees. My dad said the sidewalk was previously pretty grimy: lots of gum and unmentionable stains obscuring the stars' names. You dare not put your hands in Betty Grable's imprint in the concrete plaza in front of the Grauman's Chinese Theatre: he said you could get Legionnaire's Disease but I'm pretty sure he was kidding. All that was in the past though; it's clean now, and so the tourists came back to us, to the Walk of Fame – but so did the nut cases and exhibitionist buskers dressed as Darth Vader or Spiderman, and the homeless, and someone handing you a CD and then insisting you pay for it but refusing to let you return it – all these people are here, too.

Yes, I'm pretty sure Team 6 has started to notice that I have been washing this window for a really long time – *Why?* – they might ask themselves. Maybe I'm a nut like the woman with cat-eye sunglasses and a polka-dotted scarf who asks everyone who passes by, "What is your heritage?"

After hearing the lady ask that question all day long for the last twelve Saturdays, I long to hear an answer. But no one does answer, they just keep moving.

Team 6 has to ask me a question, any question, before I can give them their next clue.

Those are my instructions. But they don't know that. They do know that sometimes people are part of the game, but that's it. Yet they still haven't made the connection.

It kind of reminds me of this theater class I took last semester. Mr. Slikening passed out these scripts and asked us to pair up and bring in a scene, so he handed out the script to all of us—we all had to do the same scene. The scene had no explanation of characters or setting, and no stage directions. It went like this:

Character 1: Do you?
Character 2: I wish
Character 1: But maybe
Character 2: We can't know
Character 1: Yes?
Character 2: Splitting
Character 1: Splitting?
Character 2: Splitting.

So the guy I teamed up with, Caleb, had the idea to make it about nuclear physicists at Los Alamos in the 1940's; we would act out the first time scientists completed fission of plutonium. Get it – splitting? Caleb said they used their bare hands to do it - just stuck them right in the water with the radioactive stuff. It was his idea to have this major explosion at the end of the scene, and we would portray what it is like to be totally annihilated, even though the Los Alamos scientists were able to complete the first fission without dying (right then) or anything else remarkable happening. Caleb is brilliant and amazing, and anyone who doesn't think so can suck it. He doesn't smile much but when he does, he has a double dimple, one on each side of his smile. He rarely looks me in the eye, which is a relief, because I might just lose my mind looking at those big dark eyes directly. I didn't dare let on that I felt this way though. That would have been unprofessional.

When we brought in the scene, Mr. Slikening asked Caleb and I to go first. We did our scene which involved a lot of miming and gesturing – the end, the explosion, all of it must have been hilarious, but the rest of the class was hushed. They didn't know how to react.

Mr. Sickening, as we liked to call him, had a good long laugh and then explained that we had done it wrong. Apparently, we had taken ourselves way too seriously. And we had totally missed the point. The point was to develop a character with a simple need. If you knew your character and what your character wanted, the impact of the scene was complete and more effective than any gesticulations or pratfalls. I hope I get paired up with Caleb again, despite our total failure as scene partners, because otherwise he doesn't talk to me. Not that he talks to anyone, come to think of it.

Team 6 has the same problem as Caleb and I had in drama class: they take it all too seriously and by doing so, miss the point. But they're also afraid. Here they are, jet-lagged, their perfect milky-white midwestern skin getting burned by the sun; now confronted with the chaos of Hollywood and none too sure they made the right decision coming here, to mix with the mass of human life spanning unexpected forms: how are they supposed to know who is part of the game and who isn't?

Their humiliation, when they finally have to break down and call my dad for a hint, is unbearable to me. Asking for a hint cost them points and might jeopardize their chance at winning. When, they get their hint, they feel less like winners every second. I feel sorry for them, the dumb bunnies. The game is stacked against them, unfairly, in my opinion. You sometimes need a little more information, more instruction, to do your best, otherwise it's just a set-up for failure. I never learned anything from Mr. Slikening's acting exercise except that I hate acting class even more than I hate working as a clue in the Exciting Hollywood Scavenger Hunt.

The other thing is that when you take it all too seriously, and you really want to succeed, you will fail, especially if you are in the power of someone who knows it and is jacking with your head. It is an incontrovertible fact that if you care too much about winning, your puzzle-solving mind blinds your senses and discounts what you see. You look underneath or beyond what's in plain sight, just like Team 6, assuming that if the answer *is* in plain sight, it can't count, because clues are hidden. You have this presupposed notion of what a clue is. If you want to win this game, you have to not care about winning and forget about your biases. Only then will you see what is right in front of you, and give it the value it deserves. If Caleb and I had just spoken the lines and not worked on our scene at all, we wouldn't have ended up feeling foolish in front of the whole class. We would have succeeded because we wouldn't have tried so hard.

The members of Team 6 have now bumped into me at least three times each. That's nine bumps, total, from that team, the last team to find this spot. I am desperate, so even though it was against the rules, I decide to interpret "bumping" as another way of "asking a question." I speak to the last person who ran into me, this girl about my age with runner's shorts and athletic shoes and a thin hard line to her mouth.

I ask Thin Mouth, "Can you pass me that?" meaning the squeegee that had just gone flying again, but she doesn't answer or get the squeegee; she ignores me. I know she's just trying to do the right thing: don't acknowledge this stranger, don't look this person in the eye. It just brings out the crazy.

The last time I looked someone in the eye, I was eight. I was riding my bike to the finish line to hang out with my dad. Back then, I wasn't working for him and I also adored him and missed him every weekend, because that's when the race runs. He had to work the race on the weekends so I didn't see him as much as I wished. It's not my fault that I adored him, that's how daughters feel about their dads, mostly. So I was riding up Franklin toward the restaurant where my dad was waiting for that day's racers to finish. Sometimes he had to wait for hours. Anyway, I was riding my bike up Franklin toward Highland and right outside the church, there was a man with a Mickey Mouse hat and a t-shirt with a tuxedo printed on it. I looked him in the eye. He had friendly eyes. He seemed to want to play. As he smiled at me, and waved, he pointed toward himself – but not at his chest, at his groin. Yes I looked, I was only eight – wouldn't you? – and it was hanging out of his unzipped pants like a fingerling potato.

I kept riding. My eyes were now trained on the sidewalk, no longer on his eyes, his groin, or his waving. I cut the widest berth I could while still staying off the street. I wasn't allowed to ride on the street with the cars, my parents didn't think it was safe. I pretended he was invisible. I willed him to be invisible. Just as I passed him, I held my breath, pedaling furiously. He could have easily pushed me over and snatched me, I now realize. But he let me by. I arrived at the restaurant and ate too many chips too fast. Their sharp edges raked my throat on the way down. I tried to make my throat feel better by guzzling a fountain Coke that was sickly sweet and had almost no carbonation. The chips and Coke were free, part of a special deal my dad had arranged with the restaurant.

It was hard to believe that all men had fingerling potatoes in their pants. I think that might have been the beginning of my dad's fall from his pedestal, though it took a while, since he didn't hit the ground until this year, after I started this awful job. It wasn't my dad's fault really. The guy with the Mickey Mouse hat was the one who had scared me, not my dad. But there was a weird similarity: they both waved the same way: fingers stretched wide, like a clown.

If Thin Mouth had given me the squeegee like I had asked her, then I could have returned the favor with a clue. I would have confided, in a conspiratorial whisper, "This isn't the *rear window*, is it?" Then Team 6 might know: *Rear Window* = Hitchcock movie. Hitchcock was the celebrity name they needed, and there he was at our feet, in brass letters inlaid in pink marble, embedded in the sidewalk on which we all stood, in front of the falafel place with the cleanest window in Hollywood. Team 6 would have their clue, solve it, add it to their list and move forward in the game, the goal being to discover the finish line. If they would just talk to me, they could absolve me of my participation, and I would be free.

Parkinsion Who?

By Adrianne Aron

ROSIE AT THE SAFEWAY

Did she have to say that? She was over by the organic carrots. I had just turned my cart away from the spinach and was pushing past the potatoes when all of a sudden her wide open blue eyes and big teeth smile at me from under that crown of silver hair. Her crown glints in the store's bright light, and she says, Maddie, how ya doin? You look kinda confused.

I forced a laugh. Be appropriate, I told myself. My fingers gripped the steel bar of the grocery cart. Did I really say that to myself? Be appropriate? Me, the gal who hung with the beats in North Beach and danced naked with the hippies in Golden Gate Park? I, who wiggled in a conga line behind Malvina Reynolds and belted out "It isn't nice to block the doorway," and got myself arrested time and again, and I'm talking to myself about *appropriate?* In Berkeley, at the Safeway, I should be *appropriate?*

Hi Rosie, I said. I was full of apologies for missing her gallery opening. "No problem, no problem," she insisted, "long as you promise to come to the next one." There was another exhibition in the works? "Not really," she said, "but this show might move around, so you could get another chance. And you? Whatchu up to?" Rosie spoke a funny mixture of ghetto slang and educated shtetl. Of all my friends, she was the quickest to come up with a six letter word for 14-down. She worked her crosswords in ink.

What was I up to? "I've just come from the doctor," I told her, averting my glance. The sweet, fresh smell of corn husks in the bin up ahead reached me while I paused. How much should I say? I noticed that the corn had finally come down in price. After a long silence I muttered, "I got a diagnosis." She looked at me. I looked at the corn. I let go of the steel bar, then touched it again with my fingertips. "Parkinson's," I said. I watched her lips tighten over those big teeth. "Oh my god" was all she said.

Then, perceptively, she asked, "Do you trust the doctor?"

I'd checked him out on the Internet: Indian, educated in America. B.A. from somewhere in Florida. Medical school in Tennessee. Young, competent-looking, handsome—a *shayne punim* my mother would have said, may she rest in peace. But he wants to start me on those heavy medications, and I've always steered away from the pills and gone instead for the natural stuff. This young man from India wasn't exactly what the doctor ordered, the doctor being my mother, and her sisters, and the aunts before them, who all knew what the doctor was supposed to be: a nice Jewish man trained in London, or maybe Paris, or Harvard, with a specialty in neurology from maybe Albert Einstein or Mount Zion. You understand? Rosie understood.

At a moment like this, between the organic carrots and the corn on the cob, after years of marching with a hand on the hip and a fist in the air demanding equality and peace and tolerance and a better, safer world for the children, when you find out that you'll be shaking your knees instead of your fists, and your fingers instead of your fanny, there's two things you really need: a good friend like Rosie and a nice Jewish doctor.

And there's something curious that happens to you: the Yiddish phrases you brushed up on in a community college class twenty-five years ago come back to you.

"But what about your memoirs?"

Did she have to say that, too? First the *confused,* noticing I'm looking sort of lost, and now the reminder that my time might be running out. Will there be a memoir now?

I'd started the memoir in a class at the senior center, when personal stories were all the rage and suddenly everybody over sixty was supposed to shoot for a Pulitzer. Why was she asking me this? Must have come from nervousness.

"What about anybody's memoirs?" I remark, blending myself into the zeitgeist. "I'm not so exceptional, you know. We're at the end of the Gutenberg Era."

Outside, across the parking lot, on the other side of Shattuck, the green awning of Black Oak Books stretches out above the front window of an empty store. A huge sign on the roof of the building advertises Retail Space for Lease. That's what it's come to: what we once savored as a flourishing bookstore we're now choking down as "retail space." *Commodities.* In another fifty years who's going to remember books? They hardly exist anymore, except as relics in the libraries where you can look up information on things like Parkinson's Disease—though it's more efficient and probably more informative to look it up on the Internet. The Internet is a Resource, the Book is a Commodity. *Retail.*

A long time ago a reporter broke a story at the *San Francisco Chronicle:* truckload after truckload of books from the public library being hauled to the Bay and loaded onto barges to be dumped as landfill. The shock had hardly worn off before the results began to appear in Emeryville: big-box blights behind high-rise condominiums that touched the water's edge, their underground garages sunk in deep concrete foundations resting on the scrunched, battered, discarded, compacted and recycled library books that had been sold by weight to developers. The hue and cry of the scandal faded away like all those words that trailed off into the watery mire. All those sunken adjectives, those prepositions that tried and tried to hold things together, to serve as mortar, to fend off the commodification and keep the memory alive. The old Spanish fortresses had strengthened their mortar with animal blood mixed with lime, but all we've got today is failed prose: passive verbs mixed with printer's ink, dribbling away in the wet while rebar tightens up inside concrete to support the establishment of Retail. Is there a place in that mix for a memoir of an eighty-one year-old woman? Is there time, when the digital clock has already been set by the diagnosis?

My daughter studied social work. At twenty-eight she put her kid in kindergarten and put herself in graduate school to specialize in "end of life" issues. Where does the "end of life" begin? I asked her. And she hedged, like they teach them to do in social work school. "It depends," she told me.

"Well of course it depends. But what does it depend on?" "Well, it's not exactly a *time,* it's more like a *state.*"

"New Hampshire's a state," I said. "What kind of state is End of Life?" "Please, Ma, wait till the end of the semester before you ask me questions like that."

We were having that conversation in 1978, in the playground of Jeremy's Extended Care. I gave the beach ball a little kick and watched it spin over the sand: reds, whites and blues tumbling after each other, then coming to a lazy stop. At that time my question was purely hypothetical. I expected that one day End of Life issues would sneak up behind me like a ghost, slowly, whispering, "Get ready." I'd also given some thought— there's nobody in the San Francisco Bay Area who escapes this one—to End of Life Issues crashing down on me suddenly, cataclysmically, 8.2 on the Richter Scale. And that was that: it would come either as a slow advisory or a quick disaster that gave you no time to think. And in spite of the friends I'd already lost by then, I didn't have a compartment in my brain for collecting End of Life issues. All these years later, I still don't.

End of Life *tissues:* those I know about—cottony, weightless paper squares bunched up in the waste baskets of skilled nursing facilities, SNF'S, or "Sniffs," as we like to say. But you can't read them as lessons; no two Kleenexes are alike. What for one person can open the faucet for a stream of tears might for somebody else tickle a funnybone and make for a laugh. At the memorial for my friend Jim last year, his nephew Bobby started right away with the handkerchief to the eyes at the memory of Uncle Jimmy teaching him to drive when he was a kid. Up there at the microphone with flower vases hanging their bouquets over both his shoulders, Bobby was so overcome with grief he had to be helped away from the podium and Jim's cousin Laverne, next in line to share, had to rush over with her gospel song. Mike, in the pew behind me, whispered in my ear, "Catch that irony. Getting gushy over a driving lesson from a man who spent his whole life railing against the internal combustion engine!" He was right: of all the memories Jim lost in the fog of Alzheimer's, that was one he'd have been glad got blottoed. I have a hunch the same sort of thing goes for people's issues at the "End of Life": what for one is a conclusion is for another mere illusion, and what the social worker's got in mind for dealing with me might have nothing to do with me at all.

Rosie had parked her cart in front of the carrots and rested her elbows on the steel push-bar. She leaned inward, toward the basket full of groceries, and frowned at me over a roll of paper towels. "I didn't mean will you work on the memoirs," she said defensively. "I meant, will the diagnosis change what you'll be writing about."

"Ah," I said, smiling to get her off the hook, "Susan Sontag already beat me to it. I won't write about disease. Disease isn't life."

83

A grimace crossed her face. I knew what she was thinking: It isn't life; it's death.

Somehow, nothing she could say would come out right. I had to fix it for her so she wouldn't go away depressed. Using just enough irony not to sound like a cheerleader, I told her I'd only write about the good stuff.

"Then you better leave Steffan out of it altogether."

"What should I do?" I asked, "turn him into a sperm bank?"

Steffan was my first husband, the father of both my children. I was glad the subject had moved away from death, even if there had to be a cameo appearance by a bastard like Steffan to make it happen.

"Write it as science fiction! Turn him into a *mensch*." Rosie's big teeth spread out across her mouth in a crackling laugh.

"I've got to run," I pleaded. "Check the price on the corn."

Failure

By Ryann Murrin-DeSouza

Failure is like a fine wine.
It seems to get better with more time.
Failure is not a sign of weakness,
It's a sign of courage.
That you're willing to try and try,
Even if you don't win.
Tried and true,
Just keep doing what you do.
One day that Failure will get you to the place you need to be.
Failure can be a sign of courage,
Keep doing what you need to do.

351 Genre Novelist, First Chapter

Under

By Missy Kirtley

CHAPTER ONE: THE WOODEN GATE

"Shit, I gotta go," Jess Summers mumbled after glancing at her phone. At least she'd had it plugged in all night. She rolled over in the bed, reaching across her ex-boyfriend Corey's chest, and tugged the plug from the wall socket.

"What?" He asked, still half-asleep.

"I've got an appointment," Jess bounced out of the bed, and searched the room for her clothes. Panties, bra, jeans, shirt, sweatshirt, socks, shoes. She had to reach under the bed to find her other shoe. There was no telling how it got under there. Last night was a mistake.

Drinking too much, meeting up with Corey, coming back here... At least she'd had a safe place to sleep.

She was gonna have to do something about that eviction notice. Eventually.

Now dressed and still rushing, her thoughts were scattered as she grabbed a couple Red Bulls out of his fridge and her backpack from the far cushion of the sofa. "I'll call you!" She yelled back to Corey, and let herself out.

Jess' car was by the curb on the street outside of Corey's apartment building. Everything important she owned in the world was in the back of that car: her laptop, her favorite Van Halen t-shirt, her dream-catcher, and an assortment of other things were packed in so tightly she didn't have room for passengers.

As she climbed into the driver's seat, her cell phone buzzed. Jess gave another quick curse as she saw it was her sister.

"Hello?" Jess pulled the phone to her ear and slammed the door closed behind her.

"Jessica, where the hell are you?" It was her twin sister, Jennifer, on the other end and she didn't sound happy.

"Good morning to you, too." Jess grumbled, turning on the car. She was supposed to be at her sister's place right this minute, so of course her sister was calling. Jenny never gave Jess the benefit of the doubt--never gave her sister a few minutes leeway before assuming she was running late. (Which she almost always was.) "My alarm didn't go off--"

"You mean you didn't set it." Jenny correctly assumed. "Just get your ass over here as fast as humanly possible."

"Wait wait, why don't we meet there?" Jess lifted her hand to rub her forehead. There was a tension headache coming on. Or maybe it was the hangover setting in. "I'll just meet you at the hospital and we can go from there?"

"Our appointment is in thirty minutes, and I wanted to go over this paperwork with you before we--"

"Thirty minutes at the hospital," Jess repeated. That meant that she had thirty more minutes than her sister led her to believe. "Come on, I'll just follow your lead. I don't need to see it beforehand."

Jenny sighed into the phone.

"I'll bring donuts?" Jess offered in a sing-song voice.

There was a chuckle on the other end of the line. "When are you going to grow up, little sister?"

"Never in a million years." Jess responded.

"All right," Jenny said. "Make mine a bear claw. And you're waiving any right to a last minute decision change."

Jess pulled away from the curb. "Like you ever listen to my input anyway," she said with a little grin on her lips.

"Right right. Drive safe."

They both hung up. Jess tossed the phone onto the cluttered passenger seat and turned up the radio. There was a song by Ninja on. Jess loved Ninja. She sang along with the voice of the British crooner--the band hadn't been popular since she was a little kid, but whenever the music came on the classics station, Jess loved it. The guitar riffs were legendary.

"Take my heart and take my home, I'll give you all I have to give, just don't leave me all alone, you give me reason, reason to live."

Deep stuff. Jess debated getting out her iPod and putting that album on, though the classics station played a lot of Ninja. This song was nearly as old as she was. Jess grew up listening to Ninja, but loved them a whole lot more when she was younger--back when she was in high school and dyed her hair black, wore wallets with chains and a nose ring. Her mother had hated the nose ring.

Thank God there was no line at the donut shop. Jess ordered, paid with a fistful of crumpled, one-dollar-bills, and carried the pink box back to her car. Then it was off to the hospital to meet her cranky sister.

Jess really couldn't blame Jenny for being so cranky. Jenny had had a hard year. With medical school taking up her days and nights, and her husband driving his truck extra hours to help pay for it, their lives couldn't have been easy. Then adding in their mother's terminal illness...

That was something that Jess didn't like thinking about. She reached for a cd in her glove box and popped it into the player. Commercials wouldn't do--especially because it was getting close to Christmas, and the last thing she wanted to hear about was how much money she was supposed to be spending on loved ones.

Jess and Jenny didn't have any more family now their mother was gone. The twins never knew their father. He'd done one of those cliched 'going out for smokes' and never returning things. But the girls had never wanted for anything. Their mother worked hard, three jobs from time to time, and had close friends to help with their after-school care. And she was there for all the important events. There to help with homework, to cheer at soccer matches and give standing ovations for theatrical productions. Jess and Jenny's mother was the best ever. And now she was gone.

Jenny had her husband, Tom the Trucker, and Jess had--well, she supposed she had Corey the Drummer. Her ex. They'd been on-again off-again for years now, ever since he convinced her to drop out of community college and go on tour with the band. The band that hadn't made it. Probably mostly due to Jess' horrible guitar playing skills. She still kept extra set of strings in her bag, even though her guitar was long gone; traded years ago for a burrito and a ride across town. A part of her couldn't let go of the dream.

The parking lot at the hospital was practically a ghost town. Jess pulled up to the third level, as the first two were reserved for doctors and hospital staff, and easily spotted Jenny and her car half-way down the row. She pulled into the spot next to her sister, and gasped.

"Jenny!" Jess scolded, climbing up out of her car. "What are you doing?"

Jenny took one last puff on her cigarette and then flicked it to the ground to snuff it out with her shoe.

"Did you bring my bear claw?' Jenny asked, blowing a puff of foul-smelling smoke all around her.

Jess hated cigarettes for a number of reasons. One, her father supposedly went out for a pack and then never returned when she and Jenny were still in diapers. Two, her ex-boyfriend smoked, and it reminded her of him. Three, well, they were cancer-causing and smelled like ass.

"Since when are you a smoker? Gross." Jess complained, reaching into the car for her backpack and the donut box. She put the backpack on her shoulders and brought the box out, then closed her car door.

"Nevermind, where's my bear claw?" Jenny asked, moving a little closer. She wrapped her arms around herself, tightening her sweater across her chest. Jenny was wearing scrubs under the long and cozy looking sweater, her blonde hair pulled up into a sloppy bun. She had her large, hospital bag over one shoulder.

"Here." Jess responded, opening the box and holding it toward her sister.

"Thanks." Jenny reached in and grabbed the bear claw. There were another half dozen donuts in there, too, but Jenny only had eyes for the claw. She started in immediately, and spoke through a mouthful of pastry. "What, no coffee?"

"No," Jess shook her head. Coffee would have been a fantastic idea today. Warm them up and give some pep, too. Now she was thinking about a peppermint white mocha and a cranberry bliss bar from Starbucks...

"I've got a couple Red Bulls in my bag, though."

"That stuff will kill you." Jenny frowned, starting toward the elevator across the garage. "No, smoking will kill you," Jess argued. She bent down to tie her shoe--these Converse were old and falling apart. At least she had a roll of duct tape in her backpack. She could fix them. "Red Bull gives you wings."

There was no response from Jenny. Actually, there was no sound at all. Jess frowned and lifted her head. For the second time today she gasped at what she saw.

Jenny was being held with her arms behind her back. There were bearded men dressed in strange clothes, surrounding her on three sides, dragging her away. San Francisco was cold, but it wasn't cold enough for fur lined jackets and hats, pants tied with strips of leather. They looked like Sherpas on the side of a mountain without all the snow.

"Jenny!" Jess screamed.

The sherpas all turned to glare at Jess, showing off gold teeth and narrowing bushy eyebrows. Jenny struggled in their arms.

"Let go of me! Jess!" Jenny called back.

Then a dirty-looking hand was clamped over Jenny's mouth. It was clad in a fingerless glove. Jenny still squealed underneath it, but her cries were muted.

The sherpas pulled on Jenny, moving quickly despite how hard the woman was struggling against them, and brought her with them toward a wooden gate in the wall of the garage. Jess had been in this parking structure dozens of times over the last couple of years, due to her mother's failing health, and had spent many nights crying against these walls in her mother's last weeks. But she'd never seen that gate before. It was out of place, wood in a garage that was walls of concrete, and it had a strange, shimmering glow. Jess shook her head, as if expecting to shake the image from her mind.

She started off after them, breaking into a run. It was only about thirty feet to the wall, and the strange gate, but it felt like she was moving through pudding.

The gate was almost closed with the sherpas and her sister on the other side. Jess lunged the last couple of feet, stuck out her arm and thrust her elbow between the wooden gate and its frame--stopping it from closing. It wasn't heavy, and did no damage to her arm. Then she pushed it open so she could rush through.

And that's when the world turned upside down.

It was evening on the other side. There was a black sky dotted with sparkling, white stars. Everything was turning and twisting, but Jess thought she could see Jenny being dragged off--could hear her sister's whimpers and muffled shrieks as the sherpas pulled her toward... what? Jess couldn't see. Everything was spinning violently, and it was dark. Jess was now standing in a clearing on the other side of the gate which lacked streetlights and glowing windows in tall buildings on either side of the street. Actually, it lacked a street, too.

Jess managed to keep her footing, even though the vertigo was intense. This is how Dorothy Gale must have felt when the house was ripped from its foundation and tossed around in that powerful twister. Or how Alice must have felt when she fell down that rabbit hole. Only a thousand times worse. So much worse.

The pink box of donuts fell out of Jess' hands and tumbled to the ground. It remained closed when it landed, but was upside down on the dirt path. Jess could see that much as she wrapped her arms around her middle. All at the same time she was nauseous, dizzy, cold and sweating. The idea that this place—this different world she'd come into when she came through the wooden gate—was bad for her crossed Jess' mind quickly, but then she fell face forward onto the ground. Her eyes closed. Jess slipped into unconsciousness.

Prose Poem For Annie

By Jo Carpignano

Enjoying an extraordinary performance by Cirque du Soleil, enthralled by the sudden appearance of birds and butterflies above me, the acrobats soaring overhead, a reminder of my conversation with Annie just before she died. Preparing lunch on our last visit, she sighed over always wishing she could fly like a bird. Others scoffed when she mentioned this dream, she said. Soaring and gliding overhead was a foolish thing to wish. I said it was a beautiful dream, and shared the same. We talked about hang gliding over canyons, and soaring across valleys in bright striped balloons. I had once tried parasailing, I said, and told her we might do that together someday. She only smiled, knowing how short the time.

As graceful bodies glided through the air, in colorful costumes; soaring like birds, or with outspread wings rising and falling like butterflies, I thought of Annie. Watching those colorful performers, I remembered how earnestly Annie expressed her dream. Then the figure of an angel appeared, waving her magic wand, turning each bird into a star, and every butterfly into a blossom.

Fighting the overwhelming desire to rush away from the theater, I remained in my seat, let the silent tears fall, and whispered, *fly Annie, fly.*

More Coffee

By Lisa Meltzer Penn

A little caffeine, combined
With nerves like an engine that's overrunning and needs
To be kicked down and uses up all the gas and
Never goes,
Kills sleep.
Again, I let this damn poem yank me
Out of bed.

I'm awake.
So is the lamp peering over the neck of my
Chair, a spider that kneels on the ceiling, and the humming
Refrigerator downstairs.
So is my father's snore
In the other room.

Read in the Times about a man being convicted for murder
(they found out later he was innocent),
About a boy who hung himself in tree,
An article on 3-foot tall tube worms,
The presidential race.

I hear a truck
Waking up.
Another bird is up.
Stay tuned for station identification.
(I have to go to the bathroom—damn coffee.)

Sunfall and sunrise are parenthesis
Of the world.
With the steady beat
Of the crazy sun rising, I'll
Fall on the bed into sleep that finally
Sucks me down, my body
Stiff like a turned-over corpse, toes
Curled at the edge. Maybe I'll dream
Again that elephants without trunks are maneaters
Or about the time you
Crawled out from under my sheets
And back to hers.
(The wind whistled through my head.)
That spider's still kneeling on that ceiling.

Fanboys Shrugged

By Dave Strom

CHAPTER ZERO: THE AWESOME ORIGIN STORY!

SURFVILLE, CALIFORNIA. THE GEEK GUY'S COMICS AND COFFEE CORNER. MID MAY. A SATURDAY. 2:47 P.M.

"Your comic book made me cry," the Kittygirl cosplayer softly meowed. Holly Hansson sat bolt upright. She'd never meant to hurt a little girl!

TOK! Holly's pen bounced off her signing table.

KAH-LATTER! And hit the floor.

FLUR-FLUFFLE! Followed by some of her comic books stacked next to her iced mocha. Which hadn't spilled. Whew!

Her writing life flashbacked like a dying rock star on uppers, singing his memoirs in ten seconds. Twenty years ago. Four years old. Holly had screamed at the movie screen, "Punch him, punch him, WHY DON'T YOU PUNCH HIM?!?!" But that dumb movie actress just cringed against the wall while the bad guy beat up the hero and a baseball bat was only six inches away from the actress's stupid hand! From then on, Holly dedicated her life to writing stories where the girls were brave and smart and STRONG! Finally, in *The Last Super*, Holly's self-published graphic novel and personal masterpiece, The Overlady journeyed from evil, to good, to the ultimate sacrifice ... and had brought tears to big, brown, liquid, little girl eyes made oh so adorable with Kittygirl makeup.

Holly reached across the table and grasped a little gloved hand. *Ow! Realistic Kittygirl claws!* "I'm so sorry, sweetie!"

Fans in the line to Holly's table gaped. A whopping dozen fangirls and seven fanboys.

It was taking so long to build an audience. A couple of fanboys aimed phone cameras. Great, now comic books hurting kids might go viral.

The little Kittygirl smiled big and bright, twitching her pasted-on whiskers. "It was a good kind of cry!" She shoved a well-worn copy of *The Last Super* across the table and hopped like she'd drunk a gallon of coffee an hour ago. "Sign it sign it sign it please please please please PLEASE?"

"Aw!" chorused the signing line, guys browsing superhero toys and magazines, and couples sipping coffee in the coffee bar.

"Sure, I'd love to." Holly gulped sweet, creamy mocha and took the girl's book. *Wow, maybe I should hire her for future signings!*

A Japanese woman petted the girl between pointy Kittygirl ears and spoke with an accent that could bend steel with her bare tongue. "Miss Hansson, I know you didn't write this for kids. But my daughter found it in my manga stash and I can't get it out of her hands. Until now. I guess some girls like when the princess gives up her crown."

The girl's face became very serious. "Holly? Did you really put your blood in the book?"

Holly forced her smile to stay on her face. That publicity stunt had cost a pretty penny and two pints of blood and that bloody edition barely sold. "I sure did. What's your name, sweetie?"

"Katsuko Kimura." Her diction sounded well-read. And no accent. Her mommy must have been a stickler for her kids speaking as the Romans do.

Just like Holly's daddy. How she missed his sing-song Swedish accent... she swallowed a lump in her throat and signed the graphic novel, *To Katsuko, my littlest yet biggest fan. Holly Hansson.* She put another comic book into Katsuko's dainty hands. "And for cosplaying so cutely, here's *The Last Super, issue zero.*"

Katsuko's eyes went anime big and sparkly. "Wow! A prequel! I love you, Holly!" She hugged comic book and graphic novel to her chest, then tilted her head like a curious kitten. "But why did the artwork style change in issue four?"

Ugh. The infamous issue where John Glutt drew The Overlady as C-cups on page 1, then bigger and bigger on each succeeding page, until a quadruple-F two-page spread had made Holly spit her afternoon coffee ten feet. She couldn't hold onto her smile this time. "Because he drew the Oversized, I mean, the Overlady—"

Something bombastic Holly's way bellowed. "It's because a woman took a man's job!"

"What are YOU doing here?" yelled Holly at the upright baby whale filling the store's front doorway.

John Glutt's three-hundred-and-plenty pounds bobbled his belly under a red supersuit. An acre of spandex wasted. He stepped inside, turned his back, and ... BENT OVER? Was he too scared to face her, or was the moon going to come out early?

He tossed his cape aside. "Taste sticky justice!"

Wait, on his back ... he actually DID IT! Holly leaped to her feet— fluttering her homemade bat cape and knocking her coffee onto her stack of issue zeroes, dammit—and hurtled over the table. The fart was imminent, she wasn't gonna make it! She grabbed at a red-white-and-blue costumed fanboy: "GIMME!"

BTTFFFTT-KER-SPLAT! A gluey net blanketed the store. Beneath it, heaps of geeks writhed upon the floor, walls, tables, and the coffee counter.

Except for Holly! She tossed aside the fanboy's web-covered shield that had worked just like in the comic books! She flexed her long, strong legs to first charge and then kick a boat-size butt ... but the floor rushed up instead. How come Captain Patriot never got shot in the ankles?

Holly punched and flailed against gravity. Which was not impressed. A broad, bat- logoed chest bashed her face. A huge belt buckle flicked her beaky nose. Tree trunk thighs rubbed her cheek. Dark boots hit her face.

She did a fast push-up, then stood... no. She could only sit up. Her legs stayed folded beneath her, stuck in a pillow of webbing. It smelled like rotten milk, felt so sticky, so icky, like a thousand spiders creeping up her thighs. That black widow bite so many years ago that had made her for so many days and she hated crawly spiders and their HORRIBLE DISGUSTING GLUEY STICKY WEBS!

"YyyyyaaaaAAAAAHHHHH!!!" Holly thrashed and scratched and hyperventilated at the unyielding cotton candy on her legs and frantically brushed her flinching hands on her forearms to get that rotten rancid goop off but it stuck to her arms and ... and ... she stopped. For she had glimpsed THE crimefighter at her side. Panting, shaking, she looked up to the cowled face of the Batman statue. *If only you were real.*

John's voice felt nauseatingly close, even from twenty feet away. "That's right, fangirl! KNEEL before your GOD!"

Trust John to make a movie line sexist. Holly dialed her cell phone. "I'm calling the cops, Fatman!" Wait. No dial tone!

John dramatically swung his head in time with his over-pronounced laugh. "Hah, hah, HAH! Your phone is as useless as a woman mathematician!" He pulled a small gadget out of one of the dozens of pouches on his costume and placed it near the cash register. "When I dispense my morality, my Alpha-Jammer prevents rude interruptions!"

Holly asked, "You're not Arachnid Guy?" She had a better idea of what the "A" stretched upon John's chest stood for.

He strutted toward Holly like a macho walrus. "No. I am," he puffed himself up, "ALPHA MAN! With my fear-inspiring costume which is based upon my original Arachnid Guy artwork, AND my array of Alpha-Gadgets which were invented by my brother-in-law Silicon Shrub and paid for by my vast family-in-law wealth, AND my Objectificationistic code which guides me to the path of moral superiority, I hereby swear by my lust for my art that I shall never again work for the tyranny of a fangirl! I shall shape the world of fandom into MY image!"

Holly rolled her eyes at John standing over her. Still, she had to admire his expositional breath control. "What's next? Building a fortress in the shape of your head?"

John's lip curled. It did that well. "That comes later. For now, I take back from a taker!"

"I paid you what I owed," Holly snapped, "even your penalty clause!" She took a breath for some exposition of her own. But it stuck in her throat. Behind John, under webbing, Katsuko's mother frantically whispered to a young lady wearing an amazon supersuit, tiara, and golden rope.

The amazon's face clouded with rage. She yelled at John, "HEY, ALPO MAN! Your costume is WRONG! Dan Mann designed Arachnid Guy's web guns to shoot from his WRISTS!"

John turned his back on Holly. "Who DARES— ooo, a collectible!" He grabbed a nine-inch Power Girl from a large rack of large-racked superheroine figurines and stuffed it into a pouch in his cape. He leaned over the amazon lady. "It is RIGHT! As I told that worthless writer years ago, spiders spin webs from the tips of their abdomens!"

Holly reached out, just one yank on John's cape— *Grr*, too far ... then something stirred against her leg. From under her cape, a small gloved hand flicked like a snake's tongue, clawing at the webbing clutching her legs. *Katsuko!*

An S-logoed fanboy flexed his biceps against the webbing—what little biceps there were under his blue costume's muscle padding—and said, "But web shooters aren't mechanical! I saw Arachnid Guy grow spinnerets!"

John sent flecks of spittle far and wide with his derisive snort. "Only in that Philistine movie! Although my webbing is also organic ... Ooo, another collectible!" He grabbed several Chain-Mail Bikini Babe comics and stuffed them into his cape pouch.

Holly kept her mouth shut. Katsuko clawed. And those brave comic book geeks were keeping the bad guy busy as only they could!

The Geek Guy joined the fight: "At least in that movie, the costume was the correct shade of red!"

John sputtered. "Are you saying movie directors do colors better than artists?" A fangirl sneered. "Yeah, and I'm saying Arachnid Guy doesn't wear a cape!" "My Alpha-cape covers my—"

"Cover your face, stupid! Secret identity! **MASK!!!**" "I shall NOT hide my greatness under—"

"How's your humongousness gonna stick to ceilings without making the roof fall in, Captain Blubber?"

"I told you, I am Alpha Man! ALPHA, ALPHA, ALPHA!" "Gesundheit! And you couldn't alpha a puppy!"

Holly wished SO HARD she could join that debate! Secret identities had been done to death, costume color mattered, and only super snobs used the word Philistine!

Then a moronic mumble brought pin-drop silence. "So, you like, shot organic stuff out your butt?"

That seemed to have come from one of two teenage dudes wearing white t-shirts with the letter D crudely drawn on the chest. Holly couldn't tell which one had spoken, their smiles were equally mouth-breathing stupid. Holly had advertised she'd give free comic books to cosplayers. Someone must have read the ad to them.

One dude's smile got bigger. "Uh, that's why there's so much web. Cuz there was so much butt." They laughed, a monotone that Holly hoped would not lower her IQ via osmosis. "Huh huh huh, uhhh, huh huh huh!"

The S-logoed fanboy gagged. He clawed desperately at the webbing over him. "Get it off me, GET IT OFF ME!"

A fangirl chewed on her webbing covering her face. "Grr, I'll get rid of—" Her eyes bugged out. She spat like she'd found a dead rat in her hamburger. "WHAT AM I DOING?"

Throughout the store, webbing roiled with convulsing and screaming fanboys and fangirls. "YUCK!" "GROSS!" "IT STINKS!" "YOU VILE, VOMITOUS VILLAIN!!!"

"Butt web! Huh huh huh!

The Dog of Pel

By Mary Holland

Jamie Pel nailed new shingles onto the roof of his small house. He had chores to finish before the cold came and it suited him to be up here alone as he worked off his anger and irritation. The local girl, his last unofficial liaison, had slammed out of the house last night after a final volley of recriminations. The peace was welcome.

It was a beautiful clear day, with no hint of fall rain. Several years before, he'd deliberately chosen a dwelling without near neighbors in a remote corner of Pel Demesne. The locals knew who he was and steered any encroaching brickies or begging waifs away. In return, he listened to their problems and did what he could. He did what was possible. He had no Power, could not grant what he did not have, no matter what some people thought. He'd made that plain at the beginning, although Jenifer had obviously not listened. Her assumption that he'd lied to get her into his bed had made him angrier than anything else she'd said.

He finished a row of shingles and sat on the roof ridge for a rest. From there he had a clear view to the Reave Mountains in the east. This far from the demesne border the Boundary was a faint haze, almost invisible. Autumn colors had started in the trees: scarlet, orange and gold. Some leaves had dropped and the cool scent of fall was in the air. This wasn't home but it was beautiful.

He watched a hawk soar and tilt its wings, turning his head to follow the bird as it searched for prey. The hawk floated over the path to the house and then veered away, its smooth flight disturbed by an intruder. Jamie shaded his eyes. If Jenifer returned with renewed arguments, no matter how loud she yelled or what missiles she flung at his head he couldn't do what she wanted. He was tired of saying it. But it wasn't Jenifer.

Three people were coming up the path, a tall man in the lead, wearing a heavy hunting jacket with a scarf of green and brown. Pel colors. Jamie blinked. His uncle the Magne of Pel walked up the path, as if he were any prosperous tenant visiting a neighbor and not the lord of the entire demesne. Two bodyguards followed him, dressed in Pel day livery, their weapons invisible. The second guard had a small sack slung at his belt.

Jamie slid down the roof to the top of the ladder.

"We're fine." His uncle called up, answering the unspoken question. "Alexandra's entertaining guests at Pel House. Her friends; not mine. I came to ask a favor. Can you leave that?"

"Two more rows, fifteen minutes and I'll be done here." The bodyguards looked awed. Every other person in the demesne, except his cousin Alexandra, would leap down the ladder immediately. But the Magne smiled and said, "I'll wait for you inside."

Jamie heard his steps cross the small porch. One of the bodyguards moved out of Jamie's sight to the back of the house while the other watched the path.

Jamie nailed in the rows, his mind far away from his hands. The Magne had suggested this house when Jamie had explained what he wanted, but as far as Jamie knew he hadn't been here in years. Whatever favor he wanted must be serious and—if he hadn't publicly summoned Jamie to Pel House—private, although not secret. If he walked up from the village he must have traveled there by tram; he had undoubtedly been seen. Jamie gathered his tools, climbed down the ladder, and stacked the unused shingles. Three Powers knew when he'd get back to this.

The Magne had put the kettle to boil on the Power plate in the small kitchen. When Jamie entered, he was standing by the Power tap, his hand on the shielding, below the quartered square symbol of old Gallia placed by the original builder. Sixteen demesnes were now twelve but Jamie had never gotten around to covering up the bottom four. The Portall, guardians of the Boundaries, would not approve, but his uncle didn't seem to notice. The Magne had removed his jacket and his cream wool shirt was finely made.

You might, if you didn't know, take him for a wealthy man of late middle age, perhaps a retired tenant or brickie worker who had done well. Until he turned around and you saw the Power-implanted symbol of the Magne, the imblem, centered on his chest where the shirt's cut circle displayed it. There was the imblem of Pel Demesne: the profile of a standing dog. There was no doubt what you were facing, then.

"Nice clean tap. You have a good deal in reserve." The Magne pulled his hand away.

Jamie took his word for it. He'd never felt more than a faint and distant vibration when he touched the tap. Of course, he wasn't supposed to. "I don't use much. Cooking, hot water, and now that it's getting cooler, a bit of heat in the early morning. I could use a Power brick instead." As Jenifer had pointed out the previous night.

The Magne frowned. "You're not a brickie, James, no matter how little Power you use. You are a demesne heir. You will have a full tap because your status demands it."

Jamie had always been curious about the Power, but his uncle avoided discussing it. Alexandra swore he never talked to her either but she had shrugged it off, claiming she had years ahead of her to learn. Jamie wasn't sure his cousin was telling the truth. The Magne was generally reasonable, even indulgent, to his heirs. But it was true there were things he would not discuss, and he could snap your head off for asking. Cautiously, Jamie asked, "Can you move a Power tap?"

The Magne frowned again. "What's this? Are you leaving this house?" He waved his hand around the small space, "I thought it was what you wanted."

The Trolley

By Judy Jette-Hansen

It was autumn, Sky's favorite time of year. And boy did she love it, especially on her way to the trolley stop. She would run through the narrow streets, aiming for the neatly raked piles of fallen leaves.

SMACK! Up went the leaves as if they were reaching for the clouds, and then down as if bowing at Sky's feet.

Life was good for Sky. She was 12 and not a baby any more. Ma said she was now old enough to take the trolley by herself. On her first few trips Granny had accompanied her and reviewed with her "the rules," and even told her the "Wini Maples" story. But she was on her own now; she was a big girl who knew "the rules" by heart.

Wini Maples was a bright 12 year old girl from the French Quarter. She was a straight A student and her favorite pastime was reading. In fact, from time to time Wini would be so involved in a novel that she would miss her stop and be late for school. Since this happened regularly, the teachers stopped worrying about Wini being late.

On a cold winter Wednesday, it wasn't until late afternoon that the school noticed Wini was missing. Her parents confirmed she had boarded her usual trolley for school that day.

A search by the New Orleans police produced only her novel and school books, left on the trolley. The driver recalled seeing Wini seated next to an older derelict type woman. Wini caught his attention because she seemed preoccupied with looking out the trolley windows, straining very hard to see something. Unfortunately the driver did not see when Wini exited the trolley. The police department came up empty-handed. Wini had just vanished.

Each day at the Garden District trolley stop, Sky would sit and wait patiently, grasping her school books tightly and talking to no one. She would repeat "the rules" over in her head and remember Wini's story. Rule number one: "Talk to no one."

When the trolley finally arrived, she would head straight for the seat just behind the driver. Rule number two: "Always sit behind the driver in his mirror's view and don't wander off."

Sky found the trolley ride to and from school a bit lonely at times. Not many other kids took the trolley; there were mostly local adults and tourists from the French Quarter. To pass the time she would gaze out the window at the beautiful Garden District Victorians, often picturing herself as a princess viewing her kingdom from one of the large bay windows. When she gazed out, if the sun was just right, she could see the reflection of her long curly auburn hair in the window and imagine a jeweled tiara upon her head.

On a particularly nice autumn school morning, Sky found herself gazing at the Victorians a bit longer than usual. It appeared her trolley was going to sit in the same spot for a while due to mechanical difficulties.

Sky gazed at the Victorians and absorbed their splendor. She was particularly taken by the tall, castle like home just adjacent to her. It appeared to have a small glimmer coming from the attic's window. "What could it be?" Sky thought. Curiosity getting the best of her, she concentrated all her efforts towards the glimmer. The more she stared, the more her imagination started to run away from her. Could it be the reflection of a knight's coat of armor? Could it be the sun's reflection off a wicked Queens's broach? Sky kept staring and straining to see what it was. She found if she leaned way back in her seat, the glimmer became brighter. "Maybe if I walk down the trolley's aisle, I can get a better look," she thought. With that, she rose up out of her seat. As she prepared to take her first step down the aisle, WHAM! She slammed herself back down into her seat. "Are you nuts?" she thought. "What's rule number two? Always sit behind the driver in his mirror's view and don't wander off! Do you want to end up like Wini?" Sky felt herself tossing the idea over and over, as the glimmer became a bit more enticing with every thought.

Sky sat quietly for a bit, trying not to look or think about the glimmer. But she was filled with a sense of curiosity that was unbearable. It was as if the glimmer had a life of its own and was calling to her.

She tried desperately to recite "the rules" to herself, but they wouldn't come. She couldn't remember them. All she could think about was the glimmer. "Just one more look" she thought. Finally giving in, she turned and leaned way back in her seat. Almost instantly she was filled with a sense of panic, the glimmer was fading. "Oh God, I'll never know what it was." And with that, she became engrossed with only one thought as she rose from her seat and headed down the trolley's aisle.

With each step Sky took, her heart beat faster and she became more and more excited. She pushed her fellow passengers aside one after another as she traveled through the crowded car. "Get out of my way, let me see!" She exclaimed. Sky was almost in a frenzy with each step she took. She just couldn't get a clear enough look through crowd.

Then, finally a break, a young girl shorter than Sky was standing just ahead in the aisle. If she could just reach her, it would be easy to see over her, Sky thought. "Now if I can just get past these last couple of people." Just as she was about to reach the girl, she was startled by the trolley driver's voice. "OK folks, the track's clear ahead, we'll be under way shortly."

"No!!" shouted Sky. And with that she pushed her way out the exit door.

As she rushed down the trolley stairs and her feet hit the street, she felt the wind from the leaving trolley brush against her. "I've got to get over there. I've got to see the glimmer! It's calling me, I feel it." She ran down and across the street dodging traffic and pedestrians along the way. "The glimmer, I see it. It's getting brighter, warmer, and waiting for me! I'm coming, I'm coming." Sky cried.

Sky was so obsessed with the glimmer; she tripped on the curb as she ran up to the tall, castle like Victorian. Her head strained way back as her eyes scaled the structure. "The attic, it's up there, I can see it. It's so bright and warm. It's waiting and calling for me." Sky pushed herself past the rusted iron gate and dashed up the marble steps. She banged on the coarse wooden door and cranked the brass door chime.

An older derelict type woman slowly opened the heavy door. Sky pushed past her yelling "Move! It's calling me!" and headed straight for the wooden spiral staircase.

Sky traveled up four flights of stairs, sometimes skipping two and three steps at a time. Each step creaked loudly beneath her feet as she climbed. Her nostrils filled with the musty odor from the house. The woman was in hot pursuit behind her.

Upon reaching the top landing, she was faced with a large black iron door. She banged frantically while twisting the knob, but it was locked. "Let me in!" she yelled. She turned around as the woman reached the landing. Sky grasped and shook her. "Where is the key?" "Here in my hand, my child" the woman replied. "Let me in!" Sky cried. "Of course my child." With that Sky grabbed the key and swung open the door.

As the iron door flew open, a surge of ice cold air pushed past Sky. To her shock and disbelief, the large Victorian room was almost empty. It didn't contain a knight's armor or a wicked Queen at all. It only contained a girl seated in a chair facing the bay windows.

"Where is it?" Sky shouted! "Where is the glimmer"? She entered the room only to be startled by the slamming and locking of the door behind her. She tried the knob but it wouldn't budge. Sky ran across the warped floor boards up to the girl and was shocked to see a bright reflection radiating from her chest. It was a huge crystal crucifix hanging from her neck. "Is that all it was?" Sky exclaimed "A crucifix! Oh God what have I done?"

Sky was filled with a sick sinking feeling. She grabbed the girl in a panic! "Let's get out of here." "Help me!" "Do you hear me?" Sky became more and more panicked and started frantically shaking the girl.Finally releasing her in disgust, Sky then watched as the girl slid off the chair onto the floor with a thud! "Oh God, I'm sorry, are you OK?" Give me your hand and I'll help you up.

A horrible shriek came from Sky and streams of tears hit her cheeks upon seizing the girl's hand. It felt ice cold, stiff and lifeless. Sky gasped as the girl's eyes rolled back into her head and her body fell limp. "Oh my God she's dead!" Sky released her grasp and ran to the door. She began pounding and yelling. She pounded for what seemed like hours while the girl lay lifeless and cold across from her.

As the sun started to set, Sky gave up. She was cold exhausted and she knew no one could hear her screams. All she wanted was a second chance to feel her Ma's arms around her again. It terrified Sky to realize she was alone and no one knew she was in the house.

All of a sudden, the door to the room flew open and the woman entered. Sky dashed for the open door but was grabbed and thrown to the floor by the woman. She tried for the door again, only to be stopped and smashed down again. The woman pinned her to the floor and reached for something shiny from her apron pocket. It was a large silver syringe. Sky struggled with all her might but to no avail; the needle was entering her arm. Sky unwillingly surrendered to the thick numb feeling filling her body.

Her mind was telling her to fight, but she was no longer in control of her body. She fell to the floor, paralyzed.

Lying there helpless, Sky watched in horror as the woman dragged her next to the lifeless girl. The woman left the room and returned with a chair. She picked up the other girl and placed her back in her seat. She then reached for Sky, and placed her in the new chair. As she straightened Sky's hair and clothes, the woman took from her apron pocket an identical crystal crucifix and placed it around Sky's neck. She then told Sky, "You have failed, my child. You knew "the rules," but you did as you pleased. Now you must suffer the consequences of your actions. As I promised Wini, you too will never be alone. Others will disobey as well and they will join you both. The glimmer will become brighter and brighter with each disobedient child."

Sky felt her body shaking as streams of tears fell down her checks. "I'll be good, she thought. I know "the rules." I'll stay on the trolley. One more chance please. I'll be good. Oh God, one more chance please! HELP ME someone... please!"

From her chair and through her tears, Sky could see the tiny front light of the trolley as it drove past the house below on St Charles Street. She wanted to scream but couldn't.

secret san mateo

By Maurine Killough

arms that cradle water's salt
legs that stretch from marsh to hills
of oak my belly, the bay from hay colored loaf to mist-sprayed
forest a landscape of my fertile form
my roots swam deep, even before shell mounds of ohlone heart
and lips of costanoan
my seed springs diverse beauty, a secret kind
i call new strangers home
on tracks that still carry, familiar train whistle blowing
and through the wind of time,
the accent of voices change then converge into *one* language of praise
my body they relish, vistas they divine,
 my gentle sun breath turns their faces upward
like meyer lemon fruits they grow, in my green and luscious
to these home-comers, i am garden
and each afternoon is washed fresh by coyote wind
from the elegance of the bonsai, to the fragrant bay laurel
i hold you in this treasure together we live this secret this beauty
this is san mateo

Spy Town

By Robert Barrows

CHAPTER ONE

The first shot missed me by inches...

The next shot missed by a hair. The shooter was either a bad shot or a great one, or maybe I was already dead? This was going to be one hell of an election! It was open season on politicians, and this was only the Primary.

Talk about war and get killed by your enemies...talk about peace and get killed by your friends. The last guy to talk about peace is hanging up there on the cross. If he really did die for our sins, he might have died in vain.

And the fight for liberty and freedom? Well... "Give me liberty or give me death!" said Nathan Hale, right before they hanged him.

This is one crazy world we live in. We were on the verge of a new revolution, with everybody grabbing for power.

Everything you used to believe in, everything you used to hold dear, none of that held sway anymore. It was everyone for themselves and anarchy was at the door. Even the ministers and priests were preaching war, and I was the pacifist with the gun.

The press thought I orchestrated the shooting at me to help me build sympathy and support for my campaign. The truth is, I don't know who was shooting at me, or how they managed to miss. This was the age of laser guided roboguns that could always hit their target. Oh, it was still illegal to kill, but it was almost impossible to miss unless you wanted to.

I wasn't going to waste my time trying to figure out who was trying to almost kill me, the real question was why did they still want me alive?

They knew the shooting would dominate the headlines, and they knew it would give me the chance to get in front of the microphone.

It might have been my stand on defense that terrified both sides? That, plus my stand on the second amendment. They knew that inside, I couldn't hurt a fly, but they also knew I was fascinated by the history of war.

And I knew that a strong defense was essential to our safety. Quite a dilemma for a pacifist politician, but the truth of our evolution and our history was "survival of the fittest" and "might makes right!" "Political power grows from the barrel of a gun," said Chairman Mao, and if the Allies had not won the second World War, those of us who were not yet exterminated would be slaves to the Master Race.

But every domination falls prey to revolution because you can only suppress people for so long before your own lieutenants start plotting your downfall, and that's where the right to bear arms comes in. The right to bear arms is essential to our democracy...if you can live with the fact that someone might shoot your head off just because they don't like you, or usually, for no damn good reason at all.

It's not there so you can kill your wife of your neighbor or shoot up a convenience store... Thou still shalt not kill! But the Second Amendment is there so we can use those guns to rise up against and ward off oppression.

The guns are necessary. The bombs and the planes are necessary, and the submarines and the aircraft carriers are necessary and the spies and the wet work is necessary.

But is all of that armament necessary for peace?

If elected, I would have to take an oath to defend and support the Constitution of the United States, and that would mean supporting the tenets of the second amendment, but the truth is, I would like to see us ban guns once and for all.

Ain't gonna happen.

I know full well that we are a species of predators and hunters, and that the need to eat requires us to kill. As we grow more specialized in our society, we become more adept at killing.

When we eat, we let the food processors and the butchers do the killing for us. We let farmers and ranchers grow our food. If we had to hunt for food and kill it ourselves, we might think differently about killing. But as it is, we don't think about it much at all. But I do know this...I am a pacifist until someone points a gun in my face and then I become a warrior – or so I would like to believe. The truth is, I'm probably a chicken, and you know what, the truth is, you probably are, too. I was always afraid that if I were drafted and someone put a gun in my hands that I'd go crazy and start shooting everyone around me, and if that were the enemy, they would put a medal on my chest. That's exactly the man they were looking for!

But is killing in war the same as killing in murder? You bet it is! Do they prosecute you for it? No, they make you a hero.

Is there a need to defend our borders? Yes! Is there a need to kill or be killed?

Before you answer that, think very carefully about the world you want to live in. Do you want to live in a world that is always on the brink of war, or would you rather live in a world of peaceful coexistence?

You may still have to be wary of your neighbors and you may still not be sure who your friends are, but are you willing to give up your guns and take the chance?

Does a gun really make you feel more secure? Not me my friend. A gun makes me feel more paranoid. It gives me a false sense of power. It makes me want to dominate and command. It makes me want to impose my will on others and it will do the same to you. If everyone had guns we'd all be in trouble.

So what's the solution? We're at the point of a big dilemma that has no answer. If we ban all the guns, we will have to learn to trust each other. "Praise the Lord and pass the ammunition."

But is that our future? Will we really work for a peaceful and more gracious world, or do we want to be the party that's in control?

Are we condemned to a life of violence and war?

Throughout history, there have been kingdoms and revolutions and benevolent dictators and not-so-benevolent dictators and overthrown dictators and lots of dead dictators. There has been slavery and oppression, mass murder, extinction and ethic cleansing, all in the name of culture and civilization.

Wars between the haves and have nots... Liebensraum! You can kill and wound with rocks and knives and swords and arrows and cannons and rockets and bombs. Every generation improves upon the weaponry of the last. In my heart, I preach disarmament, but beware, there are those of us out there who would just as soon kill you because it's easier to kill and steal than it is to build.

So I still couldn't tell you which side it was that was trying to shoot me and miss. Both sides hated my stand on the second amendment. Both sides hated my stand on war. Both sides hated my guts and both sides might vote for me because they think I might be the easier candidate to beat in the general election. God Bless the open Primary system. It made elections into a real crap shoot.

But since I didn't yet know who was trying to almost kill me, I say, let it be. If they shoot me dead, I won't have to worry about it at all, so why waste my time trying to guess which side wanted me not quite dead.

They might have been better off if they wounded me just a little, but that would have brought on too much attention. "A miss is as good as a mile," so they say. Now I knew what that meant.

Oh, they'll show their hand soon enough and I'm sure they'll let me know what they want. It's clear already. They want to be in control and it looks like I'm already part of their plan. They need me alive, or else they wouldn't have missed. It's a good thing we have spies. Maybe the spies can make some sense of this.

Both sides were calling me subversive, and all I wanted was peace. If peace is subversive, then we'd better get used to suppression, because the feeling is that peace is unpatriotic. It's an easy trap to fall into.

If you don't like seeing people killed, you're not supporting the troops. Excuse me? War is not the natural state of man, or is it? Has there ever been an extended period of peace? The Pax Romana? How long did that last? A thousand years? Baloney! They said it lasted for close to two hundred years...if you don't count all the people who were probably killed in "skirmishes." It really lasted until people got fed up with peace.

It lasted until somebody else wanted control. I think it ended in the Hundred Years War...Who won that one? How many people do you think were killed in those hundred years? How much blood was spilled? How many wives lost their husbands? How many children were slain?

How many medals were won for killing? How many lives were lost down the drain? Who wins in that... just the undertakers.

However long a peace may last, as soon as somebody ran low on resources, back they went to the battlefield to try to steal some more. Haves and have-nots. Haves and have nots...That's the way we are programmed, We're predators you know. All this jive about civilization is not really in tune with our primal natures... We're carnivores, baby. Meat eaters. And suits and ties and dresses and clothes don't really hide our intentions, they just keep us warm. So are we destined to fight wars all our lives? We may well be. Me, all I wanted was peace... and that was a threat to us all.

Finist

By Nicholas Kotar

"There is nothing more beautiful than a fairy tale well told. Let me show you." Every evening began with these words of my father. As the shadows grew taller, Father's face transformed with the magic of the storytelling. Before my eyes stood not Father, but a Syrin, a talking tree, a maiden trapped in the body of a wolf. When the heroine narrowly escaped being eaten by the hag, her relief was my own. When the hero ignored his beloved's plea and opened the box he was never to touch, I screamed at him to stop. More than the romance and the joy of the final kiss, I preferred the dangerous parts. The darkness at the edge of beauty. The menace looming over the lovers even as they embrace in triumphant love.

One morning, I met that menace face to face.

It was a morning with no wind. On a small island like our Sanctum, where the sea winds never end, it meant a day of rest, a morning free of the hated weaving room.

Windless mornings were for my own stories, written down among the trees in the quietest part of the island, in the hills where, it was said, creatures from legend used to roam, free from the bondage of the storybook. The trees still talked, if you had the patience to hear them. What stories they had to tell! I already filled reams of paper with their tales.

As the sun rose I strode up the hill, hiking up my narrow linen shift above my already twice-scraped knees. Mother would not be happy.

The sea peeked out through the aspens' quivering orange leaves. The waters looked like the gold-flecked hide of some mythical creature, perhaps the great worm that was said to encircle the world, slowly choking it to death. It was a frightening thought, but it tickled me pleasurably with that elusive sense of darkness at the edge of stories.

As I reached the top, breathless more with excitement than the effort of climbing, I stilled myself down to my very center. At first I could hear only my own breath, the insistent beating of my heart. No trees. But I knew they would speak. They always did. All it took was a little patience. Having pulled the swan quills out of my pack, I tossed it aside and put the ampule of ink on my flat stone, perfect for writing. Soon the trees would begin.

For a long time, nothing, just the distant swish of the sea against the rocky shore. The trees' whispers took shape from the sound of the sea, gaining strength with each passing second. But something was wrong. They were jagged, harried, as though they feared to be overheard by someone. But to the eye, everything seemed normal. The trees shone in their autumn oranges and reds, the sea-creature still slept its millennial sleep, and the great tree still towered over the village center, its branches heavy with white flowers, ripe as grapes.

"You cannot possibly be real." The voice was from that dark place in the stories, the place that Father always tried to gloss over.

I looked right and left, but saw nothing. Then it struck me: the placement of the voice was wrong. It came from above.

"You are not Elía, daughter of Siloán the Shipwright of Sanctum, the isle once known as Sanctum?" A bird-woman perched on one of the thicker aspen boughs, no more than a few feet away. Before I had time to assess her appearance, her voice struck me: cold, alluring, sarcastic.

"Or are you?" Both eyebrows, thick as overgrown moss, shot upward.

I nodded. Looking at her face—so sad it would take a desert sun to dry off her tears— I felt smaller than a shrew, and no more significant. It irked me, but at that moment I wanted to do anything to please her.

She shook her head, the black hair shimmering like silk curtains. The effect was exquisite, but she was hardly beautiful. Here eyes were too closely placed to the hawk- nose to be beautiful.

"And to think," the bird-woman said, "all this time, all this way. And you are nothing more than a *girl*!"

My cheeks grew hot as the blood rushed up to them.

"I'm full fifteen years!" It occurred to me that I sounded like the little girl I was trying not to be.

"Fifteen is nothing. Not for what you are called to do." "Called? What do you mean? Who are you? Are you a Syrin?"

Actually, she looked nothing like the Syrin on the chapel wall frescoes, joyful even in their solemnity. They were beautiful beyond compare, but this one was disfigured—her eyebrows grew askew and her bird body did not seem to fit her woman's head, somehow.

"I am Gamayun."

It was supposed to mean something important. Her voice had the same inflection that Mother had when she mentioned some famous battle I never did study the previous evening (though I always promised).

"You haven't heard of me," she said. It was not a question. Gamayun turned to gaze at the sea, as though I were not standing there at all.

"Should I have heard of you?" I asked.

"I thought everyone knew of Gamayun. I sing the future."

I remembered. Gamayun was the black Syrin, the seer of all futures: those that would be, those that could be, and those that never would.

"Are you here to sing Sanctum's future?" I asked, not really knowing what I asked. When I said it, the air palpitated with the power of incantation. The trees stopped their whispers to hearken to me. A cold tremor ran up and down my back.

"No, little girl," Gamayun whispered. "*You* are."

My heart skipped. The trees stilled, but only for a moment. Suddenly, they writhed like snakes. My first thought was that the wind returned, but the branches all swung in different directions. Gamayun opened her mouth wider than seemed possible and groaned. The trees moved in time to the sound (I could not call it a song). They reached toward me, these things that were not *my* trees. They twisted, faces forming in the folds of the bark, agonized at being born. Beyond them, the sea was a creature, too large to make anything out except the hide, not gold-flecked, but green and stinking. It rose up like a wave, rising and rising over my head until the sun was eclipsed.

I ran before I realized it. At any moment I expected to be drowned in the water that was not water, to be choked by the trees that were not trees, to be turned to stone by the noise of that creature that looked like a Syrin perverted by nightmares. The sounds around me were a parody of music, disfigured like Gamayun's face. The reaching branches, now black and spiky like winter hawthorn, grabbed me and pinned me to the earth face-up. Above me, the sky was no more. The monstrous worm with the stinking hide had blotted it out. The stench was like a thing alive, choking my life out. Gamayun flew in circles overhead, her black eyes no more than holes in a pale face. I screamed.

"Look, child!" she commanded. "Your life and the life of your family depend on it!" I did not trust her, but she had mentioned my family. I forced my eyes to stay open.

The worm-hide above me began to swirl and give way like a lifting mist. Above it, or through it, I saw shimmering water, an entire world reflected in it, but upside-down. I saw our own Sanctum, its white stone buildings blackened with the kiss of fire. I saw flames tumbling from the sky like monstrous hailstones. I saw a swirling black mist, full of indistinct figures, engulf the village like a wave. I saw the water come in after it, washing it all clean. I saw the bodies. Everyone was dead.

"No, no," I whispered.

"It's in your hands, little Elía. This is the future I will sing for Sanctum, but you have the power to sing another."

"What can I do?"

The smell subsided, the light returned, the cacophony stopped. Gamayun alighted on the damp ground near me.

"You will give me the greatest treasure of Sanctum. You will give me Living Water."

My heart froze inside me. I lifted my hands at her in the gesture to ward off evil. No one could touch Living Water. It was the sacred fountainhead, the source of Sanctum's plenty. From it came health and harvest, ease of childbearing, calmness of death. If any dared to take it, they would be cursed for all eternities.

"I cannot do what you ask."

"If you do not, I will sing the death you saw in the waters. You choose, Elía. I will be back in one week."

She raised her black wings, too long for her body, and flew up like a parody of a vulture. She was no more than a speck when I came to myself. Did I just awake? All the trees whispered serenely to each other and the swish of the sea was as calm as ever.

In a dark corner of my heart, something fluttered to life. To my surprise, I realized it was pleasure. I had just experienced the menace from stories come to life, and I liked it.

The Waiting Room

By Evie Groch

CHAPTER ONE

The curtainless waiting room was not filled to capacity yet, but in an hour or two, it would be. The vast galactic scenery spread across the floor-to-ceiling viewing windows and had just begun to sparkle with stars igniting randomly against the dark void. The tinted glass returned to normal. Some voyagers sat glued to these vistas, while others engrossed themselves in interstellar negotiations on their tsaquis. Children played with their znusests until parents decided they had indulged too long and forwarded the five-minute warning signal to their devises before they shut down for an hour.

The multi-grey tones of the body-shaped furniture offered an array of seating choices for every shape, form, and size, all with attached eating and/or writing arms easily locked into place. The highly glossed rainbow-colored floor tiles formed patterns and games for the young to engage in, from hopscotch and mazes to oval running tracks encircling a red trampoline. Several travelers were shopping on line for travel comforts to be delivered to them on the craft. A few chose disposable night wear, earbud ocean sounds for sleeping, or wrist alarms.

Most were waiting for their mitz to be delivered. The droids had already circulated and taken the flavored orders for mitz for all the passengers. Aduard, now 11, had only done this twice before, but he remembered having the droid scan his encoded bracelet and had been ready to let it happen again with his outstretched arm. He was well aware that some of his ancestors had perished on earlier trips when mass space travel first became popular. This did not deter his parents from traveling this way again. Aduard's entire health profile (age, favorite flavors, avoidance foods, history of illnesses and surgeries) was scanned in three seconds. Out from behind his blond bangs, his eyes spotted the first droid rolling out with the mitz. He couldn't wait for his name to be called. Some much younger children had already started to balk as their parents were attempting to psychologically prepare them to imbibe the mitz. Those under the age of five were not required to drink the mitz, but their parents had to sign off assuming all responsibility for any negative consequence.

Aduard heard his name called, and after a nod from his father, ran over to receive his mitz. He picked up the chocolate-flavored concoction from the droid's tray and walked back to his parents, slowing sipping and savoring his rich, creamy mitz. A calmness started to spread from his taste buds to all arteries and extremities. He looked at his mitz and smiled as he compared it to the pink mitz his mother was given and the orange one his father was enjoying. This family's tastes ranged from sweet to tart, and that was all noted.

Aware that boarding the craft would commence in one hour, Aduard settled down with his znusest to play games as he sensed the mitz nourishing his body and brain. Ever since space travel improved, the side effects detested in 2400 no longer were present now. Jet lag was unheard of, and cradling was the preferred position for travelers. The magic elixir that mitz was, had a lot to do with the elimination of the side effects, but its usefulness went way beyond that. Based on the destination of the aircraft and the individual makeup of each humanoid aboard, mitz could be engineered to introduce into the brain, an understanding of the culture, etiquette, and rituals appropriate in the habitat to be visited. The volumes and tomes that travelers used to scan to familiarize themselves with the oddities and uniqueness of the alien land before traveling there were no longer necessary. There were still discoveries to be made and challenges of communication and translation, but no longer was there the need for endless study sessions and diplomatic anxiety. Aduard already knew that Kapteynians produce sounds that Humanoids cannot comprehend without assistive technology, but he was confident he would succeed in communicating once it was all hooked up. And since the discovery of the stable worm hole connecting deep space with our galaxy, light years of travel had been greatly reduced.

Shortly before boarding, announcements emanated from ground speakers reminding passengers where to look to see their disc-shaped craft outfitted for Kapteyn b. Aduard remembered studying in school that two super-Earths existed which orbited Kapteyn's Star. This star was an orphaned one torn from an ancient dwarf satellite galaxy of the Milky Way. And now they'd be heading to Kapteyn b. He had aced his test on this subject and recalled that Kapteyn b had at least 4.8 earth-masses and completed its orbit in 48.6 days. Not very long. His mind was swimming with such deep understanding and openness that there was no room for fear. He knew the droids on board would see to all his needs while the captain and remaining human crew would take them where many had gone before.

As Aduard and his fellow passengers readied themselves for boarding, unbeknownst to them, a digital set of electronic eyes scanned the passengers, matching their faces and wristbands to the approved roster while being alert to any inappropriate random behavior that marked a departure from their profile. If only these precautions had been available centuries earlier, Aduard's lineage would now not be so thin.

Although there was no basic cause for alarm or concern, the blue light on the scanning eyes blinked twice, signaling a need for human attention. One young girl, aged 12, no longer matched 100% with her profile and wristband, and her eyes were darting back and forth with signs of anxiety. A quick decision would have to be made.

Farm Boy

By Michele Jessen

"Wait Milly!" Those were the last words seven-year-old Millicent heard her older sister shouting, as they echoed back towards the chamber door. Now little Milly wished she could have her big sister standing next to her telling her what to do, helping her to explore this new world.

She froze and carefully listened. There was an eerie silence. Why wasn't there any sound? Did the door shut? Did her sister make it through before the slam? Milly pondered alone and fearful. She trudged on for a few minutes into nothingness. Slate clouds hovered around her looming. A fog of black-grey encased her as she bravely traversed forward. Milly held Sir Galahad her pet hamster, a little too tightly and stumbled, tripping one step after another. After several long minutes she spied a ray of sunshine, blocked by a grove of barren fruit trees. Sticky slush and ice crunched underfoot and she was no longer in a room but outdoors.

Gosh, I'm freezing! I should have brought my jacket. She shivered. I should have taken the satchel that Sarah showed me. I know she hid magic things in it. I'll bet it was filled with all kinds of useful objects. Why didn't I think of that?

She slumped down under a pine tree on a stump ready to cry, but stopped short at the sound of a scratchy old voice.

"Come here you pig!" The shriveled up man was screaming loudly whild chasing an oversized sow.

He asked the pig, "Just what are you smell'in at?"

Startled momentary out of her self pity, Millicent stood up and brushed herself off. She stashed Sir Galahad in her pocket. The farmer scratched his scalp with gnarled fingers. His yellow tinged eyes gave her a once over from head to toe.

"Are you my new pig tender?" He bellowed in a not-so-friendly voice. Milly sized up the grubby stick-of-a-man. He was half bent and had something like a corn pipe poking out from his mouth.

"Hey little boy, you be deaf? Come along now... I been 'specting you. Now git!" The strange shriveled up farmer swatted at her with the stick that he used to tend his pig.

Milly wanted to speak, but found she could not. For some reason she had lost her voice. His filthy overalls were caked in mud or worse. He approached her.

"Cat got your tongue 'lil boyee?" Then he mumbled under his breath,

"These farmhands getting' younger and younger. Why I've half a mind to..."

She backed away reaching towards the wall of the empty room. But this was not a room at all. there was no wall to grab onto or even a wall to back up towards. She remembered she went through the door to a magical place. Once outside of the grove of trees, there lay open farmland spread out in every direction. No structures dotted the landscape. Lime green grass and the neon pink pig startled her back to the moment. Milly looked down at her hand which still held the key and quickly tried to shove it into her pocket.

"What y'a got there worker clone?" He smacked his lips together. This little tiny old man squinted in Milly's direction scrunching his upturned nose much like his pig.

Springing forward his gangly fingers snatched at her apron and tore the pocket clean off.

"Gimme 'dat shiny 'ting." As he charged, the pig followed his lead. The neon pink swine squealed and bumped hard into Milly's legs, knocking her over onto her backside.

"Now I got ya, Don't want to work huh? Is you a sleeper or a maker? Shucks now... you's be only a young 'un. Now best be on your way to ours farm or its t' the factory for you and no sleep. Move along or I'll report you to the... "

Ignoring his strange speech, Millicent looked for a way out. A very determined pig again charged at her with abandon.

Startled by this willey pig's repeated assaults, little Milly found her voice, and shouting in her most grown up tone.

"Hey farmer Brown, give that key back. It's mine!" Milly demanded, pretending to be sassy.

"Ah so ye do speak boyee, even 'iifin its mights crooked talk at that. What are you?. .. a day sleeper or somthin?"

"Go away. I dont know what your talking about! I'm not your boy, nor do I tend pigs. Now give me back my key!" Milly put one hand out and the other on her hip defiantly. She stood waiting for what seemed an eternity.

The old farmer man stood dumbfounded by this uppity squawking child. His pig squealed at her in a conversation of its own.

Waiting for him to return her key seemed more unlikely as the seconds became minutes. Her thoughts spun in circles as she reasoned out many possible outcomes, all of which ended badly.

The only chance she had was to get away and forget about the skeleton key for the moment. So she did just that. Millicent left her portal key behind. She ran as fast as her legs would take her, cradling her pocket's contents protectively.

In what seemed like hours Milly leapt over small creeks and through the gnarled brush. The small girl never slowed down until she was sure that no man nor pig was following her.

Collapsing by a creek bed, she caught her breath and began to cry.

Why did I go through that door? I'm all alone and no one knows where I am. Reaching into her good pocket, she remembered her hamster. Carefully pulling him out of her pocket, she fluffed his matted fur and began to caress him behind his ears.

"Oh Sir Galahad. I'm glad you're with me. I knew that it was smart to take you."

"That's what I thought", the tiny creature squeaked. Hey I'm talking, not just thinking."

Millicent's jaw dropped, "What is going on...? Did you just speak to me Sir Gallahad?"

"Why yes, I think I did." The wheezing rodent practiced his new voice. "In fact I always could speak, but it came out in squeaks and grunts. I always looked for you after school. And I loved the colorful house you built for me with all the mazes and tubes."

Now he got carried away with his owner's attention and babbled on.

"Now that I have a voice... I have to tell you about that roommate you brought into my house last month. She was so rude, she ate all my food and stuffed her cheeks with my best seeds. I had to secretly forage at night while she slept. What did you call her Petunia or Priscilla ?" He scampered back the warmth of her apron pocket.

"Stop, Sir Galahad, I'm glad you can speak in this new world, but we're in trouble here. We need to get home. I have to go back now before we get even more lost."

"What, go back? Why we just escaped!" He wheezed his confusion loudly while keeping one paw firmly locked to her apron pocket.

"Well that old timer has my key. Plus, I thought my big sister Sarah would be right behind me... but I guess the door closed. I forgot the magic book about how to use the portals. Worst of all, I forgot to bring the satchel with her timepiece that she got for her 10th birthday. I know it has a hidden map of doors and names of the cities where the perfect portals are." Milly explained to her companion who scampered out onto her shoulder.

"You mean we have no way home to our soft bed of newspapers and fresh oranges? I might even like to see that annoying Petunia again sometime." Sir Galahad was now added hanging upside down from her colar for effect.

Milly questioned him. "You sound as mixed up as that crazy farmer back there. Do you want to help us get home or are you saying you want to stay here?"

"Both, I guess. Here I can talk to you. But, I like home best! Just don't forget to play with me. And don't put me into that plastic ball. He crawled close to her ear and whispered, "You never play with me anymore."

Milly thinking aloud, tried to imagine a game that would solve their predicament and cheer up her neglected pet.

She looked around exclaiming, "Come to think of it Sir Galahad, I'm hungry. So let's pretend we're spies and trace our footprints back through the snow before they get covered up. Then we can eat a nice big lunch back home. I want the spice cake mom was saving for the weekend."

"Ok. But I'm tired of riding in that apron pocket. I like the view from up here. Put me on your head and I'll hold onto your red hair. I'm a good horse rider. Kiddie up!"

Shaking her head smiling to herself Milly thought, first I'm a pig tender, now I'm a horse for my hamster. She conceded lifting her tiny charge up to her braids. Milly patted his tiny hamster head and laughed saying, "This is an upside down world. But come to think of it... I do like the fact that you can talk."

Milly began to retrace her footprints and Sir Galahad rode on the top of her head proudly. His squeaks and shouts pointed out the next set of prints, still outlined in the stiff white icy snow. It seemed twice as long to find their way back through overgrown forest. A slight mist of snow rained down covering the open fields behind them as well as the grove of trees to their right.

Sir Galahad directed her towards an abandoned structure. It was noon and the sun began to shine high over their heads. The snow had melted exposing neon green turf.

"Did you follow those horse hooves? Milly pointed down to the muddy slush. "I only have two feet, not four. You followed hoof prints, not my footprints. Now we're lost. And look at the factory."

They stopped abruptly at the sight of an oversized brick factory. Surrounding the entire structure were tiny flaps with conveyer belts leading into and out from the building. As they cautiously approached the building, they noticed rows of small doors. There were two very strange doors in particular.

The hamster broke the silence first. "Why so many doors? Those look like doggie doors."

The first was metal with a bolt and a guard posted at the door. It was covered in rust from the snow. Milly noted the door seemed a bit too low for adults to enter without ducking. Above this metal door frame, a sign was posted CLONES. SLEEPERS.

The other door was giant and had no guard. It was framed in wood and painted in a soft yellow and pale blue color. Purple flowers were carved carefully into the polished wood. Above the door frame the sign read MAKERS.

Milly asked Sir Galahad, "Which door do we try to go through, the sleepers or the makers?" There were hundreds of doors for her to choose from. She had a determined look on her face that he recognized. Milly did not wait for an answer and stared at her target door.

Sir Galahad grabbed firmly to her hair. He wheezed in protest "Milly, stop, wait!"

Past the Quartermark

By Don Rogers

Two years past the quartermark A day of celebration and ...
Perhaps a day of questions What does the future hold?
Are the years slipping away?

Well ... time is only a measurement ... of what was and what is
What is to come is still out there ... and it can be whatever you want

So on this day of celebration ... give this as a present to yourself ...
that your future belongs to you Letting time record that ...
as much as possible you made it ... what you wanted it to be

Dancer

By Karen Hartley

Two black and white photographs
Hang on the wall
Each time she walks by
They call her to remember

Those shiny black tap shoes clacking on the wooden stage
Costumes in blue, each a different shade
Sequins and maribou sparkling under the lights
Dancer wished it could happen every night

Daily she practiced her tapping
Lost in her own little world
She danced to the rhythm of her heart
While she dreamed of being
The lead dancer girl dancing the title part

In recitals she tapped and twirled
To the delight of those who watched Always wanting more
When the music stopped

There were other performances Long ago
Those photos gone
Now packed away
With memories of Dancer's stardom
And her costumes of another day

Decades later she can still recall
The applause, the lights
The sight of all eyes on her
She's tapping, dancing,   a sea of faces smiling
Hands are clapping for her
Today she can still remember it all

She's ten years old
In the pictures on the wall

Grade School Anthropology

By Suda Miller

Elsa and I rode the bus home from Curtis School when I was in fifth grade and she was in fourth grade. We were the same age; at the beginning of the year I had skipped grades after six weeks of school. I skipped grades because the teacher, Ms Badicam, got totally sick of me practicing my spit gland ejaculation technique. I managed to come across this trick by accident, but if you jerked a muscle under your tongue at the right moment and keep your mouth slightly open, you could catapult drops of saliva as far as a foot away.

Ms Badicam was a pretty, young brunette; she wore mascara and lipstick and she was the daughter of the principal, Mr. Badicam or Baddy as we liked to call him. We liked Baddy but we were also afraid of him because he had a paddle hanging on the wall above his desk. He used the Paddle when kids were bad. So we tried not to be bad.

Eddy Hansen was bad a lot and we knew he had gotten the paddle once or twice. Except in fourth grade his mother blew her brains out and after that he was mild as a dove. We felt bad for Eddy when he came back to school, so we left him alone. In those days this was about as compassionate as kids would get. Everyone pretended that nothing had happened. He looked pretty sad. Usually he looked feisty and angry, but not anymore. He didn't get the paddle after that, either. There was no cause for it.

I did spit gland ejaculation practice because I was in the front row, so I could experiment with the physics of the spit projectile without it getting on the person sitting in front of me. Also there was plenty of space between me and Ms. Badicam's chalkboard, so I wouldn't get it on her either. I have no idea why I thought she wouldn't notice my solution to being bored, but she did. One day she turned to me and said, "THAT is DISGUSTING," with such contempt that you bet I didn't do it again. But boy was I bored. Until I skipped. Then I was just behind, struggling to catch up, and suddenly had no friends. It wasn't ideal, either way.

I don't know why fifth grade was so much more boring than previous grades, but it was. Marvin and I were both offered the option to skip to sixth grade even though it was against school policy, but Marvin turned them down flat. I found out after the fact and it made me look pretty bad. Here I had left everyone in our small fifth grade class with whom I had gone through four years of school and counting, and he hadn't. The reason he declined to skip, might be because he had a rare disease which caused him to be completely hairless; no eyebrows, bald. He showed up mid-year in fourth grade wearing a plaid boater's hat. Underneath he was as bald as the surface of an eggshell. A brown eggshell. He was African-American although the correct term of that era was "black."

My grandpa wore boater hats too but never plaid. His hats were pastel solids: blue, yellow. He was six feet four and a complete racist, which was often awkward for me when he came to visit from Florida, as my best friend Nikki was black, and when she walked through the TV room where he planted himself the entire visit, he would hiss racial slurs at her like she was not fit for this earth, a pariah. Then after she was out of his sight, he would settle back into his usual genial demeanor. It was scary.

For my grandfather the boater hat worked well but for Marvin, being just a little kid, it was too jaunty to pull off. But we didn't say anything despite the fact that our school, our class, was just as full of savages as any other elementary class in 1976. That is, full of a lot of confused, half-finished beings, trying stuff out on each other that was usually mean or inappropriate just to see what would happen, or for the sake of catharsis. A whole lot of unconscious acting-out bullshit, is what elementary school was.

The day Marvin came to school, which was sometime in the middle of fourth grade, we were lectured about how we were to treat Marvin normally and not single him out because he didn't have any hair. This was during PE at the swimming pool. Yes, it had a swimming pool; I found out later the school was known for its physical education program. Not for its academics, which might be the reason for my aforesaid boredom. I attended that school because of my brother; he was not academic and probably had Oppositional Defiant Disorder, which was coined over thirty years later. Back then, my brother was known as a kid who stirred things up, got in trouble. But why did I also attend Curtis, as I never got in trouble and could have used a challenge? Since I was "easy," that is, not rebellious or difficult, it didn't matter where I went. So I went to Curtis. And I was bored. But we had a pool.

That might sound pretty nice, having a pool, but mostly it sucked, because the pool was pretty cold and there were no showers. But it was good in that I never had any fear of water. Swimming was as familiar to me as walking. But we went around coated in a thick layer of chemicals and chlorine, from the pool. When you combine that with the sodium nitrate in my bologna sandwich, and the 1970s LA smog, it's kind of a miracle I have lived to tell this tale without any serious health problems.

So that day, Marvin's first day at Curtis School, right before PE, we were all shivering in our swim suits, waiting to go in the water where it might be marginally warmer, one could only hope. Maybe it was January. That's when we got the big speech about Marvin. We had seen him with his boater hat, jeans, t-shirt; now we were going to see him in just a bathing suit. I guess that's why they decided to tell us right then, it being bathing suit time, not to make a big deal out of it.

It was a complete anti-climax. He came out of the boy's changing room. He was bald. Which was a little surprising, the kid was like an old man and at the same time, just a kid. He wore his glasses poolside and took them off only just before we went into the water.

We all got in the pool and worked on our backstroke. No goggles, the chlorine stung our eyes, but that's the way it was. I think I had calluses on my eyeballs. Nowadays my kids bitch to high heaven if they don't have their goggles for the pool. I'm like, goggles? Keep track of your damn goggles if they're that important to you. In my day — and so forth.

So Marvin stayed behind in fifth grade; he had been places and knew a good thing when he had it, and I didn't; I went ahead to sixth.

I started out talking about Elsa, but got side-tracked. We rode the bus home together. She came to Curtis School in third grade I think, and didn't make friends. People didn't like her. I don't know why the others didn't like her, but I know why I didn't like her. she tried too hard. She was also arrogant.

"I'm Basque," she announced proudly one day while we were on the bus going home.

That was as dorky as where my dad was from: Turkey. Yeah try explaining that to savage children who will make a joke out of anything. "Your dad's from TURKEY? GOBBLE GOBBLE hahahahaha." Also my name, "SUDAFED HAHAHAHA," so I started saying my dad was from Italy, which was also my dad's legitimate answer whenever it suited him, as his passport was Italian and he had lived there for twenty years. Italy didn't inspire jokes, so I stuck to that after learning the hard way that the truth was not easy.

"What does that mean—Basque?" I said to Elsa. Did they make baskets in Basque Land? "It's a region of Spain in between Spain and France. They have their own language. The

Basque Language. Their own food, their own customs. I have a basque dress. It's beautiful."

I was embarrassed for her; but I only rolled my eyes and wrote down an answer on my boring grammar worksheet. Circle the verbs: Grandpa hates blacks, wears a boater hat, knocks back a highball and watches the news.

The bus wasn't really a bus, more like a converted van. We tried to get close to Nancy the driver, because carsickness was inevitable otherwise. We lived only fifteen minutes away from school but it took an hour to get home.

I couldn't fathom why Elsa thought being Basque was important. No one had ever heard of Basqueland and no one cared if The Basque wanted to secede from Spain for the last millennium. In this town, HOLLYWOOD, what made someone special was very clear.

For example, the Bad News Bears had just come out when I was in fourth grade. We had all seen it and I in particular was fascinated not only the basic idea of girls playing baseball and being better than all the boys, but I also idolized Tatum O'Neal playing that girl who was better than all the boys. She was badass. In the movie, she made money by selling Hollywood Star Maps on the side of the road. (I really wanted a Hollywood Star Map but my mom would NEVER stop to purchase one). Then Tatum O'Neal turned up at my school sometime that year, after the film was released, but she only stayed for about six weeks. We were all abuzz. She was a grade or two ahead. After school one day I found myself playing on the parallel bars next to her. She was just a normal kid, trying to make the parallel bars fun, which was not easy, but she was also a Star. This dissonance was completely mystifying. I don't know why she didn't stick around; maybe she had to make another movie.

Also, Sean Amos was a grade below us. Sean Amos wore glasses and had honey-brown skin and light brown curly hair; the kid was never at rest; a little guy who could run fast. His father owned Famous Amos Cookies.

Then there was Michael Goulet. Michael Goulet was Robert Goulet's son. Robert Goulet was a famous singer — I think sort of like Frank Sinatra and that ilk. Las Vegas? Michael Goulet looked exactly like his father, with his white skin and dark wavy hair, and he wore a lot of velour. Also miniature leisure suits. In other words, he was like a mini lounge singer, which was strange, but he was still the son of someone famous, so we left him alone.

Then there was Robert Wagner's kids, they went to Curtis School too. They were a bit younger than me, so I'm not sure who they were. But it Was Known.

In other words, we had some brushes with fame on a daily basis, and there was nothing in the canon that added up to Basque people having special cache or clout as it were. So I wanted badly for Elsa to just pipe down about the Basque thing already. It was like she couldn't learn her lesson from the way I rolled my eyes and pretended she wasn't speaking. She kept on anyway.

I found out about thirty-five years later, that Elsa's grandfather cofounded the city of Vernon (this is east of downtown Los Angeles, straddling the LA River and convenient to Boyle Heights and South Gate), owned half the real estate there and basically ran it like an Italian City State from the Middle Ages. During this time of revelation just a few years ago, I discovered that Elsa's family still owned half the real estate in Vernon, which was mainly leased by major Los Angeles County's slaughter houses (Value Added Meat Processing, courtesy of Farmer John) but also all the Fortune 500 companies were represented there in one way or another. That only about 60 people actually lived there; the other 30,000 came there to work and then left again at the end of each day to go home, no doubt to points far away in all directions, because Vernon smelled bad, had a freight train running through it, had lead poisoning in the water, and didn't have any amenities except for La Villa Basque, a Googie-style (Mad Men) restaurant that had gone to seed. That because there were only 60 people living there, elections were a friendly matter of going through the motions and reelecting the same people, such as Elsa's dad as mayor (he was mayor from 1974-2009), because the entire electorate was basically related to or worked for the people they were electing.

And if she had said any of that to me, I think it's likely I would have been more impressed. There's even more stuff that happened to her family just in the last few years: her brother John was convicted of child abuse (he was dean at Daniel Murphy High School, one of the three or four schools that my brother attended in his checkered middle and high school career); in 2009 Elsa's father resigned as mayor of Vernon after being convicted of voter fraud (he claimed to live there, a few blocks from Farmer Johns, where they made Dodger Dogs. But they really lived in Hancock Park, an upscale classy older neighborhood full of mansions on double lots, tennis courts, pools, trees: no warehouses, freight trains, or value-added meat factories to be seen), although he was convicted, Elsa's father didn't go to jail because he was over eighty years old and in poor health.

I tried to find Elsa after discovering all this, but she hired someone to make sure she had no online presence; too much scandal I guess. But through schoolmates on Facebook, I did finally come across her. She lives in the Valley. She's deeply religious. She's a teacher. There's no mention of Vernon or being Basque anywhere on her Facebook profile. I find this very disappointing.

About Time

By Luanne Oleas

At some point, I crossed an imaginary line. Time, in my lifetime, became finite.

Suddenly, I didn't want to talk to uninteresting people, read uninteresting books, or take boring vacations.

It was as if I had x amount of time left, and y number of things to do in that time. I didn't want to eat crummy food, drink bad coffee, or write uninteresting blogs—though I probably will.

I became obsessed with maximizing my remaining time. Even while doing something "worthy," I was anxious about not getting to the next worthy thing. In short, I wasn't enjoying life.

Then I remembered a lesson I learned while traveling. If you visit an interesting place, like London for example, there are so many must dos and must sees—the Crown Jewels, Buckingham Palace, St. Paul's Cathedral, ad infinitum. No one has enough time in one trip.

So, I told myself, "Do what you can do comfortably (comfortably being the key word) and do the rest the next time." If I never returned to London, it still made the current visit more enjoyable.

I think it's the same with life. I'll do what can do comfortably, and then do the rest in my next life. If there is no next life, I'll never know. And if there is... well, perfect.

It allows me to enjoy the moment. This moment. And that's all any of us really have.

355 Memoir: Personal

Home on the Range

By Laura Deck

Hollywood immortalized the western cowboy mystique in classic television shows such as *Gunsmoke*, *Rawhide*, and *Bonanza*. Hooves pounding through clouds of dust, horses whinnying, whips cracking, cowboys whistling and chasing down runaway cows–this was the stereotype we were fed. The theme song from *Rawhide* depicted a wild west with reckless riding in difficult weather to keep them dogies movin'. It was a job for only the toughest cowboys. In 1991,

Hollywood gave us *City Slickers*, a Western film starring Billy Crystal and Jack Palance that featured a trio of urban cowboys battling mid-life crises on a cattle drive gone awry. Tough-as-nails trail boss Curly, played by Palance, teaches the dudes how to become real cowboys along with sentimental lessons about life on the open range.

I hate to burst the celluloid bubble, but Hollywood was wrong on many counts. The traditional western cattle drive does not move "hell bent for leather," and these days cowgirls are as common as cowboys. Although the goal remains the same – move a herd of cattle from pasture A to pasture B - the modern cattle drive is as much about preserving a fast-disappearing western tradition as it is about the business of transporting livestock. As semis replace horsepower and locomotives, it is more important than ever to keep the cattle drive rollin' before it becomes extinct and ends up a nostalgic footnote in some history book.

The cowboy lifestyle has cast a spell over me since I was old enough to sit on a horse. A horse topped my list every Christmas, but my sensible suburban parents sent me to horse camp in Arizona instead. Over the course of four summers, I learned the rigors of horsemanship: riding confidently at any speed, saddling, bridling, roping, grooming, and even starting colts. Wrangler jeans and scuffed cowboy boots became my second skin. With every second I shaved off my pole bending time in the weekly rodeo, my shyness retreated a little further and self-confidence soared. Loping through alpine meadows in the White Mountains of Arizona brought me endless contentment and started a life-long love affair with the western ranching tradition.

During the forty years since then, my family has made frequent pilgrimages to several guest ranches. Our favorite is Hunewill Ranch–the oldest working guest ranch in California. Six generations of the Hunewill family have kept western heritage alive on their ranch in Bridgeport, California, in the heart of the Eastern Sierra Nevada mountains. The 4,500-

acre cattle ranch was founded in 1861 by Esther and Napoleon Bonaparte (N.B.) Hunewill. In 1931, the livestock operation expanded to include guests, and the Circle H Guest Ranch was born. Guests started coming on the cattle drive sometime in the 1960s, and they've been coming every year since then.

The Hunewill family spends summers at the 6,200-foot-elevation Bridgeport ranch and winters in Smith Valley, Nevada, about 2,000 feet lower. With Bridgeport shivering under a blanket of snow all winter, the herd of pregnant Angus cows must be moved north to the more temperate climate of the high desert in the Great Basin. I was joining the 104th Annual Hunewill Ranch Cattle Drive to push 519 head 60 miles over the course of five days. Our ragtag crew of drovers – cowboys and cowgirls who drive cattle–consisted of ten Hunewill family members, five wranglers, and twenty-five guests.

While the ranch makes a few concessions to modern comforts, my days in the saddle were anything but cushy. I had a job to do, and this sense of purpose made me feel that I was a bona fide ranch hand. The wake-up bell broke the pitch-black stillness at 6:15 am on Monday and Tuesday and rang half an hour earlier each successive day. We took a break for lunch and finally dismounted around 5:00 pm. Winter hovered in the wings and made its presence known in the pre-dawn and dusk hours. Cowboy hats provide instant credibility and protect eyes from sun and rain, but they fail miserably as ear warmers. My cattle drive apparel consisted of a ball cap with a ski hat over it, a "wild rag" or large silk neckerchief blocking cold air from creeping down necks, Wrangler jeans and leather chinks for warmth and protection, several layers under a Carhartt jacket, and gloves. Function definitely trumped style.

Monday was the longest day–16 miles from the ranch to Ferdell Field. We pushed the herd from the field south of Bridgeport across Highway 395 in the shadow of the Eastern Sierra peaks. The Highway Patrol blocked the road and many townspeople turned out to watch the bovine parade. My job was to form a human fence with other riders to keep the cows from running into a boggy field. An even harder task was getting my young mare, Lorna Doone, to stand still. Horses, like cows, have the herd instinct in their DNA, and getting her to hold her position was a constant challenge. Meanwhile, the drovers riding point were spread out in a line shoulder-to-shoulder to keep the cattle from bolting through an opening. It is difficult to hold the cattle back with only one or two riders if they decide to run. The operation was reminiscent of the "whack-a-mole" game where the cows kept appearing at the unblocked holes.

After lunch, we headed north up the spine of Highway 182 and followed a dirt road along the East Walker River that meandered through willows, sagebrush, piñon, and cottonwoods. The sun was disappearing fast as we reached Ferdell field. The wranglers told us to water our horses and tie them to the picket line. In a nod to early tradition, and for the safety of the horses, Blair Hunewill and his wife Hayley, along with two border collies, were bunking in the barn overnight.

I applauded their dedication as I dreamed of the hot shower, ranch grub, glass of merlot, and Advil that awaited me back at the ranch.

The route has remained basically the same as the one used by the first cattle drive in 1909 that followed the tracks of the Carson City stagecoach during the gold rush era. Day 2, Tuesday, is the shortest day from Ferdell Field to Sweetwater Ranch stopping at Jean's Rest for lunch.

After a finger-numbing morning, the sun soon warmed the canyon and my spirits. We crossed the Nevada state line and the landscape changed to sandstone rock formations, with piñon pines clustered near low hills and clumps of wild rose bushes on the desert floor. The scenery alternated between wide, sage-covered valleys edged by rugged peaks and narrow canyons dotted with willows and the occasional scampering jackrabbit. At Jean's Rest, according to cattle drive custom, we paid homage to the drovers who have passed on, and one of the wranglers recited some cowboy poetry. Many ashes have been scattered at this solemn place.

The remaining days of the drive offered intangible riches: ample time for reflection, unhurried conversations with new friends, and a ringside seat from which to enjoy the scenery. It was refreshing to unplug and slow the spigot of life to a trickle. I gladly traded the complexities and busy-ness of everyday life for the simplicity of one task with one goal.

Whether you call it throwback, retro or vintage, the cattle drive is a western practice that deserves to be continued. Each November, like clockwork, the cows follow the North Star to Smith Valley. For the drovers, our internal compasses lead us back to Hunewill Ranch so we too can journey north, once again, with the cows. The cattle drive brings happiness and satisfaction to many, and much like the Amish barn raising, brings a community together to accomplish something that could easily disappear. As for me, I earn the right to call myself a real cowgirl.

At dinner the final evening we all raised our glasses to a job well done. Rhian from Wales captured the essence of the week when she said she experienced *eiliadau tragwyddol*, which means in Welsh, eternal moments of utter peace to treasure forever. I couldn't have said it better myself—in any language. Let's hope this cherished western tradition outlasts us all.

War Stories - 1941-1945

By Margaret Vose

War and its consequences has been a factor in my life since I was ten years old. I will never forget that fateful December Sunday afternoon in 1941, when the President of the United States interrupted our radio concert to announce the bombing of Pearl Harbor. It seemed our lives were instantly changed. The peaceful rhythms of our family life were refocused by daily directives from Washington, D.C.. My father, who was forty, tried to join the Seabees, a group of men too old for the draft, who volunteered to build overseas bases for the military. Much to my mother's relief, he was rejected because of his withered arm, an injury he acquired at birth. I believe he was very upset about this rejection of his honest patriotism.

All through my adolescent years, the war raged on. We listened to radio reports and read the papers with unsettling photos and did what we could for "our boys" so far away from our land-locked lives. We collected old newspapers, removed the tin foil wrap from dad's cigarette pack before he threw it away. We saved string and rubber bands wound into balls and dropped them off at collection centers with mother's coffee cans of bacon fat. I was never sure how that was going to help fight the war, but we did it faithfully.

Our Girl Scout troop packed small boxes with items soldiers overseas could use like a toothbrush and paste, hard candies, pencils, paper pads and socks. Father designed a Victory Garden in the backyard with rows of lettuces, radishes, beets and kohlrabi. In the middle was a large V of bright green parsley. Our Oldsmobile had an A sticker on the front windshield that indicated our gasoline allotment for the month. Government-issued coupons limited the number of shoes a family could buy. Butter was rationed so most everyone used the bland tasting, pure white margarine we mixed with yellow food coloring to make it look more like the real thing. These small family contributions for the war effort were the least we could do for our brave men abroad who were sacrificing more than anyone dared imagine. We weren't on the front lines, but as United States citizens we were blindly joined in a just cause.

In 1944, the circumstances of war presented a human face right in my seventh grade classroom at the Bloomfield Village School in suburban Detroit. Carolyn Ando, a shy 13-year-old Japanese girl with uncertain eyes, was assigned the seat behind me by the windows. We smiled at one another and Mr. Wilson introduced her to the class, suggesting we make Carolyn feel welcome in her new school. That was all he said. Carolyn was sweet, smiley and smart. Even though she looked different than the rest of us, we were interested to get to know this curious girl.

Carolyn, her younger sister, and their parents, as the result of hysteria and discrimination after the attack on Pearl Harbor in December, 1941, were swept up in the relocation of over 120,000 Japanese-Americans living on the west coast. President Franklin Roosevelt signed the directive,

Executive Order 9066. Most were U.S. citizens or legal permanent residents. Half were children. They lost their homes, possessions, and livelihoods–uprooted for four years and incarcerated behind barbed- wire under the watchful gaze of armed guards–"to protect against domestic espionage and sabotage."

When Carolyn arrived at my school in 1944, her father was garden manager of a farm owned by Devon Gables, a fine restaurant in the area. The farm grew the fresh produce used in the restaurant. That's all we ever knew. We never asked how they happened to be in our community because we probably didn't know about the relocation. Carolyn and her little sister became one of us at school, but every afternoon, a pick-up truck quickly took them away until the next morning. She never spoke about her personal life and we never met her parents.

After eighth grade in 1945, Carolyn told us she was moving to Los Angeles, California. We exchanged addresses and occasionally wrote cards and letters to one another. Her address changed several times and finally, we stopped writing, but I never forgot Carolyn. As a college student, I learned about the internment of Japanese-American citizens during World War II and was curious to know what became of the Andos. I found the last address Carolyn had sent me and wrote her a note inviting her to lunch when I visited Los Angeles in 1955. I was pleasantly surprised when she responded accepting my invitation. So, on the patio of a Westwood restaurant, sipping iced tea, enjoying an avocado stuffed with tiny shrimp, I finally heard Carolyn's story.

After the bombing of Pearl Harbor and President Roosevelt's Order, the Ando family was forced to close their successful interior design business on Wilshire Boulevard in Los Angeles and report to a government relocation center. They were allowed one small suitcase each to take with them. Apparently, Carolyn's family was well-known and respected in the area and their Anglo neighbors and friends did everything they could to help them, with little success. They packed in 48 hours and were sent away to a camp for two years. Their friends continued to seek help; finally, with government influence, the position on the farm in Michigan was arranged for Mr. Ando and his family. The children attended the public school nearby. After the war ended, the Ando family quickly returned to Los Angeles to reestablish their lives. Carolyn graduated from UCLA and joined the family business. After our pleasant lunch and childhood reminiscing on the sunny patio in Los Angeles, we said goodbye. We never saw one another again.

Eating My Heart Out

By Sue Barizon

It was the late 60s. I was a junior in high school when I first approached Rob. He was leaning against the railing in center court eating his lunch. Rob's mother loved him. I knew by the way she wrapped his sandwiches – the halves cut equally straight across, then stacked side by side "standing up" on their crusts. She wasn't stingy with the waxed paper, either. Clearly, she had mastered the tuck, tuck and fold method, an avid student of Reynolds Wrap commercials, I deduced.

Rob was tall and lean with short cropped auburn hair, freckles and a low key manner. I knew him to be smart and a bit of a loner. I was a cheerleader and since he was on the basketball team, I took advantage of my uniform to do a little research.

"I'll bet your mother made your lunch." I'd meant it as a playful inquiry, but thought it sounded a little accusatory around the edges.

He looked down at the sandwich cupped in his hand, shrugged and gave me a "Who else?" look.

"Let's see what Mama Marbleston packed for her little boy this morning," I teased.

Rob trusted that I wasn't disrespecting his mother. I knew Mrs. Marbleston from cheering her and the other basketball moms on at the Friday afternoon games. Playing along, he opened his brown paper, bag offering it up for my inspection. Mrs. Marbleston had applied her handiwork to a cluster of cucumber and celery sticks, a stack of slice and bake cookies, and a second sandwich identical to the one Rob was holding. The shiny red delicious apple was a perfect specimen – the kind seen on the teacher's desk in "back to school" ads. The two milk cartons perched on the railing came from the school cafeteria. I imagined his mother Scotch-taping two quarters to his lunch bag as a precaution, lest they be misspent on candy from the vending machines. Just as I expected, Mrs. Marbleston not only loved her son, she adored him.

"Does your Mom always remove the strings from the celery?" I asked.

"What strings?" Rob shot back.

Clueless, I thought to myself eyeing the neatly shaved celery sticks. Most guys are just plain clueless when it comes to what goes into a bag lunch.

I had become a student of bag lunches since I was old enough to notice the discrepancies between mine and my school mates. Consequently, I'd become aware of the discrepancies in the mothers who packed those lunches, my mother being the most discrepant of all. Mom suffered from a mental illness that kept her from performing the June Cleaver duties of her day. But, as I saw it, suffering was in the eye of the beholder.

Mom didn't do lunches. She rarely did breakfast, except for the occasional Sunday morning waffles. Mom's penchant for last minute dinner prep was fraught with drama usually triggered by Papa's declaration, "if you took the frying pan away from your mother, we'd all starve to death." Growing up in an Italian household, food equaled love. Mom just didn't get the equation. Her mind was preoccupied with the fantasy world she created, an escape from the routine expectations of her housewifely duties. School lunches were a daily reminder that my mother was "ill."

Living next door to Aunt Mary, Mom's sister, didn't help. My sweet Aunt made June Cleaver look like Mommy Dearest by comparison. Every day, she packed my cousins, Carla and Mark, off to school with custom-made lunches sporting the designer labels of our time: Oscar Meyer bologna, Wonder Bread, Kraft American cheese slices, Oreo cookies, Lays BBQ potato chips and Jif peanut butter ("...because choosy mothers choose Jif!"). There was the token nod to nutrition, carrots and celery scrubbed clean and uniformly cut. Although, Mark rarely ate the celery for fear his mother might have missed a string or two. His apple had to be peeled, cored, cut into eighths and dare not have the audacity to turn brown before lunch time. No ordinary brown paper bags would do for my cousins. Even my thrifty Uncle Pete sanctioned the latest trend, pastel colored lunch bags in pale green, sky blue and "baby's ass" pink.

Do I sound bitter? I'll admit my school lunch envy goes as far back as when I first compared my plain, red plastic lunch box to Mary Lou Mermen's glossy new Barbie model with matching thermos. Then, in the third grade, Johanna Giorgi opened my eyes to just how lacking I was in lunch time protocol.

"Is that all you're having for lunch?" Johanna's flippant tone caught me off guard. She sat fondling the package of Hostess Twinkies she'd been bragging about all morning. Her mother agreed to let her have the whole package if she promised to share one of the two Twinkies with a friend. At recess, she had declared me the lucky friend. The chatter at our lunch table stopped as everyone's attention turned to me. I swallowed hard to get down the last bite of a sandwich I had made myself from two stale bread ends and a gooey chunk of Velveeta cheese.

"I've got an apple," I gulped.

A little snicker escaped from Johanna's lips, then the announcement. "Too bad, Linda gets the Twinkie."

Linda Lorimer was the tallest girl in our class. I watched as her long gangly arm reached across the table emphasizing the humiliation of the trade we were all witnessing. My wrinkled apple was no match for a baggie of Chips Ahoy. I was as good as branded. I was a poor lunch-trade risk.

No wonder. Our Old World Italian kitchen sorely lacked the popular lunch making provisions of the 60s. I could cover for Mom by making my own lunches, but I needed supplies. Imported sardines packed in olive oil weren't going to cut it. The chubs of salami Papa brought home from North Beach delis were hard to slice evenly and fell out from between the bread unless I anchored them with butter. What kid is going to trade his mother's homemade snicker doodles for a set of dry, crunchy white Italian cookies called Ossa di Morto (translated, "Bones of the Dead")?

I remember walking to school carrying a full sized grocery bag sporting the store's initials in big, red letters, QFI (Quality Foods, Inc). How ridiculously light the bag was to carry save for the lone apple rolling around the bottom, bouncing off the sides like a giant pinball looking for an escape. I watched Debbie Lomalino pry open a sandwich sized container, the latest addition to the pricey Tupperware line. I marveled at the trust Mrs. Lomalino placed in her daughter for its safe return. There was the Logan family who boasted seven kids. I once asked Mrs. Logan what time she got up in the morning and just how long did it take to make seven lunches and get two sets of twins ready for school? I assumed that nerdy little Archie McFarland's thermos never saw a drop of spoiled milk. I pictured his mother emptying his lunch box the minute he came home from school, the thermos soaking in hot sudsy water while Archie sat eating milk and Fig Newtons at the kitchen table.

There were mornings when I'd wake up to the sizzle of bacon frying and the aroma of fried potatoes with rosemary and onion. It meant that Papa was home on vacation from his garbage route in the City (San Francisco). I remember as we sat finishing up our breakfast, Papa would be putting the finishing touches on our lunches. How he loved to feed us, salami, mortadella, and provolone piled so high that he had to scoop the soft center out of the French bread to keep the lunch meats in place. Then he'd butter the soft crustless scoop and throw it in the fry pan to toast along with the rosemary and onions. I saved mine for the walk to school. No one could cook like Papa.

How I savored every bite of that toasty delight as I meandered through the streets daydreaming of the lunches I'd someday make for my kids. How full they would be with all the things I wished for everyday at lunchtime. How their lunches would be the envy of all their friends. How hard pressed they would be to make a trade for my submarine sandwiches and homemade brownies. How I would pile it on thick and wrap it up with generous sheets of waxed paper using the tuck, tuck and fold method. How I'd Scotch tape their milk money securely to the inside of their trendy new lunch boxes. How someday I would send my children off to school

Moments Pass By (tanka)

By Amanda Hassitt

The river of time
Stands not still, but ever flows;
Moments pass by you –
Never to be repeated –
Treasure them while they are here.

The Seventh Floor

By Terry Toomey

One evening I decided to walk up to the seventh floor in the beautiful Cathedral Building in Oakland. A nicely dressed man suddenly lunged at me as I took the bend in the stairs where I could not be seen by anyone in the lobby. He was polite and apologized for scaring me and hurried out of the building with his hand in his pocket. Two days later, John was murdered. I wondered if the murderer was the man that almost knocked me down the stairs that evening. Unable to give the police a good description, they dismissed my thoughts because I would not be able to ID him even if he walked up and said hello to me.

I had a part time job as an answering service operator. I normally worked from 5 pm to 9 pm. The job was always interesting and so were the people whom I worked with. I didn't make much money, but I did this type of part-time work for many years.

Working here, I met people I might never have come in contact with. People like Joe, Jane and Dorothy. They talked about the most unusual people. It took me a week to figure out that these were not people they knew, but rather characters in the soap operas they all watched. They sure could have made guest appearances on the soaps they all loved; they were interesting people themselves. Joe, a gay black man, had a skunk for a pet and he walked along San Pablo Avenue in Oakland with Stripes on a leash. Dorothy was from the Deep South and had never really had much contact with white people and she was fascinated by my hair and also wanted to save Joe's soul. Jane would have been great at setting up sting operations. We would get a Berkeley Barb and decide which personal ad she should respond to. We listened to her calls on a speaker. She could be anything a pervert wanted.

When I started answering other peoples' phones, there were no cell phones or texting. The calls were routed to us and we would take messages. We answered calls for the Oakland Raiders and a television station. We connected people to their doctors. We dispatched tow trucks with our direct line to the police department. We sent nurses to peoples' homes. We had to make important decisions.

We knew a lot about our customers from the calls they got, eavesdropping and as a last resort listening to them on our trusty speaker.

It was amazing that one of our doctors, an OBGYN, had a patient whose water broke every Saturday. I guessed it never dawned on either of them that we would remember her name. A large pediatric group would talk to anyone who called them; all they asked was that we get the name of the child. One woman had a four-month-old child with an odd name. I asked her how to spell it and she did not know how it was spelled. A nurse had spelled if for her. It was almost more than this doctor could stand, although he did talk to her. The Oakland Raiders only wanted fans to answer their line. A popular newscaster would talk to his friends for hours and the smut could have been a bestseller. A family would rather have their loved one lie in fecal matter than have a black nurse come out and clean him.

The Doggie Diner next to the building was open all night. They had good chili and pastrami. The Broadway and Telegraph location also attracted the downtrodden and some crazy people. Once on a graveyard shift, I watched and listened from our window as a man talked to a manhole cover and shadow boxed his reflection in window for hours. He might have been a bit crazy. I guess I wasn't far behind him because I did watch him for at least an hour.

John was the heart of the Cathedral Building. He was the only janitor in this flatiron building for 25 years. He loved the brass elevator, the marble lobby, the odd shapes and all the nooks and crannies. Every evening he would stop and talk to us. He told the graveyard operator about his son who was into drugs. He had told the people his son was involved with, that he was going to the police. He never had the chance; he was murdered by the elevator and left on the stairs. His son was killed a month later.

Every night after his murder, the elevator would come to the 7th floor, the door would open, and the elevator would just sit there. The elevator and John's ghost waited for everyone when they got off to take them downstairs. Then the empty elevator would come back up again and wait until someone else went home. Just before 11 pm, the elevator would go back downstairs to wait for the graveyard operator.

John had never really left the building. His spirit was still there the day we closed the office and moved to a new building. Hopefully, he was ready to leave when we did, and didn't need to ride the elevator all night watching out for us and looking after his building.

Uptown Oakland is bustling; it is a dining and entertainment designation. Of course the Cathedral Building is still standing. This 1914 building is considered one of the best examples of Gothic Revival in the United States and was the first Gothic high-rise west of the Mississippi River. It was added to the National Registry of Historical Places in 1979. Like Oakland, it has changed too. There are now high priced condos from 7th floor to the 14th floor; there isn't a 13th floor. SFgate described floor seven: It features windows all the way out to the prow point of the building. The 14th floor was listed at over $1.95 million in 2008. There is no parking and the homeowner fees were $450, they have all been sold.

I wonder now if John is still in the building. I've driven by at night and the only lights I saw were on the floor where we all knew worked. It would be nice to think that he can still ride in the private, keyed elevator if he wanted to, but then again no one would know his story or any of the stories connected to the 7th floor.

Seasons Pass Speaks the Tree

By Michele Jessen

I am everything I am nothing
I am something. I am ever changing

Decades pass and I'm still me
Yet outside appearance is like a tree

Who lends itself to seasons four
Within lie buds of dreams to store

Come Fall, I grasp at a fallen leaf
Slowing fingers let go of grief

Come summer, springs my blooms array
I speak so fast, so much to say

Come spring, I rest limbs so fragile
No longer spewing wasteful prattle

Come winter's end, my sum's a stump
For snows fallen frozen heap, a lump

Now underground so wet
Reach and rise above mossy net

Escape the earth and burst through again
Squinting piercing breathing then

Peeling husk to twist and bend
Leaving seeds, a story to lend

I light the way in Dust to sparkle I hold the chasm
Wide between heavens

And what lies below to rest in warm hands
Upon sun's sweet glow

Forgive Us Our Trespasses

By Sylvia E. Halloran

The last of the choir leaves, tuckered out from a good rehearsal tonight. I hope they'll show up for the service Sunday. One of the altos offers me a ride to the train. She guides her sedan along deserted streets to the Millbrae station. I buy my one-way ticket home, slip it into my briefcase, and settle in to wait for the 9:04.

Thursday, perfect April. Warm air, trees in bloom. As I dressed this morning, my favorite DJ even promised the "leading economic indicators" were looking up. I fill up the time till the train comes savoring the day's events. It has been the kind of day that proves life is good.

The wheel-chair crowd at the retirement home sang along with me this morning, bright and cheerful. We were all Julie Andrews for a little while.

I stopped for a sandwich on the way to the park, and split the turkey and avocado on wheat with the squirrels. As I wait dinnerless now, I wish I'd kept the squirrels' share for a snack. But it's only a forty-minute trip. I'll be home in no time.

Writers in my afternoon Memoirs class carried our imaginations from Brazilian jungles to the Baltimore Catechism, stitching up a patchwork of life's little moments. Good or bad, everyone has a story.

The bench where I wait for the train grows colder and harder as the wind whips up. The warmth of the day has vanished. My sweater isn't quite enough.

A warm cat on the lap would be welcome about now. My kitties will be glad I made it to Target for their kibble. I dashed after class to snag some on sale, and still caught the "Baby Bullet" to Millbrae. It makes the 28 miles in 20 minutes.

This afternoon, as I walked uphill to church from the Millbrae station, the view astonished me; Berkeley shone across the bay like an enchanted kingdom. Tonight is just as clear. Faraway lights on the East Bay hills sparkle beyond the black expanse of water.

Choir rehearsal went well, considering it's the week after Easter. Even with two sopranos missing, we got a lot done. I filled in as I conducted, but those high Gs wore me out. I can't wait for a hot cup of tea and no shoes.

The *192* arrives right on time. It lunges out of the darkness à la *Anna Karenina*, a trio of blazing spotlights approaching fast from nothingness. The train uses the whole length of the platform before coming to rest. Weary folk slink aboard and pile into seats. I heft my music briefcase to the empty seat next to me. Just please take us home. The train resumes its ride south. No "bullet" tonight: the *192* stops at every station, 40 minutes from Millbrae to Mountain View, draining commuters like a sieve all down the Peninsula.

The next stop is Burlingame. Before we reach the station, the train slows, then stops. No doors open. Passengers begin to murmur just as an even-voiced announcement floats over the speaker.

"We apologize for the delay, folks. The train hit a trespasser on the track. There'll be about an hour's wait."

Here's the thing about announcements. You don't know what you're listening for until they're over. At first, disbelief and wonder hold the passengers mute. Then in one motion, cell phones blossom in every hand and the train fills with loud chatter from the flurry of calls.

"Some homeless guy jumped in front of the train."

"At least an hour, they say."

"Can you pick her up at the sitter's? No, I can't get there."

"I don't know why. I suppose they have to scrape him off the bottom of the train."

"Everybody's fine. Well, except for the trespasser. You know. That's what they called him. They said an hour. Like they do it all the time. I know, ick. Okay. Love you, too."

I call but no one answers. I wonder if the message I leave sounds as strangled as I feel.

Energized by nervous shock and finished with the first volley of calls, once reserved strangers now begin to joke with one another, sudden comrades in the same stranded battalion. The conductor assures the two men in wheelchairs that lifts will be available for the transfer, no worries. This train, our dear old *192*, is now guilty of involuntary manslaughter and has to report to headquarters. The conductor explains that the scheduled southbound *194* will come along in an hour and pick us up.

"We're really lucky," he continues, "being so close to San Mateo. The coroner is right there, so it won't take much longer than an hour."

Muffled sirens approach. Red and blue flashes bounce crazily across our windows. Suspended in unreality, we wait within the white glow of the train's fluorescent cabin lights. They obliterate the view outside. I eavesdrop as the conductor details part of the delay to a woman across from me. "Most of what they can clean up is behind the train."

My reflection looks queasy in the blind window.

It takes an hour, exactly their estimate. The frenzy of emergency vehicles disappears and we creep into the Burlingame station. Out of nowhere the *194* pulls up parallel just inches from our windows, heading south on the northbound track. The conductor asks us to file out the door. "Just walk to the end of this train, cross the tracks and board the other train," he encourages. We leave our light-drenched cocoon and emerge disoriented under the cold night sky. The Burlingame platform is a considerable distance from the accident site. Some of us peer back into the blackness anyway.

The silver twins loom side by side; lights and striping, windows and wheels exactly the same. We climb into the already loaded *194*, and sit where we can. The established riders are accommodating but remain detached. We refugees from the *192* belong to a secret club. The friends we made while waiting for the coroner nod in recognition as each boards. For one surreal hour, we lived our lives together. Nobody says another word.

Once emptied, the convicted *192* hustles away from the scene of the crime. "They can't," says a man leaning against the luggage rack. He wears a Bluetooth in his ear, leaving his untended mouth to broadcast to the whole car. "They got to empty it out. Yeah, everybody. Head straight to the yard in San Jose and debrief him. Drug tests and shit." We cannot help but listen until the noise of the moving train drowns him out. "Yeah. Totally. You gotta believe this shit's real hard on the engineer..."

The *194* ambles down its wrong track. At every station, the conductor combs the platform's waiting passengers "toward San Francisco" or "toward San Jose" and patiently explains single tracking. At Hayward Park we switch back to southbound rails; within uncomfortably close minutes, the northbound train from San Jose barrels past us.

Our rescue train is running 22 minutes late—the time it took to load us on. We're packed tight, but the crowd thins at Palo Alto. I relax a little when my seatmate leaves and push the heavy briefcase off my lap. Nobody has bothered to ask for my ticket.

Mountain View comes up, my stop, and I wrangle my briefcase and step off the train. The still air holds the scent of blossoms. It is warmer here than in Millbrae.

Midnight is bearing down on this once-perfect April day. Our "trespasser" fancied it a good day to step in front of a speeding train. Perfection is relative.

Shivering in spite of the balmy night, I throw my briefcase into the back of the Plymouth and plop into the driver's seat. A deep inhalation— prelude to a deep sigh—captures my old car's familiar scent and comforts me. I head home, thinking about my train adventure, grateful to be tied to earth with the gossamer thread of life.

The next Thursday, the trustees' committee paints the kitchen at church. Yellow drips speckle the *Chronicle* pages protecting the long counters and sinks. By chance I start reading the article closest to the faucet:

Burlingame Man Hit by Caltrain ID'd

A man struck and killed by a Caltrain in Burlingame was identified by the San Mateo County coroner's office Friday...No one on the train was injured... circumstances of...death...under investigation...

The man's name and address are given. He wasn't homeless at all. Three simple Internet searches take me to his funeral, his hometown, his family. He was my age. He left a twin sister, brothers, nieces and nephews. He loved California, and he loved to cook.

Everyone has a story.

What's Wrong with Judy

By Judy Grisell

My mother asked doctor after doctor "Why does my daughter walk on her toes?"

Neurologists, orthopedic doctors and our own family doctor, Dr. Skankey, pondered my physical problems. Diagnosis such as cerebral palsy was a possibility but not a clear-cut case. Multiple sclerosis or muscle dystrophy were not my diseases.

Over the years, I have had many examinations and tests. The three neurological work-ups happened when I was nine, fifteen and twenty-six. When I was fifteen, the tests were at the University of San Francisco Medical Center in San Francisco. When I was twenty-six, I was tested at Letterman Army Medical Center. All these work-ups caused me to be hospitalized for almost a week. Tests included brain waves, blood tests, and spinal taps. One test that was very painful was when they put needles put into my muscles and then ask me to move my arm or leg. To this day, I dislike being stuck. Neurologists checked my reflexes in many ways. Pins were poked in me, I followed their fingers, and my knees were hammered. So much fun!

At UCSF, the doctors suggested my disability might be functional not organic. Could a psychiatrist help me? My parents were not in favor of any psychological testing. For years, I was mad at them because I wanted to be "normal." During my stay at UCSF, I met my first boyfriend. It was so special—Richard Knapp, came from El Cerrito to take me to my Junior Prom.

When I was around nine years old, my parents took me to an orthopedic doctor in San Mateo. The medical building is visible from El Camino Real. Even now when driving past that building bad memories flood my mind "Mama, I do not want to see that doctor. He wants to hurt me," I cried. As young as I was, I knew cutting my Achilles tendons was not for me. The doctor believed it would help me walk better. Thank God, my parents were against such a surgery. That memory is almost sixty-five years old and I still feel sad and vulnerable when going past that building. When I was around nine years old, I wore lower leg braces to stretch my tendons. And for a while I wore full leg apparatus to bed. This treatment was painful and interfered with my sleep.

After I married my husband in 1968, I was treated by physical medicine doctors at Letterman Army Medical Center. Over the years, I have had lots of physical and occupational therapy. Psychiatrists and psychologists have examined and treated me. Dr. Urban, my favorite Army doctor, said my diagnosis would only be known after I died and an autopsy could be done. My daughters will know the cause of my physical disability.

After Letterman closed in the early 1990s, my doctor was Robert Telfer, a neurologist in Burlingame. For a lack of clearer diagnosis, he says that I have dystonia – a muscular disorder.

My treatment over the past sixty-five years has been lots of physical therapy and some occupational therapy. Also, I am on many medications such as pain pills, bladder control pills, and a mild antidepressant. Also, I take vitamins, calcium and pills for high blood pressure. For the past three years, I have been enrolled in an adaptive physical education class at Skyline College. My classmates have a wide variety of disabilities—strokes, post polio, accident victims, and a young man with autism. I go two days a week. I have slowed down a little and require more assistance with daily living activities. Presently, there are three ladies who come in two hours a day to help me fix lunch, get dressed, and do light housework. I have learned to cope with my challenging situation. I try to keep positive and always see the best in any situation. Naturally some days are more difficult than others but I do persevere and believe, "Tomorrow will be better." Someday, my daughters will know "What is wrong with Judy?"

Blue

By Jeannine Gerkman

Jet plane screams above
Sky blue, clean of clouds

Fuzzy sweater, baby blue, knobby with lint
Pulled from the dryer, static sparks

Wisps of blue smoke, gas flame fired hot
Icy blue glaciers calving, chilly air

Blue jays swooping, burst of feathers
Iridescent blue plays on hummingbird's throat, catches the sun

Blueberries picked fresh, still warm, explode on my tongue
Blackberry pie, flakey crust oozing sweet blue, tints vanilla ala mode

Midnight blue, silky, dotted with stars
Inky blue, stubborn, stains my fingers

Learning the Bones

By Laurel Anne Hill

My friend, Carmela, owned a large box of bones—a gift from her relatives. That's what she'd claimed moments ago. How strange. She was from the West Indies. Maybe chicken bones resided in her unusual package. Her family might have given them to her as a joke.

HONORABLE MENTION

I waited for her explanation. Or even for her to laugh. Yet Carmela, seated on a laboratory stool by the sink and across from me, instead reached into her plastic tub of dialysis tubing. She swished those flat, cellulose strips in the water. I glanced toward the racks of processed blood samples awaiting purification. It was time to transform tubes into bags.

We set to work knotting one end of each strip. Carmela told me about the medical school in her home country. Her ebony hair, not quite shoulder length, shifted as she tilted her head and spoke. Her eyes avoided my own.

"You won't believe what my family did so I could learn the bones." Carmela reached into the tub and withdrew another clear, wet tube. "They went to a graveyard. At night. Dug up a body. Granma boiled stuff clean. I kept the box under my bed."

A graveyard? A human body? Oh dear God, Carmela wasn't referring to chicken bones.

If my eyes had opened any wider, my eyeballs would have fallen out and rolled on the floor.

Wait a minute. This was the real-life nineteen-seventies, not a grave robber scene from a Charles Dickens' novel. She had to be kidding.

"I needed them for anatomy class." Carmela tied a knot. "Our school didn't have such good supplies. You people in the United States take so much for granted."

A skeleton or two lurked in the closets of most families. But Carmela had stashed a real one under her bed. Had she become a physician in her own country? She certainly wasn't a doctor here in California.

She knotted one end of more strips of tubing. I stuffed a marble into the bottom of each bag. A tight fit. We would use the weighted bags, as always, to purify test samples in a buffer-filled tank—to get rid of interfering substances. Then we could analyze for a protein linked to certain cancers.

"I get married," Carmela said, "but I still want to be a doctor. When my husband slept, I put the box on my side of our bed and studied the bones. Then one night he starts waking up at the wrong time. Reaches out, eyes closed, to touch me and feels something else." She shrugged, her mouth curving in a tentative smile. "That was the end of medical school for me."

135

Such a scene would have been hilarious in a British comedy. In real life, however, an unfulfilled educational dream was no laughing matter. How frustrating for Carmela. She must have resented her husband's attitude. And the decision must have disappointed her family, too. Her grandma had boiled those bones clean for nothing.

I once had hoped to earn a Ph.D. in immunology, but the opportunity had never arisen. I had achieved an M.S. in biology, though. My grandmother had baked bran muffins, casseroles, and created savory soups to offer me strength and encouragement. During her lifetime, Grandma had boiled more than one turkey carcass to create fragrant and tasty broth. Thankfully, she had discarded the bones as household trash. No macabre box lurked under my bed.

These thoughts returned to me twenty-five years and several careers later, when I received a phone call at work from my daughter. Alicia, in her second year of law school, expressed reservations about completing her studies. I planted my elbows on my desk and clutched the phone.

"I've learned so much," she said. "I really appreciate the opportunity you and Dad have given me. But I'll never work in some high-powered attorneys' office. That's just not me. I feel as though I'm wasting your money."

How could she talk this way? Alicia, with a dramatic arts undergraduate degree from New York University, worked hard and passed exams in Tulane University's well-regarded law school program. No easy transition. My husband and I had dug up the money to help her succeed. Boiled away obstacles. The least she could do was bury her doubts, resurrect her enthusiasm, and finish learning the law bones.

But was I thinking this way to benefit her? Or because David and I would be disappointed? She hadn't actually said she planned to quit. Did she really want to drop out of law school at all? I listened to her voice. Somewhere, under those words lay her real distress. What would reveal it? I had to find a way to provide helpful advice.

Two years ago, acceptance to Tulane had elated Alicia. Even the need for emergency surgery had not delayed her move from California to New Orleans. What had changed? Her father was in his seventies. Student loans and David's retirement account funded her graduate studies. She often called to discuss potential expenditures. Fear of family financial disaster might have fueled her current worries. Yet, was money her only concern?

I thought about our previous conversations. Alicia liked to bake cookies for friends and do volunteer work at animal shelters. Her internship this past summer had been with Court Appointed Special Advocates, an organization protecting abused children. Ambition and avarice motivated some lawyers. Alicia was sensitive to the needs of others. Did she wrongly perceive a mismatch between her personality and the law profession? Then I remembered something she had told me.

"No one takes me seriously," she had said.

I pictured her honey-blonde hair, long eyelashes and shapely figure. In teen theater, she had frequently played the sexy airhead. Did some of her current peers typecast her in this same manner? Even tease her?

Another unfulfilled educational dream could be waiting to happen.

But Alicia was perceptive and intelligent. She enjoyed her law classes. Was capable of finding a niche. I brushed back a lock of my graying hair, determined to provide the best advice I could.

"You need to finish what you've started," I said, trying to sound firm, yet understanding and motherly. "There are opportunities other than typical law offices. You just have to find one right for you. And you haven't flushed our financial security—or your own—down the toilet."

A few months later, Alicia reported she'd found a potential summer internship in New York, for a manager of bands and other entertainers. Her dramatic arts background would be perfect for an entertainment law career. This intern position could provide insight into the business. Plus some agents had law degrees, another possible choice. I crossed my fingers, toes and eyes—anything to bring good luck. Then I prayed hard.

"I love my new job. My boss is fantastic," Alicia told me on the phone one afternoon, bubbling more than a washing machine overloaded with suds. "I finally know how I'm going to use all of my education. Really help people. I can hardly wait to graduate. I can see myself doing this for the rest of my life."

Years ago, Carmela's grandmother and my own had used fundamental skills to encourage us to follow our dreams. Career doors had opened, even if not the portals Carmela and I had envisioned. Many routes could lead toward rewarding lives.

Education provided the supporting structure—the skeleton—to stretch and grasp future opportunities. But who people were and what values they treasured breathed life into the dry bones of learning, and, ultimately, into themselves. Achieving real success meant struggling and learning to unearth inner strength. It meant discovering when to boil off obstacles and how to dialyze away what interfered with seeing truth.

Achieving real success also meant lighting the lamps to guide younger generations.

I perched upon my chair, as though seated on a lab stool across from Carmela. I smiled.

Another day, another bone learned. And that was no joke.

My First Alcoholic

By Judith Shernock

In April a new boy moved to Seventh Street. He had some unusual characteristics: no mother or siblings, lived with his Dad and wore glasses which he called "specs."

Jim's face was small and freckled, his nose upturned. His clothes were either a tad too small or so overly large that the sleeves were rolled up so it seemed that his spindly arms were covered by a thick, unruly band of dark cloth.

Sometimes Jim was lots of fun. He ran very fast and never ended up as "it" when we played tag or "capture the flag." He was nine, a year older than me. At first he tried to challenge ten-year-old Eddie, for leadership of our group, but soon realized that wouldn't work and appeared to adjust to the way things were done on our street.

Though Jim was Catholic he didn't go to the local parochial school. Like me, he went to public school and we often walked there together. Twice a week my mother gave me a penny for the candy store. Jim had perfect intuition as to when those days would occur and would be waiting for me at the corner, his face wreathed in a crooked smile.

When we entered the tiny candy store with its myriad smells, colors and unending choices Jim was right by my side. He whispered in my ear; "Choose Sugar Dots."

These were little drops of colored sugar in pink, blue and yellow. For your penny you received sixty dots, ten multicolored rows of six, which Mr. Eghart, the owner, tore from a long, long paper roll on top of the counter.

"Divide them carefully," Jim warned me. He meant equally, thirty for each of us.

Jim gobbled them up so fast I felt awful savoring my candies slowly while he was gazing at me hungrily.

"Sharing is a blessing, my Mom used to say before she died."

"How old were you when she died?"

"I was five." For a second the always upbeat Jim looked a bit crestfallen and we walked the rest of the way without any of his funny remarks.

In June, the school year ended and we sang : "No more pencils. No more books. No more teacher's dirty looks."

One lazy summer day Charlie, Janie, Jim and I, were discussing whether to go hunting for scrap metal to help the war effort or to the railroad yard and sneak into the boxcars and pretend to be hobos.

Suddenly Jim piped up: "Have you ever seen a real drunk?" Three pairs of eyes turned to stare at him. "It's very funny," he continued. "They do strange things. Sometimes they even dance."

"Where can we see it?" Janie asked.

"I can show you one but it'll cost two pennies—that's two pennies each." He grinned charmingly at us.

Charlie wanted to know when we could see this unusual sight. "Sunday afternoon at two. We'll meet right here."

Janie shook her head. "I only get one penny a week... I won't have two by Sunday."

"I get a penny every day and I'll give you one." Charlie smiled at Janie who turned red. She knew how much he liked her.

"I can save up my two pennies, I thought. "No candy for us this week," I said to Jim.

Sunday at 1:30 we were anxiously waiting for our guide. Each of us had something to say about alcohol. Janie confided about her big brother, Johnny.

"He came home drunk once and Dad yelled at him that the next time it happens he'll be living on the street and not in a house."

Charlie said, "I heard in church that liquor is a sin."

"My parents say only really bad people drink and get drunk." I added.

Finally Jim came sauntering along and led us to a four-story walk up. It was built in a curious manner, becoming narrower and narrower as you approached the top. The fourth floor landing was tiny and we were all pushed together. Before us was a brown door whose paint was peeling.

"Who goes first?" Jimmy asked. Charlie volunteered.

"Two cents please." Jim's hand shot out his to collect the coins.

Charlie handed over the money. Jimmy gave a glance through the keyhole and then said "Go ahead."

Charlie put his eye to the keyhole. After a few minutes he silently walked away and sat on the steps.

"Who's next?' Jim asked.

Janie poked me in the ribs to take my turn before her. I put my two pennies into the outstretched palm and put my eye to the keyhole.

Before me was an emaciated grey haired man sitting at a wooden table on which was a bottle. He filled a glass with amber liquid, brought it to his mouth and finished the whole thing in one gulp. Then he got up, stumbled, started cursing, fell down and crawled on hands and knees back to the chair. His shaking hand poured out another glassful.

Having seen enough, I moved away from the keyhole. With a confused mind and a sad heart I sat down on the steps next to Charlie. Neither of us spoke a word or even looked at each other.

Janie paid her money and looked through the keyhole. In a shocked voice she cried, "That's your *Father*, Jim!"

The three of us silently walked down the stairs and back to our homes. Jim remained alone on the landing, tightly clutching his pennies.

I had met my first, but not my last, alcoholic. He, like so many others, was somebody's parent.

Montana Badlands - In the Past

By Pat Callaway

I went to Montana one summer. But not just to Montana. I went back in time! Far beyond the days of the Wild West. Far beyond the days of the first Indian settlers who are thought to have migrated down the old north trail from Alaska. I went back in time millions of years! Not through a time machine, but little by little, carefully scraping away at the earth with an ice pick and a brush.

Nearly 80 million years ago, during the Cretaceous Period, dinosaurs roamed among the conifers. It is thought that these creatures were wiped out locally by volcanic eruptions, the intense heat leaving only the dinosaurs' bones to be scattered around later by mudslides.

In the late 1970s, paleontologist Jack Homer discovered one of the world's largest dinosaur beds here in the badlands of Montana. He also discovered a nest of dinosaur eggs and the first-ever nest of fossilized fledglings.

Now I'm here, at the Conservancy's Pine Butte Guest Ranch, along with ten other aspiring paleontologists, hoping to make discoveries of our own. It's day four of a weeklong summer camp for adults ready to pick and scrape under the watchful eye of Karen Chin, a bona fide paleontologist (and Homer disciple) at the University of Colorado.

At the dig site, owned by the Museum of the Rockies, our work area consists of two adjacent plots, totaling 125 square feet. I claim my coveted piece of earth and kneel down.

To the untrained eye, it is difficult to distinguish a fragment of dinosaur bone from a clump of dirt or a piece of rock or calcite. Calcite, the purveyor of good and bad news, forms around both bones and rocks and brings the anticipation of discovery every time I strike it. I pick and brush, pick and brush, being careful to keep the area clean and level. "Is this a bone?" I ask over and over again. The answer is always, "No."

We break for lunch. A Townsend's solitaire flies overhead. The area is teeming with wildlife such as white-tailed deer, pronghorn antelope and prairie falcon. Grizzlies are careful to hide their presence. Coyotes howl in the distance. A Richardson's ground squirrel soaks up the last bit of sun before hibernating through the winter.

Then, back to work. I pick and brush, pick and brush, wondering if this is a futile effort. Again, I strike something hard and it feels different. I carefully brush away the soil. I can tell this is it! This is not Jurassic Park: this is not a myth: this is not a rock. This is the real thing!

I call to Karen, who confirms the finding. It might even be a rare find, part of a skull. I carefully pick around the bone. Although it's not a skull, it's an ischium, a fragment of hip bone. But as I excavate, I discover a femur (leg bone}-the largest bone we've found so far (1.8 feet) and then an ulna (arm bone). The thrill of discovering real dinosaur bones—of touching fossils that have not seen the light of day in millions of years and have never been touched by human hands—is incredible!

We dig a trench around the trio of bones. I dunk strips of burlap in plaster and carefully lay them over a thin layer of paper covering the bones so they can be extracted and sent to the museum. On the last day, our group sends 16 bones to the museum in Bozeman.

It occurs to me that my encounter with the remnants of an extinct species, brings it back only in my imagination. I reflect upon my travels and realize more than ever what a privilege it is to encounter the world's amazing flora and fauna concurrent with their existence. I want to do what I can to protect them.

The weather is chilly today. Strong winds often blow through this part of the badlands, where, earlier this season, researchers housed themselves in windproof tepees. The bare poles of the tepees, now stripped of their protective skins until next season, stand in symbolic tribute to the prized bones that lie beneath.

Diet Dilemma

By Edie Matthews

Fatty tissue has become the issue; It's so hard to stay thin.
My clothes are tight. Darn this appetite! Am I getting a double chin?
Cleaning your plate—what a mistake, But wasting food is a sin.
One little snack, is it will-power I lack? Oh, tomorrow my diet begins.
Of all fates counting carbohydrates, In an Italian pasta meal.
Pounds to dislodge, fat thighs to camouflage, If only celery had some appeal.
I always cringe when I'm starting to binge; Chocolate's my biggest addition.
How can I stop? May I'll shop. I must control this frightful affliction
Social events with tempting succulents, How will I ever lose?
I'll have my quota with a diet soda; Well, it's rude to refuse.
Big as a whale! Please hide the scale! I'm trying not to get frustrated.
It's so hard to shed this lard. How do people stay motivated?
Candies and sweets high calorie treats, Why do they have such magnetism?
Get off the log, go our and job, Maybe I have slow metabolism.
Down in the dump cause I'm pleasantly plump; Indoctrinating ads are hard to resist.
This inclination for every temptation, Seconds?... Oh, if you insist.

A Seventh Grader's Odyssey

By Jamie Miller

Nineteen-forty-eight was a good time to be twelve years old. The war was over and the demands that had kept railroaders like my dad always on the road had subsided, so he was home regularly. Consumer goods were available, and I could get on with begging my dad for a bicycle. That year, he finally admitted that I was big enough, and maybe we could afford one.

I knew exactly the bike I needed. Radio programs aimed at boys like me, plus ads in the Boy Scouts' magazine, pitched the fabulous Monark Silver King, a lovely creation with gleaming frame of octagonal aluminum tubing. Nearly 70 years later, Silver Kings still surface occasionally on eBay at astounding prices. Imagine their appeal then! A hardware store in my little town once had one in stock, and when we went shopping I managed to steal a few minutes to stop by and caress it. Unfortunately, they cost nearly 80 dollars, so actually buying one was never going to happen.

I settled on begging for one of Monark's lesser models. Monark bikes are no longer made, and the one I chose is a good example of why. Mine had a headlight powered by two D-cell batteries, with its beam weakened by cutouts on the sides of the reflector that showed red to my left, and green to the right, just in case I should meet a sailor on Main Street, in doubt as to whether to pass me to port or to starboard. It had a pressed-steel luggage rack that gave up and sank to the fender the first time I gave my sister a ride. It had a "tank" between the upper bars that included a horn powered by another two D-cell batteries. It might have been useful for warning little old ladies of my approach, except that the batteries had a habit of shaking out of place on the dirt streets of my Wyoming town. A pair of chromed bars up front seemed to suggest a shock-absorbing fork, but actually did nothing. No matter. And no matter that it weighed over 56 pounds, whereas my latest 10-speed weighs only 37. I was pleased and proud, and took every opportunity to go to town to shop for my grandmother when needed.

My destiny was obvious, even at that age. I would be an engineer, ergo, I had to take things apart and see what was inside. How, I wondered, did a coaster brake work? The design was clever, but I was shocked to learn what a light-weight grease had been used on the bearings. This was obviously not suited to the hard riding I would give it! I had watched my dad re-pack the wheel bearings in our car, so I knew what needed to be done. I found the axle grease can at the back of the garage, and re-packed my coaster brake. For good measure, I re-packed the pedal crank and front wheel bearings. Admittedly, it was harder to pedal, but it wasn't going to overheat and burn out the bearings!

I rode, that summer. Almost everyplace in town was less than three-quarter mile from home, so I rode there. To the market, my aunt's place, the park, the railroad to watch my dad take the trains out, I rode. But that wasn't enough. Bicycles were made for traveling. But where could I go? I wasn't ready for a big ride, but there were a few places to try first.

My small town had an even smaller "suburb" ten miles away that consisted mainly of a gas-station/store, a bar, and a school. We had driven through it on our way to the mountains, but never stopped to look. It seemed worthy of some serious exploring. So the town of Big Horn would be my destination.

I began my preparations. Nowadays, with a few years and cycling miles behind me, my starting kit would be a tire patch kit and pump, a helmet and gloves, and a bright, visible jacket. At twelve years old, none of this entered my mind. The first thing that I would need for my quest was lunch. I gathered up my pocket knife, matches for a fire, my army-surplus canteen and mess kit, and I secured them in the bike's basket. Now, I needed food for the expedition. I might be gone for several hours, so the food would need to keep and not spoil on the way. I knew much of the food in the house would not do, so I settled on a potato. Potatoes keep, I knew. I could slice it up and fry it in the mess kit, which featured a folding handle to keep my hand away from the fire. I was ready. What more could I ask?

Where my mother and grandmother were during all this planning is a mystery. They were usually not inclined to let me go more than a few blocks without a thorough explanation, and I don't believe that they had a clue as to the extent of my plan or it would have died aborning. Did I sneak out, give them a cover story like going to the park, or what? I'll never know. But I was soon away and on the road.

Ah, freedom! The wind in my hair, the song of my tires on the open road, the rumble of the 18-wheelers as they rolled by! And this was before I even passed the city limits. I cruised past the sugar factory with its landmark chimney and past the street where my aunt lived, and soon I passed the tall silos of the flour mill. To my right, Airport Road turned up the hill. That was the last street on the town map. I really was out on my own. I had never been out here alone before, and it was thrilling! I wasn't exactly *alone* alone, but the trucks roaring by didn't count.

In 1948 most commerce went by rail, so big trucks were rare, and there were long intervals when I could hear the meadowlarks calling from the fields alongside. I still remember their seven-note call, and I believe I could pick it out if I had a piano before me. Six miles past Airport Road, US Highway 14 turned away leaving just occasional Big Horn traffic to share my road. I rode on a little way, but I was wearing out. I decided maybe it was lunch time, so I found an inviting spot in the borrow ditch, gathered scraps of wood and grass for tinder, and set it alight. Now, how does a person slice a potato when he doesn't have a table to work on? The quick answer is "badly." No matter. I dumped some slices in the pan and held them over the fire. They went from raw white in the center to burnt black at the edges, never offering up the enticing aroma of fries at home. I kept trying, and ended up throwing the whole experiment over the fence into the pasture beside me.

Time to go home. The trip out may have been wearying, but the way back was a painful slog through the dust and heat of a Wyoming summer afternoon. Outbound, I remember the meadowlarks. Homebound, I remember sun and sweat. I made it home. I had to: no way could I admit defeat, even if I had to walk my bike home from the sugar factory. I never again rode that bike that far.

I did ride my faithful Monark to junior high and two years of high school, until I found a friend with a car, but I rarely rode it after that. I parked it in an outbuilding and ignored it. But it had done me well. Many years later, my wife and I were cleaning out the old family place and loading some antiques on a trailer to bring to California. On a whim, I loaded the old Monark on the trailer, too, and stored it away again at our California home. California's humid air is not as healthy for bicycles as is dry Wyoming's. Parts have rusted and the paint is not looking good. But one of these days, when I work my way through some of my backlog of essential stuff, I am going to take it apart and clean and lube all the parts and get a new pair of tires. Then I will see just what it was like to make that abortive ride to Big Horn.

But no way am I going to use automotive axle grease when I put it together. That stuff might have been good for combines or Conestoga Wagons, but never for bicycles. That bad choice was really the beginning of my education as an engineer. It taught me to think things through before doing something foolish: The folks who built that bike for me may have known what they were doing, after all.

Lovely Butterfly (haiku)

By Amanda Hassitt

Lovely butterfly
Lands among the flower beds
Whispering her love.

Frogmen and Snowflakes

By Kennon States

My first experience of snow is remembered, not so much for the snow, but for what preceded it. Sometime before Christmas, 1944, my mother and I left our home in North Carolina, driving by car to join my father in Fort Pierce, Florida, where he was to be commissioned as a naval officer, following the formation of and recruitment for the U.D.T. – Underwater Demolition Teams, fondly termed "Navy Frogmen." This trip came at the end of arduous weeks of training and preparation for him.

Daddy had enlisted shortly after the attack on Pearl Harbor, despite the fact that he was over thirty, married, and the father of an eighteen-month old daughter – me. He had been told that he would have been exempt from the draft. However, he felt an obligation. Because of his profession–he was in the construction industry, building boilers, hydroelectric machines, steam-powered engines, and the like–he joined the "Sea Bees," the nickname of the Construction Battalion. Despite his degree from Duke University, he chose to remain in the enlisted ranks, refusing the automatic offer of officer training.

When Mother and I arrived in Florida, we found motel accommodations in the tiny town of Vero Beach, in a row of one-room cabins, only a few steps from the water's edge. Fort Pierce, located about two-thirds of the way down Florida's Atlantic Coast, was just a few miles to the south. This was also my first memory of the seashore. But what did I know of "Vero?" To my four-year-old brain, it sounded like the word "bureau." I had a set of bureau drawers in my bedroom at home, and so we called it "Bureau Beach" for the duration of our stay.

We spent languid days, the two of us, enjoying the beach and what attractions were to be found in Vero Beach, itself, shops, the movies, the park. The beach was a delight to my senses. The balmy air and warm sun on my skin, the wet, sugary sand that squished between my toes, the smell of the salt, the dazzling blue of the ocean, bathtub temperature waves lapping up my legs above my knees. I enjoyed watching local fishermen cast their lines out beyond the breaking waves and haul in their catch of brilliantly colored fish, yellow and green and silver, some with black stripes between the colors, with their glassy eyes that seemed to wonder where they were.

We spent our evenings getting reacquainted with Daddy. Mother and I had seen him, perhaps two times, since he joined the Navy, three years earlier. He had been serving in the South Pacific, involved in deadly encounters with the enemy. Shore leaves back to the East Coast of the United States were infrequent for men in his situation.

This reunion was bittersweet, more so for my mother, who had to know, without a doubt, that his new assignments would be far more deadly than any that had come before. My parents were trying to make the most of what time they had together. We stayed in Florida about a week, perhaps five days. I'm not certain about that detail.

I do remember that Daddy came to us each evening when his long training day was finished, and we would go to some nearby restaurant and dine on fresh-caught local fish. And I wondered if they were the ones I had seen on the beach that morning. He would spend each night with us, and the three of us would rise early each morning to have breakfast together in our little cabin before Daddy left for the day.

We were never a cereal-for-breakfast family, but a box of Corn Flakes, a few cans of condensed milk, and some bananas to slice on top, lasted for the week and sufficed. I have never been able to recreate the sweet, soggy taste of those breakfasts, and I've never become a cereal eater. Perhaps it was the company, more than the food.

At the end of our stay, there was a ceremony at Fort Pierce; at which Daddy was commissioned as a Lieutenant, Junior Grade, and pinned his gold bars upon a white dress uniform. I did not attend this ceremony. I can't remember why not, nor where I was while Mother celebrated with him, but I still cherish a black-and-white photo of the two of them, standing under palm trees – Daddy smiling and proud, wearing medals already, from his service in the Sea Bees, and Mother, not exactly smiling, but proud, nonetheless, her hair swept up in that 1940's style.

The day we drove away from Vero Beach was hot and humid. I wore a sun-suit. Do they even have sun-suits anymore? Mother and Daddy wore shorts and cool tops. We all wore sandals, and we sweated formidably – it was the era before air conditioners in cars. Daddy had leave coming and would spend a few days at home with us in North Carolina.

Shortly after passing through Georgia into South Carolina, the first snowflakes began to fall. It was growing dark, as night came on quickly. The car radio informed us that a freak blizzard had struck the Carolinas. We could hardly see beyond the hood of the car, and the windshield wipers were useless, as the snow swirled wildly from all directions. The car heater was put to such use that it broke down. I remember shivering in my sun-suit. We sang Christmas carols until we arrived at home.

We would see Daddy one more, brief time before the end of the war. Then, in June 1946, Mother and I boarded a train, bound for Coronado, California, to join Daddy, as he awaited separation from active duty, and where I celebrated my sixth birthday.

But so ends my first-snow tale. None of my subsequent snows quite compares.

Visual and Performing Arts

By Evie Groch

Miss Edwards taught me British Literature on the second floor of the four-story brick edifice known as L.A. High in the early 60s. She boasted a regal, aristocratic posture and enunciated clearly in her formal English diction. As we entered the class daily, she would quickly put her recently applied makeup into the middle drawer of her institutional brown desk and walk to the podium with such pomp and measured steps that we took to imitating her behind her back. Her brightly dyed auburn hair was a bit too long for someone her age, perhaps in her mid to late forties. A shade of lipstick paler or softer than the loud ruby red color she wore would have made her appear less severe. The harsh red contrasted too highly with her pale powdered face and lent a clownish quality to her appearance.

"Now class, let our minds focus on...." was how each class started. So predictable. As we would leave, she would remind us, "Remember, when you travel to England and are about to leave, turn around and enjoy the While Cliffs of Dover." We reacted to this like we would to a broken record and mumbled "Yeah, sure we will."

Miss Edwards sat very daintily on the stool behind the podium with her open-toed shoes touching and lectured on noted British authors and literature. She introduced us to Shakespeare, Austen, Dickens, the Bronte sisters, and Thomas Hardy. At times it sounded like she had had a personal, passionate relationship with each of them – that's how intimately we felt she knew them. At first we found it hard to understand how she could be so enthusiastic about all those long dead authors whom we believed had little relevance to our teenage lives. It wasn't until I became a teacher myself and developed a fondness for authors on my own special list that I grew to understand her great love. Under her guidance and tutelage, I came to appreciate and value the works of her beloved authors. I discovered the author of *The Adventures of Tom Jones,* Henry Fielding and elevated him to the top of my list.

As I replay those classroom days in my mind, the black and white movie clips of Miss Edwards come to life with infused color, and I see a spotlight fall on her and follow her to and from the podium and around the dull green room with faded yellow shades. We, the audience watch, listen, pretend to understand, and many times react appropriately; other times tuning out entirely. The melodramatic aura surrounding her suggests a film directed by Cecil B. DeMille in which she stars a few years after her best work, acting as her own makeup artist when she clearly could have used a professional. She never has to say "line, please" as she is competent and well-rehearsed, but what she seeks and never seems to get are appreciation and applause. She's not even in the credits. No one is. She has, however, become a permanent image in my mind with a starring role in my love of British literature.

It occurred to me many years later why Miss Edwards was doing what she did as her students entered her room. She was readying herself for her role, on stage, in front of an audience. First makeup, her script memorized, her dramatic entrance, and then the show of passion for her craft. This is what a professional would do, and that is what she considered herself. I had gotten the genre wrong. I had seen her starring in films, yet I believe she saw herself in the theater.

The second time I visited England, I went out of my way to travel with my hesitant roommate to a destination she had no interest in. As we were leaving, I turned around and beheld the White Cliffs of Dover and heard Miss Edward's voice in my ear, "Well done."

Rock On

By Ellen Six

I loved my little wooden rocking chair. It had been a Christmas gift and was the only chair that was just my size and it was all mine. Of course I did let my dolls sit in it when I wasn't using it. Mother's furniture was French Provincial in style and covered in plastic so I wouldn't get my muddy shoes all over it when I climbed up to sit near an adult. But now there was my rocking chair. It was mine, all mine. It was brown stained wood and looked like it belonged in a log cabin. I was enamored with the Little House on the Prairie series so I let my imagination run to covered wagons and old-fashioned towns and it became my reading chair. I piled up my library books on the floor next to me and I was in my own world. But childhood doesn't last forever and lest I become Goldilocks who tried to force a fit and ended up smashing a chair to bits, I saw my rocking chair end up in the back of a storage closet.

After I was married, I got an adult size rocking chair where I tried to rock my babies to sleep. Surprise. The rocking motion only annoyed them and they showed me their discomfort by crying in high-pitched wails. They preferred to be driven around the block in their car seats where the rhythm of the road finally won out. So much for tradition.

I put the chair in the storage closet.

When my youngest married daughter announced that she was pregnant and that we would be having our first grandchild, my eyes filled with tears. Of course I was overwhelmed with joy about this addition to our family but there was that little nagging voice in the back of my head that kept whispering, but you're too young to be a grandmother.

Grandmothers have gray hair, my hairdresser helped prevent that. Grandmothers have arthritis and are forgetful. If you want to find a grandmother, you just look for the nearest rocking chair. As my daughter's waistline expanded, so did my vision of myself as an old woman. I would be stepping into the final frontier, the oldest generation in the family. The reality of old age was hitting me. The word grandmother made it real.

What woman doesn't worry about getting old? What about all those ads on T.V. that promise to remove wrinkles or give you softer hands without those brown giraffe spots? I'm sure that the definition in the dictionary for grandmother was old lady.

There was no doubt about it. This was a final affirmation that I was over the hill and sliding fast towards eternity in support stockings and flat heeled shoes.

But what of the joys of being a grandmother? It would be great if I could see this new child without a warning that cataract surgery would be coming and could I even hear this baby cry? Probably not without turning up a hearing aid. As for running after this child in a year, do they make a racing version of walkers? So much for a vivid imagination and too many late night commercials for denture cream and hair transplants. When did I get old?

I remember when I was growing up. I would stand in front of the mirror in my bathroom. Then I could see only the top of my head. As I grew, my forehead became visible, then my nose, my mouth. When I became a teenager, I became critical. Was that a blemish? As a young mother, a quick glimpse and a touch of make-up and out the door on multiple errands. Somewhere along the line there was the first gray hair, the first wrinkle but we mothers joked that they were badges of courage that we had earned in the trenches of motherhood. Now that word grandmother had sent me the message of elderly senior citizen. How could I have missed this reality?

The phone rang. Our daughter was in labor. My husband and I rushed to the hospital where we heard the wonderful news. It was a baby boy, 6lb.3oz. We went in to see our daughter and the baby was laying in her arms. "Mom, would you like to hold him?" There was a rocking chair in the room. I sat down and they brought my first grandson to me. I held this precious life in my arms. What joy! What elation! This was the reward of all those years. He grabbed my heart and I was his.

This little boy as he grew wanted to know when he could visit his Golden Grandma. Thanks again to my hairdresser, I was the grandmother with the blond hair, and now my rocking chair was a royal throne.

A Trilogy of Misadventures

By Jake Lucas

One

In 1948, I was a precocious youngster of eight, often looking for something to do. I had a very active mind that often got me into trouble or danger. One activity that I remember listen to the 'Lone Ranger' on the radio. After the cave was about eight feet into the hill, I started to carve out a bigger area at the end where I could sit up. Using a flashlight from the house to look at my handiwork, I could see where I needed to do more. I was very pleased with myself now that I had created my own 'private place' to hide away when I didn't want to be found.

About this same time, I read an article in the paper about a young boy in Nebraska who had almost died when a sand cave collapsed in on him. I had a nightmare about being buried in sand and going into sheer panic.

As much fun as it was to have my very own cave, I was much more afraid of being buried alive. Maybe my dream was sent by a guardian angel or maybe it was a warning from somewhere unknown—who knows for sure—but I believe it was one of those things that protect small boys from being hurt by their follies. I have no idea what happened to that cave, as I never crawled in there again. Thus ended my great cave experiment.

Two

My brothers and I had stacked a huge pile of firewood at the back of our house to last through the cold Colorado winter. One autumn day while picking up some wood to take into the house, I became curious about what might be in the woodpile. I started poking the pile with an old three-foot-stick just to see if anything was in there. I heard a rattle. All of a sudden there was a four-foot-long rattlesnake slithering out from underneath the pile. He seemed quite upset about being disturbed. He turned in my direction as his beady eyes looked straight at me. Cornered between the snake and the fence, I froze in panic.

My parents, standing about fifteen feet away, weren't paying any attention until I cried out. I think that they were startled to see my predicament. They frantically called out, "Stay still, stay still," From their tone I knew that I was in danger. Fortunately, I was too scared to even move a finger, which apparently was the right thing to do. The snake gradually lost interest and moved away.

It's amazing to me that this incident, which took less than a minute, made such an impression. To this day, I still have a healthy respect for snakes and a firm resolve never again to poke at a pile of wood, unless of course I have a much longer pole.

Three

My younger brother Sam and I were walking along the railroad tracks, looking for adventure. We came to an overpass where the tracks crossed over cars driving underneath. The gravel under the railroad ties was just the right size for throwing, so we started looking around for something to throw at. I had a thought, Why don't we see if we can hit a moving target, like a car going underneath us? This seemed like such a seductive idea that we didn't really stop to consider the consequences. We dropped rocks from the tracks to the cars below. After quite a few misses, our aim improved and I hit a windshield. The car swerved and slammed on the brakes. It finally dawned on us that maybe we had done something dangerously wrong. We flew back to our house to hide, hoping that no one would find us out.

We were very nervous about what would happen next. The suspense seemed as if it lasted forever. After about an hour or so, there was a knock at the door. As Mother opened the door we could see the county sheriff standing outside. There is nothing so intimidating to a wayward eight-year-old, as a big sheriff, in full uniform, with a badge and a gun.

Since our house was closest to the scene, he asked us if we knew anything about rocks being dropped from the overpass. I don't remember admitting anything but I didn't deny it either. The guilt on our faces told the Sheriff all that he needed to know. Mother told him that I would pay for the damages out of my savings.

I had a savings account that my father had insisted I set up so that I would have enough money to go to college. In my eight-year-old mind, I concluded that if I had to pay for the windshield, it would wipe out my entire savings and jeopardize my ability to go to college and therefore my whole future. Miraculously, the sheriff said that the man's insurance company would pay the $25 (1948 prices) to replace the windshield. As he was leaving, the sheriff said, "If you do it again, there will be serious consequences." As he went out the door, Mother turned to us and said those infamous words, "Just wait until your father gets home."

My father came home, scowling and wheezing, from one of his frequent asthma attacks. He was not in a good mood. After he heard what had happened, he took off his belt, grabbed us by the arm and swatted us on the rear end. After our 'attitude adjustment' and much crying and wailing, he had made his point. We had no desire to do that again.

After a few days, with the latest events heavy on our minds, Sam and I knew not to repeat our past misdeeds, but the agile mind of a young boy cannot be suppressed for long. As the pain (mostly emotional) subsided, our imagination gradually returned and we started to think about what we could do next.

Lone Deer

By Martha Clark Scala

Driving south on Route 495, I had my Bluetooth on so I could talk by phone with my friend, Sue. En route to a scheduled appointment with my sister Margo's attorney, I anticipated a tense rendezvous in the parking lot with Margo and her oil-versus-water son and daughter. Nearly four months prior, Margo had been diagnosed with metastatic melanoma. She took action immediately when I suggested that she get her estate plan in order as soon as possible, and used our conversations over those months to discuss the likelihood of her demise despite seeking treatment.

The papers had been drawn up but not finalized, and today was the day. My niece understood the urgency of this critical administrative task. My nephew had balked at virtually all discussions about Margo's eventual death, and complained, "Could we just focus on her treatment?" Well, no, we could not. My return flight to California was the next day and I was determined to complete what I had offered to help Margo accomplish. I also had a very strong sense that there would be no further treatment, and that the finalized documents would be needed sooner than later.

This would end up being my last day with my sister.

Sue and I discussed these challenging dynamics amongst Margo's primary caretakers in the final chapter of her brave encounter with such a devastating illness. We talked about how complicated it was to both have business to take care of and a wrenching goodbye to face.

It being a stunning October morning in Massachusetts, my eyes veered from the highway to glance at foliage turned burnt orange and fiery red by the onset of autumn. Never in any of the previous days that I did this same drive had I seen anything but trees, cars and trucks on this stretch of 495.

I spotted two deer grazing close to the shoulder, oblivious to the speeding vehicles passing by. I stopped, mid-sentence, to share my awe with Sue about this brief glimpse of such precious beings. I asked Sue if she could look up the significance of deer in her Animal Medicine book. Within seconds, she replied, "They are about gentleness, Martha." Tears tumbled out of my eyes, making my driving a bit hazardous. Yes, gentleness. There is gentleness between the two surviving deer in this family.

I had to conjure the image of those two deer in the remaining nine days until Margo's death, and afterward. Each time I remembered those two deer, my concerns about the lack of coordination or cooperation between my niece and nephew in the aftermath melted, temporarily. When I learned that my nephew had hired a lawyer because he did not trust his own sister to carry out Margo's wishes, I hoped for some further deer medicine so my niece and nephew could find a way to mediate a gentle détente.

Five weeks later, I was on another highway. Driving south on 101, the phone conversation was with my niece, this time. While she asked for counsel on how to proceed with a stalemate in attempted conversation with her brother, my eyes glanced to the right and once again, I caught sight of two deer grazing. I told my niece about the last time I saw two deer and she immediately grasped the blessing of gentleness we had just received.

A few hours later, I turned left off Highway 1 to climb the two-mile drive to the top of a mountain for a much-needed silent retreat. Shortly after the first hairpin turn, I came upon a lone deer standing right in the middle of the road. This was the first and only time this ever happened in all of my years of coming to this refuge. I stopped the car while the tears started up again. The lone deer soon darted off into hiding while I fully registered the absence of my deer sister.

My family of origin is gone but deer keep finding me. They are finding my niece, too. On a day when my niece was loading treasured items into a storage pod, she noticed an entire family of them snoozing in the afternoon sun in the meadow just outside my sister's home. Each time, the deer shower us with the blessing of gentleness. Each time, they kindle hope for reconciliation and peace.

Hiding

By Claudia Grisell

Dark shadows play upon my face, the evil left all in one place.
In the pit of my eyes, there is a darkness that I shall never be able to disguise.

Secrets rom the past and future, to never be set free.
For if you knew just who I was you would never come near me.

Regrets and sorrows shall always remain hidden in the darkness of my eyes.
Life is too short to share with people, the doom that lies inside!

Covering up sin is a part of life, because we all have some to hide.
To reveal your sin would mean sharing all the trouble you hold inside.

The Brandenburg Gate, 31 December 1989

By Henry Poor

A LETTER

Dear Ones,

Why do I write this? Show off? Insecure ego reaching out for fame/ fortune/future?

All not applicable, but, rather, a lover of history embracing a fly-on-the-wall moment which leapt for seizure.

1989 Time/Date, New Year's Eve, of December 31
Place, West Berlin.

Facing the Brandenburg Gate, and on *the WALL*. Looking through the great aperture of the Gate towards East Berlin. Some 50 feet to the right of the Promenade Avenue named "Unter den Linden" which continues through the Brandenburg Gate for several miles into East Berlin.

In the months before, from Leipzig (and Warsaw), the pressure built and eased on Berlin along with fracture of East Germany's Honeker / "Stasi" rule. I had vacation time at the end of December from airport ground operations for Pan Am at J.F.K.

Sensing where my head/heart were, Gaby said, "Well, why don't you go then?" I said, "Really? Great! The money won't be cheap, but I can keep it to $200-400."

So plans made. After Christmas I flew to Berlin from JFK, arriving on the 30th's morning.

Before flying, and consequently in flight, I planned, got music for, words to, practiced singing melody and words—in English—to the choral closure of Beethoven's 9th, Choral, Symphony. Can I, can we, how's it go, when and where are all Q's needing A's. A's were pending.

Around mid-day (morning) in the main Berlin train station I talked with the Zimmernachweiss office. They are the go-betweens for Hotels, B&B's, rooming houses. They are price/need savvy, and are street-wise about Berlin's layout, mass transportation and phone numbers.

Placed residentially in a Lutheran-approved boarding house, I got a single, with a sink, and access to a shared toilet/bathroom for $20/night: well-placed via public transport. Clean, safe and quiet. Bags placed and face washed, I headed out for "the wall."

The Reichstag is that enormous seat of German government just to the left of the Brandenburg Gate. It is (maybe) 50 feet from Unter den Linden. "Ein Deutsche Volk" is inscribed.

On the 31st, I got there about 2:00pm with my black Samsonite attaché case, a hat, gloves and long warm overcoat.

The Wall, then separating West from East in Berlin ran from behind the Reichstag, to its left, then formed a bulging arc in front of the Brandenburg gate making a 30-50 feet separation. On the right, it then ran down an avenue's east side. That avenue carries everyday traffic and has a tree-lined grassy park to the right or west side.

People were already mounting the wall (at 2:00pm) and standing on it. Maybe 7 feet high (2 meters+), it was at least that broad on top in the area giving good room for some people to stand easily (if loose packed). When tightly crowded, footing was tricky. I'm a tourist. I'm slightly social.

No one jumped up, but others on the ground pushed while some reached down to "give 'em a hand" as they clambered up.

As I talked with those I centered with, I sorted out impressions as to how I thought they might join my plan. Chatting was mostly in English, but German and French helped a lot. Those who stayed "up" really wanted to be there. Some were Romanians just loose from Ceausescu's tyranny. All had individual stories.

Afternoon turned dark, but evening's chill was offset by friendly acquaintance. The level of inebriation was minor, because those there were crowding in, and we all wanted to be there at midnight.

German New Year's Eve celebrations are laced and punctuated by a heck- of-a-lot of fireworks. Mostly there are firecrackers, second there are "rockets."

Many of them! Sometimes 50-100 are zooming all over at one time! There are always (2300-0010 o'clock) some in the air.

They go up (no problem) and they come down (ok), but don't get hit by them. You just have to be alert so as to not get hit (hurt and burned) by some, and then you're just fine. Getting "caught-up in" the celebration is fun anytime, but with "the walls" coming "down" at the time, and democracy's ascendance (like a sunrise) looming, excitement sparkled.

I muttered to a coterie of new neighbors that I was about to sing (at 2230) as I invited them to join in. We sang the melody, and anyone who knew words thereto (in any language) could contribute at will.

One time through it, the idea rolled out. Two times, the idea was catching on. Three times, maybe 100 joined in. I said, "That's it for now. Thanks. At 2330 we are going to cut loose again for 3 or 4 times, and let's all see if we can get more and more joining in on our chorus!"

Rockets glared red. Down, through, and over the Brandenburg Gate they crashed, zoomed and soared. Watch out!

West German television broadcast some coverage (2300-0015) locally in Berlin. From 2330-0005 some U.S. TV networks picked up some of German TV's broadcast feed. My son saw/heard some of this (2330-2350).

At 2330, I rolled out the melody. We weren't quiet! Accompaniment was a groundswell of celebrants readying to hop on next time we recycled the melody.

What got us is that 10's went to 100's to 1000's and at least 200,000 sang Ludwig von Beethoven's "Hymn to joy" there at that time before the Brandenburg Gate by Unter den Linden. The thrill of the music's sound, the accompanying groundswell of the growing chorus, and the call which so many must have felt of "Hey, I know that music, so let's sing!" coalesced a massive crowd towards a Mass.

Sensing mood swing, at 2340, I/we stopped. The 50-150 people right near me then joined in for 2 verses of "He's got the Whole World in his Hands." We delighted. We calmed down, a little. Time, rockets and approaching midnight pulled us along. THE SPIRIT CAN NEVER BE FORGOTTEN.

On the East side of the Brandenburg Gate, at least 100,000 people were grouped too. I heard some singing coming from there as well, singing of Beethoven's melody too. The verse which graces my mind's eye and ear is, "Teach us how to love each other, brothers to eternity!" Is that all there is to that? Sufficient and wonderful!

The Brandenburg Gate on Unter den Linden is reminiscent of Paris' Arc de Triomphe. Berlin's Gate is topped by their "Quadriga" in the arch's center. Four galloping horses pull a chariot driven by a victorious maiden Goddess. The statue inspires awe. Facing the Gate from the West or its left pedestal at the top is a pole on which the flag of the East German nation was flying.

At first, occasional firework rockets aimed at that flag nearly hit it. "Oohs and Ahhhs" of the crowd called out. East German police with rifles patrolled on the ground left. The flag flew.

I don't know how they got access, but shortly before midnight some youngish "college" students having gained access to an interior stairway, did appear on the top of the arch's left side. Some were Canadians.

The crowd whooped. The East German flag was stripped from the pole and tossed down. The guards did not respond.

Moments later, a new flag was sent up the pole. Surprise and laughter broke from the crowd. The flag was a Canadian Maple Leaf flag. It stayed for almost 5 minutes.

It was brought down and a new flag followed. Appropriately, it held a blue field with a circle of white stars. The new European flag flew over Germany. Chancellor Helmut Kohl ushered in a reunified nation whose capital city moved from Bonn to all of Berlin.

From my briefcase I brought out three bottles of beer and with one fellow singer to the left and one to the right. At midnight, we and no less than a half million others, welcomed in 1990.

After climbing up from West, to top, then down the East side of the wall, I— and thousands— meandered about East Berlin having been given a non-committed nod by the police (for several hours). Well after early morning, we went West again to our own rooms.

I felt very much part of a modern renaissance. My communal pride rose.

Telling this story recaptures some. I tell it for you and yours—you know why. Music's language can transcend, transport and move masses from neutral to sharing the lead to proceed and share again.

Music has the secret to move hearts, and bodies, then minds. That is a surprising and delightful sequence! Such a delight to realize the note which this can strike in a kindred spirit!

I'll not pretend that any portion of this or its sequelae reached perfection. I do sense that these moments celebrate a piece of the human struggle from bondage for freedom.

I found beauty and joy in sensed spontaneous camaraderie in this dynamic, peaceful midnight!

Yours, Henry Poor
Stony Brook NY

Tinder

By Amani Sheppard

"here is the deepest secret nobody knows
(here is the root of the root and the bud of the bud
and the sky of the sky of a tree called life
which grows higher than soul can hope or mind can hide)
and this is the wonder that's keeping the stars apart

i carry your heart (i carry it in my heart)"
—e.e. cummings

Some time ago, I spent a month with my mother, walking across Spain from the Pyrenees to Santiago, then on to the town once thought to be the end of the earth. There we watched the sun set over the ocean. I had begun this endeavor on the cusp of a huge transitional decision. I was very much afraid because my husband and I thought, it was about time, to consider unfathomable life-transformation, and start a family. Maybe. By the time my journey ended, I had discovered truths that changed me, and cleared the way for my next important adventure: becoming a mother.

Walking the width of an entire country entailed covering about 20 miles a day, week after week. My mother and I stayed, each night, with strangers in simple hostels catering to people walking this path. Each morning we woke up, packed our bags and went where the road, the camino, took us. At the beginning, I wondered if I had the strength to go more than 500 miles on nothing but my own two legs. There were steep climbs, there were blisters, there were dull days walking through plains so plain and endless I felt small and lost. But the rhythm, the heartbeat of the Camino de Santiago, is in the steady footfalls; in the people you meet and walk with and leave behind; and in the way each day brings beauties and trials you must travel through.

My mother and I followed the yellow arrows and scallop shell images marking the trail.

As we passed through small towns and large, the weight of my backpack lessened. In the first few days I abandoned an extra set of clothes. Then books. Soon, it was anything I could justify leaving behind—every unnecessary weight. Initially this was a tangible lesson, but as the days added and I battled a growing physical weariness, I realized there were intangible things I had to leave on the trail behind me. What is doubt except a tired thought the mind carries and carries? I had to keep walking.

Days and miles passed and my existence became beautifully simplified. Wake up, share food, share conversation, walk and walk and walk, and find a new bed for the night. Wake up, repeat. Every evening I was tired yet satisfied. I began to discover how little I really needed. I began to see I could decide what to carry with me, and what mattered. At the same time, I marveled at the truth of my mother's strength. One bleak day, I had a blister so painful it felt like a four inch nail hammered between my toes with every step. My mother became patience manifest. She carried all our food. She asked to carry even more. Her strength is so much a part of her love; her love is so much a part of her strength.

Twelve days into the journey, we arrived at the medieval ruins of the Pilgrim's Hospital of San Anton, outside Castrojeriz. A modern road runs through it, taking the occasional car under the arched portico connecting two large crumbling structures. One of the buildings was open to the sky and travelers both. I stood there in its stone skeleton and stared up at tall monastery windows, long empty of glass, yet through which I could see the vibrant green leaves of a fig tree. I remember thinking the play of the leaves in the wind and the sun, framed by the window, was its own kind of stained glass, only better. Living. Once again I thought the camino had exposed a truth: maybe we build walls to protect ourselves (and sometimes we need that) but every wall, every fear, doesn't it also keep a little bit of life on the outside?

On the twenty-eighth, day we woke with high spirits. We were just two days away from Santiago. The camino had grown terribly crowded in this final province it traveled through; yet Galicia was beautiful—lush, green, and thriving. We set out before dawn, knowing we'd have to arrive at that night's hostel early enough to get a bed. There were now hundreds of people walking, but my mother and I kept seeing the familiar faces of friends we had made. That afternoon, we reached the hostel where we planned to stay, and for the first time, we were brusquely denied. Every hotel was full. We were turned away at every inn. Stunned, we sat together under eucalyptus trees, eighteen miles of tired, and now anxious. Where would we sleep? What could we do?

We decided our only option was to keep walking. It would be another twelve miles to Santiago. We could do it. One foot after another. We found blackberries growing on the trail and we picked the sweetest ones to give to each other. As we walked we noticed the distances on the mile marker signs (our steady countdown all across Spain) now lurched, inconsistent. The numbers went up, down, up. How far away were we? I don't know. To distract us my mother taught me the lullabies she'd sung when I was a little girl. We sang together. Then we grew too tired to sing and we simply walked. Perhaps just over that next hill. We must be close. The mile marker signs vanished entirely. We passed next to stables and rested, watching the horses graze in the failing light. I saw my mom sway on her feet and I knew how tired she was. I offered to carry her backpack. She let me. One more hill. The land grew grey after the sunset. How far?

One more turn?

Finally, we came to the huge municipal hostel on the edge of Santiago. We requested beds, desperately afraid, knowing we had nothing left, should we be denied. We had walked over thirty miles in sixteen hours. The man working registration could see how far we'd come. He asked for the privilege of carrying our backpacks to our room. I blinked away tears of gratitude, exhaustion, and relief. We had arrived.

Years later, my husband and I are still trying to conceive. Battling infertility, I continue to have waves of doubt, fear, and anxiety. I see them though. I see doubt as a thought I can choose to carry or let go. I see fear as the thing that would keep me safe and closed, but at too great a price. I see anxiety as that hard section of trail—where it would be easy to miss the blackberries and sweet songs—thinking only of a dark beyond my control, and if I will be strong enough. Yet I have also learned the truth of my own strength. It is hereditary. So, to the future child I still hope to meet, I say, "I carry your heart. I carry it in my heart."

A Rush to Judgement

By Ken Owen

When love fails us
we banish it from memory with a series of charges

In sorrowful deliberations
the heart pronounces judgement victims and villains
demands for restitution

In its passing
we are quick to bury love with a eulogy of its sins
and no celebration of its gifts

In solemn days of retrospection as we wait patiently
for justice to balance the mortal scale

we search for words to capture the heights
of love's ascension and the depths of our fall from its grace

until the day gratitude arrives
to relieve our grief with one simple lesson:
There can be no failure in knowing love only success in
touching it at all

Raining Haikus

By Pastor Bejinez

Sun, unseen in sky
Missing in clouds for two weeks
No trace of sunlight

Where's your umbrella?

Clouds cover the sky
Have been nesting for three weeks
Above shade-less trees

Daddy, I said I lost it.

Mild raindrops drip and
Splash out the green from the grass
As thick mud enters

Look for it again.

Puddles flood cracked roads
Car slips and slides behind tree
And swerves out of sight

But where can it be?

Shivering clouds shake
Silent crow sits and watches
Beneath spring winged leafs

I don't know, go look for it.

Never dried oak tree
Reflects rain with spring soaked leafs
Fallen branch stays wet

I already did.

The Love That Endures

By Thomas Kirkpatrick

"We interrupt this program to bring you a special news bulletin. The Japanese have attacked Pearl Harbor, Hawaii, by air, President Roosevelt has just announced. The attack also was made on all Naval and Military activities on the principal island, Oahu."

Time stood still as the urgent voice stunned Mother and me. We had been sitting in the small living room of our apartment in Webster Groves, Missouri, that pleasant Sunday afternoon listening to the regular broadcast from Columbia Broadcasting System when the announcer had broken in.

My father, Captain Thomas Le Roy Kirkpatrick, was the Fleet Chaplain aboard the USS *Arizona,* flagship of the battleship flotilla stationed at Pearl Harbor. The United States Navy's Pacific Fleet had been home ported there more than a year earlier to act as an advance line of defense against the increasingly warlike actions of Japan. Father would have been preparing for morning church services at just about that hour. Sick with apprehension, we sat listening for more news. The afternoon wore on, the announcer occasionally interrupting the regular programming with more fragments of information. As the reports came over the air, the picture grew worse and worse.

That Sunday morning, the fleet at anchor in the protected confines of Pearl Harbor had been going about its normal business. As the first wave of Japanese aircraft swept across the calm waters of the bay, sailors aboard *Arizona* and other ships were amazed to see the "meatball" painted on the wings of aircraft they had at first assumed to be American. They knew what that symbol meant. They were under attack. Shortly after 7:55 a.m. Hawaii time, *Arizona* sounded the Air Raid Alarm, followed soon after by General Quarters. My father would have interrupted his church preparations and started to make his way to his assigned battle station, sick bay, where his duties were to assist in treating the wounded and to minister to the dying.

Mother and I went to bed that night in 1941 still not knowing the fate of my father or of his ship. The next day, December 8th, the entire nation was in a frenzy over the news and with the talk of outright war. President Roosevelt addressed Congress that day, beginning his speech:

"Yesterday, December 7, Nineteen Forty One —
a date which will live in infamy—the United States
of America was suddenly and deliberately attacked
by Naval and Air forces of the Empire of Japan."

The President asked for—*demanded* in his righteous wrath—a Declaration of War, which was quickly granted with but a single dissenting vote.

Late that same afternoon we heard a knock at the apartment door. In today's military, the practice is to send bereavement teams to compassionately break unbearable news to the families of our dead warriors. However, in 1941, such teams did not exist. Instead, when Mother opened the apartment door, she saw a Western Union courier. With a sinking heart, she took the telegram from him, opened it, read it, and then without a word handed it to me. It said:

"DEAR MRS KIRKPATRICK STOP I REGRET TO INFORM YOU THAT YOUR HUSBAND CAPTAIN THOMAS LEROY KIRKPATRICK IS MISSING IN ACTION AND PRESUMED DEAD STOP SIGNED SECRETARY OF THE NAVY FRANK KNOX STOP"

I was just old enough to know that death meant my father would not be coming home to us.

That night, as I was climbing into bed and preparing to say my bedtime prayers, I asked Mother a childish question: that must have torn at her heart. I asked, "Mommy, should I leave Daddy out of my prayers now?"

Mother, with tears streaming down her face, replied softly, "No, Tommy. You must always keep Daddy in your prayers."

The next day we heard another knock on our door. Mother, still barely able to keep the tears from coursing down her cheeks, called out through the closed door, "'Who is it?'"

A man's voice answered, brusque and businesslike,. "Are you the Mrs. Kirkpatrick whose husband was killed in the Jap attack? I'm a reporter for the Webster Groves paper and I *must* talk to you."

Mother, appalled at this callous insensitivity to our grief and need for privacy answered querulously, "I can't talk to you now." To her dismay, the man persisted in trying to gain entry, banging on the door and repeating his demanding for an interview. Mother began to cry openly, calling to him, "Please! Go away! I can't talk to you." I could only sit across the room, terrified, not knowing what to do. After many minutes, Mother resorted to the only thing she could think of. She took her bedside portrait of my father out of its leather frame and slipped it through the crevice at the bottom of the door. The reporter immediately stopped his banging, took the picture and left without a word. The next edition of the local paper featured my father's portrait on the front page with huge black headlines blaring, "WEBSTER GROVES MAN KILLED IN JAP ATTACK." The story that followed was filled with misinformation about my father mixed with fragmentary information about the attack itself. The portrait was never returned.

On January 2nd, 1942, Mother received an envelope bearing the return address "Secretary of the Navy, Washington—Official Business." Inside, as if to assuage the starkness of the earlier telegram, was a brief letter of condolence signed by Frank Knox himself. Later on, in 1943, a year later, Mother received a brief note of condolence, on a microfilm form known as V-Mail, from Boatswains Mate Second Class Thomas W. Stanborough. At the time, he was serving aboard the USS *Leigh*, but he was one of the few eyewitness survivors among *Arizona's* crew who had been aboard her during the attack. He described seeing my father at the ship's stern rigging for church when the first bombs fell. According to other eye-witnesses, a brief moment after Seaman Stanborough saw my father, a bomb dropped from a Japanese "Kate" torpedo bomber, specially modified for high-altitude bombing, glanced off the number four turret, the one closest to the ship's stern, and exploded on the deck where my father was last seen.

Seconds later, a 1700-pound armor-piercing bomb penetrated the forward deck near the number two turret. It exploded four decks below, igniting the horrendous magazine explosion that literally tore the ship apart, killing nearly the entire crew.

In that moment, the intense twenty-year and lifelong love affair between my mother and father that had begun two decades before, tragically ended. This love affair, their love, was the living embodiment of St. Paul's Letter to the Corinthians on Love:

> *"Love is patient, love is kind. It is not jealous. Love does not brag and is not arrogant, does not act unbecomingly. It does not seek its own, is not provoked, does not take into account a wrong suffered, does not rejoice in unrighteousness but rejoices with the truth; bears all things, hopes all things, endures all things. But now abide faith, hope, love, these three; but the greatest of these is love."*

During their life together, Mother and Father endured many lengthy and stressful periods of separation brought on by to my father's Navy service. The stresses of Navy life took their toll even during the times they were together during my father's shore duty. Even when together during times when my father was assigned to shore duty, the stresses of Navy life took their toll. Through it all, my mother and father were faithful to each other and to the teachings of St. Paul to endure all things with and for each other.

Would You Call It a Coincidence?

By Adrianne Aron

I was no stranger to coincidences. Hadn't I been at the scene of the car wreck where the American Studies teacher was rescued by a medic named Thomas Paine? Wasn't I at the top of the World Trade Center in New York when, amid the thousands of tourists, my 11-year-old kid bumped into someone he knew from home? Or, how about the time I was on a remote mountaintop in Costa Rica, and met a naturalist whose last job was at a summer camp in the Missouri Ozarks, the very place where I'd gone to camp as a kid? I understood about coincidences. But my encounter with Brenda bounced over the line of coincidence, into the court of spooky.

I'd received a call from former students of my grade school, who were organizing a reunion, and I thought to ask whether anybody on their list had a zip code close to my own. What a surprise! Two thousand miles and fifty-five years ago, Brenda Prager lived across the street from me, when she was seven and I was six. Now she lived across town from me, in south Berkeley. They gave me her number.

"Hello? Is this Brenda?" Is this the Brenda who lived in St. Louis, Missouri as a child? Brenda who attended Hamilton School? Brenda who lived on DeGiverville Avenue? Brenda who had a sister named Vickie? After each "Yes" my fun with this got bigger. When it got to the bit about the sister, she interrupted: "And did you know me?"

At that point I identified myself. She didn't remember me, but I remembered her so vividly, I could even describe her red brick front porch, and Vickie's amazing doll house, and the wagon her mother used to pull her little brothers around in. I think the wagon clinched it for her: if I knew about the wagon, I was probably for real.

I explained about the reunion, and gave her contact information. We talked for about five minutes, just long enough to establish that both of us had been living in Berkeley for decades, drawn to the town by its quirkiness, diversity, and tolerance for independent thought. And we both had fond memories of our elementary school in St. Louis. The next day, she called to say that her head had been spinning ever since we talked. Could she meet me? *Of course!*

It was a little like a blind date, with Frankie, my dog, as a mediator for the awkwardness. We met at a park in the hills, where Frankie could run free while we hiked the trails. I learned that her dog had died the year before. By coincidence, her dog had also been named Frankie.

"Ah, but this one is a female," I said. Oddly, so was her Frankie. It was surprising that both of us had named our dogs Frankie, and really unexpected that both Frankies were females. The only other female Frankie I'd been acquainted with was the Carson McCullers character in *The Member of the Wedding,* a book Brenda hadn't read.

My Frankie sniffed and burrowed in the woods as we hiked the park trails, crossing creeks and bridges, talking about our dogs, the one thing we strangers had in common for an easy ice breaker. The possibilities were ample: dog health, dog food, dog antics, dog parks, our attachments to our pets. I was amused to hear her say that she used to sing to her Frankie, because I'd had many dogs in my life, but not till Frankie had I ever taken to singing to an animal. I confessed my own silliness, and after a good laugh Brenda drew the line. Too many coincidences here, things were moving from surprising to strange.

"It was crazy: I only ever sang one song to my Frankie," she asserted.

That wasn't so crazy; I was a Johnny-One-Note with my Frankie, too: the same song, just that one song, over and over. Nothing crazy about that. Crazy came when it turned out that the song I sang to my dog, "You Are My Sunshine," was the same one she sang to hers. What are the probabilities of that happening by chance? We were teetering on a continuum from surprising to strange, to weird, to positively uncanny. We kept laughing, but I could feel goosebumps from the Twilight Zone on my sleeveless arms.

I wanted to change the subject, to something a little easier, a little safer. That ruled out DeGiverville Avenue, where we had lived as kids. Too much there I didn't want to talk about. Now we were both Berkeley people, and had been for a long time. I remarked that for all its changes over the years, I still loved Berkeley, wouldn't want to live anywhere else. She felt the same way. We began talking about neighborhoods—hers, mine, and one we both enjoyed: the Theatre and Arts district downtown. I loved some of the new things that had sprung up, like Addison Street: poetry engraved on the sidewalks, sculpted mosaic reptiles climbing on buildings, and the *windows!* Who would have thought of putting an art gallery in the empty windows of a concrete parking garage? "Berkeley's incredible," I said, "The windows are my favorite of all the innovations."

Brenda smiled a big toothy smile, just like I remembered from when she was seven years old. She had plenty to smile about. She was the artist who created the Addison Street Windows. Until recently she had also been the gallery's curator. Spookiness had set in.

The next day I was telling my friend Stewart about all this weirdness with this woman I'd met. As I got into the story he wanted to know her name, but the name was the least of it, and I went on about the dogs, the song, the windows, never mind the name. Finally I told him her name. He slapped himself on the forehead for an "Oh No!"

Stewart used to date her.

In the months leading up to the reunion, Brenda and I became close friends. When I began getting cold feet about returning to the place of complicated memories, she was able to reassure me that she'd be there as a reality check, to remind me that I was a strong woman who could outrun the phantoms from the past. And I was able to reciprocate the moral support by promising that if the stomach trouble she was having got worse, I'd help her get to a place to take care of it. With each other to lean on, we'd be able to overcome the obstacles to having a good time at the reunion.

At the reunion we discovered another amazing coincidence: our fathers were in the same business! Hustlers in the Jewish mafia, both of them had been wheelers and dealers in the same illicit scams and gambling syndicates. That house of Brenda's on DeGiverville: she hadn't lived there long. Without warning, Mom, Dad, and all five children were kicked out in the middle of the night. Her father had lost the house in a poker game. And there were other gangsters! Fathers of children we both knew! Some had even done jail time. Until then, I had believed for my entire life that I was the one and only kid in town who had an outlaw for a father. Now I was actually face-to-face with kindred children of the underworld, and able to see some humor in the family resemblance. We all knew who you were supposed to call in case of emergency: Morrie Shenker, the criminal lawyer who represented all the St. Louis mobsters. His niece, in fact, was one of our schoolmates, and like me, she had become a psychologist. Fancy that!

Back in the 1960s, when I was busy with anti-war protests, Brenda was going through a hippie stage, living on a commune near Cazadero. She had friends still living there, and wanted me to meet them, so we made a plan to drive up there when we returned from St. Louis. She called me on Tuesday, two days before we were to go, and said she was going to have to cancel. "I'm calling from the hospital," she explained. They were doing a number of tests for that stomach problem. It was not looking at all good. On Thursday the oncologist would go over the results with her. Would I come and be with her for that?

I was there when the doctor explained about palliative care and hospice. Six weeks later, Brenda was dead.

At the memorial held in the forest near Cazadero, I was able to share with her friends the uncanny sense I had, of having come into her life to take her back to her beginnings, so she could complete the cycle and rest in peace, accepting that it was finished.

It was the closest I had ever come to feeling that the Higher Power people talk about might actually exist.

A Single Stroke of a Pen

By Sheena Arora

I am waiting in my eighth-grade classroom for my Sanskrit language marks. This is my final grade of middle-school. Somehow, I've managed to get passing marks in all other subjects. Hindi, Sanskrit, and history need a lot of memorization, unlike math, physics, and chemistry. I've difficulty learning verb conjugations, gender nouns, and important dates. I simply need passing marks: 33/100.

I hear, "Metha, Banerjee, Nayak," my classmates surnames. Mrs. Sharma, my Sanskrit teacher, is returning our corrected answer-sheets.

Mrs. Sharma loudly announces, "Arooodaa."

In her left hand, she is holding a bundle of crumpled sheets. Her bundle of sheets has lost their crispness. I favor crisp white sheets, without any dents or marks. I've an excuse not to get my graded exam.

Mrs. Sharma senses my hesitation. She bellows, "Arooodaaaaaaa."

I bend my head until my chin touches my stomach; I hurry towards Mrs. Sharma's voice. She is leaning against the teacher's table. Her sari is gathered a little bit at the bottom, exposing her feet. She is wearing open V-scandals in red, with gold trim. Her toenails bear smudges of lilac nail polish. Her heels have lines; crisscrossing, zigzagging dirty-yellow deep cracked lines filled with black soil.

I lift my eyes to her hand.

I cross the index and middle finger of my left hand behind my back. I cross my index and big toe inside my shoes. I don't make eye contact with Mrs. Sharma. I extend my right hand. I don't have a specific god, therefore I pray to all the Hindu gods. I beg that any one of thirty-three million Hindu gods do their god-magic and get me a passing grade.

I wait to open my folded answer-sheets. I don't want my classmates to see what I know for sure will be my shame. I avoid making eye contact with my classmates. Although no one is looking and paying attention to me, yet I know what everyone thinks and gossips about me. My eyes search for my best friend—Ranu.

I see Ranu. She is sitting cross-legged on the corridor floor, outside the classroom. Ranu sees me; she waves. As I wave back, I open my answer-sheets. Highlighted by a thick dense oval in blue ink are my Sanskrit marks: 7/100.

Six sheets of my Sanskrit exam are tied with a white thread. I browse through the pages. I flip my answer-sheets upside down. I shake the four pages. Nothing works. I can't find the missing digit.

I sit next to Ranu. She enquires about my grades. I pretend not to hear her. I concentrate on straightening the pleats of my skirt. Ranu wraps her right arm around my shoulder, and shows me her Sanskrit marks: 80/100.

I should be proud of Ranu but I want to hate her as I hate my younger sister Kajal. Both of them are always first in class. I, except for the art class, have difficulty in all my subjects. I want to be like Ranu and Kajal—intelligent. Hating Kajal is easy; she snitches on me to Mummy. I can't hate Ranu. She is the only person in school who willingly talks to me.

Often I wonder, if I will be different, if I was born intelligent. My life could've been colorful. Instead, it is jet-black matching Daddy's leather belt.

Now, only bleakness lies ahead. Living is over. I'll never get to study in the adjoining high-school building. It is perfect. Its classroom walls are painted in cool-white. Its windows have borders in crimson. It has a boundary wall that is covered with vines of money plant. In high-school, I can study only science subjects. I'll not have to waste my time with Hindi, social studies, domestic science, and Sanskrit.

Failing any subject in eighth-grade will make high-school impossible. I'll be stuck in the same grade. I'll lose my only friend. I'll have to study with students who are younger than me. They will snigger at me. Everybody makes fun of Ritu Mathur, who is repeating seventh-grade. Failing Sanskrit means, no six-and-half hour escape from home. I'll be stuck with dirty-brown mopping water, and reddish-yellow dishwater at home.

Probably Mummy is right. My kismet is to be a maidservant.

Or probably, I can do something.

I can ask Mrs. Sharma for a re-test. She'll never agree to it. Or. I can plead with her. I don't think she'll increase my marks from seven to thirty-three. Or, I can not tell Mummy about my grades. Impossible. Mummy and Daddy will see my marks in the final report card. Or, I should do what Mummy thinks I might do, if I am to fail. That is, I should not go back to home. I can run away. But where? But how? Compared to the unknown, home is easy.

I unfold my answer-sheets. I re-read my marks. No miracles. Nothing has changed in the last three-and-half minutes. I curse myself.

Earlier Mrs. Sharma announced that she hasn't recorded our marks in her register. She wants us to re-check our answer-sheets, in case she made mistakes while correcting our answers. On my answer-sheets, I can't locate a single mistake of hers.

I swear more.

Suddenly, I see a way out. My Hindu gods are pointing to the path.

Mrs. Sharma always corrects the exams with red ink. This time she used a blue ink ballpoint.

I've a blue ink ballpoint in my skirt pocket. I can write a digit in front of the seven. I make the lonely seven into 37, 47. . .87, or 97. There is space between the seven and the forward slash. I can make my marks as 71, 72. . . 78, or 79. Giving myself a 37 or 47 is too low. Mummy will never believe that I received a 77 or 87 or 97. I can try for 57 or 67, my average marks.

Matching Mrs. Sharma's handwriting is impossible. If I am caught, I'll be expelled. Once Mummy sees these existing marks, she'll not let me attend school. In either scenario, my routine of cleaning, cooking, laundry, and beatings will not change.

If I fail, Mummy will slap her forehead with her left palm, and wail, "We treat you better than how people treat their sons." When Daddy finds out that I've failed, he'll blow mucus in a white handkerchief and say, "Since you were born, I knew you are nothing more than a maid."

I cannot change them. I've tried to change my dumbness. I need to change this.

Mimicking Mrs. Sharma's 2, 3. . .8, and 9 is difficult. Writing '1' is easy. Just a little tiny single stoke of a pen. It is not cheating. It is a slip of the pen.

I look around. Nobody. Or, there is somebody just like me, lurking around, thinking the same thing, and hiding behind one of the massive square columns.

Edging the corridor is our school lawn. I stand and walk towards the pile of leaves under the tree. I pick a Peepal leaf. It is shaped like a lover's heart with elongated pointed tip. My leaf is so big that it covers my entire hand. I sit cross-legged on the corridor floor. I flatten my answer-sheets on my lap. I cover my marks with my left hand. I look around. All my classmates are inside the classroom, chatting. Ranu is re-reading her answer-sheets.

I lay the Peepal leaf, with its tip pointing upwards, on top of my answer-sheets. I slowly glide the leaf to cover my marks. I pretend to read Mrs. Sharma's corrections. Gently, I lift the bottom-curved part of the leaf. I slide my ballpoint under the leaf. I scan for prying eyes. I make a quick small firm mark.

I look around. I am sure nobody saw my action. I place my answer-sheets under Ranu's. I walk back to the classroom. I give Ranu and my answer-sheets back to Mrs. Sharma. I wait.

It is done. I can't change it back. I wait for Mrs. Sharma to notice my shenanigans. I am ready for whatever that is to follow. I will never confess, no matter what.

My classmates are surrounding Mrs. Sharma. I peek through their shoulders. Mrs. Sharma is hunched over the open grey register on her table. I stand on my toes. Finally, I can read the names in her register. I scan the left-hand column for my name. Sandwiched between Sharmishtra Mitra and Shilp Gupta, I find my name. I follow the row of my name to the right-hand column. In red ink, in tiny letters, is my grade: 71/100.

I understand that I will never be literate in Sanskrit. Apart from Hindu pundits, nobody in Delhi uses this dead language. I know I am a failure. I know I am a cheat. However, I don't feel guilty. I don't have shame. All I know is that I crossed one more hurdle towards my not being a maidservant.

Reeling the Day

By Pastor Bejinez

I don't have to yawn to get through the day
Let me catch a glimpse of this fine day
Not every day do we not need an air conditioner
Or a heater to bare keeping awake

I'd like to catch a glimpse of this day
Where people want to go out and play
Without the hindrance of jackets
Nor traces of sweaters
Where jeans and shorts or skirts all o.k.
Look at those students enjoying those pages
Bathing under layers of calmness
And wearing worry free faces
As if all worries voluntarily walked away

I would like to catch this day
As if it were a random fish in the lake
Where I can take it home
Devour its energizing nutrients
Or just hang it on my wall
So when storm drenched days
Are flooding my spirit away
Or when overheated days
Are terrorizing my skin to death
I can just look up on my wall
Catch a glimpse of a great day
A trophy day
So that I'll remember
There are great days
Out in the sea full of days

Who knows if once again
We'll see such a day
So just give me like ten
Or twenty more minutes
To try and catch this fine day

Gut Instinct

By Vanessa Baker-Simon

I carried my son Jaden into the operating room, which was a large, state of the art and intimidating place. The title track to the movie Grease was playing though the speakers as the operating team greeted us. Dr. Krigsman, one of the top pediatric gastroenterologists in the U.S. who we to traveled from California to New York to see, instructed me to place Jaden on the operating table. Jaden was too weak from fasting for 36 hours in preparation for his GI scoping procedures to protest until they placed the 'astronaut mask' over his face. At this point, his hands shot up to the oxygen mask in a futile attempt to pull it off, while his legs kicked three of the operating staff until I lay next to him and sang a Blues Clues song that all four year-olds love. Within a few seconds he went limp and looked dead; I felt the tears come and a wave of nausea hit me like a punch to the chest. One of the nurses quickly ushered me out of the room, calling for assistance from someone else to help carry me out as I couldn't stand. I wish my husband were here with us, but he was in California with our 18 month old, who was on a similar medical trajectory as Jaden despite our best efforts to prevent him from suffering the same fate as his brother.

Jaden had a rough start in life from the moment of his birth as he was not breathing and had to be intubated. As a baby, he had such severe allergies to pollen that we had to place a blanket over his infant seat every time we carried him from the house to the car, or else his face and chest would welt and breathing would become labored to the point we would have to rush him to the hospital for a steroid shot. Allergy testing proved futile, as all results came back negative for any allergies. The allergy doctor prescribed a heavy dose of allergy medication and an EpiPen anyway. When we begged Jaden's main pediatrician for answers, he could only say "I've never seen this before in an infant."

After I found blood in his stool, I took Jaden to a new pediatrician, bloody diaper in tow, and showed it to him. The new pediatrician's response was "that's from an anal fissure." 'But why was the thin line of blood *encased in the stool*?' I thought to myself. A long-awaited referral to a pediatric gastroenterologist yielded no further insights; the GI doctor instead spent the 45 allotted minutes berating the medical insurance industry and handed me a sheet on calcium supplementation for Jaden—most of which were filled with dairy products (Jaden hadn't been able to tolerate dairy in my breast milk or in formula since birth). I left that appointment feeling frustrated that I took the morning off of work for nothing, but more important, discouraged that no one knew how to help my son. I knew something was terribly wrong.

While Jaden's medical issues had been obvious since birth, his development had *seemed* normal until he was about 17 months old. Over the course of approximately two months, he stopped singing songs and talking, then became obsessed with repeatedly walking up and down our step ladder one night when I came home from a business trip. This disparity was most evident at preschool. Just as his preschool mates' interest in peers and the world around them intensified, Jaden withdrew into his own world which no one could enter. While other toddlers ran around playing 'tag' or vroomed their favorite truck around the floor, Jaden would sit blithely in the sandbox, staring at nothing in particular. When we took Jaden to his primary pediatrician and expressed our concerns about autism, the doctor said that "Jaden doesn't have autism because he is affectionate with you." That confident reassurance from a well-meaning physician will haunt me forever; it also highlights how ill prepared most pediatricians are in understanding how to properly diagnose and treat autism.

A few weeks later, we were back in California and on a conference call with Dr. Krigsman to discuss the biopsy and scoping procedure results. Jaden had Inflammatory Bowel Disease with extensive inflammation in the small bowel—something that he sees with many of his patients who also have autism. Finally. After four years of countless doctors, specialists, testing, and no answers, we have a reason why Jaden has been *howling in pain on a daily basis since he was three days old*. The initial 60-day treatment course of big gun steroids prescribed for Jaden induced a roller coaster ride of sadistic behavior, an explosion of new language gains, and the first normal bowel movements of his life. But why did he repeatedly erupt in a maniacal laugh and intentionally slam his brother's head into the stairs like he was spiking a football? We wouldn't learn why until nearly two years later—Jaden had two infections, acquired in utero, that crossed the blood brain barrier and proliferated once his immune system was suppressed while on steroids. Navigating the landmine of autism, gastrointestinal disease, and the myriad of treatment issues is like peeling an onion layer—fix one thing, and there are ten other layers of "fixes" required underneath.

People say autism is a brain disorder. After experiencing it with both of my sons, spending most of my 'free' time listening to the leading researchers in the autism research field and scouring articles in the PubMed database, I can tell you that's not entirely true. Autism is a complex, multi-system disease which is triggered by an inherently dysfunctional immune system. When a malfunctioning immune system is hit with an insult (e.g., infection, allergy), it sets off a cascade of symptoms that impact the brain, gastrointestinal tract, and other systems in the body. The standard medical community is about ten years behind us autism biomed moms, and the kids they serve can't afford for them to be. Mothers should not have to become medical researchers to help heal their children because most doctors cannot. But I have.

Washed Drawings

By Pastor Bejinez

Tony was his name. You wouldn't call him Tony-boloney like you would every other Tony in the neighborhood, unless you wanted to risk getting into a fight that you'd likely loose. He hadn't crossed my mind until listening to the poem *Stupid America* where it mentioned that Latino kids are flunking out of English and Math, when they could really be a Picasso without the material to create and that it looks to outsiders that these young Latinos without a creative outlet are aggressive and angry creatures. This part not only stood in my mind, but it stepped into my memory and pulled out a story that it must have slipped onto. It's about one of my childhood classmates that not only always seemed to flunk English and Math, but every other academic category.

No one really knew how he always managed to pass from one grade to the next, but he just did. We all figured that after all the crap he would give his teachers, they just wanted to pass him after attending summer school; not have to deal with him one more year, since he always challenged himself to see how far he could go at pissing the teacher off, without getting sent to the principals' office. He didn't always succeed on his goal: once he had to spend two weeks in the office, so some of us would find ways to go to the office and say "hello" to him and naturally, he'd walk out and say "hello" to whomever went to visit him.

Well, one thing he was great at, other than picking fights, was at drawing, but no one really seemed to notice because he'd always manage to draw on the weirdest places and then have to erase them, so there was no proof that he was good or could even draw. He once pissed off our fourth grade teacher, so she made him put his head down on his desk for an hour. After that hour, she said he could put his head back up, but he said he'd rather keep it down covered with his jacket because he felt like swearing, so since he'd been unusually quiet, she said he could keep his head down until he was ready to do his work. A few wordless hours later, he raised his hand and asked if he could get up to use the bathroom. When he got up, someone noticed that his desk was fully drawn on. It turns out he was quiet and not trying to start trouble because the prior day he had seen a drawing that inspired him, so he drew it on the desk. At first most of us, including the teacher, thought he had pasted a drawing on the desk because it was so detailed, until he showed us that he had drawn it with a pencil by erasing part of it. The teacher was shocked that he was able to do that, especially in the amount of time he had, so she felt bad, but had to make him wash it out with soap and water and gave him a lecture on not drawing on objects.

That's pretty much the type of places he would draw on, or occasionally on class walls or on his parking lot where it would all get washed off. He rarely drew on paper for the reason that he did not always have material, other than a pencil and occasionally binder paper that would get ripped or thrown away by one of the ten to twelve kids, or by one of the six parents that lived in his two bedroom house whom saw paper with figures on it as junk or by one of the six to ten kids that one of the parents would babysit. That seemed to be the story of his life, so he did not bother trying to keep anything or get material that would enhance his drawings; it wasn't safe from getting tossed easily, and it was tough to come by since food and clothing for him and his four brothers and sisters was more important.

He was always a pissed off kid and it seemed as if he was most likely going to end up in jail, which was what everyone around him figured because all the beatings he got never worked on getting the anger out of him, nor helped straighten out his behavior. I hadn't really thought about it before today; he was a very passionate person about drawing, which was always disguised behind the anger he always presented everyone. Now, I can't help but think that maybe it had something to do with him being reminded that he was incredibly stupid for flunking most of his Math and English assignments, as opposed to being encouraged for something he was incredibly great at? I don't know what ever happened to him, since I haven't seen him since we were twelve; maybe, just maybe, if someone noticed how great he was, he could have gotten a chance to express his deep passion for drawing, which he protected under the layers of anger that covered his existence.

I Used to Be But Now

By Lisa Meltzer Penn

I used to conduct an orchestra

But all the sheet music turned into railroad tracks
So now I conduct a train down the tracks.

I used to squish red ants with my thumb
But now I suck my thumb.

I used to be a grown-up

But now I am orange like the sunrise.
In the evening I am a parachute
And lift the sun down the sky.

Now I am a snakeskin
Squeezed off a snake.
Like a mother,
I will regrow my insides.

The Ol' Button Place

By Linda Brown

In the early 1970's my Uncle Harold took me to see the "old Brown Farm."

Originally the cabin was built in 1841 out of logs, but various family members had looted the cabin, the tin roof had fallen, the rock fireplace had been dismantled, and many of the old logs had been pilfered as well. We visited the old Brown cemetery, and as we stopped to rest, Uncle Harold pointed across the fields and said, "Over yonder is the ol' Button Place. Some would say as it is haunted. Some would say they have heard screams at night floating across the holler."

I had come to begin my journey into family genealogy. But Uncle Harold told me he would tell me some stories that I could *not* put into the family history. He admonished me that this was one I shouldn't write about.

"Oh, you must tell me!" I enthused.

"Well, apparently after ol' man Button died, his wife went crazy and kilt their young daughter. Neighbors came over to visit to see how they were getting along without the ol' man. They said the wife was dirty and talkin' crazy. The girl they smelt, and when they found her she had been dead some time. So they sent the wife off to Farmington (the state mental institution). And, the boy, the son in the family, had apparently run off."

I listened to the story, but never wrote any of it down, as I had promised not to include it in my genealogy.

It has been some 25 years since I first heard that story and when I went to Missouri this time (July 2007), my Uncle Harold said he had a cousin he wanted to introduce me to, that he would probably have some good stories to tell me about the "old days."

Turns out Jules "Bomber" Brown was the grandson of ol' man Button. Bomber was 81 years old. He explained he got his name because when he was a young man Joe Lewis was a well-known fighter to whom they referred to as "the Brown Bomber," so his friends just reversed it and got to calling him Bomber Brown and the name stuck.

Bomber had been a steel worker and among other projects, he had worked on erecting the St. Louis Arch. He mostly wanted to talk about his steel working days and other projects he worked on. He enjoyed telling old jokes too. He also talked about "getting on the ball" to be carried to the top. We were all amazed to realize that that phrase came from the steel workers. Of course Bomber pointed out that OSHA stopped that practice a long time ago.

But the story Bomber had to tell me about the Button place brought up some old memories, and though I did not feel comfortable cross-examining him in detail, I registered his story too.

It seems his father, Jules Brown, Sr., the son of Button Brown, was the 16-year-old boy who had run away after the family fell apart. Jules Sr. ran off and joined the US Navy and never came back until he was an old man. However he never returned to the area, but instead retired farther south in Missouri (Tanner County).

Button's farm had lain fallow for years. But Uncle Jennings Brown (my grandmother Zita's brother) wanted the farm. Jennings tracked down Jules Sr. and went down to see him. He took a Quit Claim deed with him. He explained to Jules Sr. that the Quit Claim deed was for the one acre that the grandpa had donated for the Independence School (the old country school) which was no longer needed (as all the children went to town schools now), so he just wanted to keep it legal and have all the heirs to Grandpa William Brown's property sign off on the one acre. So Jules Sr. and his wife signed the Quit Claim deed and accepted one dollar for the signing.

Then Jules Sr. called his son, Bomber Brown. He explained to Bomber what he had done, and said he was happy to be done with it. But for some reason Bomber was suspicious. He went down to the courthouse the next day to read the abstract and discovered that Uncle Jennings had pulled a fast one. Jules Sr. never read the Quit Claim deed and it turns out he signed away 101 acres.

Bomber went home and called his dad to explain what had really happened, but though they both felt taken advantage of, Jules Sr. expressed to Bomber, that he had never looked back to the farm anyway, so he didn't care. And, Bomber felt it was too late to do anything once it was recorded. This was all done in 1960.

But as he told me the story he still seemed bitter about how Uncle Jennings had taken advantage of his father.

Days later, I visited with Burton Brown, a son of Uncle Jennings. He was the member of the family that kept all the old land abstracts and deeds of trust and other miscellaneous family papers. I had already made an appointment to see him and review documents before I ever heard Bomber's story.

But even though Burton had piles of blue bound legal papers for me to look at, he held his hand protectively over them and said, "Some would wonder jest why you want to see all these old papers."

I could sense that he had become uneasy between when I had made the appointment with him and my arrival; and, now I had a pretty good idea why. Both he and his brothers and his children and his brothers' children, had split up Uncle Jennings' land and Button's land. They all had houses with acreage from the two places.

I oh-so-innocently said I was just collecting information. He knew that I had already done a lot of family genealogy.

I reassured him with my story about the Carnes in Wales, and how all the locals thought we were coming back to Wales to try to collect some of the Carne acreage due to England's law of primogeniture or that the oldest living male heir inherits family land, when in fact, we were simply on holiday.

He seemed to accept that explanation and as the hours went by, he became more and more forthright. I did actually see and photograph the aforementioned Quit Claim deed. It was amazing that he let me see it. I never commented on it, nor did he.

He eventually became so comfortable with me; he showed me another relic he had which he said he didn't think anyone in the extended family knew about. It was an old rifle dated 1794, which William Brown (our revolutionary war soldier) had bought after the war to bring west with him. Burton said he had hunted with it as a child, but had recently learned its value, and that it was too valuable to use anymore.

After I drove away, I wondered if the old Button Place was still haunted, not necessarily by the crazy old woman, but rather by their collective guilty consciences.

Along the Knoll

By Michele Jessen

Black sweet soil, hyacinth bud
Awaits downpour beneath the mud

Peek and prod
Burst from sod

From moistened clay
Beneath somewhere

Sprouting seedling of rebirth
Hatching open cracking earth

Stirring deep within its soul
Unfolding hope along the knoll

Agnieszka

By Nicole Justine Cavanaugh

"I like to be assaulted by strangeness," she said, and I found myself leaning in cautiously.

Chimpanzees jumping and scratching above her tent, engulfing her in sounds and energies, soaking in the wilds of Africa. A lion's roar in the distance.

Immediately immersed, I noticed jealousy and inspiration had arisen simultaneously within me and I let them be, let them move through me.

She was weaving her stories around the Carne Asada dinner and margaritas on the table, the hot air of vacation hugging us. At her proclamation—a simple sentence that captured her so clearly—I found my curiosity pushed and I couldn't turn the light off.

"Experiences," she said, and something about the way she said it overlaid a reverence for life all around us.

Out in the Mongolian cold with cowboys. Poetry read on the dark, wild plains. The aliveness she felt.

The generosity of helping a man she barely knew get two more cows towards the fourteen needed to wed his bride with honor. How it felt to get to know him, to be a part of that.

And, another time, finding herself sandwiched in stimulating conversation between a general and an admiral at the banquet through which her marine husband cried.

When does she cry? I found myself wondering. She thinks I cry too much. This is our battle.

She was tough, thick skin covering this depth of feeling I didn't know existed for years until these stories rolled out of her on to the table this night. Her usual armor melted just enough for her tenderness and depth to be noted, and I didn't know what to do with it. Just as I began to open in response, she was covered again, a motion to the waiter for the check and an assembling of facial features that caused my heart to reassemble itself into its own armor.

I wondered how my mom experienced life with her as a big sister. Part of me already felt not good enough. Again.

Holding the struggle within me, I practiced holding the door that had opened within just a crack more than usual, to see if it would stay.

And later, as the Mexican night wind brushed itself across my face on our way back to the hotel in the open air cab, I heard the African chimpanzees in my ears, felt the cold of the Mongolian dark night in my bones, and I began to dream of the adventures I would go on, the stories I would tell.

Delight

By Mary Ruth Coffey

I brushed my fingers along the leaf of the African violet in the center of the windowsill, my windowsill, the window facing the garden of my weekend, the window of the room called Kathryn, and I breathed as my thumb and index fingers kissed the soft hair of the leaf and swam into the crevices and climbed each ridge, imagining that my fingers were hiking a mountain that extended beyond the window, into the garden, into botanicals surrounded by the strong arms of a giantess named Kathryn. With my eyes closed, I took minutes, and minutes became parts of hours, to caress just that one leaf of the single African violet and I entered again that way, the right way, the peaceful way, to live this life, in the present, in wonder and awe of just this leaf. This is what love is, when you give your time, all your time, when you invest your spirit, in the beauty of every small portion of the canvas of your lover's skin. When you take a lifetime to make love because you relish every single leaf of his body and embrace every small moment in the tiny hugs that can only happen between fingers.

I was supposed to be on an airplane, gazing out an entirely different window, one without African violets, one where I would want to strum the clouds like a harp made of cotton, but wouldn't be able to, facing a window that would only tease me, running past clouds so quickly that there would not only be no access, there would be no time. I chose to stay here at this window, with the African violets, and today, in this moment, steal time back, create a future of lifelong love, by caressing only one leaf today. With three African violets in front of me, I can make this romance go on and on, moment after moment, so I have no need to rush.

That's why I didn't get on the plane. Because I wanted this moment, here in my room, Kathryn's Garden Room, in my bed & breakfast in Sarasota, my room that has just one window with three African violets with many leaves, each different, each worthy of the attention of time. Beyond the leaves of my violets, skating over their crown chakras, through my one window is the garden of the house, where palm trees waltz a slow dance in the hot, barely visible, summer breeze. Jersey Joe, the new tabby of the estate, reigns over the garden like King Henry the Fifth, frightening every gecko that crosses the brick entryway, but never harming any of them. Joe's paws are much too big for his already quite stately body but they are as gentle as my thumb and finger on my African violet leaf, as soft as my lover's delight of every moment of my skin.

Down the brick path, around the corner from the B&B, past the old movie theater in Burns Court, on Pineapple Street is my favorite boutique, at least I think it's my favorite, although I've never been inside it because it's always closed; well, I suppose not always, just every time I walk past. I stand at the window, that impenetrable cornea, that separates me from the beauties inside, just inside that window, so close that if I had magic fingers, fingers of flame that could melt glass, or fingers with blades like Edward Scissorhands', that could slice through the pane, I could gather the mauve velvet, the antique white lace, the pale pink beads between my fingers, those fingers that made love to the leaf of my African violet just moments ago. I again searched in vain for store hours, scanning the glass that imprisoned my goddess-esque dresses, the pane that kept me from them like an airplane window. They caught my breath and kept me still and moments turned into minutes, and minutes into part of a morning, a morning I was journeying to the Sarasota farmer's market to buy, for Robert, my friend and now lover, a tomato, but only, he said, if I found a beautiful one. I drew into my mind's eye, my sixth chakra, anja, the burnt orange satin dress draped with olive green pearls standing behind the glass, and once it was there, in the place of inner wisdom right between my eyebrows, I transformed it into the most beautiful bright orange tomato crowned by the green folds of its mother, a strong, deeply rooted plant from which it had been lovingly harvested by its guardian, the local farmer, fresh this morning.

Again, no store hours, so I needed to move on to the farmer's market in search of that tomato. As I turned my body away from those dresses, my fingers caressed the glass over the only words inscribed into it – Delight. I read those words with my fingertips like a blind woman, feeling their shapes, like I felt Robert's Russian brail watch that circled his wrist just last night, taking in each character and placing them one by one onto my skin until I was wearing a dress of roman numerals, his fingers moving from one to another like the hands of a clock.

I strolled down Pineapple Street, greeting people with dogs, happy people, happy dogs, in Sarasota on a September Saturday morning, a morning whose night before, a morning whose Eve cleansed and cooled the city with storms that made swimming pools of crosswalks, wading ponds of gutters, and changed a Mediterranean climate to that of the North Americas, storms that left a residue, a morning tolerable to Sarasotans, real Sarasotans, not snowbirds who fly down in December, real people and dogs who live through the heat, and revel in the gift of September mornings washed in the aftermath of storming, cooling evenings.

I could see the tents and hear the music, and as I turned onto Main Street, the city came alive and, but for the lack of olives, I felt myself back in Provence, in Gorges, at the Tuesday morning market. I began to delight in purple peppers, ripe eggplant and honey made by local bees.

As I always am at farmer's markets, I was overwhelmed, over-awed. I love the fragrances and the colors and the texture of everything. And so, as in every city, I have to find a stand in which I immediately feel at home. I knew instantly when I saw the two racks of clothing that there was art here, and there was. The first rack I went to was the more fascinating, carrying dresses that were designed from repurposed clothing. A previous dress had been cut in half and married to a gorgeous lace tank, whose diamond shape caused a triangle directly over the pelvis in the front and the sacrum in the back. A blue tie-dyed t-shirt was now joined with a mini-pleated orange skirt, an outfit I could see Sharon

Stone wearing to the Oscars. I moved to the other rack. Perched upon the metal shoulders of recycled dry cleaner hangers, like the scarecrow of Dorothy's memoir, were old clothes, not refashioned, just old, attempting to be repurposed by sliding onto a new person's body.

In the center of this rack was a yellow dress, the precise color of Plochman's mustard, the mustard of Chicago hotdogs, a vintage, linen beauty, with eyelit snowflake cutouts resting perfectly at the clavicle bones above its chest and skirting the base of its thighs, just above the knees. The woman in the tent now came out and told me this was the $5.00 rack. Everything, $5.00. Next to the rack was a basket. She pointed to it and informed me that everything in the basket was $1.00. I put on the hat that was at the top of that basket, pulled that yellow dress onto my body, over my t-shirt and shorts and walked across the street to look in the reflection of the building as my mirror. I stared into the marble and it felt like a window, a window in which I saw myself, in a yellow dress with a small, men's hat sporting a red, white and brown stripe, and I lifted my fingers to cradle first the brim of the hat and then the hem of the dress. As I handed the merchant my $6.00, she asked me my name. I said Mary Ruth, and she opened her arms, just like Kathryn, the giantess of my room, my garden, does every day in my bed & breakfast in Sarasota, and embraced me. She said it was unbelievable because her daughter is named Mary Ruth. I asked her her name, and she said, "My name is Delight. I own the boutique on Pineapple Street."

Same Moon (tanka)

By Amanda Hassitt

It is the same moon
That shines down on me tonight,
Though you are not here.
Look up at that same moon, too,
Thinking of me, as I, you.

Three Crashes and a Wedding

By Elizabeth Fajardo

If I had one wish, it would've been to have my late father, Jack, present at my son's wedding this past June. There I was gleaming in a strapless royal blue chiffon gown, sable soft hair styled up to perfection, my silver studded heels dancing on air as Anthony twirled his proud mother around the reception floor. Yet I couldn't help thinking that our mere presence at this momenous occasion was a miracle fashioned by my guardian angel. It was nearing the end of August, 1995, when I received the call from the police at work. "Your son was hit by a car. He's okay, but we'll be transporting him to Peninsula Hospital." The rest was a blur as I choked back tears. Only three weeks earlier I had been notified in a similar way to hasten home and say one last good-bye to my dying father. "Anthony can't die!" I screamed, my heart pounding to the rhythm of my terror. Within seconds I was racing down El Camino, running red lights en route to the hospital. I arrived just as the EMTs wheeled my son out on the stretcher.

"Mom, it hurts," he moaned, his brown eyes looking up for answers. "You'll be fine," I replied, massaging his arm, hoping to disguise my fear.

A bright magenta sunset filled the night sky as I glanced outside the window of the ICU, yearning for the warmth so prevalent throughout summer evenings in Burlingame. The smell of stale hospital air surrounded me while I sat helpless and alone beside Anthony—a single monitor regulating his vitals. An IV tube longer than an eel provided limited sustenance. What would heal his emotions? I forced my eyes shut, trying to forget sickness, pain, the reminders in every corner of the drab, sterile room. Suddenly, as if in a dream, I heard my father's voice from beyond.

"Everything will be alright, hijita," Dad said in his soft-spoken, reassuring manner. With that, he vanished. It seemed so real. All I knew was that I wanted to stay asleep forever. Daylight brought new details. Witnesses said Anthony flew ten feet in the air when the vehicle struck. However, there was no blood at the scene. His skull suffered no trauma. Remarkably, the broken bones in his arms and legs could be mended. Plus, the on-call physician happened to be an orthopedic surgeon. Anthony barely missed two months of freshman year.

By April of 2001 I had become an orphan, having lost my mother to cancer. I hastily moved to Vallejo with a boyfriend, though I often felt lonely. One trying morning, as I traced the shadows of fog seeping into the neighborhood from my front porch, the enchantment transformed into melancholy. It was then I decided to drive through Mare Island in search of peace. Less than five minutes on the compound, I was on cruise control, and at the same time, on the path to nowhere.

The haze at sunrise had evaporated; nonetheless, my mind was as muddled as ever. No matter what, there was no denying the ultimate truth: Mom and Dad were gone! The grief became overwhelming when all at once I realized that I had no sense of belonging. Life as I knew it had ceased, with emptiness having supplanted love. Tears began streaming down my face even as happy memories of my childhood came flooding to the surface: reading the Sunday funnies with the family, roasting marshmallows at Rio Nido, picking blackberries on summer vacation, eating cotton candy at Playland, catching sight of the Matterhorn on our annual trip to Disneyland, making tamales with my relatives at Christmas, and listening to Giants baseball games in the backyard with Dad. Instead of turning for home, I continued straight—the image of my father appearing before me. Unbeknownst to me was the abrupt emergence of a military Humvee barreling in my direction.

Wham! The momentum sent my ruby red Nissan Sentra spinning into the stratosphere, over and over again, like a roller coaster gone wild. My body was thrust upwards, circling the top of the car multiple times as my hands flailed in the air for a grip. In all the commotion, I'd forgotten to buckle my seat belt.

"Ahh!" I shrieked. Nothing could make it stop. I bounced up again, the blow propelling my head hard against the windshield, my hands slipping like melted butter off the dashboard. *Plop!* It ended. Dizziness overcame me. My head ached in the temple but the real nightmare was the recurring sound of metal crunching metal when both vehicles collided. Miraculously, I was released from the ER without injury, no blood at the site. The car was not so lucky.

After dark on December 11, 2014, I began counting my blessings, having survived several days of rain in transit without incident. I had my health in spite of being on my feet 60 hours that week. Leaving my sales job at 10:30 pm didn't seem so dreadful when I imagined the newlyweds coming for the holidays. I waited at the red light as a slight drizzle trickled down the front window. I flipped on the wipers. The moment was as serene as a stroll in the country during a light mist. Soon I would be in bed snoozing.

Then...POW! Rear-ended, my car shot out like a dart, piercing the bubble of tranquility. My body—even buckled in—was hurled towards the windshield, just missing contact. Instantly, the air seemed to drain from my spirit, as my cobalt blue 2006 Toyota Corolla was rammed into the next lane. By sheer destiny, the street was as deserted as a ghost town. I took a deep breath, rubbed my sore neck, and pulled over to the side. The other driver, a middle-aged woman, followed.

How could this happen? I'd been so careful.

The police came, trailed by the paramedics. They checked my pulse—I passed. My vehicle, in contrast, was totaled, the trunk squashed like an accordion. The irresponsible party's pearl white Chevy Tahoe was undamaged. On New Year's Eve, as fate would have it, my insurance made it official—the Corolla would remain where all good automobiles go to die—the wrecking yard. Upon hearing the devastating news, I recalled words of wisdom dispensed by a mechanic in the local body shop when he first spotted my broken-down heap.

"You're lucky to be alive," he said. Now his sentiment meant all the difference in the world.

Days later, I retrieved my belongings from the old jalopy. Inside the trunk I discovered: Anthony's torn baby blanket, a newspaper listing Barry Bonds' homers, remnants of *Newsweek* magazine's 9/11 cover featuring New York firefighters raising our flag, dozens of shoes slated to be donated to charity, and lastly, a damp paper sack. I was about to discard my findings when something told me to empty the bag.

A wobbly object, light as a feather, fell into my arms. Wrapped within a sealed plastic tube was the golden tree topper angel I'd misplaced one Christmas. I smiled back at the beautifully chiseled creature, whose wings were spread wide, as if poised to absorb the impact of unpleasant things. And, perhaps, save a life in the process. I went home feeling safer than ever, knowing that Jack, my guardian angel, was coming along for the ride.

How I Became a Poet

By Jeannine Gerkman

Some people know exactly what they are going to do in life even as children and continue to hone their skills. I am not one of those people. I didn't start writing poetry until a couple of years ago. I suspect three different experiences contributed to my discovering this gift.

The first one started in 2002 when my husband and I moved from an English-speaking congregation to a Spanish-speaking one. I was immersed into an ocean of words I could not understand. They washed over me and then I'd catch a drop here, a splash there. Gradually, I recognized more and more as my brain unraveled the patterns and swirls. It was very disorienting, but I was able to make sense of what I was hearing as my head adapted to its new environment. We were in the congregation for close to five years and I am now able to communicate in this lovely foreign language.

Second, as a result of hormone imbalances during peri-menopause, I suffered from intense anxiety and overwhelming depression. My brain felt like it was stuffed with cotton. My thinking was blurry and I was in a state of panic. What could I do? How could I fix this? I did research and in addition to working with the medical professionals, I decided to take up Sudoku as this is supposed to help the brain. At first, I couldn't see where the numbers were to go, but I noticed if I was just quiet and waited long enough; my unconscious brain would take over and unlock the patterns and I'd see exactly where I needed to put the numbers. An added benefit was during this "Sudoku break," I would feel calm. Then I started doing crossword puzzles and something clicked inside. Clues would help my synapses come up with connections they hadn't tried before. I had learned to take care of myself and calm my panic. About this time, I started to go to Filoli as much as possible to walk in the gardens and take deep cleansing breaths.

Then my mother-in-law suffered illnesses that eventually lead her to being in our home completely helpless and dependent on our care. In December, 2011, I found myself the primary caregiver to a dear sweet woman who couldn't leave her bed, didn't know who I was (or her son either), and was panicked all the time. Her constant cry was "Help, me," "Help, me" when she wasn't actively engaged or asleep.

With this full-time responsibility of caregiving thrust upon me, I had to learn how to cope. I also wanted to help her. I found that singing to her was soothing for both of us and to our surprise, when I spoke to her in rhyme, she calmed right down. I picked up children's stories and would read Dr. Seuss's *"One Fish, Two Fish"* to her every evening. She never tired of it. During the reading, she would be calm, blissful and laugh delightedly. As soon as I stopped, she would be anxious again. Pretty soon, I was making up silly rhymes whenever I spoke to her and she loved it. Trying to find a way to ease her discomfort and make my job bearable unlocked something else in my brain. It as if I had a lump of coal inside me that was subjected to intense pressure and transformed, producing a diamond. My first official poem was in response to the grief my neighbors experienced losing their beloved cat of 20 years. I wanted to comfort them, but didn't know what to say. While mulling over this, a poem sprang from my unconscious that was just the right mix of humor and pathos. When I wrote it down, I cried and laughed and knew it was just right. Every poem I compose has moved me literally to tears or filled me with joy (or both). When it does that for me, I know it is worth sharing with you.

Dry Bones

By T.R. Poulson

Oh dry bones. . . I will lay sinews upon you, and cause
flesh to come upon you, and cover you with skin,
and put breath in you, and you shall live.
Ezekiel 37:4-6

The vet pulls out the second calf, hind legs and tail first,
and splats it near its dead twin. His hands
rip the membrane, feel the chest. He looks

for a nostril's twitch. Then he tells the girl
and her father, "If you'd called me this morning,
I might have saved this one." The girl, whose job

it was to check the heavy cows, looks from her dad's tanned face,
to the cow's round eyes, to the slick black
newborns. She's been out to the gully, seen

the dry bones of her grandpa's roping horse, her brother's
4-H steer, and others, some forgotten. Soon the cow,
swishing her tail and pulling on her halter rope,

will know. She will bawl when her four-wheeler takes
her still, unlicked calves. Now the girl,
who knows of the prophets from Bible study, resolves
never to let this happen again. But it will. It will.

Subtle Hints of Spring (haiku)

By Amanda Hassitt

Subtle hints of spring
As the buds peek out their heads –
Here and there, a bloom.

Hessie and Hope

By Jane Goold-Caufield

In the 1950s, Englewood, Colorado, a suburb of Denver, was a "Dick and Jane" sort of little town and a perfect place to grow up. Englewood had a small-town feel, and consisted of about 20,000 people living in homes built in the 1930s and 40s around a quiet downtown area along South Broadway. Life was cozy.

Mothers didn't work. Traditional family values were the norm. No one would have expected the town of Englewood would strike a historic blow for gender equity in sports. But that is what happened.

There were eight little girls of about the same age on our block: Donna, Patty, Judy, Kay, my cousins Pat and Marilynn, me, and Alice Hessel (I called her "Hessie"). Our block was an enclave of small working-class bungalows, each flanked by large lawns and front yards banked down to wide sidewalks. The banks were for rolling down; the sidewalks were for roller-skating, ka-chunk, ka-chunk, as the metal wheels grazed the cracks. We skated up and then whizzed down the sidewalk, the ka-chunks coming closer and closer together an acoustic science project.

We knew our neighborhood as only children can, and walked everywhere: three blocks straight down Sherman Street to Lowell Elementary School, one block over and two blocks down to Flood Junior High. Englewood High School was a two-block walk around the corner. On Saturdays, we walked downtown to the Gothic Theatre for the 20-cent matinee.

During the summer, the annual Pet and Doll Parade often found us entering our dressed-up pets or riding our crepe-paper-ribboned bikes down South Broadway. At my house, we played with hollyhock dolls on the picnic table in the back yard. We liked to dress up in our mother's old gowns and shoes, with some old hat to top it off. At Judy's glamorous house on the corner with the sheer white curtains, we would sit on the polished hardwood stairs and go bump, bump down in our pedal pushers. On warm summer nights we played "Kick-the-Can" or "Midnight Ghost" in the street.

But most often, we played in the vacant lot beside the Hessel house next door. In winter we played "fox and geese" in the snow. In the summer, Mr. Hessel kept it beautifully groomed like a grassy baseball diamond, and my friend Hessie liked to organize the girls into a ball game of some kind. We played kickball, softball, and "five-hundred." We were not good enough for baseball, but Hessie's older brothers were baseball players.

She practiced with them on that lot as a little girl, and finally got so good at it that she was invited to pitch for the boy's baseball team, ironically named the Old Timers League.

Hessie was not the very first girl to break the gender barrier in boy's baseball. This was accomplished one year earlier by a thirteen year old in New York named Kathryn Johnston, who called herself Tubby, after the comic strip character. Johnston was invited to join the team because she was good at hitting, but she was heckled by both boys and adults. After her first season in 1950, a new rule was made that banned girls from Little League. That rule stood until 1974, when it was overturned by a lawsuit won by a 12-year-old girl named Maria Pepe, with support by the National Organization for Women (NOW).

In 1951 then, Alice Hessel must have been the second girl to play in an all-boys league. As a nine-year-old, Hessie was the winning pitcher and first baseman for Englewood's Old Timers League. A team photo shows her on one knee at the end of the line, glove in hand, looking completely natural with her team of boys. Unlike her predecessor, she said she didn't get heckled much by the boys, because "they could see how good I was."

My friend Hessie became a local celebrity. Actually, she was royalty! Because she had taken her team to a regional championship, she became so popular in Englewood that this skinny little girl in pigtails was put up against a bevy of high school bathing beauties for Queen of the Youth Festival. And she won!

The contest was decided by the citizens of Englewood, who could vote on the streets downtown in front of the local businesses. Those high school girls didn't have a chance! The event gained the attention of the national press, and Time Magazine sent a photographer out to take pictures. A more photogenic young athlete there couldn't have been. In Time's glossy black-and white photos, Hessie is endearingly shown in baseball uniform and pigtails, sitting cross-legged on the grass, little brown fingers splayed over the ball in a perfect pitcher handgrip. Another photo shows Hessie, wearing her baseball cap and t-shirt, smiling from a lifeguard seat above the seven swim suited former contenders. And in another, she is riding in a convertible down South Broadway, waving, with her teenaged attendants in the cars behind her.

The best photo of all shows Alice Hessel being crowned during in an evening ceremony at the bandstand of a local park by none other than Bob Hope! Yes, the Bob Hope. In the photo, Hessie is wearing an unlikely long frilly pink dress and a bit of lipstick, and her normally pigtailed hair is styled in finger-curls around her face. Hope's entourage hovers in the background, and a gabardine-suited Bob Hope is seen on his knees talking to Alice, holding a huge chrome microphone nearly eclipsing his lower face, but allowing display of his prominent nose. Bob has his arm around Hessie's tiny waist as she leans away from him, smiling nervously. I knew she was very ticklish. I remember standing on the grass below, watching, as he asked if he could give her a kiss. , Loudly and reflexively, she replied, "No!" Bob mugged surprise and chagrin to the crowd, but he didn't try again. I'll bet Bob Hope hadn't had many turndowns for kisses in those days. In fact, that's sort of what he quipped afterward, in his nasally funny way.

Not long after that season, Hessie's baseball career ended. Her big brothers told her it was time to cut off her pigtails and be a girl. She grew too old for the Old Timers, and there were no women's competitive sports in public schools in those days, least of all in baseball. Title IX, the law that requires gender equity for boys and girls in every educational program that receives federal funding was not passed until 1972, and while it still has not been fully met, women's sports are now ubiquitous in high schools and colleges. Alice's niece was one of those who later benefited, playing basketball for Iowa State University. Although Alice grew up to be a rather petite woman, her athletic talents would have surely shone if she had had today's opportunities. But thanks to girls like her, the way was lighted for the likes of Mo'ne Davis, the brilliant girl pitcher who won the Little League World Series in 2014.

Even without a sports career, however, Alice Hessel's focused spirit continued to shine as an achiever in both academics and school politics in high school. She graduated from University of Colorado School of Nursing and worked as a nurse for many years at St. Anthony's Hospital in Denver. She married a music teacher and had two boys. I don't know, but I'll bet they were good baseball players.

Alice was my best friend when we were little; I called her "Hessie" and she called me "Gooldy." She was a "tomboy" and I was a "wimp,", but we had lots of fun together. She tried to encourage my interest in sports but I lacked her physical prowess and focus. Although I was happy and proud of her, I didn't know then what a significant feat Hessie had accomplished. I'm not sure she knew. She was just good at baseball and wanted to play, and the team recognized her value to them irrespective of her gender.

Time Magazine editors didn't publish her photos due to an international event that took precedence. But in 1951, the citizens of Englewood, Colorado had recognized and appreciated Alice Hessel's historic achievement, courageously breaking the gender barrier and taking her team to victory in boys' league baseball. They rewarded her with a coronation and celebration as Queen of the Youth Festival. There, she proudly presided in the triumph of skill over beauty in a local pageant. It was a history-making event for herself, for Englewood, and for all of us girls and women. Not cowed by celebrity, this liberated young woman even turned down a kiss from Bob Hope!

Waiting for the Bus in Joseph, Oregon

By Ruth Stout

My sister-in-law, Linda, and I are having a lovely day in Joseph, Oregon. Joseph is a short drive from Wallowa Lake, Oregon, where we are vacationing. We eat lunch and visit the local Nez Perce Indian history museum.

Our husbands are out on an all-day excursion, so we need to take the bus back to Wallowa Lake. The bus is twenty minutes late. Linda and I aren't worried yet. The buses here run infrequently, and apparently not on time. Linda gets up to walk around and rub her aching back. "Are you on disability?" a voice calls from the general direction of the trash container. "No," Linda answers, "I'm not. I just have a sore back."

"My names Earl. I'm on disability. Things get tight at the end of the month." Now I can see a small, gray haired, wiry man with arms stained dark as walnuts from many overlapping tattoos. He is busily pulling cans and bottles out of the trash. He also finds a Swiffer Wet Jet refill container in great condition. "Here," he says to Linda putting it on top of the trash container. "I already have a lot of these, but this is a good one. Do you want it?"

"Oh, thanks, Earl" my tender hearted sister-in-law says, "I don't need one right now."

"Ok, well I'll leave it here. Someone might want it." He quick steps across the street to the grocery store to turn in the cans and bottles.

"Linda, you are too nice, why are you talking to him?"

A cold, stranger avoiding me says, "Oh, he's harmless. Bless his heart."

The bus is now a half hour late and we are starting to wonder if it will ever come. I search my phone. There are no taxis in or around Joseph. The bus is our only way back to Wallowa Lake.

A few minutes later, Earl returns from the grocery store carrying a bag of potatoes. "These are on sale!" he says, "only $1.49. Do you want some? They are right in front of the store."

"No, thanks," says Linda, "thanks for letting me know though."

"The bus is probably coming soon," the man volunteers. "When Mary is driving, she sometimes takes Thelma or Marty to the doctor." He brightened. "Sometimes Thelma lets me sleep on her sofa. I think George might be driving today. He does hospital pick up." The man lopes into the middle of the street. "I'll just watch for it."

"Linda, he's standing in the street watching for the bus. What if he gets hit?"

"The last time we saw a car was five minutes ago. He can get out of the way in plenty of time."

"There," he shouts, "the bus just came into town. He has to go around the back way and then he'll be here."

The bus arrives and Linda walks over to the man handing him something. We get on the bus and start toward Wallowa Lake. "How much did you give him?"

"Oh, just a couple of bucks."

"Well, it looks like he could use it," I say as I hand her a buck.

"Bless his heart," says Linda, and we drive out of town.

Holiday Rituals

By Luanne Oleas

"What about this one, Honey?"

It's only one of the many disembodied voices heard in the thick forest of our favorite Christmas tree farm. That great tradition—with all its faults—still holds magic for our family. Take the kids. Search high and low for the perfect tree. A fine reason for a family outing.

"Bobby hit me."

"Stop it you two, wherever you are."

"Now look, you've gotten pitch on your new jacket. How am I ever going to get that out?"

"We shoulda taken the first tree."

"Where is the first tree?"

"You should have taken the first tree. It would have been the sensible thing to do. But then, sensible people buy trees that come in boxes and don't shed needles."

"This is a good one."

"It's pretty good. If we don't find a better one, we'll come back to it."

"Right. How are you gonna come back to it? They all look alike."

"Your mother told me to bring Kleenex and put a tissue in each tree that I was considering."

"That one is way too big."

"It's not that big."

"Where's the dog?"

We have a lot of traditions behind selecting our yearly tree. To be "The One," it must be situated in the perfect spot. That would be farthest from a) where we parked, b) where we pay for it, and c) any road, dirt or paved.

"Hold the tree. I'll cut it."

"Where's Bobby?"

"Geez, this is a terrible saw. It would be easier to chew down this tree."

"Bob-be-e-e-e-e?"

"Hold the tree. I'm almost finished."

"Bobby, where did you get that? Give it to me right now!"

191

"Don't let go of the— OW!"

"Oh dear, I'm sorry. Does your head hurt?" "Let's just get this thing back to the car."

"Daddy, you're getting it all dirty."

"Here, let me hold one end. Oh, yuck. Pitch."

"I have to go to the bathroom, Daddy."

"Oh, swell."

"Can you wait until we pay for the tree, sweetheart? I'll ask the man if there's a restroom."

"I gotta go now."

"Go behind that tree, Son."

"Not on it, Honey. Behind it."

"This thing is so heavy, we'll never get it to the road."

"We could cut off the bottom branches."

"Oh, look, it's got a bald spot. I didn't see that before we cut it. Did you?"

"You could drill some holes and insert some branches like you did last year."

"I wanted to cut down a tree, not build one. Bobby, where are you?"

"Do you think I should go back and take all those Kleenexes out of the trees?"

Ain't traditions and fresh air grand?

Morning

By Jeannine Gerkman

Bathed in sunshine
Glistening with dew
The morning has started
The day's begun anew

Children are streaming
To take their place at school
My face is beaming
I'm grinning like a fool

The air is crisp and bracing
My steps sure and strong
Whatever I might be facing
Will never turn out wrong

Stories About Patriots

By Rich Hoggan

eye before e
e before eye
can't keep 'em straight whisper again
i'm a failure
preach them stories about patriots the
ones who crossed oceans
preach again about the ones who want equality
you've lost the meaning
tell em they're protected tell em
again they're good
now everyone lets look their way
i was slapped in the face slapped for
forgetting

walk just a day in these shoes wake up
just once, forgetting you can't handle
the feeling can't cope with forgetting

1,2,3 its just that simple
what do you mean you can't do it in your head just
quit i don't have time for your failures come at me like
i'll quit
come at me cuz this strength gets in your head no i
won't quit
won't wear your labels
is this creating all men equal
is this walking with the ones who cross oceans

and now i'm in a dark hole
cuz its acceptable tellin me i'm a failure just quit
you're not good enough
look at them they don't
forget
why can't you be more like them this is not
a rap about the perfect its about the
broken
yes i'm broken
and there's o changin

I Love My Wife

By Chris Knoblaugh

Now you have to understand, I love my wife very much, but sometimes you have to laugh at her... not with her. Like the time she read that peanut butter could be used in a pinch as deep conditioning hair moisturizer, so she grabbed a giant glop and plopped it on her head before realizing it was the "chunky" kind. It took hours to wash it out and she reeked for weeks. Then there was the time she took our cat out for a walk on his leash without taking into consideration the fact that he could jump the fence in our yard while she could not.

The cat survived, but my wife was a clawed mess for a while. She grabbed his hind legs as he went over, so when she hauled him back up he lit into her. She just kept hugging him until he calmed down and realized it was not a big dog that grabbed him.

She is a very smart lady with a Mensa membership to back it up, and she sometimes talks over people's heads (including my own). She gets all excited about an idea and starts talking about it in big long streams that are hard to follow. I have learned to just smile, nod, and grunt from time to time when that happens. She thinks I am smarter than I am, but heck, I know how to grunt and nod like the next guy.

The funniest time was when she ran headlong into the four-foot tall redwood trunk and knocked all of her wind out. We were car camping at Big Basin in the redwoods. Like a ninny, I had the car doors open to unload when a raccoon the size of a Great Dane lumbered into the car. Our daughter let out a yelp, and momma bear (my wife) ran toward the car at full tilt screaming at the top of her lungs until she crashed into redwood log.

She knocked her wind out, fell to the ground, and started gasping and thrashing around. I started laughing, and the startled coon fled from the commotion. It took a long time for her to get her wind back, but when she did I caught an earful. It turns out that she thought the raccoon had our daughter. She said she never even saw the tree; all she saw was the raccoon in the car.

That woman can focus like nobody's business. I'm glad she didn't reach the car, but having seen how she handled the cat I think she could have taken the raccoon. In fact, she would have probably tamed it and taken it for walks on a leash.

How I Received My Sex Education in the 1940s

By Audry Lynch

My niece invited me to take a tour of the old Sanborn mansion. She was surprised when I said, "I actually spent a year living here during my junior year at Marycliff Academy." That started a whole chain of memories that began when I was thirteen years old. Now I am 81 so that meant looking back sixty-eight years in time.

I had won a 4-year full scholarship to Marycliff. My freshman and sophomore years had been full of wonderful experiences but my parents noticed a change in me the next summer when I turned 16. Suddenly I bloomed physically and then socially.

I discovered boys and they started appearing at our cottage every day and on the West Harwich Beach. Looking back I realize that my parents must have been surprised by all this constant activity into their usually peaceful summer. It reached somewhat of a peak on my sixteenth birthday when three different boys gave me pearls as a gift.

My parents started having a lot of private conversations. I discovered the gist of these conversations when they announced. "We've decided to let you live at Marycliff this year because we think that all that commuting is too tiring for you." "Tired" was a euphemism for bad behavior.

If my parents' goal was to isolate me from the male sex, they had picked the right place. The only male in sight was dear, old Father Garrahan, a retired priest of advanced years who occupied a loft.

Without any boys in sight, we spent a lot of time thinking and talking about them. That brings up the matter of sex education. The closest we came to that was a yearly lecture on menstruation given by our science teacher, Mére Haché. It was an embarrassing event and rather overdue.

Instead we existed in an underground of myths and misinformation. Any sort of make-up, even the palest of pink lipsticks, was totally forbidden. The underlying message was that the use of make-up to attract boys must be some kind of sin. The minute we left the school grounds the first thing we did was to put on make-up.

We didn't have mirrors so I mastered the art of putting on lipstick without one. Patent leather shoes were used as another example of the occasion of sin. Supposedly a boy could stand close to you, look down at your shoes and see the reflection of your panties. This has never been verified to my knowledge but women of my generation avoided these shoes—just in case.

Our social life consisted of two yearly dances with St. John's Prep School. One of its charms I suppose was that it was located a good safe distance from Winchester. The boys were eager but always gentlemanly. We girls attributed the latter fact to the story that we heard that the

Brothers put saltpeter in the boys' food just before the dance to calm them down.

In addition to the saltpeter, there was another deterrent to fraternization. The dances were sharply patrolled by the Brothers who kept an eye on all potential danger spots. Towards the end of the evening as the dancers grew closer, they would be startled by a rap on the boy's shoulder and an admonition to "leave room for the Holy Ghost."

I was well prepared for the Ivy League by these intelligent, dedicated women. The nuns also tried to turn us into little ladies. They demanded courtesy at all times. I've heard that in their southern academy, the girls even had to learn to play a good hand of bridge before graduation.

As a boarder the nuns suggested gently that I should emulate the fine example of two sisters who lived in the house with me. They spoke softly and walked with dignity. In fact they seemed to glide rather than walk. Of course I hated them.

Some of the girls came from wealthy families. Despite the disparity in wealth, there was no overt snobbery. One of the great equalizers was the mandatory requirement for uniforms. This eliminated all clothes competition. The uniforms consisted of blue jumpers, white blouses with Peter Pan collars, and navy blue blazers. Looking back now at our class picture I think we looked very neat and nice. As teenagers we cordially hated them.

As graduates we did very well in our college placements. By now we were a class of 12, just half the size of our freshman class. Two of us went to Harvard and the rest went to other colleges and we all graduated and one of our class became a nun.

Prom dates had been a problem for most of the girls so some male teachers at Cambridge High and Latin School had been commandeered to "find dates" for the girls for the prom which they did. The gym was decorated like a fairyland and we were one of the few girls' schools who danced to live music by a popular local band leader who was related to one of the girls.

Then came graduation day, which we thought meant the beginning of real life. The weather was gorgeous—all blue skies and rolling green lawns. We were dressed in floor length white lace gowns, scoop necks, with a blue underskirt. In our arms we each carried a dozen red roses. Looking at our picture, I now know that we didn't suspect on that beautiful day that never again would we look so young, so pretty, and as innocent as we did with the lovely Sanborn House behind us as a backdrop.

That dedicated band of French nuns had helped us to carry the light into our college and then our careers. They had taught us the simple truth of the adage that the quality of our dreams will determine its power.

...And the 11th One is Free

By Luanne Oleas

My wallet bulges with cards from local stores. They're not the plastic fantastic sorts that allow you to charge everything you don't need. They keep those away from starving writers.

No, the cards that cause my billfold to split a seam are those cheap little business cards.

Every time I visit a new establishment, they give me one. You know the scheme.

You buy a cappuccino, they give you a card. Buy ten and you get the eleventh one free. They stamp a smiley face in a grid on the back of they card as you work your way to your free whatever. Spend twenty bucks on hot water dripped through dead, ground beans and, voila! You get one free.

This catchy marketing technique knows no limits. It's at book stores, video stores, car washes, and ice cream parlors. But if you think about it, who really cares if they get their 11th pizza free?

Why can't this apply to the stuff you really want in life? If you take ten units at the local college, you should get the 11th one free.

If you buy ten gallons of gas, why can't the 11th be free?

If you enter ten writing categories at the San Mateo County Fair, well, I better not suggest it.

How about a car? Anyone who buys ten cars in their life should get the 11th one free.

This should be applied to all aspects of life. For those who want big families, the 11th child should be free. If you need multiple visits to the psychiatrist after that 11th child, the 11th visit should be free.

Now comes the big question. Suppose all of life operated on the "11th One Free" principle. Your 11th vacation? Free. Your 11th computer? Free. The 11th tire, the 11th stamp, the 11th house, all of it, free, free! FREE!!

Would every facet of society, including the world's oldest profession, benefit from this?

Certainly—though some restrictions may apply. The airline industry has it already. It's called frequent flyer miles.

If this does take over the universe, who is to say where it will end?

After all the human possibilities have been exhausted, will the Big Guy buy in? Probably.

It would be my luck. I can just see it.

I die on a busy day. I'm standing in a long line outside the Pearly Gates. Milliseconds before my unfortunate demise, two things happened.

First, ten Sisters of Charity in a rickety bus had finished five years of serving poor starving people in a third world country. As they traveled back to the convent, singing and praising their Maker, their bus plunged off a cliff.

Second, after a lifetime of refusing to reform, the world's worst serial murderer died in his cell from natural causes. (He had avoided the death penalty because he was the tenth serial murderer convicted that year.)

In line in front of me is the serial killer and in front of him are ten nuns. St. Peter passes the ladies through, no questions asked. Harry Horrible gets in because he's number 11.

Now they pull up my life file on the big monitor in the sky and scroll through it.

Naturally, I am sent downstairs for an overdue library book.

My only hope, as I approach the inferno, is that there are ten real schmoes are in front of me. And the 11th one goes free.

the big fall is coming

By Maurine Killough

we walk hand in hand toward the precipice
the big fall is coming
i can feel it in your slight distance
the gap gets just a little wider every day
your warm love does not burn me as bright
you pay less attention to me and pull away
into some place i am not invited
the pit i will fall into is like a grave
you do this every year
somehow i know if i sit it out, you will come back to me
maybe you just need time alone, time away
from me
i want you too much, you think me selfish
that i've had enough, too much of you
your steps away from me grow farther and will soon
leave me in the shadows with only your halo to flicker memories
of our hot nights together
plump blackberry days and watermelon nights
so hot to burn my skin
your kisses fade only by drops each day, but i can feel it already
i beg you, don't retreat, don't shut me out
but i know what is coming
we have done this dance before and before
it is less and soon i will have only grey where there was sun and blue
i will drop into persephone's fall
cover my vacant bones that housed your sunshine
make a cup of tea
and wait the long winter
for your return

Taking My Imagination for a Ride

By Marjorie Bicknell Johnson

A Missouri mule from Arkansas went down to Tennessee
 Hee Haw, Hee Haw, Hee Haw
Took one look at the folks down there
Said, "It ain't no place for me."
"Hee Haw," sang he, "Haw Hee Haw Hee Haw Hee."
The old mule sang, "Hee Haw."

The song was recorded on one side of a thick disk the size of a dinner plate but twice as heavy, a flat platter that would shatter if dropped. My father had several albums and a three-foot stack of loose records piled under his workbench. He would take a record out of its paper sleeve from a six-inch thick album of singles, hand-crank the phonograph, put the record on the felt turntable, and carefully place the needle arm into a groove at the outside of the disk. The polished oak box under the turntable showed a dog listening to a gramophone horn, "His Master's Voice," the RCA trademark. The 1910 phonograph didn't use electricity and it didn't have high-fidelity sound or a volume control. With a more modern phonograph in the living room, my mother had banished it to the garage.

The garage in Nevada City evolved, during the twenty-five years that my father was retired, into a long and narrow structure with two step-down rooms added behind, a bay window bulging out on the south side, and a funnel through a knothole on the windowless north side only three feet from the neighbor's fence. The funnel was a secret delight for three grandsons, who used it for a urinal. The twenty-foot long workbench held treasures such as quartz crystals and gold ore samples acquired during Dad's gold mining days. Under the workbench, a chest five feet long, three feet wide and three feet deep held replaced faucets and scraps of pipe, all things "perfectly good" that you might need someday.

The garage was so narrow that Dad's truck and Mom's sedan parked one behind the other. The vehicle in front had to be moved sixty feet along a narrow drive to the street to allow the one behind to drive out; Dad always parked in the front. My eighty-year-old father liked to sit in the cab of his Ford pickup, drink a beer, read the paper, and listen to his portable radio, but his driving was limited to moving the truck out to wash and polish it. He spent hours just sitting there, wishing he could still drive.

One day I climbed in beside him and asked, "Where are we going?"

He said, "I'm taking my imagination for a ride." And, no, he didn't want me to drive his big truck, The Green Giant, but I could ride with him if I didn't talk too much.

We sat silently. I remembered wonderful places Dad had taken me in years past: an abandoned apple orchard with a bramble of blackberries taken over by a black bear, a secret fishing hole with a three-foot trout. One day we drove across a wooden covered bridge spanning a deep river canyon along the old stagecoach route from Alleghany to Downieville with thousand-foot high hand-fitted stonewalls supporting the road. On another trip, with red dust boiling out behind, we lurched along a rutted washboard road miles from anywhere, and he showed us brilliant and barren red clay banks reflected in a cyan blue lake, a remnant of hydraulic gold mining. My father knew every back road and every deserted gold mine and ghost town from Timbuktu to Red Dog.

Dad especially liked to tell stories about rattlesnakes. He had once happened upon rattlesnakes hibernating in a cave, a hundred or so snakes tangled together in a ball. They come out in the spring to mate and to eat small rodents. Rattlesnake eggs hatch within the mother; eight to ten babies are born at once. The snakes' rattles are dried, hollow segments of skin, which, when shaken, make a whirring sound. If a snake warns you with its rattle, you will hear it, and you will run. So when I found a can of "rattlesnake eggs" in a souvenir shop in Reno, I mailed it to Dad. He called me to say that he put the eggs in the cellar and checked them every day to see if they had hatched. "But, Dad," I said, "don't you remember that rattlesnakes bear live young? You taught me that yourself. It's just a joke; you don't need to check it every day."

Dad's strokes left him a little unpredictable. He broke every clock in the house when he tried to reset them after a power failure, and he snapped off every knob on the television set because he would forget which way to turn things. But Mom took loving care of him, and he adored her. For fifty-three years, Dad never forgot their wedding anniversary, and he always bought Mom a heart-shaped box of chocolates for Valentine's Day. When my mother died unexpectedly from a sudden heart attack, it broke my father's heart. With Valentine's Day approaching, he couldn't stand the pain. He taped a picture of my mother onto the dashboard of The Green Giant and took her for a ride.

The fire truck came too late to save Daddy. If he had not put a section of garden hose from the exhaust into the cab, you might have thought it was an accident. The garage didn't catch fire, but the wooden floor under the truck was charred to a depth of two inches by the heat from the truck's overheated exhaust system.

The pile of platters remained, but the old phonograph no longer worked. The newer records on top of the pile curled and stretched into sculpted art forms, never to be heard again.

In my mind's eye, Dad and Mom are driving still in The Green Giant looking for Valhalla or wherever Welsh gold miners go, maybe a rift valley with lots of blackberries, trout, and black sand for gold panning.

mysterious jazz

By Maurine Killough

jazz, you are a mystery to me
curly notes cue up to fugues on acid
sprightly tuned colors ignite velvet fur juxtaposed with electric fusion
noodle highways drive sound from a high speed chase
to the color of cool, green avocado
striped trumpets pop like stars in your xylophone hair
jester music, you are two faced
you climb me from your creamy lips to the suicide drop of a sky scraper
jazz shaman, mystery witch, you pull me deep into your fractals
lose me in your saxophone eyes
then hang on your obtuse hooks my ears
waiting to be rescued in a wave of piano or left to drown in a Minor C
mysterious jazz, you shun convention
you spark infused parody
soothe, then confuse and take hostage our sensibilities of rhythm
and into the smoky night
of slippery hot pepper butter-love
you stand guard over the rebellious realm of
the undefinable
keeping the lock safe from the key
its mystery

Our Past Is Made Up of All Our Best Efforts

By Judithe A. Guarnera

The door slammed. I yanked it open and watched my husband of almost thirty years, tromp across the front lawn. As he opened his car door, he looked back as I stood silhouetted in the doorway.

"You're wrong you know," he said so quietly I had to strain to hear. "There was never anyone else, but you. No one. Ever." With those words, he disappeared into his car. Perhaps symbolically, the car sputtered and shook before the engine turned over and he pulled away.

Tears cascaded down my cheeks. I was once again the twenty-year old who had fallen in love with the slender young man with curly black hair, soft brown eyes, a tender, but tentative smile, who was exactly one year older than me. A birthday wasn't the only thing we shared. We both worked hard, loved our families, espoused similar political beliefs, loved children and knew how to live within a meager budget.

In four years we had bought our own house, had three of our four children and established a comfortable life style. Our frugality allowed me to be a stay-at-home mom and him to be the bread-winner. We made a good team. On our ninth anniversary we conceived our fourth child, who appeared nine months to the day later on our shared birthday. Fate seemed to be giving our marriage a stamp of approval.

My husband gained prestige and acknowledgement at his job while he pursued a college degree. He became the first college graduate in his family. When I expressed pride in his accomplishment, his eyes flattened and darkened with something I couldn't identify. I believe this was the first time I suspected all was not well. Later I realized there had been other signs I'd ignored.

Our children and their activities kept us busy and distracted us from working on our relationship. We became more financially secure, but failed to notice the seeds of discontent threaded throughout our marriage. Once the children completed their education and secured jobs, I had more free time than I wanted. I decided to step back onto a road I had abandoned when I married and gave up my dream of a college degree and a career. I found the challenges of college stimulating. Although it wasn't my intention, my choice to complete my Bachelor's degree had a profound negative effect on my marriage.

Once begun, there seemed to be no turning back. Again, relying on hindsight, I wondered that fateful day as I stood in the doorway, watching my husband drive away, how we had ever fallen in love and why we had stayed together as long as we had.

To understand how this dilemma developed, I must point out where our paths diverged. I was gregarious, outspoken, loved a good conversation, especially one with a suitable amount of controversy to jack up the interest level. Quick to say I love you, never able to stay angry, optimistic to an annoying fault, my husband, was my polar opposite—quiet, introverted, someone who refused to discuss religion or politics, content to sprawl on the couch and watch TV during the few hours he wasn't working, going to school or playing sports. I found it difficult to engage and sustain him in a conversation of any length.

John had a guttural laugh that seemed reluctant to emerge. I tried to make him laugh, but he withheld his laughter and I began to wonder what else he withheld.

We argued about disciplining our children, what they should and shouldn't do.

And we blamed each other when we didn't approve of their behavior. The tenuous thread that held us together showed serious signs of fray. Angry words replaced words of love.

We made deals to get through activities. When days had gone by without any significant words passing between us, we'd turn on the smiles when company came or a work-oriented event required us to attend together.

My studies intensified as I neared graduation. When I began working, I switched from roasts and potatoes to microwaveable meals. But we ate separately. I began to wonder if he had found someone else.

"Are you having an affair?" I asked one day, my gut wrenching.

"Yeah. What's for dinner?" he replied, head buried in the refrigerator. I never knew if his answer was fact, but I realized later he was trying to tell me our relationship was over.

When we separated, angry words became the tone de jour. We battled endlessly through the long divorce. Each of us took steps to move on and our new lives fleshed out. But the infrequent contact we had continued to hit the near-explosion range.

All the paperwork that accumulated in our divorce, served as one big tally sheet of wrongdoing that I carried in my head, long after the decree was final. That tally sheet created a major roadblock preventing me from moving on.

I joined a divorce support group. Although the support helped, I felt stuck. The group featured speakers and therapy to help us begin to rebuild our lives. What one speaker said grabbed my attention.

"Repeat after me," she began, 'in my marriage I did the best I could.'" I did as requested and heard the words echoed by others in the room.

"Now," she added, "say, 'my spouse did the best he or she could do.'" This time there was an audible silence. *The heck he did,* I thought, and imagined others thinking the same.

Because she had oozed compassion and understanding when she began her talk, the occupants of the room stayed in their chairs, albeit still in silence. She continued to make the case that, up to that moment, all of us had done the best we could. "After all," she asked, "who would *choose* to do the worst?"

I left the room that night, intrigued, but not convinced. It took a while before I could embrace that idea and forgive myself and my husband. *He wasn't the best husband for me and I wasn't the best wife for him.* But I had loved him and had intended to do my best. And I believe his intentions had been the same.

Only when I acknowledged that did forgiveness become an option.

And my past, sorry as my efforts might have been, was the best I could do at that time. The speaker reminded us not to use the past as an excuse for poor future behavior. Seeing the limitations of my past is a strong motivation to do better in the future. My past is indeed, made up of all my best efforts.

Her Tired Heart Stopped Beating

By Judy Jette-Hansen

Her tired heart stopped beating
So she couldn't pray again
And with their names
upon her lips
She left this life of pain

Then they all stood
around the grave
Unthinking never to know
How they all failed their mother
Who had always loved them so

They'll not know how
she longed for
The warmth of one kind hand
For one of them to whisper
"Ma, I love and understand"

May they never know the horror
Of dying all alone
May none of their dear children
Ever leave them in the home

Be it oh so new and classy
It's an awful place to be
Pushed away alone unwanted
On legs too weak to flee

Left alone, to wait to die
Without a friendly face
To share and bring some
comfort
To that God forsaken place

No, she never missed her dinner
And she had her room and bed
But she needed love and comfort
Now it's too late, she is dead

Memoirs Writing Class

By Sylvia E. Halloran

Heartbreak to heartbreak
The silver-haired unfold their careful stories:
Here the birth of the atom bomb, there
The time the skunk lived under the house.
Today come equal, even-voiced accounts.
Twin survivors, Axis and Ally,
Become unison doting comrades in class,
Each nursed at the breast of horror.
One dodged London's awful Blitz,
Returned home just in time to see Aunt May
And baby Teddy blown to bits.
Watched it from the garden walk...
The other lived through Dresden's death by fire
Clutched in the icy-watered Elbe
By her mother's frantic embrace
Already frozen in shock.
Sometimes come bitter or boastful tales,
Careers that munched or swallowed whole
The writers' fragile lives, devouring the long time
Between anticipation and regret.
The brave expose the ugly flaws
In those who should have known better.
They bandage the wounds with healing words; at least,
Admit with weary hope that life rolls on.
The braver meet their own failings on the page,
Write and weep, surmount, survive.
Sharp self-realization plows the stone earth
So seeds of grace may sprout in coming seasons.
Good writing, so they say, shows transformation,
Gives us characters who matter, who
Bear the change with honor and with strength.

355 Memoir: Lifestyle

The Wisteria

By Kathleen Canrinus

The sweet scent of wisteria hangs heavy in the air outside the kitchen door. It's April still. Foot-long clusters of white blossoms dangle from a mass of branches to form a canopy that stretches from the eaves of my small, wooden house to the front gate. For almost a century, the vine's floral fanfare has announced the long days and warm months of summer, though from this year on, the blooming of the wisteria will also mark the anniversary of a loss.

Throughout the winter, I worried about the old vine, its thick trunk gnarled and twisted. During the cold, wet weeks of late February and early March, I searched for new growth, picking at nodes on its grey limbs with my fingernails. I reminded myself that the vine would probably not outlive me—though no rehearsal has ever softened the pain of losing anyone or anything. At last, the first pliant buds appeared—moist and pale green inside.

Since moving into my home some thirty years ago, I have known the vine by name. But for twenty-five of those years, I could not have said whether its flowers were white or purple or whether it bloomed in summer or spring. I was too busy with family, small children, and a demanding job. Now that the children are grown and gone, and I'm retired, I find myself paying attention to things I once ignored or overlooked.

Throughout its annual cycle, I observe the vine's gradual changes. They are variable, yet predictable, and mark the passing of time kindly—unlike the clock whose hands measure shorter, seemingly disposable increments. As the foliage expands, single blossoms will begin drifting like confetti onto the pebbled walkway below the trellis, where they'll shrivel to papery detritus. Breezes and the soles of my shoes will carry them far beyond where gravity first left them. They'll accumulate among the roots of plants and trees quite distant from the trunk of the vine. I'll find them in my hair after digging in parts of the yard also ignored during decades of tending other growing things. The dried flowers will stick to a spider web in the doorway and collect in the corners of the kitchen and under cabinets; many will catch in the ridged runner rug where I wipe my feet. No amount of sweeping will keep the house free of them.

In summer, after the flowers have disappeared and the weather has turned hot, leaflets arranged on delicate stems will provide green-tinged shade along the side of the house. Eventually, the foliage will yellow, fall, and after the rains, lie gray and sodden beneath the bare branches from which it emerged. Stripped of their flesh, the thin bones of the vine will allow afternoon sun to shine through panes of window glass and warm the interior of the house. Though there are reasons to appreciate the vine in all seasons, spring has always been my favorite. Next April, however, when the vine's big show begins again, I'll watch with a mixture of emotions.

It was shortly after the clusters had begun to unfurl when my brother's wife e-mailed to let me know my brother had been hospitalized again. The subject line read, "The End is Near." He was unconscious, she wrote, and not expected to live through the day. I sat by the phone and waited for the call, but he didn't die. He was fighting, she said when we spoke. I flew to Southern California. He'd been near death dozens of times over the previous eight years, as a rare and mysterious disease ravaged his brain. I clung to the hope that my visit would end like all the others, with his return to consciousness. I did not want to believe that this was the end. He was only sixty-four. It was not his turn. He was not supposed to die before our ninety-six-year-old mother, and not before me, the first born, either.

As children, we had not been particularly close. I was the conforming, compliant child, he the one who marched to the beat of his own drum. I read and studied, and he tinkered and took things apart, abandoning them when he had satisfied his curiosity—a new radio once. After he got a driver's license, he started spending most of his time away from home, and after graduation from high school, he went to sea, like his father and grandfather before him. Throughout our twenties and thirties, we

We kept in touch by phone even when he was barely able to retrieve the words to express a thought. During fluent moments, he'd share what was hard for him. He once told me I was the only person he could talk to about certain of his fears. I supported and encouraged his heroic efforts to regain what the periodic, uncontrollable grand mal seizures would wipe out. I felt fiercely loyal to him, the way I do toward my children, but he was not my child, and when he asked if he could come and live with me for a day or a week or a year, I told him I'd arrange a weeklong visit. He told me he loved me at the end of all our conversations—even that one—and I told him the same.

After every one of our contacts, I wondered if it would be the last. Odd as it seems, I always thought there'd be more. After all, I *needed* more time with him, but he died anyway on the first Wednesday in April, at 4:30 AM, while I was lying awake in my hotel room near the hospital. His wife said he was at rest. I was not. I felt as if I'd had an organ removed without an anesthetic, a layer of skin I'd never noticed, though it had held me together my whole life. Now it was gone. And nothing about how I'd lived my life made sense.

At the memorial service three weeks after his death, I learned a lot about my brother's life and met dozens of friends, colleagues, and members of his church—all loved, respected, and admired him. I felt even sadder when I realized I'd lost a brother I knew very little about. I could find reasons but no satisfactory explanation for what had kept me from placing a higher priority on knowing and loving him better and especially spending time with him during the last year of his life. I mourn the closeness we might have had and wonder how to live with a loss so steeped in regret.

When I returned home from the memorial service, the sight of the old wisteria in full bloom stopped me at the gate. Hundreds of slender, young branches exploded above dense old growth and outward as far as the heavy clusters would permit. Others twined upward into the fronds of a nearby date palm, and still others climbed over the gutters and onto the sloped roof of the house. At almost the same moment I looked up to take in the vine, I was struck by a sorrow so intense, I gasped. The handle of my suitcase fell to the ground as my knees gave way. My only thought was that my brother would never again see anything so heart-stoppingly beautiful.

Next winter, if the wisteria shows signs of returning from its death-like state, I'll look forward to another April when the air outside the kitchen hangs heavy with the scent of its blossoms. Yet at every stage of the old vine's reawakening, I will grieve the loss of my brother. By the time the clusters unfurl again, perhaps I will have learned something about how to hold the loss of someone I only came to know after the moments we might have shared were lost to us. And perhaps when the leaves have all dropped to the ground, I will have begun to forgive myself for decisions that now seem inexplicable or worse yet, coldhearted. And perhaps as I prune back the wisteria's dark, textured new growth next winter, I will have begun to discover something I cannot yet grasp about how to live this life.

Summoning Levity

By Martha Clark Scala

I am a rectangle
in need of roundness
Squiggly lines
Thoughts going nowhere
Messes cleaned up later or by someone else
Smooth, soft sensuous journey away from
shoulds and structure
Sweaters with stains
socks with heel holes
Giggles get glory and worry blurs.

Eight Letters

By Louise Lenahan Wallace

Eight letters sent, and saved, from 1966. The postmarks span one year, lacking a day. I hold these yellowing envelopes and wonder ... as I've wondered for nearly five decades....

1965. Vietnam. A country on the other side of existence. Newspapers recounted grim war details, dutifully posting the latest casualty list. We read and prayed, grateful only that the list remained impersonal. My brothers' friends shipped out for "over there." Twice the list was not impersonal.

The War ground on. The daily casualty lists echoed their cry of anguish.

I turned sixteen that summer; my older brother enlisted in the Army. We sent packages regularly. The cookies might be crumbled, the popcorn stale, but it was, nevertheless, a taste of home.

My high school asked us to prepare Christmas packages for the soldiers in Vietnam. I fixed a box of cookies and added small oddments of holiday cheer. Following instructions, I enclosed a card with my name, address, and age.

I couldn't know how my simple, gladly-given gesture would alter my life.

21 Dec 65
Your name and address were in the package my Company received....

I hadn't really believed I would receive a response—but here one was via air mail, dateline—Vietnam. The soldier writing thanked me and the other young people for our support and thoughts. He wished more people could understand how it was for the men to be in Vietnam, giving their lives for another country's freedom. It was signed, "A thankful G.I." Thus, the sober reality of the War was brought, literally, to my lap.

And I didn't know what to do with it.

Wrapped in adolescent shyness, I didn't answer immediately, but something—his loneliness, the need for understanding of his situation—unuttered, nevertheless there, kept nudging me.

Easter approached. Inspiration struck.

A friend and I sent a joint Easter package to "my Sergeant." We cast off a large box of cookies and candies, complete with chocolate bunny, without even knowing whether he was still there. We waited, guessing at the delivery date. For surely he'd receive it and answer. Wouldn't he?

9 Apr 66
With surprise and much appreciation we received your package ...

I responded promptly, thus beginning a correspondence of a rarity I would not fully appreciate until much time had passed, and the world and I had accomplished some of the maturing we both so needed.

His letters were ever cheerful, always appreciative of hearing from me, yet gave fleeting glimpses of the feelings of an American soldier stationed in a foreign country, fighting a war not always appreciated by its inhabitants nor by his countrymen safe at home.

2 June 66

I've been transferred to a detachment further south ... things are a lot different here ... They've been having riots all over Vietnam for a different kind of government....

Sometimes, he admitted, he got frustrated with the Army but most times it was good and he planned to make a career of it.

7 Sept 66

Since I received your last letter I've been traveling around the country. I was at Phan Rang ... your letter (June 17) never reached me until week before last....

18 Oct 66

So you knew your Dodgers would win the pennant....

He assured me he didn't mind being teased about the Giants losing the World Series because, even though he lived so close he "could look into the Raiders' playing field" in Oakland, California, "my team, Notre Dame, is going great guns." He'd played professional softball in Washington State with the White Center Eagles.

In that letter he admitted he was thirty, an age far removed from my seventeen years. He had one brother, and his father, and "that's all there is in my family." I was lucky, he said, having a mother to raise me.

Because he'd be coming home soon, his "whirly-bird" days were over. The men didn't fly when their time was short.

8 Nov 66

Received your very welcome letter. I just came back from a five-day escort into "Charlie's country."

29 Nov 66

Sorry have to run. Charlie—(V.C.) is playing around again... I'm back. Would you believe it is 2:01 in the morning. Charlie hits around that time or midnight.

Always, he passed lightly over the constant danger. The loneliness, however, could not easily be concealed. His close friends had been shipped home. He hoped to get home for Christmas. He closed by saying he had a trip ahead of him tomorrow which would take three or four days. I was to "take care."

20 Dec 66

It's almost Christmas and hardly seems so here without snow or anything out of the ordinary happening. Next year I hope things are different....

He mentioned pictures he'd had taken earlier that week. If they came out good, he'd send me some. If at all possible, on his leave he'd come visit my family and me.

It's so wonderful to have someone to think of you and to send a package or even a card....

In about sixty days, he'd be in the States or Germany, but "don't think I'll stop writing, for I will not. I'll keep you posted wherever I go." He closed by telling me to "be good, and write real soon."

I never heard from him again.

Over the next months, I wrote several times. My letters were neither answered nor returned to me.

What happened?

Common sense proffered many reasonable answers: He was married and dropped our friendship upon returning to the States. He was tired of writing and decided to end our correspondence.

He was killed.

For two decades my heart refuted each of these suppositions. If he were married, he had no reason not to admit it when he told me his father and brother were "all there is in our family." With the thirteen year age difference, we were friends. That simply. That profoundly.

The very tone of his writing belied the easy explanation he became bored and decided to end our letters. If it were so, he would have told me.

I never heard from his friends that he'd been taken prisoner or listed as missing. Neither did I ever see his name on one of those neatly-typed, so impersonal, casualty lists.

There was nothing to tell me that two decades later I would live in Washington State, where he once played professional softball for the White Center Eagles. So many twists of fate make up the whole of our lives.

When my daughter was sixteen, she sent a letter when her school asked the students to write Christmas notes to the men and women in the Service. A young man in the Navy responded promptly, and with appreciation....

Thus was my life across years of silent wondering. Until one day I was thumbing through the telephone book. "Veteran's Assistance" caught my eye. Would they—could they—help? A brisk professional voice informed me cautiously there was a possibility he could be located. He put me on hold "for a minute." I stared at the trees lining the sunlit street. Five minutes later, his voice spoke against my ear. "Ma'am?"

I gripped the receiver tightly. "He died in May, 1979."

Died? May 1979? All along, he'd been thirteen years older than I—in his mid fifties now, grey-haired, creases around his eyes. *But he isn't. He's only forty-three. Just three years older than I am now....*

"He was an old-timer in the Army," the voice continued. "He was in the service for over twenty years."

So he'd made it out of Vietnam and had continued in the Army—only to die at forty-three.

I thanked the voice, replaced the receiver, and stared at the sunlit street, the sharp lines of the trees strangely blurred.

What had happened all those years ago?

Once more I conjured up—and rejected—all the might-have-beens. Except one that I had refused to acknowledge. Now, at last, I had to consider that uncertainty. Like fine-spun cobwebs in the dark cavern of my soul where it resided, I could not brush it aside. And so I faced it.

After writing that last letter, bright with the hope of homecoming, did he become badly wounded and unable to respond to my letters? If so, after recovering, did a physical reason remain that he thought it better not to continue our correspondence? During those thirteen years, did he sometimes think of me and the friendship we'd shared? Questions— perhaps melodramatic. But today, forty-nine years unanswered.

My life is rich and full. But sometimes—sometimes I wonder. When Vietnam is mentioned or highlighted in a program, I am taken back to that bitter-sweet time when I glimpsed the power of the light he carried—the dream of peace, and home.

We never met. I never had a picture to know how he looked. But I am the richer because I received those eight letters.

Chuck—my friend for always—take care. Wherever you go.

The Symphony

By Ryann Murrin-DeSouza

Ringing in my ears,
Holding back my tears.
Losing hold of the song,
Hoping, hearing, fearing,
That the end is near.
Gripping the chair,
Fighting for air,
As the end finally nears.
Listening to the tune of the violin
And the strum of the cello.
They make my body tremble.
The feeling I get inside,
My body fills with joy and excitement,
The symphony that plays inside my soul.

Liva and Let Liva

By Sue Barizon

"A woman at a casino carries a bucket of her winnings onto an elevator occupied by two big black men. She becomes frightened, fearing she may be robbed. She then hears one of them say, "Hit the floor." She reacts as though she's about to be assaulted, flinging the contents of the bucket up over her head before dropping down on all fours. The man who spoke had simply asked what floor she was going to. All he'd done was offer to hit the button for her floor. She's embarrassed. The next day she receives some flowers along with a note from the black men saying it's the biggest laugh they'd had in years. The note is signed Michael Jordan and Eddie Murphy."

I heard David Letterman tell this story on his late night talk show and laughed harder than I know I should. I pictured myself on all fours suspended over the floor of that elevator surrendering to my own preconceived prejudice. Yes, I am prejudiced, but only moderately so. The five minute "How Prejudiced Are You?" test I took online confirmed what I already knew. What do you expect from a first generation Italian-American garbageman's daughter, raised in the San Francisco Bay Area during the turbulent 60s?

My earliest recollection of race differences came from the kitchen pantry. I was well acquainted with the smiling faces of Aunt Jemima and Uncle Ben. They shared a shelf with the likes of Betty Crocker, Gerber Babies, Chiquita Banana, and Chef Boyardee. Intuitively I knew I was Italian (my parents peppered their conversation with the language); these faces introduced me to a reality outside my homogenous suburban cocoon. One time I lined up the Aunt Jemima and Betty Crocker mixes side by side, and dared Papa to give his opinion on who was the better cook.

"C'mon," he grumbled waving off the challenge. Then, he eyed my bemused mother standing at the kitchen stove stirring a pot of polenta. He pointed a critical finger at Betty Crocker. "Not that one," he said. "She looks like your mother; she probably can't make toast, either."

As I grew, the kitchen table became the classroom for teaching family values, morals, and the nuances of prejudice starting with our own ranks. I heard the Sicilians dismissed as the "Blacks" of Italy, and the Genovese teased for their penny-pinching, likening them to the "Jews." The well educated Italians who looked down their noses on the peasant stock from which we came were condemned as "know-it-alls."

My easygoing father had a "live and let live" philosophy. I often heard him use the expression when he sat at the kitchen table with his neighborhood buddies nursing their five o'clock highballs. I'd listen as the bull sessions progressed to more controversial topics of the day and inevitably became heated. The fervent switchback from English to Italian was confusing, but I was a seven-year-old sponge and soaked up the language of prejudice just the same.

I never heard the "N word" spoken in our house. Blacks were referred to as "Negre," Chinese as "Chin-e-say" and Jews as "Judah." To my senses, the Italian versions buffered the harshness of the English ones I heard on the playground. I learned to read the clues that spoke to the character of the men sitting around our table; the way Ernie Griffin averted his eyes when Tony Lucca joked about having neglected to tip the "Negre" parking attendant. How Frank Ricci gave a half-hearted chuckle and poured himself another shot. How Mario Lombardi laughed as he pilfered through his wallet and threw a dollar bill across the table at Tony, "for next time, you cheap son-of-a bitch!" Then my Uncle Pete's arbitrary "They got to eat, too." How Papa, with his hang-dog expression and perpetually broken English brought closure, "C'mon boys, liva and let liva."

Years later I learned about the pockets in Papa's prejudice. Dinnertime conversation often centered on his garbage route in San Francisco's Fisherman's Wharf. He told stories of the City in the wee hours and the misadventures shared with his partners Rico and Leoni. Papa touted the threesome's camaraderie, mutual respect, and good humor – a necessity for packing a forty pound can up a flight of stairs and sidestepping rats the size of alley cats.

One night, after dinner, Papa produced a couple of photographs from his shirt pocket. They were taken by one of the customers on his route. The first photograph showed Papa with an easy smile sitting on the front bumper of a garbage truck. A slim built man with his arms folded and his cap brim turned up sat next to him. In the second photograph the same man posed standing in the open cab of the truck. A third man, square shouldered and proud sat next to the driver, my father, who was smiling playfully from behind the steering wheel.

"Who are these guys?" I asked Papa, pointing to the two black men.

Papa tapped their faces with a pointed finger. "That's Rico and that's Leoni."

"What?" I yelped. "I thought they were Italian!"

Papa gave my mother a dubious look. She had already seen the photographs and reacted with characteristic indifference to Papa's two black co-workers. "Susan, don't you know your father's English by now? Rico is Roscoe, Leoni is Leroy."

My mother had allowed a singular experience to taint her view of her fellow co-worker so radically that the woman was forever referred to in a whispered tone as "The Negress." Legend had it, that the poor woman had the misfortune to be paired with my mother in the gift wrapping department at Macy's during the holidays. No doubt, she had reached her limit waiting for my slow-as-molasses mother to finish tying the bow on a gift for a waiting customer. The woman's audacity at having snatched the package away before Mom could "fluff up" the bow had branded all black females for generations to come as "Negresses." A term I'm convinced mother acquired   from a B movie at a Saturday matinee starring Eartha Kitt.

As a teenager growing up in the 60s, I'd monitor the telltale vein on Papa's neck bulge as he watched the six o'clock news. His blood pressure registered contempt as our generation practiced its version of freedom of speech. In his eyes, the race riots, demonstrations, and protests boiled down to disrespect for authority. However, it was the looting, physical assaults, and random destruction of property that provoked the strongest reaction from my "live and let live" father.

"You wanna march through the streets, go ahead, MARCH to Timbuktu!" Papa would bark at the TV. Next, he'd turn to us kids sitting at the table eating our dinner, and ask, "But why you wanna go break some poor guy's window and steal him blind?" Then, through clenched teeth he'd spew forth threats of his own violence aimed at the young radicals. "Dirty son-a-ma-baygos! They oughtta take a machine gun, line up against a wall and... eh, eh, eh, eh, eh, eh!" There was nothing like the evening news coupled with Papa's accented machine gun fire for venting hostility towards your fellow man.

You might say Papa got a taste of his own medicine the day I delivered it to him, second- hand. A boy I had been dating for two years had finally suggested I meet his parents. When he came to pick me up, he took me aside and broke the news that I wouldn't be meeting them after all.

"Why not?" I asked.

"Because my mother wanted to know what your father did for a living," he said. "I told her he was a garbageman."

It was the first time I could honestly say I'd experienced prejudice. Although I was the intended victim, I felt strangely protective of Papa. Incensed, I wasted no time in running to tell him all about the grave injustice that had been heaped upon both of us.

"Who does she think she is? I'm a cheerleader for Christ's sake and the sophomore class secretary. I have a 3.0. Her own son doesn't even have a 3.0! Her husband is a pasty-faced accountant, for crying out loud. You probably make twice the money he does." I ranted on, determined to show Papa how little it mattered to me. Papa listened as he sat in his Barca lounger, staring straight ahead, not swallowing or blinking. The telltale vein on his neck remained conspicuously inactive during my "moderately prejudice" tirade. When I was spent, he looked up at me with his hangdog expression and gently shrugged,

"C'mon now. Liva and let liva."

215

Writing and Demons

By Mimi Vaillancourt

Demons. I've been thinking about them lately. Because I have them, I guess. They say all writers do. But what are demons? And with only a handful of unpolished pieces (and one neg- lected blog) to my name, can I truly call myself a writer? If I am a writer, does that automatically guarantee demons? Or, does the fact of my demons resolve the 'writers status' question? Is said question, my demon?

We've barely gotten started and, already, you see the problem.

Demons, nasty little buggers. Now, I know the subject of them has been addressed before, the consensus being—demons exist because, as Fran Lebowitz says, "Writers are trying to be God, and they can't." But even if that's true and writing is some epic struggle between good and evil, are we not duty bound (as cognizant beings of free will) to try and banish them in service to our higher calling? Indeed, who better to fight the dark side than pursuers of truth and light (writers)? Why be given a brain and not use it? Clearly, we must. So I will attempt to crack this nut, quell this creature and wrestle this beast to the ground. Failure to do so, and we sink to mediocrity, destined ultimately to dissolve in the primordial ooze. Definitely not an option.

Let's start with the word itself. Demons—one of those catch-all phrases, too general and all encompassing to have any meaning. A bland, cultural contrivance of the opiate variety; a sop for the masses, keep-it-at-bay word. Don't worry, be happy! (Turn their brains off and the more we can control them!) I mean--demons--just a word, right?

One must rail against banalities of language. One cannot fight something so ill defined.

My first encounter with demons came with my decision to write a play. Fascinated with creating a world, performed live, playwriting was a lifelong dream of mine. I had tried once while still employed in a demanding job, and failed. Couldn't I be one of those people who got up and wrote for two hours every morning before work, as dedicated, Real Writers did? Not a chance. Evenings and weekends, too tired. Years went by and the dream became a diminishing specter in my rearview mirror; a second litmus test of writers, starting early in life, failed.

But rules are made to be broken (at least one, anyway). After quitting my job, I did start writing. Now, having conquered one demon, another sprang up. Good for you! With zero encumbrances, and unlimited time at your disposal, you are undertaking the most difficult and noble of activities—writing! And who better to shine a light for the rest of us than YOU? I couldn't honestly disagree with this provocation. Writing was a luxury. But there was so much real need in the world. Shouldn't I spend my time volunteering? And what did I have to say about anything, anyway? I was no authority.

Reason prevailed, and I satisfied myself that the subject of my play, the News Media (aka. Fourth Pillar of Democracy!), and writing itself (the pursuit of truth), were noble endeavors. Even for a schmuck like me. It's the brain thing. Plus, I do like a good challenge and what else am I gonna do? Demon vanquished!

Once steeped in the river of writing, however, demons morph into ever more cunning forms.

For me, they gain entry during periods of intense experience which are often accompanied by a deep questioning of, what previously might have been considered, routine, ordinary events in life. For instance, on the spectrum of human experience, a dot labeled grief, or say, death, suddenly becomes blown up and magnified a thousand fold, presenting one with a giant, alien landscape of raw emotion and unfiltered, sensory input. What had been a simple marker, a tag, has now become a new and totally immersive experience unto itself. Such heightened awareness and keen sensitivity is manna to writers, and begs exploration. The writer must press on, treacherous though it may be, and aspire to new heights.

And it is the aspiring that is the key. It literally means 'fly high'. When you fly high, you are trying to touch God, and the closer you get to God (truth), the more acutely aware you become of the dark side. You? A mere mortal? Presume to KNOW THE TRUTH? Ha, ha, ha, ha, ha! You are traversing a steep, sharp (Himalayan) mountain ridge, an arête (of crossword puzzle fame),and thus, are high up, in rarified air, walking Gods knife's edge of this known world, at the intersection (or close to) of it, and the great beyond. You are striving for the pinnacle, but your birds- eye view makes perilously clear the presumption of your quest and all that comes with it. One false step—into the abyss; complete the journey—bliss.

But we are not on a mountain ridge. We are in a landscape of our minds making, our imagination. We do not know what lies beyond. We sense the pull of truth and it guides us. But it pulls us into an unexplored world whose contours are evanescent and ever shifting, like a funhouse mirror. Truth is elusive. The closer you get to it, the more fractured it becomes. And yet, you must decide. You are, in fact, God. And you know who will be nipping at your heels in no time. You? A mere mortal? Presume to BE GOD? Ha, ha, ha, ha, ha!

Thus, artists must have a heightened awareness. The rest are sleepwalkers, cowards. Oh my God, am I being arrogant? Wait, I have an escape hatch: I haven't proven myself as a writer yet, remember? And my demons are getting to me, thwarting that effort. Perfect! The circle is closed, the problem solved. But the dark side has won. I've dodged the accusation of arrogance, but sacrificed my writing in the bargain. No! I will write! I will beat you Beelzebub! You, and all your satanic, somnambulant proxies of this earth!

And this gets at (for me) one of the most insidious forms demons take. The simple act of daring to pursue your dreams. The old 'gap theory'. When you pursue your dreams, you set yourself apart from others, creating a gap. You are no longer their peer and have disrupted the social hierarchy. This forces them to look at themselves, which makes them uncomfortable, and they seek to close the gap. There are two ways to do that. They can pull themselves up (pursue their own dreams), or take you down. Guess which one they most opt for? Cowards. And if you try to defy them, they will train their negative energy on you like a laser. You? A mere mortal? Presume to BE SUPERIOR to your fellow mortals? Ha, ha, ha, ha, ha!

Demons, demons, demons!

Okay, lets try one last route. You dig down, go inward for the truth (for your art). To get at it, you must go deep, dredge everything up at once. The good, and the bad, real personal stuff.

Then, the hard part, you sort through it. Examine every craggy, nasty bit, up close, since it is the only way to find the nuggets, the pearls. Your defense mechanisms stripped away, you are face to face with your own reality. No short cuts. No coarse sifters to hasten the process. Every granule, important. The devil's in the details (as are the jewels)! Do you have the courage to do it? Or are you (me, in this case) the coward? You? A mere mortal? Presume to be an ARBITER OF TRUTH? Ha, ha, ha, ha, ha!

Yes, my truth! Demons.

The Story Lady

By Judith Shernock

At eight years old I had four friends who were as close as children get at that age. We lived on Seventh Street in Brooklyn and the Second World War was raging. Our neighborhood was blue collar. Parents were always much too busy to pay attention to us as long as we came home before dark.

We were five together and the other children called us The Seventh Street Gang. A gang needs a territory. We decided that ours began on the corner where the Apartment house stood, past the one and two family houses where we lived, to the white house with the beautiful garden where the story lady lived.

The territory ended there because the next lot was filled with rotted trees, overgrown bushes and a derelict building known as the haunted house. Nobody went into this scary place. Certainly not us.

Every Sunday morning at eleven ,we along with many others, gathered at the story lady's home where we sat on chairs, pillows and rugs to listen to Fairy tales told in an enchanting, soft voice. This was before TVs or Library story time so none of us had experienced a magic hour like this.

A tall, thin young woman named Maude always greeted each of us at the door. She would smile and say:

"Thank you for coming."

As we left, each of us chose a cookie from a large colorful tin box. The cookie came in its own little white paper basket. They weren't the ordinary "biscuits" we had at home but something creamy and sweet, each crumb delicious.

At first Annie , the white haired story lady, read sitting up. Her lovely voice transported us to long ago and far away where each of us grubby kids could become a princess or a knight on a white horse. As the months passed her skin became paler and she read to us lying on a large bed propped up by four lacy pillows embroidered with flowers.

One Sunday morning, our hands and faces washed, our hair combed, we arrived to a sad, different Maude. She told us that the story lady had died, but we were invited to sit with the body if we wished. My friends and I chose to stay. We were served a piece of cake and a glass of lemonade.. We stared at Annie, propped up by her embroidered pillows, her cheeks rouged and her expressive hands lying silently at her sides inside the wooden casket.

When her cuckoo clock struck twelve noon, four burly men came into the room. Maude said: "Say your goodbyes to Annie. You may touch her before you leave."

I lay a finger on her hand. It was icy cold.

We waited outside watching the men transport the casket into the black hearse. When they opened the huge back doors it seemed like a hungry animal opening its jaws to swallow its prey. Maude, wearing a large black hat with a veil hurried into the vehicle. The hearse will eat her too, I thought.

As we started to walk home I noticed that Maude had left the door ajar. I wondered if it was on purpose.

The next Sunday morning Eddie, our accepted leader, suggested that we go looking for hidden treasure in the haunted house.

"Maybe Annie hid some of her treasures there. That's why Maude left the door open.

There was nothing to steal. All the important things were squirreled away in the haunted house."

Eddie told us knowingly as if he had given it deep thought.

We followed him down the block but stopped at the story lady's house. We stared at it as if we were expecting Annie and Maude to still be there.

"I bet she's in Heaven." whispered seven year old Eugene, our youngest member and a fervent Catholic.

"She's telling fairy tales to the Angels," murmured his eight year old sister Jane. She was not enamored of her religion.

"My religion doesn't believe in heaven or hell."I said. What about you Charlie? "Well my Ma is Jewish and my Dad is Catholic. They call me a 'little Jewlic" he laughed. They say when I'm 13 I can choose for myself."

"So why do you go to Catholic school with us?" Eddie asked.

"Well my Dad says I'll have somewhere to run to if I decide to be a Catholic and my Ma says I'll know what I'm running away from if I choose not to be Catholic." He smiled in his charming way. We all smiled back at him. His good humor was catching.

Eddie scowled at us." We got to get going if we want to investigate this place."

He marched forward, his freckles and red hair seeming to put out a message of determination. We followed with less bravura.

The door to the haunted house fell in with a touch of a hand. We entered and looked around. Broken furniture was covered with rotting white linen covers. Huge cobwebs covered everything. Very little light entered through the filthy windows. Just enough for us to see huge rats running across the floor.

Janey grabbed Eugene's hand and said "We're late for Sunday dinner." She ran with Eugene dragging after her.

Eddie said "We probably need a flashlight to see where anything is hidden. Lets come back next Sunday with a flashlight."

Charlie and I followed him and said to each other:"Next Sunday at eleven." The following week only the two of us returned. Neither of us with a flashlight.

As we passed the Story Lady's house I noticed that the garden where the roses grew was filling up with weeds. There was an air of abandonment starting to creep around it.

"Where are they?" I wondered aloud.

"Who knows?" Charlie answered with a sigh. The haunted house awaited us.

We decided that the best place to look was in the ground where treasure was usually buried. There was a shed with old tools but the door wouldn't open. Charlie picked up a stone and hurled it through the window, shattering the glass into a million shards.

The noise scared us and we hid behind a rotting oak our hands clutching the filthy bark. After we stopped shivering we took the shovels from the shed and began digging..

Charlie began near the house and I as far from it as was possible.

I dug and dug and then... A miracle! A flash of silver appeared. It was an old Silver dollar. I screamed and Charlie ran over. He began digging next to me and found old coins but not a silver dollar.

Finally we tired and stopped. We swore a pinkie oath not to tell anyone what we found. Charlie said, "Next week again."

Although I agreed we never did go back. The silver dollar stayed with me as hidden among my things as it had been in the earth.

Looking back I understand why we were searching so hard. The story lady died but left something precious behind. It was inside us forever. We were looking for it in a haunted house. The supernatural melting into our reality, driving us to search when something precious was lost. Perhaps the small something I found supplanted the irretrievable. Something is always better than nothing. Perhaps the nothingness was death and the silver dollar symbolized life.

Children's minds... so simple and yet so complex.

An Education on a Greek Island

By Shelley Buck

Milapota, this valley reached by donkey trail from the main town on Ios, had its own taverna. Over a small cup of thick Greek coffee there in the morning, I learned that one of the foreign travelers had gone away and that his desirable camping spot—an empty cave—was now available. I claimed it.

The cave was just steps from the taverna. It was not a real cavern, only a hole about a dozen feet deep, one of many that pocked the porous rock face behind the taverna. It had an arched entrance and a flattish floor. To reach it, I climbed the ridge behind the taverna until I was more or less above the opening, then worked my way a few feet down the slope. Small bushes on the hillside made good hand-holds, and the descent from the ridge to the cave opening turned out not to be as sheer as it looked from above. Getting back down from the cave to the taverna at the beach was not as tricky as it looked, either. I could even slide down, if I didn't mind damaging my jeans.

In no time, I learned how to scamper straight down the rock face to the taverna with no trouble at all. There, I tasted and liked *mavro*—the dark island wine made by the proprietors. This "black" wine was not really black at all, but dark red.

I drank more *mavro*. I ate island dishes, *pasticcio*, a ground meat and macaroni dish under a thick layer of cheesy cream sauce, *kotópoulo*, a golden half-chicken on a platter. Food money was no longer a problem. I had no rent to pay. I marveled that I could live in a cave and still go out for dinner.

I learned how to climb straight up the rock face to the cave. The climb required good visibility. I bought a flashlight, so that I could stay later talking with other travelers at the taverna and still make it safely up the cliff.

I drank more *mavro* and grew more agile.

At the taverna, I learned how Greeks fix meatballs with mint. I learned to love the rice pudding from the cooler case. I learned how Greeks extend the battery life for their cassette recorders by pulling out the batteries and setting them in the warm sunlight like little plants. New batteries were expensive.

I climbed back to the high village and bought a kerosene lantern. I learned how to cook in my cave, pulling off the lamp's glass chimney to hold canned octopus in a metal drinking cup over the tiny open flame. A handy hiking sock became a potholder. I bought fresh-made yogurt and ate it with island honey drizzled on top. I learned the trick of squatting in the wild to pee, keeping hidden as cleverly as any deer though the only woods around were sparse olive trees and brush amid stones.

Cave life suited me. I was going back in time. Back to before the crowded commute from the hospital in San Pablo, before the SATs and college sit-ins, the anti-war demos and summer typing jobs. Back to stone and sea and olive trees....

I had written my mother about living in the cave. Apparently entertained, she sent me some traveler's checks, enclosed inside a carefully-worded letter commenting on how exciting my life was growing. Had my enthusiastic letter home wooed my cautious mother into endorsing a life of adventure, or was she merely terrified on my behalf?

I didn't know. I cashed the checks. I felt flush. Temptation grew. Maybe I could get to India.

Movie

By Jim Stanfield

Circled by a thousand Hollywooden Indians
our pioneering pilgrim's trek begins
He plods past lengthy shadows done
by rocks and unrelenting sun
For whose amusement was this battle staged
fearless forces for the ages raged
Who am I kidding, only me
whether a featured player or an extra be
Usurping nature's ageless monument
for some feeble writer's cemetery plot
Boot hill, the obligatory, inescapable cliché
To indicate a change of place or time of day
the educated editor inserts a lap dissolve
On just such tricks does continuity revolve
The stones of wood, the iron gate
A few choice words to stay my fate
I cleared the cobwebs from the lock
to leave my mark upon the rock
Not quite anachronism free,
I fly contrails across a cowboy movie sky
Which, through the framing lens he spied
cut, the dour director cried

How An Internet Date Saved My Marriage

By Dorsetta Hale

I was on the phone with a friend when my husband called on the other line. "He's calling to tell me he's on his way home," I said.

"Really?" my friend asked. "My mom would have done anything to have my dad call when he was coming home."

According to a census survey more than half the Americans who might have celebrated their 25th wedding anniversaries are separated, divorced, or widowed.

I wasn't surprised. There hasn't been a decade that my husband and I didn't consider parting ways, but by keeping busy and ignoring our problems, we've managed to keep it together. We have a contract. We wrote our own vows and promised to stay together as long as we both shall love. Damn vows! It's like Al Pacino said in Godfather 3, "Just when I thought I was out, they pull me back in."

Everything changes when you realize half your life is over, but a midlife assessment doesn't have to be a crisis. There are women who like their names and independence as much as their husbands like theirs and they've got the credit score to prove it.

And in the event of divorce, they survive.

When I telephoned my mother that her son-in-law and I were thinking about going our separate ways, she said "Life is short," code for "I'm busy right now watching people with real problems on the Maury Povich Show."

I then consulted my best friend who turned out to resemble the woman in the Bizarro cartoon picking out a greeting card in the divorce section with tabs reading "Idiot," "Don't Be Ridiculous," "Oh Please," "You Wish," "Surely You're Joking, "Oh Grow Up."

"Dorsetta, he's clean, dependable and he's not a freak," she said as if I didn't know. "He shares the bills! He's the perfect roommate. You don't understand. It's tough out there. Last night on an Internet date, I got dressed up for Matt Damon and wound up with Pee Wee Herman. He's also married to an illegal alien who kidnapped their child and is withholding visitation rights as ransom for her citizenship."

My friend who's been married 58 years understood what I was going through.

When she has a bad day she gets no sympathy either.

Saturday night, my husband and I decided to call a truce and have dinner together. He took me to a seafood restaurant close to his office. It was large, noisy and crowded with families and casual business types. While reading the menu at our table, I noticed another couple being seated next to us. He was wearing a suit and she so was she, but it was sexy and chic.

"You look just like your picture," he said loudly.

She was black, late 30's, slender, well dressed with a really nice weave. He was white, older, mid fifties and decent looking. He was fidgeting with his silverware and began talking a mile a minute. I think even from a table away, I could hear his heart beating. Within five minutes I knew everything about him and I wasn't even dating him. He's an intellectual, makes a good living and is divorced with grown children. He doesn't like to work out but he thought she looked like she did.

"Do you work out? You really do look just like your picture. I'm not disappointed at all," he said. "And I'm totally cool with the interracial thing. I work at Stanford, which is very internationally diverse. I know I'm older than you are but that's not a problem when you have common interests. Forgive me if I'm going on, I haven't been on a date in a long time and you're so attractive. You probably go out all the time. Have you used this Internet site before?"

The mother of a family across from us shot me a look as he went on and on and we smiled. He was a nice guy. He looked good, but that whiff of desperation was more overpowering than his cologne.

"I should tell you I'm loosing my hearing in one ear, so you'll have to speak up. I don't want to miss anything you say."

The poor woman hadn't been given the chance to speak more than two sentences since they sat down. When the waitress came to take their order, his date chose salmon, the most expensive item on the menu. He gasped in sincere surprise. He had no idea he'd never see her again.

My husband totally missed everything I'd overheard during the evening. He was busy enjoying his calamari. After dinner he left a large tip for the waitress just like he does at every restaurant we go to regardless of whether we receive great service or not. As he opened the exit door for me, I thanked him for the lovely meal. In the parking lot, I stepped back beside his car, knowing he'd go around me to open the passenger side door. And he did.

On the way home riding in the new sports car he bought and registered in his name only, I began to look at my situation from don't different perspectives. I realized that no matter how long I live, life *is* short. And if I were to cruise singles ads on the Internet, I'd definitely go out with him.

Soul Masala

Eternally. Forever. Always
By Ixchel Leigh

FIRE EPOCH

*In everyone's life, at some time, our inner fire goes out. It is then
burst into flame by an encounter with another human being. We
should all be thankful for those people who rekindle the inner
spirit.*
~ Albert Schweitzer

Once again I'm reinventing myself. Scraping off the flakes, the human
ones and the dead skin. Digging further to discover what I must let go of,
in order to get to the more of me. Honest. Naked. Vulnerable. Beautiful.
Creative. Strong. Fragile. Loving.

Life is a savory and sweet mix of experiences. Life is a masala.

The reality is if you want to feel all of life, you may also feel its angst. I
keep telling myself that the pain let's me recognize the bliss, just as the
most fragrant and delicate rose is accompanied by thorns. Life is for the
fearless, not the faint-hearted. If I have the courage to step into my
greatest fear, will I loose it all?

"Has it sunk in? Do you realize that you're moving to India?"

His voice startled me out of my *reverie*, these musings. I turned to
look at the face of the man who brought me to the airport. Sitting in the
International Terminal in San Francisco I felt numb after the last two
weeks of packing up my life.

Several times I've come to a fork in the road, which created a major
life change.

Selling many of my belongings was not new to me. Things were sold
or given away.

Other items still precious to me were fostered out to different family
members and friends.

Still unable to respond to him, my eyes were fixed on a young girl with
her father. The girl must have been about six. She danced and skidded on
the floor. Then twirled and jumped into her father's arms. Her face was
bright, full and open, like an Indian rose, *jawaa*, when it gently lifts its
face to kiss the sun good morning. The sun is all that the rose sees. The
joyous and giggling young girl looked to her father as the rose does to the
sun, full and trusting, swathed in the beauty of innocence and bursting
with light. And like the *jawaa*, the young girl was fresh and vibrant, just as
the rose when she releases her sweet nectar of fragrance in prayer to the
rising sun in the morning.

Oh, I'm moving to India, to their land! My stomach took a dive. Why
am I leaving this incredible man? Why now? There were feelings inside

me, feelings blossoming of the kind of love that I had sought all my life. Sometimes it felt like I had yearned for that love for eons. What an idiot I am! Did I make the wrong decision?

"No, it really hasn't hit me yet. I was just watching that young Indian girl over there playing with her father, and I had the very same thought, Shit, I'm moving to India! Maybe when I'm on the plane it'll sink in." His arm tightened around my shoulder. Both of us silenced by our thoughts.

All of this happened so fast. Two months ago this man and I discovered that there was more to our relationship than our platonic deep friendship had explored. The fire of intimacy was ignited and pretzeled in one another's arms, we were both ecstatic. A few days later I received a phone call asking me to bring my work to India.

"For a few weeks?" I inquired.

The caller said, "No, think of this as long term. We want you here for at least a couple of years. And that's just for Mumbai. Then we'll expand to our other spas in India."

What? How is this possible? Is this a cosmic joke? How can both the man *and* the dream job offer be happening in the very same week? And the job takes me to the other side of the world!

"You must step into your greatest fear," a dear friend told me.

What is my greatest fear? The question reverberated in my mind. Then a thought shot into my brain like an arrow from an expert archer. But the arrow that crept into my mind was not alone. It was quickly accompanied by another arrow into my heart, and a twisted lump in my throat. Ending with the feeling of being punched in the stomach by the end of a telephone pole. I found my greatest fear.

For nearly as long as I can remember, I wanted to feel joy and happiness with every part of my being. I wanted to feel passion in my spirit and in my body. I wanted a relationship that stimulated: spiritually, physically, mentally, emotionally, and creatively, for both of us to be all of who we truly are. Oozing with creativity, joy and wonder is everyone's birthright. Oh my God, does this sound like a pipedream?

Life is for the fearless, not the faint-hearted. If I have the courage to step into my greatest fear, will I loose it all?

Life is like a mix of savory and sweet experiences, a masala, a combination of ingredients that takes just the right amount of expertise to manifest a worthy outcome. Birthed in India, masala is the pungent, heady, brown colored mixture of ingredients, which adds flavor to any great meal.

But what idiot created the idiom, "Variety is the spice of life?" Too much chili in the mix and you get burned. Too much turmeric and everything is permanently stained. Too many spices in the concoction and you just get confused. Just like life, a little spice goes a long way.

So I decide to spice things up and move to India! We are the sum of our ingredients; our total experiences in life, just like a masala. Masala will transmute anything and in the process an alchemical transformation occurs. The individual ingredients in the masala together ignite, and ultimately unveil, something greater. Alchemy is like a masala. In the end, you finally create something fabulous and as valuable as gold. A blah meal becomes extraordinary. Vegetables, chicken, prawns, mutton, all are immediately transformed by a concoction of pulverized spices. The dry masala, *garam masala*, is known in the west as curry powder. Spicy cardamom, smooth cumin, zesty cinnamon, pungent turmeric, and hot chili, combine together to form an aromatic and delectable sauce. These are then combined with wet ingredients: vinegar, yogurt, tomato, or water, to create the transforming sauce. We are the sum of our experiences. We ourselves are a masala.

In my life I have collected experiences and pushed myself into growth, towards the gold. Often painfully, it is so much more comfortable to stay where you are, to keep the old habits of protection or defense, the old thoughts and indoctrinations from culture or family. It is easier to resist change.

I see my collage of experiences, all of which have created the, me, of today: As a kind of soul masala, as the result of my total experiences. The many different ingredients that are deeply carried within me for all eternity are the gold of who I am today.

No Good Deed Goes Unpunished

By Greg Erion

About 50 years ago someone had the idea of embedding a message board into the wall at the front of our church. It was a solid way at the time to get the word out on various occasions like:

Sunday Night at 7:00

An Evening of Praise Songs

Accompanied by Cadwalleder Blitts on his accordion

Or

Easter Cantata Directed by Minerva Wallop Who will be "Giving Her All on the Altar"

The board served its purpose over the years, although there were times when it succumbed to various mischievous incidents like the time when the song for Sunday morning service was anonymously changed from: "Up From The Grave He Arose," **to:** "Up From the Gravy Came a Roast"

It turned out a couple of boys I the youth group thought this was an absolutely hysterical thing they had thought up on their own and weren't shy about having "altered" the message. After this, a lock was put on the covering over the board.

As time went on the board fell into disuse, then disrepair. Several years ago I mentioned to the Board of Trustees we ought to do something about it. All agreed, but as the sanctuary was being remodeled, this relatively minor project fell by the wayside. About a year ago the subject was revisited. Again there was another job claiming precedence.

The more I looked at it the more I felt taking it out would not be a big job. I told the Board that I would remove the message board and stucco over it to match the surrounding wall. I knew how to stucco having done it previously – was it 1985 or 1975? I couldn't remember but I was positive my skill level could be rekindled.

On the big day I went to work. It needs to be noted that this wall, while at the "front" of our church is also the front of our Academy, which serves Preschool through Eighth Grade. At any given moment scores of children go from the school to our sanctuary for devotions or vise versa. As they moved past me, questions came:

"What are you doing?" Answer.

"Why?" Answer.

"What sort of tool is that?" Answer.

"Is it dangerous?" Answer.

Twenty-five minutes later, I was back to work. A couple days later I came back to do more work. Brain cells were firing on all cylinders trying to recall how I had stuccoed a wall – gosh has it been 30 years? Just got going and then:

"What are you doing?" Answer.

"Why?" Answer.

"Isn't it messy?" Answer.

"Do you like getting dirty?" Answer

This time the process was deterred half an hour.

I put the first two coats up, a layer per day and the outcome looked good. Folks who didn't know the difference between stucco and staccato meandered by and offered sincerely expressed encouragement. The third and final coat had to be thin, match the surrounding wall – a more exacting process. After applying it, I realized I had failed. Cracks developed, I needed to rip it out and start over. Just then one of our teachers, an innocent young thing, meandered by.

"What are you doing?" After telling her I was stuccoing the wall, she responded;

"Well I think you are doing a fine job."

Just after she left, I ripped the offending coat down. Another trip to Lowe's to get more stucco mix. A carefully applied layer put up. My contractor friend said I had to wait a week to see if cracks appear. They didn't. I was in the home stretch. Our maintenance guy came by and asked what I was going to do next. Prime the new stucco and paint it to match the wall (we have a bucket of matching paint in the maintenance shed).

"You should prime and repaint the whole wall to make it look better."

A fatal crack appears – not in the wall – but in plans to get this project done quickly.

Sounded good; I primed the wall. An inspiration hit me. The whole front of the church was tan. Just tan. What about an "accent" wall? I had some brown tint, the trim was green. Brown and green – even I – a novice on complementary colors knew brown and green worked. Visions of Robin Hood in Sherwood Forest flit through my mind.

So I tinted some tan paint and put it up. My wife Barbara did not like it. Too close to tan. The Board didn't like it, "We can't have everyone come by and decide they are going to alter (not altar) the paint scheme. They were right (I recalled someone volunteering to paint our youth room years ago. They did – glossy black. Five minutes in the room caused one to look for the nearest cliff). The Board was right but I was in a snit. This eyesore had been there for decades. I was trying to fix things up and suddenly everyone had become an expert.

A month passed. Barbara said one day, "The Board is right." Thought about it. Went to the Board and told them the paint color I used was wrong. I'd do it the way I wanted. If the Board didn't like it I would redo it in tan. Fair enough was their response.

So armed with that directive, my confidence in picking the right color shot, I went to Lowe's. Didn't want too brown, Barbara said. She picked a not too dark brown; I painted the wall and waited for comments. One of the Board members sidled up to me after church as I was standing in front of the wall. I instinctively asked:

"You don't like it do you?"

"Mmmmm, well you mentioned brown – this is sort of ahhh pinkish."

"Funny that is what Barbara said after it went up."

Brilliant inspiration came to the fore. Her husband, Steve is a painter. He would know. I corralled him and explained what I was trying to do. Asked his advice.

"Brown"

Pulled a bunch of paint cards out of his truck and picked one. Brown. Went back to Lowe's (they were getting to know me by name). Got a can of brown and repainted the wall. Looked good except that the other colors needed to be touched up. So I redid the green trim and painted the drainpipe that came down the wall.

I was done. Or so I thought. The Principal and Secretary came by to view my handiwork. What did they think?

"Well, mmm, it looks nice..."

"But?"

"We were just thinking the other day that maybe you could paint the stucco walls brown that are on each side of the door to the Academy."

"Sure"

Did it. Was back up a few days later to get something. Saw the Secretary.

"How does it look?"

"Good, ahhh, we were wondering, no never mind..."

"What?"

"The molding around the door— could you paint it green? Sets things off better"

"Sure"

Went to Lowe's for some green trim. Did it, spent a few days touching up. Came to church the next Sunday and my contractor friend sauntered over.

"Wow! What a great job. Liked how you accented the wall."

"Thank You."

"Have a suggestion."

"Yes?"

"Well the pipe coming out of the wall – the paint is sort of faded. What if you repainted it like it originally was. Fire engine red."

"Sure"

Back to Lowe's. If they had a "frequent shopper" award, my now bosom buddies at Lowe's would have put me in for it. Got fire engine red. Some call it whorehouse red. An alternate appellation that was gradually growing on me. Painted said pipe. Contractor friend came by to say what a nice job I did. Then mentioned it would be great if the piping on the grassy area in front of the wall could also be painted. Began dreading seeing my contractor friend. Looked at the structure, not only did it need fire engine red, but a good coat of glossy black on certain parts of the pipe would be appropriate. Lowe's had glossy black. Went on my weekly sojourn to get it.

I've been having dreams I was in Italy about five or six hundred years ago.

"Hey Mike, we got a paint job for you. It's a ceiling in town. In a chapel. You could probably knock it out in a few weeks. We have a couple of suggestions…"

The World

By Ryann Murrin-DeSouza

The world,
It's what you make of it.
To make it in this world,
You have to concentrate,
On the hard and good times in your life.
But remember to do things,
That you know are right.
That is good for you and others too.

The world,
Is a great place,
If you make it that way.
If you believe,
And are true to yourself.
The world could be a greater place,
Than you would ever think,
Or ever imagine.
You only live once.

Needle-Shy

By Jamie Miller

I have a young friend I've never met. Not in person, at least. There's nothing odd about that these days: Having a long list of Facebook Friends is hardly unusual, even if we might not even recognize many of them if we passed them on the street. We know the things that our friends choose to tell us, and they may show different personalities to every friend. I know, for instance, that my young friend is a very pretty, very bright, thirty-and-a-few years old girl (a "girl" at least to me, with my 78 year history.) She has two little daughters, the younger about two. She is also what I would term an "antivaxxer," implacably convinced that getting her two girls immunized against childhood diseases would expose them to great risks, much greater than leaving them to trust in the "herd-immunity" resulting from a sufficient fraction of their age-group having been immunized to prevent epidemics taking hold. I've argued to her that this is a bad choice, that the medical community's position is quite rational, that regardless of the stories she quotes, the risks of vaccinating her girls are less than continuing as she is. She does not react well to this.

The conversation is at an impasse. I give up. I'm going to "unfriend" her and post this on an open forum. She's a lovely person and I don't want to harangue her or distress her any further, or waste any more time for either of us, but I know things that she doesn't really understand and, by the grace of God, she never will.

I remember things...

I remember a person from the county coming to our house when I was quite young and nailing a "Quarantine" placard to the house, just outside the door. I had measles. I couldn't leave and no one beyond the immediate family was allowed to enter. I remember boredom and itching that went on and on.

I remember a time when I wanted to play with a friend, but his house had a placard like mine, except it was for whooping cough ("pertussis", it's called now.) The sound of my friend's little brother coughing inside the house was the most frightening thing I had heard at that young age. The mere sound of whooping cough is terrifying. It is seldom heard, these days.

I remember my mother worrying about mumps. Not only were they painful, but she was concerned that boys my age sometimes were rendered sterile by the disease. I remember her looking into my mouth and prodding the glands at the back of my jaw for the onset of swelling. I don't know what she would have done if I had shown signs of the disease: there was no cure. But if the MMR vaccine had been around, I have no doubt that my mother would have had me first in line to get it.

I remember how my home town's swimming pool was closed at the first suspicion that an outbreak of poliomyelitis may have reached our remote corner of Wyoming. I remember the dire warnings that included pictures of victims confined in "iron lungs" and a traveling exhibit with a machine that wheezed and sighed as it alternately sucked air into its occupant's lungs and then expelled it. I remember the impression that it made on me that a person might be in an iron lung for months or years without being able to use his hands even to turn the pages of a book! We gladly accepted our sugar cubes carrying doses of oral polio vaccine, and just in case that didn't work, we were also treated about the same time with the new injectable vaccine. After the iron lung presentation, I remember that even the shot didn't seem so bad!

I remember a friend in college who had suffered from polio, and walked clumsily wearing leg braces that had to be snapped into place before he could stand. He was a jovial fellow, and I remember a conversation one day when he remarked that he had been out with his girlfriend just the evening before the onset of the disease. He had a feeling, he said, that he shouldn't kiss her good-night. I offered what I thought might be a joking comment, that if he had kissed her, maybe they would have ended up in the hospital together. He turned suddenly serious: "No. I wouldn't wish polio on my worst enemy. It's just agony that goes on and on."

I remember my wife's best friend who died not long ago. She had contracted polio back in those days before immunizations and it had seriously damaged one of her lungs. She was vivacious and outgoing but short of endurance in any sort of physical activity. Senior classes in the YMCA swimming pool became her major source of exercise. For the last few years, she was tethered to her oxygen tank. The last couple of times we saw her at her house, she sat slumped in her easy chair, barely responsive.

Polio finally killed her some 60 years after it first appeared in her life.

I do not plan to tell my young friend, the anti-vaxxer, about any of this. It wouldn't do any good: Her mind is firmly made up. It would just antagonize her. Instead, I am about to "Unfriend" her, then post this where someone who does not have an already-fixed opinion on the subject may find it convincing.

Good-bye, young friend, and God bless you. May you and your little girls never have a chance to learn in person these things I remember so clearly.

The 1990s, Golden Era of Open Mics in San Francisco

By Camincha Benvenutto

Sacred Grounds Café has always been at 2109 Hayes and Cole. Parking in that area in the '90s was difficult but not impossible as it is now. Centrally located. Serviced by several Muni lines, surrounded by apartment buildings. Small restaurants, Laundromat, boutiques. A few blocks from   University of San Francisco and St. Mary's Hospital.

That time had passed showed in the furniture, booths, tables and chairs still covered in bright vinyl of matching colors. Alba became a regular there at Bob Randolph's invitation. The friend she had met at THE BLUE MONKEY. Retired business man, still had interests in Japan, and was full of plans for the Open Mic he was managing at Sacred Grounds. A historical venue he felt enormous respect for because in the '50s the Beats had also hung out there.

A big want ads board near the entrance gave a warm touch to the place, informed the community that the Café's management had space for all their concerns and needs. The restaurant consisted of two rooms, one large, one small. A wall fashioned like a service counter separated them from a rectangular kitchen. Turn left and find yourself facing a narrow corridor and a couple of steps from the bathroom. Obviously like most public places in San Francisco in former lives, the Café had been something else—an apartment, a retail store, a warehouse.

But soon you didn't pay attention to any of that because the spoken word, the camaraderie, was energizing, delightful. Alba absorbed it all and used it in her writing, her short stories, poems. Figuring she had enough material was inspired to publish a chapbook. Did it with the help of friends. While the   readings were going with great impetus under Bob's direction, Alba's chapbook, *Where I Come From   Where I am Going/De Donde Vengo a Donde Voy,* was born. Had twenty-five copies printed. She was on fire. Sold them all in one month, which surprised Alba and every one else. Her former Professor at San Francisco State University, Dr. Michael Krasny had written her a most generous flattering introduction: *"... wants to take in continents and hemispheres. She is a woman of extraordinary vitality, passion and a hunger for life. Read her, enjoy her." Michael Krasny*

FORUM, KQED FM.

And so her life because of her writing progressed, bringing her joy putting her in touch with interesting   people, some homeless, some ladies of the night. Some Grammy winners. Some best seller authors. Her boyfriend, Alain, whom she had met at The Blue Monkey. And there were always friends ready to help, praise. Through all these Alain, smiled and when they got together made passionate love, even if they were only talking, deciding what movie to see. In between there were doubts, times

233

of silence and always her poems giving meaning to it all. So when one day their relationship was no more she had the

Then one day Bob decided to give up managing the Open Mic and passed it over to Jehanah, a regular words she had written, ...WHAT HAVE YOU DONE with the gifts I gave you?/ my body, laid down for you to explore: earlobes,/eyelashes, toes, arms, legs, breasts that I cupped /in my hands and a lovely woman, poetess. To Alba she was The Eternal Flower Girl, the way she dressed, her celebration of nature. From the beginning she made the Open Mic into an even greater success. Ran it with a smile, generous praise, and surprise to all, also a steel discipline Alba had never imagined she was capable of. And went on to publish the work of the readers with the expert, selfless help of Teddy Weiler, Jim Watson-Gove, Eleanor Watson-Gove, The Sacred Grounds Anthology (a Cooperative quarterly). The foreword said in part: The Sacred Grounds Anthology is being published to celebrate and promote the weekly reading at the oldest open mike reading series in San Francisco. This being the case we would prefer that all poems submitted for publication be read at Sacred Grounds and then presented to one of the editors at the reading. . . .

It was an exhilarating time for all involved. Alba often arrived at the Café to hear, We are being interviewed by UP, or you are famous, and a friend would brandish the Bay Guardian where, Jennifer Joseph, The Literary Critic had given her latest chapbook a glowing review which said in part: *...frames the ordinary in a way that makes it extraordinary and that is real talent.* Meantime the Anthology was published. Alba, most thankful and hard working, contributed to every issue. Some of her pieces became favorites:

From tome # 1 her short fiction, *ABUELITA ...she came to see me this morning, let me see her. For she has been dead for decades . . .*

From tome #6 her poem, *Claiming the night ...sounds, colors and streams of city lights,/ . . .*

From tome #9 her 1st person account, GINSBERG at BERKELEY ....love.../I'm the King of Men/all human son of Jewish parents./How petty that I sing of love, do I dare...?

And the last one was, tome #14 dated 2003, is another 1st person account, A GREAT ENTERTAINER, GORE VIDAL... Aaron Burr, a character of immense charm. An anti-hero. And the writer, what kind of man was he? . ..

Tome #14 Jehanah told her, We have decided not to publish the ANTHOLOGY anymore. The cost has become enormous. It made sense. Alba was grateful she had her treasured copies.

Time went on. One day, it must have been an e-mail, a notice about all getting together in Oakland to celebrate Jehanah's retiring from managing the Open Mics. Every one was to join her afterwards for dinner, which for Alba was impossible. She had to get up early for work and be alert in the court room, all day long. Alba avoids bridges, long freeway rides, but she made it that evening. The reading-celebration finished, went to Jehanah, hugged. Tears in their eyes, talked. Alba explained she couldn't stay, pressed $20 in her hand saying, Buy yourself something fun. for me, she said.

They kept in touch off and on by phone. Alba was busy with her writing life, promoting her novel, *As Time Goes By*, keeping up with all her obligations and pleasures. Jehanah was enjoying her activities nature-spiritual. And having her earlier poems reprinted.

Then, November 15, 2010. The phone call, followed by an e-mail: Her daughter just let us know, Jehanah died last night in her sleep.

Meantime, Sacred Grounds Café with its Wednesday nights Open Mic is alive and well thanks to loving volunteers. Thank you very much.

Proudly Addicted

By Jo Carpignano

I've been plagued with numerous addictions. Some were overcome, others are so much a part of me that they seemed impossible to conquer, others I treasure, and take pride in preserving.

After graduating from high school, I worked in an office with ten men, all of whom were dedicated smokers of pipes, cigars and cigarettes. Until then, I hadn't planned to smoke, but since I continuously reeked of smoke anyhow, I decided to legitimize the stench by taking up the habit myself. It was difficult at first, with the choking and coughing as my lungs objected strenuously. However, I persisted until the discomfort receded, and the habit was firmly imbedded. Continuing this addiction for twenty years, I understand completely, how difficult it is for those who smoke, to quit. Now, I empathize, but hope that I stopped soon enough.

Another of my addictions is almost as harmful, and much more difficult to control. I am addicted to food. I like to cook it, smell it, admire its appearance, feel it in my mouth, savor the taste, enjoy the chew, then gleefully swallow it. Understanding that it's impossible to stop eating entirely, I feel that I should be better able to limit my consumption. My weight, teetering on the verge of obesity, is clearly unhealthy. There have been times when I seemed better able to exercise control of this addiction. At Weight Watchers, I learned how to regulate portions, make better choices, select wisely, and engage in physical activity more often. With this regimen, there was success for extended periods of time. Then holidays arrived, and with them was the first excuse to suspend my better judgment.

Then there are those addictions I prefer not to give up. The compulsion to be neat and orderly is useful, and not the least harmful, so why should I give it up? When searching for needed items, I know where to look. When wanting to store something, I have a place where similar things are stored. My labels on boxes help avoid the need to search endlessly for something I need.

The other day, expecting rain, I wanted to find my plastic rain cap. I knew I had ordered one from a catalog not long ago. Now where would one store such a thing when the rainy season in my geographic location is so brief? My first search was in the box labeled "Travel Items." Although I found containers for toiletries, soap boxes, zippered bags, notebooks and many other items for travel, the rain cap could not be found. Since I could think of no other place to look, I gave up. Later it was found along with a sleep bonnet an shower cap in a box labeled, " Makeup and Toothpaste." Oh well, I guess it doesn't work every time. Nevertheless, I like being well organized.

The rain cap I placed in the box labeled "Travel Items" so I could find it the next time I looked for it. I put the sleep bonnet in my bedroom, and the shower cap in the bathroom.

I take pride in another of my addictions, but am puzzled by how this particular habit developed: I feel compelled to be on time. There is a clock in every room, and I own at least ten wrist watches. Each of the watches have large numbers and dark hands to assure that I'll not be late. Most of the time, being prompt is not a problem. Recently however, my favorite watch, the one with the red band (to match my red sweaters) had a sluggish battery. Although I arrived at my first meeting on time, the defective watch caused me to misjudge the time for departure, and I remained too long. Upset by this failure to arrive on time for my next appointment, I considered writing a note of apology to the individual who was inconvenienced by my being tardy. I thought better of this, when I realized that writing the letter would make me late for another meeting. This particular addiction has been awkward at times, but you may be assured that I will continue to take pride in being on time.

Addictions are habits that become ingrained over time. Although many may be harmful, and some may become annoying, there is much to be said for those that serve a good purpose. I regret that I became addicted to smoking, and my food addiction will continue to be challenging for the rest of my life. But on the whole, I take pride in many of my addictions.

Cups of Tea

By Gloria Bares

I walk next door to the home of my friend Miho bringing a small gift to her new baby. She greets me at the door smiling. Outstretched hands touch me gently.

Miho's Japanese father enters the room and kneels at the low table, shoeless, dressed simply in loose black pants, and a white shirt. He is a widower, exactly my age, and 5 foot in stature. He does not speak English. Lean, wiry, hair still black as ebony. His eyes concentrate on his hands folded in front of him.

When he looks up at me, I am ten years old again, remembering the slant-eyed, buck-toothed faces of pilots attacking Pearl Harbor, or flying Kamikaze suicide bombers. He is my enemy. A Jap infantryman marching our soldiers at Bataan, fighting in Guadalcanal or New Caledonia. At home I am scared of submarines off the coast of Los Angeles. Scared of blackouts. Proud of my father, a block air-raid warden.

Miho's father leaves. He returns carrying a round black tea tray. Kneeling at the low table, he pours tea silently from a small pot into tiny cups. He does not speak, just nods his head slightly as he hands each of us a cup, one at a time, ceremoniously. His movements are deliberate. Purposeful. Yet, no eyes meet. Steam curls lazily in the cooler air. He offers tiny pastries on a square black plate. In the plate, an elegant white flower lies on a bright green leaf reminding us of the ever-present beauty in each moment. He is calm among strangers, strong within himself.

What do his eyes see as he looks at me, his "enemy" of 63 years ago? Does he think of the Enola Gay in the sky? The mushroom cloud of the Atom Bomb? Does he recall pictures of the destruction at Nagasaki, Hiroshima? Was there a sister so burned she fears she could never be loved? A lost father, brother, cousin or nephew?

Our eyes meet as we sip our hot green tea. Old memories dissolving as sugar, invisible in my cup. Time, the ultimate steeping process, has diluted my fears. And fear is harder to find teacup to teacup.

House of Comedy

By Edie Matthews

CHAPTER ONE
Rules of Comedy

A fanfare of flashing lights and pulse-pounding music signaled the start of the show at Rooster T. Feathers Comedy Club. Over the loud speakers a voice boomed, "Put your hands together and welcome—MADDIE QUINN!" The audience's applause reverberated through the club as a trim ash-blond stepped onto the stage.

Maddie tried not to squint under the spotlight blazing down on her like a meteor from the cosmos. This would be her last chance to perform before returning to Hollywood for an audition that would determine her destiny.

RULE: Establish you're funny.

Warming up the crowd was a challenge, especially if you're not famous—yet. An unknown comic has two-to-three minutes to prove they're funny before people will relax and enjoy their performance.

When the clapping subsided, Maddie paused an extra beat until the chattering and glass clinking died down. She flipped up her collar and glanced over her shoulder like Sam Spade in the *Maltese Falcon*. "I've got a secret."

A woman sipping a Gin Fizz stopped in mid slurp.

"I found a moisturizer that really works—you know the white cream in Twinkies?"... Feminine laughter bubbled up from the crowd. Maddie continued in earnest, only a trace of glee in her eyes. "I figure anything with a shelf-life of seventeen years has got to be good for my skin." She frowned, jabbing a fist on her hip. "Men don't worry about wrinkles or gray hair. It makes you distinguished. Just one of the reasons you don't understand us. Ladies, am I right?

Say 'Yeah!'"

"Yeah," replied some of the women.

"In fact, there's a LOT about us that men don't understand. Say 'Yeah!'" *Come on ladies, get with the program—we're on the same team.*

"Yeah," came a stronger response.

Maddie lifted the microphone from the stand and began pacing the stage, revving up her delivery like an evangelical leading a revival. "Men understand why we like to shop.

EVERYBODY say 'YEAH!'"

Some of the men joined in. "Yeah!"

That's it guys—I'm not here to hurt you, just telling the truth. "You see fellas, most women were born under the sign of VISA," she slowly raised an outstretched arm, "with Master Card rising."

"YEAH!" replied the audience without prompting.

RULE: Never begin with new material.

If the new jokes bomb, the audience concludes you're not funny, and it's a Herculean task revising their opinion. Later in your set, you can try new bits, and if they flop, you can still recover. Tonight, however, Maddie smoothly segued from one bit to the another in a routine that had been polished and practiced in countless venues.

"My husband found out what turns me on. He put a sign over the bed that says: CLEARANCE!..." She purred, "Gets me hot every time." Masculine laughs trickled in and Maddie breathed easier.

"I love to shop, especially for shoes—you always wear the same size no matter how big your butt gets."

During the laughter, she took a moment to gaze over the kaleidoscope of humanity. The dimly lit club made it difficult to decipher individual faces beyond the front tables, but the laughs and guffaws from the blurred spectators in the back of the showroom boosted her confidence and her nervousness diminished. Then to her left, she spotted a chinless man with a blank expression. The Face. *Not one of those. Okay, some people take a little longer to warm up.*

RULE: Create a memorable persona.

Maddie's real life as a wife and mother inspired her routine, though not as cartoonish as Phyllis Diller or as whiny as Roseanne Barr.

"I've been married to the same man since I was eighteen!" There was a spattering of applause and comments among others. "I know, a few of you are impressed, while some are thinking, 'What kind of a PERVERT are you?'

People ask me, 'What's the key to a successful marriage?' First, we never go to bed angry." Maddie shrugged, "Well, a couple of times I kept him up for a week ... to straighten out a few things. ... A little sleep deprivation is very effective.

RULE: Make the men laugh too.

Men laugh louder, and strangely, if the men feel alienated, the women stop laughing. Maddie attributed it to a woman's protective instinct because with an all-female crowd, it was never an issue—they laughed uninhibited.

"What keeps a marriage going? *Great* sex."

The men in the audience whooped and whistled. *Of course, they love that topic.*

"The truth is my husband is the only one I've been intimate with. So I don't know." She shrugged, "But he keeps telling me," she gave a thumbs-up "he's the BEST!"

"They all say that!" shouted a woman in back.

RULE: Don't slam a heckler until he deserves it.

If you're too harsh too soon, you alienate the audience. The woman speaking out was enjoying herself and not disruptive (at least so far). Besides, the worse hecklers were men, and she was prepared for those occasions. As the heckler became more obnoxious, the audience became annoyed and eager to see him get his comeuppance. That's when Maddie queried the crowd: "Clap if you'd like this person to shut up?" Following an enthusiastic response, she'd address the culprit: "Pal, you should save your breath for later when you need it to blow up your date." People guffawed while the heckler fumed in silence.

Maddie held up a hand. "Don't get me wrong—I have a wonderful husband—he even cooks." She hesitated, "Only, he likes to experiment: He made beef stew one night, ran out of vegetables, and threw in a can of fruit cocktail." People groaned. "Right away, the kids spotted the neon cherries. 'DAD!'" said Maddie in a child's voice, "'the tomatoes are bionic.'... Call me finicky, but I don't want to eat meatloaf stuffed with Lucky Charms. ... Once when I went out of town, I said, 'Honey, for the kid's lunches there's peanut butter and tuna fish." Maddie nodded, "That's right—he mixed them! TOGETHER!... The kids brought the concoction home—and he MADE THEM EAT it." The audience groaned. "His mother said, 'It sounds healthy to me.' Oh, really? I'll make you one now. Go ahead. Chow down. *Bon appétit.*"

Maddie continued riffing, pelting the audience with the setup, punch line, and topper.

RULE: Structure jokes so they end with the "punch word."

This way the audience doesn't get the joke until you've spoken the final word.

"In all fairness, I admit I've had a few mishaps." She reconsidered, "Okay, calamities. Once I created molten lava—accidently, of course. I was trying to make chocolate candy. Forget scouring that pan; I BURIED it! Have you done that, ladies?"

"YEAH," said Miss Slurpy saluting Maddie with her drink.

"Ticks me off, cause the dumb dog still digs it up and BARKS at it. *Ruff! Ruff!*... Shut up, Sparky. ... Tattletale. ... My motto is: if at first you don't succeed—order pizza.

RULE: Establish a friend in the crowd.

This person becomes a representative that the audience that they can relate to.

"Don't get me wrong—I *love* being married." She pursed her lips, wary. "Except when my husband sends me on his *little* errands." She spoke directly to Miss Slurpy. "Like to an auto-supply store—where you don't have a clue *what* you're talking about—and there's always that guy, GOOBER, ... who tries to make YOU feel stupid. ..."

Miss Slurpy nodded in agreement.

"Right away I knew I was in the wrong store—because you fellas have cleaning products named 'Gunk' and 'Goop'?" She raised her brows quizzically. "Isn't that like having a deodorant named B.O.?... or a toothpaste named Driller?"

Maddie smiled, looking fit in snug Levi's; a black vest over a white-shirt blouse framed a red tie splattered in black like a Jackson Pollack painting. (She had a dozen variations of this outfit.)

RULE: Never step on a laugh.

Delivery and timing are as critical as the material. When people are laughing, WAIT! If you keep talking, people stop laughing, afraid they'll miss what you're going to say next. So Maddie stayed in suspended animation after each punch line until the audience was ready for the next joke.

"I don't send my husband on my little errands." She pressed her lips together, pondering. "Okay, once I did. Noooo, *not* that one. Ever see a man accidently walk down *that* aisle of the grocery store?" Nonchalantly, she strolled the stage browsing, suddenly her eyes widened as though spotting feminine hygiene products. "Yikes!" and she quick-stepped away. She stopped and glared. "It's life, men! Get used to it—I'd like to see one of your species bleed for five days and survive. That would make headlines." In the modulated voice of a newscaster, Maddie said, "Scientists are calling it an unexplainable phenomenon. Five days! And the man is still alive ..." Holding the mic in one hand and the other hand on her hip, she said, "Come on, fellas. Be a MAN! Prove your love! Slap a box of Tampax on the counter! In full view! The giant size!

Super absorbent for heavy days! The pink package with the purple posies!"

In her peripheral vision, she caught a glimpse of the Face. It was still frozen. Just like a male: He'd be falling off his seat if I were telling dick jokes, but mention periods, and he's squeamish—well at least everyone else is laughing.

"Actually, once I sent my husband on one of my errands—to buy nylons." She fluttered her eyelashes and cooed, *"Honey bun,* would you *purty* please get me the Hanes, sandal-toe, re-enforced heel, control-top, with the cotton-crotch? Poor guy came home dazed. 'Are you an A? Or a B?'"

RULE: Asking questions keeps the audience involved.

The laughter settled, and Maddie waited a beat before transitioning to another topic. "Do we have any Catholics here tonight?"

Silence.

"Don't panic. We're not hearing confessions. Oh sure, like, LOCK THE DOORS!

Tonight we're excommunicating sinners." She gestured off stage, "Father O'Malley, bring out the sackcloth and ashes!" Maddie clasped her hands in prayer and stammered, "Ba-ba-bless me, Father, it's been te-ten, no tw-twenty years since my la-la-last confession. ..."

She smiled. "Let's try it again: By applause, who survived Catholic school?" Across the showroom groups of people clapped.

"I went to Our Lady of No Mercy. ... I'll never forget Sister Gonzaga." Maddie shivered. "The kids called her Sister Gozilla. ... My grandmother is a very strict Catholic, and she loves to talk. Once she outtalked a Jehovah's

Witness. ...Followed him out the door and down the street. Tried to give him one of her own pamphlets." Maddie mimed handing out a flyer. "'Have you heard about Saint Jude? He could help you.' My grandmother knows all the Saints and who to pray to depending on your problem. Like if you lose something: pray to Saint Anthony. If the dog is sick: Saint Francis of Assisi. So I figured, if you burn yourself: Joan of Arc ... "

"By applause, how many here have kids?" About half the people responded.

"Being a good Catholic girl, I had three kids by the time I was 22." She scratched her head. "I think we had too much rhythm ... And I can't even dance ... " Maddie executed several klutzy gyrations.

RULE: Vary your gestures and use an array of tonal qualities, raising and lowering your voice, and emphasizing key words.

"You know, there are signals you've been around small children too long. Number one: you have diaper bags that match your outfits. ... How does that happen?... Number two: you ask adult company if they'd like a glass of wa-wa. ... Number three: While taking a shower, you sing 'Itsy Bitsy Spider.' Maddie snapped her fingers and began a jazzy rendition: *"Itsy bitsy spider went up the spider spout."* Snap, snap. *"Down came the rain and watched the spider out."* Snap, snap. ... "Ladies, it's time to get out of the house! I could hardly wait for my son to start school. I did my best to prepare him: 'You must be brave. You must be a big boy.' On the first day of kindergarten, he checked out all the kids! All those toys! The milk and cookies!—and he was GONE!" She sniffled and waved, "I'm leaving now." Then blubbering, "WAAAAH!" In a child's voice, she said, "Mommy, you must be brave. You must be a big girl.'"

"You need to enjoy your children while they're small because before you know it, you have TEENAGERS!" She imitated Rod Sterling, "You've lost control of your life. You're now entering the *Twilight Zone.*" She hummed the iconic theme song. *"Dee de de de—dee de de de.*

... Teenagers go through what I call the 'dinosaur syndrome.' That's when they look big, they talk big, but the brain hasn't caught up with the rest of the body. ... And I think God intentionally makes teenagers obnoxious, so when they leave home, you don't feel so bad."

RULE: End with your strongest material.

Maddie started her close with material honed and hewed in hundreds of clubs on hundreds of nights. She delivered each line like a maestro conducting the final movement of a concerto.

"They say boys are easier to raise then girls. I was inclined to agree, until my son started driving. He's had so many tickets, they put him on a time-payment plan. ... Now he uses the Highway Patrol as a credit reference. ... While driving on a new overpass I said, 'Son, enjoy it, YOU paid for it.'... And his ROOM!" She shook her head, "I think the elephants go there to DIE—Late at night I can hear them." She flung her arm up in front of her like the behemoth trumpeting, *"BBBAAAPPPHHHFFF!"* She called out, "TARZAN! We've found it—the lost graveyard of the elephants!"

RULE: Conclude with a callback to a previous joke.

242

Like a running gag, a reference to a previous joke empowers the material.

"A burglar broke in my son's room and left a vacuum cleaner. ... Under his bed I found his Yogi Bear lunch pail from the THIRD GRADE!" She fanned the air. "The thermos still had MILK in it. ... But," she gave the A-okay sign, "the Twinkie was all right!"

The audience's laughter and applause rained over her, and she felt refreshed and euphoric. This was the response she needed at her LA audition to become one of the regular performers at Quip's Comedy Club and move her career in striking distance of success.

The house emcee, a young man in a red tuxedo t-shirt, vaulted onto the stage. "Let's hear it again for MADDIE QUINN."

When Maddie reached the back of the club, the Face exited the restroom. His demeanor was as wooden as a ventriloquist's dummy. "You were really funny."

"Oh, thanks." Was it possible he'd had a root canal and the Novocain hadn't worn off. Her worse nightmare would be an audience filled with frozen faces on the night of her audition.

She entered the green room, a small waiting area for performers painted the same shade of green frequently found in mental institutions. An assortment of half-empty beverages and a partially eaten plate of nachos cluttered the table.

"Nice job," said Artie Harris, the headliner, waiting to close the show. "Is that your audition set for Quip's?"

"More or less, what'd you think?"

"You'll get in. They love clean material—it works on TV."

"Hope you're right. The problem is LA audiences are so jaded." She sipped some ice water. "Have you ever auditioned for Spyder Byrnes?"

"No, but I heard he's an jerk." "That's what worries me."

"How long have you been in LA now?" He reached for his guitar. "Almost a year."

"You down there by yourself?"

"Yes, but there are eleven other comics living in my building."

He twisted the tuning pegs, his head cocked sideways, strumming and listening. "Is that where Stu Patterson lives?"

"He's across the hall from me! He's the one that told me about the building!"

"I've been there," said Artie. "Off Sunset Boulevard? The Bellevue?"

"The Belvedere," she corrected.

"That's it. I need to move to LA. You have to go there to make it in this business. Any openings in your place?"

"Not right now."

"Do me a favor." He dug out a business card, a caricature of himself holding an oversize guitar. "Call me when there's a vacancy."

"Sure," said Maddie. "We're always trying to move in another comedian."

"So you're divorced or ..."

"No, I'm still married. My husband just lives and works here."

"He doesn't care you're living three-hundred-and-fifty miles away in the same building with eleven other guys?"

"We've got an arrangement."

"Really." His eyes narrowed, appraising her from tits to toes.

Pig. But she kept a poker face. "I have one year in LA to succeed." "How long do you have left?"

A rush of panic slammed her like an oncoming bus, but she managed to say. "One month, two weeks, and five days."

Squirrel in the Intersection

By Luanne Oleas

CHAPTER ONE

"Years and years and years ago."

That's how Alice Hopkins' grandfather started every story. She could still hear him saying those words, even now, at 50, seated behind an oversized receptionist's desk. There was another phrase she could remember him saying too. "I hear screams of death."

Now, Alice worked at a high tech company with people from all over the world, but the screams-of-death tale was uniquely American. It was always her favorite, and her relatives were rabid storytellers. Those yarns kept her grounded in the gold rush mentality of Silicon Valley.

The "screams of death" story started when Alice's ancestors left Michigan in a Calistoga wagon and headed for Missouri to join a wagon train. On May Day 1857, her great-great-great grandparents and their two daughters left St. Louis for California. Another daughter was born somewhere between St. Louis and Salt Lake City. They never could say exactly where, just in "The Plains."

When Alice was younger, she had imagined those young girls on the adventure of a lifetime. Maybe one of them had dirty blond hair, like Alice, and the same slight gap between her two front teeth. Later, after having her own daughter, Alice wondered how difficult that long ago birth must have been.

The story was full of Old West details about meeting Indians and sharing a meal with Buffalo Bill Cody. According to the story, he loved Grandma Garrison's biscuits. Alice's grandfather always digressed at this point in the story. He would tell about he and his grandmother, years later, visiting Buffalo Bill's Wild West Show and going backstage where Buffalo Bill himself had remarked, "Them was the best biscuits I ever et."

Alice used to hate it when her grandfather had gone off track during that story. She had wanted to hear the part about "screams of death." At other times, she didn't mind hearing his tall tales about his youth in San Francisco. She liked knowing that he had snuck into the 1915 World's Fair and flown with the great stunt pilot Wiley Post. Just not in the middle of her favorite story. Eventually, he would come back to the wagon train saga.

"They trusted the Indians more than the Mormons," her grandfather would insist. They would invite the Indians into the campground and trade goods with them. The Mormons were a different story. They weren't real Mormons, her grandfather had claimed. He called them "Jack Mormons." Utah was still a territory back then, which made it an ideal hideout for anyone avoiding federal marshals. Some of those fugitives even called themselves Mormons.

The phone rang, disturbing Alice's recollection. She answered it, redirected the call to Technical Support, and stared for a moment at the eight-lane intersection outside her office. Her long curving desk, wide windows, and overstuffed leather chairs meant she had the biggest office in the building. But the lobby was empty now, and she was soon recalling her grandfather's words again.

The wagon train made it to Salt Lake City in September. The intended route was to head south across the desert to southern California, but Great-great-great Grandma Garrison had a change of heart.

"I won't go that way," she had said. "I hear screams of death."

Alice's grandfather said her premonition must have been very convincing. Four other wagons left the original wagon train with them. The Garrison's smaller group took the Oregon Trail north, arriving in Portland around Christmas time. The rest of the train continued south without them. All but the children were killed in the Mountain Meadow Massacre on September 11, 1857.

The lobby had been deserted most of the morning. No one had been through since the mailman at 9:30. Now, Alice could sense someone coming, and collapsed the solitaire game on her monitor. Two seconds later, Jack entered the lobby and tossed a dollar on her desk.

"I could kill Tech Support. Get me outta here, Alice."

Jack was a Product Marketing Manager for I-S-Cubed, the startup where they worked. He was one of the few people there who wasn't younger than Alice. He was responsible for a product (code-named "Spidey") scheduled for release next month. Alice understood his frustration. He wasn't the only one in the building on eggshells about Spidey. The future of the company was riding on it. She picked up his dollar and started to tell him she could make no promises about winning. As usual, she couldn't get the words out. Jack seemed to have that effect on her.

"You're holding my future in your hands," Jack said with a wink. He nodded at the dollar Alice held, and she smiled, still wordless. She noticed his eyes twinkled, even when he was angry. She wished they didn't.

"Promise me we'll win," he added and exited the lobby.

Gee, no pressure, Alice thought. She slid his dollar into an envelope marked "Lottery" in her top drawer. Then, she added Jack's name to the list of players for the next drawing. He was number seven on the list. Alice's name was always number one. She looked at his name for moment, not noticing what was wrong at first. Then, when she did, she quickly scratched out the name she had written. "Bob."

It was an odd mistake. Jack wasn't anything like Bob. Bob liked libraries, walking the dog, mowing the lawn, and splitting firewood. Jack, she imagined, liked red cars, drinking, and gambling. They were nothing alike. After 29 years together, Bob was her forever love. There would never be another. She still missed him every day, though he had died two years ago.

Alice tended to blush when Jack was around, and it infuriated her. Deep in her heart, she knew she couldn't take the hurt involved with having, and possibly losing, someone else. It was best not to even entertain the idea. Next time she got butterflies when Jack was around, she vowed to pinch herself until she bled. That was pain she could handle.

Alice's people may have come to California in the Gold Rush days, but they weren't miners or gamblers. No get-rich-quick schemes attracted them. They were farmers, butchers, and bartenders, part of the support system for the wild risk-takers settling the state. Even her husband Bob had been a locksmith. She came from a long line of people who never believed they would be rich, but who always believed that with hard work, they could get by.

She closed her desk drawer and looked out the window at the intersection again. Traffic in the eight-lane junction appeared worse than usual. There were always a number of "almosts" on any given day, and sometimes the real deal. Occasionally, Alice would sense it coming. She would focus on a car before it cut through the intersection, almost knowing it would run a red light. She would whisper "no," as if she could stop a pedestrian stepping into the path of a car making a quick right. Just then, an inattentive driver screeched through the intersection. Alice gasped, her shoulders tensing enough to touch her short hair, and she noticed why the latest "almost" almost occurred.

There was a squirrel in the middle of the eight-lane intersection. He would run in circles when cars began crossing, and then freeze in the middle when there were no cars. Alice sat up to watch the little guy. Joe Li entered the lobby and followed her gaze.

"He crazy animal," Joe said, a non-native speaker. "He going to get it." Joe walked to the far side of the reception desk, watching the squirrel but talking to Alice. "Bet you ten bucks." Alice knew he struggled with English—he wasn't the only one at the company who did—but hearing him use slang made her smile.

"No way," Alice answered, wishing she could ignore the ringing phone. She answered it, and in a single breath said, "I-S-Cubed. How can I help you?" She hoped it was a call she could just transfer to another line. But no. It was some recruiter, mining for software developers. After six months on the job, Alice recognized them right away. They asked for people by job title, not name.

"I'm sorry," Alice said. "I need a name. I only have names and extensions. Not titles." The caller pleaded for a minute and then hung up.

Alice returned to staring out the window with Joe Li. The hopeless plight of the squirrel had them riveted. Joe wasn't acting like the same Senior Developer from upstairs who rarely said two words. Actually, he usually said three words to Alice. "Here's my dollar." He was a regular player in the company's pool of people who attempted to win the state lottery. She could see why. He even was willing to bet on the fate of a squirrel. But so was Noreen, the company's technical writer, who had entered the lobby.

"I would wager $5 that squirrel perishes before the light completes a cycle," she said. Her clipped British accent defied the fine features inherited from her ancestors in India.

"Okay," Joe answered, pulling a five from his wallet. He was more animated than Alice had ever seen him. But then, Noreen, who chatted with Alice on a regular basis, had never been so brutal. She always sounded so tech savvy and well spoken, Alice often felt in awe.

Alice would have bet—if she did that sort of thing outside of the weekly lottery draw— that Noreen was right about the squirrel's life expectancy. Alice's finances since her husband's death didn't allow it. They both had counted on Bob working 10 or 15 more years. Their ability to pay off the mortgage of their former house relied on those extra years of income. Now, if she wanted to keep her little apartment and still put her daughter through law school in Boston, Alice had to be cautious with every penny.

Noreen had explained once that 'Alice' and 'Bob' were the two names used in most technical user manuals—the same names as her and her late husband. They came from the expressions "Person A" and "Person B." It seemed believable to Alice. She and Bob had met in a small town, but spent their married life in fast-paced Silicon Valley. She had been there long enough to know it was unlikely that motorists would care about the life of a squirrel. They would push you aside in the vegetable aisle, steal your parking place, and be your friend to climb the corporate ladder. That squirrel was doomed.

Occasionally, someone would hold the door for Alice or make eye contact and share a smile. It always surprised her, and right now, the drivers seemed to be exhibiting that unexpected behavior. Cars swerved around the intersection, trying to miss the little guy. The squirrel was running circles around the manhole cover in the center when Nazir entered the lobby.

He was eating an apple. Alice noticed a curious look on his face when he saw the three of them staring out the front window. He looked like he hadn't slept in three days. But then, he was responsible for the company's computer infrastructure. He always looked like that.

"Good afternight," Nazir said with his distinct, middle-eastern accent. He pulled a dollar from his pocket. "Get me out of here, Alice." She held his money in mid-air, turning her attention back to the squirrel.

"Holy cows," Nazir said, focusing on the squirrel. "Allah... did you see that?"

A car attempting to make a left turn had swung so far around the squirrel that it nearly took the front bumpers off the cars waiting at the red light on the opposite side of the intersection.

"He's a goner," Alice whispered, hoping against hope that it wasn't so. The light changed, and another set of motorists entered the intersection, doing their best to avoid the squirrel.

"Oh heavens," Alice gasped.

"He's dead meat," Joe Li added.

"Hurry," Noreen said and bit her lip. "Run—" Nazir started. "Not that way."

The squirrel was now streaking between and under cars, his bushy tail straight out behind him.

"I can't bear to watch," Noreen said, but she didn't turn away.

Just then, a police car arrived and parked in the middle of the intersection, lights flashing.

Cars squealed to a halt, some narrowly missing the patrol car. When all the cars had frozen in place, the officer stepped out of his patrol car and charged the squirrel. It took a few tries, but he finally herded the squirrel toward the curb and into the planned "open space" that graced one corner of the intersection.

"Well, I'll be darned," Alice said. "I wouldn't have given you a plug nickel for his life." But in her own mind, she knew, just like her great-great-great grandmother must have known, that miracles can happen.

"What's 'plug nickel'?" Joe Li asked.

Dreams

By Elaine Mannon

In thin places Boundaries dissolve
The spirit whispers

The curtain ripples
Fleeting images In morning light

357 San Francisco/Peninsula Writers Club: Writer of the Year Contest

Short Story Class
Class 363-01

Short Story: Best of Show

Literary
Exhibitor
of the Year

SF/Peninsula Writers
Writer of the Year

In Plain Sight

By Anami Sheppard

Akina Tanaka's new uniform is the popularized and inaccurate ninja costume, rendered in hot pink. She's naturally shy and unused to being stared at, but part of her job is posing for photos with tourists from all over the world. They ask her to smile or to look secretive. By the end of her first day, masking her discomfort has given a furtive quality to all her smiles.

Akina finds that her favorite part of her new job at the Iga-ryu Ninja Museum is preparing its main attraction, the Ninja House, for tours. The building is more than 600 years old, and requires cleaning each morning. She sweeps the tatami mats with the traditional hemp palm broom, seeing in her mind's eye the series of hands that have held it before hers. Strong, skilled, yet ordinary-looking hands.

Akina sweeps, gentle on the tatami. Swish, swish, swish. She gathers the dead dust to where she crouches. Gratitude settles in her as she cleans each shadowed corner with care. In this way she pays her respects to those who came before her, who chose to live like ghosts so they could protect others.

Akina has only worked there a few days when the manager summons her. She is directed to the top level of the museum and led down a narrow hall to a windowless office where she waits among some newly acquired relics. The manager surprises her by entering from a different sliding door. She catches a narrow view of living quarters beyond, before he shuts them. He is efficient, commending her dedication and then offering her more responsibility. He hands her a navy blue ninja costume.

They begin training her to give tours of the Ninja House. They tell her she must study so that she can answer any question about the ninja of the Iga clan. Later, another tour guide, Mineyo, whispers to her while they lunch in the park. She says the manager will test Akina in secret. He will send his cousin, a museum night guard, to take the tour and ask the most obscure questions. If she doesn't have the answers she'll lose her promotion. Akina embraces Mineyo, thanking her for her kindness.

"We need the help. There's a new Tokugawa exhibit coming in two weeks. Never seen before. We will be very busy." Mineyo blushes, "Please, do not let on that you know you're being tested."

When Akina gives her first tours she enjoys boasting of the house's clever secrets.

She demonstrates hidden escapes, covert lookouts, and the false facades. At the end of each tour, she pries up a floorboard to reveal a hidden weapons cache. For the finale, she grabs a throwing star and speeds it into the opposing wall. Thunk. The tourists blink in unison. She has moved so quickly they're uncertain if she threw it. They look back and forth between her and the star sticking out of the wall. They love it.

There is a board placed on that wall, with the score marks of thousands of throws.

But who would ever notice that Akina always hits the same spot?

On the night of the shadow moon, Akina goes out wearing a suit of dark blue. She is amused at how similar its shade is to her museum costume. This however, has 40 secret pockets. They hide fortified mirrors that serve as armor, weapons and tools of varying sizes and functions, some explosives, and three types of poison. One of those poisons is for her, should she be discovered.

Yet she is confident she will have no problems. She was born to this.

She breathes deeply then begins to climb a stone wall that stretches taller than the trees. She climbs using nothing but her hands and feet. At the top, where it grows impossibly smooth, she uses two small metal spikes. Each awl is barely longer than the length of her palm. She wedges their points between the stones then drags herself up. She makes no noise; all her motions are precise. Finally, she climbs down to the other side and pulls herself into the shadows to wait.

Akina knows right away when the manager's cousin is on her tour. No one has ever asked so many questions. She is cautious and correct, making her voice calm enough to soothe her own impatience.

"How did the ninja disguise themselves?'

"In plain sight," replies Akina, noticing that his lips are the same shape as his cousin's. "They often wore the clothes of farm laborers to appear as ordinary men. There were many disguises though, depending on what suited their assignment. As a komuso priest the ninja could hide his face. As a merchant he could talk to many people and gather information. As a flamboyant player in a noh troupe, he could gain access to enemy castles."

"Why do you keep saying 'he'? Were there no women ninja? If so, then isn't it strange for you to give the tour?" For the first time he smiles—it transforms his face—bright and impish.

Akina notices a second too late that he has stolen a smile from her. She steals it back, answers with a straight face, "There were some. We know little about them. It is supposed they were useful as concubine spies, or perhaps servants who were well-positioned to leave doors unlocked for other ninja. As you can imagine it is hard to piece together a secret history. But--" Akina swallows. Her pride dares her to venture beyond what she has memorized. "It is the art of the ninja to hide in the open. And it is rare for a man to truly see a woman, isn't it? It could be women were the finest ninja, and that is why we know so little of them."

He has opened his mouth for another question, but closes it now. A small frown appears on his forehead. He looks at Akina. "I suppose a man's mind is always clouded by what it wants to see."

Akina nods, taken aback by his perception. Had she wanted to see him as simple and had her own mind clouded? For the rest of the tour, she notices he pays new attention to her answers, as if sifting them for clues. She sticks to the book.

When the tour ends he puts on his shoes. He stands under the eaves on the ground, several feet lower than Akina. Quietly and with great sincerity he admits his family connection to the manager. He apologizes for his deception and tells her his name is Tesuma. Before he leaves, he bows to her so deeply she can see his heart.

On the night of the shadow moon, Akina edges just beyond the view of the security cameras. She climbs the second wall to a third story window that has been left cracked open. She lifts it and has no trouble fitting through.

Akina is deadly quiet as she makes her way to the top floor and arrives at the sliding screens of the master bedroom. They make no noise, opening under her gentle touch. On a futon across the room a man and woman sleep intertwined. On the ceiling a painted dragon watches.

Akina enters, silent as the nighttime fog.

Akina has worked at the ninja museum for two full weeks when Tesuma asks her to go to dinner with him. She says she must focus on her work. They count on her to do a good job, no distractions. But the next day everyone sees him bring her a bento lunch.

She cringes to see how he has exposed his feelings for her, and she finds she must go with him if for no other reason than to protect him from embarrassment.

Akina sits with him beside the bright blue hydrangea bushes in the park. From somewhere unexpected, a cool breeze weaves through the hot July afternoon.

He tells her of his ambitions, the wide-open future. He is young, honest, and sweet as a clear mountain stream. She is surprised by how much she enjoys hearing him laugh. If she didn't have a thousand miles of her own to walk, they could build a life together.

On the night of the shadow moon, Akina passes through the bedroom and into the small windowless office. It takes her thirteen minutes to find the Tokugawa book she needs: Basho's *Narrow Road to the Interior*. The book is beautiful but Akina doesn't hesitate to slit inside its cover. Her thin fingers reach in and pull out a tissue of paper. Her hands quiver. She reads the list of names and when she sees her own, real, ancestral name, she wastes no more time. She crumples the paper and places it in her mouth. She works her jaw at the same time she mends the book cover perfectly. She swallows. It catches in her throat for one thin second before vanishing.

On her way out she listens to the sleeping couple breathe in harmony. She bows to the silent dragon.

The next morning Tesuma comes to Akina's house with two white calla lilies. She doesn't answer the door and he waits for thirty-six minutes on the steps. When he leaves, the flowers have been in the sun so long they feel warm to the touch. She puts them in a blue vase.

In her tour voice she speaks to herself. "Ninja live by a strict moral code. They are celibate. They neither eat nor drink to excess. They are vegetarian. They train their minds. They sleep only on the left side, to protect the heart from an attack."

The two lilies stand silent witness. They bear no secrets, they simply keep tender company with one another.

On Akina's last day at the museum there is a celebration to wish her luck in the big city. Mineyo cries and promises to visit. The manager shakes his head, "We had so many customers impressed with your tour. They believed you were a real ninja."

Tesuma asks to walk her to the train. Outside the station he waits with her in a gentle silence. When the time comes, he finds the courage to lean in with that sweet smile, hoping for a goodbye kiss.

Akina feels some secret fragility caught in her throat. She knows if she were strong she would kiss him. She would believe such things don't matter--that they, too, are a play of appearances and assumptions. But she has reached the limit of what she can pretend. She can not, except she must, guard against the selfishness of her own heart.

She brings her chin down. "I'm sorry," she says before vanishing like a ghost into the night.

The Gentleman Caller

By Nancy Horton

On one fine summer's day, A young man came to town.
A man independent means, Was the story goin' around.
So I set my cap for him,   (too late I was to find)
The same did for me.

Our meetings I tried to seem casual, l was told, too many for decency.
No one complained about his daily promenade,
In front my garden gate.

On one fine summer's day, There stood my Gentleman Caller.
At once I showned him into my pallor,
I ladylike offer him the only chair,
He gingerly chose the sofa. There I started wonder "
Is he really the man for me?"

His jacket had no buttons, His shirt I saw no sleeve,
His stomach started to grow right in front of me.
His pant legs rose up like my window shade,
Just stopping at his knees.
My eyes popped wide open, When his hair began to slopen.
I can't tell you then or now, Why he's the man for me?
Straight to the preacher, We went to see.

The years have been many, And many more to come.
The children few, But, just enough.
All schooled and well married. Now, their little ones foot steps,
Echo in the hallways and on the steps.
Sometimes, by the fireplace, My mind often wonders,
Was I the spider or the fly?

Packed Away

By Kimberly Schultz

Katherine sat in her wheelchair in the middle of her empty living room desperately holding back her tears. An invisible breeze blew dust balls across the worn hardwood floor like tumbleweeds rolling through a desolate desert. Back when Katherine was more mobile, she never gave dust balls the chance to form. Her house was immaculate. But with age came more aches and pains; and just recently, her confinement to a wheelchair.

Her eyes skimmed the barren walls that held faint discolorations where all her pictures were hung. Her children's masterpieces drawn with crayons of their stick figure family were all gone. The photos she hung with great care that told many adventurous stories – a sunset picnic of her family in the Grand Canyon and captured moments in front of the enchanted castle in Disneyland – were all packed away in a box simply labeled, "Mom's Pictures" somewhere in someone's garage. "You can't take everything to the nursing home," her son, Thomas, said when he was packing away her things. When her children first started packing up her things, Katherine made sure all of the big brown boxes where labeled. But as her children uncovered more and more items of Katherine's scattered everywhere, things were thrown into unlabeled boxes.

"I'm probably never going to see any of my things again," Katherine muttered to her daughter, Liz. Liz responded by giving a tight-lipped smile while she fumbled for words that would reassure Katherine that this move was the best for the whole family.

"Are you ready to go grandma?" came a voice from behind Katherine, startling her.

"Not yet. Would you be a dear and push me into the front bedroom?" Katherine whispered. "I'd love to take one more look before we go."

Mindy struggled with the weight of her grandma's wheelchair but managed to turn her around and slowly push her down the hall. As she pushed, the floorboards creaked under the weight of the chair.

"These damn floorboards," Katherine said with a calming smile. "I could never sneak down this hall with all the creaks."

Every Christmas Eve when her kids were young, she'd lie in bed, staring into the pitch-black room, eyes wide open, waiting for them to fall into a deep sleep so she could put out their goodies. Her husband's snoring would almost always lull her to sleep, but she fought to stay awake. Once she thought they were in a deep sleep, she'd sneak down the hall like a ninja holding bags and bags of Christmas presents trying to avoid the floorboards that creaked under her weight. "Did Santa come?" her daughter, Liz, sleepily asked one year, emerging from the dark of her room, stopping Katherine right in her tracks. "Go back to sleep, Honey," she said, urging her back into her room.

"Why are you smiling, Grandma?" Mindy asked.

"When your dad and aunt were teenagers, I could always catch them when they were trying to sneak out of the house with these creaky floorboards." Katherine knew her youngest grandchild didn't fully understand, or maybe it was just lack of caring, that made her answer her with a quick "oh," before she took off down the hall leaving Katherine alone in the silence that filled Liz's old room.

Katherine's eyes wandered the empty room. *Where has the time gone?* she thought, grief-stricken. The tears she had fought to keep from falling finally escaped, burning a wet trail down her cheeks. Her body violently shook with every sob. The sharp pain in her chest came fast and hard and almost knocked her out of her chair. She put her hand to her chest until the pain subsided. She continued to look around the room. Her swollen eyes found every memory made in that room – the dent on the closet when Liz fell into it while dancing; all the tack holes in the walls from years of Liz's posters of music bands from Adam Ant and Duran Duran in the 80s to Metallica in the 90s.

Katherine didn't hear Mindy walk up behind her. She only knew she was there when she felt her granddaughter's hand on her shoulder. "Are you okay, grandma?" she asked. Mindy's dark brown eyes resembled her own. There was sadness in them. Katherine knew the sadness was for her.

Katherine reached over her shoulder and touched Mindy's small hand. "Can you take me to your father's old room down the hall?" As she rolled past her own bedroom on the way to Thomas' room, Katherine looked away. She could not bear going into the bedroom she had shared with her husband of 50 years. Life was conceived in that room. It was also where her husband decided he was done fighting cancer and passed away.

Once in Thomas' room, Katherine took in a deep breath and exhaled. The pounding in her chest echoed in her ears muffling her hearing. Katherine closed her eyes. The pounding played like the beating of Thomas' first drum set that Katherine and her husband made the mistake of putting in his room.

"Okay, mom," Thomas said, his voice echoing off the empty walls. "The van is all loaded. We are ready to go."

"I'm not going," Katherine said. "I belong in this house."

Thomas sighed. He leaned down in front of her and took her hand in his. "You have fallen down the stairs far too many times, mom," he began. "You don't eat. Not to mention the health hazards growing in your refrigerator." He stood up and started wheeling her out of the room. "You can't take care of yourself anymore."

Katherine felt defeated. "Push me into the living room. I just need a moment alone before I leave my house forever."

"A moment, mom. I'll give you that. Then we have to leave. It is a long drive to the nursing home." Thomas walked out the front door, shutting it behind him.

Katherine slowly looked around the quiet, lifeless house. The hum of the refrigerator silenced. All her magnets from all of the places that she visited with her family that once filled its front were thrown in a shoebox lost in someone's garage. The dining room table was gone. There would be no more Thanksgiving dinners served there. The spot in the living room where the family Christmas tree sat year after year would forever be vacant. A violent sob erupted from within Katherine causing her to shake. Silence stung her ears. Coldness surrounded her, swallowing her up in its emptiness. A slight pressure began to form on her chest, getting heavier and heavier until it was too much to bear. Katherine gave into the pain that gripped her limp body and let go. Katherine turned her lips up into a small smile as she closed her eyes forever.

The Tout

By Jim Stanfield

What a beautiful, golden October day. The pungent mix of smells — hotdogs, hay and horse manure — both familiar and palpable, mingled with the crisp colors. The nip of fall and the sounds of the race track blended with all this to produce a peculiar surrealistic reverberation of pleasurable sensations. It was the kind of day that made you glad to be alive. It feels more like home to me here than it does in my apartment. What a lonely place that came to be after my second wife left me. I hope Snickelfritz does okay today in the eighth. I could use the purse.

I'm Burney King. Snick is a gelding. I've had him for a year now. I have a barber shop in town. When I'm not here at the track, I'm there cutting hair. I drive a Caddy. I think I've done pretty well for myself.

My buddies and I watch the races from a special section of the turf club reserved for owners. We usually invite this character, Ralph, to join us on occasion if he promises not to regale us with religion. Ralph is a regular at the races. No one could remember when he had not been here. His brand of crazy seems benign. Most of us put up with him for his entertainment value alone. Lately though, he has gotten on this religion kick; memorizing and spouting jeroboams of bible verse. A dower scowl has replaced his previously ever-present smile. And now, according to him, the world is coming to an end.

"Hark, you sinners. The end of days is approaching! It's not too late to repent. And in those times there was no peace to him that went out, nor to him that came in, but great vexation were upon all the inhabitants of the countries."

"Christ, you can say that again. What are you talking about?"

"And Jehoiachim the king of Judah went out to the king of Babylon he, and his mother, and his servants, and his princes, and his officers. And the king of Babylon took him in the eighth race. And let it be said that Malibar will win in the first race followed by Marigold and Ann's Dandy."

Well, this is a new twist; predicting the winners of the race along with his pronouncement of doom.

Now Malibar is not a bad horse. The racing form has her going off at

5 to 1. She placed in her last race. A lot of people will be betting her for that alone. But the simple fact is that if a horse finishes that well in the previous day's race it will have been run to exhaustion and will need a few days to recuperate. They run them easy for the next couple of races. It's common practice. That's what I tell my jockey to do. No horse wins two in a row in two days.

I love the pageantry of the jockeys in their silks. The horses are led to the starting gate, and they're off. They are getting there, getting there, and it's Malibar, Marigold and Ann's Dandy. Ralph got it right!

Without referring to the racing form—had he memorized that too—Ralph solemnly proclaimed:

"And Joshua the son of Nun sent out of Shillim two men to spy secretly, saying, go view the land, even Jericho. And they went, and came into a harlot's house, named Rahab, and lodged there. And let it ring out that it shall be Mimsey, Fairlane and Solid Gold, one, two, three!"

That's how it went down, folks!

"Yada yada blah blah blah." Not that it mattered to me, but this makes all three picks predicted correctly, two races in a row. What are the odds?

Back in my handicapping days I would return home empty-handed after spending hours pouring over the Racing Form calculating every indicator in the book. I would use percent change in the posted odds between six minutes to post and two minutes to post. I would look for a horse's energy level, sweating or agitation in the paddock. I bet against the bias of the track handicapper. And using every trick in the book, I still couldn't consistently pick a winner.

Nobody gets it right all the time. I know just how hard it is. That's when I wised up and bought Snick. He has been my payday ever since. I still handicap, nickel and dime, just to keep my hand in but I know how hard it is. Just nobody gets it right like this. This is nuts!

A small crowd had gathered around our new tout to see who he would pick next. We had taken to calling him Nosty, short for Nostradamus.

"Why don't you bet on them yourself? You could make a fortune?" I asked. "That's not the way to salvation."

In handicapping it's all about statistics. Statistics and probability. In statistics there is this thing called the theory of runs. If you have a large enough sample size, say all of the races at all of the tracks, then just about anything can happen if you wait long enough. In a million coin tosses you might get a hundred heads in a row. The overall average will come out very near fifty-fifty, but there is that run of a hundred heads staring at you. Maybe that's what's going on.

For my money, it's got to be Corky in the third.

But Nosty had a different take. "I am Alpha and Omega, the first and the last: What thou seest, write in a book, and send it unto the seven churches to shew unto his servants things which must shortly come to pass for the time is at hand. This just isn't your day, King. It'll be Crown Jewel to win, Rudolph to place and Santa Claws to show."

Amazing! Ralph got three for three in the third race.

A lot of smart money goes in near post time to pull down the odds on the horse you liked to the point where the payout is no longer worth the risk. It is better just to set these races out.

I'll just bet Ansonia, with the good indicators going off at 8 to 1 and ridden by a less well-known jockey, to place. This has worked well for me in the past.

"And I saw, and beheld a white horse: and he that sat upon him had a bow; and a crown was given unto him: and he went forth conquering, and to conquer. Prismacolor, then Cloppelganger, then Ansonia. Judgment Day is at hand."

"Nostradamus speaks again!"

"What are you talking about? My name is Ralph."

Can you beat that! Cloppelganger beats Ansonia by a nose to place; both of them breathing Prismacolor's dust.

On average, only one out of three times does the odds-on favorite win. The favorites are usually bet down to nearly even money. Overall, the odds of any given past winner, winning two non-consecutive races is one in five. In order for a bet to make any sense, the horse has got to go to the post at 5 to 1 or higher. Usually the odds are less. If nothing else stands out from your indicators it is best just to be a spectator. Keep your money in your pocket for the next race.

Nosty screwed up his face in a vituperative scowl and proclaimed, "And I saw in the right hand of him that sat on the throne a book written within and on the backside, sealed with seven seals. Who is worthy to open the book, and to lose the seals thereof... And no man in heaven, nor in earth, neither under the earth was able to open the book, neither to look thereon... The root of David has prevailed to open the book, and to loose the seven Seals thereof... Dump Truck first, Squeaky Clean second and Ain Darka runith third."

Nosty did it again!

Between them, the top three jockeys win about half the races. That means between them all the other jockeys, win the other half. As many pickers that bet yesterday's winning horses there are half that many more that bet the best jockeys thereby lowering the odds on their mounts so the odds they end up paying are less worth the gamble.

When betting the nags, you narrow the field first before trying to pick the winner. Apply the negative indicators in the process of elimination and see what's left. Of the horses in the sixth race, four of them scored good break-aways out of the gate in their previous outings, but Inverness finished first yesterday so she's out. Gee Willakers and Charlie Horse both faded badly at the three-quarter-mile post so they're out. That leaves Amazement. She had a good break and is a good closer. I'm betting her to win.

Nosty was quick with his prediction: "I know thy works, that thou art neither cold nor hot: I would thou wert cold or hot. So then because you are lukewarm, and neither cold nor hot, I will spew thee out of my mouth. And that the shame of thy nakedness do not appear, be zealous therefore and repent. And behold a throne was set in heaven, and one sat on the throne. And he that sat was to look upon like a jasper and a sardine stone.

And there was a rainbow round about the throne. And verily Harass will win then Obstreperous places then Alpo will show."

Good grief. He nailed the sixth race in a row.

"Nosty, when did you say the world is coming to an end?" "The Ides of March!"

"That's not from the Bible, that's from Shakespeare!" "Doesn't matter."

Always go to the paddock to check the body language of the horses. Folks at the OTB miss out big time by not being able to do that. I don't have favorites. It is best not to get emotional about the horses you bet on. I only have one horse to love. But I never bet on Snikelfritz. That way when he loses I'm not all that angry with him.

Okay! This race has got to be different. The crowd is betting the so-called obvious favorites and the odds on these geldings are sinking in response. All these Samuel K Suckerbetters love yesterday's winners with the net effect of bolstering the odds on my pick, Applejack. It makes me queasy that they're putting him in gate eight, but long ago I figured that betting gate numbers was a dead end.

Nosty has really developed a following. All the people within earshot are beginning to take notice of his phenomenal string of successes. Boy, this really sucks. With all these people piling on the bandwagon, it's killing the odds on all the best picks. Lucinda should be going off at 20 to 1 but with everybody within earshot of him betting on her, she is only paying 7 to 1.

I have to give the nod to Gilda's Gail to place here in the seventh race. I see Nosty likes her too. For once we are in agreement so I'll wager a double sawbuck on her to come in second. The main thing to always remember is that you are not betting against the horses, you are betting against all the other bettors.

The streak is holding. Gilda's Gail put a good chunk of change in my pocket.

I'm on my way home. I'm going to get drunk and watch the late show. Nosty predicted Royal Flush, Oofty Goofty and Snickelfritz to show.

I bet them all, just exactly as he called them. Snickelfritz came in first. Demetri came in second and Maxie Mouse came in a length behind at third. The future, it seems, is veiled in mystery. Even for Nostradamus.

Remnants

By John Hotson

I wanted a coffee and a scone, preferably cranberry. The sign read *Premium Outlets— One Hundred and Forty-Five Stores—Next Exit*. Garlic greeted me at the highway exit, the resident air pollutant of the city named Gilroy. I wondered if I'd carry the scent when I left.

The mid-morning coffee line looked long. I stepped behind a young woman and admired the speed of her two thumbs on a phone screen. Ahead stood another woman in a baggy sweatshirt, resting her right hand on a wheelchair's back handle. Next to her a child's left forearm lay still on one armrest, while the opposite arm moved through the air without apparent purpose: extending, pronating, curving, rising, flexing and rotating with the fingers and hand turned outward. Foam, secured with duct tape, covered the right armrest.

A new podcast downloaded on my phone while I waited. The women in the sweatshirt ordered and turned the wheelchair, revealing a child dressed in pink who she pushed with one hand while holding coffee in the other. I recognized the woman's posture and the lip. She had gained weight, but still walked with her ears and hips aligned and shoulder blades down. Her lower lip still pouted. Kim noticed me, stopped, almost spilled her coffee, stared at my face then waved. I nodded back and forced the sides of my mouth up, my polite smile that in pictures looked part snarl.

After picking out a scone, I walked to the counter where Kim topped her cup with milk. I noticed my left palm moving, rubbing up and down my thigh and brought it to a halt. My breathing felt a bit stiff and hurried.

"Teddy—you've cut your hair and your beard's gone. You look all professional," she said stirring her coffee.

"Got a job," I didn't know what else to say, You look ten pounds heavier. Your child's dress is pretty. Too bad she's disabled. "How's Ron," came out.

Kim looked down at her daughter. "He left us a year after Charlotte was born. Divorced me, not for another woman, he just quit us." She sounded tired and looked a bit blotchy.

I wasn't surprised that Ron had left. I never liked him. Never understood why Kim said NO to me and YES to him.

Her gaze moved up to my face, "You're still in the Bay Area?" "Live in The City, near Mission Bay. Work in biotech."

"The barista called, "Ted, medium nonfat latté."

"Do you have time to sit with us and talk for a while? I'd love to chat. It's been so long since I've seen you." Kim said.

A small round table divided us. Kim stationed Charlotte to her right. I pulled my scone from its bag, broke off half and offered a piece.

"No thank you. I brought a bagel from home and animal cookies for Charlotte." The child's head tilted up and toward her mother, her mouth half-open, lips tense and distorted, released a slurred, grunting sound.

Kim leaned over and put a cookie in her mouth. "Yes sweetheart. You heard the cookie word."

"Does she understand what we say?" "A few words."

"Her right arm is always moving. Does she ever get to rest?"

"Only when she sleeps, otherwise it moves on it own. Charlotte was born with a bad brain and has no control over half of her body."

"What can . . . what does she like to do?"

"She likes to look at colorful pictures and go on trips with her stuffed monkey." A long- armed monkey made out of worn socks, grayish brown except for an off-white face and blue button eyes, sat in the child's lap.

Kim put a straw into her daughter's mouth. Charlotte sucked in milk, coughed and splattered the monkey. Kim wiped with her napkin then said, "Did you ever marry?"

"No. Never found someone who'd say 'yes" to me." The words tasted sour. "Do you have a main squeeze?"

"You mean a girlfriend. No. And you?"

"I haven't dated much since Ron left," She looked at her daughter again. "Charlotte's my usual date."

I bit into the scone, watched Kim scrape her fingernail along the tabletop and thought, *The unexpected can hurt.* Instead I said, "Are you going to your reunion this fall? Ten years right?"

"I may. You remember my graduation?"

"Absolutely. You received your degree and then you left. The last time I saw you was when you crossed the stage at commencement."

"Did you get my letter? I tried to explain about Ron and me. You never responded."

"I was in the middle of my thesis and generally not responsive." I remembered the sound of the shredder ripping her letter into strips.

I thought we could still talk, meet for coffee. Like now." "So you could show me your engagement ring?"

Kim touched my hand. Her touch felt tactile, skin on skin. "You're still angry. I'm sorry. I was very fond of you," Kim said.

"Oh, the fucking 'fond' word." I moved my hand to my jaw, a fingernail between my teeth, stopping more verbiage. Kim gave her look, the, *I'm so disappointed in you,* look. I remembered that face. God I hated the pose. My eyes shifted to Charlotte, otherwise I'd reply with my, *Don't give a crap,* stare.

"Do you still drive the blue Ford van with the broken air conditioner?" Kim said. "It expired. Transmission went. Wasn't worth fixing."

"We had some good road trips: Yosemite, Pinnacles, Mendocino redwoods, Point Reyes.

Good days and nights traveling in that van."

She included night traveling. Did she mean following a truck's lights on an otherwise dark, lonely road, pushing for home, anticipating a shower and bed at the end of a trip. Or did she mean in the back of the van, parked in the darkness of woods, my fingers under her t-shirt tracing the ridges of her ribs, then down along her bare hip and on to her thigh. I said, "I remember the cave in Pinnacles... forgot the name. The one on the west side."

"Balconies Cave."

"Right, our phones provided the only light. I left behind part of my scalp in the ceiling.

You tripped and scrapped up a knee."

"And afterwards you played your blues harp when we limped back to the van. Do you still play?" Kim said.

"No. Learned a few rifts and how to bend notes, then my interest faded."

"You played *Amazing Grace* . . . and I liked your rifts. You could move from one right into the next."

I sipped my coffee and watched her gaze, not at my eyes, but lower. "It's called a soul patch," I said.

"A what?"

"The tuff of hair below my lip. It's called a soul patch or a jazz dab." "Why did you grow a soul patch?"

I not going to say: so I'd look different, not so plain, so average, to interest women. "It's just a phase. Trying it out."

"It makes you look like a Ted. In your beard you were a Teddy."

"Is there a difference?"

"Don't know. I played with Teddy's beard. I don't know Ted . . . but I'd like too." "What do you and Charlotte do on your dates?"

"In the summer we go to art and crafts festivals. Eat ice cream, look at the paintings, the wood toys, join the crowd walking pass the booths and listen to bands scattered along the way. Charlotte likes to watch people dancing."

I smiled at the girl. The fingers on her right hand spread apart. "Still go to the theater?

You took me to A.C.T. once. Some bewildering play. I only remember chairs on the stage and the gray lighting. "

"Probably a poor choice on my part," Kim said. "Still go to such plays?"

"I'll watch them at home. The library has some on DVD. I don't get to the theatre much.

Are you dating?"

"A little."

"What she like?"

"It's more a they, than a she."

"All female?"

"Did I ever give reason to think different?"

"Well, you live in San Francisco, your not married, you sport a soul dab and all that. Just asking." She reached across the table and pressed her fingers into my chest. "You still lift weights."

I nodded, looked at my watch and finished my scone.

"I kept all your letters. They're tied in a bundle. I think you were the

only person who sent me handwritten letters . . . and on good stationery. "
Kim said. She pressed a hand down on her knee to calm its quivering.

"Makes you think about what you going say before you write. No editing or spell-check."

"It was so personal and private. And you sealed them with a heart stickie. I opened the envelopes with a paper knife so I wouldn't rip the heart."

I stood. "I need to go. Supposed to be in Monterey for lunch. You and Charlotte have a great day." Kim's lips enacted a smile.

"Wait just a second, please." She took out a pen, wrote on napkin and handed it to me. "It's my phone number. Please call. It was so good to see you. I'd love to talk again."

"Sure. Great. Thanks," I put the napkin in my shirt pocket and waved goodbye. That night I sat in my hotel room, a single light on, looking at Kim's phone number, thought about our meeting that morning and remembered a decade back. The next day the housekeeper took Kim's napkin out in the trash.

The Long Road Home

By Carolyn Donnell

Inspired by Cesar Vallejo's Black Stone Lying on a White Stone?
A prompt from National Poetry Month 2014

May I rest in a field of bluebonnets on a sunny day.
I can already remember the mockingbird's song.
I will lie in Texas. I won't mind any more.
On a Thursday, like today, in springtime.

It should be a Thursday
For that is the day I write these words.
I have seen my mind in a saddened mood
And feel myself today on an island, alone.

They will say Carolyn is dead. They put her away.
She was never good enough.
Kept her down with their unkind words.

My witnesses the flower-strewn fields A blue Texas sky
The purple-hued thunderstorms And the long road home

358 I'm Dying to Tell You: Mystery Novel Chapter

Righteous

By Ezra Barany

CHAPTER ONE
Winneba, Ghana

Disarming a bomb isn't so hard. What's hard is disarming a bomb that hasn't been found yet.

In my living room, I sat at the desk carefully working one of the wires of my device into a perfect ninety-degree angle.

There are so many different ways a bomb might detonate. By timer, by pressure, by proximity. But if it's triggered by a remote signal from something like a cell phone, the bomb's location doesn't matter. All that matters is that the signal doesn't reach the bomb. How can you stop a signal? Make a device that releases the same sort of signal as the phone except in a way that interferes with it. When the two signal waves combine, the phone's wave and your device's wave, the wave peak of one hits the wave trough of the other and they cancel each other out. Like flat-lining a sound wave. Good noise-canceling headphones work that way. Flat-line the outside noise and you can't hear the noise. So flat-line the phone's detonation signal, and the bomb won't explode.

I had to line up everything on the device just right or else the device's signal wouldn't cancel out the phone's signal. Or worse, my device would trigger the bomb too early.

Outside my house, the growl of a large vehicle idled into silence. I peeked through the slit between the wooden boards on my windows. An unfamiliar van was parked out front. David Moore, my friend and the vice president of my company, stepped out of the van and pointed out to two men in white uniforms which house was mine. I bet they knew I was close to finishing my device and wanted to stop me. That didn't worry me. I knew how to handle them.

I turned off the lights. Squatted in the darkest corner of the living room. With the windows boarded up, the lack of light in the room hid me well. A moment later I heard the knock at the door.

In a sing-song falsetto voice I called out, "Who *is* it?"

"Nathan," David's voice shouted through the door. "Open up. It's important."

"More important than taxes?" I asked using my regular voice now.

"Nathan, please."

"I'm not home right now. Please leave a message after the beep. *Beep!*"

"Nathan, open the door."

I said nothing. "Nathan."

There was some muttering outside and then a loud bang crunched against the door. A piece of the wood frame busted. They were working on kicking down the door.

"That's okay," I called out. "I've been meaning to get a new door. One of those lovely hand-carved things with a stained glass design."

The next kick came with a crack and flung the door open. The uniformed men stepped in and paused, probably to get accustomed to the darkness.

That pause gave me the opportunity to attack first. I pounced high and lead my fall with my elbow into the first man's face. His nose released a cracking sound, and he fell backwards. The second one came at me from behind, but I elbowed him in the gut. Looking behind me, I placed a kick to his shin and he dropped to the floor as well.

"Nathan, stop!"

I held my fists close to my face ready for the third attacker and saw it was David.

"Nathan, why do you think I called them? What would be in it for me?"

"You're just trying to stop me from deactivating the bomb."

"What bomb?"

Anger spilled into me. "You know damn well what bomb."

"Nathan, you're just having one of your delusions." David looked sincere, the way those bushy eyebrows of his practically lifted off his forehead. "Alright, just for the sake of argument, let's say there is a bomb. What specifically clued you in to its existence?"

I thought about it. There had to be a specific clue, a precise piece of evidence that made me aware of the threat. But the more I tried to grasp that clue, the more I realized the evidence was never there. The knowledge of the bomb just came to me. Like dream knowledge. When I dream, my dream knowledge can reveal facts true to the dream but false in reality. Someone I may have never met before can be my brother, according to my dream knowledge. Someplace I may have never seen before can be my old high school, according to my dream knowledge. On rare, treasured occasions, my dream knowledge lets me have a dream of a world where my girlfriend Sophia doesn't exist, and I don't feel so alone without her.

In this case, my dream knowledge told me there was a bomb. The problem? I wasn't dreaming.

David gestured to the living room mirror. "Look at yourself. You're a mess."

In the broken mirror, I saw the fractured features of my unkempt brown hair that reached past my long neck. My t-shirt had more stains than my driving record. Though the mirror couldn't reflect it, I imagined my scent wasn't much better to bear. The men in uniform weren't criminals. They must have been wards from a hospital. David put his hands on his hips. "What would I gain from putting you in the mental hospital?"

"You'd take over my position as CEO." But as I said the words, I knew that would never be his motive.

"You know I never wanted that much responsibility."

"True, but you'd be good at it."

David sighed. "Think about it. Think about how you've been handling the company lately."

I considered the logic of it all. The pieces of the jigsaw for my logic didn't fit. The puzzle pieces for David's logic fit well. I had stopped taking my meds several months ago, and during that time I found more and more enemies. But now, considering it this way, I realized all my enemies may not have been enemies at all. The only true battle I had left to fight was against my own paranoia.

Crap. Fighting people was easier.

"Alright," I said. "Let's go." I left my house and walked to their van. The wards followed behind me, one limping, the other holding a handkerchief over his bloody nose.

Beauty and the Bum

By Stanley Gedzelman

Here they come, beauty and the bum.
Her sparkling gown, his shirt spotted brown.
Her glorious train, his tie's faded stain.
Her visage divine, his pants bottoms shine.
Her beauteous soul, his sock's gaping hole.
Her shoes fitted neat, his dun sneakered feet.
Her slow regal walk, his jacket's caked chalk.
She passes by and every man whistles.
Ladies wince at his minefield of bristles.
How can she take him anywhere?
But when he's there she glides on air.
Floating on a bubble immune to his rubble.
Cause under those rags he's loving and trim.
And that is why she can't live without him.

Customary Madness

By Bernadine Fornesi

In the 1930's, Italian families gathered in the house basements of South San Francisco on Saturday nights to sing and dance to the music of their homeland. An accordion, drum, clarinet and a bass fiddle provided the evening's entertainment. The concrete floor had been sprinkled with polenta meal, so dancers' feet would slide easier. Wooden benches lined the walls where mothers with babies and toddlers sat. They gossiped about the weeks' activities while bouncing children on their laps.

One corner of the basement was set up as the refreshment center. Jugs and bottles of wine in various sizes, lined an oilcloth table. Two or three different brands of whiskey, a large tub of ice, and several brands of soda crowded the table. A large coffee urn perked in the center, and would be ready for the older Italian men who only drank coffee royals.

The noise from inside spilled out onto the sidewalk, where families walked in the gathering twilight before the fog from the ocean hung a white shroud over the city. The laughter and music they heard enticed them to enter basements, even though they didn't know the owners of the houses. They always found somebody inside they knew, and were welcomed as they joined in the festivities.

The only man in the community who owned a bass fiddle, was a smallish man who measured five feet in height. He had no family in this country, and lived alone on the second floor of an apartment building in town. Each Saturday, around six o'clock in the evening, the next-door neighbors heard the thump, thump of the bass fiddle being dragged down the stairs of the apartment, supported by the smallish man. Once he reached the sidewalk he bent over, and eased the bass fiddle onto his back, holding it by placing both arms backwards on the instrument as he started walking up the Avenue. When he heard music and laughter coming from a basement, he entered amid a chorus of "Franking made it." The men in the basement removed the bass fiddle from his back, and placed it upright in the corner with the other musicians who were starting to play. Franking made his way to the refreshment table and poured himself a glass of wine.

Franking drank his wine in two or three gulps, and walked to his bass fiddle. He was dressed in misshapen dark trousers held up by wide suspenders over a checkered shirt with frayed collar and cuffs. His black suit coat hung almost to his knees, and he wore a pair of red arm bands to keep the long sleeves of the coat pushed up from his hands. Two buttons were missing from the coat, and he had buttoned the one remaining in the wrong buttonhole, forcing the coat to hang uneven in front. His sparse hair and two-day-old beard were turning iron grey. His few remaining teeth were crooked and stained from coffee and wine.

The small man joined the other musicians and, spun the bass fiddle around a few times to the delight of the crowd. He started drawing the bow back and forth across the body of the instrument. The music produced from the group, who had no training in the instruments they were playing, sounded pretty good, and dancers started shuffling around on the polenta strewn basement floor. Some danced with children in their arms; others had little daughters whose shoes were planted on top of their father's feet dancing with big smiles on their faces. One jovial man in the group always danced with a filled glass of whiskey placed on top of his head.

He never spilled a drop as each of his partners glanced upward, nervously.

Franking, the bass fiddle player, fortified himself frequently during the evening with glasses of wine. After playing for two or three hours, his arms and hands weren't gripping the bow as they once were. The bow sometimes got pushed into the sounding hole of the instrument, and he tugged to remove it. The effects of the wine were slowing down the small man's movements, and the strings of the bow were becoming quite frayed. One last sweep across the strings, and the bow became lodged in the opening. Franking started teetering back and forth as he fell to the basement floor clinging to the bass fiddle, which fell on top of him. Everybody laughed and kept right on dancing. The small man took a short nap with the fiddle.

The older Italian men sitting together on the benches sported felt fedoras, and some had handlebar moustaches. Occasionally they twirled the outer edges in an upward motion. Dry, Tuscany cigars were lit by the old men, and women started complaining about the stench from the smoke curling upward. It was said that if you blew smoke from a Tuscany cigar on a fly in a room, he would immediately drop dead to the floor. The Italian women were fanning the smoke away with tea towels while holding their noses, and berating the smokers. The smokers didn't seem to suffer any ill effects, continued to smoke, and ignored the women's complaints.

At midnight, platters of pasta appeared from the kitchens above the basements. Crusty French bread and sliced salami were carried by the women, and placed next to bowls of grated cheese on a table. The noise abated as everybody started eating. Franking was urged to the table, and ate a plateful of pasta along with more wine. He now had drunk enough wine to believe he was invincible. He always started an argument with the largest man close by. His eyes wandered to other people, never looking directly at the person he was accosting. His small head wobbled on a thin neck, reminding one of an infant whose muscles haven't fully developed. A forefinger went back and forth like a metronome, and his opening remark was, "You think I be big fool?" This was repeated a couple of times until he got a response from the over-sized man.

"You had too much vino, Franking. You always think you be strong as Primo Carnero."

After this exchange the small man threw caution to the wind, and in a high pitched wavering voice said, "You betta shuta-up or I gonna give you one pretty soon!" Everybody laughed, knowing Franking couldn't punch himself out of a paper bag.

The musicians were putting their instruments into their cases. People were lifting their sleepy children, carrying them outside, and walking toward their homes. "See you tomorrow at the I.C.F. picnic in Saratoga after mass," was heard often, as people departed from the basement.

The man whom Franking had attacked verbally, picked up the bass fiddle, and grabbed the small, belligerent individual by his suit coat, pulling him to the sidewalk. "I can't carry both you and this fiddle. One of you will have to walk, and I don't' see legs on this thing. I'll help you up your apartment steps, and then you get yourself to bed." Franking mumbled, but followed along meekly behind the man and the fiddle; occasionally taking one step forward and two steps back.

At the bottom of the stairs leading to his apartment, Franking waited clinging to the iron banister, as the man with the bass violin on his back, opened the door to Franking's living quarters and pushed the instrument inside. He looked down at the little man standing at the bottom of the stairs, "Do I have to carry you up too?" He sighed as he retraced his steps down the stairs. Throwing the slight man over his shoulder, he trudged back up the stairs and placed Franking on the unmade bed in the room.

As he closed the apartment door he heard one last, "You thing I be big fool?"

The large man chuckled, and shook his head as he descended the stairs "I don't know why we all put up with your nonsense." Looking up at the closed door of the apartment he said in a loud voice, "See you tomorrow at the picnic."

So, the customary madness of a Saturday night ended, but would resume on Sunday at the picnic in Saratoga, in the true tradition of Italians of South San Francisco.

Weak Moments ~ Mexico City, 1958

By Sonia Meyers

The streets screamed. To be a passenger on the public buses that shrieked past was to risk being unnecessarily fondled by old men. At the market, a pair of thieves worked their way through vendors' stalls. One ordered a spicy heap of mango on a stick as a diversion while the other reached for the cash box. And of course, there were the simple folk who had been living in the city too long. The elderly men who would be better off set up in a small, quiet country town instead set up their chairs outside their apartments and watched the daily commotion. They watched lives pass by as if at a movie theater, as if the people were extras in the made-up tales they told to one another.

Mexico City was hectic. The only way to survive was to learn how to live within the chaos. Citizens from other states soon began flocking into the city limits. There was always work available, but for most it would scarcely allow a decent life. Those less fortunate were blessed to afford a studio apartment bordering crowded streets where people hustled at all hours. As the Torre Latinoamericano building was built downtown, so was a measure of hope. It reached beyond the tops of the surrounding buildings; the peak pointing to the sky fueled the people onward toward the modern world. It was a city on the move, and Josefina, born and raised at the center of it all, was skeptical it was only a means to an end. At this moment, she simply aimed to get her daughter and two young sons across the street to her aunt's house.

She had gathered the children from her home with urgency, wiping sweat off her round forehead. The heat was breaking her down. Josefina scanned the way with her bulging, brown eyes. Short, dark hair curled itself tightly into small bunches on top of her head, preventing useless strands from dangling in her face. Three months pregnant with a fourth little one on the way, she was terribly nauseous and could barely get out of the house with the kids, who clung tight to her sides, much less stomach a bite to eat—which was all she had in her house: one bite. She could not remember a time when she had extra food for the next day.

As she waltzed across crosswalks on her bony legs, the toothsome smells of fresh sweet bread swirling about the air from the bakery was enough to ignite her growling tummy. No amount of nausea could keep Josefina from devouring a dozen sweet rolls if they were to ever reach the palm of her hand.

Her husband was working in Nevada through the Bracero Program that the presidents of the United States and Mexico created between the bordering countries. It began as wartime assistance and grew so that Armando was merely one of nearly half a million Mexican men legally hired to work in the United States. It was a fine time for the Braceros, with laws becoming more relaxed. Business owners provided more opportunity for employees by sharing their profits, better providing for their country. It trounced the illegal migration men faced, and it worked for Josefina. Armando was gone for nine months out of the year and she didn't need him at home. She would rather suffer her hungry stomach than endure his chauvinistic demeanor. Josefina held together the small studio along with their three children by way of working a few shifts at a nearby restaurant to supplement the income she received each month from Armando, which never carried the family to the end of the month. Everyday was a struggle. Rather than confront the faces of her hungry children, during dinnertime hours it was often easier for Josefina to see them playing on the swings at the park.

Too young to grasp the reality of their ravenous situation, her children appeared happy enough. Graciela, the oldest at seven, had her mother's tight curly hair and a feisty manner that hinted at oft-hidden bravery. She presented strength only when necessary. When the boys used their growing brawn against, her away from their mother's scrutinizing gaze, she dug her fingernails deep into their eyelids to further ensure the natural order of things, she was the oldest and they were younger. The boys, Edgar, who was five, and Rogelio, ten months younger than his brother, were fighters, though it was usually amongst themselves that they fought. Josefina knew the boys would be okay, they had the spirit of their father, who could go days without food or water and labored more than twelve hours in a single day. Armando was the strongest man she knew. No one could push him around, not even his wife. But Josefina was the foundation where the family found stability. This she knew.

After a long day of work on his latest job in the U.S., Armando dressed himself up and walked to the local bar for a well-deserved drink. His face, neck, and collar appeared charcoal from working under the intense sun. He sauntered into the bar with his unmistakable swagger. With an index finger pointed up in front of his dark face, he turned to the bartender. As best as he could pronounce in his broken English, he said, "One high bowl." It was payday, and he had money for alcohol.

"Excuse me?" the bartender snapped, lines of disgust layered across his forehead. "What did you say to me?"

Despite the bartender's condescending tone, Armando raised his finger again and repeated, "One high bowl."

"I can't understand you, and I don't serve Mexicans." The bartender dismissively turned away and continued wiping the shot glasses he was stacking on the bar.

Never one to back down, Armando challenged him. "Oh, you don likey Mexicans?" His tone was secure, sarcastic.

Armando craved to be heard throughout the bar. By-standers shifted in their seats uncomfortably. The bartender dropped his shoulders with antipathy and slowly faced Armando. "No, me no likey Mexicans.

Get the hell out of my bar, you filthy wetback!"

Fellow Americans swiveled around in their barstools to face the commotion. It wasn't unusual for Mexicans to walk into an American bar, but it was uncommon for them to bare cockiness so bold as to question authority.

Armando caught sight of the bartender's pyramid of perfectly placed shot glasses. With utter grace and no hesitation, he swiped his toned, brown arm across them. They crumbled and broke across the bar, crashing to either side of the counter. The bartender fearfully covered the top of his head with his white rag and slunk below the bar. Armando stared at the bartender, waiting patiently for him to look up. When he finally reached the depth of Armando's dark eyes, Armando told him with in a most composed tone, "Fuck a-you mother. You understand now."

Without flinching, Armando turned on his boot heels and stalked out of the American bar without so much as a glance behind him.

This was the latest story Armando shared with Josefina. She was the only one to hear of his escapades in America. "No, Armando! You didn't!" Josefina gasped, afraid he would soon get caught and deported if he kept up such defiant behavior.

Armando was sitting back in the familiar brown leather chair of his brief returns to Mexico City, waiting for something to eat. "Si, I did," he said plainly, without turning to face Josefina. He simply stared off into the distance of their small space and reveled in what he thought was a brave performance.

Ready to vomit in her early months of pregnancy, Josefina thought about Armando as she struggled across the street, her weary brown sandals slapping the hot pavement. The thought of him drinking in his risky adventures as if they were moments of triumph, make her sick. He may share his stories and send his money, but she knew they were not friends. Friends smiled at one another.

She had a few hours to clock in at La Rocketa, her sister's restaurant, and she needed her aunt to watch the children. They are good kids, Josefina reminded herself, more for her benefit than anyone else's. The struggle of poverty and motherhood wore on her and she knew the next day would only bring more difficulties.

Josefina couldn't leave them at home with Luz, who was much farther along in her pregnancy. It was Luz's first child, and she was already terrified of her growing belly and the anxious thought that she would be a mother at 16.Josefina had met her at La Rocketa a few months back. As Josefina waited on her in one of the booths, she could feel the life being sucked out of this lonely, nameless girl. She saw the sorrow fill up her young soul so that her eyes clouded over with complete despondency. For reasons Josefina couldn't understand, the girl immediately opened up to her: "It's that I'm pregnant and I need to abort my baby."

The girl threw her head down and circled it with her arms like a halo. Letting her arms encompass her fallen head, she cried onto the table. Perhaps in that moment of despair she reached out to whoever would listen, and Josefina, a complete stranger to her, would.

Josefina went to her side and whispered, "What's your name?" "Luz," the girl managed to say.

"You don't need to abort your baby."

"I do," Luz cried. "I don't know where the father is."

"Did he run off?"

"No," she wept. "I did."

Josefina learned that Luz was from up north in Durango, and escaped with fear dragging at her heels. She couldn't face her family lest they disown her. The Maya family was well to do, and it would shame them to hear of her promiscuity. That left her with one option: to run away, as far away as possible. Then she could have an abortion and return home a new woman, leaving it all behind to start anew. So she left.

"You can't kill the baby," Josefina pleaded. "You just can't."

She knew only one thing in this life, and that was to help those in need. It was clear the girl wanted to keep the baby. Otherwise, she would have already committed what Josefina believed to be a crime; it was her staunch belief that everyone deserved a chance.

"You don't know my family. They would kill me," she sobbed. "I'm better off getting rid of the problem and moving on, but I don't know what to do."

Josefina remembered a time when she needed extra cash to take Rogelio to the doctor's office. He had been increasingly lethargic for days, which she had initially attributed to laziness. But then she found blood in his stool and could no longer blame his attitude. Armando's mother refused to loan her the money. Severely dehydrated, it was by the grace of God Rogelio made it through. Thinking of her son's plight and her own desperation then, Josefina assured her. "I can help you."

"How?" Luz stared up at her with wet, hopeful eyes.

"I will let you stay with my family, if you promise to keep the baby."

"Then I can't stay." Luz fell back in her seat and gathered her tears in her hands.

"Please, do not take the life away from this baby. I will help you." Josefina could see Luz's hands trembling. "Please, let me help you," she begged. "I can't. You can't help me."

And just as soon as Luz came into Josefina's life, she slipped out the booth and vanished out the restaurant, leaving the doors shuddering on their frames. In weak moments, decisions are often made based on emotion. Had Josefina been weak, none of her children would have existed and she would never know love. She wanted to convince Luz that the world needed strong women like her to raise babies, but there was nothing Josefina could do. She once was a young mother, and she knew what people said.

It took only one day for Luz to return. She stood at the entrance of La Rocketa, eyes red and so puffy she could barely see. But she didn't need sight to feel. Without pause, Josefina took the girl into her arms and Luz decided to accept Josefina's offer. That day, Luz shared the small studio apartment that was the home of Josefina and her three young children. Luz had developed beautifully and accepted a chance at love, but Josefina knew she couldn't burden her with the kids.

Josefina reached her aunt's home and rapped on the open door, "Hola, Tía," she shouted from the city sidewalk. Josefina could smell the grain of fresh golden corn smashed in the stone molcajete her aunt used to prepare tortillas. She made the best tortillas in that part of the city, sold them at all the nearby markets, and traded them with her neighbors in exchange for fresh garden produce.

"Hola, Josefina," her aunt said. "Are you bringing your kids again?"

"I have to work just three hours. Do you have time?"

"No," her aunt scoffed. "I have to go to the store and visit con mi Madrina." Rosa's thin, curvy build made her a magnet for all men, but she chose a life of service, which often left her grumpy.

Rosa walked down the foyer to meet them at the door, wiping her hands clean on the sides of her apron. Seeing the distress upon Josefina's face, she quickly changed the subject of childcare and said, "Aren't you feeding these children?" She took Graciela's face in her hand. "Graciela, you're so skinny." A little embarrassed, Graciela's face sunk down to her chest. "And these boys, Josefina. How are they supposed to grow up to be strong men with just skin on their bones?"

"They're okay, thank you, Tia Rosa," Josefina politely said. "We have to go. I have to go to work."

"Where are you going to take them?" Rosa asked. "To the restaurant? Are they going to take orders and bring out the food?" Rosa laughed. "You know Miriam won't let you."

The boys were attempting to taunt Graciela, who gave each a quick kick to the shin. They yelped.

Josefina didn't have an answer. She couldn't take them to La Rocketa, but she had no one else. Armando's mother was repulsed by her. When she and Armando were first married, her mother-in-law told her son that Josefina was hideously ugly and asked him why he couldn't have found a prettier girl to marry. Josefina, standing there in their presence, was left without words. She tried to smile, but she was better off not showing her semi-toothless grin. She settled for her natural under-bite and lowered her head in shame.

Now, standing with Rosa, there was nothing she could do. She waited a few moments to consider her non-existent options.

"Oh, just leave them here!" Rosa barked at her. She grabbed the children by their shoulders and pulled them inside her home.

"Oh, thank you, Tia Rosa. Thank you so much, I won't be long. I'll be right back. In three hours, I promise," said Josefina, already running down the street. "Just go. And don't be late!" Rosa yelled down the street.

With that she shut the heavy wrought iron door. The sun was searing that day, but she didn't want the kids running out into the busy streets

274

where dark men would sooner take the children and flee on a bus to the country.

"Don't touch anything!" Rosa yelled at the kids as she slammed the second wooden door, locking it tightly.

Havasupai Rising

By Chris Knoblaugh

The car rattled along Highway 95 as Raven struggled with incoming Las Vegas traffic. Motorcycles roared past in herds of 10-20 bikers, truckers hauling double loads blasted her with tidal waves of wind as they rushed past, and her fellow lost tourists hit the brakes over and over while looking for their exits. The beads of sweat on her brow were from a combination of 108-degree heat and sheer terror.

She had not expected the old rental car to have a faulty air conditioner. Her grandmother had told her Arizona would be hot, but since she had never been to Supai herself she thought she would also see Las Vegas over in Nevada before heading into a culture she had only heard about. She had also not expected her grandmother to pass. Her grandmother was supposed to be her guide to this culture, but the heart attack had taken her. Raven was on a mission to explore her American Indian side, and would be an immigrant into her own culture's lands. She let out a little scream as a semi came too close while it passed her; the car even shook in the truck's tailwind leaving her completely unnerved.

Meanwhile, her husband slept like a peaceful baby in the passenger seat. She could have choked him, if she had had the courage to release her white-knuckled grip on the wheel. As it was, every ounce of energy poured into keeping the rental car in her own lane. Vacation? Maybe, but at that moment she was fighting an epic highway battle fought by many on a daily basis. Just another of the multitude of hopefuls spilling into the casinos in search of a little luck and a break, she was overweight, middle aged, and tired. As luck would have it, she was headed for much more than she ever imagined.

Back in her youth, when she wrestled with how to spend her future, she worked as a database builder organizing mountains of news and medical information into searchable text. When the Internet first began, she used Arpanet to send files of information to other research centers long before the Web or browsers ever came into being. She was one of the original spinners who wove knowledge from information, seeing patterns of light and shadow reminiscent of a weaver's loom. That was how she thought: in patterns. Some patterns were bright and hopeful, while others sank into dark decay. She tried to focus on the light images, both to keep her own spirits up and the spirits of those around her. Her grandmother had said she had "the sight."

Her ability to focus was impeccable. Scant shadows of implied relationships were quickly traced, analyzed, and categorized. Always looking, always seeking, she hungrily sought more knowledge on a myriad of topics. Relentlessly curious and tirelessly patient, she pecked though facts and assembled them into interpretive patterns – tiring both friends and family with her constant analysis and stoic composure. Her grandmother had said she would have made a good weaver. Her grandmother had said a lot of things.

Right now, however, panic filled her as realized she had missed her freeway exit. She could see the distinctive shape of her casino in her peripheral vision as her car crept forward in the snarled middle lane, a solid line of trucks occupying the desperately desired exit lane on the right. No breaks appeared in the line, and no opportunities to escape the crowd occurred. She was stuck in the middle of everything – traffic, life, and the day at hand – as her husband snored away beside her in the Vegas sun.

Belmont Hills

By Jeannine Gerkman

Most poems are about emotion
This one is of place
The neighborhood around us
The vistas that we face

Our oak is dropping acorns
Like missiles on the deck
The squirrels are scurrying after them
Our backyard's a wreck

There's a gentle murmur of traffic
As background for our street
The scent of apples ripening
And footsteps at my feet

My dog halts at storm drains
Hesitation always there

Is it the metal grid that grates
Or a hint of raccoon in the air?

We climb up Monte Cresta
And then descend Monserat
Along our route trudge children
With backpacks big and fat

Some days we startle
Does with wet noses
Staring at us through the mist
Maybe a fawn or two behind
them. You get the gist

This place means beautiful
mountain and I'd say its name is apt
'Cause as we walk these hills
With beauty we are wrapped

Fairy Garden

By Kimberly Schultz

Celestial awkwardly stood in front of the classroom fiddling with her fingers. *Fingers, please work for me today,* she thought nervously. Her wings stiffened. They darkened from a bright pink to a deep red like they always did when she was nervous. She concentrated on the spell she was about to perform in front of her entire class. Three fairies in the back of the classroom sat huddled together giggling. Celestial knew it was because of last week's explosion. Miss Flitter put a flowerpot in front of her and told her to do the spell for flower growth.

Celestial awkwardly stared at the pot and wished she could be like all the other fairies in her class. All Candylyn had to do was point her finger and out from the dirt grew a beautiful African violet. When Sweetess tapped the flowerpot, a beautiful rose grew.

Celestial tapped the pot and something bloomed all right. Slow growing dirt-filled vines awkwardly emerged from the dirt. The vines grew fatter and fatter with dirt as they grew up toward the ceiling until... POP! Dirt dusted every inch of the classroom, including Miss Flitter. The whole class laughed.

So today, Miss Flitter stood in the back of the classroom. Celestial concentrated on the flowerpot in front of her. It took her weeks to learn a new spell, unlike all her fairy classmates who learned new spells in minutes and were already using them. Celestial wiggled her finger at the flowerpot, but nothing happened. She stood in front of the fidgeting class of impatient fairies wishing she knew a spell that would make her disappear. It felt like forever, but she was finally saved by the dismissal bell.

The entire class zoomed past Celestial and right out of the classroom. While Candylyn and Sweetess flew by her, they giggled. Celestial stood in front of the empty flowerpot longing to be like the other fairies.

"Maybe tomorrow," Miss Flitter said looking disappointed.

Celestial wandered out into the meadow. Fairies flew all around the meadow dancing and singing. Candylyn and Sweetess held hands as they flew out of the meadow and into the forbidden forest. Curious where they were going, Celestial ran into the forest after them. She jumped over dry leaves and fallen branches so that the fairies would not hear her. *If only I could fly as well as them! They wouldn't even hear me!* Celestial thought. But the faster she ran, the more noise she made.

Candylyn and Sweetess stopped in mid-flight, turned around, and spotted her. "Go away, Celestial! Go practice your spells!" Candylyn said as she pulled Sweetess into the shadows of the enormous trees.

"But you shouldn't be out this far!" Celestial shouted. Celestial knew she should go tell someone, but she didn't want to be called a tattletale. She started walking back to the meadow, but stopped when she heard a loud crash. In the far distance, she heard Candylyn and Sweetess calling for help.

Celestial started to run, but her legs were not fast enough. She tried out her wings, but she did not raise high enough off the ground. So she took a deep breath and tried again. This time, her wings began to flutter – at first her wings beat against each other very slowly, but the more she tried, the faster her wings moved. She flew up into the air, bouncing off a tree or two before finally gaining control. She weaved through the trees and right out of the forbidden forest.

Fear dropped her to the ground when she saw that Candylyn and Sweetess were trapped in a fairy garden in the backyard of a human's dwelling. All her life, adult fairies have warned her about humans. "Stay away from the fairy traps!" her parents warned her. She even took a class all about avoiding the enchanting spells these gardens cast over fairies.

Celestial knew she had to help Candylyn and Sweetess. Her wings slowly brought her back into the air. She cautiously moved between the shadows of the swaying trees to get to where Candylyn and Sweetess were trapped. When the fairies saw her, they reached through the solid bars begging her to help them.

Celestial became hypnotized by the beauty of the garden. She wanted to run through the gravel pathways that lie between luscious bright green grasses. She wanted to frolic in the miniature houses that were positioned throughout the garden for her enjoyment. Her eyes locked on the beauty of the clear waterfall made of the bluest rocks. And the fragrant flowers were absolutely divine.

"Celestial!" the girls screamed. "Look away!"

Celestial struggled to close her eyes and break the spell this garden cast on her. When she opened her eyes she was able to focus. She flew over to the cage and fumbled with the lock. "I can't open it! I have to go get help!"

"There is no time!"Sweetess said. "You have to use your magic! Our magic does not work in here!"

"I can't," Celestial said sadly. She was embarrassed to admit that she was the only fairy in their class that learned differently than all the other fairies. "I don't know any spells yet."

"Do your best, Celestial," Candylyn said softly. "You are better than you believe you are."

Celestial took a deep breath and closed her eyes. She tried to remember a spell—any spell that would help the fairies out of the cage. She tapped the cage with her finger but nothing happened. Candylyn and

Sweetess huddled together in the back of the cage and waited as Celestial concentrated. Celestial wagged her finger again and the cage turned into dirt-filled vines that exploded, leaving Candylyn and Sweetess covered in dirt.

They wrapped their arms around Celestial giving her a tight hug. "You did it!" Candylyn cried. "I knew you could!"

The fairies returned back to their meadow deep in the forest and were never tempted by fairy gardens again. The next day at school, Celestial stood in front of the classroom in front of an empty flowerpot. She was not nervous or scared. Candylyn and Sweetess sat in the front row encouraging their new fairy friend. "You can do this!" Candylyn whispered. And Celestial did. She cast a spell that grew a beautiful daisy.

Seems No One Writes A Sonnet Anymore

By Nanci Lee Woody

Seems no one writes a sonnet anymore.
Who shall compare thee to a summer's day?
You'll find no simile nor metaphor
Except in my sweet words. I'll show the way.

I want, I need, the fourteen metered lines,
The A-B-A-B rhyming scheme. No free
Verse odes splaying across the page, like crimes
Of modern art. Such words come not from me.

Your bard of love begs forbearance. I pen
Occasional clichés. My love is blind!
Yet you, my dear, will find now and again
My words come from the soul into your mind.

Today, always, 'til winter's upon us,
You'll find my love when you read this sonnet.

One Fog-Knit Night

By Bill Baynes

1.Weldon

Weldon wasn't happy.

He lay with his whole company, his family and friends, more than a score of them, basking on the dock. Cinnamon, his favorite wife, was draped across his broad back, her pup right next to her. His brother Sergei stretched across his rear fins.

Burps, grunts, gaseous intervals, gossip – hard to tell one from the other. The tourists kept ticking their little lights. A normal afternoon on Fisherman's Wharf.

But Weldon was out of sorts. The flashes irritated him. He couldn't get comfortable. He could hardly turn his head. The big bull was as affable as the next guy, but this was truly annoying

He was sick of chilling with the sea lion colony. Every day the same individuals, the same quirks, the same habits. Everyone was totally predictable, right down to the next whisker twitch, the next belch.

He was bored with them, with all of them, with everything.

Nothing to do but perform stupid tricks for those grinny, ugly humans looking down from the crowded pier. Odd colors, obnoxious odors—they irked him.

Normally he was the loudest, the biggest clown, the strongest wrestler, the wettest splash. He was the one the people came to see. It usually amused him to amaze them with his antics, his blares and boasts. Now he could barely muster a yawn. He had lost his bluster.

His mind was turning to chowder.

He lay there, glaring at the humans. They watched him and he watched them.

They seemed so happy, most of them, but always so busy. They were always in motion. Didn't they ever get tired?

Weldon was. He was worn out from doing nothing, from being on the bottom, both physically and mentally. It was the most washed out, squashed and wasted, the tiredest tired of all.

He yearned for adventure. He needed something to do, something new. He wanted to go somewhere he'd never been, to meet someone he'd never seen.

But how can you meet anyone under a ton of sea lion blubber?

Cinnamon squirmed higher on Weldon's back. She always wanted to be on top of the pile. She was constitutionally unable (and certainly unwilling) to take her turn on the bottom like everybody else.

The nerve. Weldon liked the sun as much as she did. He felt he deserved a share.

Monotony made him touchy. He rippled his back.

Her pup rolled across his neck and hit the wood with a wet thud.

Weldon was actually a pretty gentle guy, but he was big. Really B-I-G. When he belched, waves formed. When he sneezed, fish swam into rocks. At least, it seemed that way... almost.

Jumbo, that's what Weldon was, and that's the way he expressed himself. His sadness was limitless, his anger volcanic, his boredom... flat all the way to the horizon, uninterested, uninteresting, the yawn that ate all existence, mind-numbing B-O-R-I-N-G.

Sergei slid to the end of the deck and slapped Tomany, hunting for a little fun.

They tussled and skimmed along their fellows' backs, grappling and slipping and grunting, until they both spilled into the bay. They made a considerable splatter, prompting a flurry of "ohs" and camera flashes from the sightseers.

Weldon wrinkled his snout and passed gas in comment.again.

Sergei sleeked back onto the dock and flopped across Weldon's rear flippers.

"They're such losers," he snorted.

Mpff. What did he know? What did he think he was?

Cinnamon wiggled her front flippers and hit Weldon in the face. That did it.

Weldon had had enough. Just because he was the largest and the smartest didn't mean he wanted to take care of everyone else. Right now he was more inclined to take some time for himself.

Crowded, chowdered—he couldn't put up with it any more. He couldn't even snooze in all this confusion. Enough of all this sociability, this geniality, this creature closeness. .

"BAH!" he barked and made a massive shrug. "OOF! Off!"

Sea lions slopping in all directions, he erupted and registered his displeasure. "ROAARR!!"

The humans applauded. Weldon shook his head in disgust, hurled himself off the pier and boogied down the bay.

He was a wonderful swimmer, fastest in the herd. He churned through the water, large enough to leave his own wake. Halfway to Alcatraz, he paused and looked back toward San Francisco.

He could hear a faint buzz that he never noticed when he was closer to shore. The people onshore swarmed like schools of mackerel with no predators to control them.

What was going on up in those hills? Were the humans enjoying themselves? All the activity—so glittery and exciting, so inviting—it seemed ceaseless.

It made him sleepy just to watch it all. He took a nap, floating upright with the tip of his nose out of the water.

When he woke, he swam alone for the rest of the day. It felt fine to be away.

Separate. Radical.

He could feel the pull of the herd, imagine the familiar feel of sea lion skin sliding against his, but he resisted it. When was the last time he'd spent several hours apart from the cluster, not lying with everyone on a slimy dock or floating together in a raft of bodies?

After dark, he fed his fill. He bobbed in the waves of the Bay and stared at the city again. Slow time. He enjoyed the solitude. The fog was rolling in. He could scarcely see the soft twinkling lights.

After a while, he noticed that the buzz had died down. The lights had stopped moving, though they were still on. Might be the time to investigate.

He cruised toward shore, propelling himself effortlessly, completely comfortable in the water. He climbed on some rocks and inspected his surroundings.

Quiet. Empty. No people. No machines. It was pleasant and damp. It felt safe.

Weldon skidded down to the ground. He brought his hind flippers under his big body and leaned onto his front flippers. Swaying from side to side, he wobbled forward into the heavy mist.

He had some exploring to do.

Arriving on Kulangsu

By P. John Anderson

Once in Kulangsu, looking for my father, looking for my mother, trudging over old fish bones, surrounded by deep blue sea -

"Hullo!" two boys hanging out the back of the electric tour bus, laughing already even before I parrot my reply.

"Hullo! Nǐ hǎo!" They nearly fall out. The bus sweeps on past Hope Hospital as it was once called, long ago.

No pause, no commentary for this old shell.
But I have seen it, watched it grow some more skin of brick veneer.

The birth-place reborn and I born again, invisible amongst the violins that will come—how sweet to become a music museum.

"Let's go see the sunset from the mountain—you know, Rìguāngyán - Sunlight Rock."
At our feet, the islet slowly sank in cool fire.

The Drawing Lesson

By Nanci Lee Woody

My new schoolhouse was a red, square building with a bell on the roof that clanged so loud you could hear it for miles. Twelve of us kids sat at desks in one big room. A wood stove stood in the corner and shelves close by were filled with books. And we were lucky, our teacher reminded us, to have a piano she played for us daily.

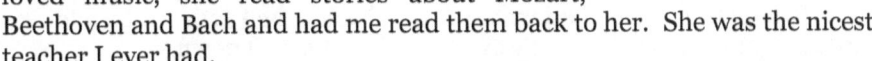

Miss Andrews noticed I had trouble reading and stayed after school to help me. Since she loved music, she read stories about Mozart, Beethoven and Bach and had me read them back to her. She was the nicest teacher I ever had.

She taught us about art, too, and one day told the class our parents sacrificed a lot for us and we could do something for them in return. She wanted us to draw a picture of something our parents cherished that we could give to them as a gift.

Later, I told my brother, "You know how Mom and Dad always listen to that *Ninth Symphony* record with the big chorus at the end? Our teacher wants us to draw something special for them, so I've decided to draw Beethoven."

"He going to sit for that?" Henry asked.

"He already has." I opened my library book. "See? I'll draw one of these."

He thumbed through the book until he found a portrait he liked. "Says this here was painted in 1820 by Karl Stieler. Pretty good artist, I'd say."

He studied the painting. "I used to draw a bit. I was pretty good if I do say so myself."

Henry left me at the kitchen table with my drawing pad and when I heard, "From out of the past comes the thundering hoof beats of the great horse, Silver!" I knew he had settled in by the radio. I began a rough sketch that wound up looking more like a cartoon character than Beethoven. I crumpled the page and started over.

Henry returned. "This doesn't look anything like Stieler's painting." He ran his finger around Beethoven's face. "Don't you know about shading? I hope you're not planning on handing this in."

I tossed my pencil at him. "You do it, then, if you think you're so good."

He sat down cocky-like and made a quick sketch, putting the eyes, nose, mouth and long hair in place. Finally, he put the dimple in Beethoven's chin, drew the musical score in one hand and a pencil in the other.

He handed the drawing to me. "Don't say I never did nothing for

283

you."

I put Henry's Beethoven on the nightstand by my bed and admired it all weekend. I knew it would impress Miss Andrews so, on Monday morning, I signed my name on it and headed off to school. I left it on her desk.

The next morning, I gasped as she taped Beethoven's portrait to the blackboard. "Look at this, class. Nellie, here, just a fifth-grader, is our very talented artist."

She smiled warmly at me. "Come on up here."

My heart thumped practically out of my chest as I stood beside her.

"I'm hoping you won't mind re-creating your work of art for us," she said. "You mean, draw it again?" Everybody watched as I tried to make a Beethoven like Henry's. When I got to the details, I was in trouble. Miss Andrews went on with her lessons, but asked me to stay in front of the class until my drawing was complete.

By lunchtime, I had a terrible stomachache. As I finished by adding a few squiggles for Beethoven's wavy hair, she let me sit down.

When Miss Andrews dismissed the class, everybody filed by my drawing, giggled and made smart remarks.

"Hey, Nelllll-eeeeee. Wanna draw my butt?"

When we were alone, she asked if there was anything I wanted to tell her. I shut my eyes tight, shook my head.

"Nellie, I very much like the drawing you did today. But that other drawing, that's obviously not your work."

Now the tears gushed out.

"Have you listened to Beethoven's music?" she asked.

"Just the *Ninth Symphony*," I mumbled, trying to hold back the tears.

"Then imagine how Beethoven might have felt if some other person got all the credit for writing this magnificent work."

"I can see you feel badly," Miss Andrews continued. "Maybe you'll want to talk to me tomorrow."

I had trouble falling asleep that night, worrying that Miss Andrews wouldn't like me. After some hard thinking, I knew what I had to do.

I got up early and left with a canning jar tucked under my arm. Along the way I picked at least a hundred flowers. At school, I filled the Mason jar with water, put the flowers in the jar, spread them out like mom did, and placed them on Miss Andrews' desk.

I wrote, 'I'm sorry I lied about the drawing' on a piece of notebook paper, signed 'Nellie' and tucked the note under the beautiful dandelions in the Mason jar, hoping Miss Andrews would forgive me.

Blackberry

By Luanne Oleas

One day, a tiny black kitten, not much larger than a squirrel, appeared at Blackberry Farm Park. He was so scared, no one could get close to him. Everyone wondered why he was there.

Where was his mom? Would he survive all alone, so small, and living under a bridge?

It was almost summer. The days were warm and the park was full of people. Some worked there. Some came to picnic and swim or play in the creek. In a way, it was a wonderful place for kitty to grow up.

Some days, the kitten even managed to forget how alone he was, with no mother or brothers and sisters. After all, deer, raccoons, rabbits, and other animals lived in the park.

Most mornings, school children walked or rode bikes through the park just before a bell rang. He would hear the same bell in the afternoon, and the children would reappear. But then, many days went by when the bell didn't ring, and the children didn't pass through the park. At first, the kitten felt lonely, but then, he noticed more families came to the park and cooked food over open fires and that smelled wonderful.

At night, he would crawl under his bridge and the crickets would sing him to sleep. He liked their song much better than the chorus of coyotes that echoed from the foothills down through Blackberry Farm some evenings. He tried to make himself very small on those nights and squeeze even further under the bridge.

Workers at the park called him Blackberry, but he didn't know why. He didn't know he was in Silicon Valley where Blackberry phones were made, and he didn't know he lived at Blackberry Farm.

He drank water from the creek when he was thirsty. Sometimes picnickers gave him leftovers or the park staff gave him food, but not always. Sometimes, he was so hungry, he would gather all his courage and steal a chicken leg from an unwatched barbeque grill.

His meals were irregular until a grandma started coming to the park one day. She would leave food for him and he would eat it after she left. One day, she even brought him a ball. He had never had his own toy.

Each day, when she brought him food, she would call him the same way. "Blackberry! Kitty-kitty, meow. Kitty-kitty meow. Blackberry!"

He would run to greet her, so matter how far he had wandered from his bridge.

He learned how to climb a tree. He showed the grandma that trick. He liked when she talked to him. She even would dangle a string and he would play with it. Before long, he let her pet him.

Blackberry noticed it seemed colder when Grandma left in the evening. He thought she took the warmth when she left. He didn't know the weather changed. He only knew summer. And coyotes.

One night, the coyotes left the surrounding hills and followed the creek into Blackberry Farm. Bone-chilling yowls announced their arrival. He was so afraid, he climbed a tree, and stayed there all night.

The next day, the workers at the park put away the tables and chairs, waved to each other, and said good-bye. The grandma came to the park, put him a box, and gave him to one of the workers. Blackberry had never been in a box before. He was scared.

The young man told the grandma he wanted a pet. When he took the kitten home, his parents told him he couldn't keep the cat. He took Blackberry to the animal shelter. Blackberry had never been locked in a cage. Doors slammed. People yelled. Dogs barked. It was never quiet. He crawled to the very back of the cage and wished he was under his bridge.

How could he ever get back to Blackberry Farm? He didn't know where he was or where the sky went. He felt even more scared than when the coyotes ran through the park.

A whole day passed before he heard a familiar voice. "Blackberry! Kitty-kitty, meow. Kitty-kitty meow. Blackberry!"

He didn't know how the grandma found him, but he was glad she did. She took him to a nice warm house and didn't lock him in a cage.

At night, the crickets sang him to sleep. Each day, he could hear the bell that used to call all the children. It was like being back at the park, but better. He didn't worry about the coyotes anymore. He just fell asleep in the grandma's arms and lived happily ever after.

Gettin' Outta the Bronx

By Dave LaRoche

It started like this, ya' see. Morey, he came up to me one day and said, "Jake, we're gonna be rich. We don't have to do much and when it's over we'll go to the Bahamas and loll around on the beach. The broads there, they'll serve us drinks with those funny umbrellas, and the sand'll be whiter than Coney. It'll be warm, Jake, warm through da whole year—all of it just like we been talkin' about for years. Whadda ya say, you in?"

Morey and me, we go way back. We ran the storm-sewers in the second and third grades, boy scouts together for almost a month. Even in high school though the tenth when both of us got tossed for pantsin' the daughter of the algebra teach. Well, she was a prudish kinda dame just needin' it. and what the hell, everybody was doin' it.

Double dates? Yeah, we did those too when we was lucky enough to boost a car for the night.

We played stickball in the alley on the same team, shared cigarettes and beers, and later on, nookie—when we was with the sharin' types, a'course. Good friends would be a big understatement.

We always wanted outta the Bronx, so I says, "Sure, Morey, is it legit?" "I think it is," he says.

"Doncha know?" I asked.

"Didn't ask," he says, "but it'll get us outta da neighborhood. You still achin' to go now, aintcha?"

And the deal was we'd sell this life insurance to the ancients at some lo-ball rate, no questions asked about age or body condition. Morey, ya' see, he'd hooked up with this shyster down on the east end who'd ginned up this deal with official looking policies—gold seal, fancy borders and all. Lookin' pretty kosher I'd say. And the best, we'd keep two-thirds a' the initiation fee and the entire first premium, both payable at the time a the signin'.

So I say to Morey, "Are these real policies?"

And Morey said, "Like I told ya', Jake, I didn't actually ask. The deal was sweet and I didn't wanna queer it with no stupid questions."

Well, I thought, we didn't know that they wasn't.

I figured on it a little and concluded that in all the ways I could think, I was Morey's best friend, and if I had a few lonesome doubts about the policies, they was overcome by our long association.

A beach in the Bahamas didn't bother me much neither.

So we go around the neighborhood knocking on doors, up and down the narrow stairs, crawlin' over tricycles and roller skates, listening to kids yowling, dogs yelpin'. Kitchen pots bangin' from being tossed by somebody's ol' lady due to watchin' basketball, their throats goin' dry and they wanting another beer. And we sold some of those policies and pocketed two-thirds a' the initiation fee and the whole first premium, which, incidentally, was nothin' to sneeze at.

The thing was, no physical examination was required, no restrictions on account a smokin' or drinkin' or havin' TB. Previous denials was not a problem and everyone qualified. The ancient ones, they jumped at it.

Yeah, it was pretty easy once we got used to it, and we was pickin' up some good dough. And, you know, most ancients, they don't read too well and have problems with hearin', but they seen we was from the neighborhood, and them needin' the payoff to handle their burying, they forked over the cash. A lot of 'em thanked us—cookies and stuff.

They was to send their monthlies to a box at the post office down in the Queens, "Sunset Insurance." And I suppose the shyster was there behind the box, just sittin' back on his laurels and checkin' out the travel brochures. Well, everybody wants ta get outta somewhere.

It mighta been a shitty situation and to be truthful I had my suspicions. But when they came into my head, I just pushed 'em right out with the notion that we'd be at this only as long as it took to get a small stake. We all gotta live, ya' know, and I guess we thought it best to do it in a might warmer climate.

Morey. He delivered the applications and the third of the fee. I never saw the shyster then and didn't like to ponder about whether the whole thing was on the up and up. What I thought about was those broads with the drinks in the Bahamas.

So, one day we knocked on this door way down at the end a' the street. A man answered. He was dressed good, in a brown suit and black tie, and he didn't look as old as he shoulda, given what we'd heard on the

287

street. Ya' see, before we'd even climb up a stoop, we'd scout out the place with a candy bar or some gum—"marketing research," Morey called it. A well-placed Baby Ruth would bring us the lay of the land from kids around, and we wouldn't have to waste no time.

Anyways, this guy, he says, "I know you dopes. Seen you hangin' around here and there—not doin' much. Knew your old man, Jake—what a bum he was." Well, I didn't take well to that, though I knew it to be the truth—no helpin' what your old man was.

Now I don't want any a' your insurance," he says. "It's not that I don't trust you, it's more I'm not ready. So how much are you makin' with that insurance scheme of yours? Step in here, you guys

—now, you wanna make some real dough?"

Morey said sure we was open, and a'course, bein' best friends, I nodded. I mean the guy says he knows us though I never seen him before.

He disappears into the back of his flat for a minute, this guy dressed to the nines with a bulge under his coast, and returned with a bag—a black satchel with a mean lookin' lock on it.

"All you gotta do is deliver this bag," he says. "The guy there, where you're to deliver it, he'll pay you five big ones."

Bein' the skeptic I am, I ask 'im. I says, "That's a lot of money just to carry a damn bag."

"It's a very important bag," he says, "needs a courier, and I don't have the time either to deliver it myself or call in a professional service. You want the five or not, no quibbling."

Okay, so we grabbed the bag and took off for East 159th Street, the five hundred sounding good. The Bahamas was around the corner, and we could stop with the insurance gig earlier, which'd make me feel better.

We're on the way over there when Morey says, "Wonder what's in this here bag, Jake? Must be somethin' important to pay us all that dough just ta carry it."

"So whatta we care?" I say.

"Think about it," he says. "Could be we won't need the five big ones." So I thought about it, like he says, and it don't take long for the light to come on.

"Look," I say. "Whatever's in there is ill-gotten or we wouldn't be carryin'. And more," I say, "if it's ill-gotten, you know who's gotten it and it ain't Mother Teresa. Me, I wanna go to the Bahamas, not to no early grave."

Morey was quiet. I could see he was figurin' on it—mixin' what I had to say into what he was thinkin'.

Then I says, "Anuder point is this. If we was to do a good job here with the carryin', could be we'll get to do more. Five-hundred big ones, now and then, would get us outta the Bronx in style, and that much sooner."

Well, that seemed to make sense to Morey and there was no more talk about what's in the bag.

We get to the address, Morey rings the bell and right away a greasy lookin' fat guy in an undershirt and black baggy pants answers the door.

"Oh, I see ya got the bag," he says.

"Yeah, we got the bag, where's the five-hundred?" Morey says.

The fat guy, ya' see, he didn't smell so good, was thinnin' out something terrible on top, though he made up for it with all the hair on the rest. He hadn't shaved for a couple a days and he must've had a bum ear.

"Five-hundred?" he says. "What five-hundred? There ain't no five-hundred," and he reaches for the bag.

Morey stepped back. "No dice," he says. "We get da five for deliverin'. For coming all da way up here wid this crummy bag. It was his promise, ya' see, the guy at da other end. No five, no bag, that's the deal."

The fat guy, he looked disturbed. He scratched the back of his head and some flakes fell off on his shoulders.

"Shit," he says. "Okay, c'mon," and he opens the door wider and beckons us in.

The place smelled jus like he did only more. Took your breath away, I'm tellin' ya', though nicely furnished with marble tables—a nice divan and some brass trimin's here and there. So we entered, sorta cocky I guess, thinkin' about the beach in the Bahamas and how we was soon to be big-timers, throw around some real cash, smoke a cigar. He closed the door there, kinda quiet.

"Now looky here, fellas," he said, "I don't have five-hundred. I don't know what the other guy said but he was full of it—an' ya' shouldn't a believed him. Maybe I could rustle up fifty bucks for your trouble, but that'll have ta do ya'." He reached out again for the bag, and again Morey withdrew.

Now this guy, he was breathin' kinda hard, and actin' sorta nervous like. The sweat was gatherin' on his brow and I could see his skin was startin' to glisten under the hair on his arms.

"Look, pal," Morey said. "Ya' think we rode in on a truck? You get up with the full tithin' here or we leave wid da bag."

Without a word, or even a gesture with his eyes, ya' know, the guy pulled a gun from his black baggy pants and thumped Morey hard on the side of the head. Knocked him clean to the floor, stone-cold out and the bag alongside. On the way down, his head—well it's hard for me to see it again, but Morey's head cracked loud against the coffee table there.

We dove, the fat guy and me, but being a bit younger and quicker, I got there first and I grabbed the bag. 'Course the policies got dropped on the floor.

"Look, buddy," I said, once I'd recovered composure, "Morey's my best friend. You can't be whackin him around like that. Now give us the five we're due and we'll leave ya' the bag and get outta here."

The guy seemed infuriated now, sweatin' heavy through his undershirt, it beading up all over his arms, eyes red and bulging and he's approachin' hysterical, I thought.

"Alright! Goddammit," he said. "You look to your friend and I'll get you the money."

As he started his turn toward the back of the apartment, he lunged over to whack me one. 'Course, by now I was wary, saw it coming and ducked. He swung so hard that his hand smacked the doorframe and he up and lost his balance along with the gun.

"Umph, goddammit!" I heard him say on his way down.

As he busied himself regaining his feet, I dove for the gun and got it snugly in my hand. But as I rolled over to face him, he up and grabbed ahold of one a those free-standin' ashtrays and came at me again. So I fired.

Well, I ain't so cozy with guns and the bullet missed the fat guy entirely, ricocheted off the coffee-table and right into Morey who was whoozy, just gainin' consciousness there across from me on the floor.

"Holy shit," I muttered as I turned to look at Morey. He had a dark hole below his eye and a lot of blood and other stuff on the back of his head and more on the floor.

Well, I got to the phone and dialed 911 while keepin' the fat guy at bay. Now that he knew for certain that I'd pull the trigger, he got less aggressive. The fact is, as I'm dialin' he's straightenin' the house. Picked up the ashtray and laid the policies out on the table. With the authorities comin' I suspected he wanted to show a good front.

The EMTs came, and right after the beat cop, then the homicide guys—and whadda ya' know, the fat guy was connected. In the commotion of it all, and the cops doggin' me—askin' a lot a questions I didn't know how to answer, the fat guy, he'd put on a shirt and ditched the bag somewhere. On the way to the station he rode in the front seat of the cruiser—me in the back behind the grill. "Ya' wanna cigarette?" the driver says to him. "Too bad ya' got roughed up a little."

A'course the gun wasn't registered, serial number gone—just the kind a' gun I woulda owned, if I owned one, and the story he told sounded reasonable, even to me.

We'd come to sell him insurance, he said, and he came to know it was a scam. And he told 'em, he said, while we was with the applications and policies spread out on the table, he ducked outta the room and dialed 911. There was a tussle, he said, and while he was talkin' there on the phone, I drew the gun. As we grappled, it went off and Morey was shot. The fat guy was lucky to be alive, ya' see, cause right after the shootin' the cops arrived. The bag I kept yellin' about was nowhere to be found. 'Course no one was lookin' very hard.

Morey was pronounced dead on the way to Our Lady's Memorial and, given my "questionable history," the desk sergeant said I might as well have passed along with him.

So, there I was, caught in the consequences a sellin' those policies, and then later there, standing in the drizzlin' rain, cuffed to one of a couple a precinct blues as a part of a small gatherin' that had gone to put Morey away.

I told 'em I'd give 'em no trouble, that Morey was my best friend, life long since playin' in the sewers and at least they could allow me his buryin'. I was from Morey's neighborhood, they said, and we'll all get to go if we wanna.

So I'm, checkin' over his hole in the cemetery there, listenin' to the preacher drone on and wonderin' just what was had happened—indicted for killin' my best friend and thankful to tears that the shyster stepped up to the funeral tab. And I'm thinkin' then, all we ever wanted was to get outta the Bronx.

Oh yeah, you wanted to know about the well-connected fat guy? It's kinda ironic, ya' see. My guess is both he and the brown suit was chiselin' the family and we just got caught in the middle. And I'd bet, if I was a wagerin' man, they's both in the Bahamas with the contents a' that bag, lying on a white sandy beach where the broads serve you drinks with those funny umbrellas—like me and Morey wanted to do.

And as it turns out, me too. I'm getting' outta the Bronx like I'd hoped to all a' my life. How's that, ya' might ask.

Attica, they say—it's upstate New York.

Drrrag and the Tooth Fairy

By Carolyn Donnell

The little dragon leaned against his grandmother on the old couch in the den and inhaled the lavender she kept in a bowl on the coffee table. "Grandmother, I have a question."

"Yes Drrrag?" She wrapped one wing around his shoulders. "It's about something my friends told me."

"The ones from your imaginary adventure?"

"It wasn't imaginary." He looked at his Grandmother. She loved him but she didn't always believe everything he said. He shrugged. "Yeah, those guys. They told me there was a tooth fairy, said they put their teeth under a pillow and the tooth fairy would leave money for the tooth."

Grandmother Dragon laughed. "Oh Drrrag, what a story! I wish I could get money for all the teeth I've lost. I'd be rich."

"What do you mean? You have all your teeth."

"Yes, but they're not really mine." Grandmother Dragon put her paws in her mouth and twisted her fingers around. Drrrag heard a squishy sound and then, with a pop, she pulled her teeth out of her mouth.

"Grandmother!" Drrrag's eyes got very big. "Your teeth. Oh, what happened? Are you OK?"

"Don't worry darling." She made a funny smacking sound as she talked and couldn't pronounce her THs. "Teese are falsssh. Some old dragons have temm."

"False teeth?" Drrrag looked closely at the teeth set into pink plastic she held in her paws. "I know now that everyone loses their baby teeth and grows new ones. But I never heard of false teeth. Dragons can have lots of different kinds of teeth then?"

"Tat's right."

"That's neat." He watched her wiggle her teeth back into her mouth. "But I still want to know about this tooth fairy thing. Are you absolutely sure there are none?"

"Well, teere was an old, old story I did hear once. Why don't you go talk to your Uncle Mushmush?"

"You mean mother's Uncle?"

"Tat's right. He's tee oldest dragon in our family. If tere's ever been a toof fairy story he would know about it. And take cookies. He loves cookies." She yawned. "Run along now. I need a nap."

Drrrag gave her a hug and tiptoed away.

Uncle Mushmush was very old and couldn't fly that well, so his cave was at the lowest level of the dragon house. Drrrag knocked loudly on the door. Uncle Mushmush was hard of hearing too.

A trembling voice came out from the dark entrance. "Whhooo's there?"

"It's me, Uncle Mushmush. Drrrag."

"Drag? Drag who?"

"Drrrag. You remember me. My mother is Derrrena. I brought some cookies."

"Cookies? Ah, your mother. Derrrena. She is my favorite niece. Why didn't you say so? Come on in."

Drrrag walked slowly into the dimly lit corridor. The aroma here was more like old socks than lavender. Drrrag wrinkled his nose.

The old dragon sat by a fire, a red shawl draped around his bony shoulders. He pointed to the cookies and then to the table next to his chair.

Drrrag placed the platter next to his uncle and stood, shifting from one foot to the other.

The old dragon took his yellowed set of teeth out and placed them in a glass on the table. "Mmmm." He mashed the soft cookies up with only his gums. "Scuse me, boy, for not putting my teef in. I don't like to use tem any more tan I have too."

"My grandmother has teeth like that too. I just found out today. I didn't know there was such a thing as false teeth."

"Not many dragons have tem. Teef are important, but expensive. Your new ones are growing in, I see."

"Yes, they are. Actually that's what I wanted to ask you about. Well, not the teeth, but about a tooth fairy."

Uncle Mushmush coughed and spat out cookie crumbs. "Aach! What did you say?"

"Tooth fairy. Grandmother said if anyone knew anything about it you would know."

The old dragon glared at Drrrag. "Where did you hear about toof fairies?"

"From friends."

"What friends? No one around here has fairies in teir memories."

"So there is a tooth fairy?"

"Well..."

Drrrag stamped his foot. "Uncle, I need to know!"

"Tey haven't been around since I was a very small dragon."

"What happened Uncle? Tell me."

"Was an argument. My father refused to leave teef out unless the fairy left a great treasure. The Toof Fairy got angry and never returned. Tat was a very long time ago."

"Oh no! And I really wanted to find one."

"You're first baby teef are already gone anyway, why would you want to find a fairy now?"

"Just because. I want to know. Please help me."

"All I remember is the old legend." Uncle Mushmush closed his eyes and began to recite. "If you wait by a stream on a night when te moon full. If your heart is pure, if you wish all night, have pity on you, a Fairy might."

Drrrag moved closer to the old dragon. "Uncle, did you ever go to the stream?"

Uncle Mushmush sighed. "Many times, but no one ever appeared."

"When is the next full moon?"

"I believe it's tonight." Uncle Mushmush blinked and squinted at Drrrag. "But you aren't tinking of going out, are you? You're much too young. I forbid it. You just go on home now."

"But Uncle ..."

"Not anoteer word. Scat! You'd better be home when the moon rises too. If I find out you disobeyed, I may find I have a little fire left." He began to cough again and a trickle of smoke drifted from his nostrils.

"I'm going home. Now!" Drrrag ran from the cave and up to his mother's house. After supper he sat in his bed, looking out the window. The moonlight was so bright it filled half the room. Drrrag tiptoed over to the window and stared in the direction of the stream. Moonlight at the edge of the forest illuminated an opening in the underbrush he had never noticed before.

He couldn't stand it any longer. Slipping on his shoes and grabbing his long sweater, he crawled out the window and made his way toward the woods. Strange noises surrounded him. He shivered. He slipped his wings through openings in the back of the sweater and pulled it on, buttoning it up to his chin. Moonlight lit the pathway to the stream. A little waterfall added its rushing sounds to the nighttime song of crickets. He sat down on the sloping bank by the water and wrapped his arms around his knees.

"I wish with all my heart and with all my might, that the Tooth Fairy will hear me and come here tonight." He rocked back and forth as he repeated the verse over and over again.

The moonlight turned the water to liquid silver. Drrrag thought he saw a shimmer, but when he looked again he could only see water. Just the moon's reflection, he thought. He repeated the verse again. He was cold. And he was hungry. "I wish I had brought some of those cookies for myself," he mumbled.

"So do I."

Drrrag jerked around so hard he almost fell over. "Who said that?"

"Me."

Drrrag heard a sound like a large bumblebee. He turned his head slowly. Close to his right ear was a pair of silver wings beating fast, surrounding a delicate body dressed in a shimmering gown embroidered with tiny pink flowers. A matching band of pink flowers held her long pale blonde hair out of her round little face. The golden hair was long enough to sit on. Tiny pink shoes on her feet and a purple silk bag hanging from her belt completed the costume.

"Who are you?" Drrrag whispered.

"Who am I?" The soft rose above the wings' vibrations. "You called for me. That's who I am."

"Me? You mean . . . Oh! You're the Tooth Fairy?"

"That's right."

Drrrag narrowed his eyes and looked at the tiny flying creature. "You look too small to be a Tooth Fairy."

Tooth Fairy's wings vibrated faster. "And you look too small to be a Dragon."

"I'm a very young Dragon. I just lost my baby teeth not too long ago." He opened his mouth and pointed to the new teeth that were coming in. "See?"

"Ahh. Well, I'm a very young Tooth Fairy." The fairy flew around in a circle above Drrrag's head. "But where are your baby teeth? I don't see a pillow anywhere."

"My teeth fell out a while ago. I didn't know about tooth fairies then."

"What? Everyone knows about tooth fairies."

"Not us dragons. Only my uncle remembered anything at all. He said there was a fight. A long time ago."

The fairy flew to a nearby bush and sat on one of the larger leaves. "My mother told me some story like that. But I didn't believe it."

"Well it's true. My uncle told me today. I may be the first one to wish for a long, long time."

"Yes. I was told that no one wished any more. But when I heard you tonight, I came to see for myself."

Drrrag smiled. "I'm so glad you did."

"But why? I can't do anything about teeth that are already gone."
"No?" Drrrag's smile faded. "Nothing at all?

The fairy shook her head.

Drrrag frowned. "But that's not fair. I didn't know."

"Sorry, but it's not my fault. Those are the rules. You know about rules."

"Yes, I do. That's OK then. I guess it was worth it to find out that you are real."

"Wait." The fairy's wings began to vibrate and she flew straight up off the bush. "Since you wished so hard, I might be able to do something for you. But you would have to help me with a task first. Do you have another wish, besides money for your teeth?"

"Another wish?"

"Something you really want."

Drrrag scratched his head. "Well..."

"Just ask. If I can't do it I'll tell you."

Drrrag stood up and opened his sweater. "I really hate this silver color I'm changing to." He flapped his wings. "The best dragons are gold. Can you change me to gold?"

"You don't like silver?"

The fairy shook her head. "I think it's beautiful."

"Silver may be OK for a tooth fairy like you, but gold is best for dragons. Can you make me gold?"

"You're sure that's what you want?"

"Yes. Yes!"

"Okay. But like I said, first you'll have to help me."

"Sure. But help with what?"

The fairy flitted around Drrrag from side to side and head to toe. "You look like a strong dragon."

Drrrag raised his left arm and tried to make a muscle appear. "I am strong."

"Good. I need help moving a tooth."

"A tooth? You need help? I thought fairies just waved a magic wand or something."

"Humph!" The fairy brushed by Drrrag's ear. "I wish. And this is not an ordinary tooth either. It belongs to a giant."

"A giant? How big?" Drrrag held up his arms. "Bigger than I am?"

"Oh yes. Much bigger. If you can't do it . . ."

"Hey! I can do it. Sure. I'll help you."

"Ok." The fairy started to fly away. "Let's get on with it."

"You mean right now?"

"Yes little dragon. Right now. The tooth is ready as we speak. Has to be tonight."

"Oh. Ok, I guess. Where is this tooth?"

"On the other side of the mountain."

Drrrag stood on his tiptoes and looked through the line of trees. "That's too far. It will take too long."

"What do you mean? You can fly can't you?"

Drrrag gave his wings a feeble flap. He shook his head. "Oh phooey."

The fairy landed on the bush again.

Poppy and Hyacinth

By Anne Jayne

CHAPTER ONE

Poppy Patel, age 10, sat by the window of the manager's apartment in the Occidental Hotel.

Her head was bent over a placemat she was hemming for the school fair, and her long dark braids brusd the table. Beside her, Hyacinth, age 7, was patiently gluing yellow lentils and beans on a picture of a kitten she had drawn, making yellow and brown stripes on its back. The window overlooked Mission Street in the big city of San Francisco. Wisps of cold fog blew past the hurrying people below them, but Poppy and Hyacinth felt safe and warm with Mama beside them, her knitting needles clicking, and Papa at the Hotel registration window, ready to rent rooms to people who came up from the street,

When Poppy was only one year old, before Hyacinth was even born, the family had come on an airplane from far-away India to be hotel managers for Papa's Uncle Gautam.

Uncle Gautam had called Papa's father, Armetesh, on the village phone.

"Brother Armetesh, send one of your sons to be my hotel manager. It would be a good opportunity for him." Drought was making it hard for cotton farmers in India, so Papa and Mama had decided to join Uncle Gautam in America.

The Hotel buzzer sounded.

"Who is there?" Papa asked into a tube connecting to the front gate below.

"It is Joseph and Aunt Rebecca." These were very welcome guests! Papa pushed a button to open the iron gate, and in a moment Aunt Rebecca and teenaged cousin Joseph could be heard coming up the stairs.

"Look what I've brought you!" Joseph held out a shoe box. He took off the lid to show a tiny kitten with yellow and grey stripes. She looked like Hyacinth's picture! Poppy and Hyacinth were amazed!

"Meow," the kitten said and backed unto a corner of the box.

"My friend at school needed a home for this kitten." Joseph said. "I thought you two would like it"

"Oh, how beautiful!" whispered Hyacinth. She reached into the box to gently touch the kitten.

Aunt Rebecca sat down heavily in one of the chairs.

"This may not be to your liking, Mary Amita," she said to Mama. "You do not have much space for a cat."

"She can help by catching mice," said Joseph. "She can sleep on our bed", said Hyacinth.

"Please, Mama, can we keep her?" pleaded Poppy.

Papa came over to look at the small kitten. He stroked her back with one of his fingers. His eyes met Mama's and he smiled.

"Well, perhaps we do need a way to prevent mice from living here."

Poppy and Hyacinth squealed with delight. The kitten was soon sitting in Poppy's lap with Hyacinth bending over to smooth her fur. They named her Kitty. That night she slept between Poppy and Hyacinth on their bed.

Kitty investigated every corner of the apartment. She climbed on top of every shelf and table. She lapped-up the milk mama poured for her, curling her tiny pink tongue. Poppy and Hyacinth said good-by to her each morning as they left for school. When they returned, Kitty licked their hands and faces with her rough little tongue. She slept beside them every night.

The day of the school fair arrived. Poppy had finished hemming two matching placemats Hyacinth had glued beans and rice and lentils onto her picture.

"It is a picture of Kitty!" she said.

She had made a frame from the thick cardboard of a grocery box and colored it yellow to match Kitty's yellow stripes. Mama put two jars of pickles she had canned into a small box.

They were ready to go.

Papa must stay to watch the hotel. He took two dollars from the wallet in his back pocket, and gave one to Hyacinth and one to Poppy.

"You can each buy something you like." He told them. They hugged him in excitement. Mama and the girls walked down the hallway steps to the hotel door that opened onto Mission Street. As they opened the iron-grilled gate, Kitty suddenly dashed past them and out onto the busy sidewalk.

Poppy and Hyacinth made so much noise that Papa came down the stairs. "Kitty has run away!" they wailed.

"I'll get her. You stay here."

Papa pushed past the iron gate and looked for Kitty. He saw her standing against the wall a few feet away, near the Bueno Comida Café. The owner of the café, Jose Manuel, opened the door.

"Kitty, Kitty," he called and reached for her, but Kitty backed away and ran down the sidewalk, dodging beneath the feet of passersby. Papa followed but Kitty kept ahead, out of the reach of his arm.

Poppy and Hyacinth stood in the hotel doorway. Hyacinth was crying, and Poppy was calling "Kitty! Kitty!" Mama set down her packages and put a comforting arm around each of them.

Halfway down the block stood Harry Smith, a homeless man who sometimes stayed at the Occidental hotel when his pension check came in the mail. As Kitty flew past, he bent down and scooped her up in his hands.

"Whoa there little fella!" he said to her. He held her up and showed her to Papa who was running down the sidewalk.

"Thank you!" said Papa, out of breath.

Harry walked back with Papa to give the kitten to Hyacinth. She could feel Kitty's heart thumping in her chest.

With many thanks to Harry, Papa took Kitty up into the hotel. Poppy, Hyacinth, and Mama holding their packages, began again their journey to the school fair.

The fair was fun! The school raised lots of money. Mama's pickles and Poppy's place mats were sold. Poppy used her dollar to buy the picture of Kitty which Hyacinth had made. They put it on the wall above their bed. Hyacinth used her dollar to buy a pair of socks for Harry Smith.

Uber Girl and Wonder Boy

By Missy Kirtley

Uber Girl and Wonder Boy Meet Dirty Jack

Maryanne and Tobias Watkins are normal children. They live in a regular house, they have a good-sized yard, they eat family dinners together. Maryanne and Tobias Watkins have two normal parents; Mr. and Mrs. Watkins.

Every day Maryanne and Tobias Watkins get up in the morning. They brush their teeth, they eat breakfast, they go to school. After school, Maryanne and Tobias Watkins come home. They do their homework, they walk the dog, they feed the cat.

Mr. and Mrs. Watkins are very proud of their son and daughter. Maryanne and Tobias are very well mannered, get good grades in school, and do all their chores. All in all, the family is very happy, healthy and normal.

As most normal kids do, Maryanne and Tobias have a normal bedtime. They brush their teeth, wash their faces, and then head to bed at eight o'clock. The cat curls up on Maryanne's bed, and the dog sleeps with Tobias.

Maryanne and Tobias Watkins are completely normal, except when they're not. You see, Maryanne and Tobias are regular children by day, and super heroes by night. Under the names "Uber Girl" and "Wonder Boy" Maryanne and Tobias face villains most nights, vanquishing evil doers and helping their local police department.

When the secret phone rings, Wonder Boy and Uber Girl spring into action. They answer the call from the Police Commissioner, no matter what time it comes in. It's their sworn duty to help protect their neighbors from the forces of darkness, and those who would be nuisances to the general public.

So far, Uber Girl and Wonder Boy have thwarted The Giant Crab (who wanted to fill all the bird baths in the city with salt water), Warrior Man and his Tiger Friend (who were trying to steal all the frozen chickens from the local supermarkets) and The Obnoxious Hugger (who they simply asked to refrain from hugging random people on the subway).

When Maryanne and Tobias change into their superhero outfits, become Uber Girl and Wonder Boy, then leave their bedroom through the window, they leave their cat, Smoochkins, all by herself on the bed. Little do Maryanne and Tobias know that Smoochkins herself has a secret identity. Smoochkins is actually "Kitty the Smooch," a secret agent in the Organization for Villainy. She has her own secret agenda.

Jack Williams is a likewise normal child. His hair is never tidy and his clothes are always stained. Jack has two arms and two legs, one head and two eyes. He is a very average boy. Jack is similar to Maryanne and Tobias. He is the same age, and has a pet of his own.

Jack moved with his mom and his dad to the opposite side of town. Unlike Maryanne and Tobias, Jack doesn't have any siblings.

Much like Tobias and Maryanne, Jack does a lot of things that normal kids do. He plays baseball, he reads books, he feeds his hamster. The main difference between them is that Jack hates to be clean.

Hamsters, unlike cats, have no problem with owners who are untidy. Jack's hamster, Mister Twitchy Nose, has his own living space with cedar bedding and toilet paper rolls. He doesn't care if Jack never takes a bath.

Baths are the bain of Jack's existence. So much so that Jack has started to call himself "Dirty Jack." Dirty Jack hates baths.

A few nights ago, during an abnormally cruel and unusual scrubbing session, Dirty Jack decided something must be done to solve the world's cleanliness problem. He brainstormed, and planned, and soon he had the answer.

The Dirt-O-Ray! It will make everyone and everything dirty! Using some child like ingenuity and a combination of 85% dirt to 15% water, Dirty Jack created the ultimate weapon in the fight against cleanliness.

Making things dirty will make Dirty Jack very, very happy. Unfortunately, and unbeknownst to Dirty Jack, Mister Twichy Nose reports to the Panel Aganst Evil Doers, or PAED. When he became aware of Dirty Jack's plan, he alerted the Police Commissioner.

The Police Commissioner is a confused man in a Bow Tie. His office door is blue. The Police Commissioner didn't waste any time before contacting Uber Girl and Wonder Boy. They were the best Agents for the job of stopping Dirty Jack's plan. It wasn't the first time the Commissioner used the signaling device after bedtime.

Wonder Boy and Uber Girl rush out of their home to answer the Commissioner's call, and Kitty the Smooch leaps into action. He contacts the Organization for Vilanny to let them know that Wonder Boy and Uber Girl are on the way to foil the latest Dirt Scheme.

At the Commissioner's office, Wonder Boy and Uber Girl arrive to find the Commissioner pouring over blueprints. The fear, he tells them, is that Dirty Jack will be attacking with his Dirt-O-Ray from City Hall, which is at the heart of town.

Wonder Boy and Uber Girl go over the blueprints themselves, and decide the best plan of attack. So long as Dirty Jack doesn't know they're coming, they have a good chance of stopping him and disabling the Dirt-O-Ray.

There isn't much time, so Uber Girl and Wonder Boy have to prepare quickly for battle! Dirty Jack prepares for battle, too, knowing that he's going to face the goody-two-shoes.

On top of City Hall, Dirty Jack prepares his Dirt-O-Ray. The machinery needs a few last minute tweaks and adjustments as the weather conditions make dirt-ifying the city a bit more tricky than he had originally anticipated. He'd used a lot of buttons and switches on the machine.

Suddenly, Wonder Boy and Uber Girl show up on the scene! They spring into action, to try and stop Dirty Jack's evil plot. Uber Girl hits Dirty Jack first with a hairbrush and a toothbrush, and Wonder Boy moves straight to the Dirt-O-Ray.

Uber Girl runs her comb through Dirty Jack's hair! And takes a bar of soap to his face! She uses wet wipes on his fingers, and a lint roller on his clothes! And Dirty Jack just stands there and takes it.

Wonder Boy works at the machine, looking at the Dirt-O-Ray's buttons and switches. He's never been that great with machinery, so he starts to push buttons, trying to turn it off. A panel opens to show that there's a timer counting down!

"Why won't you fight back?" Uber Girl yells at Dirty Jack.

"You're so beautiful," Dirty Jack says to Uber Girl. "I can't fight such a pretty girl." But it's just a distraction, as the timer ticks down!

Uber Girl gives Dirty Jack one final rinse with a bucket of water, and he falls down onto the ground. Then she runs across the roof to where Wonder Boy is still frantically trying to stop the Dirt-O-Ray. She steps in front of him and clicks a few buttons, and the Dirt-O-Ray stops counting down, with only two seconds left on the timer!

Dirty Jack climbs up from his spot on the roof and sneaks away, dripping wet and squeaky clean, while Wonder Boy starts to smash the Dirt-O-Ray to pieces. Uber Girl turns just in time to see Dirty Jack's cape disappear through the door to the stairs.

Back in the Police Commissioner's office, Uber Girl and Wonder Boy are being thanked for their good work. The Commissioner gives them a plaque, and they all pose for a photo. It'll be the front page news in the newspaper in the morning. Hot off the presses!

After the reporter and photographer leave, the Commissioner turns to Uber Girl and Wonder Boy. They don't know who this new villain is. They wonder if they'll see more of him. Uber Girl, with a blush, secretly hopes that they do.

The kids go back home and sneak into bed. It's very late, and they're very tired. They'll both have to get up early in the morning to have a good, solid wash before school.

Dirty Jack arrives home to his own place and pulls his cape off to toss it aside. There's a light blinking on his computer, and he opens up the message program. There's a message there from Kitty the Smooch, and Dirty Jack leans in as he reads...

Morning comes. Maryanne and Tobias are exhausted as they get up and go through their morning routine to get ready for school. They have a test today!

On the bus ride, Maryanne and Tobias discuss Dirty Jack. They wonder what other dubious schemes he might come up with. What else might he try to make dirty? Hopefully, Mister Twitchy Nose can keep them informed of Dirty Jack's plans so they can thwart them.

After waiting for her class to settling down in their desks, the teacher announces they are to welcome a new student. He's a transfer and he's excited to meet everyone and make friends. When she steps to the side to reveal the new student, Maryanne and Tobias gasp. The new kid is Dirty Jack.

Ruben's Tales of the Amazon Jungle

By Audry Lynch

Introduction

Ruben lived in a little village along the mighty Amazon River. The river was big and brown and reminded Ruben of the fierce anaconda, the most feared of all the snakes in the jungle. It was powerful and unpredictable. It could be calm as a lake or produce waves and dangerous eddies during storms.

The river brought good and evil. He knew people who had drowned in it. But it also brought the big ships with the tourists who bought the masks from the village housewives. They also gave the children candy and gum and pencils for the village school.

Each morning when he woke up, Ruben's day involved some time with the big river. Sometimes his mother asked him to bring pails of water from it for her cooking. Sometimes his father took him with his brothers to catch fish from it for their dinners. Sometimes he led tourists from the boats up the muddy slope to his village. Every night before bedtime he took his daily bath in it.

The Amazon River governed his daily chores but it was the Shaman, Don Jose, who also controlled much of Ruben's life. Don Jose was the Shaman of the village, its oldest and wisest man. People even from other nearby villages came to him all day and night to ask questions to inquire about good and bad spells, and to purchase little bags of his herbs.

Don Jose fascinated Ruben. As long as he could remember, he had visited the Shaman every day of his life. He watched his visitors come and go and listened to every word that he could overhear from their conversations. Finally, Don Jose asked him to come along on his trips into the jungle pharmacy as Don Jose called it. They collected herbs and plants together while the Shaman explained their many uses to Ruben. Sometimes Ruben thought Don Jose could cure anything.

Shaman means Teacher, and Don Jose was the best one Ruben had ever met. At first Don Jose told Ruben about all the plants and animals in the Amazon Jungle. As they walked on the green slippery carpet of the jungle, Don Jose pointed out dangerous plants and the hiding places of poisonous snakes. At dusk, the songs of the birds and insects became louder and Don Jose explained to Ruben each sound in the Jungle Symphony.

Like most children, Ruben loved stories. The best times that he could remember with his Father were when, after a hard day of wild boar hunting, his father would relax by telling stories around the fire while his Mother cooked the meat. Ruben knew that Don Jose told some very special stories about the animals and creatures of the Amazon. Finally, he had the courage to ask Don Jose to tell them to him.

"Yes, Ruben," Don Jose replied, "I will tell them to you. But, remember they are special and secret to our village. Only share them with boys and girls who will appreciate them." Ruben decided that he was one of those special people so here are amazing Amazon stories that he heard directly from Don Jose.

Tale # 2 — La Tanrilla (Sunbittern Jungle Bird)

"There was a handsome man young man in our village named Roberto," the Shaman began. "Even as a child he seemed to be the best at everything he did. He swam the fastest and farthest, caught the most fish, and killed the most animals of any boy in his age group. Everyone admired him. When he grew up, the girls in the village all giggled whenever he spoke to them. All of them dreamed that someday Roberto would ask one of them to be his wife.

"Roberto liked all the girls as friends but he only loved one of them, Maria. He wanted her to be his wife but Maria had other plans. Her family had relatives in Iquitos, the city on the Amazon where the boundaries of the three great countries of Brazil, Peru and Ecuador come together. She had dreams of living there with them.

"We all know that it's a terrible mistake to leave the jungle," said Don Jose sadly. "People lead happier and healthier lives here than in the city but Maria's mind was made up. She wouldn't listen to anyone who didn't agree with her decision, even her parents.

"Finally Roberto came to me for advice. 'Please help me, Don Jose,' he begged. It was then that I thought of the legend of a little amazon jungle bird," said Don Jose. "I told Roberto what it looked like. It is a small bird but it has long legs. When it is nesting, it is dark and not very attractive. When it spreads its wings it has a beautiful combination of gray, white and black feathers. The bird lives along the shores of the Amazon, so I commanded Roberto to find one, kill it, and bring it back to me."

"Wasn't that cruel?" Ruben asked Don Jose.

"Sometimes these things have to be done when something important is at stake," explained Don Jose. "In a few days Roberto returned with the body of the little bird. He watched in amazement while Don Jose buried the little carcass. "Come back in a week," Don Jose ordered Roberto.

When Roberto came back a week later, Don Jose dug up a leg bone of the little bird. It had a hollow hole in the middle so that a man could hold it up to his eye like a telescope. "I want you to hide in the jungle brush and look at Maria through this leg bone. Legend tells us that a woman will be attracted to the man who looks at her through this bird's leg bone."

Roberto believed strongly in the wisdom of Don Jose so he did as he was told. Every day he peered at Maria through the leg bone. Each time he did it, she turned around, smiled, and beckoned him to join her.

Each day they took long walks together in the jungle and long swims in the Amazon. In a few months Maria forgot all about leaving the jungle to go and live in Iquitos. Instead she and Roberto decided to get married and stay in the village.

"Do you know who that story is about?" Don Jose asked Ruben. While Ruben thought of an answer, Don Jose told him, "It was your very own parents," and he enjoyed watching the surprised look on Ruben's face.

A Carton for Barton

By Stanley Gedzelman

Barton hated reading. "Why bother? We can talk to our phone and it answers any questions we have."

HONORABLE MENTION

Poor Barton! School had reading assignments and maybe even worse, writing. "I can always see the movie, so why do I have to read the book?"

You could argue with Barton until you were blue in the face and get nowhere. Barton's parents weren't particularly dedicated readers so when they told him to read he chose to follow their actions instead of their words. In his extended family only Uncle Jesse loved to read. Jesse was his most interesting uncle by far. He was very funny but also intriguing, and provocative. He had tons of jokes and stories and was a warehouse of facts and figures, a fount of information. He was always reasoning through problems and inventing things, at least in his mind. Barton loved his Uncle Jesse, but that wasn't enough to get him to read. Reading was hard, hence boring. Video games were also hard at first, but Barton loved them and had mastered most in his enormous collection. If he wasn't outside playing some sport, he was indoors killing monsters and seeking treasures.

Then Barton turned ten. How excited he was when a large carton arrived for his birthday. It came from Uncle Jesse. What could be in it? It was far too heavy for video games. Barton should have guessed. He should have read the stamp saying "Media Materials" but since he wasn't much of a reader he hadn't.

Instead he began to tear the carton open. As soon as he had ripped open one corner he peeked inside and... spied a book. Clearly, the whole carton was filled only with books. Barton picked up the box and carried it across the house to the door to the cellar.

The cellar was dark, dingy, and musty. Dust accreted into planitesimals on its cement floor. After the previous owners of the house had been robbed they bricked up the outside entrance. And for added security, they riveted a metal sheet that covered the cellar door so that even if you managed to get into the cellar, which was impossible, you still could not gain entry to the house. Moreover, this filthy, unfinished cellar was a cluttered mess used solely for the oil burner and for storage of anything that needed to be forgotten.

Barton opened the cellar door and heaved the box of books down the wooden slat stairs. It made a series of bangs before crashing on the cement floor.

Barton's mom heard the noise and came running. "What did you do, Barton?"

"I am storing old books."

"Well don't just throw them down and leave them for someone to trip over. Go downstairs and put them out of the way!"

Begrudgingly, Barton went down into the cellar and looked for a place to stuff the carton. All the shelves were stuffed but on one corner of the dusty floor was the Flexible Flyer, a magnificent old sled that he loved when it snowed and that his mother rode on when she was a girl. He gently lowered the carton pretty on the precious sled but even so, a microburst of dust still rose around it.

Then Barton climbed the wooden slat steps and lo and behold, he discovered that the heavy cellar door had closed behind him and automatically locked. This wasn't the first time Barton had locked himself in the cellar. So, peeved at the lousy door, he banged on it and screamed for his mother, until she heard him and let him back upstairs, after, of course, he removed his shoes.

A week or so later, Uncle Jesse called. "Did you get the birthday present I mailed to you?"

"Yes, Uncle Jesse. Thank you for all those books."

Have you started reading any of them, Barton?"

"I am real busy in school right now, Uncle Jesse. I'll read them this summer."

"Barton, its October. Summer is ten months away, and those books can help you in school. That's one reason I got them for you. You should at least look at them now."

"I will, Uncle Jesse, I promise. I just need some time."

Several months passed and because Uncle Jesse didn't bother Barton again the books were happily forgotten.

Now it was winter. A blizzard had just begun. Barton's parents raced out to go shopping, miles away in town because they knew they would be stuck at home for days. "Would you like to come shopping with us, Barton?"

Barton hated shopping for anything but video games almost as much as he hated reading.. "No, I'll stay home."

So Barton stayed home. Then the snow began to fall real heavily. The intensity was so great Barton could not see the Clackson's house 200 feet away. About two hours after the snow began, Barton's parents called. "Barton, we are stuck in town and will have to stay in a hotel. Go over to the Clackson's and spend the night with them!"

"Mom, I can't see their house and the wind is screaming. I can stay home alone for one night. I am OK. I promise."

"Well, Barton, we may not be able to get home tomorrow either. It may take us an extra day."

"That's great, Mom! I mean it's OK. Besides, there won't be school tomorrow. I'll be fine. I can make Mac and Cheese for dinner."

Barton's mom was real worried, but Barton's dad wasn't. So they finally agreed to let Barton stay home alone with the normal instructions to be very careful and don't burn the house down and don't die while they were away.

Did Barton have fun that day! He went out for a short time, but it was colder, windier, and snowier than he had ever felt so he soon came in again. This was a perfect day for video games. He played for hours and just before he finally fell asleep around midnight he noticed that the Clackson's house was still not visible.

The next morning, it was still snowing but not so heavily. Now, at last, he could see the Clackson's house. It was completely white. So was everything else. The view outside was weird. The house seemed to have sunk several feet into the ground. Barton went to the front door and wedged it open. Snow sifted into the house. It was real deep.

Barton went back to his video games and played until noon. By that time the snow had stopped and the sun had come out. It was blindingly white everywhere, like a fairyland. Suddenly Barton remembered the Flexible Flyer sled in the cellar. The hill behind the house was just perfect for long, fast runs. Barton raced down the slat steps, slid the carton of books off the sled and carried the sled back up the steps.

As he approached the top step, Barton noted his error. The cellar door had slammed behind him when he had raced down to get the sled. Now he was locked in the cellar with no one home to open the door.

Barton tried to turn the locked doorknob. Then he smashed the heavy door and kicked it until he was exhausted. But despite all these valiant efforts the door and its knob did not budge. Then Barton got a bit smarter. Maybe he could unscrew the doorknob. After all, there was a tool chest in the cellar. But luck was against him. Of course, the screws were on the other side, for even at ten years old, Barton instinctively knew Murphy's Law. Furthermore, he had left his cell phone upstairs.

Barton was out of ideas. He was stuck. When he realized this, his feelings of frustration, anger, and fright morphed into a recognition of facts. He was going to be stuck in the cellar until his parents came home and that was all there was to it. He was surprised and proud he didn't even feel like crying. Then again, he was ten years old so why should he cry? It was what it was.

As reality took hold, he began to think about what to do with all the time he was going to have to spend in the cellar. That carton of books presented his only option. He actually felt thankful for it.

Barton dragged the sled with the carton to the base of the stairs right below the cellar's brightest light bulb. He sat down on the sled and began to open the carton and remove its contents. Out came a dictionary. Ugh! How dull! Next was an atlas. That was almost as bad although he did like geography. There was *Oxford History of the American People* by Samuel Eliot Morison with such small print that only children could read without glasses and only adults could understand with them. (Years later he would fall in love with that book.) The boring books seemed to keep coming until one with the title, *The World's Greatest Stories*. That was the book for Barton.

Barton scoured the book for pictures and there were plenty of them. One caught his eye. It showed a giant Cyclops sleeping on his back on the ground of a cavern surrounded by sheep and goats. A number of what seemed like miniaturized men were holding a pointed pole like a battering ram, which was clearly aimed at the Cyclops single, giant eye. It was a tale from the Odyssey. Barton began reading in his stuttering manner, of course. But the tale was so compelling he didn't even think of bemoaning his stunted skill. Then his imagination began to work in ways that video games never had inspired. Barton could feel and see what was happening. From those video games, Barton was no stranger to gore so he was not queasy at all. But he sensed he was reading an original. He was fascinated by Odysseus's ingenuity, telling Polyphemus his name was "Nobody," getting Polyphemus drunk so that he would fall asleep, impaling and boiling his eye, and escaping by clutching the rams' stomachs.

Barton was disappointed when the story was over. He started reading it again. Then he remembered that he had heard the story before although he didn't recall all the gory details. His Uncle Jesse had told him when he was six years old.

As Barton reached the point where Odysseus and his men gored and sizzled out Polyphemus's eye, he was struck by a sudden revelation of an ancient memory. One time when he was visiting his Uncle Jesse, he had inadvertently locked the bathroom door on the way out. Jesse had taken a paper clip, straightened it and poked it in the small hole in the center of the doorknob. He poked several times, explaining to Barton that inside was a release latch and you had to aim right to hit it. Finally, he heard a click and the doorknob turned.

Barton raced up the stairs. "Wow, the doorknob has a hole!" He then raced down and over to the toolbox and found an ice pick that seemed thin enough to work. Bounding back up the stairs, Barton was overjoyed to find it was just thin enough. He began poking in and out and, CLICK! The doorknob turned like butter and Barton was free.

Triumphant, mature Barton walked regally down the stairs, returned the ice pick to the tool box, put the sled back in its place in the corner, repacked all the books except for the book of stories and gently placed the carton back on the sled. Carrying the storybook under one arm, he slowly climbed a few steps but stopped deep in thought. Then he turned back downstairs. "My room has plenty of space for all those books."

Promises Gone

By Carolyn Donnell

I wrote the first verse a while ago
About promises pledged, but now I don't know.
The roses that came with the guarantees made
Have dried like a desert long after the rain.

He said "I should have been there back then.
You shouldn't have been all alone to fend.
I swear to do what I can from now on."
And other promises that are now gone.

I knew it felt like a dream that day.
Those pledges melted like mist on the bay.
At the first sigh of woe they were gone in a flash.
Doors slammed with a resounding crash.

Yes, he got sick and that was bad.
But instead of faith he panicked and ran.
Took back everything he said that day
And tried to make it all go away.

He died last week with it all undone.
Stubbornness runs from father to son.
Broken hearts now bleed anew.
Old wounds reopened with promise untrue.

I should have finished the first verse when I could,
'cause now I can't stand to look if I would.
The first inspiration has become moot.
And left in its place are ashes and soot.

Foster City, CA Before the Drought

By Lisa Meltzer Penn

The California sun, our Marilyn Monroe of weather has called for a break, a little privacy for a change, cover of gray.

A week of rain, a steady beat. No flux, no false promise.

My weather app displays five miniature boxes of raindrops and produces another box each day.

In the upstairs weight room of the PJCC, my thigh muscles tense and flex astride the adductor machine.

I watch through the window as the outside layer of gray grows softer and softer, the surroundings ever more indistinct. The weight room seems to be inside a dream.

The flat brittle field puddles the rain. A flock of geese roves through the newly sprung weeds, feather edges growing misty as they pull the greening up and out of the ground.

The adductor is set up to face its foster twin, the abductor, metal plates pressed together in forced companionship,

a thing and its reflection. "Did you see?" I blurt out to the woman facing me. I point behind her at the windows.

"I know," she says, turning back, blowing a wisp of hair off her face, "It's despicable, isn't it?"

"No, it's beautiful," I insist.

"Huh," she says. "I thought I left all that behind."

It turns out we share wet and muddy east coast roots. Different towns. Maybe that's why our knees and voices almost, but don't quite, touch. We finish our reps and trade machines.

She faces the window now, and I am her reflection

With a final set of repetitions, I bequeath my wishes to her Push out: rain. Back in: soft gray

Push out: possibility. Back in: magic

Outside, of course, it is wetter than it looked from above, not just misty. I unhinge my soggy umbrella.

The spring pops up violently

The gangly geese on the grass don't look up from their smorgasbord. Tail feathers point to the sky and beaks jab in and out of the earth.

Their winged and waterproof bodies were made for this day.

Like the geese and the softening ground, I adore and revere the rain. A breathy echo of Marilyn calls,

"A smart girl leaves before she is left."

In this moment my sneakers and umbrella lose the last of their imperviousness and the rain soaks through.

The Unexpected

By Pat Callaway

The red sun shown as a torch of gladness,
But the silent sea was a sign of sadness.
Its silver cloak shown as stars in the night
With colors of orange, blue, grey and white.
A cloud moved across its pathway of sky.
It moved very cunning, slowly, and sly.
As the sun disappeared behind its horizon,
I heard a rumble like great herds of Bison.
The sky turned purple with great streaks of gold.
There were flashes of lightning and low and behold ... .
A silvery streak flew from out of the sky.
It thrashed and it thundered as it flew past by.
The rain fell in hails as very small stones.
The sea roared and hollered and let know its moans.
As I grasped to my little boat it glided and swayed
And I dripped wet with sallow foam as I was sprayed.
The sky was now wanton with puffs of dull smoke,
And the moon shone through eerie, weary, and it bespoke.
I was cut and I was bruised as the waves plunged onto me.
A nightmare had arisen from a silky, sullen sea.
And then a spark I saw flash from afar.
It looked as if it were a bright falling star.
And the sky changed to a silvery white,
And then back to its dullness with little or no light.
I shivered and felt hollow and soaked to the bone.
 Never before an experience like this had I known.
With a fire a distance away in the hills,
It lit up the sky like fireworks and thrills.
The night was a decade that lasted an hour.
The sky and beyond was full of great power.
The treacherous sea pushed me near to the rocks
That stood there proudly like ships at their docks.
And the wind kept on blowing and hurling me South.
And I saw a great whirlpool with its vacuuming mouth.
And it pulled the debris down its dark tunnel dream
As the wind whirled with fury and with its scream.
And again thunder roared with. its deadening sound,
While the sky turned purple with death that I found.
For no longer could be heard my wailing plea.
A nightmare had arisen from a silky, sullen sea.

361-01 Free Form Poetry, 54 years or younger

Stock

By T.R. Poulson
— *after William Carlos Williams*

Back at the farm a heifer,
so much sleeker than the others,
depends on the alfalfa field up on
the hill beyond the red fence.

She prances as rusty wheel bearings creak.
The loaded barrow nears the pen.
Her first calf, glazed with birth,
glistening with rain,
shakes off the water
and stands on wobbling legs beside her.

He must sell by next year's white frost,
or she'll be replaced with chickens.

Brave

By Nicole Justine Cavanaugh

A green sprout, small and brave
claiming space among the brown
crumbling around her

I want to be as brave as that little plant
silently making a statement:
I am growing and –

Please don't step on me.

Poetry Before Language

By Michele Jessen

Before words were uttered
And thoughts were spoken
I was there

The poem
The song
The rustle

At the dawn
At the sunset
When shadows cross short overhead
I form language on my tongue
And whisper your name
Poetry

Summertime

By Jeannine Gerkman

Wet splashes from the pool
The smell of chlorine
Children's laughter
Bees humming in clover

Succulent peaches
Juices sweet and sticky
Dripping down my chin
Tangled hair, untamed

The pop of ice cubes melting
Cups slick with moisture
Gin Rummy and Go Fish on the dusty porch
Salty potato chips

Purple cherries bursting with flavor
Sun out way past dinner
Blackberries stain our lips
Mosquitoes circling

Heat waves rising from asphalt
The smell of burnt rubber
Flip-flops slapping

Portrait in a Windy Frame

By Lisa Meltzer Penn

Pretend you knew everything, and stood in the ocean up to your knees rolling with a kaleidoscope the world around a hundred million times, wishing on the side you had already done your laundry.

Imagine the scratching noise outside the window is the reflection of your fingers on your head. Don't forget that old guy who invited you in for a glass of grapefruit juice and sat you down and gave you forty minutes worth on the history of agoraphobia, then untied your feet from the chair, but halfway to the door tied you up again and showed you forty family photo albums.

Go for a walk.

A brown leaf scuttles after your sneaker like that huge-pawed brown mutt with a tongue on the side that met you two blocks from your house three days in a row and followed in front and on the third day on a street you hadn't been to in four days, a man on a ladder against the front of a house stuck out his paint brush at you and said, "There's a leash law here, you know."

Bad news. Your car was stolen. Your bicycle is rolling, the house has been eaten, the sounds you make, stolen. Pretend someone else were you, and you were on the moon watching the ocean lay still.

Did you ever wish you could return or backspace or clear? Pretend to be the mailman, the ice-cream man. Pretend your grandmother could knit sweaters. Remember to write a tribute to that lady the day after the 4th of July who told you of a man in the grave, a son in school, the dirty laundry, and the round-eyed mother on the next floor who when you knocked would open the door with the chain.

Pretend you like mushrooms or raw onions, or cobwebs on your face. Imagine you are grace. Pretend you lived across the street or down the block or in your feet. When the tide rolls in, curl your toes, open your nose. Pretend you are rare and well done. Pretend you are all done.

Good news. Your bicycle has rolled back. Your backyard has sprouted a second set of bedrooms and beds and kitchens and dens, and the stolen, rolling ocean licks the salt from where it has run into your navel, from behind your ears, and with its tongue, returns your sounds and holds you to its ear.

Imagine this sky tonight, sun setting, moon and mountains rising, gray-greens framing this memory like hair. Your car must be zapping through Nevada by now, with your laundry in the back seat.

361-02 Free Form Poetry, Senior

Best of Show: Poetry

Gladiolas in a White Vase

By Evie Groch

How do they prance while standing still?
They parade rooted in a vase
as they pose in the light's prism and smile a rainbow's colors.
They need not yell nor jump to sing out meaning.
Silence of awe is louder than declarations of beauty
and longer remembered.
I live in their moment, meditate on what they emit—
grace, style, spirit.
I take their serenity for my calm, return to it when
I stumble on doubt.
Gladiolas in a white vase—
my icons of strength, innocence, and pride.

So Here I Come

By William Baldwin

So here I come, bouncing across the sand
On flying crutches, like some strange bird
With sticks for wings, rushing to catch you,
Frantic with longing; laughing, shouting.
Haven't seen you lately, can't let you get away.

I need you, you know; I need you desperately.

The Oddball Dancer

By William Baldwin

For forty years he dances, dances,
Sweeps round the hall to irregular rhythms
Of Balkan music, leading or following
The line of dancers
On Friday nights or off on trips
To dance workshops.
Five-four, seven-eight, nine-eight,
Even, at times, twenty-five-sixteen,
Convincing his relatives the record is skipping,
Puzzling them with leaps and squats and slaps.
They wonder why he doesn't dance the polka.

The Invisible Synagogue in Lima

By Evie Groch

Guido walks the three of us from our
hotel on Sunday
to take in the small synagogue sitting in
a sleepy setting.
—You can't miss it—they all said, but had
he not walked us,
we would have missed it.
A pale blue one-story building encased in a
steel-rodded outer gate-windows covered.
It sits silently in the calm of a cool morning
—devoid of symbols, markings, name plate, signs of welcome.
Locked, shuttered, cloaked in anonymity.
Our gut fills in the story,
and we are saddened to understand the need
to hide as in centuries past.

Worship

By Martha Clark Scala

Two pew neighbors, kid sisters,
take turns at creating
a comfortable lap for each other.

One, slightly more strawberry blonde
than the other,
covers her sibling with a stunning Ellen Tracy scarf,
tucks her in for a bedtime story,
pulls the hair out of her eyes, and starts a small braid
with the long, uncombed hair of her sister.

Sea Dreams

By Lisa Meltzer Penn

I'd like to fly, thought
The boy, sneakers
Tumbled on the dock; he wiped
Hair off his face.
The gulls can Love this place,
Why can't I?

He watches them day
After day.
The sea becomes greener,
The sand, waves, and clouds he
Squints into,
Gulls graze on fish.
Breeze sweeps cool
On his back where the
Undershirt and shorts don't meet
And he hugs his knees loosely.

Dibbledy-Dabbledy-Doo
He says, and drops
A pebble from his pocket, closes his eyes,
Drags a toe through the water.

361-03 Structured Poem, 54 years or younger

Long Hair

By Michele Jessen

How short the time of long hair will last
Grandma is holding hands with her past

Miniature baby brushes laid out on velvet at her birth
To await her fuzzy sprouts soft scalp, caressed in mirth

She speaks of auburn golden locks to brush
With gilded handles, matching mirrors to trust

She limps along with a short snowy curt cap
Recalls her youth of lovers stroking a playful tap

When she swung her locks across her back
And lifted thick tresses to tie braids in tracks

Preparing, pretending her crown still there
As she braids my long hair with such delicate care

Again. Again.

By Frank Saunders

Spring conceals its cruelty far below its daffodils.
Beneath the verdant frailty
an ancient, restless movement builds.

The residue of buried roots, of tangled tendrils left to rot,
still holds the moldy skin of fruits that long ago have withered.
Fraught with memory, they stir again.

Unbidden, they begin to grow
and choke the fragile shoots.
Spring rain gives life to bones from long ago.

We return to cut the weed
that threatens every newborn seed.

361-04 Structured Poem, Senior

Honor Student

By Dorsetta Hale

You are born
and I am more than a wife.
Your little face mirrors
the love of my life.

You are nine months
and walking on your own.
Most often you hold my hand anyway
to show that you're not too grown.

You are two
and run twice around the track
chasing down your father
before I call you back.

You are three.
The world is your playground.
You question, laugh and experiment.
Even at three, you astound.

You are four
reading bedtime stories to us.
We are so proud and
you enjoy all the fuss.

You are five.
The school years begin.
I hold back tears sensing some kind of end.

You are ten.
Too old for pigtails.
You give up hugs and goodnight kisses.
The mushy stuff has gotten stale.

You are thirteen
and want your hair straight.
Going natural was of my generation.
An old subject you hate.

You are sixteen
and forget both Mother's and Father's Day.
Too busy with school and friends,
making your own way.

Villanelle for a Coffee Queen

By Evie Groch

On alcohol I am not keen
I am not even tempted
I have a broken drinking gene

There, now at last I have come clean
I crave not scotch, want no vodka
On alcohol I am not keen

My whiskey-bringing friends I screen
They all can drink their fill at home
I have a broken drinking gene

So much hard liquor I have seen
At my wedding so long ago
On alcohol I am not keen

Still unopened, sealed and obscene
Bottles stand in our cabinet
I have a broken drinking gene

But you could tempt me with caffeine
I'm not a total Philistine
On alcohol I am not keen
I have a broken drinking gene

The River That Sings

Ken Owen

Time will make
The grass lay down
Under my feet
As I make my path
To the waters edge
Of the river that sings.

Time will make
The pain lay down
Go fast asleep
On my journey
From the quiet place
To the river that sings.

Time will make
The wind blow down
My troubles and sorrow
Will fall like stones
To the side of the road
Of the river that sings.

Time will make
The trees bow down
And give cool shade
As I listen and fill
My open heart with song
From the river that sings.

(Inspired by the story of the Yuchie Tribe of Muscle Shoals, Alabama)

362-01 Persuasive Essay

Whack-a-Mole

By Stanley Gedzelman

Whack-a-Mole is a game with five circular holes. Moles pop up from random holes at random times and you must whack them down with a large hammer. But they come faster and faster and you ultimately can't keep up. Much like the moles in the game, extremism is a pop-up feature of being human even if it is inhuman.

Extremism enables tyranny, and tyranny institutionalizes extremism. This feedback loop pops up all over. Communism in Russia was followed by Nazism in Germany and Fascism in Italy. Japan went on its own racist rampage. After World War II, Communism spread to new centers, particularly China. More recently, it has bubbled up from within Islam.

Converts to extremist ideologies are often people who are both aggrieved outcasts and authoritarian by nature or nurture. Because extremist ideologies are driven by a certain type of psychology, they are identical at their root despite enormous apparent differences. No wonder Hitler found far more of his converts not from the mass of people in the middle but from the ranks of Communists.

The Far Right starts off by being exclusive. Their misfits want recognition in the privileged race they belong to and would eliminate all 'impure' outsiders. The Far Left starts off by being all-inclusive. Their misfits are the 'impure' outsiders who preach a world of comrades but want to eliminate the privileged class or race they can't belong to. Once in power, members of both sides force everyone they don't exterminate to be docile and servile. In the end, they're all exclusionary and tyrannical.

Ideologies based on race and religion have greater staying power than those based on elusive qualities such as the Brotherhood of Man. Race may be ill-defined but it is something you can see. It is overt and fixed from birth. It never disappears. Religion is based on and requires the invisible. This compels it to be even more authoritarian.

Extremism is activated by rousing the grievances of the aggrieved. The United States, beacon of freedom to the world, has done a good job of it. American foreign relations have too often been propelled by greed rationalized by paranoia. Strange, how we care most about Democracy in oil rich lands. (Vietnam held promising oil and mineral fields.)

When the Gulf of Tonkin Incident was first announced it was suggested that the Chinese Communist juggernaut was involved and certainly that we were under attack by North Vietnam. This made USA involvement in the incipient Vietnam conflict appear as a righteous cause. As the weeks and months passed China was never mentioned again. That was curious.

American politicians used the Domino Theory to justify combating Communism. Presumably, any hamlet that fell to Communism would start a chain reaction that would spread across the globe. We were in mortal danger. We were staunchly upholding Freedom. Such was the claim.

What were the facts? We backed a series of corrupt, autocratic leaders and an incompetent South Vietnamese army. We were there "to train them so that they could learn to defend themselves." Strange that the opponents, their brethren to the north were so capable, evil, and determined. In the end, despite our turning much of the country into a crater field, dedication driven by extremism emerged triumphant. Gross slaughter did continue after our exit from Vietnam, though it was no worse than during our presence, until the Vietnamese exhausted themselves. Ironically, in the horrendously violent process the Vietnamese actually performed a great good by ousting Cambodia's Khmer Rouge. The USA loss did not cascade any dominoes. Today, Vietnam is a peaceful, beautiful tourist destination, a model of "Capitalist Communism."

Thirty years after Vietnam we launched a search for weapons of mass destruction in Iraq. Once again we were fed the identical horror stories and prescribed the identical, unworkable solutions. We did eliminate a horrendous tyrant, a real causes for celebration. But once again we backed the corrupt and incompetent in the name of Democracy while rousing the greater and more effective dedication of extremists and dismantling Iraq's feeble infrastructure.

With Islam, as with any God-based religion, extremists are far more durable. Communism is religion without God. It is doomed to die or at least evolve. Islam has an unwavering God. It is one more religion founded on intolerance and slaughter while brandishing its inflexible "truth" as a moral monopoly.

What should we do about the Middle East and its extremism? Do we engage, as we seem to be doing, in a perpetual state of low-grade war such as Rome conducted against its "Barbarians" from the time of Marcus Aurelius (also for precious resources). Aside from providing training grounds for our troops and military technology, that is no solution.

What we should do in the Middle East is exactly what we were ultimately compelled to do in Vietnam—get out. By continuing our persistent but timid band-aid meddling, the best we are able or willing to do is whack a small mole in their giant molehill. And in the process we are creating even more moles by vindicating and stoking and reaiming their grievances—toward us. Our presence will only prolong tragedy. It may sound inhuman, but let them slaughter each other until they exhaust themselves and whack their own moles.

History has shown that tyrannies don't survive long once they export war. But the cost of allowing Germany and Japan to arm before World War II was immense. So we would err by allowing any tyranny to develop its own deliverable advanced weaponry while we have the strength to stop it.

Our international meddling should be necessary, decisive, thorough, and hopefully, rare. We should not cry wolf to satisfy an agenda. We do weaken and alienate ourselves in the world's eyes when we meddle continuously and indecisively.

Solutions are certainly not simple. Santayana wrote, "Those who cannot remember the past are condemned to repeat it." Given unchanging human nature, those who do remember the past may suffer the same fate.

The Dream Can Survive If –

By Rudie Tretten

The key to American progress, 'tis said, is education – particularly a university education. That's what my folks thought and taught me and my brother back in the long, long ago.

They weren't the only ones who thought that way. It was federal and state policy. The GI Bill guaranteed veterans of World War II financial support as they pursued higher education. For Californians, there were free community colleges. The fee for attending the University of California was $35 a semester in spring 1949. And that huge sum entitled students to top notch medical care at Cowell Hospital, psychological services and copies of the 5 day a week Daily Californian, the top newspaper in the East Bay. (In the interest of transparency, I worked there as a sports writer and editor for several years.)

I could not afford the current $7,000 plus annual tuition without loans and scholarships. Another barrier for prospective students is the state's financial problems. If the budget limitations proposed by the governor are adopted, over 7000 applicants will be turned away this year.

That is not the way it ought to be. Back in the fifties and sixties, California was a vibrant, forward-looking state that offered a top-notch education system from kindergarten through graduate school. We built a splendid highway infrastructure and a water system that served our biggest industry, agriculture, and a growing population.

California was number one.

And now? California schools rank 46th in the nation in per pupil spending. Take a ride on our freeways, highways and roads and count the bumps, pot holes and traffic jams you encounter. Water rationing is a real possibility with our current drought (one or two storms do not end a drought) and global warming.

It all takes money and that takes leadership to raise the public willingness to invest in the future. Where does the current state government propose to generate financial support? Naturally it's the easy way—increase gambling revenues from Indian casinos. Let's gamble on the gamblers to pay our way.

Gamble is no longer a word in the official lexicon in California. It's gaming. Nobody gambles (except in illegal gambling joints). We game. Gambling may be a sin; gaming helps reservation economics and the state budget.

Once upon a time, we acted as a community to meet our local needs. We used our taxes to make our lives better. Now, talking about a tax increase is akin to talking about gambling. We don't do it and if some poor soul is caught using the word he or she is banished.

Yet gambling is what we are doing with our potential for the future while our leaders refuse to lead. It's easier to propose cuts to currently under-funded programs like education and medical care than it is to present us with a process/program that will result in improvement in the lives of Joe Sixpack and Agnes English teacher and their children.

We have survived an international crisis. This has had a negative impact on California's finances and is certainly a restraining factor in approaching the issues delineated above.

Perhaps we are in the midst of a reformulation of that old chestnut, the American dream. Why should our kids do better than we have done? Why should the lives of the poorest among us be our concern? Why should we be concerned that the rich are not only getting richer but that the gap between them and us is a growing chasm?

As a child of the Depression, I came to understand that, if enough of the little folks can get their act together, they can protect their interests and expand our democracy.

Where, oh, where, are the truth tellers and the leaders who can articulate the dream and the ways in which it can become reality?

Washing Away Mountains at Malakoff

By Marjorie Bicknell Johnson

A gold pan is shaped like a pie tin with a base larger than a dinner plate. The miner shovels river muck into the pan, adds water, and swirls the contents. Next, he pours out muddy water and lightweight debris, adds more water, and repeats the swirling action until only black sand and gold remain.

If his claim yields handfuls of nuggets, he gets rich. Otherwise, he moves to a new location or learns to reclaim gold dust.

During the California gold rush, miners discovered an ancient river channel buried under a hill near Nevada City. To get to the gold, they had only to remove the mountain.

In 1853, Edward Matteson did just that. He directed jets of water under high pressure through a canvas hose and a giant iron nozzle, called a monitor, to the gold-bearing paleogravels and washed the entire hillside down through enormous sluices.

Early placer miners knew that the more gravel they could process, the more gold they were likely to find. And the small stuff? No problem: use liquid mercury from the quicksilver mines at New Almaden (Santa Clara County) and cyanide to dissolve and separate gold from black sand and other impurities.

Hydraulic gold mining operations sprang up throughout the area, especially at Malakoff Diggins, eleven miles from Nevada City. As much as 100,000 tons of gravel per day disappeared, and miners built a 7,847-foot tunnel through bedrock to serve as a drain.

Entire mountains were lost.

That drain dumped mine tailings into the South Yuba River, flooding and destroying vast areas of farmland in the Sacramento Valley as well as inundating the communities of Yuba City and Marysville. Silt flowed all the way to San Francisco Bay, impairing navigation on the Sacramento River.

For crows, the park at Malakoff is only 11 miles from Nevada City, but the recommended route on paved roads is a 50-minute drive. The old road, no longer maintained, carried the stagecoach through North Bloomfield to Allegheny along a canyon wall hand-built by Chinese coolie laborers in the 1850s. The wall is a marvel; no mortar was used, and rocks are hand-fitted against a nearly vertical wall a thousand feet above the Yuba River.

Today, scientists continue to study long-term effects of the mercury dumped into the water and introduced into the ecosystems. More than 125 years after the cessation of hydraulic mining, very little life has grown back into those water-blasted mountains at Malakoff Diggins State Park. Man created the remaining huge cliffs and colorful rock formations in just a few decades. Mother Nature would have taken many millennia.

Back then, farmers sued the hydraulic mining operations in the landmark case, *Edwards Woodruff vs. North Bloomfield Mining and Gravel Company*. In 1884, Judge Lorenzo of the United States District Court ruled in favor of the farmers and banned hydraulic mining, declaring it "a public nuisance."

California valued clean water and agricultural land more than gold. Now, in a similar issue with *fracking*—a method of oil extraction that uses a lot of water and leaves a wasteland—will we value water above oil?

The Pain of Passion

By Evie Groch

Perhaps it was an omen that in my junior high school journalism class I was selected as proofreader for the school newspaper. My eagle eye caught typos, misspellings, and grammatical inconsistencies in all the writing pieces before we went to press. I took my role very seriously and forced many rewrites.

"Who cares?" you might say. "That's such tedious work. Boring!"

But for me it was a solidification of my interest in grammar and its unique kind of beauty, a beauty not many appreciated. It's like beading a necklace. Certain procedures are required, but how you select and arrange the beads is completely your choice and can be as creative as you want. It must be like the beauty math teachers see that eludes the rest of us. Many of us do math grudgingly, as many do grammar, but those who have found their passion, their undeterred interest, will forever travel in good company.

My friendship with grammar began in the fifth grade, when, after a particular grammar lesson, everything fell into place for me. The clarity facing me was astonishing. I had been given the secret code, the key that unlocked it all. I loved the predictability and formulas that structured language and provided challenges to play with. How far could I stretch or bend the rules and still be legal? I was probably the only one in my class who actually enjoyed parsing sentences. I'm not even sure if that word is still in use today, but I believe it was and is a legitimate and effective way to teach and learn the concepts of grammar.

The most fun I have with language and words is to create puzzles, puns, and jokes based on semantics. The one-upsmanship in a series of punning rejoinders thrills me no end. *Games Magazine* liked some of my challenges and published them. I was euphoric.

Lest it go unnoticed, I must put it out there, as any world language teacher would, that most native English speakers don't learn about their own grammar until they study a foreign language. To build transitions from one language to another, you must have anchors, and if they don't exist, they must be created. Once created, you can place a bridge across them and walk the learners over it where connections can be made. Having laid down the bones of one language prepares you to conquer others.

We all know people who are highly allergic to perfume, cigarette smoke, or certain foods. We understand their challenges and try to lessen their exposure to these substances, even through legislation at times. I'll never convince anyone, except perhaps another grammarian, that I experience a visceral reaction similar to that of these individuals when I'm part of the audience at a conference, watching a PowerPoint, reading a handout, or listening to a presenter and come across an egregious grammatical error either in print or orally. My eyes and ears go immediately to the errors before I can stop them. I cannot receive the intended content or teaching until I deal with the errors and correct them in print or make a mental note of the oral infraction to share with the presenter in private, only if it is welcome. It always has been.

Mama Cora

By Dorsetta Hale

You know I didn't bring you into this world
to be mistreated and abused.
Don't let me hear
someone made you feel worthless and afraid.
Don't let me hear
somebody is trying to dim your light.
Don't let me hear
someone has left bruises where no one can see,
but if I do hear
and later you see me crying
believe they are proud tears
because you were brave to say,
"I knew if I told you,
you'd do something."

Best of Show: Essay

Seeing Jerry Winters

By Katie Burke

March 26, 2015

While riding home on Muni just now, I seized with fear when a rough-looking, impaired-by-something, elderly man yelled "Excuse me!" several times, at a woman who was perched across the aisle from me, on the aisle-adjacent side of a two-seater, her neighboring window seat being empty.

So loud was this man's voice, and so angry his tone, that several people in my Muni carriage immediately looked on, presumably to help the woman should this become necessary.

Though she couldn't possibly have missed hearing him, the woman clearly didn't realize he was addressing her; she neither looked in his direction, nor exhibited the telltale signs of a seasoned San Franciscan consciously avoiding trouble on the bus. She seemed genuinely lost in her book, and totally oblivious to the scene unfolding around her, in which this man had already cast her as a main character.

Finally, he shoved his face up to hers and bellowed again, "Excuse me!" She calmly looked up at him, moved to the window seat, and tried to resume reading.

"You're rude!" He screamed. "I said 'excuse me' four or five times, and you just IGNORED ME!"

"I did not ignore you," she countered. "I didn't know you were talking to me." "Bullshit! You were RUDE! You IGNORED ME!" he insisted at top volume.

Now every eyeball in the Muni carriage was on them, as he screamed at her at adjoined-Muni-seats range, spit flying out of his mouth and onto her face with every sentence.

"Well, you're spitting on me right now. Don't you think that's rude?" she asked.

"What the fuck does that have to do with anything?" he asked, appearing shocked at what he obviously believed was an abrupt change of subject.

"If you're not going to admit that you were RUDE," he continued, "then I'm just WASTING MY TIME!"

"I wasn't rude," she said.

"Yes, you were. I said 'excuse me' FIVE TIMES," he said, apparently testing whether a solid "five" would hold more sway with her than his previously asserted "four or five."

"Listen," she said, her voice suddenly softer. "What's your name?" Sticking to his principles, he replied, "No. You were rude!"

"What's your name?" she repeated, looking into his eyes.

"No."

"You're seriously not going to tell me your name?" she asked, with the mock-exasperated smile of a person who can't believe her spouse is doing that annoying thing that she or he always does.

His eyes instantly lost their edge, coming into color as a muted blue.

He pointed at a sign over the seats in front of them, the one reminding riders to vacate those seats for seniors and disabled people. Using his inside voice for the first time on this ride, he said, "You know, that is the stupidest sign."

"Why?" she asked.

"Because I'm old and disabled, and people are just rude. They don't move out of those seats, anyway. They just act like I'm not here."

"What is your name?" she asked again.

Silence.

"Well, I'm Susan," she offered.

"I'M JERRY WINTERS!" he yelled, though this time beaming pride, not hatred, into the atmosphere with his impressive pipes.

His name sounded familiar to me, though I was not sure why.

The two continued chatting, his tone and facial features gentle. He seemed suddenly aware of his surroundings, and of her.

"She's pure class," said a man and fellow onlooker about Susan, to no one in particular. I nodded, as the bystander and I exchanged a look of admiration for Susan, and I choked back tears.

Susan and Jerry spoke for another few minutes, learning that they had both lived for some time in New York and both miss it terribly, but both love San Francisco so much that neither has any regrets. The same commentator said, again to the air before him, "Wow. She's special." I had to fight the tears harder this time.

Jerry departed the bus at the bottom of Dolores Park. The man who'd been verbally high-fiving Susan said to her, "You're amazing." Several people chimed in, each sharing some variation on the theme that, in her shoes, they would have handled the situation abysmally. One would have been terrified. Another would have "lost it" on Jerry. A third would have gotten out at the first stop following the initial "excuse me." (And these are San Francisco residents. Who ride the bus. Late at night. A veteran crew, you might say.)

"But not you," said Susan's cheerleader. Then he started clapping. The entire carriage immediately joined in, all of us applauding Susan for the next ten seconds.

Then another man said to Susan, "You have ... empathy skills."

Susan replied, "Well, yeah. You just have to extend grace when you can."

I departed the bus at the top of Dolores Park. As I walked the park's high perimeter toward home, still marveling at Susan's compassion, I reflected on the power she had, and used, to put Jerry at ease.

Jerry had told all of us in that Muni carriage, in no uncertain terms, that he wanted desperately to be seen, and was sure no one was meeting that expectation. So he was going to yell until someone saw him. He would write everyone off as rude until Susan told him he mattered, that he had a name, and that, by the way, he could stand to be a little less rude himself.

As I unlocked my front door, I realized how I knew Jerry's name. One weekend evening seven years ago, I was at Caffe Trieste in North Beach with my dear friend Gayle, saying goodbye before she moved from the Bay Area, to embark upon her pastoral work in Winnemucca, Nevada.

I was so sad to see Gayle go, yet excited to pack in one final marathon catch-up with her. I had recently begun pining away for an on-again, off-again love interest whom I had bid farewell for good 2.5 years before. Out of nowhere, I could not get him out of my head, and I looked forward to hearing Gayle's insight on the situation, having come to rely on her deep wisdom over the years.

Jerry Winters approached us that night. Well, he was really there for me, but he let Gayle stay at the table while he regaled me with several life stories. I remember wanting Gayle to myself, but listening to Jerry Winters anyway, because I sensed that he needed me to hear him.

He introduced himself by his first and last name, just as he did with Susan tonight. When he walked away, Gayle laughed, shook her head at me, and said, "Well, you have a new boyfriend now!"

I just searched my archived emails for Jerry's name, betting that I had referenced him in a follow-up email to Gayle after she moved. Indeed, I had.

I must have given him my business card at the coffee shop, for the solo family law practice I was operating at the time. Referring to our Caffe Trieste date, I had written: "I had a blast. And so far, the coast is clear on communications from Jerry Winters. I think I dodged that bullet. Maybe I'll get some interesting, Caffe Trieste-based referrals out of the experience ..."

When Jerry Winters started in with Susan tonight, my first and second thoughts were that she might need her fellow Muni passengers to intervene, and that I had dodged a bullet by sitting where I had, and not landing where she was seated, with the man whom I didn't yet recognize as Jerry Winters antagonizing her.

All of us, I guess—you, Jerry Winters, and I—just want to be seen and heard. We scream and spit and accuse our way into it, until someone looks us straight in the eye and says, "I see you. I hear you. Now knock it off, Jerry Winters, and tell me something about yourself."

The next time I find myself shouting inside my mind that I am invisible, that I am inaudible, and that everyone is rude, I'm going to remember Jerry Winters, that friend I made seven years ago and saw again tonight. I will relax my eyes and lower that voice in my head, make myself heard, and tell my neighbor something about myself.

And though tonight proved that a compassionate ear is only those few steps away, I'm sure I will be surprised when I find one.

(I changed Susan and Jerry Winters' names, for whatever privacy they might desire.)

Steinbeck and His Wives

By Audry Lynch

It may not be a great literary question—but at least its human—to wonder about the effects of a great author's love life on his writing. In the case of John Steinbeck the love life was extremely varied and turbulent. It included early experimentation, college sweethearts, three wives and several Hollywood stars.

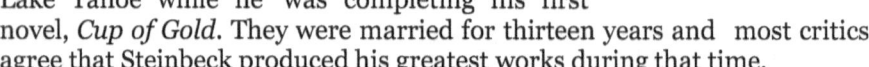

Steinbeck's first wife, Carol Henning, followed this early pattern of emotional/financial support for her husband. She met Steinbeck at Lake Tahoe while he was completing his first novel, *Cup of Gold*. They were married for thirteen years and most critics agree that Steinbeck produced his greatest works during that time.

They lived in the family cottage in Pacific Grove and, with the exception of a small monthly allowance from Steinbeck's father; Carol worked at a variety of jobs to support Steinbeck while he wrote. When she came home at night, she corrected his manuscripts—spelling, grammar, and sequencing—and then typed them and made sure they were mailed to New York publishers.

When it came time to research the plight of the migrant workers, Carol joined Steinbeck's trek to the Arvin Camp in Bakersfield, California. She was such a vital part of this expedition that resulted in the classic, *The Grapes of Wrath* that the dedication reads "To Carol who willed it." She is also credited with choosing the title from the "Battle Hymn of the Republic."

The divorce from Steinbeck was torturous and there were many allusions to his adulterous behavior with Gwyn Conger who was to become the second Mrs. Steinbeck. When I met Carol near the end of her-life, she was well advanced in bitterness and alcoholism. During the Steinbeck marriage she had discovered she was pregnant, but John had urged her to go to Mexico for an abortion. The job was botched, led to an infection and a hysterectomy, and no hope for motherhood. Carol said sadly, "John decided early in our marriage that we would have books instead of babies. When he left, he had the books and I didn't have the babies." (Same interview)

His second wife, Gwyn, had the babies—the only Steinbeck offspring, Thom and John the fourth. At the time he met her, Gwyn was a beautiful, red-haired singer on her way to success in Hollywood. Instead she opted for marriage to Steinbeck. Shortly after the marriage, Steinbeck left for Europe to cover World War Two for The Herald Tribune. The marriage was short, six years, and stormy and filled with accusations of extracurricular affairs on both sides.

Gwyn had not been featured in any Steinbeck book except the dedication to *The Wayward Bus*. A meeting with her gave me the chance to ask her what it had been like to be married to a famous author and she replied, "My function was to take care of the house, answer the phone and keep the kids quiet while John stayed locked in his room writing. (Personal Interview, Steinbeck Conference sponsored by San Jose State University, 1971.)

In one letter he complained to an old friend, A. Grove Day, that he would never become involved with another actress. He didn't find another actress but his third wife did come from the film colony—Elaine, who was married to the actor, Zachary Scott, at the time. Like Steinbeck's other wives, Elaine was a bright, talented woman in her own right. She had a career as a set designer until she married Steinbeck

This last marriage endured for nineteen years and was the one where, reportedly, Steinbeck finally found marital happiness. Ironically, this time of domestic peace did not produce his greatest literary output. Instead he became a national and international figure, the friend of such luminaries as President and Mrs. Johnson, the Kennedys, and Adlai Stevenson. Again ironically, he won the Nobel Prize during this time and produced a backlash among critics who dubbed him a "has-been" writer.

Like Gwyn, Elaine did not figure in Steinbeck's literary efforts. After his death, she made her own contribution to the Steinbeck literary legend. He was always a prodigious letter-writer; Elaine collected these letters from all over the world, sorted them and selected the ones that would present a good chronology of his life. She worked on this with a young writer and Steinbeck protégé, Robert Wallsten. The project produced a book called *Steinbeck: A Life in Letters*.

Even though this marriage was happy, it also had its trouble spots. Once in a newspaper interview Elaine reminisced: "He was a manic-depressive, like many artists. He was selfish and jealous. I may have wanted to kill him at times but I was never bored." (*Women's Wear Daily*, Sept. 2, 1975).

Steinbeck's relationships with women show us a very complex man. Or, conversely, do writers turn to writing because of a lack of fulfillment in human relationships? Perhaps, Steinbeck, himself, answers this enigma the best. Once while ill in a San Francisco Hospital, he passed the time by writing down some aphorisms. After his death, his old friend and noted columnist, Herb Caen, quoted them as a form of eulogy. One stands out: "Art is a scream of loneliness." (Herb Caen, *San Francisco Chronicle*, 1968).

Each of Steinbeck's wives helped him to "carry the light" of his literary talent to readers all over the world. Carol provided the prodding and the self-sacrifice to ensure his early success. Gwyn supplied the quiet home life he needed to continue that success. Elaine was the gracious companion who travelled all over the world with him to enjoy the final fruits of his literary success. They all made contributions to the prodigious output of an iconic writer but one is left wondering, "Was it ever enough?"

In one letter he complained to an old friend, A. Grove Day, that he would never become involved with another actress. He didn't find another actress but his third wife did come from the film colony—Elaine, who was married to the actor, Zachary Scott, at the time. Like Steinbeck's other wives, Elaine was a bright, talented woman in her own right. She had a career as a set designer until she married Steinbeck

This last marriage endured for nineteen years and was the one where, reportedly, Steinbeck finally found marital happiness. Ironically, this time of domestic peace did not produce his greatest literary output. Instead he became a national and international figure, the friend of such luminaries as President and Mrs. Johnson, the Kennedys, and Adlai Stevenson. Again ironically he won the Nobel Prize during this time and produced a backlash among critics who dubbed him a "has-been" writer.

Like Gwyn, Elaine did not figure in Steinbeck's literary efforts. After his death, she made her own contribution to the Steinbeck literary legend. He was always a prodigious letter-writer; Elaine collected these letters from all over the world, sorted them and selected the ones that would present a good chronology of his life. She worked on this with a young writer and Steinbeck protégé, Robert Wallsten. The project produced a book called *Steinbeck: A Life in Letters*.

Even though this marriage was happy, it also had its trouble spots. Once in a newspaper interview Elaine reminisced: "He was a manic-depressive, like many artists. He was selfish and jealous. I may have wanted to kill him at times but I was never bored." (Women's Wear Daily, Sept. 2, 1975).

Steinbeck's relationships with women show us a very complex man. Or, conversely, do writers turn to writing because of a lack of fulfillment in human relationships? Perhaps, Steinbeck, himself, answers this enigma the best. Once while ill in a San Francisco Hospital, he passed the time by writing down some aphorisms. After his death, his old friend and noted columnist, Herb Caen, quoted them as a form of eulogy. One stands out: "Art is a scream of loneliness." (Herb Caen, San Francisco Chronicle, 1968).

Each of Steinbeck's wives helped him to "carry the light" of his literary talent to readers all over the world. Carol provided the prodding and the self-sacrifice to ensure his early success. Gwyn supplied the quiet home life he needed to continue that success. Elaine was the gracious companion who travelled all over the world with him to enjoy the final fruits of his literary success. They all made contributions to the prodigious output of an iconic writer but one is left wondering, "Was it ever enough?"

The Deathsinger

By Sylvia E. Halloran

When Eleanor Hadley first noticed her gift, she dismissed it as coincidental. Certainly she could not admit to herself that what was happening was her doing. And mostly, folks were kind enough to avoid pointing out the connection. But as the body count rose, she could no longer deny the nature of her talent. In some way she did not understand, Eleanor could dispatch people by singing to them.

Now, many would agree that they have heard types of singing that are torturous if not downright murderous, and Eleanor had studied long and hard to avoid that path. Her first attempts in weekly voice lessons were enthusiastic but unremarkable; she practiced scales and arpeggios and Italian art songs every day and never discovered how to relax her tongue. Her teacher had promised the career of a Wagnerian soprano as the fruit of her diligence, but really, after all those years and all that money, she had mastered only the ability to breathe without moving her shoulders.

Her next teacher, a retired church soloist and mother of five, hinted at untapped greatness. In addition to vocal exercises, she coaxed some actual music from Eleanor.

Small arias and snippets of oratorios entered her repertoire. Wagner reigned far, far away from the teacher's cramped living room with its orange carpet and tiny spinet. Relieved of the looming threat of Isolde, Eleanor could at last be comfortable with what she could sing. She entered a few competitions and performed in church when they couldn't get anyone else.

But nobody died.

By chance, Eleanor met her teacher's teacher, a legendary woman grown godlike in Eleanor's eyes by her own teacher's blatant adoration of the woman. The opportunity to work with this flamboyant icon inspired Eleanor, and she scraped and borrowed to afford the costly hours. Week after week her confidence grew, and the gold that her first teacher had promised so many years earlier became once again a visible speck in the streambed of Eleanor's song.

The operatic stage remained eons from her reach while Eleanor's own years accumulated. The dreams of youth grew weary. To survive the looming sorrow of meeting old age with unfulfilled potential, she planned a rollicking birthday recital for the church where she worked—a review of the music that had delighted her first fifty years.

The birthday program was a collection of everything that Eleanor had

333

loved to sing: infant lullabies she had cooed along with her mother, and songs they had shared together on road trips, hymns to honor unknown grandmothers, snatches of Gilbert and Sullivan and a couple of favorite college solos. As a lark, Eleanor included a set of old time-pieces, to provide her church friends a window into her hobby of singing for convalescent homes.

Within these old songs lay the first hint of her true vocal power, although everyone treated it as an unhappy accident at the time.

The small church was filled with family and friends. The recital began as scheduled. Eleanor told stories to weave the story of her musical journey together. She sang competently, as always, with that hint of gold and the ever-elusive breakthrough still taunting her. The pleasant afternoon fulfilled her hope for celebration in the face of approaching old age.

Concessions are made as dreams die, and Eleanor grew increasingly aware of this as the program neared completion. After overextending her way through an unforgiving scene from *Lohengrin,* she caught her breath and, with relief, launched into the final sing-along set, with one complication: as she finished "Till We Meet Again," Mrs. Lafferty from the 10:45 service slipped off the pew and crumpled to the floor, peaceful and dead as a person could be.

Eleanor's recital was finished, which was lucky. The hubbub that followed enveloped the rest of the afternoon. Following the departure of the ambulance, the reception in Fellowship Hall was well attended and highly animated. Every conversation focused on the efforts to revive dear old Mrs. L. and what a beloved and faithful follower she had been for all of her 89 years. No one mentioned Eleanor's voice or the program.

The distraction of Mrs. Lafferty's unexpected demise tempered any possible triumph on Eleanor's part concerning the recital. The daughter flew in from Minneapolis and arranged the memorial service. Mrs. Lafferty had specified that, when her time came, she wanted Eleanor to sing. Eleanor rehearsed the Twenty-third Psalm with the organist and ironed her navy suit. She never considered for a moment that she might be dangerous.

Mrs. Lafferty's memorial service drew a very small crowd, mostly choir members and ladies from the Quilter's Guild. Her daughter sat in the front row with the pastor's wife, who chuckled as the eulogy revealed a wild and adventurous girlhood quite contrary to the old saint in retirement.

The time for Eleanor's solo came. Its familiar words of comfort reassured her as well as her audience. She finished the last phrase. People in the pews smiled and nodded in approval and appreciation. Mr. Collier, the choir's portly tenor, nodded off and rested his chin on his chest.

The Pastor commended Mrs. Lafferty's soul to God and invited all present to the reception in Fellowship Hall. They sang the closing hymn, and everyone proceeded across the plaza to black-olive-and-cream-cheese sandwiches and strawberry punch.

Everybody except Mr. Collier, that is, who remained sitting quietly in his seat in an attitude of prayer. It wasn't like him to ignore sandwiches.

Eleanor did not stay for the reception; there was still laundry to do and some weeds under the camellias to pull. She went home and did not learn until the following Thursday evening that her sole tenor had expired at the service for Mrs. L. It was a devastating blow.

The shock of losing two older parishioners within a week kept conversations lively at Sunday's coffee hour. Oddly, both people had succumbed during events in the Sanctuary. In its whole history, the church had never before been the actual scene of death. Well, old Arthur Kellogg had suffered that heart attack back in '69 on clean-up Saturday before Easter. But everyone agreed it was not the same thing at all.

Eleanor tried not to think too much about the deaths. She continued working on her upper range. Some days she felt conflicted about singing. She wanted to succeed but really could not measure success. She feared recognizing in herself one of those deluded wannabes pursuing a futile goal.

No reason existed for her to continue her studies. No auditions were appropriate to her age. The goal of the operatic stage became increasingly less attainable as she recognized that singing opera is for the young.

However, her range of nostalgic music mushroomed as she found more places to sing. Sight-reading the best music of Tin Pan Alley for rooms full of wheelchair-bound ancients involved only a little effort, yet gave her a real sense of doing good. All the convalescent homes in the area welcomed her; she developed a devoted following among the Activities Directors and their flocks of forgetful grandmas.

It was during one of these visits that Eleanor realized the growing regularity of final departures amid her audiences could no longer be dismissed or ignored. Her third victim that month slumped into her cupcake at a sing along party the Wednesday after they buried Mr. Collier. Eleanor finished *"Your Buddy Misses You"* and the old dear left to meet her maker with frosting on her nose. The next day a frail, halo-haired sweetie in the front row at Pilgrim's Rest slipped away during *"Let the Rest of the World Go By."*

At Eleanor's visit the next week, a nurse diverted her from the door of the dining hall where the piano waited. "Could you come with me for just a minute?" the nurse asked, motioning down the hall. Eleanor followed her along the corridor to a small private room.

As they approached, a chilling moan soaked the air. The nurse inclined her head slightly toward the doorway and introduced her patient in low tones. "This is Mrs. Sawyer, Eleanor. She has pancreatic cancer. Her only child was killed in a car crash twenty years ago. She lost her husband last year to prostate cancer." She looked at Eleanor with a level gaze. "Would you sing to her, please? She loves Irving Berlin."

Eleanor stared at the nurse with emerging understanding and backed away from the doorway. The nurse never varied her hopeful smile and gazed into the room.

Eleanor's eyes unwillingly followed the nurse's sightline. The woman's wasted frame held the thin blanket in straight, defined ridges.

Heartbreaking sighs rode every breath. Mrs. Sawyer's bleary eyes met Eleanor's. The briefest of smiles touched the woman's papery lips.

Eleanor stepped toward the bed. As she took the woman's hand, the fragility she sensed went far beyond the delicate lacing of tendon and vein. Eleanor willed her breath to behave. Leaning close to the woman's cheek, she began, *"I'll be loving you always, with a love that's true, always..."*

The old ballad tempered her voice. With an even whisper, she sang so quietly and close to the old woman's ear that the air barely stirred as the words poured out their promise: *"Not for just an hour, not for just a day, not for just a year, but always."*

Mrs. Sawyer answered with a rattle as the breath left her. Her taut body relaxed and she was gone, just like that. The nurse, who had waited nearby as Eleanor had approached the bed, said brokenly, "Thank you. She was my favorite. I was so afraid she would have a long time to suffer."

Eleanor felt dizzy, elated and completely empty. "You're welcome," she murmured.

She walked back up the corridor to the dining hall and discovered that she could not make herself enter the wide door. She was suddenly frightened of herself, of her voice, of whatever had just happened. She didn't dare sing for people if...

Eleanor choked on the warm air outside the dining room door. The flowery scent was designed to mask the persistent odor of waste and death. A gentle hand touched her shoulder. She turned to it.

"You have a great gift," the nurse began. "You bless the suffering with relief. You are the boatman that carries them across the river to where they need to be. By some kind of grace you can heal their souls and set them free." The nurse pushed the door open. "Your public awaits."

Reluctantly, Eleanor walked to the piano and set her music down. She looked from wall to wall in the clean, institutional room and rested her gaze on the audience of wheel chairs filled with quiet, diminished bodies. Discolored feet poked out from under fleecy throws. Wispy hair swathed nodding heads. A few sparkling eyes peered with interest at Eleanor, and suddenly she was filled with an all-consuming, dimensionless love. She played a gentle chord on the piano and began her important work: *"Shall we gather at the river where bright angel feet have trod?*

Beyond Wonder

By Rudie Tretten

Wonder Woman was born in December 1941. Not a good month for her native land.

But just as the United States went on to victory in World War II, Wonder Woman went on to triumph over evil doers in the comic book stories detailing her life.

There was, however, a real wonder woman whose life story begs for capitalization—WONDER WOMAN.

Eunice "Judy" Seaton Mongan's career has included teaching on an Indian Reservation, service in the Red Cross in World War II, teaching high school English and drama, and being the oldest member of the Peace Corps when in her eighties. There's more she has done but the list illustrates commitment, not to rounding up the bad guys, but to making the world a better place for all of us.

For example, desiring to "do something to help the war effort" in World War II, she learned to fly so she could apply to join the Woman's Air Force. She succeeded as a pilot but found she wasn't tall enough for the Air Force, so she volunteered for the Red Cross.

She and 20,000 others, primarily soldiers, went to England on the Queen Mary. Seventy-seven Red Cross personnel were there with Judy. Most were assigned to London headquarters near Marble Arch.

After the war she was assigned to Bremerhaven in Germany to assist GI's on their homeward journey. In 1946 she returned to the U.S. and spent time with her family in White Salmon, Washington. She then visited a cousin in San Francisco. She got a job at the White House Department Store and was then recruited as a model. She accepted this job. In January 1947 she applied for and was offered a teaching position at Jefferson High School in Daly City.

Comic book Wonder Woman has not been much for romance. Judy's life has been much more real. Judy Seaton married Jefferson's divorced principal, John Mongan, a little after ten years in her return to teaching after the Red Cross and modeling experience. Their marriage was the blending of two Americas. Judy describes the cultural gap bridged by their love.

"I had a lot to learn from John. I grew up in this little village, Protestant, and with a very simple life... and I was with a man who was first generation Irish Catholic in a big cosmopolitan city where there were all kinds of activities"

John died of heart problems in 1966. During the eight years of their marriage, Judy "learned a new culture." A significant part of that culture involved Irish family life. Her background had not prepared her for the high energy and demands of the Irish family and the open displays of grief upon the death of a loved one.

In what she described as "a way of holding on to John" she went back to teaching at Jefferson. Much of her work there centered on drama and she produced two and sometimes three shows per year.

She developed close relationships with the actors and actresses who performed for her over a nine-year period that earned her a sabbatical leave.

And off she went. The small-town rigidly Protestant child had been cosmopolitanized by her marriage into a woman who wanted to experience the world. She started in Brazil then went to South Africa. A good part of her time in that rigidly segregated society she spent driving a VW bug over difficult roads and desolate sections of the nation. She stopped for a time to visit Kruger National Park and the wild life living there. All of this she did by herself.

"I told you. I'm a very strong woman."

On a subsequent journey to Africa, she did a twelve-day camel safari. She also spent time in Ethiopia and Egypt. Later came the Seychelles and Nairobi. So on to the seventies and eighties. In 1982 she joined the Peace Corps for a two- year assignment in Liberia. She was 70 years old. Still too young to step back from her service-oriented life.

On returning from Liberia, she noticed a newspaper ad for a teaching job in Japan. She applied; she got it and spent a year learning about still another culture.

The coup de gras: in 1992 she applied again for the Peace Corps and was sent to Hungary to teach teachers. Eighty years old and the oldest serving member of the Peace Corps.

Judy stayed in Hungary for three years. At the end of her Peace Corps assignment, the Hungarian College where she worked asked her to stay for one more year, and she did. Asked why she had continued her active, engaged life, she responded:

"Well, I guess I just have always had a great curiosity about other parts of the world and I think that the thing that is the biggest driver in my life is learning. I have this tremendous curiosity..."

That desire to learn is not restricted to faraway places. After one of her stays overseas, she came home to find that her kitchen was in bad shape. She couldn't afford a contractor so she got two books and "I learned how to do it."

Bill has not been mentioned on these pages. He and Judy have been "a number" for over a quarter of a century.

He graduated from Whitman two years before Judy and is now 104 years old. They got together at a Whitman Alumni meeting. For several years they commuted between his home in Honolulu and hers in San Francisco. They lived in the house with the remodeled kitchen.

She said it herself, "I am a strong woman." There are many attributes that could be attached to "strong." That strength enabled her to carry the light! She died at age 102 on March 6, 2015.

Nursing Homes, Pilfered Lives

By Carole Taub

The image from her ghost-like figure was incredulous and sucked the breath out of me. I walked into her sparse room with a tentativeness like I'd never quite felt before. This had been our first encounter.

What lies beneath her milky skin is a mystery. Mostly.

They don't tell me much. So it's always a time for discovery. If I'm lucky she throws me a golden nugget of information. I'm supposed to be placid. I try.

But silently, beneath my skin, I'm screaming.

Did she like coffee in her *before now* life? As much then as she does now? I've learned the signals that make up her pseudo happiness. There are so few. Coffee is one of the highlights though. The mere mention of it and her face lights up as if on cue.

George Strait is her favorite singer, and she says to me without a moment's hesitation, *handsome*. I stole *this* precious nugget, digging deep, looking around, like a pilfering cat. Her concern for my possible fatigue is ongoing, questioning me on the matter every few seconds.

Tired? She slurs. Sweetly she tells me I'm pretty. I return the compliment. But she shies away from the idea only to schmear it over with *fat*.

Sitting beside her corpse-like body I take her hand in mine. I stroke her creamy skin. And then I try gently to pry her hand open. It's not locked, yet she can't open it. Her nails are nasty, long and beginning to bend like Howard Hughes'. *Why don't they cut your nails?* Another blank stare. I try to open up her hand. *Tell me if it hurts*. And she nods her head in agreement. It doesn't hurt. But the smell is repugnant, like rotted cheese. *Don't they wash your hands?* She slurs that they don't care.

What was she like before? Her claim of having had two husbands leaves me in want. I'm filled with hope that one day she'll tell me if she had children. And being the ideal volunteer, I try not to ask.

I can't. I'm told not to ask. Still I cave. Maybe one day she'll feel that she can trust me enough. But I soon realize that I'm reading too much into this; she's like a child and has no idea what trust is anymore. One day, might she tell me things without my probing? But this is one of those *time will tell* stories. Yet I question how much does she have? I bring her a pair of pearl earrings. And I gently place them into one of the three sets of piercings she has in each ear. I hand her my mirror. She studies herself, like she's in wonder who she sees in the reflection.

An attendant comes into the room carrying two cokes. She placed one on *her* table, and the other on her seemingly comatose roommate's table. And then she left. No eye contact. No greetings. Her cold chill left a trail as she walked back into the hallway. *She* looked at me shaking her head, slurring *diabetic*. I immediately emptied the Coke in the toilet. Tossed the can into the garbage.

Returned to her bedside. That's when I asked her how long she'd been there?

Unable to walk, an ongoing scrimmage with words and thoughts, incapable of doing anything, she'd been robbed of her independence. And her struggles were only getting worse. She'd been there five years. Pride and dignity? It's there beneath her milky warm skin.

Weekly I make my appearance. Automatically affixing my *blinders*, and giving her my all. Arriving at my scheduled timeslot, I check in at the desk, sign my name, attach my volunteer sticker onto my shirt, and I'm off. Down the sterile hall, squeaky clean linoleum floor, bordered by barren walls, passing a wheelchair here, the blank face attached to a slumped body, unaware that I'm a passerby. No waves. No smiles. No uttering words.

Still as I cruse down the hall, I graciously smile, look them in the eye, acknowledge that they are there. That they are still alive. And yet I wonder why? They appear more like living ghosts. Their life has been sucked out of them. And all that remains is absolute emptiness.

Passing the nurses station I see another band of wheel-chaired inmates. Again blank faces, voices that moan, and bodies that continuously jerk and beg. Again there are no smiles. No blinking eyes. No life.

I meander a little further down the hall and I've arrived. And there she is again, a massive blimp-like figure molded into her chair. The kind with wheels and a brake to boot. The kind with an elongated extension to rest her lifeless legs. That will ease her here and there, but in actuality nowhere. Her look is asking me, *Am I dead yet?*

Reminiscent of a death sentence, she's a lifer. No chance of parole. There for the long haul. Till death does she part. And that feeling of uncertainty hovers each time I take that infamous walk down the hall to her room.

Will she be there? Is she still alive? Would they even tell me? Not to bother coming because her sentence is complete? Discreetly, they watch me. Intently. The overseeing powers. "Haven't seen you for a while; where have you been?" And I only shake my head and flail my arms. Never having missed one of my scheduled visits I think that to be strange. As the good volunteer, I'm there every week.

Sitting in my living room, studying the adorned walls, fireplace, candles, I am rich with a hovering peace. What does she have?

Striking a match, I light the candle in front of my Buddha. Then unroll my yoga mat and stand erect in the very front. Taking a breath I close my eyes, hands at my heart.

What does she have?

She's trapped within the confines of her existence. Her teeth have yellow stains. Her breath is foul. Is that all she has?

So who really cares, and am I actually doing anybody any good? I'm certainly not prolonging anyone's life. Not really bringing joy and happiness into the equation. The energy I put forth is truly in vain. Perhaps I'd be better known as the observer. Am I simply doing something to satisfy myself, giving back to the community? What purpose am I serving?

My time is up for this visit. I touch her arm that looks like creamy mashed potatoes. I smile and watch as she jerks around again and again. I used to wonder what she was looking at? But I've come to understand she sees nothing. Although I question whether she's hoping to get to the *other side*. And wonders how much longer must she stay?

I continue to go. The visits are arduous. And the reward is closing in on zero. As are the benefits. Her earrings were pilfered. I think the employees like me though. They smile at me.

Bells and Smells

By Evie Groch

In a room that could compactly seat 35 to 40, she sits alone and works on papers. Her pen scratches out notes in the margins, and the ruffling of placing papers at the bottom of the pile marks her progress and encourages her to continue. A random bell sounds between the predictable ones and heightens her sensitivity. A few muted footsteps mingle with running ones and scurry down the hall amid squeals and cursing. This is not a safe haven as backpacks smack into doors and walls, leaving an echoing chaos in a structure built for order.

Spring smells drift into her room through the partially opened windows—the freshly mowed grass the noisy institutional mower left behind—the occasional sweetness of field flowers. She focuses on the disharmony of clustered bees easily able to enter through their screenless openings. She could be out on a picnic doing her avoidance dance and swatting them as their buzzing deafens her, but instead she's sensitive to the clicking of her pen scrawling across ruled papers, several of which she must uncrumble and flatten by hand without the use of an iron to press them open.

The turn of the doorknob to her room awakens in her the anticipation of the young bodies about to enter, many thunderously tripping over themselves to dump their books on their desks and steal a few extra minutes of gossip and whispers before the tardy bell. It finally rings, and the odors of perfume, bubble gum, hair spray, cologne and after-shave pour in on pounding tennis shoes. She inhales it all and lets it fuel her into action.

363 SHORT STORY

Note: We have included all categories of Short Fiction, General Fiction under 55 years, General Fiction Senior, Sci-Fi Senior, Mystery 55 or younger, Mystery Senior, Historical, and Humorous.

Campsite 39

By Kimberly Schultz

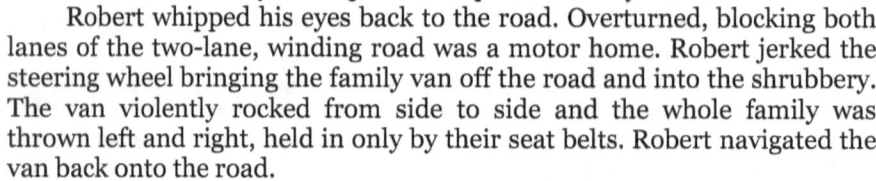

"I'm going on a camping trip and this is what I am going to bring..." Robert tapped the steering wheel trying to remember what Jennifer said for the letter a. The family made it all the way to the letter p in this game of memory. "Oh, yes," Robert said with a smirk. "I remember now. An apple," he said with a grin, taking a look back at Jennifer through the rearview mirror. Jennifer giggled.

"Robert! Watch out!" Karen screamed from the passenger's side of the car. She grabbed a hold of the dashboard ready for impact and squeezed her eyelids shut.

Robert whipped his eyes back to the road. Overturned, blocking both lanes of the two-lane, winding road was a motor home. Robert jerked the steering wheel bringing the family van off the road and into the shrubbery. The van violently rocked from side to side and the whole family was thrown left and right, held in only by their seat belts. Robert navigated the van back onto the road.

"Is everyone okay?" Robert yelled out of fright, not anger. Sobs erupted from the back seat as Jennifer began to cry. Karen opened her eyes and saw a blur of greens and browns before her eyes adjusted and sent the message to her brain that they did not crash. Redwood trees flew past them as the van drove along the road as if nothing happened at all.

"Yes," Karen whispered clutching her racing heart. She looked back at Jennifer. "Are you okay?" Jennifer shook her head up and down.

The state park was only 10 miles up from the crash site, but it felt as if it were 100.

Robert gripped the steering wheel with both hands, his knuckles white, as he cautiously drove the van along the winding road. Karen couldn't lift her stiff arms from her lap to block the sun that was streaming through the windshield and burning her lap. Although her legs were on fire, she sat back in her seat, eyes watching the road.

Robert slowly turned into the entrance of the state park and pulled the van to a slow stop at the ranger station. A sharp pain stabbed through his chest as he finally exhaled a long, deep breath he realized he was holding in since the near crash.

"Can I help you folks?" a tall ranger with a large, brown hat asked leaning into the van.

His name tag read, "Rick."

"We have reservations to camp here tonight," Robert said, his voice shaky.

Ranger Rick looked into the back set at Jennifer, then at Karen, and finally at Robert. "You folks okay?" Ranger Rick asked. "You look as if you have seen a couple of ghosts."

Robert explained the near collision with the overturned motor home just down the road and Ranger Rick said he'd call it into the sheriff. He reached into the van, taping a small yellow piece of paper with their campsite number, 39, to the windshield."

"No wood seller on duty tonight so you are on your own," Ranger Rick said. He hit the top of the van with the palm of his hand. "Have a good night." Then he disappeared into the ranger station.

Campsite 39 was located in an isolated corner of the park away from any other campsites.

Overgrown bushes surrounded their site leaving them in seclusion. By the time Robert pitched the tent and gathered fallen branches for their fire, the sun sank behind the canopy of Redwood trees, casting eerie shadows throughout the site.

Karen sat in front of the campfire shivering. The orange glow from the fire illuminated her sunken eyes and downward lips. Jennifer sat in the dirt with a shovel and collected dirt in the light of the lantern placed right next to her.

The roar of a truck engine overpowered the sound of the crackling fire. Robert looked toward the road and saw Ranger Rick's pickup truck slowly pass their site. The truck was dark inside, but Robert thought he saw a ghost-white hand reach out of the driver's side window and give a wave.

"Can we have s'mores?" Jennifer asked, getting up from the dirt and pulling at Karen's arm. Karen looked at her daughter's face and noticed that the glow from the fire did not reach her face. Her daughter's pale face was transparent. She pulled Jennifer closer to the fire to see if the light would reflect on her face, but it didn't. Jennifer's skin was as pale as the smoke that rose from the fire.

"What are you doing?" Robert yelled. "She is too close to the fire!" He grabbed Jennifer's hand and brought her over to the table.

Karen couldn't take her eyes off her daughter's pale face as she stood next to the fire roasting her marshmallow. The only sound that of a crackling fire.

Crunch, crunch, scrape. The sound erupted from the black night. Crunch, crunch, scrape. As the sound grew louder, Robert and Karen's eyes pulsated black as they looked into the night trying to make out any shape. Robert jumped up from his chair and grabbed the marshmallow fork from Jennifer. "Heyyyy," she whined.

Crunch, crunch, scrape. It was coming from the direction of the road. A small, white light that moved with the sound of each crunch and scrape appeared and floated toward them, growing bigger and bigger.

"What do you want?" Robert called out. His voice evaporated into the darkness.

Crunch, crunch, scrape. As the light approached, a shadowy figure appeared. "Just stopping by to see if you have enough wood for the night," a male voice answered.

Robert put the fork down and walked over to the figure that now came closer. An older man stood in front of them with a bright light attached to his hat. He walked with a stick to hold himself up. "I'm the wood seller."

"Ranger Rick told us that you were not working today," Robert replied, his heart finally slowing down.

A puzzled look came across the old man's face. "Did you say Ranger Rick?" he asked. "Yes," Robert replied.

"You must be mistaken," the old man said. "Ranger Rick died two weeks ago. We have no ranger on duty over the weekends." He started walking toward the road then stopped. "Although," he said as he turned around. "People do say that they still see his pickup truck doing the rounds at night."

Robert and Karen listened to the crunch, crunch, scrape slowly fade away as the old man walked down the road.

"I want to go home," Karen said.

"I am sure there is a reasonable explanation," Robert said, not sounding too convincing.

A rustling sound erupted from the bushes behind them. Fear shot through their bodies like an electric shock. Karen grabbed Jennifer and fell into the tent; Robert was right behind them.

As Robert zipped up the tent, he saw two big raccoons emerge from the bushes and scurry over to the picnic table. Robert breathed a sigh of relief.

Robert and Karen lie still in the dark tent. Jennifer, tucked in the middle of the couple, slept. They listened to the sounds of the raccoons' feet walking across the picnic table. The two raccoons growled as if talking to each other.

"Do you hear that?" Karen whispered. Before Robert could answer, the sound of Ranger Rick's pickup truck roared through the night and pulled to a stop at their campsite. Robert and Karen froze, holding their breath until the truck pulled away.

The next morning, Robert threw everything in the back of the van and the family rushed out of the campsite, past the empty ranger station, and back onto the winding road.

The wood seller hobbled to the ranger station, saw the pickup truck parked outside the station, and walked in. "What are you doing here?" he asked Ranger Ted. "And why are you wearing Ranger Rick's jacket?" he asked.

"Wife and kids are out of town for the weekend," Ranger Ted responded. "And I can't find my jacket so I am wearing his."

The morning news played on the small black and white TV in the ranger station. The two stared in disbelief at the newscast that flashed pictures of the campers in Campsite 39. "A family of three died at the scene yesterday when their van collided with an overturned motor home on Highway 1, bursting into flames, killing the family instantly," the news lady said.

Homicidal Blueprint

By Bernadine Fornesi

The list was completed. Two blonde heads hovered over the piece of paper in the bedroom of a neglected old house on the outskirts of Chicago, and studied it. In careless childish printing it started with... "Ten Ways to Bump Somebody off Without Getting Caught."

Number one on the list was the rat poison kept on the shelf in the garage at the back of the house. The two sisters, Betty and Millie gave this one much thought. "How much do you think we would have to put in his pancake mix to kill him?" asked Millie the ten year old.

Betty, the older sister by two years, appeared thoughtful as she replied "Well, we could read the directions on the box and multiply it for Howard. He's a big rat."

Second printed suggestion was the sleeping pills that were left by their mother when she became ill. Remove the sleeping pills from the bottle and place them in the wine jug he keeps on the kitchen table. "I don't know if that would kill him, it might just make him sleep at the table all night," Betty sighed as she looked at her sister eating a stale cookie.

"When we get rid of him, I don't want there to be too much blood. I get sick when I see blood," said Millie as she shook her shoulders in fright while brushing cookie crumbs from her dress. "I like the idea of taking the light bulb from the basement stairs, and if he's drunk enough he could fall, and break his neck. I don't think there would be too much blood that way."

"Yeah that might work," Betty said.

They continued reading down the list. Number five on the list was to cut the brake line on his old Ford pick-up truck. "Do you know where the brake line is?" Millie asked.

"Not really. I think it's underneath the car somewhere. But we better scratch that one since we don't know too much about the workings of a car."

"Now I really like this one," said Betty, "Spray Raid Ant Poison on his mashed potatoes. He might not notice the Raid because he says we're rotten cooks." Both girls giggled, and put their hands over their mouths. The list was folded and put under the mattress as they heard the sputtering

345

of the pick-up truck pulling into the driveway.

Howard was a sorry stepfather to the two girls. People called him the town drunk. The four bars in town knew him well. He was able to run a bar tab for a short period of time until the owners cut him off for nonpayment. He couldn't hold a job for more than two weeks. He had to travel farther from his house to find work. The girl's mother had married Howard nine years ago when their father ran out on them. Howard offered them a place to stay in his home when he found them huddled inside an old car close to the park. He wasn't drinking as much then, just on weekends, and he had a steady job at the car factory. When Howard proposed marriage to their mother, she figured this was the best way to give her small girls security. It worked well for a short while until Howard decided he liked the booze better than his family life. His personality changed... he was a mean drunk.

When their mother became ill and was taken to the Community Hospital, she never returned.

Betty and Millie only had drunken Howard to look after them. He expected them to do all the household chores, and cook for him as their mother had. "What the hell is wrong with you brats? Can't you cook an egg without a crust on the bottom?" His hand swung swiftly against the side of Betty's head. She ducked the next blow and Howard fell into the kitchen chair. He lifted up his cup of coffee and took a sip as he yelled, "MY GOD, THIS TASTES LIKE TAR! If you stupid brats don't shape up I'm kicking you out. You came with nothing, and that's how you're going to leave... with NOTHING!" The girls ran into their bedroom and hid behind the clothes in the closet hoping Howard wouldn't follow them with the leather strap he used frequently on them.

Snow started falling the following evening. It was cold in the house. Howard had turned the furnace off when he left the house in the afternoon searching for more alcohol to fuel his insatiable thirst. After walking the few blocks from school, the cold air greeted the sisters as they pushed open the front door. "Get a blanket Millie, and I'll make us a peanut butter sandwich." They sat eating the sandwich with the blanket wrapped around them.

"Do you know how to start the furnace in the basement?" Millie asked.

"I don't think so," Betty replied, "but we'll go down and look at it." They fumbled around with the handles on the furnace in the basement, but decided they couldn't restart it. On the way back up the stairs, Betty reached overhead and unscrewed the one light bulb. "No sense in giving Howard any light to walk down the stairs if he decides to turn the furnace on."

True to form, Howard came home around two a.m. His noisy entrance into the house woke both girls. They heard him utter an oath as he slumped into a kitchen chair. "Damn it to hell, it's cold in here!" The chair scraped against the floor as he rose and staggered toward the basement door. "Got to turn on that damn furnace." He opened the basement door to darkness, "Where the hell is the light?"

In the sister's bedroom they heard a loud cry and a thud, then silence.

The girls looked at each other, and Millie said, "Do you think he could have fallen down the stairs?"

"I hope so, said Betty, let's go see." Betty took a few steps down the steps to the basement and screwed the light bulb on.

Howard lay at the bottom of the stairs. The girls came slowly down, and looked at Howard. "Do you think he's dead? But his eyes are open, maybe he isn't dead." Millie was shaking her head in disbelief.

"Sometimes dead people keep their eyes open, but he's dead alright. It looks like he broke something that can't be fixed. Go next door and have Mr. Patterson come over and take a look."

Mille hurried up the stairs and yelled back at her sister, "I told you this was the best way to get rid of Howard. And I didn't see any blood either."

The funeral was small. At the cemetery Howard was lowered into the ground as Betty and Millie kept handkerchiefs over their mouths. But it wasn't grief they were feeling. It was to hide self-satisfied grins of no regrets, and deeply felt joy at his passing.

On the other side of the cemetery, the girls stopped at their mother's grave, and pulled some weeds away from the small headstone. Partially covered with vines and dirt, the sisters saw strange scratching on the cement headstone. In bold printed letters were the words... WELL DONE

Serenade

By Lisa Meltzer Penn

Robbie gazed up at the side window of the suburban home where a soft glow filtered out of the edges of a blank, white blind. Swollen purple knuckles with tiny pinpricks of white refused to bend. Robbie looked out to the city lights in the distance—bright, tiny lights, inconsequential for him—they didn't illuminate him; but the sky—here was his inspiration; his hand trembled and the long, thin fingers finally bent a little. The doctor had said to keep them splinted for another two

weeks but Robbie didn't care. They had healed enough to play simple chords, and this time he had been more careful loading the folding ladder into the old station wagon. He frowned a little at the absence of the sliver of moon and scattering of shining stars that were supposed to accompany him. But the sky stared back blankly; only a few distant stars were perceptible from behind the gray and although the moon must have risen by now, it was nowhere to be seen. He shrugged. It didn't matter. This was the moment.

Robbie hoisted the ladder and it came to rest against the wooden shingles. With guitar slung over shoulder, red rose between lips, he ascended. The ladder was shaky and when Robbie moved his left foot and then his right, the hinges creaked like the steep, paint-chipped stairs leading to the attic storeroom.

He missed his footing once and the whole ladder swayed to one side and strained for the ground while Robbie grasped at a rung, stabbing a hard splintered piece of wood into an Injured finger. He grimaced, rested for a moment to remove what he could of the sliver, and then continued to the top. But the rose had fallen to the ground.

How he'd get down again he didn't know, but that wasn't important. He was here to serenade Laura.

Supported by a ladder rung with one leg, the other wrapped around the narrow ledge at the top of the ladder so that he was part sitting, part squatting, part standing, but mostly just all twisted up and facing the road more than Laura's window, he positioned the guitar precariously across his lap. With shoulders hunched and elbow pointing to the sky, he played. He sang the lyrics of his love and the clear notes of the guitar and his voice spread up as far as the moon. It felt good to sing like this! Laura must be lying on her pillow, enjoying the promised music. It was all right. She could relax and listen. He could wait for her to raise the shade. He could wait.

He sang. He sang his rendition of "Greensleeves."

A warm breeze swept through the trees, shaking the branches, rocking the ladder. Robbie didn't worry too much. He was getting used to the motion and if he fell, he fell.

Laura had first brought up the idea of the serenade. She was joking about his new-found passion with guitar and said that someday he should come to her window like a Spanish serenader. Then she laughed, her passionate hazel eyes appearing a rich jade. But a smile crept up Robbie's cheeks. Here was an idea. After that he would talk about it once in a while. One week he would say, "I've been working on those songs. You'll get that serenade one of these days." And the next week he would ask which window was hers or what time her parents went to bed. Laura would laugh kind of nervously and he could tell that she didn't quite know if he was serious.

Last week he had told her that his finger was almost better. "Should be better by … oh, I guess … Tuesday or Wednesday, maybe Thursday."

"That's good," she said, her eyes fixed on something behind Robbie's back. "How did you hurt it anyway?" she asked, breaking her stare.

"Oh, I just had a little accident," he replied, and looked up, blushing a little with his secret.

He figured he always would get pretty much what he wanted out of life. At least he'd try. And not like those spoiled brats that whined and begged and got everything from their parents. He'd do it on his own, and he wouldn't waste time with all that material garbage like clothes and video toys. None of those insincere people either. Just give him his tapedeck, his guitar and Laura and he'd get along just fine.

He wondered what was taking her so long to acknowledge his presence. She should be expecting him; it was Wednesday. Maybe she was in the bathroom or something. Or maybe just waiting for more music.

He remembered their date. She had kissed him quickly and thanked him for the evening. "Anything for you," said Robbie, and paused. She smiled for a moment and reached for the doorknob. "Yeah, I guess I'd do just about anything for you," continued Robbie, little spasms going through his chest. "I guess I've loved you since I first saw those hazel eyes one day after school.

She stared down at their feet.

After a long while and a couple of "Well's" from him, she looked up. "Please don't love me," she said in a low voice. He was a good buddy but, not this. Heh, big deal, he thought, his eyes beginning to water. But she looked at him with solemn eyes and he kissed her. It was the most thrilling moment of his life.

Perched at the top of the ladder, Robbie stared at the window. His fingers gripped the cool, damp sill and he looked into his own reflection. Hadn't Laura heard the beautiful music he had poured forth? There was no sound, no shadow rising against the shade. But she must have heard. He knew her bed was near the window. He had asked. His palm rested against the rough shingles. The only sound was the soft dripping of water off the roof, a chorus of crickets, and the frantic wail of a siren in the night.

Where was she?

A hand was reaching under the blind. Robbie gasped. He checked his balance and a grin spread over his face. The panel rustled and wound up and Robbie's eyes were shut in the sudden light.

"Laura?" he whispered. He knew she wouldn't be able to see him in the dark. His eyes opened a slit into which entered a pink-bathrobed woman with the graying hair flattened on one side of her head—Laura's mother. She squinted into the darkness, through Robbie and under him. Robbie's eyes opened very wide. Brighter than the moon, the overhead light illuminated the forest-print bedspread of jeans, towels and a green t-shirt. His smile dropped.

"Who's out there? Who is it?"

Robbie wrapped both hands tighter around the ladder and stared at Laura's empty pillow. Mrs. Kelly looked through him again: his eyes fell to the quiet road.

"Who's out there?" Her face had the grouchiness of disturbed sleep.

He sighed. "It's Robbie Ames."

The woman started back from the nearness of the voice, hitting the wooden bedframe and landing kerplunk in the heap of cast-off clothes. Suddenly she saw the face and shoulders at the window.

"What are you, nuts? What are you doing up here? You'll get hurt!"

His injured hands gripped the ladder even more tightly, pressuring the pain in sharply. He tried to steady his breathing. "I came for Laura."

From the next room, a medley of bedsprings creaked and a hoarse voice asked what was going on, who was out there.

Robbie remembered Laura telling him that her father had such a bad voice that they wouldn't let him sing in church.

"Donald, why don't you get in here and help me instead of lying in bed and you wouldn't have to ask so many questions?"

349

No thank you. He would rather go back to sleep.

Robbie's legs were beginning to cramp and one foot, the one wrapped around the top of the ladder, was falling asleep, pinpricks racing across his toes.

Laura's mother turned back towards him. "Well," she said, "you've probably succeeded in waking up the whole neighborhood." Shaking her head, she pushed the window open more. "I'm sorry Robbie, but Laura's out. Let me help you get off that thing. You're making me very nervous!"

Robbie sighed again. Mrs. Kelly pushed the screen up and he handed the guitar through the window. He disentangled from the unstable structure the legs which wouldn't coordinate properly, and with a knee on the ledge, pulled up the rest of his body, careful not to kick over the ladder. He brushed his bruised fingers over the discarded t-shirt as he stepped down into the room.

Robbie thought he heard the father's coarse, irregular breathing from the master bedroom.

Mrs. Kelly's eyes stared fixedly toward the window as Robbie wiped the hair out of his eyes and the water from the guitar with the ends of his shirt.

"Now," she said, "why don't you go home and call Laura tomorrow?"

Laura... Laura... he thought to himself. He couldn't finish the sentence even in his head. The corners of his mouth twitched. Mrs. Kelly was rambling on about some guitar player in her past.

Speaking as little as possible, Robbie hung the guitar over his stiff shoulder and followed Laura's mother down to the bottom of the stairway where she held the front door open for him. He walked across the porch, back around to the base of the ladder and looked up. The light in Laura's room was not on anymore. He hunted in the grass for the fallen rose. Picking it up, he cradled it in his swollen fingers.

Robbie reloaded the battered wagon and stood under the sky. He knew where the moon was supposed to be, and after staring at that spot for a long while, he thought he made out a hazy sliver. The melody of "Greensleeves" played through his head with no words at all.

Clipped Wings

By Cheyenne Wiseman

I poise my hands above the keyboard. They begin their irregular heartbeat of a dance, creating lists and adding numbers to documents about pet supplies, that apparently were more important to the world than my own time.

Then the day is gone. My wrists ache with carpal tunnel syndrome and somewhere for someone my work has made a change.

On my way home, I am stopped by a young boy, who stands glass-eyed in front of a sporting goods store.

"What are you doing?" I ask, out of curiosity. Normally I would walk by, but I am feeling pensive.

He points at a polished-looking baseball glove. It is four hundred dollars. "Isn't it nice? I'm savin' up to buy it."

I give a half-nod. "But why? You can get a regular one for forty or fifty dollars... " His gaze leaves the display to shoot me a confused response.

"Why? Well, Major League players don't have fifty dollar gloves... "

"But you're not in the Major League."

He scratches his head. "I will be! When I grow up... "

The boys prattle on about baseball. I leave when my wrists ache to be iced. My mind is turning in circles. Does that boy know how low his chances are of getting into the Major League? How many millions of others are holding the same dream, how many others are better than him and will always be better than him?

I tell this to my boyfriend, and he laughs. He works at a clinic, as an apprentice specialist for some aspect of the body I could never understand.

I ask him if what he is doing is what he imagined himself doing when he was a child. "Of course not." He laughs again. "I wanted to be a giant robot."

I sit in the sofa with bags of ice, surfing the channels on the TV. What about these people? Did the Viagra voiceover lady feel sad at how her life had become?

I close my eyes and drift back to when I ran around playgrounds with simple thoughts and feelings. How I was sure I could save the world, become a change in history like my role models of Gandhi and Princess Diana.

Where did that all go? When did I forget my dreams? I feel a sudden longing for the sky.

My dreams from my youth creep back to me. I am hit with such an incredible wave of nostalgia that I begin to cry.

"What's wrong? Another TV movie?"

I get up and go outside. I tell my boyfriend that I do not know how to explain it.

I feel like a child again, standing under a mural of stars and creating shapes out of the moonlit clouds. I imagine myself lifting from the earth and floating up until I can see the horizon curve. It is so vivid I feel myself swaying.

When I was a child my dream was to fly. My heart lay with Peter Pan and his fairies, and I wished every year on my birthday candles to sprout wings like the lucky heroes and heroines of my favorite books. I had read somewhere that everyone desires to fly at sometime in their life. However, if there was such thing as a personal calling, then this was mine.

With sudden joy I speed inside and lean over the computer, forgetting the pain in my wrists. My fingers shake as I type. It all comes back to me: the time I sprained my ankle jumping from the monkey-bars, the week I was in trouble for opening the bird cages at the pet store, my love for my high school engineering class...

A sense of loss engulfs me. *I've lost a good eight years of my life*, I think in dismay. I find it: the flight school I always dreamed of.

The next week I quit my job. As a final declaration I sneak into the company's testing warehouse and free all the wild test subjects. I feel nine again.

However, when some of the birds only flutter in hops, I realize their wings are clipped.

This is how I ended up with thirty birds in our apartment, I explain to my boyfriend. He is not amused.

"Can't they fly again?" he asks one morning as I feed them seeds, ironically from the same company they had come from.

"Yeah, but it'll take a while. They've lost the muscles for flying."

At the end of the month, when my paycheck does not come, my boyfriend learns of my life's new direction, and he is furious.

I cannot convince him of the flight school's appeal, or of my personal calling to the air. I enroll anyway, and look into housing near the school.

The months roll by on square wheels; the birds have all healed and flown off, and summer has revealed itself once again. It is an anxious time. The school commences in September, and after my initial enthusiasm has faded, I am thrown into doubt as my intentions begin to materialize, and my boyfriend's staunch disapproval does not help.

He refuses to move across the country. He tells me I will be back within a month.

When the day comes, I move as if in a dream. It has not yet dawned on me that I am leaving, even though I am packing my suitcases.

My boyfriend quietly gives me his goodbyes. I see it in his eyes that he believes I am abandoning him.

For a minute I am close to forsaking it all, setting down my luggage and falling into his arms with relief that I did not leave. We could get married and be happy.

But I would always feel a tugging whenever I turned my head to the sky.

He asks me again not to go. His anger bubbles up and he threatens our relationship. I am crying, but I shake my head.

"Then go. Just go," he says, turning. "I thought this was a joke. Don't come back, then."

"Hey, come on... " I whisper, backing to the door. It is open.

He lunges as to grab me, and yells at my back. "There're no woman pilots, you won't make any money. You'll come begging to me!"

I run from the apartment and take a taxi to the airport. I am still wiping my eyes while I wait for my flight. I feel that my boyfriend is right, as I watch people walk past me. How can they all be so confident, I wonder?

I know, I have read online, about how slim my chances are of success. Maybe the gender I was born into was fate's way of letting me know I should not be a pilot.

As my mind spirals, a hand taps on my shoulder. It is a homeless man, who has taken the seat beside me. An unwashed smell emanates from his clothes and his hair is pulled back. A guitar rests in his lap.

"Miss, yal'right?" he asks, with wide eyes.

My untouched layers of doubt collapse like dust, and I confess myself to this man, who listens intently.

Then, the man launches into a song. For a reason unknown to me, I smile. The song is ridiculous, about talking animals and morphine addicts, but it is the release I need. The music ends with a peaceful strum. "My father owns a company," he says. "Every day when I was growin' up he'd tell me how much he expects o' me, since I'd one day take over from 'im." His eyes fall to the guitar. "But my passion was always in music. When he wanted me to start workin' with 'im, I said 'no sir' and insisted on playin'. He cut me off completely."

I ask him why is he telling me this. Is he not upset with how his life turned out?

Small echoes reach me as he fingers the strings of his instrument. It is only then that I notice its long, deep scratches and chips in the woodwork.

"Miss, I've never been so happy in my life. I was lost at first an' made many, many mistakes, but I've beat it all. Playin' music is how I prove myself worthy o' being alive."

This hits me somewhere, hard. I begin to see this homeless man in a different light; he wears the aroma of freedom and plays his personal calling on his guitar. He is a hero.

I feel lifted, and my wings unfold once again as another song about pop-idols and marching trees fills the airport.

I am boarding my plane. Glancing around with wide eyes, I come to the realization that the people are not confident as I had thought; rather, they walk with an air of repetition. It makes me sick.

Flight school has started and I am at a loss for money. I am hired at a local garage to work the front desk as a part-time employee. I have fun working here, and the mechanics teach me about cars. I learn about how planes work at school, but at the garage I learn more.

One of the mechanics has worked as a pilot for a major airline, but was fired after the discovery of a minor heart condition.

"It's a risky business, what you're aiming for. Never any promises."

By the end of the year, I can be trusted to fix small car problems, and I help out whenever business is slow in the front.

Going to school, studying, and the garage consume my daily life. After six years, I am graduating, and nerves are high. I am close to obtaining my license, yet also far from my dream job.

I am putting an engine together with my mechanic friends, laughing and joking, when one of them turns to me and with a serious tone says,

"Y'know, you could become a certified mechanic, within a year." He adds that I will always have a job here.

I am surprised. Before I had realized, I had become comfortable in my side job. It would be so perfect. So easy. I could come to the garage all day with the others, and be happy.

My pilot job is only a shadow in the distance. It will be another five years at the minimum before I qualify for an airline.

I am reminded of the boy at the sporting goods store. There will be pilots who are older, have more experience, and fit the mold of what an airline is looking for.

I fly home to visit my family. They are thrilled to see me, and I begin to recount my experiences, but it is without enthusiasm.

I go on a walk. A certain magnetism pulls me to my old street. It is morning and the light reflecting off the columns of windows narrows my vision.

As I approach my old apartment, my hands shake in my coat pockets. The memories of my departure are overwhelming. If I close my eyes I can convince myself I live here and that I am leaving for my desk job, anticipating all day the warmth of a meal on the table, with my boyfriend laughing at something I said, and the sky still a forgotten notion, far away.

A breeze touches my face and the illusion is gone. I look around. There is an old woman across the street, and a mill of bees swarming a tree behind me. On the fence dividing the apartment complex from another, a bird is preening itself. As it flies off I catch a glint of metal and remember the birds I had cared for. I never could remove the company's identifier rings from the birds' legs. *It is so graceful in the air*, I think. I turn around and do not look back. The air lifts my soul. The notes of a familiar song fill my head, and I begin to run. I have a lot to tell my family.

Surgery

By Jarmila Skalna

During the summer, I would help Amy stir strawberry jam in her kitchen. One time, I asked her why she labeled the jars 1, 2, 3, 4, instead of writing what was inside. She explained that she wanted to know later if any of them were missing.

One day, I had to take Amy to the hospital. Her pant legs swooshed as she walked slowly toward me.

"When I'm sick," she said, feeling her seventy-eight years, "I always think of those women pioneers who came to settle the west. They didn't have time to feel sorry for themselves or seek help from a psychiatrist."

"It's always good to think positively before surgery," I responded. "Now let's go. We're late."

As we walked out through the gate, Amy turned back to the house. "Oh, would you look at that tree!" she enthused. "Isn't it gorgeous!"

"Yes," I agreed, noticing how the long branches were intertwined, as if they were sailing in the sky.

"That's a Deodora cedar," she instructed me. "Once, some Neanderthal working on my yard told me he could cut it into the shape of a pine tree. The branches were too long, and the fallen pine needles were damaging the roof and plugging up the gutters. But I said, 'No way! It's a cedar, and it's beautiful just the way it is.' In Italy I saw them everywhere."

"Okay, Amy. Let's go. Otherwise, we'll be late." I gently urged her toward my car. She walked a couple of steps and stopped again.

"Look at this praying mantis on the leaf! I love her! She likes to watch me through the kitchen window. Look at how she tilts her head to the side, as if she were listening. And her legs are bent, as if she's praying."

"She's lovely, Amy. But let's go."

"And how well she blends in with her surroundings! She looks like a stick." Amy clearly wanted to be heard. Finally, in the car, she started talking about two Danish ladies down the street who had died recently. One was ninety-five, and her sister was ninety-two. They had had a good life. Both drank a little whiskey and ate good food.

Amy turned on the radio, saying that sometimes it helped her to feel better. Then she would know where the sun was shining in the world and where it was cold.

Thinking that we might need papers at the hospital, I asked if she had any sort of proof of her birth. She answered that she had some pictures of herself. I told her that pictures were not proof, since they could be falsified. She gave me a strange look and didn't say anything until we got to the hospital.

As we entered the building, a man wearing a sky blue uniform was pushing an open cart with two skeletons on it, covered by a plastic see-through tarp. Amy asked in disbelief, "Are those skeletons real?"

"Yes," the man answered, giving her a fleeting smile. She hopped after the cart, saying again, "Can I ask you to pull back the tarp just for a second? I've never seen a real live skeleton before." The man hesitated for a moment, and then, with a slight nervous air, uncovered the skeletons.

"Wow!" Amy said. "Were they treated with something?"

"No, just scrubbed and cleaned thoroughly."

"I didn't know our bones were so smooth and yellowish, like plastic. If that's how we really look, we're attractive skeletons!" The man gave her a short smile and went about his way.

"That wasn't smart to see the skeletons before surgery," I said. "Maybe they were the two Danish ladies from your street."

"I don't think so," Amy mumbled, slowing her walk. "What surgery? They're just going to take a small sample of my skin and send it to the lab."

"But since it will shed blood, do you think they'll put you under anesthesia?"

"I'm not a princess. They'll just give me something local. Everything will go well. You'll see."

The young doctor introduced himself as a student in his last year of medical school. After sitting Amy down in a chair, he numbed her upper lip with an injection and proceeded to cut a small sample of skin from the left side of her mouth. Amy seemed to be concentrating, as if she were stirring strawberry jam. To avoid watching the surgery, I stared out the window. Two angels carried me across the river to the land of the dead, where two Danish ladies were pouring whiskey.

"Life is good here," they said, turning to me. "And the neighbors are better. Stay with us." I refused their hospitality. I have to take Amy home.

I turned back to the doctor, who was frantically shaking a bloody gauze in the air. "Did you see that piece of skin I just cut out?" he asked. "It has to be around here somewhere."

Amy opened her eyes and answered irritably, "I wasn't scrutinizing your every move, doctor. My eyes were closed."

He shook his head and started on the first stitch, mumbling nervously under his breath, "Such a nice sample I had. I did it so well. It has to be around here somewhere."

"I didn't swallow it, doctor," Amy was annoyed now.

"I don't understand," the doctor mumbled on his fourth stich, by now completely discouraged.

"And who's supposed to understand? Am I supposed to understand?" Amy replied out of the corner of her bloody mouth. The doctor completed the fifth and final stitch. Then he got down on his knees, looking worn out. Amy struggled to kneel down next to him. I joined them, too. We all searched in different corners. But there was no sign of the skin.

The doctor, drained of energy, said, "That's okay, Mrs. Roisen. Go home and rest. We'll wait two weeks and do it again."

"Doctor," she said, "don't forget to bring a video camera next time. And sterilize your shoes when you get home. Maybe my sample is stuck to the bottom."

Two weeks later, everyone at the hospital greeted us like old friends. The doctor apologized again. "After you left last time," he said, "everyone here was looking for that sample. No one found it. It was so strange. That's not the first time, either. Sometimes they even lose samples in the lab, and we have to do everything over again."

"My friend here," Amy said, nodding toward me, "wants to write something about this whole fiasco."

"Just don't put my name in it," the doctor whispered alarmingly. "I might never graduate."

"Don't worry," I said. "Maybe we should go to another hospital next time?" The doctor turned red and said warmly, "I assure you that Mrs. Roisen won't pay a thing for these two visits. They will be completely free."

"Five free stitches," I said playfully. "What a bargain!"

Pluto's Republic

By Jack Rosman

Beneath his standard issue army helmet was nestled a pair of sunglasses with round, purple frames, not unlike those worn by Sir John Lennon. If your gaze were to continue a little further south, they would find the words "War is Hell" tattooed on his neck in jagged handwriting. Judging by the work it would seem that the artist responsible had received most of his tattoo training in prison. He showed up to Basic Training looking like GI Joe's socially inept stepbrother. His scrawny forearms awkwardly poked out between the swathes of white t-shirt fabric. His jeans were awkwardly too tight exposing his twig like legs until they ballooned out into his oversized black skate shoes. The only thing well-kept about him was his high'n'tight hair cut that looked as if Uncle Sam himself was his barber. I think his name was Jared but nobody ever called him that. Instead, he had one of the more unique nicknames of our unit. He only spoke in vague phrases tinged with philosophical musings, which, no matter how you figured it, just made no damn sense.

"A man is just a man, man." He preached to us, as we bitched and moaned about Sergeant Kennedy, a particularly ornery drill master. "He who throws rocks in a glass house is the first to worry about paper cuts."

"What the fuck is that shit?" Sterling hissed as he walked away.

"Dudeman is trying to sound like Pluto!"

"Who?"

"You know. That old Greek guy. With the beard, who always talked philosophy."

"Plato."

"What the fuck ever."

From that moment, Jared (or whatever) was known as Pluto. Mostly to give Strerling shit, but also because it kind of fit him. Pluto was an odd entity of the Disney world. He was a dog, but so was Goofy who was personified as a human. Pluto just didn't fit. That's what we thought about our Pluto. He just didn't fit, despite his clear desperation to. But he had a nickname and I think that was good enough for him. He continued to bounce around camp, mumbling his little phrases.

"Hey man, just believe in yourself" He told a particularly chunky soldier who was throwing up after our daily march.

"Shut the hell up." The private heaved out between upchucks.

Physically lackluster and socially at edge, he was an uncharismatic guy. Nobody knew where he was from or what he did before he enlisted. Maybe that was a good thing–it added to the enigma he had become. We still don't talk about him much, mostly when guys in other companies happen to know he was once with us.

"What was he like? Anything like on TV?" They would ask shortly after their eyes lit up with realization that we were the famous 52nd company.

Nobody really knew how to answer that. For one, he hardly got to know him ourselves. The only reason he was very memorable was because how much shit he took. The drill sergeants had a field day with a private who, never seeing a minute of action, deemed it necessary to get such an aggressive tattoo on such a public body part.

"What the hell yew know 'bout Hell boy?" They screamed at him as he finished his 500th pushup of the day. He would never answer them directly, but give one of his trademark phrases such as "Takes one to know one, sir." He was never very popular with the upper brass.

I honestly don't think he would have survived the duration of Basic Training. Myself and many others agree that what happened was for the best. He just didn't fit the mold of a solider. Most of us were athletes and felt natural on the drill field. He could hardly run in a straight line. The army would have chewed him up and spit him out. Some members of our company were a little irked that such a ready target for their jokes had disappeared. But I think the sergeants were thankful such a distraction was gone.

It happened around midnight the first Friday night of boot camp. It wasn't the blaring alarm that ripped me from the depths of sleep back into existential awareness. It was the flashing lights leaking under my closed eyelids that tipped off my snoozing unconscious that there was a body attached to it and I would need to be returning soon. The funny thing is that, to this day, I'm still not sure if there was an actual fire or if it was just a drill. I do know that firefighters showed up, regardless.

As I made my way out of the barracks, the flashing light of the alarm temporarily blinding me every few seconds, I tripped over something. Cursing under my breath, I turned to see a writhing form under my feet. It was Pluto. His eyes were rolled up into his head. Foam poured out of the taut slit his mouth had contorted into. His body shook uncontrollably. I had seen seizures before, but none as bad as that one. I put his head between my legs like I had been taught in first aid training. There he laid until the Sergeant Kennedy came storming in, wondering why his line was two shitheads short. He dropped the attitude when he saw Pluto's flailing limbs. As we shut the door to the ambulance, we were all quiet for a few minutes. Sterling was the first to break the silence.

"I hope he's okay and everything. But what kind of an idiot enlists in the army when he knows he has epilepsy?"

I had no answer for him. Sergeant Kennedy was livid. As were his superiors. It was not long until we got word that Pluto had been kicked out of the military for lying on his medical form.

Dishonorable discharge.

"Little shit is lucky we didn't bring him up on fraud charges." Kennedy spat. "He thinks he won't see any flashing lights on a damn battlefield? Could have gotten somebody killed."

The question remained: Why? Why would he lie? We were about a month away from full-on battle simulation with plenty of flashing lights. He clearly would have been exposed then. Pluto did seem like one of those mislead southern kids who confused military trivia with patriotism. The kind of kid who would read Gun World magazine and could list off multiple kinds of military helicopters with his southern drawl. He probably had multiple family members serve, and had dreamt of enlisting since he first shot his BB gun at the tender age of five. There were a few of those in our platoon. Few in every platoon, I hear.

We didn't hear from Pluto for a few months. And even then, I don't think being on the cover of Time Magazine counts as hearing from somebody. Apparently some "Maverick" reporter had heard of Pluto's discharge and had written a story criticizing the military's prejudice against epileptics.

"He always leads crusades against those who hurt the disenfranchised." Somebody told me later. "Pluto's story is SO in line with his brand."

I had seen pictures of the guy and I would have guessed his brand was metro sexual guido, but what do I know about journalism. The writer got promoted, Sergeant Kennedy got fired, and Pluto became a national celebrity. Human Rights groups cried out against the injustice. Newscasters put up unflattering pictures of Sergeant Kennedy and condemned the prejudice of the US military. Websites like EliteDailey and Buzzfeed posted articles with titles such as "Why The Military Are Huge Assholes To People Who Have Seizures." All the politically active college kids from my home town put photos of him as their Facebook Cover Photos with captions like "Support Pluto" and "If he wants to serve, than let him serve." Sargeant Kennedy received death threats. Members of our platoon were called out for Hate Crimes. It was one of the biggest controversies of the year, until Kim Kardashian farted on The Today Show. Then people seemed to forget all about it.

All of these people seemed to turn both a blind eye and a deaf ear to the fact that that a battlefield is no stranger to prolonged flashes of light. They didn't seem to hear the argument that if Pluto was on the battlefield, it wouldn't be too long until he was writhing on the ground in the fetal positon drooling like an infant. A grown man reduced to a useless blob because of what he had been taught was an injustice that just didn't get as much ink as some think it should have. But hey, what do I know about journalism.

Through out it all, Pluto appeared fairly neutral. He never actually said anything negative about the army. He never mentioned Sergeant Kennedy by name. He never really said anything. He would just smile and give one of his bullshit philosophical ramblings. I had a sneaking suspicion that he didn't really understand what was going on. Maybe Pluto was a little more than just a weird guy. In every public appearance he gave, he remained in his army greens. The same glasses and an open collar, drawing attention to this tattoo. I found an article on a gossip site stating he had gotten "shading done" on it by Los Angeles' Dr. Woo, one of the most renowned tattoo artists in the world.

"War is Hell," he stated bluntly to Katie Couric, who was hanging on to his every word. "But... isn't life itself hell?"

This made her cry on the air.

"I don't get it man. What the hell does that even mean?" Sterling asked as we watched in the barracks.

"Nothing." I told him. "It means nothing."

We were stationed in San Diego when we heard about the film being made about him. It didn't take long for the Oscar Buzz to start flurrying around Daniel Day Lewis' gripping portrayal of an epileptic soldier. Danny Devito was cast as Sargeant Kennedy. I wondered who was playing me. In the mail, a choice few of us got invitations to the premier in LA. Many threw their's away in disgust. I admit I was too intrigued not to go and made the trek up myself. I got to the Chinese Theatre around 6pm, just as the paparazzi were marking their territory. It was another hour before Pluto rolled up in a chauffeured Aston Martin. He waved over the crowd towards me. I tried to wave back but was shoved out of the way by an adoring paparazzo.

"Move asshole." He grunted as his flash light up like a hand grenade. He joined the growing throng of reporters than began pushing the boundary of the velvet rope. They hounded the line of celebrities making their way down the carpet. Some who starred in the movie, others who were just there to show their support for such a noble cause.

"It's such a great story," Ryan Gosling told an E! News reporter. "I think it's the responsibility of great art to expose social injustices."

I caught the last half of Jessica Chastain's interview. "...I just think it's wrong of the United States military. If Pluto wants to die on the battlefield because of an unavoidable, preexisting medical condition, than that's his damn right."

When Pluto finally made it onto the red carpet, it was beginning to get dark. As the photographer's turned to capture his arrival they also mounted flashes on their cameras. As the bulbs popped around me, I was forced to close my eyes. The bursts of light continued to make an impression on my covered iris' regardless. It reminded me of one other time when blaring light interfered with my eyesight.

Oh God.

My eyes snapped open just in time to notice Pluto's rolling back into his head. He collapsed right on the carpet. His head shaking violently. Foaming at the mouth. I shouted at the top of my lungs but nobody seemed to notice. I pushed my way through the ocean of people but it was too much. The whole time, the paparazzi kept flashing away.

Finally, Jennifer Lawrence noticed he was down. But poor J-Law had neither the medical expertize nor the experience with high-octane situations to handle a seizing man. Pluto died in her dainty hands. Not one of the paparazzi moved to help, instead the influx of their flashes worsened his seizure. Pluto had always dreamed of dying on the battlefield, weapon in hand, defending his country. Instead he died in the arms of a blond starlet, wearing a borrowed tuxedo, as millions of photographers were snapping images to be used on Internet click-bait articles for years to come.

The coroner's statement said that the flashing cameras made his attack escalate to the point where his shaking broke his own neck. He was photographed to death. Somehow the media didn't seem to pick up on this point. They didn't even mention a cause of death. Instead, they concentrated on how he was unjustly kicked out of the military and died on the eve that his story was being told to the world through the art of cinema. Poignant.

I really didn't know Pluto as well as I would have liked, but I nonetheless felt like I had lost a comrade. The EMT's had told me I had saved his life that night in the barracks, and I guess that made me feel responsible. Maybe that's why I was so angry at the lack of attention his death received from the media. Even those that did mention his passing failed to acknowledge the fact that it was the doing of their own profession.

Death by paparazzi. Helluva way to go.

Good Art

By Nicole Justine Cavanaugh

Good art starts a conversation,
punctures the lining of the being to get to the soul.
You don't need to "like" it.
(What does that mean, anyway? Warm fuzzing feelings? No.)

If it brings up the mess inside of you,
vomits you out for you to see something new or lurking: Bless it.
Good art may ruffle you,
Stretch your brain to popping,
Set your tongue to twisting in nasty remarks: (oh, God! that is SO ugly!)

Life's ugly sometimes.

What part of you are you avoiding?

The Boat Ride

By Valerie Stoller

Jorge stepped onto the splintered planks at the water's edge. The wooden dock swayed under his bare feet. Callused skin on his soles as good as sandals. Sí, tough from years of working in boats and salt water, the mangrove swamps of the Yucatán. His world, the only life he knew.

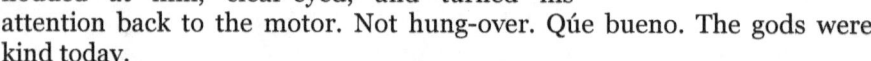
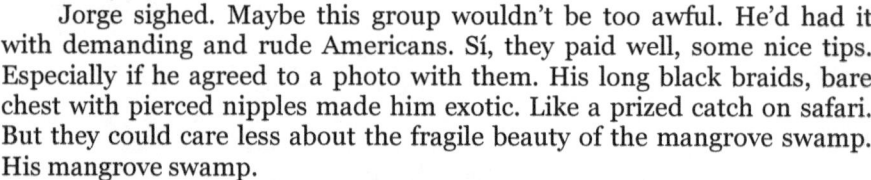

He'd been assigned the thirty-foot boat, seating for six tourists, plus Jorge, the tour guide, up front, and Oscar manning the motor. Oscar nodded at him, clear-eyed, and turned his attention back to the motor. Not hung-over. Qúe bueno. The gods were kind today.

Jorge sighed. Maybe this group wouldn't be too awful. He'd had it with demanding and rude Americans. Sí, they paid well, some nice tips. Especially if he agreed to a photo with them. His long black braids, bare chest with pierced nipples made him exotic. Like a prized catch on safari. But they could care less about the fragile beauty of the mangrove swamp. His mangrove swamp.

How he wished he could just hop in the boat without them. Make Oscar rev the engine and race out to where the lagoon's clear fresh water merged with the salty jade-green gulf. Just him and nature undisturbed. Tranquilo. Close to the Mayan Gods of Water and Earth. Chac and Mam. He would bless the water as his grandfather had taught him.

"We forgot to bring sunscreen." A man's voice. "Do you have any extra?" Jorge snapped out of his daydream. The question came from one of the middle-aged men in the tourist group that had followed Jorge to the dock. The guy's legs, poking out below khaki shorts, were pale and hairless, never exposed to sunlight. Rich American businessman, cooped up in an office all day, breathing recycled air and big city pollution. Out of his element here. Jorge squinted up at him.

"Yeah." Jorge reached into his bag and pulled out a full tube. What if he'd said no? Let the guy burn like a tortilla over an open flame? He'd probably sue the tour company. Jorge tossed the sunscreen to Milk Legs, who fumbled to catch it with both hands. Should make him pay extra for it.

The one kid in the group wore ear buds inside bright red fleshy ears that stuck out under his baseball cap. He stood off from the others, back turned. Already sunburned. Too mad about being dragged on a swamp tour by his mother to listen to her warning about the fierce sun.

Jorge walked over to the boy. He tapped the kid's shoulder to get his attention. "Vámos, muchacho."

"Ow." The boy ducked away from Jorge. Must be sunburned under his shirt too. "What do you want?" He was maybe twelve, trying to act so cool. "And my name is Simon."

"Okay. Simon." Jorge made eye contact. "You have to put sunscreen on now.

Before we get in the boat. Let it soak in."The boy's mother handed Simon a large orange tube of Banana Boat. She flashed Jorge a grateful smile. Happy to let Jorge be the boss, deal with her son.

"That's the rule," Jorge added. "Gotta keep the stuff out of the water later on when we swim. It's toxic to the fish."

"Fine." Simon rolled his eyes. "Whatever."

He smeared the white goop on his ears and face, and handed the sunscreen back to his mother. Then he pointed to the 3-inch wood carving that pierced Jorge's left ear lobe.

"What's that thing in your ear?" Simon waited, not taking his eyes off the earring. "Does it hurt?"

"No," Jorge said. "Unless I do this."

Jorge tugged on the large earring, stretching his ear lobe down, and grimaced like it hurt a lot. Messing with kids on the boat ride was fun.

"Ow." Simon stared at the earring. "I'm never gonna get a piercing." He rubbed his own ear lobe. "Unless I get a diamond stud. Like Kanye."

A little younger than Miguel, his own son. But already with that same attitude. Like they knew it all, and life was just a big bore. Yet Miguel would walk onto a soccer field and come alive. What made Simon come alive? Not being stuck on this boat ride with a bunch of grownups in the middle of nowhere.

Jorge smiled at the boy. "Yeah, well, okay. Vámanos. Let's go."

The group settled into the boat and fastened their life jackets. Jorge pushed off from the dock, and perched on the bow facing them. He nodded at Oscar, who gunned the motor and headed the boat out towards open water.

Jorge inhaled the briny damp air. His body relaxed into the familiar rhythm of the slap-slap vibrations as they flew over the water. Wind pushed his braids up like two antennae searching for a signal. Simon held one hand on top of his baseball cap, the other dragged through the water, splashing an iridescent spray straight up at his red cheeks.

"How fast can this go?" Simon yelled over the noise of the motor. He grinned and wiped his wet face with the back of his hand.

"So, you want to go faster?" Jorge smiled. These boat rides made a person feel alive. "Hold on, everyone."

He waved at Oscar, gave him a thumbs-up and braced his hands against the bow. The boat lunged forward, sped across water the color of lime juice mixed with coconut milk. The dense deep green foliage of the mangrove swamp beckoned on the horizon, islands of untouched jungle. Soon the trees' thick gnarled roots came into focus, twisted and overlapping in the loose sandy soil. Nature's precarious balance, miraculously resilient.

"Okay, amigos." Jorge stood up. Oscar slowed the boat to a crawl. "Míren. Look around you. What do you see?"

"A lot of stupid trees." Simon, his smile gone, had teenage boredom perfected. "Can't we go fast again?"

"Later we will, hijo." Jorge nodded at Oscar who cut the motor. A large black and white bird squawked at the intruders and flew over the boat towards the ocean. Tiger heron, Jorge's favorite.

"But now I want to tell you a story about survival. The mangroves and my ancestors, the Mayans, have a lot in common."

Jorge studied the boy's face. The ear buds hung like limp noodles around his neck.

His eyes were wide open. Bueno. He was paying attention.

"There are three different types of mangrove trees. Black, red and white. Named for the color of their bark." Jorge reached across the bow of the boat and grabbed a branch, pulling them close to the tree. "This is a white mangrove." Jorge nodded at Simon. "Pull off a leaf."

"Okay." Simon plucked a dark green leaf and held it between his thumb and finger. "So what?"

"See the white crystals?" Jorge asked.

Teaching was his favorite part of the job. Even though he knew these tourists would forget his words once they flew home. But right now he held them captive.

Especially Simon.

"What is it?" Simon's eyes fixed on the leaf. "Some kind of weird stuff, you know, like magic mushrooms?"

"Hmmm, well, let's find out." Jorge couldn't resist. "Could be poisonous." Sí, the kid was definitely not bored now. "Taste it."

Simon looked back at his mother. She glanced at Jorge, scanned his face like she was reading his mind and then nodded at her son. Simon shrugged, stuck out his tongue and licked the crystals off the mangrove leaf. Then he scrunched up his face.

"Yuck. Too salty." The boy spat over the side of the boat and threw the leaf into the water. He glared at Jorge, ready to throw him overboard. "Are you trying to kill me?"

"Ha. Very salty, sí. Exactamente."

Jorge raised his hand to high five the boy. But Simon scowled and wiped his mouth, then sat down and drank from his water bottle.

"Did you know mangroves have grown here for thousands of years? They are survivors. Like the Mayan people. We too have survived. In spite of wars. And greed." Jorge let that idea sink in.

Everyone in the boat was paying attention, touching the mangrove leaves, tasting the white salt crystals. How could he keep Simon interested?

"These trees have adapted to a hostile environment. Their roots bring ocean water up into each branch." Jorge held up a single leaf coated with crystals that glinted like tiny diamonds. "Every day, the trees secrete salt out through their leaves. Over and over.

Otherwise the trees would die."

Simon sat quietly, rolling the water bottle between his fingers. Then his eyes returned to Jorge.

"You know what?" The boy's cheeks flushed a deeper red. He looked at his feet. "Oh, never mind."

"What?" Jorge asked.

"Well..." Simon twisted the water bottle. "It's kind of like the trees are crying." The boy grabbed the brim of his baseball cap and pulled it down over his forehead.

The boat rocked back and forth, bumped against the twisted roots of the mangroves. Another heron flew overhead, delicate wings striped black and white against the cloudless sky.

Perfecto. Jorge leaned back on the bow, trailed his fingers in the warm water. He had been about the same age when he felt that sense of discovery. His spirit now so connected to the trees, his callused feet deeply rooted to the earth, his tears shed like those of the mangroves. Tears of despair, tears of wonder, tears of joy.

"Sí, hijo." Jorge reached out and placed his hand on Simon's shoulder. "Like the trees themselves are crying."

Haunted by the Past

By Edie Matthews

Up early, Mary Ann spent the day negotiating LA streets running errands to the bank, the cleaners, the dentist, and the market. By three o'clock, she finished her last task and inched along Santa Monica Boulevard. In front of her, a red double-decker tour bus bellowed black fumes.

She rolled up her window, watched for a break in the gridlock, and merged into the right lane behind a black Camaro. The traffic came to a complete halt. She glanced out the side window and realized she was atop an overpass. Below, the never-ending vehicles on the Hollywood Freeway roared by. Her heart began to race. She gripped the steering wheel, forcing herself to stare at the Camaro. The fender was mangled and a taillight bashed in. Despite her closed windows, she could still hear the drone of engines below. As long as I don't look down, I'll be all right. "Don't think about it," she ordered. A crescendoing blast from a diesel truck shook the bridge and rattled Mary Ann's nerves. "Oh, God... " She clicked on her blinker and scanned the left lane for an opening in the boundary of cars jammed together. Trapped. Nowhere to go.

Above a layer of slate-gray smog blocked the sun; ahead a purplish building stood out like a bad bruise.

She was six again, her hair in a perennial ponytail, playing with Bonnie Sue, the little girl who lived next to the freeway in a house overgrown with thick palm trees and dark ivy. Bonnie Sue was an only child who lived with her mother and grandmother. When the girls played together, Mary Ann took charge and organized their activities: paper dolls, coloring, roller-skating.

That summer Bonnie Sue's grandmother suffered a stroke and was hospitalized. One hot drab day in the middle of July, a carload of relatives from some place back East arrived in an old Dodge, here to visit their ailing grandmother. The family included five children, two shy young girls about Mary Ann's age, and three teenage brothers, loud and brutish, who tore around shoving and wrestling with each other.

Mary Ann gathered the girls into a circle, all four kneeling on the sidewalk. She threw a handful of silver jacks on the concrete in front of her.

"This is how you play," she said. She bounced a red ball and grabbed up a jack and caught the ball.

"That looks hard," said the youngest, a girl with unkempt brown hair and a small tear in her dress.

"You can use both hands," said Mary Ann. She demonstrated, this time bouncing the red ball with her right hand and picking up a jack with her left. "First you do onesies, then twosies, then threesies until whoever gets the highest amount without making a mistake wins. We'll practice first, and then I'll only use my left hand to make it fair."

"We're not playing that stupid game," said Dwayne, the oldest brother. He peered down at them. His face was covered with acne, and nicks from a clumsy shave.

Mary Ann glared back at the stocky teenager. "No one invited you to play."

"Oh yeah, this is my cousin and my sisters." He jabbed his chest with a thumb. " You need my permission to play with them."

"It's a free country," said Mary Ann. "They can play with whomever they want."

Dwayne kicked her jacks into the gutter. "You'd better do what I say." The three other little girls cowered.

Mary Ann rose indignant, her arms akimbo. "You're not the boss of me."

"You wanna bet?" The brute picked her up and strode towards the freeway.

"Put me down, you big bully!" Mary Ann struggled, but his arms clamped her to his chest.

Dwayne continued walking until they stood on the bridge above a mass of speeding automobiles. Mary Ann heard the rush of traffic. He leaned over the gray metal railing and held her out over the freeway. Hot fumes gusted up from below. Mary Ann froze.

"You want to go to the hospital and visit my grandmother?" he asked. She grabbed his shirt.

"Do as I say or I'll drop you."

She held her breath and began to pray. Angel of God, my guardian dear...

"Who's the boss?"

Ever this day be at my side—

"Who's the boss!" he demanded. His teeth were yellow and his breath smelled rancid. She whispered, "God is."

He snickered. She saw clusters of blackheads across his nose. Suddenly Dwayne tossed her up. Mary Ann felt herself airborne. Her life went into slow motion and she visualized herself plummeting, crashing on the roof of a speeding car, then hurled onto the asphalt, and hundreds of cruel tires crushing her body beyond recognition. She never remembered him catching her.

"Honnnkkk!" blared a yellow Hummer behind her. Mary Ann gripped the steering wheel and gasped for air. She refocused and saw that the Camaro in front of her had moved on. She pressed the accelerator and tried to erase the ordeal seared in her mind. But she knew she never would.

Stalking Elizabeth George

By Valerie Stoller

There I was last night, in line at Books Inc. waiting to get my books signed by Elizabeth George. She's my absolute favorite mystery writer. I want to write just like that. Her characters are so real. Sometimes they talk to me. Just a whisper in my head. I have to be really quiet to hear them.

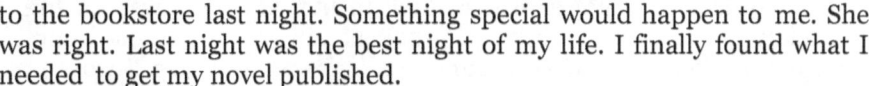

One of them spoke to me yesterday when I was eating breakfast. Barbara Havers, Inspector Lynley's sidekick. Tough and smart like me. But not as pretty, and no sense of style. She told me to go to the bookstore last night. Something special would happen to me. She was right. Last night was the best night of my life. I finally found what I needed to get my novel published.

I'd decided to wear my favorite jeans and the Mexican embroidered shirt I'd swiped at the flea market. I love that shirt. The design has flowers that look like snakes up close. It's my new good luck charm. Not that I really need any luck. Turning forty last week made me even stronger. My powers get me whatever I want.

By the time I got to the bookstore Elizabeth George had already finished her talk. Damn. Stupid traffic. Hadn't she known I was coming? Maybe she was afraid of me. She never did answer those messages I'd left on her website. No problem. I was close now. I was ready for her.

Elizabeth sat behind a large wooden table at the far end of the bookstore. She wore a lime green sweater, black skirt and red sandals. But her hair. Oh my god.

Elizabeth had dyed her hair this ugly shade of red. Made her look cheap. And that lipstick
was all wrong. I'd suggest a better color when we met. Like the Red Blaze by Revlon I used. It'd look great on her, too. I owed it to her to be honest. After all, we were two of a kind.

I smiled and turned to the lady standing just behind me. She wore a silver necklace with a hand-carved turtle totem. My fingers itched to touch it.

"I call that a torty," I told her. "That turtle you're wearing. It's very magical."

I leaned forward and stroked the turtle. Ms. Torty smiled like she was faking it and stepped back. Too close for comfort, I guess. She must have sensed my powers.

"Did you know," I asked, "that Elizabeth George is really a witch?"

"Uh, no," Ms. Torty replied. She glanced around the store. Maybe she knew I could just put a spell on her. Then *adiós*. Goodbye Ms. Torty.

"How do you know that?" She gave me a funny look. "Not the broomstick kind of witch. A real one," I told her.

I stared into the lady's eyes. No blinking. I used my mental spirit sensor to read her aura. A lot of orange and blue energy. Nothing as strong as mine. I kept staring. I liked watching her squirm. Finally she turned away from me, opened her book and pretended to read. Don't mess with me, Ms. Torty. You know I'd kick your butt.

God, I was getting antsy. I counted at least twenty people still in front of me. My body began to vibrate. I had to find a way to get centered. My powers were rising. I needed to let my spirit out. But not here in line. It wasn't safe.

"I'll be right back," I told Ms. Torty. "Save my place."

The lady looked at me and frowned, then nodded. I put down my stack of books and hurried over to the bookstore's magazine section. One of the cashiers watched me. I felt his eyes on my back as I sat on the floor and grabbed a copy of Bon Appetit.

By now my entire body was generating tiny sparks of energy that flew out of my skin. My power was coming to life. My body was on fire. I picked up my hair with both hands, pulling and twisting it into a fat braid. Oh, that felt better. I looked around. No one was watching. I closed my eyes and inhaled. Muttered the incantations that took me to my secret world.

Five minutes later I was back. I knew what I needed to do. I'd heard Barbara Havers' whisper voice reminding me why I was there. I slipped the magazine under my shirt and walked back to the line. The energy in my body pulsated in a steady hum.

Ms. Torty had saved my spot, nudging the pile of books forward with her foot.

She gave me an annoyed look.

"I thought you might have left." She sighed. "This line is taking forever." "Thanks for keeping my spot." I looked at the turtle necklace. "Such a nice torty.

Can I have it?"

"What?" Ms. Torty's eyebrows shot up. "Can you have my necklace?" People around us looked up from their cell phones.

I nodded. Take it, said the whisper voice.

"Why on earth would I give it to you?" Her voice went up a few more decibels.

She shook her head.

"Never mind." I faked a smile. "I was just kidding."

You bitch. I could rip that off your neck and paralyze you before you knew what hit you. Don't tempt me. You have no idea who you're messing with.

Her eyes darted around. Like she knew what I was thinking. How powerful I am. "Is there a problem here?" The man's name tag identified him as Jim, the store manager. He smelled of cologne and breath mints. He smiled at me like a flight attendant determining if there was going to be trouble on the plane.

"Oh gee, thanks, Jim," I purred. "We're fine." I could tell he wanted me. But he wasn't my type. His aura was mud brown. Too boring.

"Just tired of waiting." I looked him in the eye. "Too bad we can't clone her. You know, two Elizabeth Georges."

Jim shrugged his shoulders. He glanced at Ms. Torty who rolled her eyes like she was not with me, not crazy like me. He was about to say something else, but his pager went off and he left. Good. If he only knew what I was about to do.

Ten minutes later I arrived at the table in front of Elizabeth. She looked pale and worn out. Her red lipstick had smeared and left smudges on the water bottle she sipped. She'd spent all her energy on everyone else. Perfect. I was ready.

"How would you like these signed?" She picked up her pen, poised over the title page. "Made out to whom?"

"I just want your name," I told her. Not really. I needed her talent. I stared down at the author, focusing my power to make her look up.

"They sell better that way." I waited. "I bet you already knew that." "Yes, I do."

Then she lifted her gaze and looked me in the eye. Now. I held my breath and stared deep into her mind. I hunted down her talent and merged. We were one. In an instant it was over. Elizabeth George blinked and the spell was broken. But not before I'd gotten what I wanted.

"Are you okay?" The author put down her pen, frowning. She didn't look so smart anymore. Yes. Probably would never get published again. "You look a little flushed. Do you need to sit down?"

"I'm great, thanks." I smiled for real this time. "Could you hurry up and sign these now?" I pushed the pile of books closer. I needed to get out of there before she tried to snatch her talent back. I didn't want to hurt her, but the whisper voices were chanting in my head. Get out. Now. You have books to write.

She stared at me like she knew my secret. Too late, Elizabeth. She picked up the pen and signed her name.

I grabbed the book. My novel would be so much better than hers.

"By the way, that lipstick is all wrong. Do you wanna try mine?" I flashed my Red Blaze smile, and opened the next book.

What Are *Tampones* For,

By Pastor Bejinez

My mami never told me what tampones were for. I didn't know I wasn't suppose to use them to throw at my stupid primo like's they were bombs. How was I suppose to know she was going to smack me so real good with the cinto that hangs on the bathroom door, till the red got off her face? I's still can't believe I's got beat so much till I turned redder than her face, cause I don't see why's she needs all those tampones so bad cause my mami's too careful to ever cut herself and she don't have a marido to beat her when she does something wrong, so's I can't see why she got so mad that we wasted four of them to play guerra like's we were Rambo trying to kill everyone we saw. And it's not like's we were blowing up adults with them or doing any tarugadas like that. Me and my primo were so good, we's only blew each other up with those tampones, and not even the other kids. It's not like's we broke anything or made a big mess cause we only used four tampones. I thought maybe she should be proud cause we were careful not to break them into hundreds of pieces like they were stars shinning all over the piso she cleans everyday with la escoba. I thought she should be proud cause tampones are the perfect weapons cause we can throw them so hard and not break some ones stupid masetona. I thought maybe she should be proud cause we blew each other up for hours and not even got a scratch on us. Plus my primo said tampones are used to soak up blood, so's if we gots ourselves hurt enough to see sangre, we's could use them to stop our cuts from bleeding all over the piso. I's still don't get it, cause my mami never told me what tampones are for.

Crazy Sally

By Sharon Killingsworth

Even over the sound of her horse's galloping hooves, Sally could hear the deafening roar of the bulldozer as it ripped and tore apart the side of the employee's living quarters. When she reached the three-quarter pole, she eased the colt into a ground-covering lope, then stood tall in her stirrups and pulled him into a long-trot, then a jog, and finally down to a walk.

"Nice ride, Sally," Peter Goldstein yelled as she neared the out-gate. "Think he's ready?"

She nodded and unsnapped the chin strap from her Caliente helmet. Sam, Goldstein's head groom, grabbed the brown colt's bridle. Kicking free of her irons, Sally slid easily off the worn exercise saddle as Sam led the horse back towards the shedrow. "He's ready," she said, ripping the helmet from her head, releasing a cascade of wild red hair. She walked briskly past Goldstein, past his thousand dollar blue sports coat and ostrich boots. She pulled her slim, five foot frame as tall as she could and hardly gave him a look, not much interested in anything else he had to say. Like the others, he thought she was crazy.

"See you in the morning," he called after her. "Got eight horses for you."

Horses, horses. She had eight or nine or ten horses every morning. So big deal. He was still calling after her, but she wasn't listening. The sound of the bulldozer blotted out everything.

Past Shedrow Number One she walked. Past Shedrow Number Two. Buddy Atkins called to her from an open tack room in Barn Four, but she ignored him. Past the blacksmith shop, past the canteen, past the laundry.

The crashing, ripping noise grew louder and louder. Before her, in the early morning sun, the monster stood. Big. Yellow. Ugly. It raised its claw-like yellow trunk and smashed down onto the roof of the narrow, two-story building.

Why did they have to do this? Why did they have to tear it down?

"Stay back, Miss!" the monster's operator yelled. "This is a hard-hat area."

Sally slammed her helmet back on her head, red hair spiking out in all directions. There. She watched for a long time, her insides shaking. She shivered in the coolness and ran the zipper of her maroon vest up to her throat. It didn't take long to diminish what had once been hers and Tommy's into a pile of broken boards, plaster, and jagged metal. The sun was half-way to noon when the dust finally settled over what once had been their home.

Sally couldn't sleep. Her wide-awake green eyes stared at the alarm clock beside her bed— 3:30 am. Finally, almost time to get up. Flinging the quilt off, she swung her legs over the side of the bed. Every muscle grabbed as her toes reached the small braided rug. She'd been riding horses too damn long. Almost all of her forty-five years. Too many falls, too many buck-offs, too many broken bones. She pushed herself to her feet and stumbled into the shower, then dressed quickly.

The reflection that stared back at her from the small, round mirror with the crack down the middle wasn't someone she knew. She pulled a brush through the wiry red hair and looked again at the woman staring back at her. Wrinkled, sunburnt skin, freckles turning to liver spots, gray threading its way through the redness of her hair. Even the bright red was fading to a not very pretty shade of grayish-orange. She stuck out her tongue. "Ol' witch," she spat, turning away. "You deserve everything you got."

Sally's beat-up Ford pickup chugged up to the back gate and a sleepy-eyed security guard motioned her through. The employee parking lot was already starting to fill. Mornings started early at the track, a day's work needing to be done before the training track closed at 10:00 am.

Coffee. That's what she needed. A nice hot cup of coffee and a visit with Loretta. Sally headed towards the canteen, her boots scuffing up dust as she walked down the aisle between two barns.

"Sally."

She stopped dead, her green eyes darting around. Nobody in sight. The tack rooms dark. "Sally?" the voice came again.

A small gasp escaped her lips, the smell of alfalfa so strong in her nostrils she could almost taste it. She folded her arms tightly around her, feeling the early morning chill for the first time that day.

"I'm home, Sally."

A sob grabbed in her throat. "Tommy?" No answer. "Tommy?" She spun in a circle, looking, looking. Huge sorrowful eyes peered out from every stall. They nickered and stomped. Priceless knees banged against stall doors.

Lumber rattled. She turned towards the heap of rubble at the far end of the shedrows. Her boots moved quickly down the aisle, closer and closer to what had once been her tiny apartment, her home. Their home.

The huge, yellow monster was asleep, its jaw-like trunk rested in a pile of dirty straw. Sally moved past it and stepped carefully into the maze of jumbled boards and metal.

"Sally . . . Sally . . . Sally," the voice echoed again and again.

Then she saw him, his form pale in the still darkness. He was dressed in jeans and sweatshirt, the ever-present, green baseball hat still covered his straight, dark hair. Oh, he looked so good.

So young. She twisted a strand of hair around her finger, almost afraid to breathe. He looked the same, exactly the same, not one day older.

He looked up and smiled that enchanting smile of his, the same smile that had melted her heart thirty years before. His hand raised in a salute and he motioned to her, calling her closer.

Her heart pounded. "Where have you been?" she asked, stumbling forward. She tripped over the remains of a tattered mattress and almost fell. "Why did you leave?"

He just smiled. He held something in his hand, something shiny and white. He waved it at her.

"Why did you leave?" she asked again. Her boot slipped and she fell to her knees, the edge of a splintered chest-of-drawers cut into her leg. She uttered a small cry, and when she looked up, he was gone. "No!"

Scrambling wildly over the debris, she waded her way to the spot where he'd stood. "Tommy," she cried, feeling wetness on her cheeks. "Please. Come back."

A sudden gust of wind. Something white fluttered. She reached down, her fingers closed tightly around it.

Lights were on in the canteen when Sally burst through the door. "He's back," she cried, collapsing against the linoleum counter. She slid onto one of the red-padded stools and stared wide-eyed at the gray-haired women behind the counter. "He's back, Loretta. Tommy's back."

"That's not possible, honey," Loretta said, a kindness in her voice that Sally had grown to love. Loretta was her friend, her only friend. Loretta never, ever called her 'Crazy Sally' like all the others.

"Look." Sally pulled the picture from inside her jacket. With shaking hands, she laid it on the counter. "He gave me this."

"Let me get you a cup of coffee," Loretta soothed. Hot, steaming liquid poured from the glass pot into a Bay Meadows mug.

Sally's finger pounded up and down on the photo, and she spun it around so Loretta could see it clearly. "Look."

Color drained from the older woman's face. Rosy cheeks turned gray as she studied the crumpled 'win' photo. The El Camino Stakes, 1980. The smiling jockey was Tommy Kragen, the horse, Silent Sleeper. "But this is impossible," she whispered. "They went down that day." She looked up at Sally. "They never finished the race."

Sally shook her red head furiously and grabbed the photo from Loretta's hand. "Didn't die... didn't die." Her green eyes stared straight into Loretta's. "I told you, he's back. Been hiding in the old quarters. When they tore it down, he didn't have a place to hide anymore."

Loretta reached out a hesitant hand, but Sally stuffed the photo back into her jacket and spun herself off the stool. "Gotta go,'" she yelled, running to the door. The screen banged behind her as she jumped down off the porch. Then she was running, running. She heard Loretta calling after her, but she couldn't stop.

She ran to Barn Eight just as the morning sky started to gray-up. Sam had the chestnut colt saddled and seemed to be waiting for her. She darted into the tack room and pulled her hard-hat off the hook.

"Gimme a leg up," she ordered, slamming the helmet onto her head.

"Mr. Goldstein's not here yet, Miss Sally," the old groom protested, the whites of his eyes shiny against the darkness of his face. "Maybe we should wait."

"Leg up."

He did like he was told, like she knew he would. "Don't worry," she whispered, slipping her boots into the short irons. "We're just going for a little gallop."

Only one other horse on the track. A black colt. Sally squinted her eyes against the slowly rising sun. The black was on the backstretch, galloping as if in slow motion. Oh, she knew that horse all right, the long, flowing stride gave him away. She knew the rider, too. Tommy and Silent Sleeper.

Maybe, just maybe, if she rode fast enough, hard enough, she could catch up with them. Before they reached the three-quarter pole, before Sleeper's leg snapped. Before they went down.

Weenie Roast

By Marjorie Bicknell Johnson

My husband Wayne's first steady job was in the kitchen at a six-hundred-bed tuberculosis hospital far from town in the California foothills. In those days, TB had no cure; patients were not allowed to leave and children were not allowed to visit.

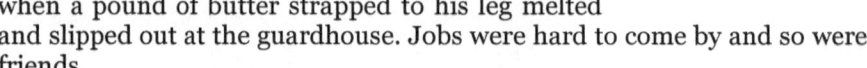

Employees worked split shifts for the minimum wage; packages and bulky jackets were inspected at the gate. One poor fellow lost his job when a pound of butter strapped to his leg melted and slipped out at the guardhouse. Jobs were hard to come by and so were friends.

On one summer Tuesday, Wayne's only day off, I jumped into our old Chevy coupe with a sense of high adventure: Wayne's new friend Fred, another kitchen worker, had invited us to spend the day. I was excited about meeting somebody, anybody, actually.

Fred lived far into the hills in a cabin leased for a dollar per year in return for keeping out poachers. The gravel road forked into dirt byways with ruts so deep that two wheels of the Chevy stayed on the center hump to avoid scraping the oil pan. When we forded a creek, the tires ran over a concrete base, the water not deep enough to swamp the engine if taken slowly, just as Fred had described it.

Three dusty miles later and after bumping through a dry creek bed, I saw a small cabin with metal chimney and tarpaper roof and set up on stilts, the walls rough unpainted lumber. The driveway circled around it as did a barbed-wire fence, completely covered with towels and shirts and draped clothing, and beyond those, discarded tires, pipes and wires, rusted and blackened coil springs from the rear seat of a car or maybe from a sofa. Wayne parked behind a polished sedan and a dented pick-up too dusty to distinguish the color.

Three children, all with dirty round sunflower faces and ragged petal hair and heads flat in the back, played in the dirt yard. They turned to stare, and a tall man ran towards our car. A smiling round-faced woman wearing jeans and a man's shirt waved from the doorway. As she came closer, I saw that she had several missing teeth.

Wayne's friend Fred, lanky, popping brown eyes in a lean face, brown hair starting to recede, beamed as he introduced everybody. "This here's my wife, Zora." He pointed at each person in turn: Chuckie was five; Linda, four; and Stanley, almost three. I didn't meet the baby until we went inside.

"Come on in and set a spell," Zora said. She pumped up a kerosene camp stove and put ground coffee and cold water in the bottom of an enamel coffeepot. When it boiled, she dropped in an eggshell left frombreakfast to settle the grounds. Flies swirled lazily, crawling across dried-on egg yolk on the unwashed dishes. The walls and ceiling were painted glossy dark green, the floor medium gray, and a drugstore calendar hung from a sixpenny nail. The baby lay flat on her back in a crib, sleeping and sucking on a propped-up bottle; when she awoke, she stayed there and watched the flies. Zora plunked the coffee cups onto a Formica and chrome kitchen table across the room from an upholstered chair and a matching filthy couch. I thought of my mother's spotless windows and snow-white tea towels and hoped boiling would kill whatever germs my stomach acids didn't digest.

Somewhat later, Zora needed something from the store. Outside, Fred pointed out his automobile's polished wooden dashboard, shining brass knobs, and leather seats; I saw my reflection in the bumper.

"Zora's father won it in a poker game," Fred said. "Have you ever ridden in a Rolls Royce?"

Wayne said no; I had never even heard of one. Four adults, three children and a baby all piled into the car, the smaller persons sitting on laps. Zora nodded toward the junk heap and told us Fred took that-there wire out of the TB hospital on a garbage truck, hid it in plain sight, he did; she reckoned he could fix nigh on anything.

Zora charged the groceries at the country store—their account balance was more than two weeks' pay. She packed everything into cardboard boxes, lots of boxes: disposable playpens for babies who wore diapers only at night to keep plenty of fresh air on those tender bottoms, she said. The boxes went into the trunk. The men sat in the front; the rest of us sat two deep.

On the return trip, Fred braked hard, waved his arm, and pointed. "See that? See that big king snake there?"

"Let's catch him," Wayne said.

The men jumped out and dashed after the rapidly departing reptile. Fred snatched the snake behind its head with his right hand and grabbed its tail with his left. "Ever see a king snake and a rattlesnake fight?" he said. "The king snake always wins."

Wayne opened the trunk and Fred dropped the three-foot squirming snake into a grocery box. King snakes aren't poisonous, but I wasn't keen on getting acquainted.

Back at the cabin, the men carried in the boxes of groceries, the snake still in one of them, and went out to catch a rattlesnake.

"They'll never find one," I said. I didn't volunteer to unload the boxes.

"Fred says he's gonna bring home a rattlesnake, I reckon that's what he's gonna do," Zora said. "Let's wash up some dishes, let the men unpack the groceries. I don't want nothin' to do with no snake."

We finished washing that mountain of dishes, and darned if Zora wasn't right. The men drove back in the pick-up, red dust twisting behind them, and Fred came in carrying a covered bucket.

"Wayne got us a rattlesnake, just pinned him behind his head with a forked stick and picked him right up," Fred said. "Now where's that king snake?"

Fred and Wayne emptied everything out of the grocery boxes, and not very neatly, either, but the king snake was not there. They looked under everything and moved piles of clutter around. No snake.

"He must have crawled out of the box," Fred said. "It couldn't have made a dash for the door or the dog would have let us know."

"It must be in the springs of the couch, no other place it could be," said Zora. "I'm not settin' there 'til you find that snake."

"Ever see a dog kill a rattlesnake?" Fred moved the bucket to the front yard. I was glad to see it go outside; Zora didn't need a second snake hiding inside the house.

"This old dog is really fast," Fred said. "Knows how to kill a snake by instinct."

"What if the snake bites his nose?" I asked. The men laughed at me.

"Take the kids into the house," Fred said. He uncovered the bucket, swung it up and over, and tossed out the snake. Immediately, the rattler coiled up. "Get 'em, Jake, get 'em, boy!"

The dog moved in, jumped back when the snake struck, grabbed it behind the head, shook it hard, and dropped it in the dirt. The dog barked and ran around the rattlesnake, both of them darting in and out. The snake coiled again and struck, the dog jumped out of the way. The dog caught the snake and shook harder. The snake wriggled and slithered; the dog attacked a final time. The dog pulled back and his drooling tongue hung out. The dying snake still twitched.

Fred wanted the rattles; he called them buttons. "Be careful, the fangs from a dead snake can still get you. One time somebody changing a tire, he ran his hand around inside to find the nail that blew the tube, but it was a snake fang. Real nasty. The guy sliced his finger with his knife, sucked out the venom, but got it into his rotten tooth. Went right into his brain, poor sucker died."

Fred loved to tell stories, but I wasn't sure I could believe him. Zora pumped the camp stove, fried up a pound of hamburger meat and boiled potato chunks, floured up the hamburger grease and made lots of gravy. I opened up a can of beans. "You and me, we have to make a meal out of nothin'," she said. "Maybe they'll hunt for somethin' better than snakes next time you come on over."

That evening, I was glad to get home to our two-room cabin. We didn't have refrigeration or hot water, but we didn't have flies.

A few weeks later, Wayne and Fred planned a hunting trip. I thought they'd bag squirrels or a rabbit, and we could make a stew. This time when we approached Fred's cabin, the same collection of laundry decorated the barbed wire fences and more wires were strung under the house. Their beds, dressers, tables and chairs sat outside. Three kids and a dog wrestled on a lumpy couch, adding a layer of mud and cookies over urine stains. Fred was outside, working on his truck.

Wayne called out, "Hey, Fred, why the barbed wire under your house? Zora need more space for laundry?"

Fred stood up and brushed himself off. "Keeps the goats from butting the flor."

"You have goats?"

"Used to. Damned goats got under the house at night. Look it here." Fred pointed to the roof of a junked car. "See them dents and wrinkles? Them damned goats, they liked to jump up on the car, dance on the roof. We had to get rid of them goats."

"Hey, Zora," Fred called out. "We got company. Get on out here."

Zora appeared at the front door with the garden hose in one hand. "Cleanin' house," she said. "I'm just about done." She had hosed down the walls, ceilings, and floors, but she couldn't sweep the water out the door. "Darn floor slopes the wrong way."

The broom flew out the door and Zora dashed back inside. All at once, three shots rang out and water spilled out behind the stilts; she had put three 22-caliber holes right through the floor on the low corner. After a while, we carried everything but the couch inside and went to set a spell over muddy coffee.

Zora held her infant on one hip and pumped the camp stove to heat a bottle; wisps of hair escaped from her barrettes. She fixed more coffee, boiling used grounds in an old kettle; dregs filled the bottom half-inch in my cup.

"Babies, all they know is eating, sleeping and pooping, but I love them all," she said. "I think I'm pregnant again."

"I'm pregnant, too," I said. "I only lasted in the hospital kitchen three days—I threw up every time we cooked eggs."

"It's a bitch, isn't it?" Zora, only twenty-three, already missing several teeth and getting heavy, liked to talk about having babies. Would I be like her in a few years?

Two cups of coffee later, the men returned with a buck, meat for a week, but not for tonight—Fred said the carcass had to hang. Hunting season or not, I knew they had no licenses. So the guard against poachers was himself a poacher as well as a board and wire and who-knew-what-else smuggler.

"Hey, Zora, what's for dinner?" Fred wiped his face and hands on a towel plucked from the fence.

"Weenie roast. Need some sticks."

"Come on, Wayne," Fred said. "Let's find us some willow. You can't use poison oak or you blister your stomach."

I wondered where Fred would build the fire. Wayne trimmed branches while Fred rolled and twisted newspaper and threw a bucketful of liquid onto the couch. Washing it, this time of night?

Fred lit a match and threw out a newspaper torch.

Vroom! Flames exploded. The blazing couch lit up the front yard— another sofa skeleton for the junk pile—but I had little appetite for hot dogs roasted over its embers.

One Day's Work

By Mary Van Tamelen

SAILOR

I loved the sea long before I ever saw it. There was a picture of the sea in our upstairs hall—so I had some idea of what it might look like. And Lake Michigan was almost a sea, with real undertows, and shores so distant as to be out of sight.

But the sea I loved was vast, had whales, and storms, and dead calm, and ships with fo'c'sles, mizzenmasts, hawsers, and heaving to, peopled with mates and bos'ns and captains shouting "ahoy," and "avast," and "aye, aye." I didn't know what any of it meant; in complete ignorance and unfettered joy, I read every sailing book in the young adult section of the Holland Public Library.

Why was it such a delightful dream to me—the idea of going to sea? First, I think, because it was different—I wanted to try everything. Then, on a deeper level, because I wanted to escape, to get away from worries, obligations, tensions, constraints. A ship has such definite parameters—in space, and also in time. The sea is elemental; past and future are of little import in a man-made structure on an enormous ocean controlled by forces of nature. It's where man—and woman, too—comes face to face with God.

I must have had some sense of some of this when I started reading these books, for the dream has never left me. (Otherwise, Howard Pease was a more captivating writer than any others I'd read.)

One girl in our class in high school, Caryl Curtis, had a sailboat, and I tried hopefully to be her friend, to no avail. So in spite of living two blocks from Black Lake, and five miles from the big lake, sailing was tantalizingly out of my reach.

I first saw the ocean when I was in college on a trip with speech contestants; I first crossed the ocean in 1957, married with two children, on a big ship, The Fair Sea. This was hardly a sailing experience, rather a cruising experience with all the distractions of cruising to become accustomed to: we were in first class, my sister Sally was in tourist; we could go to her, but she couldn't come to us; we, with our two little girls, were invited to eat at the Captain's table; Gene's father died during the trip; we had months in England to look forward to. So I hardly gave a thought to the lack of sails or to being one with nature.

I first sailed on a yacht in 1960, and then I felt it again slightly, the lure of the sea. But that, too, was hardly a sailing experience for me: we had a captain and cook, we were with Nancy and Morris Kupchan, partying, going to or from chemistry meetings in the Caribbean, fretting about children left at home, learning to snorkel. After a few more yachting experiences, always learning just a bit more of the lore, navigation, terminology, and methodology, one day I saw a course in sailing offered at Foothill College.

Yes, I had always wanted to be a sailor. Didn't I have among my favorite books Moby Dick, The Captain, Survive the Savage Sea? Yes, didn't I love my yachting experiences? Yes, weren't my ancestors Dutchmen, connected with the sea? Yes, didn't I like exploring underwater with a snorkel? Yes, wasn't every sailor I met someone worth knowing?

So I took the course. It was great. True, sometimes I rammed the little boat into the dock. And sometimes I wasn't sure whether to push the tiller toward the sail, or away from it. I never overturned the boat, and I did learn the rigging and the language.

With my husband's encouragement, in fact at his suggestion, I bought a boat.

Buying anything is always a chore for me. What kind of boat do I want? Something big enough for two, but one I can manage alone. A catamaran or a single hull? Single, I guess. For racing? I doubted it. How will I haul it? On top of the car seemed too overwhelming, so, by means of a trailer. How do you haul the trailer? With a trailer hitch, which has to be permanently installed on the back of a car. Both the boat and the trailer need registration—another area beyond my ken—and insurance. Where will I keep it? Down next to the carport, with a cable locking it to a tree. And a tarp to keep the rain out.

Did I really want to be a sailor? I knew I was not as strong as the sea. What are the rules of the sea and did I have to obey them? Having gone this far, I supposed I should know them, so I took a course sponsored by the Coast Guard, and learned a smattering amount about the power of water and wind, regulations, and navigation.

My sailing teacher, Vinny Bieberdorf, had started at an older age. She took me out with her on the bay a few times. So yes, I did want to be a sailor. I loved sailing.

That was my refrain for several years, wherever we went. At home, I'd take friends out on my bright red Banshee and we'd sail back and forth across little lakes or reservoirs. In St. Lucia, a friend arranged for me to take a small, almost hand-made dinghy out one afternoon, and I sailed back and forth across Vigie Harbor, carefully not hazarding forth into Castries Harbor.

I loved sailing. So once in St. Lucia I took my sister out from the Cariblue Hotel into the real ocean, in a Sunflower. I forgot for a moment how to rig the mainsail, but it soon came back to me and we went out. The waves, well, they must have been all of two feet high, but at times they obscured the shore, and I was soon relieved to head back. And another time I took her out on the San Francisco Bay, where we had been warned that 50 minutes in the cold water could be fatal, and the water began filling the boat from the stern. This had never happened before, and no one had mentioned what ought to be done next. Well, my sister bailed like mad with my handy calabash shell—a nice touch, I'd thought as I put it aboard, a bit of St. Lucia in my boat at home—and we did make it back safely.

Yes, I loved sailing. And so would my son. Peter was happy enough to go out with me on occasion. Once when he was sailing, I threw out the calabash shell and said, "Man overboard." He did the right thing, came about smartly, but the calabash shell did the wrong thing, and sank.

From the beginning, Peter was more comfortable in the boat than I. After a heavy winter rain, he and I hauled the boat into the driveway, only to find that not only its well, but also its sides (the waterproof hollow part that keeps it afloat) full of water, and the fiberglass of the boat bending and flexing with the slosh of water inside.

"My boat is going to break in two!" I panicked, but Peter calmly and sensibly took charge, and all was well.

I loved sailing. So when my son-in-law Dominick—who really knew and loved sailing—came, we went out in the bay and he sailed that Banshee the way she was meant to sail. We raced the other boats in the bay and cut off their wind, and heeled exhilaratingly. That was the most invigorating fun I ever had with that boat. When another sister came to visit, I took her on a nice windy day to Lexington Reservoir, and the wind was so strong it broke the gooseneck while I was rigging the boat, so we never even put it in the water. Then that had to be fixed, and it was interesting because the manufacturers of the Banshee happened to live on the next street over from us. They were most kind and helpful.

I really love sailing, but by that time I was launched on my political career, so I sold the boat.

I toyed with the idea, over the years, of offering to crew on a small boat going across an ocean. I'm sure Adrian Dronkert would and could arrange for me to go to sea somewhere—really to sea, without a hired captain. And the lure is there: wind and water and the boat and I. Parameters. Alone with God. A test, a timeless test, of myself in nature.

Many years later, on Marigot Bay in St. Lucia with the Koops, after restless days of rain and limited activity because of Howie's health, I looked down over the warm water in that small bay and thought, why not? Wind surfers were speeding across; the breeze was brisk. There weren't too many yachts passing through. The small boats were there for the asking. And Ginny was willing.

So I took to the sea again. Old lady that I was, with an even older lady as my responsibility, I set out to sail, remembering carefully to check the rigging, which way to push the tiller, which lines did what. The boy in charge of the boats waded out with us, and unfastened us from the mooring.

Heading out across the narrow channel, we whizzed along, heeling smartly, until too quickly it was time to come about. Warning Ginny properly, I took us about; we caught the wind even more strongly than before—and capsized.

Ginny was all right, thank God, and I knew what one was supposed to do after capsizing: stand on the keel and pull the boat upright. With effort, that works. However, it's difficult to get back into the boat. Exceedingly difficult. It makes an ungainly picture, a good-sized woman struggling to get a leg up over the side of a tiny, tipping sailboat. Fortunately the boat boy appeared in a motorboat, and pulled Ginny aboard that. He then wanted me to come with him, too. But no, I wouldn't. I loved to sail, and I was not one to abandon my boat. I struggled back inside. Ginny and the boy chugged off, and I got my bearings again, and my lines untangled. Checking my position, I tightened the sheet—and capsized again.

A Frenchman came by in his little boat and offered to help. Thank you, sir, but I am becoming quite adept at righting a sailboat, if not learning to scramble in gracefully. Very, very carefully, I tacked obliquely back to the mooring area.

My antic had greatly amused the lunch crowd at Dolittles Restaurant. I think they applauded when I got back, fastened the boat to its mooring, and shamefacedly dripped to shore.

I still love to sail, but I don't think sailing is the ideal career for me.

Why Gladys Stuben Turned to a Life of Crime

By Luanne Oleas

Gladys was short with brown hair and brown eyes. In fact, her ex-husband used to say she was "five foot two with eyes of poo," which was just one of his sayings. He was her ex. She had kept the best he had to offer—his four kids—not that he fought for custody. He was reliable about his one-weekend a month with them, but less so about child support and alimony. Gladys figured his latest girlfriend spent that money.

It wasn't the missing payments that drove Gladys beyond the brink. It wasn't even when three-year-old, Billy—with his bed-head wisps of blond hair and enormous blue eyes—had gotten up early, plugged the electric frying pan into the wall, and cooked a scrambled egg on the floor. (It was safer than when he had parted the dog's tail and stuck it into the wall socket.)

Gladys' insanity also wasn't caused by her 16-year-old daughter. Samantha—"Call me 'Sam', Mo-o-o-m"—had purchased a bus ticket to Salt Lake City and made hotel reservations for two at the Marriott there. Gladys found the Priceline.com receipt while pulling seven-year-old Franklin's hands out of her daughter's makeup drawer. At that point, Gladys wasn't been sure if her daughter's clandestine rendezvous 1,000 with an Internet stranger or Franklin's affinity for lipstick and eye shadow was more disturbing.

Kids will be kids. Gladys knew that. She hadn't even gone bonkers when rear-ended on her way to work by an uninsured motorist. She even maintained her sanity when she found out the office air-conditioning was on the fritz.

Her road to ruin didn't really start until she picked up her paycheck and discovered it was $100 short. After one email, four phone calls, and an in-person visit to the payroll clerk later, she got an explanation. The frustration over that fiasco hadn't improved her attitude, nor had the reason they gave for the missing money. They had deducted the money because Gladys took time off to drive five-year-old son, Norman, to the ear, nose and throat guy to have a wing nut extracted from his ear.

"But I'm a salaried employee," Gladys protested, standing beside the payroll gal's desk. "You can't deduct an hourly amount from my check."

"Your manager insisted," the payroll gal said. In that instant, Gladys had a vision of herself holding a pistol to the side of her manager's fat head, and telling him to get down on his knobby knees—if he could find them beneath his swollen belly. She imagined him begging for mercy in his lispy voice.

"It was the second time you took time off for a medical visit last month," the payroll clerk said, bringing Gladys back to earth. Were they counting the pregnancy test for Samantha against Gladys too? At least that had come back negative.

A lot of things seemed to be coming back negative for Gladys lately. She had given up on having a social life. Most of the guys paired with her by vMatch.com proved to be worse than her ex, especially that one that Franklin had been so attracted to. The attraction wasn't mutual.

"How can he do this with all the overtime I put in?" Gladys asked. She had worked every weekend that her ex had taken the kids for the last year. She wasn't that dedicated to the company. Working extra hours kept her from going to vMatch or TableforSix when she had extra time those two days each month.

"Overtime is expected from salaried employees," the clerk answered. Her phone began to ring and a stack of papers fell from her desk. "You'll have to discuss it with your manager." It was the ultimate brush-off.

"Or my manager's manager," Gladys threatened before walking away.

Of course, those discussions would have to wait. Her manager and his manager were in Paris with the sales team.

No, none of that drove her over the edge. It was an egg.

It happened after Gladys left work. She drove safely from the office parking lot to the grocery store to grab something for dinner. That was the routine on her Fridays off from parenting. Her ex would pick up the boys from the after-school program. Samantha—Sam—would spend the night with her BFF, and then meet her dad on Saturday morning.

Gladys needed just the essentials. Eggs, milk, spaghetti, no beef. She breezed through the checkout stand. She was loading her groceries into her minivan when she noticed liquid leaking from the egg carton. Inside, a lone egg sat in the middle of the dozen, its shell broken and dripping. That did it.

It wasn't a grand, noisy freak-out with screaming and hand-waving. No door-slamming or while gestures. It started with a slow, steady muttering of curse words as she got into the driver's seat.

"Putrid pond scum duck-faced futher mucker."

She was so enthralled with her diatribe that she almost forgot to stop at the ATM. Her abrupt maneuver through traffic nearly killed a pedestrian. She slammed on the brakes just in time. Her parallel parking job by the curb outside the bank stunk. No matter. She wouldn't be long. She reached under the seat looking for her purse, but found Norman's favorite toy. The life-like handgun his father (the duck-faced futher mucker) had given to their five-year-old. Who does that? She stuffed it in her purse, planning to toss it into the garbage by the ATM machine.

There was a line. Of course, there was a line. And someone was making some long, involved deposit to boot. She waited and waited until she finally got up to the machine and entered her PIN.

"Funds not available." Those words on the display hit her like a brick upside the head.

She had funds. She knew she had funds. Her paycheck, though short, was directly deposited into her account every other Friday. And this was the Friday that it was supposed to be there.

She grabbed her card and headed into the bank, 30 seconds before they were going to close. She walked up to the teller and started to explain, opening her purse to retrieve her bankcard. That's when she saw the gun. She pulled it out and pointed it at the teller's nose.

"Give me all the money you've got," Gladys said. "And make it fast. Don't push any alarm buttons either."

Two TV screens projected her image, thanks to the surveillance cameras. She had the pleasure of watching herself go crazy. The teller with the name tag "Alicia" hadn't moved.

"NOW!" Gladys shouted, which drew the attention of the next teller, named-tagged "Barbara." "You too," Gladys added, waving the realistic toy handgun between the two of them. "I need a bag too," she said. They were both shaking and opening their drawers. "Make it plastic," Gladys added, as if she were still at the grocery store. Alicia and Barbara looked up momentarily, and then went back to piling money on the counter.

"I didn't want to do this, you know," Gladys said. "I couldn't access my account from the ATM." Gladys heard herself rambling on like one of those shopping-cart people who talk to themselves while pushing all their worldly belongings. "My funds weren't available," she continued, in a quiet voice. "My boss took money out of my check because I took my kid to the doctor."

"Will this work?" Alicia asked, holding up a garbage bag. "It's the only plastic we have."

Gladys nodded and Alicia dropped stacks of twenties into the bag. Then she paused and looked up at Gladys, still pointing the gun.

"What?" Gladys said when she caught Alicia's staring from behind her teller-issue, narrow glasses.

"Nothing," Alicia stammered. "I just... I mean, me too."

"You too what?" Gladys asked.

"They took money from my check this week," the young teller said under her breath. "My baby had a fever."

"Yeah, well, this wouldn't be happening if my ex had paid child support OR alimony this month," Gladys started, as if Alicia or Barbara cared.

"My ex didn't send a check this month either," Barbara said, increasing the speed with which she pulled money from the drawer.

"Really?" Gladys said, lowering the gun for a fraction of a second and then lifting it again. "I mean, put it all in the bag. Don't forget the hundreds."

"Yes," Barbara said. "He's such a jerk."

"I wish I could just rob my manager instead of you two," Gladys said.

"That's okay," Alicia said, not shaking as much. "At least you are robbing my manager, the dork. I needed that money. My little boy's birthday is next week."

"Oh?" Gladys said, forgetting herself completely. "How old?"

"He'll be three on Wednesday," Alicia said with a sigh. Gladys realized the teller was just one broken egg away from bank robbery herself. "How about if I get some money from another drawer?" Alicia offered.

"I guess," Gladys said, feeling faint. But Alicia had started pulling money from the next teller's open drawer before Gladys answered,

"Good idea," Barbara said, moving to her left. "Let me get you the bills in this drawer too."

Gladys watched the two girls pile more money in the two plastic garbage bags. They were so full, they would be hard to carry. Gladys looked around, but didn't see anyone but the two girls. She heard voices coming from inside the vault.

"That's enough," Gladys said.

"Are you sure?" Barbara asked, just beginning to unload another drawer.

"Yes, I'm sure," Gladys answered. "Come down here," she said, motioning with the handgun to the far end of the counter. The two tellers, now smiling, carried the two bags full of money to the handicap access counter and handed them over to Gladys.

"Wait," Alicia said, running to back of the room before Gladys could stop her. Alicia popped the surveillance video out of the machine and handed it to Gladys.

"Uh, thanks," Gladys said, backing away from them. She dragged her two heavy bags to the double glass door exit.

"It was a pleasure serving you," said Alicia.

"Have a nice day," added Barbara.

Gladys remembered putting the two bags in the back of her minivan. She didn't remember the drive home. She pieced it all together the next morning when she work up on the couch, fully clothed. Two empty wine bottles sat beside her. She snuck out to the garage in her bare feet. The big bags were still sitting in the back of her van.

The bank robbery made headlines, but Gladys was too shaken to read the story. She took a shower, got dressed, and waited for the cops to break down her door. She waited all weekend, afraid to leave the house, but they never came. Her husband returned the kids Sunday night.

"Hey, there," he said, standing on her front porch. The kids entered and plopped down in the living room. He handed Gladys two backpacks and a half-eaten cotton candy. "I think Norman's getting a cold. Maybe you should take him to the doctor."

"Sure," Gladys said and started laughing. Her husband gave her a strange look. He didn't understand, but then, he never had.

"Hey," he said, stepping away from the porch, then stopping. "Some guy robbed the bank over by your office."

"Some guy?" Gladys asked.

"Yeah, smart guy," her ex added. "Even took the surveillance tape. The tellers said he looked like Tom Hanks."

"Really?" Gladys said, laughing again. The kids started fighting over the remote control, but that didn't bother her.

"Yeah, he got away with a fortune," he said, walking back to his car where a blond was waiting. "I could use a little of that."

"Yeah," Gladys said. "I bet you could." She couldn't close the door fast enough.

Blue Man in Morocco

By Linda Brown

In 1999 I went to Morocco. It was an Am Photo planned photographers' tour. Because it would be such a long flight, my friends suggested flying to and staying in New York City on the way. Dolores, Myra and I stayed in one suite. It was an older run-down hotel set up more like apartments.

We saw Brian Dennehy in the lobby. He was acting in a remake of "Death of a Salesman" at the time. I didn't recognize him at first but he seemed familiar, so I smiled and nodded at him. I must have looked familiar to him or at least looked like a fan; he waved and smiled as though we were old friends but continued out the door. My friends were astonished and peppered me with questions about Brian, but I had to admit I'd never met him.

We stayed a few days, ate in delis, went to a play, and wandered around the city. It was in February so the skies were dismal, all the architecture looking defeated.

We flew via Frankfurt and then into Marrakech. We stayed in an enclosed high-end tourist resort. Although it was beautiful, we never toured alone. We always took a group tour bus. We visited Marrakech and walked through the market square, the medinas and the exotic side streets. I could hear Sting's song "Desert Rose" echoing in my mind. The colors and the smells of food, leather goods, woven materials, and crowded streets were overwhelming and intoxicating in the way only a foreign country can be.

Once during free time in Marrakech we hired a taxi to take us to a museum not on the tour's list. It was definitely an "E" ticket ride whizzing through passageways where the taxi almost scraped the sides of the buildings. The driver drove with one hand on his car horn to warn people to jump into doorways, or side streets so he wouldn't run over them. With scowling faces looking in at us, we felt like the personification of "ugly Americans."

At the end of the day, we sat high above the market square and watched the sun go down and listened to the call to prayers. Our photo guides had hired local guides to join us on the bus rides and in the meeting places to lecture us on local customs.

One field trip was to Essouiria, the fishing village on the coast renowned for its white buildings and blue doors reminiscent of Santorini, Greece. Fishing boats and nets reflected in the water. Sea gulls screamed. It seemed an odd place to be in what one generally thinks of as a desert country. Finding places for our large group to eat seemed to be a major concern on each outing.

Another field trip was into the Atlas Mountains. Photographers groaned with the lost opportunities as we passed picturesque huts, goats with attendant young goat herders, scenes in beautiful light. But there was no place to stop on the narrow, winding road.

The Am Photo tour guides assured us that we would stop in a genuine Berber village and we would be allowed to take all the photographs we wanted. Our guides explained that the headman of the village had been paid a sum to allow this and that we did not have to pay any individuals. However, apparently no one explained this to the villagers as they all hid in their houses, grabbed their children to come inside, and slammed shutters as we walked along. Travel photos are not as interesting to take if there are no indigenous people in them.

The photographers got back on the bus and voiced their anger to the tour guide.

But she assured us as we hunkered back down into our comfortable air-conditioned bus, that next we were going to stop for lunch and be able to enjoy the prearranged native dancers.

It was clearly a designated tourist trap, right down to selling local pottery along the road. Because I sweat a lot I always wear a bandana. The young teenager pottery salesman really wanted my bandana. He was eager to trade any one of his ugly jugs just to own the bandana. I needed the bandana, so I didn't trade with him.

The food was good and the dancers were interesting. Even in this jaded tourist spot we attracted swarms of curious children. My little white haired friend Myra loves children, she is about their size, and so she never intimidates them. They surrounded her and began to ask questions, but with their hands out. I interpreted it as begging as we had experienced so much begging already. But Myra continued to try to communicate with them, even trying her rudimentary French which some of the children seemed to recognize.

After lunch our guide promised us a special treat. We were going to stop to photograph a local flea market. Shoppers and merchants were set up under makeshift tents. Some merchants still continued to arrive with

386

their wares tied onto donkeys. It was dirty, dusty, and no one wanted you to take his or her picture. They turned away or held something in front of their faces.

However, everyone wanted to sell you something. One approach was to hand you a bracelet or necklace as a "gift", but then they wanted to haggle with you about the price. I was not interested in shopping, I was on a very tight budget and not particularly interested in souvenirs. The Moroccans were way too aggressive for me. I understood from history that being on the coast of Africa it had been on trade routes for ships and caravans for thousands of years. I believe it was actually Moroccans who invented haggling.

I was not very photographically inspired, either. I tried for a few long shots. I was never very good at people close-ups anyway. Also, when you are photographing you sometimes lose sense of what is going on directly around you. I had politely refused several aggressive merchants. One man all dressed in blue suddenly rushed over to me demanding, "You must pay me! You took my photo!"

I was astonished. I had watched him haggling with another woman on the tour, but had not even bothered to look through my lens. I had not taken his picture.

"You did! You did! You must pay me!" He was insistent.

Years earlier, when I had taken SCUBA training the first important scenario that they teach you is that when you get into a scary situation, you cannot panic. If you panic when you under water and breathing a canned air mixture, you will breathe too deeply, and you will die. You cannot breathe deeply. You must train yourself to breathe shallowly, and consider your best options. Then the instructors proceeded to do Pavlovian training with us. The minute we had an adrenaline surge, we had to count to ten, breath shallowly and consider our best options. Many times in my life, this training has come in handy.

In the mountains of a strange country, with no particular travel aides close by, and with the Blue Man coming way too close to my face, I began to panic a little. Biologists will offer you fight or flight options, but my SCUBA training allowed me to breathe shallowly and offer a reasonable explanation to him.

"I never take anyone's picture without permission, and I never pay anyone to take his or her picture. That is a choice I have made for myself and in respect to anyone on the other side of my lens. I did not have your permission; I did not take your image."

Next he tried the trick of handing me a bracelet as a gift. "This is for you. I want you to have this."

"No, I do not want it. I do not have the money for it." Next he said, "I am a Blue Man. Do you know what that means?"I looked at him in his blue outfit, but his non-blue skin, and said, "No you are not." Never being comfortable with short explanations and not wanting to be entirely rude or appear to be uneducated, I said," I read about the Tuaregs or Blue Men of Morocco. I read it was the dye in their clothing that leached out and turned men's skin blue. Indigo was at one time very expensive, so for the Tuarges, it was a sign of wealth to have blue skin because of their expensive blue died clothing."

His eyebrows rose, but he nodded his concession.

Next he said, "I am a very poor man, I have made no money this day to buy food for my children. And I have three hungry children waiting for me at home. A few dirham would mean nothing to you, madam, but everything to me and my hungry children."

I said, "Well, I can understand that, but I truly do not have any money."

He took on a wheedling tone, "If you do not have dirham, I could take some of your American dollars."

I was still in my reasonable mode, "I need to explain something to you. Not all Americans are rich. Some of us are quite poor but we have scrimped and saved just to come on a tour."

I told him I had no money on me. I pulled my pockets out to show him I really only had a few small coins.

He just shook his head.

"This is not good. I would be glad to walk you back to the bus so you could borrow money from your friends."

I said, "I don't borrow money."

I had slowly been walking back towards the tour bus, and the Blue Man had been crab walking beside me, continuing his wheedling. We had collected an audience of interested old men. Obviously everyone knew the Blue Man.

"But," he continued, "Why did you come to Morocco if you are not going to buy anything to help our economy?"

I smiled and said, "So I could meet interesting people like you."

He said cunningly, "I like you. I will make an exception for you. You can charge it." I was so stunned by his remark I could not say anything.

He assumed I didn't understand. So he made the motion of sliding the handle on a card imprint machine.

"You know snick-snick!" He demonstrated.

I burst into laughter. "You take charge cards? I thought you were a poor man wandering from flea market to flea market trying to scrape out a living."

He shrugged and conceded, "Well I do have a store in the city, but sometimes I like to get out in the countryside."

I couldn't stop laughing. The crowd was also enjoying this exchange. I said, "No, you need to be a standup comedian."

"Huh, what's that you say? Co-mee-jun? What is this Co-mee-jun?"

I said, "Someone who tells stories to crowds of people and makes them laugh. I think you could make more money being a comedian."

The crowd was delighted. Here we were somewhere in the outback of the Atlas Mountains, as the local guides had informed us, each of these grubby looking people could speak more languages than I could enumerate. And, they very clearly understood and were enjoying the conversation going on between the Blue Man and me. Finally, the Blue Man graciously suggested that I take his picture to remember him by and insisted on giving me his business card so I could visit him in the city.

I did not take his photography, I did not look up his store; nor did I ever buy any jewelry from him.

The Quest

By Lisa Johnson

Life puzzled John. At age ten he brooded over missing pieces, pieces he felt had been stolen from him. He knew that everybody had a mother in the beginning; and if his mother was not dead, because his father said she was not dead, then why was she missing?

John started letters to her: Dear Mother. Or: Dear Marla, (for that was her name) I saw your picture in Grandmother Marian's book. You are beautiful (a word he never used). When he tried to ask Grandmother Marian about her daughter, she got very quiet and sad. Once, when she was out of the room, John sneaked a photo from the book and stuffed it inside his shirt. It was of Marla as a teenager, wearing a short skirt, holding pom-poms, squinting into the sun, her long hair the color of the sunlight.

John had only known Grandmother Marian for about a year. She'd appeared one day, out of the blue; said she wanted to get to know her grandson. From then on, once or twice a month he spent a weekend at her apartment in San Francisco. Even though she was kind of old, she took John to fun places: the zoo, movies, Giants games, to fancy restaurants. Grandmother's blonde-grey hair, pulled into a bun, made her eyes look very blue behind her big glasses.

At dinner one evening he blurted to his father, "Well, if people have sex to get babies, why do they give them away?"

His father poured more milk into his glass as if he hadn't heard John. Then he looked John right in the eyes, "Most people don't have sex for the purpose of getting babies. They have sex because it feels good. Babies are sometimes an unwanted consequence."

John stabbed at the food, which he'd separated into neat little piles. The word unwanted stuck in his head.

"Is there something else you wanted to know?"

"Well, what about Rosalie and Dolores?"

"What about them?"

John held his breath. "Do you wish they'd have a baby?"

"No," his father stated flatly. "But I'm glad I have you. If that's concerning you. Although you can be a nuisance." With that his father reached over and lightly punched him on the arm.

"Where'd she go?" John blurted.

"I'm not sure. Back East, I think."

"She didn't want me?"

His father studied him. "It's not that she didn't want you, John. It was the responsibility she didn't want."

"I'm not that much trouble."

"That's a matter of opinion," his father teased.

All of John's life, or as long as he could remember, he'd lived in the country, on this ranch with his father. Rosalie, his father's friend, reminded him of how fortunate he was. She pointed out how his father had grown up poor, in a big family, in an over-crowded house, in a tough neighborhood in the city. And John tried to feel more fortunate (he did love Pogo his horse and his two German Shepherds); yet he still envied the little boy his father had been, to have brothers and sisters, noise and activity. Compared to so much space and silence.

"Yes, my little friend," Rosalie lectured, "the grass only seems greener on the other side of the fence."

Whenever Dolores came from the city for a weekend, as soon as his father was out of sight and sound, John informed her of Rosalie's presence during the week, elaborating about Rosalie's great cooking and cleaning. John enjoyed watching Dolores' amber eyes flash, her hawk nose flare. "Do tell, Mr. Big Shot, Mr. Know-It-All."

John looked forward to Dolores' visits; with her he could vent his venom because he knew Dolores disliked him. She didn't try to please him, nor did he try to please her. With Rosalie he tried.

"Guess what, Dolores?" he asked on her last visit, "I'm doing a special project for school. It's called My Roots."

She ignored him. He asked slowly, "Do you know how to spell Scandinavian?"

Dolores closed her lap top computer, "I do," she said, "but surely you're not claiming to be Scandinavian?"

"I can," he said defensively. "My Mother was."

"Do tell, I thought she was German. She considered herself a superior race."

With those words John's pulse leapt. This was special news: that Dolores might have known his Mother. Trying to be cool, he inquired, "Where did you see her at? What kind of voice did she have?"

Dolores watched him intently; John tried not to swallow. He wouldn't dare let her think he was nervous. At any moment John expected her to return to her computer and sullenly ignore him. Instead she said casually, "She was a blonde prima donna. Pearls didn't flow from her mouth when she spoke and the earth didn't tremble at her step."

John felt as though she'd jerked the chair out from under him. He wanted to hit her. "I bet my Dad thought she was special."

"Your father's not always as intelligent as he thinks he is."

"I guess I know that," he shot back, "he lets you hang around." To that Dolores surprised him with a burst of laughter. John despised her, with respect; she had known his Mother.

Somebody phoned from San Francisco to tell them Grandmother

Marian had died.

John hadn't seen her since Thanksgiving, two weeks before, when his Dad had driven him to the city to spend the holidays with her. Together he and Grandmother had made pie and cornbread stuffing. They had sung silly songs and played games; they had not gone out.

The school bus dropped John by the ranch mailbox. He checked for mail, but there was nothing. He stepped deliberately into mud holes all the way to the ranch. His two big dogs rushed to greet him, finished covering him with mud. In the driveway, under a cluster of scrub oaks, parked cozily next to his father's truck, was Rosalie's van.

As he passed through the kitchen he mumbled a response to Rosalie's greeting. "That is John, I assume, underneath that blanket of filth? You remind me of Pigpen in the cartoon. You know the one I mean?" Rosalie always tried too hard to be nice.

"Yeah," he muttered. "Where's my Dad?"

"He's on the phone."

John had important things on his mind. He dropped his back pack onto a chair and sat down on the stone hearth of the fireplace where a small fire crackled. He watched Rosalie putter about in the kitchen that overflowed into the family room where he sat. A big window at the back overlooked the barn and corrals. He thought of the window overlooking the street at Grandmother Marian's small apartment. Thinking of her made his eyes sting.

"Rosie," he said pleasantly, crossing to stand before her. "Is there anything I can do to help you?"

"The first thing you can do, my little friend, is clean yourself up." She gave him a big grin.

Rosalie, though a large woman, was always neat. She wore bright colored tent dresses that mostly hid her big bosom and her big bottom.

John washed in the kitchen sink, taking advantage of this time alone with her. He hung back to give her space, so as not to offend her with his dirty clothes. Then he began, hesitantly, "Did you hear the sad news, Rosie? About my Grandmother Marian?"

"Yes, John, your father told me. I'm sorry."

"Yeah," he went on slowly, "I sure would like to go to the rosary."

"Your father said there won't be one." She paused, as if it were of the utmost importance. "She was of a different faith."

"But I need to go to whatever she's gonna have," he spewed nervously and moved closer. He spoke in an intimate tone. "Don't you see, Rosalie? I need to go. I have to go. Will you drive me? I'll give you all the money I've saved."

With one hand Rosalie continued to stir something in a pot; but she stared at him and he knew he had her attention. He plunged on. "Will you, Rosalie? Please. Please."

"When your father comes out we'll discuss it with him. I'm sure when he sees how much it means to you he'll agree. I'd be more than happy to drive you, of course, without your generous offer," and she gave him a sweet smile.

"No. No, you can't tell him. It's our secret. You're always saying how much you want to be my friend. Well, now's your chance."

"Sounds like blackmail, John. You know I can't do something like this behind your father's back."

"Please. Please. Please," he begged, "just this one time. I have to see her just this one time."

"But you can't see her, John," she said severely. "It's to be a closed coffin. A cremation. Do you understand what that means?"

John was beyond patience now. "No, no. Not Marian. Marla. I have to see Marla."

Rosalie looked baffled. "Who is Marla?"

"Her girl." He rushed now, excitedly. "I figure she's sure to be there for her own Mother's thing."

"I see." Rosalie stopped stirring and set the spoon aside.

"Will you, huh? I'll love you for it, Rosie." John took her hand and kissed it loudly.

His father appeared then, behind them. "What's brewing? Devil's soup?" John let go of Rosalie's hand.

"John and I have something important to discuss with you," she said.

"All right." His father glanced from one to the other. "What is this something important?"

"Ask your child."

"Shut up," John shouted.

His father looked startled. "John, stop that kind of talk." To Rosalie, he said, "I've asked you not to refer to him as a child."

Rosalie's voice quavered. "You act as if he's a barroom buddy. Except he doesn't have the privileges of a buddy. And you won't let him be a child. It's time to decide which he's to be, because the child needs a mother."

"I don't need her," he shouted, "I just wanna look at her."

John woke long before dawn. It was cold and his throat hurt when he swallowed.

He had apologized to Rosalie, but he'd refused to eat dinner. Now he felt weak and drained of defiance. But he had no time for food or repentance. He dressed hurriedly in his heavy jacket and a wool cap, stuffing all his allowances and gift money into his pockets. When he was safely out of the house, he put on his boots, whispering to the dogs to be still. Rapidly he crossed the same muddy fields he'd covered the day before. He reached the edge of town just as the sky turned lemon-grey.

At the small Greyhound bus depot John panicked. Although he was tall for ten and could pass for older, the man behind the counter eyed him suspiciously. Then, dismissively, he sold him a one-way ticket to San Francisco. On the bus John felt sick to his stomach. He tried not to think about what he was doing, or what he would do if Marla was not there. He thought of his father, of what he would do when he found him gone. He would go to his school, enter the classroom, his black eyes searching, towering above everyone, running his hands through his black hair. John had refused to talk to him about "the problem," shouting, "Leave me alone," before storming off to his room. But now John was seized by a sharp longing for his father, such as he'd never known before, a longing equal to his fear of the unknown.

The bus groaned as it struggled into the traffic and fog of San Francisco. At last, with a sigh, it halted. John waited for the other passengers to depart before he stood.

Then with the uncertain courage of a soldier who enters battle for the first time, John trudged forward.

Aisle of Death

By Nanci Lee Woody

One tiny pill daily kept Winnie's blood from clotting normally. Bruises appeared mysteriously on her body. Her nose bled profusely with the slightest sneeze. Yet, as George reminded her, she was better off than the neighbor's elderly mother, suffering from dementia and sitting alone under a tree in the back yard with a tiger-striped cat, seemingly her only companion, on her lap.

"Ready to go outside, Win? It's a lovely evening."

George poured wine, took Winnie's hand and, as they stepped onto the patio, an ugly but familiar scene greeted them. The neighbor's muscle-bound mutt slammed against the fence, barked unceasingly. Winnie touched her forehead. "I can't take this again."

Alone, George watched the dog bare its fangs, growl ferociously until a hand yanked at the collar. "Everything's OK, boy. Daddy's here."

"Everything is not OK, 'Daddy'," George screamed. "My wife had a stroke last year and can't even relax in her own yard because of your crazy mutt."

"He's a rescue dog," the neighbor yelled. "He can't help it."

"Can't help it? What's wrong with you?"

"Nothing's wrong with me. He's afraid of strangers."

"I'm not a stranger, you idiot. I live here."

"You're an intolerant asshole!"

Red-faced, George sputtered, "And you're the neighbor from hell." The dog bared its teeth, snarled viciously.

"You've got to avoid stress," the doctor told Winnie. "Find a soothing hobby." Winnie took up bird watching, sat in the back yard with her binoculars and field guide.

Her favorite was the California Quail, with their little hats—the cutest birds in the world. They scurried along the ground, babies trailing behind, taking refuge in the rockroses at the yard's edge.

So like today, with the dog inside and binoculars in hand, she relaxed in her lawn chair and breathed deeply. But her reverie was immediately truncated when she heard a cacophony of bird squawks. "Oh, no!" Her head jerked around to see that tiger-striped cat, belly close to the ground, head thrust forward, tail twitching, ID tag dangling.

Winnie bolted out of her chair, raised her arms, flapped her hands. "Sssssss. Go away." The cat stayed in its attack mode.

Winnie heard a "gobble gobble gobble," saw two hens trailed by fluffy chicks enter the yard.

Winnie rushed toward the cat. "Get out of here. Ssssssss. Get!" The cat did not move, crouched lower.

Winnie picked up a rock and threw it. It missed, and brazen, the cat stayed put, tail twitching.

"Damn you." She thought about the billions of birds that cats slaughter each year, picked up another, bigger rock, took aim and flung it as hard as she could. The cat didn't make a sound when the rock clunked into the ground nearby right before it slipped to safety through the fence.

That evening, George remarked the cat was present every day, that he hadn't considered it a problem in comparison to the dog.

After Winnie gave him a long discourse about the killer nature of cats, she looked into the eyes of her husband. "If there hadn't been an altercation with the neighbor, I could appeal to him, couldn't I?"

"You think he'd care about your birds?" George scoffed. "That jerk couldn't tell a sea gull from a blue jay." He lowered his voice. "But he could identify a dead cat."

"What are you saying?"

"It's outlawed now, but I've got some left over d-CON in the garage. All you have to do is mix it with cat food, and Bam! Cat's dead."

The next day, Winnie scattered birdseed and watched the quail mom and dad with eleven chicks emerge from the rockroses. She focused her binoculars, instantly saw a flash of grey, heard the distinctive sounds of bird distress fill the air, watched the cat pounce into the midst of the quail family. Winnie, heart pounding, chased after the cat only to see it, chick hanging limp in its jaws, drop the dead bird at the old woman's feet.

Now the sounds of distress came from Winnie.

The Home Depot sales associate's nametag identified him, ironically she thought, as 'Tom Ferrell'.

"What do you have to kill a large rodent?" she asked. "How large?"

"Well, like a raccoon." She held out her arms to show how big.

"Follow me to the Aisle of Death," Tom said. "We have lots of final solutions." He led her past the weed killers, traps for bees and gophers, and ant and bedbug poisons.

"These here are glue traps," he confided. "Rats step onto the surface and that's the last step they'll take. Feet stuck."

"Well, what then?" Winnie asked.

"It's up to you, Lady, what you do at that point."

Winnie winced. "What are my other options?"

"It would help," Tom said, "if I knew exactly what rodent it is you're wanting to kill."

Winnie hesitated before she said, quietly, "A fat, feral cat."

"Wild cats aren't usually fat, ma'am. And a cat's not exactly a raccoon, now is it?" He waited for a response he didn't get. "To answer your question about options, I'd suggest you buy a large trap like this here, capture the cat, and haul it off to the pound. That'd be about $90 with tax."

"Ninety dollars! I don't have that kind of money to spend on a trap I'd use one time."

"Well, then, since money's a concern," Tom said, "we have your grandmother's old-fashioned, inexpensive rat traps. You put a little peanut butter on this spot right here, and thwack!, this part of the trap crashes down over the rat's head. Breaks its neck."

"But would that kill a cat?" Winnie asked.

"The traps are designed for rats, which are smaller than cats, aren't they? So I can't rightly say," Tom answered.

Winnie stepped closer to him, spoke in a near whisper. "Do you know about d-CON?"

"It's a pretty potent anticoagulant, Lady." He put his hands over his stomach, closed his eyes, tipped his head to one side before he went on. "Once a rat eats it, it'll slowly bleed to death. Internally." He opened his eyes, looked at Winnie. "A lot of the old d-CON products are outlawed for sale. Rats are now protected by the government."

Winnie glanced at the dark blue bruises on her own hands, clasped them behind her back.

Later, Winnie pressed the microphone icon on her cell phone. "Siri. What's the best way to kill a cat?"

"Let me check that. OK. I found this on the web," Siri answered.

There was a website for the cage-like traps Tom Ferrell had mentioned. The downside to the cages, besides the expense, was, if left in the sun, the captured cat could fry, dehydrate, suffer terribly.

Another website pointed out that poisons don't always work on larger animals. The best way to do away with a cat? In short, shoot it.

Checking the website for the Society for the Prevention of Cruelty to Animals, she decided she couldn't call SPCA because they'd surely contact the neighbor who would seek revenge on George.

A reviewer on one cat-killing website wrote, "Cat's ancestors are lions and tigers, so naturally they kill. They keep the mice population down, so why not accept them as they've evolved?"

But Winnie could not accept that cats were thriving with the help of their humans while many bird species were declining precipitously.

The final article she read confirmed that Tom Ferrell was right. Some forms of d-CON were outlawed by the government with the support of her favorite wildlife organizations because anticoagulants were found in 70 percent of dead wildlife tested.

Winnie couldn't sleep. She imagined a hawk eating a d-CONned rat and suffering a slow, painful death itself. She hoped a poisoned cat would be too big to be nabbed by a hawk or an owl. But what if she was wrong?

She thought of the quail chick, hanging limp in the cat' s jaws and realized her birds would never be safe as long as the irresponsible neighbor let his cat roam free, so it was either the cat or the birds.

She got up. On a paper plate, she carefully mixed more d-CON pellets than recommended with cat food. "Bam! Cat's dead," George promised. She placed the poison concoction by the back door. If she felt the same way in the morning, she'd set the plate in the back yard by the rockroses.

Winnie took her own anticoagulant pill. "d-CON for humans," she thought. Visions of unstoppable internal bleeding flitted through her mind when she returned to bed. She hoped the tiger-striped cat would die quickly, wouldn't suffer at her hands. She thought of the helpless turkey and quail chicks, the rapidly declining songbird population. She pictured in her mind the neighbor's elderly mother who nobody except the cat paid any attention to.

She could not sleep.

Sixty and Sacked

By Lawrence Pratt

Dave Burk pulled into his usual spot in the firm's parking lot and, as his brain shifted out of "commute mode", found himself deep in thought. "Sixty years," he spoke to an otherwise empty car, "and nearly ten years with the firm," the latter milestone tinged with a tone of regret that he knew was growing by the day. But the recent Independence Day weekend with his family celebrating both the holiday and his birthday on the 4th put a bit more spirit in him.

Having time away from "the digs" on his special day was always a plus.

Dave reflected on his sixty trips around the sun—he was the first male in the family to make it this far. Poor longevity was the scourge of the Burk male line.

Exiting the vehicle, Dave made an unhurried walk to the firm's Silicon Valley headquarters security door. He made the best of a convenient flex-time policy and was usually the first one in the parking lot, beating heavy traffic in the process.

Dave worked as a technical writer and trainer, and carried the title of Staff Logistics Specialist. He made no apologies about having successfully avoided any formal management position and was considered by many as a dependable "old salt."

Once inside, he was greeted by the night shift security guard, Colin Adams. "Morning, Dave," Colin said. "How was the long weekend?"

"Pretty nice, Colin," Dave replied. "How was yours?"

"Pulled a couple of double shifts so some of the younger guys could spend time with their families. Gonna take some down time when I get off at eight."

"Well, enjoy time off while you can get it," Dave remarked.

"Always," Adams responded. "By the way, the first pot of coffee is brewing."

"Thanks, I'll get some decaf going in a bit," Dave commented, making his way to his cubicle.

As Dave began his routine of loading e-mail and making the decaf, he couldn't help but feel resentment towards the firm in its outsourcing for Security and Facilities.

"This damned place has more money than God," he muttered, "and the suits won't spring for decent wages and benefits for these people. Retirement won't come too soon."

Settled at his desk, Dave slogged through his e-mail, not really looking forward to the day. There was always at least one unpleasant fire to put out and usually more after a long weekend.

If it wasn't for the last minute, nothing would ever get done around here, he mused.

Among the missives, Burk was pleasantly surprised to find no fires to put out and not even a routine project to start. With the end of the calendar half hitting just before the long weekend, sales had worked the staff like rented mules to squeeze maximum billings by June 30. Things were still quiet and it looked like he was going to get a free ride through the first day or two of the week. The only odd thing in the mail queue was a newly scheduled teleconference with the department director at the home office out of state—an event to be held in one of the firm's conference rooms instead of everyone simply monitoring things at their desk. Dave always preferred the latter option as he could mute his headphone mike and catch up on Facebook and personal e-mails, largely ignoring the mindless drone of PowerPoint.

It looked like he had another two hours or so of dead time before the nine o'clock unknown. It gave him a chance to meander the building and do a little socializing with some of the engineers and IT gurus.

By 8:30, the other three members of Dave's team arrived, read the e-mail about the teleconference, and "replied-to-all" with their acceptance. Like Burk, none of them had received assignments for the new quarter. This was far from the norm and speculative tension spread through the group.

"So," asked Deb Thomson, the site's team lead, "anyone think they're going to shut us down and outsource our work to other offices?"

This was the worst-case scenario for the local group but all had long known it was a distinct possibility that the four had often discussed. It would be a lot cheaper for the firm to close the local group and farm things out to Texas or India. It was an all too common Valley story.

"Well," chimed in Sue Twist, "it's only twenty minutes to 'post time' so we'll know soon."

"So, does everyone know the basic rule of getting laid off?" asked Pria Khoa, the group's jokester.

"No," Dave replied with a roll of his eyes, "but I'm sure you can't wait to tell us."

"On your way out the door, grab all the toilet paper you can carry and anything you can sell on eBay," she replied with a grin.

It was enough to lighten the group's mood for the next few minutes. Entering the conference room, they noticed Steve Jacks, head of local human resources, standing by a desk with a small stack of identical portfolios. The words "good morning" emanated from the teleconference screen and everyone looked to see the face of Barbara Jenkins, their director in Texas. They all knew this was the end of their time with the firm.

"Oh, crap," Dave said out loud, not caring who heard him. "We're screwed." Given his recent thoughts about the firm, the old adage "be careful what you wish for" flashed through his mind.

Every tech worker in Silicon Valley knew the environment – you either have been laid off or will be laid off. It was more certain than Moore's Law. The most important question was, what's in the severance package?

Despite this knowledge, each of the four experienced a few seconds of personal panic and attempted to process the inevitable that their time at the firm was over.

From this point forward, it was human resources' job to get the termination portfolios processed and the people packed up and out the door as quickly as possible. Not always an easy task.

The four quickly accepted their collective fate, some with a bit more composure than others. Despite her glibness of less than thirty minutes ago, Pria's eyes welled with tears and she began to quietly cry.

For Dave, it was a time of quick number crunching. Sixty and sacked – just about the worst timing for getting laid off in an area that had little more than a thinly veiled contempt for anyone over forty.

No matter what was in the severance package, it would never be enough to carry him to full retirement or Medicare, two milestones he had only vaguely thought about until now. Even early Social Security was two years away and taking that step would be the first move to an impoverished retirement–not a viable option. In contrast to Pria's reaction, Dave felt under siege.

Only Deb Thompson offered a terse comment.

"We've given the firm some of our best years and it comes down to a small stack of termination folders. It's a crappy deal," she concluded as she faced Jenkins' face on the screen.

"Yes, it is a crappy deal," Jenkins acknowledged, "but we all know it's part and parcel of any job in Valley tech. Now, the sooner we move through this unpleasantness, the sooner we can all move forward."

"Your 'unpleasantness' is our major life upheaval," Thompson snapped. "Be warned that I'll be looking for any deficiencies in the severance paperwork that gives me an excuse to sue," she challenged. "Now, we can move forward."

The director and HR rep had expected this and stayed on script. Barbara and Steve knew the next hour or so would be the worst of the year for them but it was just part of the job. Each of the four assumed a seat at the conference table and received their packages. It was Jack's turn to speak.

"Despite any feelings the four of you might have, the severance package is much better than most in the Valley. Overall, you'll be continued on the payroll regarding pay and benefits through the end of September. Effective October 1, you'll each receive a cash payout equivalent to one week's pay for each year of employment, company paid COBRA medical through the end of the year, and full vesting of any outstanding stock. Now, let's go through the packages in more detail."

Over the next hour, the group slogged through the process with a few more questions and more than a few more tears. When it was over, they returned to their cubicles to pack up their personal possessions. During the conference, facilities had dropped off packing boxes for each now "former employee." As they packed, the group made sure each had the others' e-mail addresses and phone numbers as well as promising to stay in touch, network, and provide references for one another. While they'd soon be competing for the same jobs, life in the tech world was better if you didn't make any enemies.

Clearing out, Dave was amazed at the unused junk he found stuffed in the back of his desk drawers. He, like the others, threw out more than he boxed up. In the end, his decade with the firm fit into two small cartons.

Burk held off calling his wife until things were final and he was literally out the door. He wasn't sure how the conversation would go and didn't want to add this to the already unhappy atmosphere in the building.

Shortly before noon, the four were little more than administrative memories to the firm as they said their goodbyes in the parking lot. It was then that Dave called his wife who was getting close to her lunch break.

"Laid off?" Cathy Burk asked in disbelief at the news. "What do you mean 'laid off'?"

"You know—canned, axed, terminated, sacked, kicked to the curb," he replied in slight bemusement at his wife's shock and disbelief.

"How could this happen?" she asked, knowing full well such things happened all time but not to them. A successful technical editor in her own right, Cathy and Dave had always moved upward in their profession. This was a first layoff for the couple.

"Standard operating procedure around here," Dave replied. He went on to tell Cathy about the details of the severance package. "We've been lucky to dodge this bullet as long as we have."

"Yeah, I know," Cathy remarked, slowly accepting what couldn't be changed. "So, let's meet for lunch and start cobbling together a Plan B. I'll take the rest of the day off and we can get our bearings. With the solid severance package, unemployment, and my continued income, we'll have some bumps but I don't see any need to panic."

"Done. How about our usual spot and you buy?"

"Deal, my impoverished and unemployed husband," Cathy said. "See you in fifteen."

Dave loaded the boxes into the trunk of his car, a thousand to-do items firing through his brain–update the resume, set up accounts on various job sites, maybe even training in the newest skill sets. This last item would be a must as ten years with the firm had left him with a somewhat parochial and company-specific set of skills that he was certain would not be an ideal fit for the demands of what awaited him. This change would be difficult but not impossible. The cruise the couple had planned for fall of next year was definitely off the table.

As he closed the trunk of the car, Burk focused on the two boxes. All this time and so little to take out the door. But, he reflected, maybe the most important things of the past ten years couldn't be packed in a box.

Strangely, his biggest regret at the moment was that he never had a chance to say goodbye to Colin Adams.

The Once and Future Queen

By Carolyn Donnell

Roanna stared into the flames from the stone hearth at the hunting lodge. Streams of light spread across the shadowy floor. Recurring images played before her eyes. She was riding her favorite white stallion, her unbound chestnut hair flowing in the wind. The groomsman from the royal stables watched from afar. The flames flickered and the scene changed to the bedroom inside the lodge. She watched as her pale lithe body  intertwined with the darker, sinewy limbs and raven locks of the groomsman. They twisted and turned together in the fluid movements of lovemaking.

Roanna blinked, breaking the spell. It had been a vision in the flame long enough. Today it would become reality. She stood up and unbound her braids. Auburn-gold tresses cascaded down her back, past her waist. Bits of silver and gold woven into her silken robe caught the light from the fire as she placed one hand on the mantel and turned toward the door.

"Enter," she answered to the knock. The door opened. A smile slipped past her lips as the black-haired groomsman stepped inside.

Owain entered, his head bowed. He was an obedient servant, at least to Roanna, his Queen. She was considered their rightful ruler, not her husband, the usurper who only sat on the throne because of his forced marriage to the Queen. Owain had been sent to the castle by his uncle for knight's training. His family, only slightly lower in rank than Roanna's, was related to hers through his maternal great- grandmother and the Queen's great-grandfather, the high King Albion himself.

"Owain." Roanna's voice sounded hoarse as she spoke his name.

Owain kept his kept his eyes on the floor. "My Queen," he said softly. He had been hesitant to make this journey of obedience. While it was obvious to anyone who knew him that he had been in love with Roanna since his first sight of her, she was still Queen and he, only a subject.

"Owain." The Roanna's voice rose, more insistent.

Owain raised his eyes. The flickering firelight behind the Queen reflected throughout her hair and spread a glowing aura around her. He stood speechless in her presence. His queen. No. She was more than a queen, she was a goddess. And she had called for him.

Roanna moved toward the massive canopied bed.

Owain found himself still rooted to the floor, frozen in fascination.

"Owain." This time the sound was more like a kitten's purr. With her back to the bed, she unclasped the jeweled brooch that held the front of her robe together, revealing a glimpse of bare breasts and a triangle of red-gold curls.

Owain found his feet and hastened toward her. "My Queen," he whispered. He took her chin gently in his hand and lifted her face toward his

"Owain, my name is Roanna." She shuddered as she leaned into the kiss.

Her apricot-tinged fragrance permeated his senses. His uncle's warnings fled into the firelight.

Roanna's robe fluttered to the floor. Owain's clothing followed. He threw the coverlet off the bed in one motion. Their bodies melted onto each other's.

Roanna's firelight vision became reality.

BOOM! The massive wooden door shook the room as it hit the wall. Owain jerked back from Roanna, but before he could retreat, the King's guards were upon them. One swift slice of shining steel separated the couple. Owain rolled to the floor, trailing his lifeblood as he fell.

The swordsman sneered at the sight, then looked back at the Queen, who had drawn the bloodstained covers around her naked body and retreated to the far corner of the expansive bed. "If it were up to me," he snarled, "you would follow him now, but my master has other plans for you." He spat on the bed as he wiped his sword on the silk covers. Without another word, he turned and left. The room shook once more as the door slammed shut.

Roanna heard the sound of a key in the lock. She threw the covers aside and leapt to the floor.

Cradling Owain's head in her hands, she cried out, "Owain, don't leave me."

His eyelids fluttered. He gurgled, "Cooo...lea-an," and slumped into oblivion.

Roanna's cry rose to a wail. She threw herself on his lifeless body. As his blood seeped into her skin, she thought of the dagger in the drawer of the table beside her bed. Perhaps it would be best if she joined Owain now. Her impatience to be with him had given her husband, the King, an excuse to be rid of her. She had betrayed her people for a moment of desire—a heavy blow to the carefully laid plans to rid the kingdom of the hateful tyrant who ruled over them. Roanna sobbed in despair.

A massive stone by the fireplace slid silently to one side. A tall figure in a hooded robe came through the opening, followed by a maiden, the Queen's lady-in-waiting.

The hooded figure motioned toward the bed. The maiden grabbed the quilted coverlet and rushed to Roanna. She tried to pull the Queen from the limp corpse.

"Come now, my lady," she whispered in the Queen's ear.

"No," Roanna moaned.

"Come away. There's nothing you can do for him now. You must come away. Look. I've brought a friend."

Roanna turned her head to one side and saw the slippers, then the robe and finally the painted blue face staring down at her. "Cuileann," she gasped the high priest's name, frantically wrapping the quilt around her naked body.

The priest knelt down and placed his fingers on Owain's throat. Shaking his head, he motioned to the lady-in-waiting to bring another coverlet from the trunk by the bed. With Owain's body encased, the priest carried the body back through the passage behind the hearth and down a dark hallway lined on one side with cubicles covered with heavy velvet curtains. After placing the body in one of the cubicles, he continued to the end of the hall, where a slit in the tower wall allowed a glimpse of the courtyard below.

Cuileann gazed at the low jade-colored mountains that rose behind the field. Their ancient homeland, now ruled by the usurper, spread out before him like an ocean of green. A sigh shook his body. As he had feared, Roanna had not been patient. She had inherited her grandfather's looks and his pride, but not his wisdom. Now the plans would have to be accelerated. He hoped fate would be on their side. Back in the chamber, he slipped a packet of herbs to the maiden and motioned to the jug of water.

Roanna awoke to the sound of trumpets in the distance. She sat up in bed and found her lady-in-waiting sitting quietly nearby.

"What ... " Roanna started to protest.

"Shhh." The maid put her finger to her lips and then pointed to the foot of the bed where Roanna's royal blue gown was draped. "Hurry. Time is short."

The trumpets sounded again, announcing the opening of the games. "Why?" Roanna started her question again.

"The games have been moved up to today."

Roanna jumped at the deep voice of the high priest. She gazed at the imposing figure and then nodded. This was all her fault. She hoped they were ready.

The threesome slipped through the secret passageway and down to the arena. The knights met Roanna at the southern gate. Today they would declare her Queen in her own right before the people, as ancient custom dictated. If the people approved, they would banish the usurper according to law. Armed soldiers loyal to her and the ancient bloodline waited in the wings.

The gates opened. Another trumpet sounded. Roanna, mounted on her white stallion, accompanied the royal procession into the enclosure. The people rose to their feet in cheering approval. Roanna smiled, waving to her subjects.

When they were a third of the way across the arena, the East and West gates slammed open simultaneously. The King's soldiers poured in, their dark horses stomping and snorting, ready for battle. Roanna had been betrayed.

The cheers of the crowd turned to screams. The people tried to run, but found the exits barred by more of the King's mercenaries. The sounds of clashing metal rose to a fevered pitch. One squire lifted the Queen from her mount and onto his horse only a second ahead of a piercing sword. The two escaped as far as the stables.

Roanna slid down and looked back at the squire. His face was expressionless as he slumped in his saddle and fell in slow motion to the ground. He had taken the blow that was intended for her. Twice in one day someone else's blood had covered the Queen.

The roar of the slaughter grew louder. Roanna looked out between the cracks in the stable door. Peasants, dirty and ragged even in their clothes for the games, were trying to flee. She glanced around, the taste of terror rising in her throat.

Then she heard the sound, a high whistle soaring over the din of destruction. As she listened, the air in the stall began to pulsate. The word "Peasant" came clearly into her mind. Her grandfather's last words to her, many years ago, rang in her ears.

"You must become as your subjects. Only then can you be a true queen." Roanna stared distastefully at the layer of filth at the bottom of the stable. "No," she cried aloud. "I am Queen."

The howls from the massacre outside grew louder. She hadn't thought she would ever have to take her grandfather's advice so literally, but on this dismal day she understood that poverty, and even filth, would be the only safe disguise.

Quickly, she tore off her royal trappings and retrieved her dagger from the pocket of her cape.

The high-pitched sound continued to ring in her ears as she removed her dress and ripped her undergarments and then chopped off her long flowing hair. She thrust the bundle of garments and hair under the hay at the back of the stall and gathered handfuls of mud, manure, and straw, rubbing the noxious mixture all over.

The whistling sound stopped. Roanna looked up from her grimy task. An image of the high priest flickered next to the door. His right hand pointed up toward the North. Roanna looked out the door of the stall. A roaring sound preceded a swell of fleeing peasants and farmers. She lowered her head, threw a horse blanket around her to further hide any remnant of royal attire, slipped into the crowd.

Suddenly the air began to shimmer around her. She felt her body tugged upwards, away from her people and her land. She floated briefly in the air above the scene of destruction. The velocity of the magnetic pull increased, and she found herself being sucked down a long corridor of light.

Cuileann watched through the crystal. Roanna had failed the first test. Her desire, pride, and lack of patience had subverted their goals. They lost the battle that day. He watched darkness creep over the land and had started to look away when a silver edge of hope appeared. He watched Roanna discard her royal robes, whack off her own glorious hair, and spread filth on what was left. She had overcome her regal pride then, enough to escape this world. Cuileann breathed a sigh of relief. Roanna had a long way to go, but she had taken the first step.

He continued to watch the struggle and saw the winding road ahead. He couldn't see the end of that road, or what lay in between, but he knew now that Roanna would be high Queen again. Some time, in some future world, when she was ready, when she had mastered the lessons she needed to learn, he would beckon her home, to her rightful place and Owain would join her there.

But it would not be today.

Sophia

By Jarmila Skalna

Sophia had a relatively smooth life in America and had confidence in herself, never hesitated to do anything just because, at first glance, it looked as though it would not work out. She did take one big risk when she opened a small café in San Francisco without knowing how to cook. She decided to make sandwiches, but as the weeks went by, fewer and fewer people came, and she didn't know what was wrong. One customer told her that she was putting too much mustard between the slices of bread, and people could not swallow them. So, she started putting in less mustard, and people started coming back.

Now, in retirement, she found satisfaction in helping a few families with cleaning and with their pets.

We were good friends and one Sunday morning, she called me, very upset.

"Could you help me out? I'm in the hospital."

I jumped at her words. "What happened?"

"A cat bit my leg."

"How come?"

"The neighbor's cat likes to come to my patio every day and eats all the food I put out for my cat. When I tried to push her away with my foot, she bit me, and my leg got badly infected.

Tomorrow, I'm supposed to help a woman with her thirteen cats. Obviously, I can't go there, but I don't want to lose this good job."

"Do you call taking care of thirteen cats a good job?"

"It's easier than taking care of thirteen people, I guess."

"I'm not so sure." Nevertheless, she soon had me promising that I would substitute for her with the thirteen cats.

The next morning, I drove to the northern part of town. Following a narrow street up a hill, I arrived at a beige house, where a woman in a long white medical coat opened the door for me. A pale baby in a pack on her back observed me with curiosity. Without a word, the woman led me to a spacious garage on the side of the house. From high atop their wooden perches, the cat's eyes watched me suspiciously. I felt my face turning porcelain white. Sophia had told me that the lady was a veterinarian and tranquilized the cats with drugs. These were wild beasts briefly transformed into housebroken kitties with the touch of a needle every morning.

I was beginning to doubt my old belief that friendship with animals is better than friendship with people.

One black cat made a strange sound as she arched her back. A scream formed in my throat, and then escaped. The woman appeared with her expressionless face, and I caught a glimpse of her baby lolling its head apathetically. The woman coolly observed the situation, and then, without warning, a ghastly roar burst from her throat. I felt the heat rising in my stomach. The cats jumped briskly over me, leaping and pouncing. They darted through the open door and disappeared into the tall golden savannah behind the house. If someone had taken a picture of me right then, my chin would have reached the middle of my chest.

After cleaning up the emptied-out kingdom, I ran from the crazy household straight to the hospital.

"Sophia," I said, "I can't do that job anymore. It scares me to death. I'm beginning to believe that those cats are not far removed from wild lions." Sophia's thin lips curled into a wan smile. She pushed down her blanket, revealing a bony right leg that ended in a mottled purple-black ankle.

"Oh, my God!" I cried. "Your leg is turning black. It looks awful!"

"That's why I've decided to go home. Here they just sit back and watch me die, doing nothing. They've even started talking about amputation."

"Amputation!" My voice was quivering.

"I need you to go to one more place tomorrow," Sophia said. "There's a very sick young woman. Her name is Andrea. She and her six parrots need help."

"What will I do with her six parrots?"

"Clean their cages and give them food and water. Taking care of birds is easier than taking care of cats." As she started to move her leg back under the cover, she hissed, "My God, this is painful!" I left her with tears in her eyes.

The next morning, I drove forty minutes to Andrea's apartment building, which was at the edge of a lagoon. When I got there, I took the elevator to the third floor and rang the bell.

Nobody answered. I tried the door, and finding that it was open. I walked in. In the heavy air, Andrea was lying in a bed like a heap of mud. Her parrots were sitting around on a white bedspread like eager children. Andrea slowly raised her pale white hands, and the parrots landed on her swollen arms. She brought them closer to her face and kissed their dull beaks. Then she smiled silently and closed her eyes. While she slept, I opened the window, and the parrots flew out, following the call of a faraway drummer. They circled the lagoon and then returned, reminding me of the pair of orioles that had been coming to my garden for the last five springs. They always came to the same bush, carrying its red berries away to their nest in a tall spruce nearby.

I did my work quietly and let Andrea sleep. When I left, her parrots were also sleeping, but now in clean cages, which I covered with dark blankets.

When I got to the hospital, Sophia was not in her bed. A nurse explained, "She was a very stubborn woman. She signed the release papers and called a taxi to go home."

When I got to her house, I found Sophia crawling on all fours.

"I am not going to let them cut off my leg!" she said. "I've been soaking it every hour in very hot salt water and it feels better."

I cooked dinner for her that night. As I left, I promised that I would go to Andrea's place again.

Surprisingly, when I arrived the next morning, a woman welcomed me at the door who told me she was Andrea's mother. She talked quickly, her hands darting to-and-fro as she knitted a blue sweater. She had adopted Andrea when the girl was five years old, she said, and was always proud of how smart Andrea was in college. She pointed to two framed diplomas on the wall. But now, at thirty-five and sinking fast, her daughter and six parrots were too much trouble and too much money. The mother was going to take her back to New York.

I did my work and said goodbye to the women, taking the parrots with me in a cage to Sophia's house.

"Jesus!" Sophia shouted, covering her mouth with both hands when she saw the birds. "I've just saved my leg, and now you want to give me birds!"

"I'm sorry," I said.

Sophia opened a window to let the six parrots fly out. They never returned.

The Whaleships Lost Boat

By David Hirzel

May 18, 1843. On board the whaling ship Rachel, below the equator in the vast Pacific Ocean, two thousand miles west of Chile. Two young seamen are talking between themselves.

"The captain was right to pick up the three boats to windward. Three boats would have been lost to the night, maybe forever. Three boats, fifteen men. Some of the best."

"They were to windward. The fourth boat to leeward. He could have picked up that one in a trice, and gone for the others."

"Not in a trice, and you know it. A matter of hours to find it—you know we'd lost sight. A matter of hours, then beat to windward for the other three. Night would have fallen before—if ever—they were picked up. Your ought to know better. We shipped at the same time, same age. Boys we were then, men now. And yet you think yourself better able to judge things than the captain. The mate."

"Perhaps. Maybe. Maybe the wind would have turned."

"This is a whaleship. We don't trade in maybes. 'Tis hard enough to deal with the vagaries and troubles that we have."

"We'll never find that fourth boat now. Five good men and a boy. The captain's own son. His youngest."

"That's as may be. We've fifteen aboard now, that would not have been had we followed your course."

"Fifteen to the good, five to the lost. A hard bargain. Not one I would have wanted to strike."

"So be it. And so be it. Hush. I'm done talking about it."

In truth there was nothing more to be said in the matter. Thank God the first mate had spoken sense to Captain Gardiner. "'Tis the only thing, sir," he had said. The captain had gambled on a cruel covenant and had lost. Three boats—his own son in the third—he had sent a-rowing to windward, after a pod of whales sighted three miles off. Were the whales well-struck, there might have been thirty barrels of oil for the ship. A good bargain, that, there for the taking.

When a fourth whale showed to leeward, a white one, and sparm a that, it was an easy sail for the reserve boat to get within striking range. "Lower away the reserve," he had said, and put his own second son in it, the better to teach him the trade. Peter was but a boy, barely twelve years of age.

The boat sailed off, struck the whale, or so it seemed from the ship. There was a flurry, a chase. In the turmoil neither boat nor whale was to be seen. That was not an uncommon thing, but once out of sight there would be time to run them down.

The Captain Gardiner had made his Nantucketer deal with the devil, and been handed a choice of his own making. Which son to save, and which to leave to his fate? Peter, or Thomas? He prayed for guidance, but

God answered him not. It was the first mate who spoke the only wisdom. "You must save the most, who you can."

And so the Rachel began her tortured twisting route, tacking this way and that to windward. Before the tropic night closed over her for good, she had the tree boats, their crews, and the captain's son, Thomas, safely back on board. She cut loose the three fast whales and their thirty barrels each of good sperm oil to the sharks and the seabirds, turned on her heel and with all canvas flying sped to windward, eastward into the starlit night toward the spot where the reserve boat had last been seen. On deck her try-pots burned hot and bright on strips of blubber, a beacon to the missing men. Behind her, a broadening ribbon of black velvet between the two slowing streams of phosphorescent light that marked her wake across the Indian Ocean.

In time the sky ahead grew brighter, roseate and golden light spreading quickly, and the brilliant sun leapt into the undiminished sky.

"All hands off-watch, into the tops wi' ye! All of ye." The mate's voice betrayed no undue urgency, for once no anger. It had no need of such. Every man and boy was keen to spot the reserve boat. She must be still afloat, somewhere nearby, waiting to be picked up.

"Look there! Three points the starboard bow, about a half mile!" All heads turned, but only a few eyes saw.

"I think not," said one to his shipmate, in a low voice lest he be heard and called a doomsayer.

"Lower away!" and off went the boat, all oars straining, hither and yon as the signals flew from the Rachel's maintop, calling for the lost reserve boat. But no answer came. A night and a morning had passed, and many miles west and then back east, since she had last been spoke. There was no knowing at all if the ship had come back to the right place. Or not.

"Sail ho!" 'Twas true. There was another ship cruising these seas, a good six miles to windward.

By the look of her, another Nantucketer. The mate called from the deck, "All hands make all sail! Lively now! The helm, make for yonder whaleman!" A rattle of lines in the blocks and stu'nsail booms through the irons, a flutter of canvas unfurled, and the Rachel turned eastward again, gathering speed as she went, coming abreast the stranger in half an hour.

"Lower away!" Number two boat with the captain in it closed the gap quickly. A voice came across the water from the stranger.

"Hast seen the white whale?" In answer Captain Gardner sprang to the chainplates of the Pequod and climbed to the deck of that ship, there to be seen in earnest conversation with her captain, gesturing wide sweeping motions with his arms, holding out his hands in entreaty.

He had gone to ask the Pequod's aid in searching for the Rachel's lost boat, that the two ships might sweep the seas in tandem two more days before, if they must, abandoning the search.

Captain Gardiner received his answer. One did not need to hear the words to know that his pleadings had been denied. Visibly he crumbled, turned, climbed back down the chains, and fell rather than jumped into his boat.

The Pequod loosed her sails and sped away. The Rachel resumed her search, alone, probing the open sea under the unrelenting sun, chasing at shadows and combers, ever-hopeful for a time not for a whale to strike, but her lost boat for to find.

An hour after the second day's dawning, a shout came from aloft. "A boat!"

"Where away?"

"Three points the starboard bow!"

From the deck, "I see it not."

Another voice, aloft. "No boat, but something made by the hand of man and not God."

The mate cried, "Aloft! All eyes one it, whatever it may be! I swear the man that loses it will be a dead man to me." The breeze would not favor the Rachel. "Heave to! Lower away number two." No further orders were required.

The captain wanted to go in her. "Captain, if I may. Stand by. Make not your living son an orphan. And should we save the one that was lost, let him be reunited with his own father." No further words were needed.

Sharp eyes on deck made out a many, a living man, half dragged and half climbing into the distant boat. "He lives!" The stoop went out of the old man's spine. "They're towing something along behind, something in the water. 'Tis no boat... "

Eager hands pulled the man up onto the deck, hauled him aft, laid him out still breathing over the grating in the shade of the awning. He was not the captain's son. He was the lone survivor of the wreck of the Pequod stove in and sunk by the white whale. He had floated these two days not in a boat, but on a coffin.

Yes, a coffin.

Superstition plagues the whalemen. "Shall we bring his coffin aboard, sir, or let it float until it sinks, perhaps to lie beside whatever man it is intended for?"

Either was a bad choice. To sail with a coffin must surely bring ill-luck, death and shipwreck to the vessel that ships it. As it had plainly done to the Pequod. Or, cast loose and freed from its intended purpose, it might drift forever. Never to be recovered by the ship that set it afloat, and so haunt her and her men forever. In either case, for the Rachel, there would be no escape.

Another bad bargain with the devil, and however the hand plays out, no good can come of it.

Once again the captain heeded his mate's advice, sound as it must be, the least of two evils. At the very least it might save one more, as it had already saved one man, should the need arise. A combined luck, ill for the loss of the ship, and good for the seaman who might be saved. As this one from the lost ship will be, and those of the missing reserve boat will not.

"Up into the frames with it, into the place once held by the other boat. And I'll hear no talk," says the mate, "no more of the matter, not on board this ship if we sail three months more, or three years."

More than one voice says, in a whisper heard by no one, "Ill luck follows us, then."

The after davits swing outward, the sheaves turn noiselessly in their blocks, and with an uncommon sucking sound the Pequod's coffin rises from the water one last time. The man on the grating turns fitfully under the cook's tender hand. He will survive. Aloft, the topsails roll out from their bunts and the Rachel slowly gathers way, seeking no more the children she will not see again.

The Light at the End of the Tunnel

By Thomas Kirkpatrick

His long, slender fingers flew over the keyboard, their bony tips pounding down on the keys like so many tiny hammers. David Enright, PhD. rushed to finish the last module of computer code he needed to conduct the most important experiment of his academic career. His piercing blue eyes stared at the monitor out of a narrow face, topped by an unruly mop of black hair, unblinking, intent on capturing his work without error. When he had finished, he leaned his slight body back in his chair and inhaled a deep breath. "Now," he thought, "we shall see if this works."

David Enright was a physicist and a computer scientist, a brilliant researcher at his state university's main campus. He had always been a classic Type A personality. For a number of years, he had been studying how to measure time and slice it as finely as possible. He had constructed an exceedingly complex apparatus in his laboratory and linked it to the university's super computer. His latest round of experiments had yielded spectacularly promising results. He believed he had discovered a way to slice time in such minute pieces that even the motion of subatomic particles could be frozen in place. David intended to demonstrate this incredible result with a milestone experiment. He conducted what software developers refer to as a Unit Test on his latest code module. When he was satisfied it worked, he was finally ready.

David was seated in front of a giant screen driven by the supercomputer, on which he expected to visualize the result of the experiment. He held his breath for a moment, anticipating the scene he hoped would unfold on the screen. He pushed the ENTER key. The experiment proceeded. He began seeing what he had predicted. He had frozen the subatomic particles in their tracks. Success! He was exultant. All those years were paying off, at last!

But as the results unfolded, David noticed something that surprised him, an incredible and totally unexpected phenomenon. On the screen, he saw what appeared to be a two-dimensional slice of the universe. "Where on earth did that come from?"

As he watched this result continue to unfold before him, he felt himself being drawn into this slice of Universe. In wonderment, his eyes wandered across this image of the cosmos. He seemed to be navigating around, ranging over the entire universe at will. His mind was feverishly trying to find an explanation. In science, researchers often stumble across unexpected results. Sometimes, the unexpected turns out to be far, far more significant than the expected.

His curiosity and excitement grew rapidly as he played like a small child with a shiny new toy. And yet, in the back of his mind, he was aware that this result was so far out that he was bound to be disbelieved, and even ridiculed if he spoke about it, let alone tried to publish, so he decided to remain silent for the time being.

For some days afterward, he was content to just go exploring. Each time he entered his slice of Universe, he would go off in a different direction, just observing with wonder and awe what he was able to see. But then he began to wonder what lay outside the boundaries of his Universe. So, next day, he deliberately approached the edge of what his senses, primarily his visual sense, could perceive. To his utter amazement, the boundary was not simply like hitting a wall, or dropping off an edge. Instead, he saw grayness and nothingness. He moved forward. The grayness began to surround him like a tunnel. His ability to see his slice of Universe started growing dim. Ahead of him, far away, he saw a point of light. David had a powerful, disquieting sense that something was there. Alarmed, David retraced his path until he was well inside his slice of Universe. He traveled back to his laboratory and found himself sitting at the control console again.

Next day, David approached an old friend, Professor Aaron Horowitz, a fellow faculty member, a Professor of Philosophy in the Humanities Department. "Aaron," he said. "Can I tell you about an experiment I've been doing?"

"Of course,' Aaron replied. "Come on over to my office." The two settled into the comfortable armchairs Prof. Horowitz kept in his office. Aaron was the total opposite in personality and style from David Enright. He had fought a weight problem most of his life, and lost. His round, friendly face spoke of a personality quite relaxed and comfortable with itself, deeply introspective and contemplative, again totally unlike his hard driving friend David. One would never expect these two to be friends, so opposite were they. However, when they had met at the Faculty Club a dozen years earlier, they had hit it off immediately, and over the years had become fast friends. "Now then, tell me what you've been up to, David."

David described his amazing discovery, and what he had been doing with it. Needless to say, Aaron was captivated. He asked many questions, and became especially fascinated when David told him about his probing of the boundary of his slice of Universe. When David described the gray tunnel and the point of light at its end, a vague worry crept over Aaron, but he said nothing, just continued to listen as David spoke on. After David had left, Aaron decided he should keep their conversation confidential for the time being.

After a time, David recovered his sense of scientific detachment. He became even more curious about what might lie "out there." The next morning, he entered his laboratory, fired up his experiment, opened his slice of Universe, and entered it with his consciousness as before.

This time, he was going to probe as far as he could outside the boundary, or at least what his senses told him was a boundary.

After he had entered, he pondered how he was going to do this. Finally, he decided to simply take a run directly at the boundary at the highest rate of speed he could imagine. When he did so, he found, to his pleasant surprise, that he was able to keep going much further than he had the first time. He became aware that he had totally lost touch with his slice of Universe. He knew it was back there, but he could see nothing of it. Instead, he became aware that the tunnel of "grayness" was not getting darker and more pervasive as he had expected. Instead, things were getting lighter and brighter. The only discrete thing he could sense was the point of light, far ahead. He saw nothing recognizable as belonging to his worldly existence, no shapes, no sounds, nothing. He continued moving. The point of light became unbearably intense. Suddenly it hit him: a deep sense of foreboding. David felt more afraid than ever before in his life.

Later, he realized that "afraid" was scarcely a strong enough word. Stark terror and dread were more like it, and even that was really not adequate. So, David began to wish mightily to return back to his slice of Universe. He willed himself to move backward down the path he had traveled to get to where he was, wherever that might be. Gradually, the brilliance began to fade and the grayness returned. Eventually, he saw the first signs of his slice of Universe appearing. Breathing a heavy sigh of relief, he continued. As he had done before, he willed himself back to Earth, to his laboratory, and back out of his slice of Universe. He found himself still sitting as he had just before the experiment began running. Shaken, he switched his experiment off and left the lab.

Quickly, David walked to the Humanities building and knocked nervously on Aaron's door. "Aaron, can I talk to you for a minute?" Professor Horowitz could see that his friend was deeply concerned about something.

"Of course, David," he replied. "Come on in and sit."

As David described the events of the morning, Aaron became more and more concerned.

Finally, he stood up, walked to the wall of books lining his office, took a volume off the shelf, and sat back down next to his friend. David was surprised to see that Aaron held in his hand a copy of The Bible. "Aaron, is that a Bible? I always thought you were Jewish."

"I am that, David. I want to read you something from what you Christians call The Old Testament." Now, David was only a nominal Christian. His parents had made him go to Sunday School when he was little. However, he hadn't set foot inside a church since he left home to go to school. Mildly bemused at his friends naivete', Aaron went on. "David, aren't you aware that your Old Testament is actually the ancient Hebrew Scriptures we still use today? The early Christians simply added their own books and called them the New Testament. So, I can read you something from either the Hebrew Scriptures or the Old Testament and you'll hear the same thing."

"Well, OK," replied David, feeling a little embarrassed, since this was the first time in his life that realization had ever struck him. "What does that have to do with my experiment, though?"

"I think it might have a great deal to do with it, David. Do you remember the story of Moses encountering God on the mountain in the form of a burning bush? Here, let me read the story to you." With that Aaron Horowitz began to read from the ancient book of Exodus, in which Moses recounted how he felt when his curiosity led him to examine the burning bush and he realized he was in the very presence of God. Aaron read:

When the Lord saw that he had gone over to look, God called to him from within the bush, "Moses! Moses!" And Moses said, "Here I am." "Do not come any closer," God said. "Take off your sandals, for the place where you are standing is holy ground." Then He said, "I am the God of your father, the God of Abraham, the God of Isaac and the God of Jacob." At this, Moses hid his face, because he was afraid to look at God.

Aaron continued, saying, "I've always believed these scriptures vastly understate the real fear and trembling Moses must have experienced at that moment." He paused then to allow the implications of the scriptural passage to sink in for his friend. After a moment of silence, David's eyes opened wide.

"Aaron! You don't think I was approaching God, do you?"

"I have no idea, my friend. I know you've always been an agnostic, at most. Does God exist? I've always believed so. But, no one can prove so. Forgive me for sounding like the philosophy professor I am, but isn't that why humankind needed to invent the concept of faith? I'm struck by the similarity between your experience and that of Moses. You both were scared out of your wits. That suggests to me you both might have had the same experience–a near encounter with God himself."

After that, Aaron remained silent. David sat quite still for many minutes, scarcely breathing while his mind came to grips with the unthinkable. Finally, he could contain himself no longer. His eyes grew moist. Tears began to trickle down his cheeks. Then he began to weep uncontrollably, and stammered, "My God! Aaron! What have I done?" Neither man spoke then. Aaron simply reached out and gripped David's hand in his. The two friends sat together, while David wept his humbling tears of remorse.

Later, David dismantled his experiment and erased his laboratory notes. Neither man could ever bring himself to speak of that day again.

The Final Stage

By Judith Shernock

IMAGO

Have you read Metamorphosis by Franz Kafka? Once read, never forgotten.

Gregor Sampsa hates his job and works only to support his sister and parents. One morning he awakens transformed into a large insect, trapped on his back, unable to turn over. Eventually he adjusts to this horror. His family forced to fend for themselves, develop a great anger towards Gregor who is now helpless. This turn of events leads to his death.

The novella is considered one of the great works of twentieth century literature.

This story has been referenced because of a strange happening on my porch where Pikachu the grasshopper lived. His name refers to one of the well known Pokemon people of the Japanese Manga comic book fame. The word "pika" is the sound of an electric spark and "chu" the voice emanating from a mouse.

Our Pikachu was named by my seven-year-old grandson, Ilan, who found the five legged grasshopper in our yard and put him in a jar that we filled with grass. Pikachu refused to eat. We researched the matter and found that of the 8,000 species of grasshoppers only one is 'morphaus phagus' (eats only one specific plant). Pikachu must be fed the leaves he was found among.

With the new diet of Calla Lilly leaves, he thrived.

Over the weekend we were very busy and our pet was neglected. On Monday, when we looked, the grasshopper had grown so much that we put him in an aquarium tank. We gathered large handfuls of leaves to feed him. His once tiny droppings had become the size of fingernails.

Ilan went home and I attended to the insect on my own. Passing the cage, I felt there was someone staring at me. Were the creature's bug eyes throwing accusing looks my way? Was my imagination working overtime?

The next day, exiting the house, I heard a distinct voice saying: "Where is the boy ? He must be here when I morph. He is my master."

This sentence was followed by a racking cough. Terrified, I went inside and locked the door. The answer to all things is to be found on Google. The word Grasshopper went into my search box.

This is what I found:

"In 1971 the world is plagued by SHOCKER, a terrorist organization that plans to conquer the world by turning people into Cyborgs. Only one person escapes, Kamen Raida (Masked Rider) who becomes a grasshopper-like man and eventually, a folk hero. He is so well known in Japan that his statue stands outside Bankei Studios, the most famous of Japanese movie studios. Kamen Rider, in one of his many battles, saves another person who also turns into a grasshopper-man and the two become a heroic fighting duo."

Reading further I found that Shocker's ideology is derived from Nazism. The initials 'SHOCKER" stand for Sacred Hegemony of Cycle Kindred Evolution Realm. There are hundreds of episodes on Television and in Comic books about the daring duo of Kaymen Riders.

Was my Pikachu morphing into a Cyborg, that bizarre combo of animal and machine? Was he a relative of Kaymen Rider? How had a three legged grasshopper learned to talk? Why did he need my grandson before he morphed?

I was more curious than scared and decided to watch through my window. I called in sick to work and took up my vigil.

As evening approached there was a crashing sound and the cage shattered. A large person with Grasshopper wings slowly emerged. He was clothed in a bright green body suit and ran out the gate to the street. The thing was limping, since one leg was shorter than the other. His screech shattered the silence: "Master, master where are you?"

That was my last glimpse of Pikachu. If it weren't for the broken glass on the porch, it would have seemed like a nightmare. Somewhere in this world there is a strange creature I helped to create. This is both a frightening and exciting thought.

When a being we nurtured morphs into another and then goes his way, we are left wondering what has become of him? Does he preen in the sun or hide in the shadows? Has he become a Kaymen Rider or a SHOCKER?

If Kafka were still alive he might have given me an answer.

Tile Store

By Lisa Meltzer Penn

The contractor informs us it's time to make a trip to the tile store. We need to choose what stone to use for our new bathroom.

On the showroom floor, faux rooms are arranged as bathrooms and kitchens with cutaway walls. To our children they are playhouses, low walls on three sides, open on the fourth.

While the children busy themselves playing, Seth and I get our education in stone and tile. Our store guide is an earthy, loamy sort who moves through the aisles with a warm intimacy that belies the sharp qualities of the stone surrounding him. As he leads us around the store, he reels off names of the different types of stone as though they are mantras. "This is slate, this is travertine, this is marble, this is granite." By the second pass we are familiar with Unfading Green Slate, with the distinctive porosity of travertine, and Italian marbles with names like Bianco Spino, Calacatta Carrara, Calacatta Borghini. They roll off his tongue. He points to Layla and Gil. "And see that mosaic pattern behind your children? The other stone is quite plain but that mosaic makes the bathroom. The marble accents come from our own quarry in Macedonia, Greece."

It is local stone from far away, I realize.

"Choose a special stone and pattern for the accent," he adds. "You will need a theme. This moment or that around which to build your fieldstones."

For our bathroom, he means. All this for a bathroom. The travertine fieldstones come tumbled or edge-cut, smooth or pitted, we have seen. The pits can be left as they are or filled in with different shades of grout to either blend in or contrast.

When I wonder aloud if maybe we shouldn't do something simpler after all, our guide patiently instructs us on natural stone's innate static properties. "That's why highly polished marble is so popular in public lobbies," he says. "It might look slippery, but really it is the synthetic stone that is more likely to cause a slip and fall."

After what our guide calls a "fly-through" around the store, Seth and I cozy up to an abbreviated breakfast bar in one of the faux kitchen houses. The barstool swivels and my knee bumps Seth's under the bar. "Ouch!" I say.

"Sorry."

I rub my knee. "It's just a little sore. I'm only icing it once a day now? Did I tell you?"

He rests his hand on my knee.

"I really don't want to have another surgery." I confide in him. "The orthopedist said the ligament is partially torn again, but if I'm careful I'll be okay." I trace the edges of the tile at the lip of counter in front of me. What I don't mention is that ever since I tore my ligament again I can hear the voice of a Siren once again. A voice from my past. My old guide. I look down at Seth's big hand on my knee. I put my hand on top of his and look into his gentle face.

Seth leans in, almost bumping my knee again. "This is the closest we've gotten to a date night in months," he says.

I laugh. "I know. You're right, I'm sorry. I'll be glad when we're finished and we can put our house back together and not have to focus on tile and paint."

Gil sticks his head through the open side of our kitchen house. "Found you!" he says gleefully. Layla appears behind him and rolls her eyes. "Gil, lunch is ready!" she says bossily, holding out a sandwich made of squares of tile, and leads him away.

"Don't go too far," I call after them. But we can hear their voices just fine through the open rooms, over the short walls of those little worlds within worlds.

"Don't worry," says Seth. "This place is like an amusement park for them."

"I think everything is."

"That's the beauty of kids," he says. I look at him, the father of my children, my one true love. He leans over and kisses me. I remember what it was like before they arrived, when it was just the two of us. There's always a price to pay. But I'm happy.

Most of the time I'm happy.

I start to say something, but just then the loamy tile store guide returns with a little tray holding two cups of pale tea and two cartoon straw cups with water. "For the family," he says, and sets it on the counter. "Have you decided what you like?" he asks.

"Not quite yet," I say.

"Take your time," says the guide. "There's no rush." He bows slightly and slips out of the open wall.

"We'll have a date night soon," I assure my husband, squeezing his hand. "I'll call a sitter. It's just been so hard with everything going on and things all over the place." It feels nice to hold his hand.

"I'll leave it to you, Elizabeth," he says. He picks up one of the teacups and takes a sip.

I smile at his usage of my complete name. He's known me through almost all my names and incarnations. Not Lizzie, but everything since. (Including Beth, what I called myself when I first met the Siren.) I shake it off.

"So, what do you like here?" I ask.

"The black and white basket weave," he says. "That's still my favorite."

"I like that, too," I say. "But it's a little fancy for a kids' bathroom. I'm thinking golds and browns and evergreens. Like the fall woods for my old secret room."

"That's right, your secret room won't be secret anymore," he says.

"No," I disagree, "It will still be secret in its way. Cabinets and drawers and hidden pipes. Things will get lost and hidden. Stuff is bound to fall between places.

"Well, I don't know what's secret about kids brushing their teeth and spitting in a sink, but go for it, Ella. You may as well be happy with it since we're going to the trouble. And you spend more time in the house than I do."

"I like the golden tiles he showed us. And the unfading green slate."

"Hmmm," he says, and we sit quietly for a minute. Seth flips through a catalog on the counter. I take a sip of hot jasmine tea. He's right. We haven't been together much lately. The crews of men are always in the house. And after them, the dust, the shopping for sinks and cabinets and colors and tile. Afternoons, I spend alone in the living room, icing my knee, peering into the island while listening for the voice of the Siren who might have something of importance to tell me, and resting against the sofa cushions.

Well, the island is my past, part of who I am. Though something is different about Beth and Jasper now. Something is different about how the island calls to me. But my bond with Seth is what counts the most.

Seth helped me come up with Ella for a name. He said it reflected a lot about me.

He knows me better than anyone. But, sometimes he still forgets.

I run my finger along the textured backsplash of the faux kitchen. I note that the accent strip is composed of tiny seashells. In its center is a disc of creamy white stone and blue tile the size of my hand. Unnoticed to me previously, a figurine of a mermaid has been artfully composed in its center. This mermaid appears a lot like how I imagine my Siren to look, but with a fish tail. Most people naturally assume a Siren is the same as a mermaid. They're wrong.

Now that I am looking, the stone mermaid's eyes seem to examine me curiously as well. Suddenly I hear the Siren's voice in my head. Look closer, she says. I'm right here! I startle and look up instead. Seth is drinking his tea. I hear the kids' voices in the background. I swing my gaze back to the mermaid. This is not my favorite aspect, the Siren laments in my head. No wings in this form. They were taken—that's another story. You can find it in your myths. But this is a good disguise.

I am not accustomed to hearing the Siren's voice in public places. This is not my living room or the ferryboat or the island. I briefly wonder if I am going crazy, hearing voices in my head. Almost as quickly, I dismiss the concern as cliché. The much more surprising conclusion is that the marble mermaid in her adornment of seashells is one of the Siren's personas. Just as I have many appellations and incarnations derived from Elizabeth, so has she from Siren. I chuckle.

In my head once again, the Siren begins to recite: Three sides closed, one open. On the open side where your children travel in and out, you may question what happens. But you cannot question the closed sides, Beth. The mysteries stay.

"Why are you calling me Beth?" I whisper. "I'm Ella now."

In the beginning, then. You were Beth. Or Bet. Or Vet. Languages were fluid then. You were a container, a house. Can you remember?

Just then, the store guide reappears through the open wall. "Do you like her?" he asks.

I look up in surprise. Of course, he's talking about the rendering of the mermaid. He could not have heard the Siren's voice anymore than Seth could. "It depends on the day," I answer the store guide. "Whether I like her, I mean."

He nods. "The mermaid is quite popular," he informs us. "But not many people bring her into their bathrooms."

"Then where do they bring her?" I ask, suddenly wanting desparately to know. "Oh, gardens, covered terraces, open kitchens like you see here.

I almost start laughing. The kind of laughing that unmonitored can flip over into crying. I can't believe I'm having this conversation with a stranger. And so, I get ahold of myself and ask for several tile samples of stone to bring home with us. Some of the striated green marble squares and some golden travertine that together will feel just exactly like the woods and the paths through them. There are woods like that not far from our house, along a reservoir. There are woods like that on the island, too.

I turn to Seth. "Let's look at them at home and come back when we have a decision."

I swivel the barstool around while we wait for our materials. I shoot an appraising look of my own at the stone mermaid on her disc. The Siren in one of her many forms. As many forms as I have.

Beth, whispers the Siren again in my head. The infinite. The beginning.

I shake my head. My hair brushes over my neck. This was is not what I bargained for on this shopping trip.

Seth has collected Gil and Layla. Our guide returns with the samples in a little cloth bag and ushers us to the front of the store. As we walk through the doors, our kids trailing behind with a few trinkets of their own, I wonder how it will all turn out. The tile samples clack at my side in their bag.

Reginald Van Flautmeister, Esq.

By Thomas Kirkpatrick

Reginald Van Flautmeister awoke with a start from his late-afternoon nap. He sat up, yawned, began rubbing his sore, aching muscles, then stood up from the granite slab the management liked to refer to as a couch. It was one of the few furnishings in his star's dressing room at the Pachataukwa County Repertory Company's playhouse. This, he reflected, was definitely not Broadway!

His dressing room did actually have a star tacked on the door, though one point was slightly the worse for wear, and one of the tacks had come loose, allowing the star to dangle at a rakish angle. But, nevermind, it was a star, after all. And he was the star, so he deserved it.

It was just before 6:30, plenty of time to dress, apply makeup, and begin his vocal cord warm-ups. Presently, a stagehand knocked on his door, announced curtain time in ten minutes, and left.

That night's performance of The Lark's Revenge went well, he thought. His local costar's delivery was just a bit off tempo, but, what could one expect from amateurs. By and large, he had seen worse, so he soldiered on. Then, it happened. Penelope Whistleman, his female lead, did something quite unexpected. In the final scene, during their passionate stage clinch, she whispered in his ear, "Reggie, I love you." Then she proceeded to give him a most untheatrical and most prolonged big, wet kiss, directly upon the mouth, not just the usual near-miss, the audience was supposed to take as being real.

The curtain fell, the audience applauded lustily, the actors took their bows, then Reginald hurried to his dressing room, removed makeup, changed into his street clothes, and readied himself to leave. But before he could escape, there came a knock at the door. He opened it to find none other than Penelope Whistleman standing there, a shy smile on her face.

"Weren't you going to at least say goodbye, Reggie?" She gave him a disappointed look, then went on. "I was hoping we could have supper together, before you have to leave tomorrow."

Now, Reginald Van Flautmeister was what some would call an Aging Lothario. He had at one time been in the movies, just as his press releases claimed. Of course, it was only a bit part in a long-forgotten B-Movie. You know. The kind the movie theaters used to run on the same program as the Main Feature. As he claimed, he had a speaking part. "Madam will receive you in the drawing room, Sir," he had intoned, trying to give his best imitation of what he imagined an actual English butler sounded like. These days, he made his living as a touring "Star" of the stage and screen, a fiction enlarged upon shamelessly by his agent, Benjamin Burriss, of the Burriss, Burriss and Burriss Talent Agency.

Reginald expended considerable time and attention on trying to stave off for as long as possible the deleterious effects of aging. He slept at night with a chin strap, his face covered in a sort of slimy substance promoted as an anti-aging creme. His graying hair and moustache were regularly treated to a recoloring wash. He had some years before invested in having his somewhat dingy teeth fitted with brilliant white porcelain caps. For a while, this did seem to provide him with a quite effective distraction that kept others from noticing the unfortunate sag appearing in the area of his jowls. He wore a kind of corset whenever in public, including of course when on stage.

This hid his otherwise quite noticeable tummy bulge.

"Why, Penelope! How nice of you to drop by. I'm so sorry. I should have said my goodbyes, but I was distracted, I guess. I do have plans for the evening, my dear, but it was kind of you to invite me. Perhaps next year? I'll be returning in the Spring for The Masterful Manchurian. I hope to see you then, and I hope to have the delight of starring opposite you."

But, Penelope, being a lady of great directness and little guile, was not one to be put off so easily. With no hint of embarrassment, she replied, "Reggie, did you hear what I whispered to you in the final scene?"

Reginald, his mind racing, hesitated in formulating a reply just a moment too long. Penelope went on. "Reggie, I meant it. Our work together these last weeks was absolutely inspiring! I knew our love scenes weren't just make-believe. I felt your warmth. I sensed what a good soul you have."

Reginald Van Flautmeister had been accused of many things during his lifetime, but having a good soul was most certainly not one of them. While he had indulged in a good many casual dalliances, the very thought of a serious entanglement caused his insides to instantly turn into a giant ball of ice. He smiled wanly, then replied, "My dear, I'm immensely flattered by your kind words. I have formed a very high opinion of you—as an actress and colleague upon the boards—but in my profession, it has always been my lament that serious feelings are a luxury not available to me."

"Reggie, don't be silly! I could be your muse, your constant companion and comforer, your strong right hand, whatever you need of me!"

"Oh, Lord," thought Reginald. "This is not going well! What am I going to do to get rid of this broad?"

Miss Penelope Whistleman, it should be noted, was not a half-bad looking woman. She had strawberry blonde hair worn in quite attractive curls, not too long. This gave her a deceptively soft and feminine look, a look that hid a certain steely resolve, as Reginald was about to discover. Reginald had, in fact, flirted with the idea of making her his next conquest du jour. However, he was in the habit of making the first move. Her preemptive move had thrown him completely off his stride, so he had instantly abandoned any thoughts he had entertained about that.

Penelope was, in addition to being the town's perennial leading lady at the Repertory, the proprietress of a nice little Bed and Breakfast, located in one of the better neighborhoods. This establishment she had inherited from her late mother several years previously. Her mother had shown up in town some years before, with more than enough cash to buy the B&B outright. She had immediately changed its name from its previous rather mundane moniker to—ready for this?

– The Shady Lady Inn.

The good townspeople, when they witnessed the new shingle being hung, were scandalized. Immediately, a great deal of whispering behind hands began taking place. The elder Mrs. Whistleman was reputed to have been involved in every sort of unsavory activity, including having been the Madam (the Madam!) of a brothel in that bastion of sin, New Orleans. All of the notoriety hurt the inn's business not one whit. In fact, people came from far out of town, asking the local folk, to their great embarrassment, how to find the Shady Lady. In short, Mrs. Whistleman had a winner on her hands. When she finally, mercifully, and none too soon, passed away, the townspeople breathed a collective sigh of relief.

However, whatever hopes they might have entertained were soon dashed by the arrival of Mrs. Whistleman's daughter, Penelope. Everyone held their breath waiting to see whether she would undo the affront to the neighborhood by changing the B&B's name to something more "suitable." She didn't even consider it, seeming to revel in the notoriety even more than her mother had. And so, the town resigned itself to having to live with the stain on their reputation.

Back to our story. Penelope knew instinctively that Reginald was lying through his dazzling white teeth about being previously occupied. So, she grabbed him by the arm, walked the hapless Reggie out the stage door into her auto, and drove to the Shady Lady. She had arranged with her cook to produce a scrumptious meal, then discreetly leave for the night. Reggie, in a state of increasing panic, scarcely remembered the following day what he had consumed. He had barely escaped by pleading extreme exhaustion after the evening's performance.

When he arrived at his hotel, the desk clerk handed him an urgent message from his agent, Benjamin Burriss. Reginald was too shaken by his close encounter with sure death to respond that night, but did so the following morning.

"Hello, Reggie!" shouted Benjamin in his usual ear-shattering bellow. "Baby, I got to talk to you. It ain't good news, I'm afraid. You know those next four engagements we had lined up for you? Well, they all cancelled."

"What? Why?" countered Reginald.

"Baby, it's just the word's got around about that business in Toledo. You know what I'm talking about, don't you?"

"Oh, for God's sake! Are people that small-minded they would actually cancel on me over some little thing like that?"

"You got to remember you're in flyover country now, Reggie. People there take these things real serious. And not just where you are. It's all over that part of the country. I haven't been able to get you a single booking, and it ain't because I ain't trying, either. Baby, I think you're in big trouble." Reginald thought about this for a minute or two before answering his agent, prompting Benjamin to ask, "Reggie. You still there?"

Reginald lied, "Oh. Yes. I've been thinking lately about maybe making a career change, Benji." Indeed, he had spent the last ninety seconds feverishly doing just that. As the conversation wore on, and as Benji's statements became increasingly discouraging, Reginald's thoughts turned increasingly in the direction of Miss Penelope Whistleman. Well, she is a rather attractive lady, he thought, as a plan began forming itself in his mind.

And so it came to pass that Miss Penelope saw the object of her affections, Reginald Van Flautmeister, Esq., walking up the steps of her establishment. She practically ran to the front door in answer to his ring, flung it open, and gave him another of those big, wet kisses on the lips. "Oh, Reggie," she exclaimed. "I somehow knew you'd be back. We need to talk. Come in and sit."

To make a long story short, that was how Reginald Van Flautmeister, aging lothario, late star of Broadway and Hollywood, currently on tour, came to settle down to domestic tranquility in a small town in flyover country. He even became something of a local celebrity, taking over the directorship of the Pachataukwa County Repertory Company. In short order, he and Penelope were married, he moved into the Shady Lady with her, and the townspeople once again harbored hopes that the name of the Shady Lady Inn would at last be changed to something more "suitable."

Reginald never even gave it a thought.

The Turkish Summer

By Sally Shunsky-Hernandez

The opening of the compartment sliding door on the train startled me. My head jerked up and I was looking into the face of a fellow with a full head of spiked, black hair. He wore glasses with thick black frames and a bright red polo shirt that was a great contrast to his hair. His smile was a timid one and he nodded at me. I moved closer to the window, sliding over the four seats on my side. He sat opposite of me and close to his side of the window. We communicated with nods and guarded half smiles. According to my schedule, we were destined to arrive in Istanbul at ten o'clock, Thursday, the following morning.

I had boarded this train in Munich on Wednesday at 4 pm and was confident that I arrive in Istanbul the next morning. Mr. Red Shirt had joined me around midnight as the train slowly traveled through Yugoslavia. I made many wrong assumptions on my first trip to Europe in July, 1968. First, it was hot and arid. We rode with the window open halfway as the heat and dust of our journey poured into the compartment and over our bodies. I assumed that the outside night air would be refreshing and help in cooling off the compartment. When I accepted this assignment with the American Friends organization to do volunteer work overseas, I didn't know where I would be sent.

That spring and summer, there was a massive mail strike in France and it affected all foreign correspondence. There were 28 volunteers from the United States. We were all to receive our assignments when we arrived at the Friends headquarters in Luxembourg and then it was our job to notify friends and family. None of my fellow volunteers knew where our assignments would be and once we received them, we couldn't communicate the news to our families. (This was a million years before cell phones were born. The more affluent workers could call home direct or collect but I was in the category of volunteers who did not possess access money. I had actually borrowed the $650.00 donation to the AFSC from our church credit union to take this trip.)

My second wrong assumption was that I was capable of reading train schedules. I believed we would arrive in Turkey on Thursday am but no, I missed reading the schedule properly by twenty-four hours. This train was due to arrive in Istanbul around 10 am on Friday after we traveled a whole day through Tito's country and then another ten hours through Bulgaria. One memorable thing was seeing camels being out in the fields just as we saw cows roaming in Michigan.

Third assumption, I never heard of transit visas, which were required for travel through Bulgaria. I assumed that the border crossing would be as simple as crossing from Michigan into Canada. When we reached the border, several uniformed armed guards with rifles by their sides appeared in the doorway demanding our visas. Mr. Red Shirt had his, but from the look on my face these two guards knew that I was their victim. If you didn't have a transit visa, you could purchase one from them with Turkish lira or $20.00 American cash - I had neither. I negotiated to use an American Express traveler's check and they gave me my change in Bulgarian currency. Finally, the guards left the train and it moved forward into the night.

Around one am, the train stopped at a small town and two Bulgarian residents joined Mr. Red Shirt and me. They were dressed modestly and my traveling companion leaned over to me and whispered in his best English that they were peasants and I should guard my belongings carefully until we left the train. He indicated it was apparent that these two fellows were lower class by how they wore their shoes. The back of each shoe was bent inward and they walked in their shoes like a pair of clogs. These two kept to themselves for the next nine hours, the duration of the night.

Grrrgh. was the only sound I heard but it was loud enough to wake me from my dozing state. My train journey which had begun in Munich on Wednesday at 4 pm ended at 10 am, Friday morning in Istanbul. The dirty sweat was still running down my forearm to my wrist. I was so warm that I kept dabbing a damp Kleenex to my forehead. Then I realized that the noise in my eardrums wasn't only the squeaking brakes of this train. Now, I could hear people speaking in several languages outside of our train car. I couldn't tell what was being said but I was sure that someone was complaining about the warmth of this July morning.

Even though it was only ten o'clock in the morning, I swear that the temperature had to be in the high 90's. I saw a thermometer outside as we pulled into our resting space in the yard. It read something like 32. Then I realized that I was in Turkey, a Celsius nation, and I couldn't convert fast enough. I only knew that I was dying of the heat, my clothes were wrinkled, clinging to me and icky with sweat. I wanted to leave this compartment quickly and locate a hotel room where I could indulge in a cool bath. I left the compartment on the train with my knapsack, sleeping bag and tote bag in search of a place to stretch out. I took a moment to pause and look at the walls of this old train station. They were covered with decorative, mosaic tiles. Each square was prettier than the one next to it. I never studied Turkish history or its architecture. Miranda, another volunteer that summer with the AFSC (American Friends Service Committee) had mentioned Turkey when we received our assignments in Luxembourg the week before. She said that Turkey was her primary choice of places to be assigned. I stated on my application that I didn't have any preference. I only said that I wanted to work in Europe. Well, Miranda was assigned to Poland and I was assigned to Turkey; which is partially in Europe.

As the train rolled into the station, minarets from the various mosques were visible. When we pulled into the Istanbul station, everyone dispersed quickly. Going through customs, I did catch a glimpse of the two fellows from our compartment as they pulled bright, shiny metal machetes from their luggage. The custom officials pulled them aside as I wandered through with my backpack and tote bag. I never saw them or Mr. Red Shirt again. I often wonder what became of him.

Now, all the unloading passengers from the train were herded into lines. Our luggage and belongings had to be inspected by the customs personnel. The lines were long and my body decided to sweat profusely. The man asked me several questions in English and when he decided that I wasn't smuggling anything, he marked a large "x" in white chalk across my backpack. It was almost noon when I was permitted to leave the building. It was time for noon prayers and the call to prayer rang from the various locations across the city. It was my first hearing of this call that happens multiple times throughout the day in Muslim countries. As I left that line, I vowed to check out the beautiful mosaic art work on the train station walls on my return trip to Munich. My summer adventure continued as I walked out to the curb in search of a taxi.

The Istanbul Hilton Hotel was my destination. Somewhere I read about them being kind to college students. I caught a cab outside the train station and took a ride to this luxury hotel. The lobby was filled with sunshine streaming in from glass windows encircling the mezzanine level. Straw shades covered all the windows on the first floor. I was hot, sweaty, dirty and obviously not clear of mind as I entered that lobby mid-day on Friday, July 10, 1968. The place was packed with clean visitors from around the world who smelled good. My presence was not adding goodwill towards folks who traveled from Michigan.

The fellow at the front desk swallowed his smirk and quietly informed me that yes; they do welcome students but not midsummer. "Can't you see that we have an abundance of guests here already?" he quietly said.

"I am exhausted, tired and sweaty. I need a place to sleep for one night, please," I begged. "I've been on the train from Munich for two nights. I only need a room for a day and a half." I quickly explained that I was to meet my group from the American Friends at Roberts' College on Sunday at noon when we would be transported to our summer assignment. "Well," he finally said, "you can use the cabaña room near the pool but it won't be available until 11:30 pm." It was noon and I just wanted to melt into a puddle in front of that counter. For an instance, I wished that I was back in Detroit doing nothing exciting.

He sensed my state of being and suggested that he knew a lady who ran a boarding house nearby. He telephoned and said that she did have a room with community bath privileges. Kindly, he found a taxi for me and gave the address to the driver. The lady met me in the driveway and helped me register, carry my bedroll plus tote bag to the second floor. It was cool in her house and I thanked the heavens when I reached the second floor and located the bathroom. It had a huge old fashioned white tub with legs but I went directly back to my room and collapsed atop the comforter and closed my eyes.

Loud shouts woke me and I realized that the evening prayers were

425

being said over an outside speaker on the building next door. Looking out the window, I realized that this was an old neighborhood and quite picturesque. Grey cobblestones covered the narrow streets. All the structures visible from my window were made of gray stones. I took a cool bath before I ventured out for a stroll. I didn't go far because I wanted to keep track of the boarding house where I was staying. I went to bed very early that night and slept soundly only to wake at 6 am for the call to morning prayers.

The community breakfast was being served when I ventured downstairs. Their delicious breakfast consisted of hot tea, cheese, bread, olives and honey. I smiled and nodded to the other visitors but only spoke with the landlady because she was the only person who spoke some English. On Sunday, I would receive my summer work camp assignment so I only had Saturday to explore Istanbul. I waved goodbye to the landlady, stepped briskly onto the hot cobblestones and began my summer adventure of 1968.

Nina in Bed

By Frank Saunders

He stopped the car just inside the open garage door so his wife could get out. She smiled at him. "I'll warm up the leftover soup, okay?"

"Sure." They had made the soup together last night, Eileen covering the carcass of a roasted chicken with water and spices, as he added some chopped carrots and celery. He watched her as she moved gracefully through the door into the house. He really did love her, he thought.

He parked the car and stepped outside, his long thin body unfolding like a carpenter's rule, all bent arms and legs, slowly straightening.

He poured glasses of water for the two of them, and took his seat at the table. She brought bowls of soup and slices of crusty bread.

"I thought," he began, slowly and with some hesitation, "that I might go over this afternoon and see Nina. It's been a while." He added in his thoughts, Not since Helen's death.

"Can I come?" asked Eileen. "I'd like to see her, too. You know, I've been a little worried about her. The last time we were there, she was talking about one of the staff–a young man–who was helping her bathe. I couldn't tell if she liked the attention or was upset by it."

"Hard to tell," he answered. "She's such a tease. Always laughing. And always too much lipstick."

"At ninety-four, she ought to be able to dress however she likes. But we all have a sense of dignity." Eileen had a successful law practice handling auto accident and workers' comp claims. "I always think about elder abuse, in these places."

"Unlikely." He spoke more sharply than he intended. The board and care home was four blocks away, in their residential neighborhood. The family only took in four residents at a time.

"The building's up to code and it's always spotless. She's comfortable there, while her hip heals."

Nina had fallen, suffering bruises and a small stress fracture in her right hip that made walking and standing painful. Her doctor had recommended six weeks of recovery, and Robert certainly couldn't care for her at home.

"I miss her at church," said Eileen, picking up the dishes. "I can see her sitting on her little cushion in the choir, smiling and singing along."

"She's such a wisp of a thing," he said. "She looks so fragile. Her skin looks like wax paper, like it would tear if you rubbed it hard." Nina's thinly covered veins traced a roadmap across her skull and face, pulsing slightly with her heartbeat. "I stand next to her, sometimes, watching so nobody pushes her over."

"I'll be ready in a minute." Eileen disappeared into the bathroom. He returned to the car, backing it out into the driveway and reaching across to open the passenger door for her.

As he waited, his thoughts turned to his sister, Helen. Her last months had presented a series of crises, inexorably worsening, options narrowing. Dying at sixty-four, she had lived a long life alone in her one-bedroom apartment with her television and her cat, independent, stubborn, smoking. She ate for solace as much as for sustenance, with obesity and inactivity leading to diabetes and heart disease.

Midway across the country, he could only support her by frequent telephone calls and letters. He remembered with warmth and sadness her simple sweetness, her reminder calls every Fourth of July to change the smoke detector batteries, and her boxes of candies assembled with love at Christmas.

Her life, like her thought process, was structured and concrete, untroubled by complexities or abstractions. She travelled by bus to the grocery and to her doctor appointments, known by name to each and every one. Events moved slowly in her small community, and people looked out for each other. The local social services office had attached to her file, long ago, a diagnosis of schizophrenia, adult onset, uncomplicated, allowing her to receive subsidized housing and a minimum of support.

She had collapsed in her bedroom, managing to call 911 and to say "I can't breathe!" before losing consciousness. Paramedics broke open the front door and rushed her to the emergency room. "She was that close to dead," they would say later. "We had to bag her in the field before we could transport her."

He remembered with quiet pain the telephone calls, the consultations as her only living relative and as her "designated attorney for health care", as listed in the notarized advance directive that Eileen had prepared for her.

Helen's cardiologist, Dr. Kincaid, had called him on his cell phone one afternoon, catching him as he was returning from his afternoon lectures at the university. "Dr. Brentwood, we think we can give her a year if we replace her mitral valve. We're trying to decide between a porcine valve – a pig valve – and a Teflon ball and cage. Do you think she can she inject herself with a blood thinner, like maybe Coumadin?"

He had remembered Helen's reluctance to test her blood sugar with a finger stick, unless under extreme persuasion. "I don't think so," he had answered.

"Well, that rules out the artificial valve. Without Coumadin, it would probably throw clots. So the pig valve will give her a year."

He had assented to the surgery, on Helen's behalf and with her complete approval. He had visited her frequently during the last year, watching the slow progression of congestive heart failure, of fluid retention, of impending kidney failure.

"Hi, Maynard," she had said cheerily during one stay in the hospital. "They took out thirty pounds of water. Don't I look a lot lighter?"

Helen had agreed to move to a convalescent facility nearer to the hospital, and it was from this bedroom that she was taken for her last time to intensive care.

Flying out again, he found her lying in a darkened hospital room, unable to speak because of the respirator tube, restrained with IV setups and monitor leads. Her eyes, he thought, looked pleadingly into his own.

"May I talk to you a moment?" Her attending physician, Dr. Reynolds, drew him aside. "Her advance directive says 'full code', all measures necessary to preserve life. Is this what you think she really wants?"

Maynard closed his eyes to clear his thoughts. "Let's ask her," he finally said. The physician nodded. They entered the room.

The doctor spoke somewhat formally. "Helen, this is Dr. Reynolds, and I'm here with your brother, Maynard." The physician paused, emphasizing his words. "Do you want us to remove the breathing tube?"

She nodded her head vigorously.

"Do you understand that you'll have trouble breathing on your own, and that this may hasten your death?" The doctor spoke gently, softly and very clearly.

Helen closed her eyes for a moment, then looked directly at her brother.

She nodded her head, decisively, unmistakably. The hint of a smile appeared, more in her eyes than anywhere else. He felt his own tears.

Dr. Reynolds turned to him. "Give us a few minutes to remove the respirator. With your approval, we're shifting to palliative care." Maynard nodded again, and left the room.

When he returned, the respirator, IV stands, and monitor leads had disappeared—almost magically, it seemed to him. Helen was lying under a neatly folded sheet and colorful coverlet, her eyes closed, breathing irregularly. "We've given her a sedative," said a nurse, smoothing the coverlet. "If she appears to be in any pain, we can give her morphine drops under her tongue." The nurse gently closed the door.

Minutes passed. The room was still. He held her hand. He told her much in his mind, without speaking.

Her breathing suddenly became more labored. Her brow wrinkled. He called the nurse into the room. The nurse took Helen's pulse, turned to Maynard, and said quietly, "It's time."

The nurse filled a dropper with liquid from a vial on the table, parted Helen's lips, and released the liquid under her tongue. Within seconds, Helen's agitation was gone. Her breathing slowed. She took a deep breath, then another. Her breathing slowed again, then stopped. The nurse silently left the room. After a while, Maynard followed.

"Here we are," said Eileen brightly, as she jumped into the passenger seat and closed the door. "Do you think they'll be done with lunch?"

"Hope so," he answered, putting the car in gear. He drove the few blocks to the home, half-listening to Eileen's relating a conversation at church, half-lost in his own thoughts.

They walked together up to the entrance, and he pressed the doorbell. He had been there before, but had forgotten the small sign that said "Knock, don't ring–elderlies are sleeping." Frowning, he muttered at himself as the door opened, feeling embarrassed.

"Hi," said Eileen cheerily, from behind him. "We've come to see Nina. How's she doing? It's such a nice day."

The attendant, a small woman, said something in heavily accented English. He looked at her, unable to understand, and turned to an open binder on a table in the entryway.

"They want us to sign in," he said over his shoulder to Eileen. He signed his name and time of arrival. He was aware that a second woman had joined the first, both talking animatedly with Eileen.

Looking past them, he saw the open door to Nina's bedroom, her bed just inside and against the wall, Nina lying on her back with her head toward the door. Sunlight played on her face. She was looking at him, eyes open, smiling with recognition.

"Rosella says she's asleep," said Eileen, from behind him. "We should come back later."

"But she's awake!" he said, his words lost in the chatter. He moved a few steps toward Nina's bedroom. The volume of the voices rose. One of the women stepped in front of him, gesticulating, unintelligible. He felt someone touch his arm.

"They have to get her ready," said Eileen. "She has to go to the bathroom."

He heard Eileen's voice clearly, louder than the other two women, who were talking excitedly. He began to notice a ringing in his ears. He looked past the women toward Nina's door. He saw Nina's skull-like head hanging off the bed, staring at him upside down, her arms thrown wide, her lipstick-reddened mouth hanging open. He shook his head violently to clear it.

"They want you to wait in the living room," said Eileen, steering his elbow. Stumbling slightly, he nodded and turned toward the front room. He walked toward a chair, leaving the others behind.

Entering the room, he noticed a man standing on a ladder.

"Excuse me," said the man, gesturing with his hand. "I'm taking some pictures for a brochure. Would you mind waiting over here?"

The roaring in his ears became louder. He felt his eyes opening wide, his mouth parting. He turned back to the women.

"I'll come back later," he said, struggling to sound reasonable. "This is a bad time."

All three began talking and gesturing again. "She'll be ready in a minute," Eileen exclaimed. "We can wait."

He felt panic pushing him between his shoulder blades. Panting, he rushed for the front door and ran down to the sidewalk to the car. Jamming the key in the ignition, he gunned the engine and pulled out of the parking space.

Remembering Eileen, he stopped, began to back into the parking space. "She can walk home!" he thought, furiously, and jerked the car forward again. In the mirror, he saw Eileen walking quickly down the sidewalk. He hit the brakes again and stopped, gripping the steering wheel, rigid with anger and fear.

Eileen swung into her seat and slammed the door. "What was that all about?" she demanded. "Why were you acting like an asshole?"

He floored the accelerator, the car leaping ahead down the deserted street. Rolling down the window, he yelled outside at the top of his voice, "Asshole! Asshole! Talktalktalktalktalk..." Panting, incoherent, he threw the steering wheel left as he rounded a corner, slamming Eileen against the passenger door. "You want to hurt her," a voice said in his head.

Approaching the house, his agitation became a little less. He pulled up behind the garage, opened the door, and rushed inside, leaving the engine running. He stumbled up to the bedroom, shut the door. He stripped off his shoes and pants, climbing into bed and pulling up the covers. He curled into a ball on his side. His heart slowed. He slept.

When he awakened, it was morning. He was alone. He showered, shaved, dressed. Opening the bedroom door, he heard Eileen talking on the telephone.

"I don't know," she said. "I think he's awake ... No, I don't think so." He walked downstairs. She stood, facing away from him, still talking.

"Maybe," she said. "I really don't know..."

He found his battered brown briefcase, moved toward the garage, muttered "Sorry," and left. He drove the short distance to the college.

Climbing the stairs, he entered the classroom and placed his briefcase on the table. The classroom became quiet.

Looking out at the faces of the students, he recognized a feeling that he had had before, a feeling that came in that brief moment before the teaching began, when the room was silent with anticipation, when the students were looking at him expectantly, mouths parted, waiting to be fed.

He held the feeling a moment longer, gazing at each student in turn, drinking in the pregnant silence like cool water. He took a breath, and began to speak.

Parking for Angels

By Ellen Six

"Kyle hurry up. You'll be late for baseball practice."

"I'm coming, Nay. I'll be right there."

But five minutes later, he was still finding something to do.

"Kyle, come on. We have to leave right now."

Renee always dreaded the afternoon when she would have to drive her little brother to baseball practice. He was always playing with his favorite toys and he could never be ready on time. She hated being late because she knew that there would be no parking and she would spend ten minutes circling the lot looking for a space.

"I'm coming."

Kyle piled all of his equipment into the car, climbed in, slammed the door, buckled his seat belt and they were off, finally.

But of course, it was stop and go traffic and by the time they got to the field there wasn't one parking spot left. Renee started her usual drive up and down the rows but there was nothing in sight. Finally, in desperation she pulled into a spot with a blue handicapped sign.

Kyle shouted, "Nay, you can't park here."

"But Kyle, it will only be for a few minutes. I'll just walk you to the field and I'll be right back."

But Kyle kept saying, "No you can't park here. This spot is for angels."

Renee was puzzled. "Kyle, what are you talking about?"

Kyle kept repeating, "Nay, this is parking for angels. We can't park here."

Just then a neighbor, Mrs. Mitchell, came walking back to her car to get some water. She could see how Renee was upset and she asked if she could help. She agreed that parking could be frustrating. "I can walk Kyle to the field for you," she said. "You just go home and come back in two hours. I'll wait here with Kyle when practice is over. He is great friends with my Ryan and by then the parking lot will clear out."

Kyle gathered his equipment and Mrs. Mitchell took him by the hand and they headed towards the field. Renee, gratefully drove out of the lot and headed for home. When she got home she had over an hour and a half until she had to start back.

She went to her room, turned on some music, got out one of her schoolbooks and lay on the bed to study but in a few minutes she fell asleep. She started to dream. She felt like she was floating through the air. Suddenly, she felt like she was heading straight up toward the ceiling and out into the sky. She was floating in the clouds. The mist started to clear and the clouds parted and she was standing in front of golden gates. Could this be heaven? They were tall golden bars and she could see a garden on the other side. She must be dreaming. Her brother had said something about angels so maybe that was why she was dreaming about them.

She felt peaceful. It was a beautiful dream. Just then, the gates opened and an angel walked out. He was dressed in white. He was surrounded by a bright light and he had beautiful wings on his back. This is the picture she always saw on Christmas cards.

Just then the angel spoke.

"Yes, I am an angel and yes this is just a dream but many times when we dream we can travel to different places and we can learn new things so today your dream has taken you to heaven."

The angel escorted her through the golden gates and she walked down a golden path and she saw a line of little angels with little wings.

The chief angel explained that these were all the children who were waiting to be born.

The angel said that their parents had been waiting for them for almost nine months, hoping and praying for the day when they would finally be able to see them and hold them but there was only one last thing to do before they left heaven to go live with their earthly families. They were to go to the Lord, one by one, and He would put His arms around them, kiss them, and bless them and tell them that He loved them. He would say, "Remember me until we meet again." Then they would walk over to an angel who would remove the wings from each child because they would not need these on earth and then he would lead each child to a cloud and place them on one that would gently float them to earth to meet their parents.

But then Renee noticed that one little boy was so excited that after he got his blessing he ran by the angel and started to fly toward earth. But his wings were so heavy that when he got to earth they had hurt his back and the doctor had to tell the parents that this little boy would not be able to walk. The parents could not see these new baby's wings. They held him and loved him but they didn't know that when he was growing up and he had pain that it was because his wings were too heavy.

Then the heavenly angel showed Renee some other children who had not waited for the cloud to take them to earth. One little girl was so excited that she ran out through the gates of heaven and began to fly but then she started to fall too fast. She became frightened and covered her eyes with her wings. When she came to her family, she was born blind but she still had the light of heaven shining in her eyes.

Another little boy who tried to fly and couldn't wait also started to fall and he covered his ears. When he was born he could not hear his family's voices but he could still hear the music of heaven.

The book fell off the bed and Renee woke up with a start. Where was she? It was her room. What a strange dream. She looked at the clock. She had an hour until she had to pick up her brother. She remembered her dream. It seemed so real. She knew what she had to do. She found some colored paper. She got a pair of scissors. She started to cut out paper wings. She got some tape and took these with her to the car. She drove back to the school parking lot. She pulled into the handicapped parking space and took her tape and reached up and taped paper wings on the back of the blue symbol of a child in the wheelchair. She drove to the next handicapped parking spot and taped the wings on the symbol. She did this with the four spots in the lot and then she went and parked the car in the street in the neighborhood. She walked back to the parking lot and stood in the spot with the handicapped sign, which was now her angel sign and waited for her brother.

She saw him coming with Mrs. Mitchell and his friend Ryan who was in a wheelchair. When Kyle saw his sister, he started to run toward her. She grabbed him and hugged him and she pointed to the sign. She said, "Now everyone will know that his spot is parking for angels."

Mom. I Forgive You

By Sharyl Weinshilboum

Mom, I forgive you for getting pregnant at 17 and married while you and Dad were still in high school

I forgive you for blaming me for giving up on your dreams of going to art school

I forgive you for letting me cook my own TV dinners and go to sleep listening to the radio I forgive you for spending time cleaning and doing needlepoint instead of reading to me

I forgive you for only noticing me if I was holding a trophy or a report card full of As

I forgive you for letting me mother my little brother and robbing me of my childhood

I forgive you for pushing Dad to take jobs he hated so he could buy you a house that was too big I forgive you for yelling at us because the dog pooped on the carpet and making us clean it up

I forgive you for pulling my arm, telling me I was stupid, that I couldn't do math or paint a picture

I forgive you for your unhappy life and for pushing me as far away as you could because you were uncomfortable with closeness

I forgive you, almost

800 Notre Dame de Namur Scholarship Winner

Scholarship Winner
Notre Dame de Namur

The Fearless Latina

By Elizabeth Seter

She looks into the mirror, in her face, a sense of longing
She looks deep into her reflection, her eyes seeming to say
"Stop prolonging" Blonde-Brown hair, light skin
If only they knew, she thought with a grin
If only they knew of my Latino pride
This is not seen by her appearance, but this love of her culture she
    cannot hide "
You are Hispanic?" they say, "You shouldn't even think of college."
She asks "Why?",
They respond, "Because you have no knowledge!"
"They are immigrants. All they bring to America is crime.
Why do they even try? Honestly, they are wasting their time."
She sees these stereotypes, disgusted, for they are lies
For she hears the cries
The cries of the Hispanic culture
For the culture is being preyed upon by vultures
Defy the stereotypes, go to college, lead others
Yes, this is how she will put misconceptions to smothers
Times must change
Don't you think it's strange?
How we are all judged by our looks?
To some they see Hispanics as crooks
"Look at me! Everybody thinks I am just white, but they just
    assume."
Little do they know her cultural pride is in full bloom
Seen for her light complexion, not her Mexican heart
She is a piece of art
In her heart she yearns to eradicate all negative divisions

View one another as equals, lead future generations, these are her
    visions
She asks "Where is the cultural pride?"
Why must everyone hide?"
She says "Let's celebrate diversity"
"Think," she claims, "Of how we could all rise above adversity"
Racism in the streets, schools, and hearts of many, it is everywhere
    you turn
This is what makes her stomach churn
She does not desire an elaborate house or expensive car
This girl does not dream to be a star
So many Latinos rose above injustice, however, their work is not yet
    done
She wants to instill pride in all, she thinks of future generations, her
    future daughter or son
Who can change the negative mindset regarding Latinos?
She says "I volunteer!"
She stands before you, a Latina with no fear

Acknowledgments

Carry the Light is a community endeavor. There are dozens of people involved in its creation. The staff at the Event Center log in the literary entries, others download and print them for judges, then receive the judging returns and catalogue the results. Each entry is evaluated in its own literary category. Then there are people like me who download the entries again to prepare the stories, essays and poems for publication. All of this happens in short order!

The book is assembled so quickly (two weeks!) that errors can occur—particularly when the formatting doesn't hold from the author's pen to the contest email service, through the pdf conversion and reconversion back into Word, then to book form, and through the printer's system. Very strange things can happen. Wendy White, Kimberly Schultz, and Brenda Yodice, a small but mighty force, did their best to spot lines that are incomplete, missing, or other software mischief. Please forgive us if we missed something. Next year, maybe you can help us!

I want to especially thank Matt Cranford, San Mateo County Fair & Festival Manager, and Bardi Rosman Koodrin, creator of the Literary Galleria with her husband Boris Koodrin, for all they did to make *Carry the Light* a success.

This year the Fair's literary entries increased by 100, consequently, the book is over 430 pages—over 197,000 words and 20,000 lines of type! We'll probably need new rules next year to decide who, what, and how much get published. But we followed the rules made months ago and tried our best to publish at least one entry from every person. We failed in a few places, but judging from the amazing size of this volume, we have succeeded beyond our wildest dreams.

Congratulations to all of the winners and to all who entered and shared their stories with the community. It is only through the written word and storytelling that we can reflect and see ourselves as we are and how we could be. Story sets us apart from the beasts of the field. It lifts us to new heights. I truly hope you enjoy Volume 4 of *Carry the Light*.

Tory Hartmann
Sand Hill Review Press

Note: All of the volumes of *Carry the Light* are available from Amazon.com or may be ordered through your local bookstore.
Carry the Light, Vol 1 ISBN: 978-1-937818-05-0
Carry the Light, Vol 2 ISBN: 978-1-937818-19-7
Carry the Light, Vol 3 ISBN: 978-1-937818-25-8
Carry the Light, Vol 4 ISBN: 978-1-937818-33-3

Index